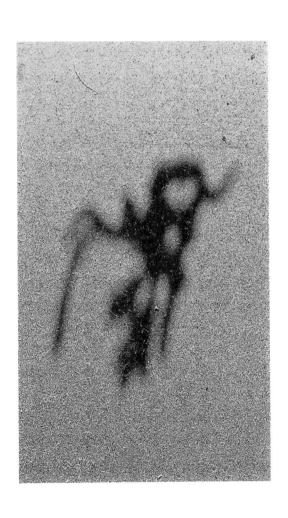

Welcome to Eormengrund, a world where the magic of a mind has more power than Smith, Wesson or Winchester. Get ready for an adventure of epic proportion, where nothing is totally what it seems.

Nancy Campbell

Remember the ORIGINAL definition of masterpiece: it's the piece done by a journeyman to prove himself worthy of promotion to master. It's not the pinnacle of a career: it's the beginning of a career.

Linda Pfonner, aka Wylfcynne

ISBN978152131723 Copyright1-515-8313271 May17, 2017 by Nancy Kay Campbell

From the Shadow of a Dream

The Cost

TABLE OF CONTENTS

Sacrifice	5
The Note	10
An Enemy Identified	13
Gathering Lucy	17
The Battle for the Portal	19
To the McCarthy House	24
Broken Spirits	27
From the Shadow of a Dream	32
Second Chance	33
Jessie's House	36
The Rabbit Hole	40
The Snake Lady	43
Night Terrors	44
Winifred James, Damage Assessor	50
Exit Strategy	51
Distant Thunder	54
Knock, Knock	56
The Crystal Cave	58
Polly-Wanna-Demon?	64
On the Eve of War	68
Tea Time	73
Whispers	77
Of Mice and Mentors	84
Pella Durett	89
Close Call	94
Harvest	99
Muster	105
Pony Rides	109
The Giant's Fingers	114
Deductive Reasoning	117
In the House	120
Choices	127
The Siren	129
Coming of Age	132
The Substitute	137
The Mission	143
The Seneschal	148
Broken Promise	152
Healer's Worth	156
At the Crossroad	162
Stakeout	165
To Kill a Demon	167
The Offering	170
Hot Times in Claxbury	174
One Door Closes	177
Revelation	180

TABLE OF CONTENTS, CONTINUED

Another Door Opens	181
Kimala	183
Northbound	188
The Gift	191
Snatched	194
Cold Storage	199
Preparing Marand's Prize	201
A Face in the Crowd	204
The Healer of Il Chatel	208
The Gambler	214
Into the Darkness	218
A Lady's Chambers	220
Demon Number Sixty-eight	223
Confidence	228
The Deal	231
Above and Below	236
Maggie and Amos and Altay and Sje	240
Reality Check	244
Strange Bedfellows	246
A Change of Direction	250
A King's Chambers	254
Climb	258
Mushrooms at Two Thousand Feet	261
The Making of a Warrior Queen	263
One Man's Vision, One Little Girl's Nightmare	266
Little Brown Jug	267
Flashback	271
A Mother's Love	274
Mercy	276
On Wing	279
The Last Thread	283
...and Prayer	285
Bird's Eye View	287
The Road to Arandia	291
First Blood	294
Engaged	296
Smart Fish	298
Shell Game	300
Duel	303
In the Service of the Kings	307
End of the Line	315
Vengeance	316
Reunion	318
The Rightful Lord	323
War Cry	326
Homeward Bound	328
The Crystal	333
Last Leg	334
The Sleigh Bed	336

1 Sacrifice

In the darkness they waited, the spring day nearly forgotten here beneath the green earth of Eormengrund near the base of Kimala. The wards above them had been removed leaving them alone and seemingly vulnerable to wage a battle only they knew they could win. Years of tedious manipulation and more blood than either of them wanted to remember had led to this moment. Sword and Shield, defender and protector, were at the peak of their respective powers. If ever there was a time to capture the Lord of Demons, it was now.

Brilliant glimmers of gold, silver and blue filled a clear crystal placed on a pedestal in the center of the room, energy ripe for the taking, energy painstakingly siphoned from them both and from Wylfcynne. Wylfcynne had conceived this plan years ago and given almost everything to the stone in an effort to save Eormengrund. Before her and Wulfhaeled, Ahleri had opened a door that could not be shut. But that is a tale for another day.

The crystal was sealed when it could hold no more. Each of the three erased their unique signature from the offering, the signatures that would under any other circumstance allow them to retrieve what was theirs. The power in the crystal was free to whomever would claim it; free for anyone save those who placed it there. To them, the crystal's precious content was lost forever.

Above them, darkness blotted out sunlight. Something descended into the room. It hovered directly above their carefully baited trap creating unmoving shadows on the walls around the room. The Sword raised his hand, signaling the demon's arrival. The Shield fidgeted in the corner, eager to join the fight, knowing that she must wait for the right time else all would be lost. Their prey was too conceited not to rise to the bait. He wanted Kimala. But he was no fool. He never traveled alone. With him was surely a host of demons even Sword and Shield could not hope to defeat. They feared their master and would not dare challenge his claim to the power. Yet a prize as great as this would be a delicate matter to claim.

"Go!" a silken voice commanded.

A lesser shadow broke off from the darkness and floated to the stone floor where it took the form of a man. He was dirty, hairy and wiry with a long tail. The Sword's lips tightened as he recognized Beh from a vision that had shone him a bitter reality. He was Fot's servant. The great one had come.

Beh paused, his eyes darting back and forth, scouring the room for hidden dangers. The Sword stood still within the shadows, visible to those who knew where to look yet unseen to the demon. Beh took one hesitant step toward the crystal. Then another. When he was three feet away from it, he dove. He placed his hands on either side of the prize without touching it, a wide grin on his distorted face.

The Sword smiled widely as his own shadow came to life.

A blade of fire, the Sword of Light, exploded from his fingertips and he lunged toward this lesser demon, driving him away from the crystal. Beh hissed. The sound of metal against metal ground out in the room as the demon drew his weapon. He ran at the Sword, blade held aloft but the Sword neatly turned the attack aside and grabbed the demon by the neck. With ease, he grasped the wrist that held the sword and turned it away. It clattered to the floor.

"Have mercy!" the demon begged.

"Myranda asked for mercy," the Sword told him. "She was my ambassador and you sent her back to me in pieces. My vision witnessed her murder at your hand. At least I gave you the opportunity to fight for your life." He touched the demon's mind.

Beh cried once in surprise, a second time in fear, then went limp in silence. The Sword released the lifeless shell of a body. It fell to the floor with a soft thud. Without another thought, he turned his attention back to the crystal and the greater enemy he knew waited there.

In the center of the room hovered the massive lord of demons, Fot. The Sword waited as the demon took human form. Unlike Beh, he was a handsome man, though he towered over normal men. His green and red eyes flashed eerily in the darkness.

"The crystal belongs to me, Fot," the Sword lied. "You have no claim to it."

"Power belongs to those who have the strength to take it," Fot replied. As the Sword had formed a blade of fire, so the demon formed a great blade devoid of color save the red flame glinting its edges.

A shower of sparks flew from the two great blades as they clashed for the first time. The Sword stepped backward, then forward, then whirled, his body responding automatically, as years of practice had taught it.

Parry, thrust, touché, parry, parry, thrust; Sword and demon performed a deadly dance. The Sword sidestepped a well-placed jab, sacrificing the cloth of his shirt in order to catch the demon across his sword arm. The demon roared, adeptly shifting his weapon from his right hand to his left.

"You fence well for a man," Fot snarled, "but you are no match for me."

The Sword did not answer. He jabbed at the demon with his right hand, an attack that was easily turned aside because it was expected. Then he ducked and rolled on the floor in a tight ball. He came up underneath Fot's arm, holding the red sword away from them both and stabbing the demon in the chest with a dagger made of metal.

The ██ scales nearly turned the blade aside, yet the action caught Fot unaware. He took an off-bal██████████ ██rd toward the corner of the room where the trap waited to be sprung. In an instant, he r█████████████ out of reach of the net. The Sword was there to meet him.

████████████████ one another and the Sword struggled to hold his weapon steady. He ██████████████████ but he did not need to. Fot breathed acrid breath into his face, █████████████████ inches from the demon's eyes, their swords locked at the █████████████████ of another kind arose.

█████████████████ before him had ever dared. He had a chance to █████████████████ He held the green and red eyes with his own and

█████████████████d. Fot's memories flew past him, memories of the █████████████████ him. Fot knew he was there. The demon laughed at

█████████████████ cost him his concentration and his weapon slipped. █████████████████ of Light up almost too late to turn away a deadly strike. █████████████████ping for more sport. Perhaps I can help."

█████████████████ the Sword by his shirt and tossed him aside as if he was █████████████████ed hard and tried to come up gracefully, but his body was █████████████████ggish. He drew from some inner source and rose to face his █████████████████er, else Eormengrund would fall.

Fo█████████████████m, tip pointed to the ground, the wide smile back on his face. "Tired so soon,█████████████ed to the glowing crystal. "If you had arrived earlier, perhaps you could have used that c█████████ you may have been a worthy opponent."

The Sword stood, feign███████dy legs and began to circle. Fot mirrored him, step for step, unwittingly being maneuvered into their trap.

"I am not done," the Sword answered. To his right, the Shield stirred. He shifted his eyes ever so slightly. *Not yet.*

"Ah, but I am no longer amused." Fot replied, still unaware of the other danger hidden in the shadows. "Prepare to meet your goddess, little man."

The Sword raised his blade and roared. He raced forward, blazing blade held aloft. He ran past Fot, making the demon turn and follow him into the corner of the room. The colorless blade swung easily at him, but the Sword thrust it to one side.

"You have trapped yourself in a corner, little man," Fot chortled. "I had respect for your style, but it appears you have made a grievous error. Well enough. This game has become tedious." He advanced in steady, deliberate strides.

The Sword waited. He shifted his weight back and forth, balancing on the balls of his feet.

Fot lunged at him and their blades met, man and demon locked in a physical power struggle. The Sword removed the dagger again from his belt. He took a deep breath and shifted his body so that Fot suddenly fell forward. The smaller metal blade found its sheath under the black scales, as Wylfcynne had told him, deep in the flesh of the demon's underarm. Ruthlessly, the Sword twisted the blade, dragging it downward with as much force as he could muster.

Fot shrieked. He turned toward the injury and the motion was just enough for the Sword to slip past him, out of range of the net.

"I will tear your limbs from your writhing body, little man," Fot threatened, "and send your parts back to your people!"

The Sword whirled his weapon in a circle before him, holding the demon in place. "Now!" he cried.

The Shield exploded into the battle igniting the wards she had so carefully set. Silver fire flew from her fingertips flashing throughout the room igniting her intricate web. Before he could think or act, Fot was ensnared.

Realizing his mistake too late, Fot clambered toward the shrinking exit only to find his way blocked by a triumphant Sword. With all his might, Fot thrust at his enemy in a futile attempt to escape. He withdrew into the shrinking sphere of light, barely able to swing his sword. The web sucked down around him, ensnaring him in a prison of light. He roared and charged, his sword ineffectively striking the tightening net.

"Get back!" the Shield yelled.

"Close it!" the Sword yelled back.

Her fingers flew in patterns long practiced. The trap was almost sealed. They were going to win.

The power that defined the Sword coursed through him and he took on the golden aura of the blade that he carried. He placed the fiery tip on the netting. The gold intertwined with the silver of the Shield and the red of the demon himself.

"You are the Sword!" the demon whispered.

"I am," he replied, "and she is my Shield." He allowed himself a satisfied laugh as he watched the Shield continue to work her magic. "And now, I will give thanks to the Lady for giving us this victory." He knelt on the stone floor, both hands resting lightly on his blade as he assumed an attitude of prayer. He bowed his head.

Fot roared and with one final lunge, sent his sword through the shrinking opening to strike the kneeling Sword. The great colorless blade met his enemy's skull, slicing through his flesh and into his soul. He staggered back into the room and slumped to the floor.

"Eron!" the Shield cried. She took one hesitant step toward him, her task unfinished. Fot seized the moment and thrashed within the web in an attempt to break the bonds holding him.

"Close it," Eron whispered. His head fell back on the stone floor and he lay still.

The Shield swallowed hard and steeled herself to her task. She pulled the net tightly around Fot's hand until the demon's sword disappeared. Fot shrieked and pulled into his jail. The only thing left for her to do was to cinch the web down and Eormengrund would be safe for a while, the hierarchy of demonkind thrown into chaos as others battled to take Fot's place. Demon and webbing were the size of a small ball of yarn. She carefully placed it on the floor and raced over to the fallen Sword.

Blood burbled from a jagged gash that ran from his forehead to just above his ear. Around it, his black hair was singed white. She tried not to look at the wound too closely, afraid of what other damage she might find. She turned his head up so she could look into his face. The eyes staring back at her were vacant, yet he was still breathing.

"I'm sorry," she said and without hesitation or permission, she entered his mind.

Chaos. Memories and visions flew around her; he was in the Crystal Lake, water closing in over his head and light all around him, ecstasy, their child holding a story book, a king dressed in steel plated armor, decorated with winged serpents in gold and a golden circlet upon his brow, charging up the mountain on a small grey stallion with a host of warriors and a thousand other things. The images were moving so fast that she couldn't make sense of them. She had to get past here, had to get to his injury, had to save him.

Into the working part of his mind she passed. Rivers of energy flowed mightily against now weakened walls that no longer held them totally in check. Energy poured from a huge fracture, his life force emptying onto the ground in front of her and flowing away.

"No!" she gasped.

She drew on her own power and forged a huge shield. She pressed it over the wound, stemming the largest tear. Instantly, it melded with the flow behind it, sealing the rift. She took a step away from her handiwork holding her breath, her eyes searching her handiwork for signs of weakness. Her heart was pounding as she ran her hand over the patch. She felt nothing untoward there, nothing indicating her ministrations would not hold.

"Thank you, Lady," she murmured.

Something bright gold flashed to her right. She swallowed hard. The blow had shattered the wall and the river of energy that defined him was oozing through it from dozens of places.

"No!" she whispered.

Without hesitation, she drew again and again from her own stores of energy to fortify the damaged wall. Each time she finished one patch, another fracture nearly as large caught her attention. She gritted her teeth and for what seemed hours, she created patches and sewed fissures together with silvery threads of energy.

Suddenly the air around her freshened as though a summer breeze had blown a door open. The feeling was familiar. It washed over her, relaxing the tension in her muscles. She leaned into the wall, resting her forehead for a moment on the cool stone and allowed herself a smile. Before she felt his hand, she knew he was there.

"Stop."

She turned slowly around to find him, dressed in long black robes trimmed with red. The fire was gone from his eyes, replaced by a peace she had seen on too many faces. Horrified, she pushed him away.

"No! I can help!" She resumed her work patching the leaking reservoir at a fevered pace, leaving him to watch from behind.

"You weaken yourself to save a dying man," he argued quietly. "You are my people's only hope now. Save your energy."

"It is mine to give," she said, pulling away from him to position another patch.

"Your oath is to my people," he told her, his voice echoing the peace she had seen in his eyes, "not to me."

"You swore an oath as well, Sword!" she snapped. "An oath to me and to our child!"

The river roared behind the fractured wall and the hair on her arms prickled with his power. She abandoned finesse and slapped patch after patch over the leaks, creating ugly but functioning bandages. He took her gently by the shoulders and turned her around to face him, ending her patchwork.

"Yes, I was the Sword. I can no longer defend. You are yet the Shield. You must go on."

"Not without you," she cried softly.

"There will be another Sword," he continued, his voice soothing but firm. "I am broken. You alone stand between this fragile victory and chaos."

"But--"

"The future of my people rests with you."

"But--"

"Fot never travels alone; you know that."

"Eron, I--"

"Do not fail me on the brink of our enemy's defeat." Dark brown eyes met green ones, pleading for understanding. "You have sworn an oath," he commanded softly. "Fulfill it."

"I...I can help! Please let me help," she begged as tears clouded his image, "please...what will I tell her? You can't...you can't..."

He took her into his arms, drawing her tightly to him, feeling the beat of her heart and the warmth of her skin. He stroked her hair, and drank in her scent, praying that if this were the end, he would take this memory of her with him to the next world. Unnoticed, he shed a single tear. "I love you both," he whispered, not knowing if she heard his words. Without waiting for a response, he released her and allowed his image to fade away.

Reluctantly, she left his mind. In the net, the demon lay quietly, a smile akin to triumph on his face.

"Pity," Fot chided. "He was almost a worthy opponent."

"Shut up." She shrunk the net until it was the size of a hen's egg then shoved it and its contents into a small, prepared container. Uttering a well-rehearsed incantation, she sealed him inside. With dread in her heart, she turned her attention back to the Sword.

The brown eyes were no longer vacant. She dared hope.

She raced to the wardrobe that had hidden her and flung open the door. Inside were a number of cloaks. She grabbed two and ran back to Eron, cast one over him, placed the other gently under his head. She used a corner of it to put pressure on the jagged wound trying to stop the bleeding. His blood oozed through the material, red with flecks of golden light, flecks that few others could see, alarming her further.

"Eron," she said, trying not to let desperation slip into her tone, "I'm going to try something."

He did not respond.

With one hand, she kept the pressure on the wound. With the other, she wove a small piece of the same netting she had used to catch the demon. She raised the cloth and threw the net onto the jagged cut. Like magic, it clung to the edges of the wound. The bleeding stopped.

She sank back on her heels by his side, now shaking. In the dim light, he looked more dead than alive. A lock of hair lay on his forehead and she reached over to push it to one side. His hand shot out from beneath the cloak and grabbed her with such force that she cried out.

"Take him," he whispered.

Her heart skipped a beat and she paused. "He will keep," she answered.

He closed his eyes, the lids quivering like a tiny leaves in a windstorm, but his grip tightened. He sucked in a huge breath. "Take him!" he shouted.

She looked around the room, searching with every sense available to her for any danger that might befall him. There was none. She grabbed the crystal and the demon. "Okay, I'm going."

The light inside the room shifted as clouds passed between earth and sky and he unwillingly drifted toward unconsciousness. The ground beneath him was cold and hard and he shivered. His head should have hurt unmercifully. He ran a hand over his wound. He felt nothing.

Time passed. Nothing changed. He did not want to give in to the darkness but peace was descending on him. As Wulfhaeled before him, he had completed his task. Another Sword would follow. He only hoped there would be no uprising until his successor was trained.

A hand slipped into his, and he opened his eyes. The Shield was there. She brushed her lips against his forehead.

"Safe?" he croaked.

She nodded vigorously. Tears glistened on her cheeks, though she was trying to smile. "With the others."

"Portal?" he whispered.

"My homeland is safe."

"Our child?"

"Safe."

He managed a smile. "She is a beauty."

"Be sure to tell her that yourself the next time you see her."

He pointed up toward the bright light that was spilling into the chamber. "They come…" he breathed. His hand fell to the floor.

"Eron?" she called. "Eron!"

His eyes flickered shut.

Through the crack in the earth above them, a host of lesser demons stole the light of the spring day once more. The Shield pulled the wounded man into her arms. With one smooth motion, she encased them in a tiny, warded bubble.

The lesser demons took a moment to assess the situation. Seeing their greatest enemies cowering beneath them, they launched into an awkward kind of victory dance. They pummeled her bubble, their fists creating thunder in the space beneath it. The Shield did not care. She held the Sword close and rocked back and forth chanting:

"Please don't die… please don't die…please don't die…"

2 The Note

Jason McCarthy pulled the parking break up on the old VW and shut off the engine. The house in front of him had been listed as "darling" when Aunt Jessie bought it from the hermit years ago. Leftover from an age of cotillions and slavery, it was a second home to him, a place of refuge, serene and quiet where he could bring his problems and let them work themselves out as he sampled Jessie's cooking or explored the grounds with his brother Kenny, sister Anna and their cousin Lucy. Jason was leader to them. He enjoyed being considered mature, even if it was only by this young tribe.

Being independently wealthy, Jessie had a lot of time on her hands. She was reclusive, though not unapproachable for family and friends. The arts were a passion for her, particularly song and dance. She would make up routines for the children to perform and they did so with glee, laughing and twirling and sometimes improvising, much to Jessie's chagrin. There were warm cookies fresh from the oven, consumed on the swing on the front porch with a cold glass of milk while playing checkers or cards or just watching the world go by.

Through the VW's open window, a slight breeze tugged at his jacket interrupting his memories. He got out of the car and walked toward the house. Something seemed different today, though he couldn't put his finger on what that was. Jessie's vintage Mustang was parked on the cobblestone drive instead of in the garage with her van. The top was down. He whistled.

"Someday," he promised himself.

At the age of nearly twenty, he had his BA in business hanging on the wall of the apartment he shared with his best friend, Ric Hawkins. They had proven they had the brains to do whatever job came their way. They had even opened a small business servicing computers and helping people with their taxes. It paid okay, but Jason knew he could do better. All he had to do was convince someone, anyone, that he had the maturity to accompany the brains he'd used to get his diploma. Getting that point across was hard to do, though, with only peach fuzz on his chin. And he had to admit, he was somewhat lacking in the social graces, having had very few dates even though Jessie had taught him how to dance.

"Oh well," he said aloud. "At least I'm not flippin' burgers somewhere."

The walkway to the house was comprised of flat, irregularly shaped stones. As Jason made his way over them, he let his imagination run wild, filling it with stories of slaves and their great escapes and southern romances, something he'd never admit to Lucy. He passed the swing where his cousin was fond of sitting while making up her own stories about cotillions and rebel soldiers. He had fun teasing her about it.

"That's odd." The front door beyond the screen was shut. When he tried the door, it was locked.

He knocked. "Jess? Lucy? It's Saturday!" He held a hand up to keep the glare off the window and peered into the house. There was no activity.

"Jessie?" he called.

No answer.

He reached into his pocket, retrieved his key, and slipped it into the lock. The tumblers obediently fell away and Jason stepped inside.

"Jess? Lucy? I'm here!"

Absent was the smell of sautéed onions, seared meat and freshly baked bread. In fact, the air inside the house was uncharacteristically stagnant, as though no one had been inside for a while. It was the second Saturday of the month. Lunch on Jessie, just like always.

"Jessie!" he called, making his way toward the kitchen, crime scene scenarios racing through his overactive imagination.

Pots and pans hung from the ceiling in the chaotic order that defined a good cook, but nothing graced the huge six burner stove. Beneath the rack on the granite countertop lay a single envelope with his name on it. Jason breathed a sigh of relief.

"I was starting to worry," he said.

He slipped his finger under the flap and slid the note out.

Jason,

I know this is very sudden, but I must go away for a while and I can't take Lucy with me. I tried to call Martha, but I couldn't get hold of her and things, well, things are happening too fast. Lucy is with Winifred, but she can't stay there indefinitely.

I don't know how long I'll be gone; months, maybe longer. I've activated the plan we talked about.

Jason gulped. He never expected her to activate "the plan." With a few well-placed pass codes, Jason would soon be in charge of Jessie's fortune. Martha McCarthy, Jason's mother, would take over raising Lucy for the short term and longer, if necessary. Martha was a lovely person, a responsible mother, but couldn't balance a checkbook much less manage millions of dollars. Money was Jason's forte.

I must go. Take care of my baby. Tell her I love her more than my own life. That's why I have to go.
Love,
Jessie
P.S. Mind the snow globes. They may be cheap, but they are precious.

There was a rust colored smudge midway up the note. The crime scene scenarios reappeared. He read the note a second time, trying hard to ignore the smudge. Nothing changed. Mom was first in line for the plan.

"Hello?"

"Hi, Mom."

"Jason! How nice to hear from you! Did you get the brownies I sent?"

The weight of the world suddenly lightened. "Yeah, and Ric says thanks. He even saved me a couple."

"That boy is too skinny," Martha McCarthy laughed, "but he'll fill in soon."

Jason laughed too, and the house got a little warmer. "We'll both be fat if you keep sending treats."

"Good. How's the job market?"

"Just got better. Sort of. Jessie's gone again and this time she asked me to be fulltime manager of her money." He related Jessie's note to her. "Mom, you know we set up this plan in case there was a catastrophic event of some sort. There's a red smudge on the note that looks like it could be blood or something. Do you think I should call the police?"

"Don't be silly, Jason," she said, but her tone was suddenly worried. "Jessie's always been a free spirit, though a bit of a drama queen. She's forever taking trips when we least expect it and leaving us very little in the way of explanation."

"She's never asked me to take everything over for her!"

"Maybe this is a long adventure and she just wants to keep her finances safe," she continued. "You know, she did get herself pregnant because she wanted a real live baby like Jason."

"That story would be a lot more believable if you didn't use it on Anna and Kenny, too."

"When they get a little older, they'll figure it out."

"Don't change the subject. That smudge could be blood!"

"More likely it's just paprika, Jason," she replied. There was an air of nervousness about her statement, as if there was something she knew that she wasn't saying. "I don't think we need to panic. Jessie can be a tease sometimes. I would think you, of all people, would remember that. She's been that way ever since she was a little girl. It's always been amazing to me that she held on to that lottery money like she did. You know, I thought she'd fritter it away on silly stuff, but she's done a very good job with it."

"I will take good care of it," he replied.

"Yes, and I'm very proud of you for helping her. Thank goodness you've got your father's head for business! Managing money is not in the Perrymore bloodline, I'm afraid."

Jason tried to relax as his mother went into the old tirade that always seemed to come up whenever there was a problem with Jessie. He flopped down in an easy chair next to the fireplace, listening to more of the lottery diatribe. With his free hand, he picked up one of Jessie's tacky souvenir snow globes and shook it. The plastic snow fluttered around a figure of a farmer and a donkey on either end of a teeter-totter. Angry eyes suddenly stared back at him. He blinked and they were gone.

"Jason?"

"Yeah, Mom. I'm here. Sorry," he said, staring intently at the globe as the farmer was hoisted back into the air. "I'll go get Lucy," he added absently.

"That's a good idea. I really don't want to impose on Miss James. She's so good with the children. I do so appreciate your aunt for sharing her with us."

He set the snow globe on the triangular shelf with the rest of them. "Why all the cloak and dagger?"

"I really don't know, honey." She sighed. "We'll just have to wait for her to contact us, just like always."

"Yeah, I guess. You know, someday I'd like to go on one of those adventures."

"Ask her."

"You know, I might."

"You do that!" Jason imagined his mother's face smiling at him. "I'll put fresh linens on your old bed and let Anna and Kenny know Lucy's coming. They'll be thrilled!"

"Okay."

"Jason?" Her voice was soft in the way that all mother's voices coo when they speak to a frightened child. Jason heard it and, even though he was an adult and wasn't living at home anymore, he felt relief wash over him.

"Yes?"

"Make sure the house is locked up before you go to get your cousin, okay? No one's likely to steal that silly collection of snow globes, but there are other things that might catch a thief's eye."

"Okay, Mom. I'll lock up."

"And don't worry." Across the airwaves, he could see his mother smiling. "Jessie's just like that. I'm sure she's okay."

"I hope so. Bye."

"Bye."

Jason shut the phone down and sighed. It was time to start earning his stipend.

Methodically, he went through the entire house making certain all the windows were shut and locked and anything that would look even remotely tempting to a thief was well out of sight. He checked all three doors before closing the front one behind him and sliding the dead bolt into place. He tested the door. It was locked.

The vintage Mustang convertible was waiting for him on the drive. He flipped through his keys until he found his copy and then slid in behind the steering wheel. Jessie's keys were already in the ignition.

"And Mom was worried about locking the house up," he murmured. He turned the key and the little car roared to life. Jason's heart raced with the engine. He contemplated taking this car to go and get Lucy, but instead drove it back to the garage and locked it inside.

"Maybe later," he told himself as he got into the VW and headed down the drive.

3 An Enemy Identified

"There!"

His Majesty King Tersan d'Jeleste, Lord of the Western Marches, Commander of the Armies, and the Hand that Wields the Sword looked up the grassy plain leading to the base of Kimala to the place where his standard bearer, Rudlo, gestured. The day was brilliant. Fluffy bright clouds hung in the sky above the mountain. Yet at the point Rudlo marked, a tempest raged.

"I see it, Rudlo," Tersan answered. "Would that we could have come sooner."

He scanned the mountainside from the point of the storm to the place where he sat upon his small grey stallion and then back to the plain that was Jeleste. The horse strained against his reins and pawed at the ground impatient for the battle to begin.

"Not yet, Greystone," he murmured.

Immediately behind him was a host of mounted warriors, their horses snorting and trumpeting. Some of the horses wore heavy plates of armor while others, smaller mounts like Greystone, wore only light chain mail designed to allow the animals to perform swift, precise attacks. The more heavily armored animals formed ranks and ran over the enemy's infantry. Tersan had to be able to move between his companies and either kind of mount would do. He was fond of this particular stallion. The horse had instincts.

The mounted Jelestine companies were divided into three sections, a cavalry captain at the head of each. In the distance, the infantry marched to join them, their shields glinting in the noonday sun. By Tersan's estimate, it would be near nightfall before they arrived at the site of the tempest. Unseen behind the infantry, a small caravan of healers traveled. Light flashed in the tempest and shortly afterward, ominous thunder rattled the air around them, demanding the king's attention. A decision had to be made.

"If we wait for the infantry, there is a good chance the Kilmari will be finished by the time we arrive," he mused. "If we proceed, we risk putting the horsemen on the ground to fight a battle for which they are not fully prepared."

"Yes, my lord," Rudlo answered.

"I am sorry, Eron," he said aloud, "I should have come sooner. Let us hope it is not too late." He turned to Rudlo. "I have chosen our path. Send word. There is no time to wait for the infantry."

Tersan nudged his horse into a gallop while Rudlo trumpeted to the infantry. Behind him, the cavalry fell into a well-ordered line.

They closed the open distance to the base of the mountain in a matter of minutes, slowing just before they entered the woods. There, a woman waited, mounted on a small horse, with sturdy legs and coarse hair. A tight smile graced her sweat-stained face.

"Tersan!" she cried, omitting his title. "At last!"

"My lady Pixil," Tersan began formally, "in the name of the kingdom of Jeleste, I present you my allegiance. Upon my sword, we shall join your fight against your enemies. We have come to the aid of the Kilmari at Lord Eron's request--"

"There is no time for words of chivalry," she interrupted. "This way!" She spun her horse back into the forest. Tersan followed.

The path was narrow and steep but the footing was good. Tersan rode beside her at an easy trot.

"Eron's messenger only asked that we come in all haste," he stated. "What happened?"

"Sword and Shield laid a trap to catch Fot, greatest of all demons. They did so in the portal room that leads to the Shield's world. The risk was great, but the reward was greater." She smiled grimly. "Fot is not among the demons."

"Demons?" Tersan asked. "It appears the old stories are true. Is this Fot dead?"

"That is unknown. To kill him would require a great deal of power. However, he is easily recognizable. We can assume that Sword and Shield have captured him as they have captured others." She paused, her face grim. "We know not the fate of Defender or Protector."

"Eron and the Otherworlder?"

"Yes. We waited outside the portal for a signal. But we were not entirely prepared."

"What happened?"

"A swarm of demons rushed the entry. We did not have time to set the wards to block them."

Tersan nodded. The rhythm of his horse's hooves sent waves of energy through him. He was ready.

"Tocar led an elite force of Kilmari to retake the portal," she continued. "We saw an exodus of demons, and the swarm was turned back on our forces. The portal was retaken." Pixel paused. "I have had no contact with Tocar for more than a day. From the patterns of the fight, we know they still hold the entry and no clear successor to Fot has emerged. As planned, this chaos works to our advantage."

"We fight an undisciplined enemy?"

"Exactly. They have no established leader and without such, they struggle for power as individuals, not as a cohesive force. I am certain that is the only reason they have not breached the portal and most probably, why we still live." Her grim smile returned. "Our forces are not large enough to mount an outright offensive, so we have resorted to guerilla warfare tactics. But with your help, we can put an end to this."

"This portal leads to the Otherworld?"

Pixil nodded. "And to other places of power as well. We cannot allow the demons access to either. Tocar and his men are gifted warriors and he knows how to use their skills, but they are still men and men have limitations. They cannot last indefinitely."

Tersan nodded. "Eron took on the mantle of the Sword, once a symbolic title, to protect the kingdoms of Eormengrund from demonkind. Up until now, I still believed demons to be the fodder of legend."

"Ahleri opened the door. Wulfhaeled began the fight after him. For good or for evil, we now deal with the consequences of our greatest defenders' actions."

Tersan glanced down at the steel plated armor he wore, decorated with winged serpents in gold and then looked at Pixil. The Kilmari queen wore leather jerkins that offered little protection against anything. It was a wonder any of them survived.

They reached a meadow and fanned out in it, letting the horses take a small break. A stream flowed down the middle, merrily gurgling over river rocks in its course. Tersan crossed it with Pixil at his side and together they rode up a small rise. For the first time he saw the almost invisible silver circlet on her brow indicating her rank. Pixil was a queen but she was also a soldier. Things were certainly different in Kimala.

The tempest was much closer now. Tersan estimated they had come more than halfway in a very short time. Four mounted Kilmari broke through the timber to greet them. Their leader was a young man who looked remarkably like Pixil.

"Lady," he said, his head dipped in respect.

"Cynthal," she replied. "News?"

"Lord Tocar still holds the portal," he answered, "and Prytal was advancing along the eastern line. Elama holds the forces to the west but the southern line I fear is breaking. We tire." He stopped but there was something unspoken on his young face.

"Tersan and I will ride with haste to reinforce the southern line," Pixil said. She tilted her head to one side, her eyebrows raised and her voice soft. "Is there something else?

"Mother, Eron…" He steeled himself. "Eron has fallen."

Pixil sat up straighter in her saddle. "You are certain?" she said.

Cynthal nodded. "Through his vision both his seneschal, Parry, and Tocar saw the demon Fot imprisoned. Lord Eron was offering prayer to the Lady when Fot launched a final attack from within his bonds."

"Fot attacked when Eron was praying?" Tersan said, his eyes wide.

"Yes, your Majesty," Cynthal answered. "There is no honor for the Lady among demons."

"To some, honor has no place on a battlefield, my son," Pixil said, "nor does overconfidence or arrogance. Eron made a grave error. You do not give thanks to the Goddess for delivery from your enemy when your enemy has not yet been delivered."

Cynthal nodded to his mother, then turned to Tersan. "My Lord, you have come in our darkest hour."

"You have indeed, Tersan," Pixil agreed. "We must go on the offensive now," she stated, launching into her attack strategy. "You have three captains?"

"Yes," he answered, "Letou, Astar, and Gorltay."

"Good. Then we shall attack from three sides. Tersan, you and I will take Letou ride straight up to the portal, from the south. Cynthal will take Astar and join forces with Prytal on the eastern line. Parry will take Gorltay to the west to join Elama."

"And who will cover the north? Tocar?" Tersan asked when Pixil said no more.

Pixil shook her head. "Tocar has no other duty than to prevent the demons from breaking through whatever wards he and the Shield managed to establish. We cannot allow the demons access to the mountain. The lake—the lake cannot be accessed."

"What lake, milady?"

Pixil paused. She stared at him carefully assessing something. Tersan stifled the urge to shiver. "No one to the north," she repeated. "We will drive them back to their home."

"We cannot win the war if we do not fight."

"A trapped animal will fight with fury if there is no hope of escape." She let her statement sink in. "We offer them an escape, a way to go home. We minimize our losses and live to fight another day."

"It is not wise to allow your enemy to escape."

"The balance of power has shifted," she answered. "There are other mighty demons but as I have stated, no single demon has yet emerged to take Fot's place. If we allow them to leave they will fight amongst themselves for a while, all vying to become Lord of Demonkind. That gives us an advantage we can use long after this battle is won."

"Removing Fot has sent them into this much chaos?"

"Sword and Shield baited their trap with power," Pixil replied, "power that can be used by anyone. This is the reason they remain here. If one of them can find their way into the portal and retrieve that power, he can use it to elevate himself to fill Fot's position. This will unify them into a force we are not ready to fight. We cannot allow that to happen. Their continued chaos is our goal."

The tempest darkened the sky in front of them. Men's and women's voices cried out in the distance, but Tersan could not distinguish bravado from fear.

"Tersan, Your knowledge of demonkind is somewhat lacking, but you are well versed in the fighting ways of men," Pixil acknowledged quietly.

"We are." He looked straight ahead, knowing what he had to admit. "But we have never faced this enemy before, not even in lore."

"Understood." Pixil cleared her throat. "Demons are difficult to kill. An arrow point blank to the eye, mouth, nose or ear will likely kill. Anywhere else only wounds them."

"Point blank?" Tersan repeated.

"They are not human, Tersan," she said. "Arrows from a distance are like hailstones to them. They are annoying but do little damage."

Tersan nodded. "Each man in the cavalry was once in the infantry. We will adapt."

"Good. Swordsmen will do slightly more damage. Puncture wounds are more effective than cuts. The demons have remarkable recuperative powers and can heal themselves in minutes."

"How do you deal with such an invincible enemy?" Tersan asked.

"As I have said, we let them go so they fight amongst themselves." She pointed to the swirling cloud. "We have never faced so many at once, in recent memory or in lore." She let that sink in. "The time has come. Say your farewells."

Tersan turned Greystone to face his troops. They waited quietly for his address as Tersan galloped the length of the cavalry He returned to a spot in the middle where his captains waited.

"Men of Jeleste," he began, "we ride into Kimala to face an enemy that is not even known to us in legend. However, your skills as warriors will defeat them. An effective wound is into their eyes, ears, noses or mouths with arrows, swords or knives. A strike to the body may wound, but will not kill."

Tersan was met with silence and steely-eyed glances. There was no fear in them.

"We do not seek their deaths, we only wish to drive them from this mountain. Their master has been taken and without him, they fight as individuals. Because there will be no organized attack, we have the advantage."

"We will create a corridor to the north, an open passage to send them home," Pixil told them. "There, they can and will fight amongst themselves until a leader emerges, leaving us in peace and able to better establish our defenses. So, when they head to the north, let them go.""

Tersan pointed to his captains one by one. "Astar, go with Cynthal, Letou, with Lady Pixil and myself. Gorltay, you will accompany Parry. We will drive the demons from this land!"

A cheer went up from the ranks and Tersan pointed to the dark cloud. He reined the little stallion in tightly. The horse reared and plunged as he pivoted in the air, nostrils flaring. The king drew his sword and led his men into the tempest.

4 Gathering Lucy

Jason turned right onto the winding highway at the end of Jessie's long drive. Winifred James lived in a small cottage on Jessie's grounds. He wasn't certain if she rented it from Jessie or if she had some kind of long term lease on it or if she was simply a guest. Now that he was in control of Jessie's finances, he would be able to find out.

"Not that it will change anything," he said aloud.

He made another right onto a gravel drive, then drove up a short hill to the white cottage. Lucy was sitting on the front porch reading her cherished book and probably dreaming of dances and runaway slaves.

"Some things never change," Jason muttered as he got out of the car. "Lucy!"

"Jason!" She jumped up and ran for him, throwing her arms around his neck in a great hug. "Mom said you would be coming to get me if she couldn't."

"Yeah," he answered, his mind flashing back to the kitchen, "she left me a rather cryptic note."

"Cryptic?"

"You know, short."

"Oh. Yeah. I knew that." She looked sad.

Jason grinned. "Been having fun then?" he asked.

"Well, I like Miss James and I don't mind her snakes," she answered as though trying to convince herself, "but I'd rather be with Aunt Martha and Uncle Ted."

"And Anna and Kenny?"

She grinned. "Yeah. Only I wish we could play at my house." She leaned over and motioned for him to come close so she could whisper a secret. "I've found a new tunnel!" she said excitedly. "It's almost right under the house--"

"Don't you dare take them into one of those tunnels!" Jason exclaimed.

"Oh Jason," she said. "You're such a baby. Just because you got stuck last year—"

"Stuck? I nearly got killed! I was running out of air when they found me."

"There was plenty of air in there," she replied. "You just got scared."

"Any normal person would have been scared," he countered.

"I thought it was kind of fun," she said.

"That makes one of us." He frowned at her. "Those tunnels are dangerous, Lucy. Haven't you figured that out?"

"You sound like Mom."

Jason shrugged. "Why don't you go get your things and I'll settle up with Miss James. Then we can get going," he said. He leaned over and whispered in her ear, "I don't like snakes either."

Lucy giggled. She ran into the house. Jason followed.

"Miss James! Miss James, Jason is here!"

"So soon?" An older woman appeared in the doorway to the kitchen, dishtowel in hand. "Come in, Jason, come in!"

Jason followed her inside. He looked around the room, hoping he wouldn't see what he knew he would see. A great white snake basked in artificial light on a piece of driftwood beside the fireplace. Except that his eyes remained open, he looked asleep.

"How good to see you!"

Jason smiled politely. "Good to see you, too, Miss James," he said.

"I'll be right back," Lucy called from the stairway. She thundered up the steps and disappeared.

"Ah, you youngsters have such energy!" Miss James said. "Would you like a cookie? Just out of the oven, still warm."

Jason bit his lip. Miss James was a great sitter, but usually a lousy cook. "Maybe just one," he said, not wishing to be impolite.

"Fine! Come in here and I'll pour you a glass of milk to go along with it." She walked back into the kitchen and Jason followed.

The cookies sat on the countertop, chocolate oozing from the center of each one. It smelled like they might be reasonably good. Miss James motioned for him to sit. She placed one of her treats on a plate, poured him a glass of milk and put her offerings in front of him. He nibbled at the cookie. Salty, but not bad.

"How is it?" she asked. The look on her face was priceless.

"New recipe?" he asked, reaching slowly for the milk. He took a couple polite sips, wanting to down the whole glass.

"Yes. I'm trying it out."

Jason nodded. "They're pretty good, but I think the recipe calls for a little too much salt."

"Oh dear," she said. She took one of the cookies and tasted it herself. Her brow crinkled as she rolled it around in her mouth trying to dissect the ingredients.

"Can I take a few home to Kenny and Anna?" he asked a little quickly.

Miss James nearly burst with pride. "Why of course you can!" She busied herself putting some of the cookies in a paper bag. With a wink, she handed them to him. "My ego does not bruise that easily, Jason," she said, still smiling.

"No, they really are good!" Jason protested. "Just a little salty."

"There is nothing better than honesty from a young person," she answered, pushing the milk toward him. "I appreciate it."

Jason ate the rest of the cookie quickly and drained the remainder of the milk. He started to wipe his mouth on the sleeve of his shirt, but Miss James offered him a napkin to use instead. "Thanks," he said.

"You are welcome." She picked up her salty treat and studied it. Her look was so intense that Jason nearly laughed. Lucy was banging around upstairs. She would be back soon.

"Miss James, do you know where my aunt is?" he asked.

Miss James put the cookie to one side. "Jessie's gone on a sort of vacation," she said rather sadly. She was choosing her words very carefully, speaking slowly.

Jason took the note out his pocket and handed it to her. "She left me that note," he said. He pointed to the red smudge. "Mom says that's probably paprika or something," he continued. "I thought it looked like blood."

Miss James nodded but she did not laugh nor did she smile as she read the note. "Your mother is a wise woman, Jason," she said. She handed the note back. "Jessie told me she might be gone for quite a long time. She asked me to keep an eye on her house. It looks like she told you the same thing."

"Yeah, but where'd she go? She's got a cell phone. Why didn't she call?"

"Maybe she did not want to be disturbed," she said kindly. "I cannot answer your questions, Jason. Please, do not mention your fears to your cousin. You would only worry her. She has a very active imagination and she would think the worst."

"Yeah, I've noticed." Jason sighed.

Lucy popped into the kitchen with a small backpack. Clothes were sticking out of the pockets along with her old book. She stood in the doorway. "Thanks, Miss James!" she said. "I'm going to stay with Aunt Martha and Uncle Ted for a while. Call me if you hear from Mom?"

"I will, dear," Miss James said, "and you do the same!"

"Okay. C'mon, Jason!"

Jason followed his cousin as she bounced out the door. "Thanks, Miss James," he called over his shoulder. "Send me a bill?" he said with a shrug.

"Of course, dear."

5 The Battle for the Portal

It was difficult to travel quickly through the woods, constantly swerving and slowing to avoid trees, but Tersan kept moving, managing a steady canter. From deep in the forest, bows twanged, steel clashed against scale, and the screams of the dying supplanted all the calming sounds of nature. They were about to burst from the forest into the field of battle when Tersan halted them. A few quick gestures, and the ranks spread out into a line, four horsemen deep and fifty wide. Around him, the royal guard prepared for the coming fight, tightening buckles and adjusting saddles, reseating their lances and loosening their swords in their sheaths.

"Pixil," Tersan started, "send word to have your people retreat into the forest when they see my standard."

Pixil sat silent on her horse for a few brief moments watching him. "Doing so leaves Tocar and the portal vulnerable."

"Your men have fought long and hard and need respite, if only to retreat to the trees to provide archery support. Our defenses will not be broken, just different."

Pixil slowly nodded. "Understood." She disappeared into the forest.

With a gesture to Rudlo, Tersan pressed his heels lightly into Greystone's sides. The stallion lunged forward in a motion so practiced, it was as easy as breathing.

Behind them, the solid wall of horseflesh and warriors formed ranks that had never been broken. Tersan had just enough time to note the relieved look on a Kilmari face before his cavalry burst through the lines of the beleaguered defenders and slammed, full tilt, into the lines of the enemy.

The first thing the king noticed was the stench. The scent of a hundred herbs overwhelmed his olfactory sense, mixed in with the stink of rotting meat and, above all the rest, the smell of lavender and garlic. Screwing up his face against this most unusual assault, he swung his sword hard at a hideous, scaled head.

The razor-sharp steel bounced off the hard scales, jarring the king's arm. The blow would have easily sliced through flesh and bone, but instead the impact nearly jerked his sword out of his hand. The demon cocked his head and Tersan could have sworn there was a smirk on his ugly face. It lashed out with a grey hand, black talons reaching for Tersan's face. The king parried instinctively, smacking the talons aside with the edge of his blade. The demon howled, a furious battle cry. It hurled itself at Tersan, its wings spreading to engulf its prey. Ducking a second swipe, Tersan caught the scaled wrist in his gauntleted hand. The motion propelled him forward into the face of his adversary. He thrust the tip of his blade into the demon's left eye. The hideous creature howled again, and this time Tersan knew it was with pain. He yanked his sword free and stabbed into its other eye. The demon threw itself to the ground, bucking and convulsing as it shriveled up and died.

Tersan glanced around, taking in the battle in one quick glance. His men were fighting hard, split into knots of five or six taking on single demons. Already at least a dozen armor-clad bodies lay unmoving on the grass, their mounts racing to the relative safety of the forest. From the trees, the Kilmari sent wave upon wave of arrows into the fray. The assault had little effect.

"Sound withdrawal!" he shouted to Rudlo. A second later, the trumpet rang clear across the battlefield, and the cavalrymen turned their horses around. In an odd dance, they galloped as fast as they could back to the tree line, leaping over fallen comrades and a very few shriveled black husks that once were demons.

"Tersan! What are you doing?" Pixil rode up alongside him, her face screwed up with fury.

"Keep your men in the trees!" he yelled at her.

They pushed passed the Kilmari defense and crashed into the underbrush of the forest. He could hear their jeers and cries of dismay, but he had to ignore them. This was war and he had to use his forces to everyone's best advantage or they would be lost. He hauled back on his reins and his stallion's hooves skidded in the deep loam of the woods as he spun the horse around.

"Reform on me!" he shouted, as the horse beneath him pranced in place. It took no more than a minute for his men to reform their line. It was shorter now than it had been bare moments ago. Gritting his teeth, Tersan raised his sword. How much shorter would it be by the end of the day?

"Forward!" he shouted. Rudlo's trumpet repeated his command, and off to his right, somewhere in the deep woods, a second Jelestine trumpet sounded.

They charged through the Kilmari defenses and the jeers became cheers. From the west, Gorltay led the second flank of the cavalry, an attack the demons were not expecting. The enemy turned, a disorganized mass of confusion, to face this new foe. They had no plan. Tersan allowed himself a wry smile.

Again they fought, and again they withdrew. On the third charge, Astar joined them, and they hit three sides of the enemy at once. As one, the three arms of Tersan's cavalry charged then retreated, then charged again. With each attack, more armored bodies remained behind, but the number of black husks beside them was steadily growing. The demons broke their relentless attack on the portal, spreading themselves more thinly across the battlefield now, their tactics changing from offensive to survival relying on only their strength without a battle plan. The portal's Kilmari guard was now visible, a group of five or six men, heavily armed with swords that seemed to be dipped in fire. More and more scaled bodies leapt into the sky and fled to the north.

"They're breaking!" Astar called. "By the Lady, they're breaking!"

Years of studying battle tactics and practicing skirmishes taught Tersan to continue this strategy. Fewer of his men fell with each charge and the way north was becoming dark with fleeing demons. As they pounded their foe for the sixth time, the number of fleeing demons diminished and the remainder were becoming organized. In the heat of battle, they appeared to have chosen a leader. The tide of the battle shifted in their favor due to the prowess of an individual demon. Tersan gritted his teeth and prepared himself for a change in tactics that could end this battle if he succeeded or end his life if he failed.

On the seventh charge, Tersan ducked low over Greystone's neck, plunging directly into the densest gathering of demons, where the only battle savvy enemies surrounded their newly appointed leader.

Black wings beat all around him, but he drove his mount toward the very center of the swarm. Ahead of him, the largest demon he had yet seen turned its full attention to this one insolent threat. In a single motion, it reared back, and swiveled to face Tersan fully. It paused to let out a deafening war cry. In that moment, king and horse slammed into the beast.

Tersan's sword had all the weight and momentum of a racing war-horse behind it. He stabbed at the demon's chest, and felt the scales break this time under the impact. The steel slid deep into the creature and stabbed out the other side.

The demon roared in agony and tried to pull the sword out of its chest, yanking it instead out of Tersan's hand. Its head jerked backward and came down with tremendous force, trying to snare the King in its teeth. Tersan shifted quickly to one side in time to save himself from the lethal blow. The demon's tooth pierced the golden breastplate and ripped a superficial slash across his flesh. Tersan wrestled his dagger from its sheath as the demon threw his head back, jerking Tersan out of his saddle. The demon flung his head back and forth violently shaking the king like a child's toy in a dog's mouth. With a well-timed slash, Tersan cut through the tethers of his breastplate, freeing himself from the demon and landing just behind the demon's head.

The huge creature lurched and flapped its wings desperately, trying to reach Tersan, but the king held on, waiting one more time for opportunity to present itself. The demon turned its head toward Tersan. The king buried his dagger to the hilt into the monster's eye and gave it a vicious twist. Black blood spurted from the wound. Tersan prepared to take out the other eye, but the creature jerked away from him and he fell to the ground with a jolt. With one last lurch of its wings, the demon died.

For a moment, the battleground fell silent. Then, with a dreadful, keening wail, the demons broke. The darkness of hundreds of wings turned the sky black, stealing the light of day. Tersan ducked instinctively as the fleeing force churned up the dust of the battlefield. Then the sun burst onto his face. The battle was done. Tersan hauled himself upright and surveyed his surroundings.

Scattered here and there, were perhaps two dozen black-scaled husks that were once demons. At least a hundred men lay dead around him. Bodies of great horses lay dead and wounded in the open field, some standing pathetically like quivering statues, waiting for direction. The Kilmari queen was right. The world had new enemies in it and he needed to learn their ways. He was certain he would face them again.

Tersan gathered Greystone's reins and led him away from the fallen demon. He paused to pat the steed on the neck and briskly checked for injuries. The horse was not visible injured. He tossed his head, ready for more.

"Not today, Greystone," he said, rubbing his mount's neck gently. "Rudlo!"

The standard bearer appeared before him, on foot and leading his own uninjured mount.

"Go and tend the horses," Tersan said as he himself prepared to tend the human wounded.

"Are you certain, sire?"

"Yes." He smiled grimly. "No one else has your skills."

"As you wish, sire." He took Greystone's reins and led him away.

"Astar!" Tersan called.

"Astar has fallen," someone answered.

The news hit him like the stench of a demon but he would mourn later. "Letou!"

"Here, my lord."

Tersan looked at his captain. He was standing, but only barely. Blood covered his face and his flesh hung away from his left arm. "Lie down," Tersan snapped. "Gorltay!"

"Sir?" The silver haired man was free of his helmet and still held his bloodied broadsword in his hand.

From the edges of the forest, the Jelestine infantry was pouring. The enemy was gone, now. There was no one left to fight. But the wounded...the wounded were many.

"Clear a place for the Healers from Bel Haven. Organize the men to bring the wounded to them on this side of the field and the dead--" he paused to take in a huge breath. "Take the dead to the other. Remember them to a man. None are without families."

"Yes, sire."

"Then prepare a funeral pyre."

Gorltay started barking orders to the captains of the infantry. Jelestine and Kilmari responded to his commands and moments later, chaos turned to order. Tersan had chosen his captains well. Now, he had his own work to do. He moved to help the wounded.

He started across the short distance to Letou. As he moved, his chain mail raked against his chest, aggravating his wound. It was annoying, but there was little bleeding from it. He could assess it later. Others had greater needs.

Letou lay in the dwindling shade of a huge tree, his page fidgeting nervously at his side. The lad had stripped his master's armor off and was looking helpless.

"Give me your shirt, son," he said to the boy.

Obediently, the lad removed his shirt. Tersan wiped the black blood off his dagger and used it to tear the garment into strips which he used to bind Letou's arm. He pulled the cloth tight around the mass of torn muscles until they once again resembled a limb. There was not much blood loss. In that respect, his captain had been lucky. Still, he would more than likely lose his arm.

"There are others whose needs are greater," Letou said as he pulled the wounded arm across his chest.

"Lie still," Tersan instructed him. "The healers are coming. You," he said to the page. "Go to the healer's wagon and get him a blanket."

"Yes, your majesty," He scurried off and quickly returned with a blanket. Letou stared straight ahead. Tersan knew he was reviewing the battle.

"There will be time for evaluation later, Captain," he said. He clapped him gently on his good shoulder and left him in the care of his page.

Between the wounded and the dying, the king of Jeleste walked, praising all, offering what comfort he could. Some looked at him with gratitude as they slipped from this world into the next. Tersan closed their eyes and offered prayers to the Lady for their safe passage and for the families they left behind.

The healers of Bel Haven swarmed through the wounded that Gorltay had organized. A priestess of the Lady walked among the dying, offering compassion. She knelt with Kilmari and Jelestine alike, preparing them for their journeys. Master Penrose, First Healer of Bel Haven, had brought her and Tersan was glad that he did.

When there were no more souls in need of prayer, Tersan left the wounded. He would return to them later. Now, he had another task to attend to.

The king found the body of Astar lying under the massive branches of an ancient tree. His captain's head had been severed but his men had replaced it. Tersan knelt beside the fallen soldier and offered a prayer of thanks for the life of this man.

"Build a funeral pyre," he said to Astar's honor guard of one Kilmari and five Jelestines who had been posted there by some unknown authority. None wore the fallen captain's livery. Not far from him, his page also lay lifeless. Tersan retrieved the boy and laid him beside his captain. "They deserve the honor of being sent to the Lady on the field where they died for her people."

"Yes, sire."

Tersan regarded the two one last time. The sun was low on the horizon, casting pale pink light on the captain's armor. His golden hair surrounded a face that had not aged enough. Astar would not easily be replaced. None of them would be.

With a sigh, Tersan looked up to the small opening in the side of the mountain that they had successfully defended. A tall man with black hair dressed in the Kilmari's traditional black leather was circling the portal, his lips moving silently.

"Eron?" Tersan said though he was too distant from the man to realistically be heard.

The Kilmari queen suddenly appeared at his side. "No," Pixil answered. "He is Prince Tocar. They are brothers."

"Brothers? In all the time Eron and I spent together, he never mentioned he had a brother," Tersan said. He sighed. "I suppose that Eron is a prince, too?"

"No." Pixil gave a short laugh. "Eron was King, until he decided to become Sword. That is when he abdicated to me."

"King? Eron? He never mentioned that, either."

"The fact that he was once king does not alter what he has become."

"And you are his sister?" Tersan asked. The conversation was starting to give him a headache, something the battle and the carnage had not succeeded in doing.

"No," Pixil answered. "In fact, we are only distantly related."

"Your ways are strange, indeed." He watched Tocar for a moment, determined not to ask any more questions that would lead to confusing answers. The Kilmari prince kept circling the hole, his hands moving up and down as he silently spoke. "Has he lost his mind?" Tersan muttered, knowing he would get an explanation.

"No," she said patiently. "He is replacing the wards on the portal room."

"Wards?" Tersan asked, instantly sorry that he did. He asked for an explanation and Pixil was going to give it to him. He hoped it would be short.

Pixil gave him a sidelong look. "You do not have wards in Jeleste?" she asked.

"Not that I am aware of," he answered. "There seems to be much about Kimala that I neither know nor understand. Perhaps one day you will enlighten me?" he asked, hoping to avoid the coming lecture.

"A ward is a barrier of energy." She paused. There was more to her explanation; he could see that. But there was something else that she wanted to say.

"Your ways are not familiar to me," Tersan said, trying to be neutral. A wave of reproach struck him. He should have accepted Eron's invitation to visit Kimala. He had gone to Calshara and Marand's city of Il Chatel. But he had not been to Kimala.

"We will gladly teach you our ways." She nodded to the hole Tocar was still warding. "And you must teach us yours as well. I was uncertain of your tactics." She looked him straight in the eye. "I thought you retreated to save yourselves. I was wrong."

"Your people held the line while we reformed to mount an effective offensive," he said. "I regret that there was no time apprise them of the battle plan."

"As do I." She flashed him a smile. "But we did adapt."

Tersan almost breathed a sigh of relief as he returned her smile. "You did indeed."

"Tersan," she started again, looking out at the healers as they continued to tend to the wounded in the field below them, "I owe you my thanks. Had you not come, I fear...I fear we would have fallen."

"We should not have left you alone so long," Tersan said. The demon's horrid smell resurged in his memory. "The enemy you fight would turn his attention to Jeleste if Kimala ever fell."

"Let us hope that day will never come." She turned toward the mountain and pointed to a place where four Kilmari worked alongside three Jelestines. They were waving to the pair to join them. "Come. The way to the portal room has been cleared. I fear what lies in its depths."

He turned to accompany her and she stopped. With one hand, she pulled back his chain mail and jerkin to expose the demonic wound.

"It is nothing," he told her.

"Perhaps you should look again."

Tersan looked down at his ribs. A crusty scab had formed over the wound but black pus oozed all around it. It smelled a little of lavender and a lot of rotten flesh. Tersan's jaw dropped.

"You have many things to learn, Majesty," she said. "The poison has an easy antidote." She pulled a small pouch from her belt and gestured to a large uprooted tree. "Sit, please."

Tersan sat.

"It is a simple balm," she explained. She applied a thin layer of the ointment. It foamed up on the wound, instantly turning the black pus to a clear gelatin. With a small piece of cloth, she wiped the length of the cut, removing the pus, scab and horrid smell with a single swipe. Then she handed the balm to Tersan. "If you see any more of that pus, apply this again. Demon venom is treacherous," she warned. "Even a small amount can claim the life of even the greatest warrior."

"Thank you," he said, tucking her gift away.

"You are welcome." Her face turned grave. "Now, come. Tocar is waiting."

6 To the McCarthy House

Lucy switched the radio on and cranked up the volume until the old speakers crackled in protest. She was singing just loud enough to be heard and was so far off-pitch that Jason nearly cringed. Instead, he turned the volume down and put the car in gear.

"Don't you like my music?" Lucy asked.

"I like it just fine, as long as I can actually hear it," he answered.

"You're such an old fogey. I bet you'd rather hear one of those old musicals like Mom likes."

"'Old fogey'?"

"That's what Miss James says. She likes my music."

"I'd rather listen to something that at least has a melody." He grinned at her. "But I don't really care. Pick whatever you like; just don't blow my speakers. I don't have the money to get new ones."

"Oh. Sorry."

"How long have you been at Miss James'?" he asked.

"Since last night." She flipped open her book and started studying the pictures. "Mom said she had something really important she had to do."

"Yeah. It looks like she'll be gone a while."

"She travels a lot, you know, and sometimes, I get to go, too. But she's been acting funny--you know, different."

"Different how?" Jason asked. The note was barely a bulge in his breast pocket but it felt oddly heavy. He shifted in his seat. The feeling didn't go away.

"Kind of sad, I guess."

She opened her book again but he could tell she wasn't reading it. "I hate it when she goes away like this and leaves me behind!" she blurted out. "I'm not a little kid anymore!"

"I feel the same way, Lu," Jason said.

"She's always running away like that and then we don't hear from her for weeks. It isn't fair!"

"Didn't you just say that you get to go with her a lot?"

"Yeah, but not since Christmas!"

Jason sighed. "Your mom's not an average mother by any stretch."

"I wish she'd grow up." She looked at the road ahead of them. "My friends' mothers won't let them come and stay with me because they say she's so unpredictable," she continued. "All the kids in school think I'm weird because she's weird."

"She's had a very different life, that's for sure," Jason agreed.

"You mean because of me?" Lucy was looking at him again.

"No. Mom says you're every mother's dream child."

"For all the good it does." She slumped in her seat and pouted. "I don't get it. I get good grades, and don't cause any trouble. I help her with her computer and I don't ask for much."

"You always ask for a horse," Jason reminded her.

"Yeah, but she's never caved on that one. I did get riding lessons, though. I'm a good rider."

"So I've been told." He downshifted the car to get up a hill. "Miss James hinted that she knows where Jessie is."

"She's in Eormengrund with my father," Lucy blurted out. "He's been hurt and she has to be with him for a while."

"Eormengrund? I thought that was a fantasy land she made up for bedtime stories and the like."

"It's real. I've been there." She turned her head and stared out the window. "Miss James got a phone call in the middle of the night."

"And you listened?"

"That house is too small not to hear everything." She fidgeted. "When Miss James realized I'd been listening, she told me about my father, that he'd been hurt in Eormengrund." A sigh escaped the thirteen year old. "Daddy and I haven't done much together. That was supposed to change when Mom got back this time. She said he would be coming with her and then maybe staying."

"Uh huh," Jason said.

Jason stilled the urge to ask anything else. His mother would be better suited to address this. Jessie's obsession with this fantasy land to the extent that she included Lucy in it and had even invented a father for her made him angry. They were getting close to Jessie's house.

"Do you need anything else?" he asked.

Lucy shrugged. "'Depends on how long Mom's gone. It's only Saturday and I packed enough clothes for a couple days. Aunt Martha can bring me back next week if Mom's not home by then."

"You know she won't be," Jason said.

"I can always hope." She sighed. "I guess that's why I don't have a horse."

"What?"

"There'd be no one home to take care of it."

"Oh." He drove past Jessie's driveway.

The remaining half an hour to Martha and Ted McCarthy's home was spent in comfortable silence. Jason tried unsuccessfully to ignore Lucy's awful singing. Jessie didn't have the voice of an angel, but at least she could sing on pitch. Lucy must have her father's genes when it came to music.

Finally, Jason turned on to Bellington Place. He drove past the carefully maintained homes until he got to a white two-story home with a minivan and a very nice sedan in the drive.

"Dad got a new car," Jason said jealously.

"He does that a lot," Lucy answered.

"It's a tax write-off." Jason switched the VW off and handed Lucy Miss James' cookies. He got out, opened the trunk and shouldered Lucy's backpack for her before reaching for the small bag she also had. He felt rather like a bell hop at some hotel, but it was the proper thing to do for a lady, even a young one.

"Thanks, Jason," Lucy said.

A woman stood at the front door, waiting for them. "Lucy!" she called. Martha McCarthy opened her arms wide as Lucy raced toward her. She embraced her niece then gathered her son into a hug.

"Ted?" she called through the open door. "Ted, come and get Lucy's things, will you?"

"I can take them upstairs, Mom," Jason said.

"That's very sweet of you, Jason," she replied. "We were just about to sit down to dinner. Can you join us?"

"Miss James sent dessert." Lucy hand the paper bag to her aunt. "Jason told her there's too much salt in them."

"Jason!" Martha looked critically at her son.

"She said it was a new recipe," he replied sheepishly. "They aren't bad. They're just salty. And I can't stay. Ric's got two computers coming in tonight and I need to get Jessie's things organized."

"I can send food home with you."

"What're we having?"

"Meatloaf and mashed potatoes. Kenny wanted green beans and Anna wanted peas. You can have either." She grinned. "Or both. Sliced tomatoes, sliced onions and a bit of green pepper." She held up the brown bag of cookies. "And cookies for dessert."

"Sounds great," he said. "Is there enough for Ric?"

Martha laughed. "Of course. Lucy, run along to the kitchen and fix yourself a plate."

"Okay, Aunt Martha." She left for the kitchen.

"Mom," Jason started after he was sure Lucy couldn't hear him, "Miss James told Lucy that Jessie and Lucy's father were in Eormengrund and that Lucy's father had been hurt very badly and that Jessie wouldn't be coming home for a while. I wish she wouldn't encourage her to think like that. It's just not right."

Martha paled, but quickly regained her composure. "It was bound to happen, Jason," she said quietly. "I'll talk to her about it."

"Is there something I should know?" he asked.

"No, no, it will be okay. Go on upstairs with Lucy's things. I'll have your food ready when you come back."

Jason took the suitcases to his old bedroom, the last door on the right at the end of the long balcony that overlooked his parent's pristine living room. He always wondered why they needed such a formal place.

They rarely ever used the room, which was just as well. He detested walking to the bathroom at the other end of the hall in his pajamas when there were people around.

When he got back downstairs, he walked into the dining room where most of the family was already eating. "Hi, folks," he said.

"Jason," his father replied.

"Thanks for bringing Lucy!" Anna said. She was so innocent. Jason wondered how long that would last.

"You're welcome."

"She's going to read to us tonight," Kenny said.

"Yes, from that same old story book," Ted said. His eyes were twinkling. "Right, Lucy?"

"Yes, Uncle Ted."

"I'm going to have to read that someday," he told her.

Martha whisked into the room holding a brown paper bag filled to the brim. "Jason, here's your care package," she grinned. "I put some more brownies in it. There really weren't enough cookies to go around."

"Thanks, Mom."

"What's the rush?" Ted asked around a mouthful of meatloaf.

"Jessie asked me to look after her affairs while she's gone and I want to get started," Jason replied. "Ric's got a few customers coming over tonight as well. I can help with the easy stuff."

"Customers. Good." Ted wiped his lips with a paper napkin. "We're barbecuing tomorrow, if you and Ric want to come for dinner. It's almost the beginning of summer, you know."

"It's still spring, Dad," Jason replied with a grin. "You just like to grill."

"True. One o'clock?"

"If we can. I'll call, okay?"

"Okay."

Jason waved a hand at them. "Bye."

"Bye," they said in a disorganized chorus.

Before he reached the front door they were already discussing how they were going to get all the kids to their various schools on Monday morning. He heard his parents laugh at a joke Kenny made up and then ask Lucy about her riding lessons. Things weren't always calm at the McCarthy household, but they were always comfortable.

The air outside was crisp and cool. Winter was not quite ready to release its hold. He placed the bag of food into the VW, turned the engine over and backed out of the drive. In fifteen minutes, he would be home and ready to set Jessie's request into motion.

7 Broken Spirits

By the time Tersan and Pixil reached the portal, it was nearly dark. Below them, the lush green valley was dotted with campfires and funeral pyres. From this distance, it was difficult to tell them apart.

Tocar was walking around the portal in slow, deliberate strides, his hands moving much faster than his body. Tersan saw flickers of light emanating from the prince's fingertips. If he cocked his head just right, he thought he could see an intricate web being woven over the non-descript hole in the mountain. Before he could fully focus, the image was gone. Tocar stopped and stared long and hard into the king's eyes, his hands now frozen as if he had been turned to stone. He wore a strip of cloth around his head, blackened in the near darkness by his own blood. In the starlight, his face was gaunt, dark circles under his eyes. There were other bandages around his limbs and torso, evidence of a hard fought battle. He finally released his stare with a slight nod and resumed his work.

"Tocar?" Pixel asked gently.

"The wards are reset," he answered, his voice thick with exhaustion. "Sword and Shield yet live," he whispered. "My brother has suffered a head wound. Healers have just descended the stair." He let his hands fall to his sides. For a long moment, he stared at his handiwork. "I chose the portal over him."

"You did what you had to do to keep Kimala safe," Pixil replied. She gathered him by his shoulders and eased him to the ground before Tersan could help her.

"Sleep now, cousin," she told him. "It is safe." Obediently, he closed his eyes and slept.

She waved a hand at the woods in front of her and motioned to her own guards. Tocar's small group of men was just barely discernable. They sat on the ground, leaned up against the trees or lay on the cool grass. "See to them," she ordered. "The king and I will go alone from here."

"Yes, milady."

"Tersan?"

"I follow your lead, milady."

The stairs that led to the portal room were uneven and sometimes unseen as they descended. Tersan heard her light footfalls in front of him but could not always see her. Instinct demanded he draw his sword, even in the close quarters within the stairway; trust requested he leave it sheathed. He reached down to place his hand on the hilt, just in case the need was there. But the sword had been lost, inserted through the demon he had defeated and then flung out onto the battlefield. He followed unarmed and uneasy in the darkness.

The stairway was long and steep and bent back on itself at least twice that Tersan counted. Pixil was light on her feet and swift. Though he was having no trouble keeping up with her, he felt the toll the battle had taken on him. The stair broadened and turned one last time, opening into a starlit chamber. Shadows fell on the walls lengthening and shortening in time with the woman sitting on the floor. Slowly, she rocked back and forth, cradling a body in her arms. Light emanated from his head, illuminating her face, a familiar face saturated in grief.

"Jessie?" Tersan asked. She looked up at them, never ceasing her slow rocking motion.

Shadows formed beneath her heavily lidded eyes giving her a gaunt and unhealthy appearance. Tears wetted her cheeks and she did not try to hide them. With a slight nod, she acknowledged their presence before returning her attention to the body she cradled.

A black leather-clad arm flopped limply on the cobblestone floor beside her. The limb moved with her tireless rhythm, but not on its own. Lord Eron, Sword of Kimala and Protector of the Outland, attaché to the Lord of the Western Marches lay pale and deathlike in her arms. Jessie stopped her incessant motion and wept.

"Oh, Jessie," Tersan breathed.

Pixil knelt placed a comforting arm around her. Tersan stood to one side waiting respectfully for her to regain her composure. Just beyond the two women, a slighter man knelt, searching through the small canvas bag of a healer which bore the emblem of his office, First Healer of Bel Haven, the hand that keeps the Shield. At his side was a beautiful young woman Tersan recognized as Sila Atin, his protégé and a Healer of the First Order.

"We are too late," Tersan said softly.

Eron's hand flexed.

"He is not dead!" Jessie yelled. "Help him, Penrose!"

In an instant, both healers knelt on the floor beside Eron.

"Sila, bring me light!" Penrose barked.

Tersan snatched a torch off the wall and made his way over to the group. Sila Atin gave him a curt nod and took the torch from him. She held it above them so her master could see.

"Let go of him, Jessie," Penrose coaxed. "I must see his wounds."

Gently, Jessie eased Eron off of her lap so that he was lying on the floor, flanked by the royalty he served and with whom he was allied. She laid his head gently on a bloodied cloak with her equally bloodied hands.

"There is only one wound," she said flatly. "Fot sliced through his skull and into…into his soul." She smoothed the hair off Eron's forehead. "He couldn't turn the blade away. I--I wasn't fast enough to close…" She shuddered. "I wasn't fast enough..."

"There is no fault," Penrose assured her.

Tersan shifted so that he could see their faces. The source of the eerie light was now clear. A glowing silver stripe ran from the right side of Eron's forehead to a point above his right ear. Penrose reached down to touch it, his hand pausing just over the glow. He pulled his hand back and looked at Jessie.

"I need to know exactly what happened," he said.

KILL ME!

The command reverberated through Tersan's body, nearly throwing him off-balance. He searched the dimly lit room for the voice's owner. Nothing had changed.

"Fot did it with a single stroke," Jessie was saying. "We set the trap. We caught the demon."

"Yes, yes and Eron was wounded. What have you done?" Penrose prodded gently.

"Inside his mind…the wall was fractured…I tried to fix it…"

DID YOU NOT HEAR ME, KING OF JELESTE?

The voice was deafening; no one else heard it.

Eron? Tersan asked in his mind.

KILL ME SO ANOTHER CAN PROTECT OUR PEOPLES!

In an instant, he was entombed in a web of light.

"Did you think I wouldn't hear you?" Jessie snarled. Her words were directed at the Sword.

Let me die!

"Why? So some other guy can take your place?" she snapped back. "Surely we can spare some time now to save you!"

Duty…

Tersan tried to move within the bubble but he was held immobile. His already taxed muscles twitched with the effort it took to fight the energy field. He coaxed himself to relax.

"If you've got enough power to attempt to influence the actions of a king, you've got enough power to heal yourself," she snapped. The others looked confused. "Eron asked Tersan to kill him so that another can take his place. I can't allow that."

"Lady Jessie," Penrose started, "please think about what you are doing."

"You have limits, Lady Jessie," Sila Atin reminded her unkindly. "Your power is for defense, not protection."

"Oh yeah?" Jessie replied. "Watch."

Suddenly the light around Tersan brightened. It came closer to him, sending an uncomfortable wave of prickling energy over his entire being. He struggled now, but he could not move. The web tightened ever so slowly around him, constricting his ribs until he could only take the tiniest of breaths. Blood pounded in his head and he fought to stay conscious.

"Jessie, enough," he heard Penrose say. "He will not harm Eron. You have my word."

"He isn't one of your people, Penrose," she answered. "He isn't bound by your word."

"Then ask him."

Tersan? he heard inside his head.

Won't harm he managed. He heard the sound of a bow being drawn and he saw starlight glint off the tip of Pixil's arrow.

"Enough blood has been shed!" Pixil's muffled voice stated. "Please, Lady Jessie!"

Tersan was suddenly on his hands and knees on the ground. He sucked a huge breath into his aching lungs. The power that nearly crushed him still prickled his skin. It was a power never before used in this way, frightening in its efficiency, a power never before questioned, a power Jessie used with skill and finesse. She was the first Otherworlder to be chosen as Shield. Perhaps they had unleashed a monster. Perhaps, not. Time would tell. He sat on the stone floor and flexed his hands. The sensation slowly dissipated.

She shifted her attention to Penrose. "What now?"

"I must do a reading, enter his mind to assess the damage and determine a course of action."

"He loses control," she whispered. She pointed to a shattered table and chairs that lay crumpled in a corner of the room. As she turned, Tersan noticed an ugly bruise beneath her right eye.

"Eron, I only wish to touch your mind. It is my sworn duty."

Tersan noticed the barest of nods. An instant later, Penrose closed his eyes. Underneath the lids, they were moving violently in every direction. In the stillness of the portal room, it seemed no one took a breath for a long, long time. Finally Penrose jerked away and clutched his forehead. He turned to Sila Atin. "I require palapaca and some yeltin."

"Of course," she answered smoothly. "And heterra?"

"A good idea for later. Retrieve that as well, but not yet. There is an order that must be followed. You know that."

"Yes, my Lord."

Penrose stared after her as she walked over to the stairway to retrieve the large satchel she had left there. He sighed heavily. "She is the best healer in Bel Haven, excluding Aramat and myself. But when it comes to Eron, her heart rules her mind. She never got over losing him to an Otherworlder."

"Or not becoming the Shield. She lost that to an Otherworlder, too. She can be a real pest." Jessie leaned over and whispered something in Eron's ear. He nodded. She reached under her bodice and pulled out a crystal filled with brilliant lights. She handed it to Penrose. "This is the power that lured Fot here," she said. "Keep it safe. Use it as you see fit."

Penrose tucked it under his shirt.

Sila returned with a small jar of ointment which she handed to Penrose. Then she positioned herself opposite Jessie by Eron's head.

"Thank you, Sila," Penrose told her. "Tersan, secure his shoulders, please. Sila, I need you here beside me to assist."

Sila shifted away from Eron's head behind the healer to a place closer to his waist.

"Jessie, you need to remove your bandage. Demon venom is in the wound and it must be purged."

"Without it, he'll bleed to death!" Jessie protested.

"Who is the healer?" Penrose asked calmly. "The palapaca will neutralize the venom and the yeltin will stop the bleeding."

"You're sure?"

"Yes. Now, please."

Jessie sat back on her heels, arms outstretched in front of her, palms up. Eron's jaw clenched and both of his hands balled into fists. Slowly, she pulled her hands back toward herself. Blood spurted into Tersan's face.

"Remove your bandage very slowly, Jessie," Penrose coached. "It is tearing flesh with it."

"Okay."

Penrose deftly applied palapaca, then yeltin to the wound as the silver tendrils flowed back toward Jessie. He smeared the ointment from the inside of the wound to the outside, briefly exposing the blackened edges. As he worked, black turned to red. Eron jerked under Tersan's hands, but the king held him still.

The room crackled with golden power as Eron lashed out with his mind. The broken wardrobe took to the air and crashed beside Sila. Splintered pieces of wood scattered across the floor and neatly folded clothing flew across the room taking on the appearance of wraiths. Sila screamed and moved closer to Penrose until she almost touched him. She held the jar of yeltin steadily in her hands though her face was white with fear.

"Yeltin," he yelled over the din. Sila Atin held the yeltin. "Tersan, hold him! It will only take a moment!"

Tersan put his full weight behind his grip and still Eron writhed. Penrose shifted so that he was above Eron's head with his right hand over Eron's ear. He wedged the Sword's head between his own knee and hand. Eron bucked under Tersan's hands and snatched his hand away from Jessie. He was mouthing words that Tersan did not understand.

"No!" Jessie yelled. She raised her hands but before she could start to do anything, Pixil stopped her.

"Give them a chance, Jessie," she said, holding the slighter woman's hands at her sides.

"He's going to kill them!" Jessie screamed. "Let me go!"

"Patience!" Pixil said sternly.

"He's calling for the Sword so he can defend himself!"

"Give Penrose a chance!" the queen commanded.

Eron stopped struggling and lay still. His breathing returned to normal and he relaxed under Tersan's grip. Penrose continued his work, meticulously applying the yeltin to the wound, pressing the edges together until they held and all that was left of the once gaping skin was a thin red line. Penrose ran his fingers the length of the wound, methodically checking for seepage.

After what seemed an eternity, Penrose smiled. "That worked better than I imagined." He turned his attention to Jessie. "I do not believe we will be long without the Sword, my Lady," he told her. "Your work inside his mind was exceptional. But it is good that he stopped you."

"I would give everything to save him."

"I know," Penrose answered. He gave his patient one last critical look and nodded. "He should sleep until we reach Bel Haven and perhaps a bit longer. Now, Lady Jessie, let's have a look at that bruise." He guided her to a quiet corner where the light was better.

Sila retrieved several of the cloaks that had been scattered about the room and brought them to Eron. Too carefully she placed one over him, taking care to tuck the sides in. Tersan looked away, embarrassed for her. Eron moaned.

"Do not fret, my lord," she told Eron. "I will ease your pain." From somewhere under her own cloak, she withdrew a jar filled with a dark colored ointment.

"Perhaps you should talk to Penrose before you use that?" Tersan suggested.

"The order was set," she answered, smearing the ointment over Eron's face. The stricken man relaxed. "See, Your Majesty, he benefits from the heterra."

Tersan looked closely at Eron. He did, indeed, seem more tranquil. But his teeth were chattering. Tersan grabbed a couple more of the cloaks and took them to where the man lay. He folded the cloaks and placed them beside Eron on the stone floor, then pulled the Sword over on his side and positioned the improvised mattress beneath him. He let him roll back gently.

"That was a fine idea, Majesty," Sila said. She smiled sweetly at him.

She is a healer, Tersan told himself. She was a beautiful healer. She was a woman healer. Why had he not noticed her before? He started to say something when Eron lurched.

His eyes flew open and he began to retch. Sila looked at her patient helplessly.

"He is not supposed to do that," she said, still staring at Eron. "The palapaca should make him sleep at least until we reach Bel Haven. Penrose said so."

"Do something, woman!" Tersan said.

Sila stood stock-still. "Why is he doing that?"

"Penrose!" Tersan yelled.

"Get him on his side!" Penrose yelled back.

Tersan pulled Eron toward him. The convulsions eased in the short time it took Penrose to cross the room to them. Eron was breathing hard and drenched with sweat. Penrose took one look at him and turned on Sila.

"What did you do?" he demanded.

"He was in such pain!" she said, still paralyzed.

"Heterra? Damn it, woman! He was sleeping!" Penrose shouted at her. "Keep him still, Tersan." He ran to his bag and dumped it onto floor and began to search.

Beneath Tersan's hands, Eron came to life. "Easy," Tersan said.

"Eron?" Jessie said from across the room.

Eron's eyes fluttered open. He looked at Tersan and through him. His chest heaved with exertion and he struggled to get to his feet. Tersan helped him rise. Eron smiled wickedly. He placed his feet shoulder-width apart and let his arms fall to his sides, palms forward. Very slowly, he raised them until they were chest high, palms upward.

"Tersan, duck!" Jessie warned.

With lightning speed, Eron brought his hands together and the Sword of Fire erupted into existence. He laughed as he took a swing at the un-armed king. Tersan leapt backward and then dropped to the floor and rolled. The sword smashed the stones where he had been standing sending fragments into the air.

"Eron, stop!" Jessie yelled.

Eron ignored her and turned mechanically toward the king, slashing at him almost as though he was a sack target instead of a human being. The strokes came so close that Tersan could feel the heat from the fiery sword. He leapt away from the others and found himself trapped in a corner. Eron laughed hollowly. Tersan had nowhere to go and they both knew it.

"Stand still, Tersan!" Jessie yelled. A silvery shield appeared in front of him. Eron stabbed at it ineffectually. He looked from his sword to Jessie's shield as though he could not believe his stroke was stopped. Like a man possessed, he stopped trying to kill Tersan and attacked the shield. Again and again he struck but each time, he was denied. Furious, Eron doubled his effort. He screamed like a wild animal denied his prey. His chest heaved and he stumbled more and more with each thrust.

"Now what?" Tersan asked as Eron took another stab at him.

"We have to remove the heterra," Penrose answered, still rifling through his bag, "before he kills himself from exertion."

"How?" Tersan asked. Even though he was safe, he still cringed with each of Eron's strokes.

"It is my responsibility," Sila said.

"No, Sila! Wait!" Penrose said. He rose from his hunt, a leather flask of something in his hands, but he was too late.

Before anyone could stop her, she raced forward holding a cloth in her hand. Eron laughed. He turned on this easier target and slashed at her robes, setting them on fire. Then he stood back and laughed as he watched her burn. Penrose abandoned the flask and threw Sila to the ground. He furiously beat at the flames until they were out and the young woman lay on the floor curled up in a ball sobbing, her hands pawing at her own face.

"No!" Jessie cried. She released her shield and Tersan tackled Eron.

The king pinned his ally to the floor. The fiery sword grew shorter as Eron's strength waned. It finally waggled ineffectively before disappearing. Like a trapped animal, he clawed at Tersan, trying to turn and attack, but the king was larger and stronger. "Now what?" Tersan said.

"He said we have to get that ointment off," Jessie said. She boldly came forward, cloth in hand. "Eron, you must hold still," she cooed. "It's only a cloth, see? Hold still."

For one brief moment, Eron held still. He waited for her to come close to him, tilting his head into her hand. When she placed her other hand on his shoulder, he relaxed. Tersan unconsciously loosened his grip and Eron twisted viciously away. He let out a blood-curdling laugh and snatched Jessie up by her waist. With one huge effort, he tossed her across the room. She fell into the stone wall with a sickening thud and slumped to the floor where she lay very still. Tersan lunged for him and they tumbled to the stone floor together.

Eron struggled against the king, still laughing. He wriggled away and turned to face Tersan with vacant eyes. Tersan waited. The Sword lunged forward at him but his timing was sluggish. Tersan took him by one arm and swung him around. He flailed and Tersan grabbed his other arm so that now Eron's hands were both pinned behind his back. He sank to the floor, thrashing weakly now against the man who held him. Penrose appeared, flask in hand. He poured the liquid over Eron's head. Almost instantly, the Sword lapsed into unconsciousness and Tersan eased him gently to the floor. Penrose knelt beside him, panting. He pulled up an eyelid, then shook his head.

"What in the name of the Lady just happened?" Tersan asked.

"An error of grievous proportion," Penrose answered, "made by an overzealous healer. The Lady has not smiled upon us this day."

8 From the Shadow of a Dream

"We cannot move forward until he is ready."
"But how long will that take?"
"He has come from the brink of death. He needs time."
"The war is nearly upon us."
"And the time we have had to prepare for it was bought by his blood and the blood of his kin."
"The few of his kin who are left will fight without him."
"Yes, I know. The army of the East fears him."
"If he rides at the head of our forces, we have a greater chance of victory."
"The army of the East knows he lives and that has stayed their hand until now. I shall not wait until pride overtakes reason. But I owe him this. We owe him this."

Lucy woke with a start. The conversation played and replayed in her mind. She could not see the two who were speaking. Only the man in the garden was visible, a man so fragile yet so strong. Worry lined his rugged face, worry accompanied by fear. With a start, she recognized her father. She threw back her covers and raced for the window, certain he would be outside her window in the shadows.

Autumn moonlight brightly lit the tiny yard of the house she had come to live in some six months ago. There was no visitor there, not even Mrs. Adams' old cat. The conversation played in her head about this man, her father, who had given everything, who was so deeply respected and so terribly haunted. She wondered what demons plagued him.

With a sigh, she closed her eyes, hoping to resume the dream, searching for answers.

9 Second Chance

The seasons hung between summer and autumn on a misty grey morning when the Sword finally walked alone through the garden of Bel Haven. The events of the spring still clung heavily to him. He made his way between the trees, pausing to cup late-blooming dicantus flowers gently in his hands. His gait was steady and purposeful though there was pain etched on his features, pain his body bade his mind ignore. His mind was not listening.

From beyond a stone wall, his healer and the king he served watched his movements with critical eyes. From a high window within the House a woman also watched, hopeful and alone.

"The dicantus trees bloom well this year," Penrose said without taking his eyes from the Sword. "It is good to see him among them."

The man in the garden took a few steps forward. If he noticed that the two were watching, he paid them no heed.

"We cannot move without him," Tersan replied.

"I cannot release him. He is not ready. Not yet." The words were spoken softly, sternly.

"How much longer will it take?" Tersan drummed his fingers on the wall, teeth clenched lightly.

"He has come from the brink of death. He needs time."

"Time, time--it is all that you ever tell me," the other growled. "The army is ready and winter will soon be upon us! I have no desire to put on a show of power in a snowstorm."

"The time we have had to prepare was bought by his blood and the blood of his kin."

The Sword took a hesitant step forward, stumbling slightly. Both onlookers leaned toward him in a phantom attempt to help him remain upright though they were far too distant to realistically help. The weary man righted himself and shuffled forward to appreciate the next blossom.

"The few of his kin who are with us will fight without him," Penrose offered.

Tersan was quiet for a while, never taking his eyes off Eron, evaluating his every move. He would protect the seemingly fragile man who stood in the garden with his life. As a king, however, he had to balance reason with personal wants, to use whatever tactics in his command to maintain peace even if it meant using an ally and a friend as a weapon.

"The power of the mind is sometimes mightier than the power of any sword," he told Penrose. "The army of the East fears him. If he rides at the head of our forces, we may have no need for bloodshed."

"The army of the East knows he lives!" Penrose replied with a smile. "We have made certain of that, have we not?"

"Well, yes. I have sent emissaries to every region that relies on the Sword and Shield for protection." A calm wind sent the fragrance of the dicantus flowers toward them and despite his best efforts, Tersan relaxed. "The story of Fot's defeat by Sword and Shield is becoming the fodder of legend. Marand was poised to attack, but with the demon alliance in chaos, he is on his own."

"Then rumor of Eron's survival will serve as well as his presence," Penrose reasoned. "Perhaps better."

"Rumor. Ha." His hands clenched into fists as they rested on the garden wall, the spell of the delicate fragrance broken. "There are spies everywhere, Penrose. Word will reach Marand of this broken man."

"I shall not wait until pride overtakes reason." Penrose grasped the king's arm, capturing his complete attention. "I owe him time to heal. We owe him time to heal."

Once again, the delicate scent hung in the air between them. "Perhaps we do owe him time to recuperate, but there is more at stake than the well-being of one man, no matter who that man may be. Our army grows tired of shining shields and sharpening blades. Some are eager to fight, others to return to their families." Tersan allowed himself a sigh. "I miss my children as well."

The man in the garden plucked a flower from the dicantus tree and was cupping it almost lovingly in his hands.

"He has come a long way in the months he has been here," Penrose mused, "but his journey is not over."

Tersan pointed at Eron. "Tell me truly, healer, is that a man you would fear? A man who shuffles through flowering trees, sniffing blossoms? He needs to get back to at least riding a horse!"

"Each day brings him closer to rediscovering the Lady's gifts."

"Yes, yes, you have told me. 'Once he rediscovers it, he must learn to control it again.' I've heard the speech."

"It is evident that I need to repeat it because you become selectively deaf each time I mention it." Penrose tapped the top of the wall with his fingers. "These things take time."

"Since the demon was vanquished, Marand has not been idle. He wants the Paranjothi mines," Tersan answered, "and he has gathered together an army to take them."

"Why not let him have the mines? No gems have been mined there for a long, long time. Surely there are few left."

Tersan grunted. "If it was only the gems, perhaps an agreement could be brokered. But the mines are vast, large enough to house an army in secret, launch a very effective campaign. There are many exits that lead deep into Jeleste and even to Lesser Kimala. Yet there are few openings to the East. The mines are easy to traverse. To lose them to Marand would yield him a tremendous strategic advantage,"

"I did not realize."

Tersan pointed to the man in the garden. "Eron did. He sent Tocar to tell me nearly a year ago. I thought little of it then." He sighed. "My hesitation nearly cost us everything. But that has changed. The winds now blow in our favor. Our armies are rebuilt and ready to strike. With the Sword riding at the head of our forces, our enemies will tremble."

"Tremble?" Penrose laughed. "He is mortal, Tersan. I think you rely too heavily upon myth. Besides, we have sent emissaries to negotiate peace, have we not?"

"Yes," Tersan returned evenly, "yes, even now, Tocar is in Il Chatel." The man in the garden plucked a second flower from the tree. He lifted it to his face and then twirled it idly between his fingers. "Mobilizing the army now, while our enemies still believe he is not mortal, gives us advantage in negotiation. We need to move before the demons find a new leader and resume their alliance with Marand."

"We have only recently emptied Bel Haven of the victims of war," Penrose snapped. "I have no desire to fill it again." Without another word, he turned away from the man in the garden and returned to the House of Healing, their home these long six months.

"Nor do I," Tersan answered after Penrose was long out of earshot.

The blossom was shaking in Eron's trembling hands; his face darkened. The muscles around his mouth plucked his lips into a smile and his eyes widened. The whole of his body shook, sweat staining his clothing in spite of the cool morning air. He took three awkward steps forward cupping the flower carefully between long fingers. With great effort, he set it down on the stone wall and took half a pace backward.

In the light breeze the blossom began to twitch. The man stared at it, his mouth forming words he did not voice. Tiny muscles in his forehead jerked as he bent his head down concentrating on the flower. He lowered his hands on either side of it, his eyes now black under a furrowed brow. The bloom trembled. Slowly, he raised his hands into the air. The flower rose between them, its delicate petals bending backward as it moved. He held his hands gracefully in front of his body, palms tilted slightly upward ready to catch the blossom if it fell.

Tersan's pulse quickened. Long had it been since Eron had flexed his mind in this way. The king took a hesitant step forward, but halted. The Sword was on the verge of remembering his power. This was not the time for interference.

The flower floated at arm's length above his outstretched arms. Lightning sparked between his fingertips and the petals changed from pristine white to a pale gold. Tersan stared at the flower to be certain his eyes were not deceiving him. The preamble to the Dance of the Sword was complete. Eron had to keep the blossom safe while performing a complex set of exercises with the Sword of Light.

Eron laughed, a genuine clear laugh. Sweat glistened on his forehead and his arms shook. He brought his hands together so quickly they were a blur and a blade of flame sprang from his fingertips. The flower he had been holding aloft dropped but settled in the air, a tiny distance above the blade.

"Yes," Eron breathed. The single word carried across the courtyard to his audience of one.

In the time-honored tradition of the Sword, he danced with the flower, twirling to the right and then to the left, responding with cat-like grace. The blossom floated above the sword, joining in the dance, drifting up and down on the air as the man turned, twirling body and weapon so fast that Tersan could no longer tell where flesh ended and sword began. It glowed with a new life created by the man who wielded the sword, floating just above the flaming sword, its existence dependent on the sword's creator. Eron focused on the dance, certain of every movement as he protected the blossom above him.

High above them, a bird of prey screeched. The call broke his concentration and he miss-stepped. The blossom fell on the sword where it burst into flame. The Sword of Light disappeared leaving the man who wielded it to sink to the ground.

"Penrose!" Tersan yelled as he ran toward the garden.

10 Jessie's House

Jason ran a finger over an old frame that housed an even older photograph. A cherubic child smiled back at him with eyes so intense they seemed alive. For a moment, he thought he could hear a contented gurgle. A shiver ran the length of his back. He resisted the urge to simply replace the picture on the untended stone mantel. Instead he brushed off the accumulated dust with his sleeve. Satisfied that the spot was now clean, he returned the photo.

"This place is a mess." He looked away from the photo and surveyed the rest of the cluttered room. People inside frames of silver and wood stared dully back at him. They were scattered over tabletops and shelves, on window ledges and end tables. No flat surface was left unadorned. A triangular set of shelves stood in the center of the room, matching nothing. It was filled with cheesy snow globes, the cheap kind that came from tourist traps, housing tiny figures and plastic snow. On a whim, Jason picked one up and brushed the dust off of it. The two figures inside, a farmer and a mule, rocked back and forth on their teeter-totter smiling toothily at him.

"I'm sorry, Jessie," he said aloud, rubbing the top of the snow globe with his already soiled sleeve, "I should have come up sooner and kept the place cleaner."

"Good grief, JM, would you give it a rest?" Ric Hawkins leaned inside the doorway, his lanky frame silhouetted against the setting sun. He was holding a video camera loosely in his hand. "The insurance company could care less if there's dust on the pictures. You're more obsessed with dirt than Felix Unger. It ain't right."

Jason raised an eyebrow but he was trying not to laugh. "You never seem to mind me cleaning our place, Ric."

"That's because chicks really hate a messy apartment."

"Chicks? You mean like women?"

"Please."

"What women?"

Ric heaved an exasperated sigh. "The ones who bring us work. You know, from the campus."

"Oh, *those* women." Jason snorted. "Like keeping a clean house ever makes a difference to them. They wouldn't notice if we had a week's worth of dirty dishes in the sink and hadn't dusted--" he blew a second cloud of dust from an end table "--in a month. They've got money and they want you to undo the stupid stuff they've done to the fancy machine Daddy gave them for school. And they're willing to pay handsomely to keep Daddy from finding out they're complete idiots. How many times has that blonde been back for downloading the same virus?"

"Um, six I think."

Jason laughed. "She might have the body of a goddess, Ric, but there's nothing in her head but air."

"If you can be anal about cleaning, I can dream, can't I?"

"Yeah, but I should think with an IQ as high as yours, you'd be able to do a reality check every now and then." He sucked in a huge breath and blew another layer of dust off yet another table. "Yuck."

"Speaking of reality checks, JM," Ric said, waving to the house, "it's just a little dust. It's not like there's fruit rotting on the counters or rats nesting in the furniture."

"You know, that smudge that was on that note could have been blood," Jason said with a shudder.

"So you said," Ric answered.

"We haven't heard from Jessie. Not even a post card."

"So I've heard."

"Lucy doesn't know whether to be mad or scared."

"Your aunt is a nut. I'd be mad if I was Lucy."

"Where do you think she is?"

"How should I know?" Ric raised both eyebrows and shrugged. "How many times have I told you not to worry about it? She left a note and obviously had a plan in place should something happen. Since when does an accountant have an overactive imagination, anyway?" He held up the video camera. "Where would you like to start?"

"Wherever you like." Jason shrugged. "Furniture, I guess."

Ric ran the camera systematically through the living room, taking pictures of everything. Jason sank into an easy chair still holding the snow globe. For some reason, this particular one fascinated him. It had appeared the day Jessie disappeared. He shook it up and watched the tiny pieces of faux snow float down lazily while the mule and the farmer bounced up and down on their teeter-totter, grinning maniacally.

"Miss James still thinks Jessie's on some kind of really long vacation somewhere," he mused.

"The Snake Lady?" Ric asked from behind the still working camera.

"Yeah, that's what she told me. But Lucy insists that her father has been injured somehow and that Jessie has to stay with him until he recovers."

"Their stories never change. There must be some truth in them."

"Maybe. I feel sorry for Lucy. Her mom created a fantasy world and a fantasy father and Miss James keeps reinforcing the story." A second picture on the mantel caught Jason's attention. He pocketed the snow globe and crossed the short distance to get a closer look. The man stared back at him with eyes so intense they seemed to look into his soul. Jason moved to his left, then back to center and to the right. No matter where he stood, the man was staring at him. "You know, these pictures give me the creeps."

Ric lowered the camera and laughed. "Just the pictures? This whole house makes my skin crawl." He paused and Jason watched as he visibly shook. "But it's more exciting than creepy. This place would make a great haunted house."

"Only you would say that."

Ric grinned. "Well it would. You were saying something about the Snake Lady?"

"Yeah. Miss James. She's Jessie's only real friend up here." Jason crossed the living room again and pointed out the window to a white cottage nestled between very old trees on the adjoining hill. "That's her place over there. Her cottage belongs to Jessie. I keep looking for some sort of written contract between them, but I can't find anything. She used to come and stay with Anna and Kenny every once in a while when my folks were out of town. She's, um, interesting. Jessie left Lucy with her right before she disappeared."

Ric was standing beside him, looking down at the cottage. "I had a snake once. Mom made me give it away after she found it curled up in one of her pots."

"I should hope!"

"Snakes can be quite affectionate, JM," Ric said, returning his attention to his video camera. "Someday I'd like to meet her. Did anyone ask her about your aunt?"

"Yeah, the cops did." Jason sighed. "She babbled something about Jessie visiting a foreign country, but no one ever heard of the place. I think she's a little left of center. Don't forget to get the poster collection."

"Poster collection?"

Jason pointed to the walls. Framed bills advertising old movies and Broadway plays hung from floor to ceiling on the east wall. "Those are worth a lot," he said.

"Maybe to a collector," Ric answered. He videotaped them anyway. "I guess that's where you get your obsession from, eh?"

Jason nodded. "Jessie used to watch musicals over and over and over again to get the dance steps from old movies. Then she'd teach them to us kids when it was raining and we couldn't go outside and run amuck. It was fun."

"You have a weird family, JM," Ric said. "But then, I suppose dancing with your relatives beats getting trapped in some old cave."

"Tunnel, Ric, it was a tunnel. From the underground railroad." He shuddered but managed a laugh. "But you're right. Dancing wins hands down over wondering whether you're going to die alone in a hole. Jessie says it's a way to become cultured. The ladies love a man who can whisk them onto the dancefloor and do something besides sway back and forth. You should try it."

"Drama does become you," Ric snorted. He shut the camera off and walked over to the fireplace, the camera resting idly in his hand. He picked up one of the pictures. "So, what are you going to do with it?"

"With what? The house?"

"Well, yeah." Ric held up the picture of a baby peering out from under a blanket. "He's got your nose."

"He should." Jason took the picture and held it beside his face. "He's me."

"You haven't aged a day," Ric told him.

Jason laughed and replaced the picture. "I don't know what I'm going to do with the house," he said with a sigh. "I have to ask Lucy. After all, it really is hers. I'm just in charge until she turns twenty one or Jessie comes back."

"Must be nice to get paid for being a caretaker."

"It's more work than it looks like," Jason protested. "Now that I've really gotten access to everything, I'm amazed at how well she's managed her money. Lottery winners usually end up wasting their millions. Jessie not only kept what she won, but she made it work for her. She's doubled her fortune and that's not counting what she spent on this place." He grinned. "She pays me well, but I'd like a real job."

"Yeah, I can see you in a suit and tie, driving to work, punching a clock, like you ever have." Ric grinned slyly. "You know, chicks really dig a place in the country."

"For crying out loud, Ric, is that all you ever think about?" Jason shook his head. He dug in his pocket and removed the snow globe he had stuffed there but the spot he had removed it from on the triangular shelf had somehow filled itself back in. Without thinking, he placed the globe back in his pocket and picked up a fireplace poker. The metal shank was delicately engraved with beautiful etchings. Jason twirled it around slowly, watching with fascination as the early evening sunlight glinted off the shiny letters embossed on its hilt. "You know, Jessie lived with us up until she got lucky with that lottery ticket. She said she always loved this place."

"If I won that much money, I think I could find a better place than this."

"Eh. She likes it. But she did sew some wild oats after her win."

"The plot thickens."

"Yeah. She never introduced me to Lucy's father. Not that I'm complaining, but I think Mom and Dad met him." Jason stopped twirling the makeshift fire place utensil-turned-baton.

"Any idea what happened to him?"

"Not really. Jessie just said she didn't want to 'expose' Lucy to 'his world' until she was older. Now it's become a bit of a fantasy for poor Lucy." He resumed his investigation of the utensil. "But they were a riot to have around. I loved coming up here to visit."

"Until the little incident with the tunnel?"

"You just have to keep bringing that up, don't you?"

"Yeah." He grinned widely. "And I'll continue to bring it up as long as it bothers you."

"They're dangerous, Ric." He picked up another of the snow globes and shook it. This one had the Golden Gate Bridge in it. Huge flakes of plastic drifted around inside it, settling on the plastic bridge. He placed it back on the shelf. "I'll never understand why she liked these tacky things."

"Seems like she could at least afford the upscale versions. You know, glass, sparkly faux-snow, maybe a music box for a base?"

Jason waved the poker at the fireplace. The wall took on an odd light, but immediately returned to the dull slate grey it had been moments before. He put the poker under his arm and placed his hand on the stone as if he could see it better by touching it. "That was weird."

"What?"

"I could have sworn that changed colors." He tapped the stone lightly and it resonated with a musical tone. "Interesting…"

"You're imagining things again, Mr. Accountant," Ric said. He sat down on the hearth, his back against the wall. "This is a pretty cool house, even if it is creepy."

"Yeah, it is." A poster of Errol Flynn as Robin Hood caught Jason's eye. He raised his left hand up in the air behind him, brandishing the poker as though it was a sword, imitating the actor. He twirled and tapped the mantel on the right, then took a step backward, shuffled and tapped on the left.

"Good Lord, JM, put that thing down before you hurt someone!" Ric protested.

"You don't like my footwork?"

"Well, actually, you look like you could use a little practice."

"Then I've come to the right place." He pointed to the floor. Inlays of slightly darker wood of varying geometric shapes were set randomly into the floor among the thin planks running the length of the room. Jason pushed the odd shelf containing the snow globe collection in front of the door, effectively clearing the dance floor. He then centered himself on a rectangle directly in front of the fireplace. The snow globe in his pocket shifted uncomfortably and he dug it out and tossed it to Ric who caught it easily. He bowed his head and started humming.

"I've got to get this on tape," Ric said. He stuffed the globe in his own pocket and swung the camera into position. "This'll make great blackmail material at your wedding."

"Or an audition tape," Jason replied as he tucked the poker smartly under his arm and turned away.

"For an accountant?"

Jason ignored him. He placed the tip of the poker directly in front of him on the floor and leaned forward on it with a jaunty tilt to his head. He tapped the floor twice with his makeshift cane and spun around in a precise circle then swung the poker like a baton as he carefully followed a pattern on the darker wood. Then he bent over and took three steps backward, his feet neatly landing within the squares. He hummed an unnamed Broadway tune from a show he had long ago forgotten, never missing a beat as he whirled across the floor. He whipped the poker out and struck a rounded stone to Ric's left.

"Hey, watch it!"

"Precision!" Jason exclaimed as he hit a second rounded stone to his friend's right. "Now, for the finale!" he said as he spun around and lunged toward the mantel intending to bounce off the stone and finish with a backward flip into the living room.

The stones changed to a transparent grey. This time, Jason didn't notice. He was too busy trying not to fall any further down the hole that had suddenly opened up to swallow him.

11 The Rabbit Hole

"JM!"

Jason hung on to the metal hook of his makeshift cane with every scrap of energy he could muster. He could see Ric above him, his lanky body halfway into the hole as he clung to the poker's handle in an attempt to keep Jason from falling further down the hole.

"Hold still!" Ric yelled.

"Don't let go!" Jason yelled back. The surface was slick, but it had a slope to it. He wriggled around to find a position to climb. "If I can get my feet under me, I might--"

His feet wind milled on the slippery surface and he slammed against the wall with just enough force to yank the instrument out of Ric's hands. He was plummeting down a steep slide. Behind him Ric yelled something unintelligible and there was a big thud. Wherever he was going, his best friend was going with him.

The slide was steep at first, then leveled off a bit, then plunged again like an unruly roller coaster. Down and down they slid, the wind caused by this wild descent drowning out their terrified screams. The light from Jessie's living room disappeared leaving them in total darkness as the tunnel twisted sharply to the right and then to the left. Jason thought there was some light ahead as the pitch steepened again. He let out a surprised shout and the tunnel spat him out onto a cold stone floor. The fireplace poker clattered to the ground and then Ric was deposited beside him like a scud missile. The globe popped out of his pocket and landed on the floor.

Jason tried to still his pounding heart. "That was some ride!" he said, trying not to let his fear show.

"Yeah, I'm okay, thanks for asking," Ric answered irritably as he reached inside his back pocket and withdrew a mangled cell phone. "Man, I just bought that!"

"Insured?"

"I repair these. Why would I insure it?" He looked around the cavernous room. "Where are we?"

"Under the house, I guess." Jason rose warily then offered a hand to Ric to help him up. "You've been asking to see one of the tunnels."

"This wasn't exactly what I had in mind," Ric answered. With Jason's help he pulled himself up and dusted off his hands. "Pretty cool, though."

"This is a lot bigger than any I've ever seen."

"This isn't a tunnel, it's a cave." Ric pointing up. Pink light glowed on a twenty-foot high wall. "I imagine after sunset it'll get mighty dark down here."

"Ever master of the obvious, eh?"

"Just trying to be practical. It's almost dusk."

There wasn't much to look at in the Spartan room. Apparently at one time, the place had been furnished, but now there was little left save broken remnants of wooden tables and chairs. The room smelled of old bricks that had been too long in a wet basement and the air was oppressively still. There did not appear to be a door leading anywhere, but directly opposite the chute was a gaping opening that led into darkness.

Ric was examining the chute that had deposited them there. He stuck his head inside and touched the walls with his hands. "JM, your aunt's a nut. What the hell kind of booby trap is this anyway?"

"If she knew that was there, she would have told me." He closed the distance between himself and Ric slowly. "She knows how I feel about those tunnels."

"This is a cave, JM."

"Whatever. But there still has to be a way back," Jason answered. He started searching the wall beside the hole. "Even if it was an escape for slaves. They wouldn't just let them get down here and not have a way out."

Ric turned his attention fully to Jason. "JM, what if your aunt fell down that chute and couldn't get back up?" he asked.

"Well, then how could she have left a note?" Jason asked.

Ric nodded his head. "Good point."

"Let's just try to find a way back to the house, okay?" Jason said, peering up into the chute. He couldn't see past three feet. The surface was slick, as though it had been polished.

"Sure."

"Maybe we can climb." Ric crawled inside and was re-deposited on the floor in short order. "Apparently there's another way," he mumbled, rubbing his backside with his hands.

"Still master of the obvious, eh?" Jason grinned. "We could sprout wings and go through the roof."

"Right." Ric pointed to the yawning hole opposite them. "I'll bet that's the exit."

Jason shuddered. "I'm not good in caves, Ric."

"It can't be that bad," Ric answered. "Somebody put furniture down here."

"Yeah and then destroyed it," Jason answered. Something on the floor caught his eye. He knelt down to get a better look at it. On a neatly folded piece of material, a thin stream of gold spilled onto the stone floor where it slipped between the cracks and disappeared.

"JM," Ric said quietly, "have you got YOUR cell?"

"Of course! Why didn't I think of that?" he answered. He stood and reached into his pocket to retrieve his phone.

"Because you're not master of the obvious?" he grinned.

Jason flipped the phone open with a flourish and paused with his finger poised, ready to dial.

"When are you going to get rid of that Methuselah and get a real phone?"

"Says the man whose phone was destroyed in the slide." He stared at the keyboard and frowned.

"What's wrong?" Ric asked.

"No signal." He looked around. They were nearly surrounded by solid rock. "It's this cave."

"What about next to that chute?"

"Good idea." Holding the phone so he could watch the bar code, Jason moved toward the center of the room. The bars surged and retreated and surged again. "Come on, come on, give me something I can work with here…Yes!" He thrust a triumphant fist in the air as two bars remained rock solid. Then he hesitated, staring at the keyboard again.

"Now what?" Ric asked.

"I can't remember the number for the Claxbury Police department," he said, still staring at the phone as though it would give him the answer.

"For cryin' out loud, give me that." Ric snatched the phone out of his hands and poked at it three times, then handed it back. "9-1-1. Simple."

Jason held the phone to his ear and shook his head. "I don't think this is an emergen--"

"9-1-1. Do you require police, fire department or medical emergency personnel?"

Jason put his hand over the phone. "Police, fire or medical?"

"What is this, multiple choice?" Ric answered. "Well, I'm not hurt."

"Me neither."

"And nothing's burning."

"Right." He uncovered the mouthpiece. "Police, please," he said.

"Sir, your call…breaking up. Can…give…your location?"

"T-3575," he rattled off automatically.

"Jessie Perrymore's place?" the operator said.

"Y-yes." Jason paused. Small towns truly were amazing. "My name is Jason McCarthy. I'm her nephew. We were cataloguing the house for insurance and, I don't know how to put this, really, but my friend Ric Hawkins and I seem to have fallen under the house and we don't know how to get back."

"…repeat?" she offered.

"Help," Jason answered. "See, we--"

"You're break---up."

"I can't hear you! We need help!" Jason heard the panic creeping into his voice.

"Police…on… Stay………com……"

As they watched, solid rock filled the chute in, leaving a tiny opening at the top.

"What the-"Jason pushed on the wall. Nothing budged. "Did you see that?"

"Neat trick," Ric observed with admiration. He ran his hands around the stone where the opening used to be. "There's got to be hinge or something here. Lots of air coming through that hole."

"Well, good. We won't suffocate while we wait for help." Jason held the phone up to the small opening. "Full battery, no signal."

"Looks like we've got two choices," Ric said.

"Oh?"

"Wait for help or find our own way out. Unless your aunt shows up to show us the way home."

"Right." Jason started across the floor. Something crunched under his foot and he jumped back. "What the …" He bent over and picked up the cracked and now leaking snow globe. The farmer and the mule still grinned toothily as the water oozed from the cracked plastic. "You know, I'll never find another one that looks like this."

Ric laughed. "We can only hope it was one of a kind," he said. "Is it broken? Or just cracked?"

"It looks cracked. Maybe a little glue will fix it. Catch." He tossed the globe to Ric. The plastic bubble landed solidly in his hands.

"Dang!" he said, tossing it from one hand to the other.

"What?" Jason asked.

"You didn't tell me it was hot!"

"Hot?"

"Yeouch!" He dropped it and it shattered.

A puddle formed on the stone that should have run off to one side or the other and disappeared between the cracks. Instead the liquid stood in a pool like red-tinged mercury, growing ever so slowly in height. A tendril of black smoke floated toward the crack in the roof and took on the image of a serpent. Brilliant green and red pinpoints of light formed its eyes.

"My bonds are severed!" it hissed in a definite male voice. "I am free!"

The serpent spun. The air in the room spun with him, whirling faster and faster until it seemed a gale force. The two young men grabbed hold of one another, trying to keep their balance. The serpent swooped down on them and Ric swung at it instinctively with the poker. The metal struck something solid and it let loose an ear splitting shriek. The body spun into a thin strand of black smoke and headed to the hole in the wall leading to Jessie's house. It slid through the opening, disappearing in an instant.

"Where…what…" Ric was stammering. He pointed to the floor.

The tiny flakes of plastic snow lay scattered like so many pieces of confetti. Instead of floating in a pool of water, they were melted into the stone along with the still grinning farmer and his mule. In Ric's hand, the fireplace poker was glowing white.

12 The Snake Lady

The white snake bathing in artificial light on the driftwood beside the fireplace raised his head and flicked his tongue. Winifred James looked up from her needlepoint. The wind had shifted ever so slightly within her cottage home.

"Yes, Alvyn, I felt it." She put the needlepoint aside, her heart racing, and reached for her cane. She did not need it to steady her gait but it always made her feel better to hold it in her hands. Thus armed, she peered out the living room window hoping to see nothing that did not belong. The valley was as calm as ever.

"It must have been the wind, Alvyn," she said searching the forest for signs of disruption, "just the wind…"

Moonlight blanketed the mountain, the conifers swaying slightly in the ever present breeze. Winifred clicked off the light and waited for her eyes to adjust to the night. An owl swooped down and disappeared into the forest, a coyote howled in the distance, and on the edge of the grassy meadow that spread out nearly a quarter of a mile beneath her window, she could see a small herd of deer grazing undisturbed. On the thread that was the highway, a set of headlights passed and she watched it travel through the trees for a solid minute before it disappeared behind one of the many hills that comprised the mountain. Something caught her eye and her heart skipped a beat. Smoke was rising from Jessie Perrymore's house.

"Jason called earlier to let me know he would be there this weekend," she reasoned. "He must have built a fire."

Against the moonlight, the smoke rose black and ominous, crowned with an almost imperceptible red halo. She caught her breath and held it praying to the Lady that what she was seeing was not real. Instead of rising, the top of the plume arched downward over Jessie's chimney and slithered across the rooftop.

"That is no normal smoke!" she whispered. "Polly!"

The plume split at its end forming a mouth and bowed quickly forward. Two eyes appeared, brilliant green with red specks. The smoky creature searched the valley before finally resting on her. The mouth flicked a tongue at her and grinned widely. *Daughter*, it mouthed before sliding back down the chimney. Winifred's blood turned to ice. Beside the fireplace, Alvyn hissed.

"Oh, Jessie, what have we done?"

13 Night Terrors

"No!"

Jessie sat straight up in bed. Her heart hammered in her chest as she tried to force her body into waking from a sound sleep. Where was she? The walls were barren and there were unoccupied beds lined up all around her in neat rows. Ghost-like beings in flowing white robes drifted toward her. *Healers*, a voice inside her head insisted, *they're healers. Eron's calling... You have to get up. Now.* Wearily she shook off the last remnants of sleep and rolled off her bed.

"Eron?" she said quietly.

The man whose side she had not willingly left for the last six months sat on the edge of his own bed cradling his head in his hands. He was moaning softly, pressing the heel of one hand against his temple while keeping Sila Atin at bay with the other. The brown jug that held Eron's special concoction, a wicked combination of alcohol and magic, was glugging some of its contents onto the floor at his feet. Visions were a gift for some, a power for others and Eron had once been a very powerful man. He had been trying to reconnect with the power the Lady had gifted to him since it was lost at the portal, though he was loathe to admit it. He vehemently claimed he did not want to keep the title of Sword. Jessie knew better.

"Lord Eron," Sila Atin started, "you must lie down."

Sila Atin had been true to her word. She was never far from him. The healer was a pest, Jessie thought, a well-meaning pest but still a pest. For all her drooling over him, though, she seemed to understand the depth of Eron's loss almost as well as Jessie did.

"Lord Eron, you must lie down," the healer repeated,

"Out of my way, woman!" he croaked, ignoring the healer as he rose somewhat shakily. "Jessie!"

Sila Atin put herself directly in his path. Eron simply picked her up and set her to one side, his attention fully focused on Jessie.

"My lord, I must protest!" Sila said, trying to pull him back to the bed. In the effort, her carefully coifed hair fell away from her face, exposing a barely discernable white scar. She looked away quickly, smoothing her hair over the imperfection so it was hidden.

"Protest all you want," he snapped over his shoulder, "it will not change what I have seen." Rarely did Eron listen to any of the healers unless he wanted to, but he was equally rarely rude to them. "Jessie!"

"I'm right here, Eron. You don't have to shout. You'll wake everyone in the House."

The night was going to be a long one; his eyes had visibly darkened, though whether that was the sign of a vision or the sign of too much drink, Jessie could not be certain. Eron thought what he had seen was real; just like it had been last night and the night before that and before that. The only difference tonight was that damned concoction. It had the side effect of inebriation, something Jessie intensely disliked. She wondered how long it would take her to convince him this time that they should all go back to sleep.

"He's back!" Eron whispered into her face, his breath hot on her skin.

"Who's back?" she asked.

"Fot! I saw him!"

"There is no demon here, Lord Eron," Sila Atin assured him from behind.

"Do you *see* a demon here, Madam Healer?" Eron snapped without looking back. "Of course not. My Shield has seen to it that Bel Haven is more than adequately warded."

Jessie sighed. His comment was an unintentional dig pointing out to Sila that Jessie had been chosen to be Shield and not her. Eron was concentrating so hard on getting back to who he was that the subtleties of curtesy were often forgotten leaving Jessie to sometimes have to explain.

"You were dreaming, my lord," Sila Atin insisted.

The healer had a point. "She's right, Eron," Jessie told him with the same patience she had used every night for the last month, "it was only a dream. That swill makes you see things that aren't real. You know that." She shrugged out of his hold and attempted to ease him back toward the bed but he would not budge.

"It was not a dream!" he said. He caught her eyes. "It was not a dream!" he repeated, commanding her not to look away. "Not this time."

Jessie schooled her body into as calm a state as she could. She told herself that she had to be vigilant, not to doubt him. She should not ignore the chance that his gift might be returning, even though her body was begging her to tell him that whatever it was, it would keep until morning. She dipped her head slightly, following the protocol Sword and Shield had established many months ago.

"You have had a vision?"

"Yes!"

She sighed quietly. "May I do a reading, my lord?"

"Yes, yes, of course!" Like a small child, he bounced on the balls of his feet as she readied herself. Offering a heart-felt prayer to the Lady who was his goddess and whose power Jessie had learned to respect, she nodded.

With a deep breath, Jessie forced herself to relax. She had permission to enter his mind now. If he had seen a vision, the veil would be gone and he would meet her as she entered to show her.

Eron took Jessie's hands, gently entwining her fingers in his own. The clear outline of his features sharpened slightly as clarity fell over the room. Jessie took in a sharp breath. The veil had fallen.

Jessie found herself alone in his mind waiting for him. True, with no veil, she could wander about on her own, but if he had truly had a vision, he would have to guide her to see it. Long moments passed. Jessie waited. Then she waited a little longer. Finally she shook her head and broke the contact.

"There was nothing there, my lord," she said. "It was only a dream."

"No!" he shouted. "You must try again!"

"Eron," Jessie implored quietly, "I have tried. And please, lower your voice. I'm standing right here."

"Why? Who are we bothering?" he returned hotly. "We are the only persons inhabiting this hall, my lady, or had you not noticed?"

"You are bothering me," she said, her voice just above a whisper, "but you're also bothering your perpetual audience of healers."

"The vision--"

"This house is the safest place in all of Eormengrund, I have seen to that, though I can't get you to move to a more private room because you think this one is more easily defended."

"Please, Jessie!"

"Well it works two ways, Lord Sword," she continued in spite of his protests. "Because you want to stay here in the Great Hall, we are attended by a plethora of healers, who think you are dangerous."

"Dangerous? Me?" he whispered back. Pretended madness tugged his lips into a smile. "I am supposed to be dangerous, my lady, it is part of the facade, or do you not recall?"

Jessie rolled her eyes. "That's not what I meant and you know it. Nobody has forgotten what happened in the portal room. Sila makes sure of that." Without giving him time to speak, she continued. "And what about today? In the garden?"

"Me practicing the Dance of the Sword has nothing to do with this!" he growled.

"Anything you do has to do with this!" she countered. "Just producing the Sword of Light is something most people have only heard of in legend," she argued. "To see it done is awe-inspiring--"

"Why thank you," he smirked.

"But then you had to launch into that dance."

"I am required to practice."

"You failed to protect the flower."

"If that cursed bird had not screeched as I was nearing the end, I would have finished! It happens."

"Perhaps in private it happens," she answered rather more sharply than she intended, "but not where impressionable people can see what you are doing. Public displays are supposed to be perfect. You forget who you are!"

"Who I *was*," he corrected.

"Who you *are*," she insisted. "The last time I checked you hadn't passed the title on and," she resisted the temptation to scowl at him, "it appears you are not dead."

"If another was trained, I *would* pass the title on. Since there is not, I have to practice." His eyes were flashing.

"Then you are the Sword?" she hissed. "Not some pretender? Make up your mind!"

"My Lady!" Sila Atin charged. She had left the rest of the healers in a larger circle behind her. "Lord Eron is not a well man! He needs rest!"

"What he needs is to decide who and what he is," Jessie snapped. She turned to the healer. "What he doesn't need is for you or anyone else to coddle him. Including me."

"Jessie," Eron started, "the vision?"

"The vision. Eron, I ..." Jessie hesitated. The veil. She looked away from him and closed her eyes.

"You saw something!"

"The veil fell," she answered. "I tried, Eron, but there really was nothing more."

"Then it was a vision!" He grinned so widely she thought his face would break. Then he rested his hands on her shoulders and gave her a curt nod. "We must try again!"

"Yes, the veil fell. There was nothing more."

"Lord Eron," Sila interjected, "you need rest. Perhaps in the morning, you'll realize that it was just a dream."

"There is more!" Eron insisted. He drew in a deep breath. "A simpleton and a jackass!" he whispered into Jessie's ear.

Jessie's heart skipped a beat. He had not seen the prison she had chosen for Fot. "H-how did you know that?"

"Two young men in the portal room," he continued. He dipped his head and took half a step back, entwining her fingers again. His already darkened eyes turned black and held hers. "We must try again. Even if only part of it is a vision, it is too dangerous to ignore."

His voice was hypnotic in the candlelit room, his breath warm and comfortable on her face. "Still yourself."

One by one, her senses blended with his as both lowered their defenses. When they were one, she again entered his mind. The veil was gone.

This time, the room was filled with memories. It was not the disciplined place she had first enjoyed many years ago, but it was not in disarray as it had been when he lay dying on the floor in the portal room. A memory of Lucy giggling while holding a stuffed bear whizzed by her, uncontrolled and misplaced.

This time doors were open. Without the benefit of a guide, she decided to move toward the golden river where his power was stored. Her huge silver patch was now bordered with Eron's gold. Smaller patches of silver remained intact, some intertwined with gold, but far more repairs were only gold. Although there were places where the once fractured wall slightly bulged, none of his power seeped through. In spite of what he claimed, the Sword had not given up. He was rebuilding.

A gentle breeze buoyed her up and propelled her forward through the eddies of his memories. Fairly certain that she should allow herself to be moved, she floated with the tide.

Children laughed at the base of Kimala as they skipped stones across clear blue waters. She heard herself laugh and caught his memory of the first time they kissed under a starlit sky. She blushed as she remembered the rest of that night. Now Lucy was holding up a five pointed star at her fifth grade Christmas pageant. Then Fot roared, hurling bolts of molten stone at them. Jessie's shield absorbed the blow but the force of it sent her backward. She could see the sweat on her own brow as Eron charged forward with the Sword of Light. The demon's anger was unleashed and he hurled himself at them.

"Eron!" Jessie cried. A bolt of light bright as lightning temporarily blinded her and the memory changed.

She blinked hard, trying to clear her sight. She was underwater, her life ebbing away. She couldn't breathe, couldn't hear and her limbs refused to move. She was cold and hot at once and her head was swimming. She couldn't even scream.

Eron slipped his hand into hers and the images vanished. "I am sorry," he whispered.

"What the hell was that?" Her mind told her to gasp for air, but her body didn't need it.

"Only a memory." Eron sighed. "I have not thought of that in many years."

"It could have killed me!"

"I survived. You would have, too." He stroked her hair. "Are you ready?"

She sucked in a breath. "I am."

"Come."

They had arrived at Eron's view of the portal room. The silvery web of her ward still held above them, but there was noise in the chute leading back to her living room in Claxbury. It shimmered and one young man flew threw it followed quickly by a second, both landing hard on the floor.

"That was some ride!" the first one said. Jessie stared closely at him.

"Jason?"

"Yeah, I'm okay, thanks for asking," the other said irritably as he rolled over and brushed off his hands. He was looking around the room wide eyed. Jessie recognized Jason's best friend, Ric. *"Where are we?"* he asked.

"Jason!" she called.

"They cannot hear you," Eron answered calmly. There was relief in his voice but there was an edge of something else as well. "I have already seen this. It is in the past."

"Under the house, I guess," Jason continued. He rose warily then offered a hand to Ric to help him up. *"You've been asking to see one of the tunnels."*

"This wasn't exactly what I had in mind," his friend answered. *"Pretty cool though,"* he added.

Jason shuddered. *"This is a lot bigger than any I've ever seen."*

The scene faded.

"Eron, concentrate!"

The images reformed. The two were standing close to one another now, pointing toward the ceiling dumbfounded. A wisp of black smoke hung in the opening there, a serpent stretching as it flicked its tail in whip-like fashion.

The scene faded again and Eron lurched as he shifted things in the mind they shared. Once again the room came into focus. This time it was crisp and clear. She felt the cool air of the cave on her face and smelled its dampness. She could hear the boys breathing and her skin crawled with an energy she recognized and feared.

"This is no memory!" she gasped.

"Shield us!" he ordered.

"My lord, no! Someone get Penrose!" Sila shouted. "Separate them!"

In one elegant arcing motion, Jessie summoned her Shield and a dome of light covered them. Outside, she saw Sila working her fingers in familiar patterns, mouthing words from a language few among the living knew. She was trying to break through the shield and she was using the correct sequence of incantations and manipulations to do so. If she succeeded, their link with the portal room would make the Great Hall vulnerable to whatever Jason was facing. There was no time for explanations. Jessie ignored her. The Great Hall became distant, the healers' voices murmurs.

Jason was gripping the fireplace poker and it was glowing silver with the spell Jessie had invoked upon it. On the floor were tiny bits of plastic floating in a puddle of water. Her heart lurched as she looked for and found the plastic images of a farmer and a mule astride a now defunct teeter-totter. They were embedded in the stone. Jessie sucked in a deep breath. "Oh my God!" she said aloud, "Jason!"

"Aunt Jess, is that you?" He sounded frightened and excited at once.

"Yes, Jason!"

"Where are you?"

A whirling wind descended from the hole in the ceiling. It smashed the already shattered furniture into the walls, splintering what was left. Jason and Ric huddled in the center of the storm, out of harm's way for the moment. The vision dimmed.

"Eron, concentrate!"

The vision cleared. "Aunt Jessie?"

"Fot! He's broken through the wards!" Eron shouted in Bel Have. "Shield them!"

"Jason, stand together and hold still!" she shouted.

They put their backs together so they were looking in opposite directions. Jessie raised her hands, her fingers moving with lightning speed as she formed a silvery sphere of protection around them. Fot reared his head and came crashing down on the webbing, throwing them to the floor.

"What the hell is that thing?" Jason yelled.

"We can't fight him from here!" Jessie said, juggling her web as another blow crashed in on it. At Bel Haven, her body sagged against Eron's and he held her upright.

"We have to reset the wards," Eron answered at Bel Haven, "with him on the outside or he will find his way in to your world and Wylfcynne will not be able to stop him! He is still in the snake stage--"

"Quit analyzing and do something!" she shot back.

"I am trying. I...lack the power."

"You have the power! I saw it!"

The arms that steadied her were gone and she swayed, nearly losing her balance.

"You should be able to activate the room wards if I can lure Fot above them."

"How?" she shouted in frustration.

"Open your mind," he answered, "and the Lady will hear you." A soft golden glow filled the portal room and Jessie's skin tingled. "No distractions now," he murmured, "I must not err..."

"It is time to pray to your goddess, little men," Fot hissed. He roared and they clapped their hands over their ears, cowering away from him.

"Goddess?" Jason shouted.

"This hardly seems the time to engage in a theological debate!" Ric answered. "That thing's trying to kill us!"

"Yes, yes, you do need killing," Fot replied, "but there is that pesky obligation of payment for my release."

"Payment?" Jason asked.

"Obligation?" Ric chimed in.

"Humans. Always neglecting their schooling," Fot replied silkily. "I may not be able to kill you, but there is a place where I can imprison you, as the Otherworlder did me. First, however, we must remove you from your egg. Let me see... what would be the best course of action? Ah, yes."

"Lady, please help me!" Jessie whispered.

The demon's eyes glowed as he made his way to the sphere. He placed two hands on the protective dome. The mighty head bent toward them and he blasted his sickly scented breath against the webbing. Surprise registered on his face.

"I see you, Shield," he said, his voice silken and chilling. "No Sword? His goddess did not grant him life? A shame, I am certain. What--"

"I am here, demon." The Sword appeared as a ghostly figure beside the sphere. Power crackled through the air as he ignited the Sword of Light. He slashed at the demon, splitting scales in half across his chest and forcing him to step away from the sphere.

"You were almost worthy last time, little man," Fot said.

Without waiting for a response, Fot struck. Eron was ready. His sword flashed in a blur and Fot spread his wings, obscuring Eron from Jessie's sight. Fot's body bobbed up and down, a shadow against the light of Eron's sword. She could hear Eron moving. He was breathing in stereo, both in the portal room and at Bel Haven. There was a thud as flesh met flesh and Eron let out a yelp.

"Jessie?" Jason asked. He sounded terrified. "That man...What happened to him?"

"Hang tight, Jason," she answered. It was time to test the defenses she had been developing.

Maintaining the sphere with one hand, she summoned power into the other. A fireball formed in her hand. She puckered her lips and blew. Her weapon shot across the room striking Fot's back with such force that he staggered. He whirled to face her, revealing Eron's ghostly image. He was struggling to stay upright, his sword still blazing in front of him. Fot laughed.

"You have been practicing," Eron breathed into her ear at Bel Haven. "Thank you."

"Any time," Jessie whispered back. She shifted her attention to the boys.

"You may have the power to be present in a vision," Fot observed, "Even to fight. But your energy dwindles. I will deal with you later."

Fot folded in his wings and slithered across the floor where he coiled his body around the sphere like a snake getting ready to strangle its prey. He turned his head to look inside while flicking his tongue. He opened his jaws as wide as possible revealing fangs and razor sharp teeth. Jessie turned her head away from his noxious breath. He sank his teeth into the webbing of the egg and tried to rip it apart.

Jessie gasped. At Bel Haven her hands were bleeding.

Fot laughed. "Is something troubling you, Otherworlder?" he asked silkily.

"You can't harm them!" Jessie said defiantly. "They released you!"

"So one of the Otherworlders has done her schoolwork. How quaint." His whole body encircled her sphere now. With a smile, he constricted his grip. Jessie's hands were frozen in place.

"Jessie! Help us!"

"See how the Otherworlders beg for help."

"JM, what the hell is that thing?"

"I don't know, Ric," Jason answered, "but whatever it is, it's got something against us!"

"You see, Shield," Fot continued as the pressure steadily grew, "I have no intention of killing them. No, indeed. But a little pain might be in order." He opened his mouth wide and sunk his teeth into her web. Ric howled.

The fireplace poker was glowing in Jason's hands. With a concentrated effort, he plunged it through the sphere and into Fot. Both the demon and Jessie shrieked, but Jessie stood fast. Fot released his hold on the sphere and spread his wings wide. From behind, Eron struck a second annoying blow. Fot wheeled round to face him.

"I am not as fragile as you, little man," Fot said.

"You can't even draw your sword, demon," Eron taunted.

"Maybe not yet, but I can destroy that shield!"

"You've tried," Jessie chimed in. "You don't have the strength!"

"I will crush you!"

Fot flapped his wings and rose into the air above them all. The great wings occluded all light from above, leaving only the glow from Eron's ghostly image, the fireplace poker and Jessie's sphere. Higher and higher he rose until he had passed beyond the cave's opening.

"Now!" Eron shouted.

Jessie flung her fingers open wide, casting the webbing of the sphere upward so that it caught on Tocar's wards and multiplied, sealing Jason and Ric inside the room and the demon out. Fot crashed down on the webbing with all his might, but he simply bounced off. Jessie allowed herself a sigh of relief and a laugh. The demon's powers were not enough to break through. Not yet.

"Jessie?" Jason shouted. "Jessie, if this is an adventure, I don't want any part of it!"

Eron's body sagged against hers in Bel Haven. "I--I can't maintain this much longer. We have to go for them…bring them here…safe here…" Eron's fingers were digging into her flesh as he fought to keep the rapidly dissolving link open.

"Jason, stay where you are!" she shouted to her nephew. "I will come for you!"

"But Aunt Jess--"

"Stay put! I'll come for you!" she said.

Jason began a tirade of protests but they were lost to Jessie. She was back among the eddies of Eron's mind, hurtling toward Bel Haven.

14 Winifred James, Damage Assessor

Winifred James glanced around the cottage one more time just to make sure everything was in order. Alvyn was still perched on his driftwood, basking in the artificial heat. He was resourceful enough to hunt for himself, if he needed to. The other of her two pets, Polly, was curled up in a silk pouch Winifred had tied around her neck.

"I am sorry to have to leave you, Alvyn," she told him, "but someone has to keep our home protected until we return."

Alvyn flicked his tongue and continued to bask contentedly in his light. With a twinge of regret, Winifred picked up her walking cane and passed into the early evening darkness.

Along the ribbon of highway visible from her porch she could see flashing lights heading toward Jessie's house. *Things* were being set in motion that might break the bonds of *things* they had protected. *Things* that might be released were a threat to this world. She had to be certain *things* remained safe.

"I hope we did not make a catastrophic mistake," she said aloud. "However, it is best not to worry over what has not yet happened. Let us go, Polly."

She made her way to the van Jessie had given her, opened the door and got in. After throwing her cane between the seats, she patted the dashboard affectionately. Jessie told her there was no soul to this metal creature, but Winifred found that difficult to believe. Beasts of burden always worked better when given incentive and this one, after all, had always responded positively to her commands.

"Nice Caravan," she cooed. As the engine purred, she mentally reviewed how to cue the beast. Being inside of something rather than being on its back had been a bit disconcerting at first, but the feeling vanished when she finally accepted the fact that she was not going to be digested.

"We are not going far, Caravan," she told her metal beast, "just to Jessie's place. If you are good, when we get back, I will suds you down and put a nice, warm cover on you." She patted the van's dash gently once more and then scratched it under the steering wheel. With a firm hand, she slid the van into gear.

The world of Jessie Perrymore was not so unlike her own. The trees were a bit shorter here, the air not quite as crisp and the creatures a bit too tame. Still, it was not a bad place to live, all things considered.

"Stop your daydreaming," she told herself. "We have work to do."

The snake in her pocket shifted and stuck its head out. "Yes, Polly, we have work to do."

15 Exit Strategy

Jason rose slowly from the stone floor using Ric for support. Then he offered a hand to his friend. Ric was shaking, but he took the hand and stood. He pointed up. Above them, the shimmering light that had formed the egg that protected them was clinging to the edges of a narrow opening. Beyond, pin points of starlight were visible.

"Wow," Jason said.

"What the hell was that?" Ric asked. "Damn thing bit me," he added, rubbing his cheek.

"Jessie's got a thing for adventure vacations," Jason mumbled. "Somehow, I don't think this is one of them. Man, it's cold in here."

"Again, I'm okay, thanks for asking."

"We've got to get out of here," Jason said as he walked across the room.

"Now who's master of the obvious?" Ric commented. "It looks like our only choice is through that cave."

Jason rifled through a pile of debris and pulled out a cloak. "At least we won't freeze." He tossed it to Ric and picked up a second one for himself.

Ric shrugged. "Whatever works. I feel like a refugee from Lord of the Rings."

Above them came a whistling noise followed by a crash. The entire room trembled as the force of the crash sent splinters of wood skittering across floor. Jason stumbled and fell, gracefully rolling to one side and coming up on one knee. He grabbed a sturdy round stick from among the debris and used it to right himself.

"What the--" Ric was saying. He was sprawled on his back pointing up.

Jason followed his finger and gasped.

It was perched on the webbing. Huge green and red eyes stared. Beneath the eyes, a tiny forked tongue flitted, bright red in color. Rows of teeth appeared as the creature's lips parted and the yawning hole of its mouth opened, dark and abysmal. It snapped shut with a smack and the serpent winked at them. The barrier sank as it flexed itself to take flight. Then, it leapt upwards and disappeared.

"Somebody needs to give that thing a breath mint," Ric mumbled.

"Breath mint?" Jason shouted. "You're worried about his breath? Seriously?"

The whistle sounded again directly above them like a train coming down a track at full speed. Without thinking, Jason grabbed Ric by the arm and dragged him out of harm's way just as the ceiling crashed into the floor where he had been lying. The webbing snapped back into place like a trampoline, leaving pebbles where there once was stone. The thing roared so loud that Jason slammed his hands over his ears.

"That way!" Jason pointed to the yawning hole at the end of the room. He snatched up the discarded fireplace poker.

"Why...?" Ric asked.

"It's glowing and where we're going looks pretty dark. Now, run!"

In the relative safety of the cavernous opening, Ric leaned against the wall shaking. "What the hell is going on?" he gasped.

The demon screamed. It crashed to the floor again and again the ground shook.

"Hell might be right," Jason said, turning his friend into the darkness. "RUN!"

Oblivious to anything else, they ran. Huge rocks slammed to the ground behind them, effectively sealing the way home.

The poker was still glowing and Jason handed it to Ric who held it in front of him like a torch. The path was wide enough for them to walk abreast but Jason hung behind. Fresh air occasionally blew in their faces from somewhere up ahead. His heart beat faster and his breathing quickened. The demon was hammering away at the ceiling in the room behind them, sending echoes down the rapidly shrinking tunnel. Suddenly, it stopped. Ric pulled up so fast that Jason ran into him.

"You don't suppose it broke through?" Ric asked.

Jason drew in a huge breath. "We'd better hope it didn't." He pointed to the dimming poker. "Our light is nearly out and I don't think it would be a good idea to travel down here without seeing where we're going."

On cue, the poker went entirely dark, sending their other senses into overdrive. Jason placed his hand on the tunnel's wall, trying to reorient himself. The rock was cold and slimy and the slime came away on his hand. He recoiled, but quickly put his hand back on the rock relishing its grounding effect more than being grossed out by the ick. Beside him now, he could feel heat emanating from Ric's body, hear him breathing. Somewhere close by, he thought he could hear water running.

"Hey, Ric," he started, "can you see anything?"

"As much as you. Wait--" Something soft smacked Jason in the face. He could hear clothes rustling. "Trade shows… so many gadgets… Yes!"

A tiny beam of light, laser sharp, filled the tunnel with dim light.

"Credit card flashlight," he said. "You never know when something like this will come in handy."

"So much better," Jason agreed with more than a little relief. "I hear water. Do you see any?"

Ric waved the tiny beam slowly back and forth. When it hit the sides of the tunnel, it illuminated their path. When he flashed it directly ahead, the light disappeared. "No water. But it looks like we're going downhill. If we can find your water, we can follow it to maybe a larger body of water, like a river or something. That will be our way out!"

"Well, we sure can't go back, even though Jessie said to wait." He laughed. "She's alive!"

"Are you sure?" Ric answered. "We never really saw her."

"It was good enough for me." He took a step forward and held out his hand. "Mind if I go first?"

"Claustrophobia getting to you?"

"A little. The sooner we get out of here, the better I'll feel."

"Lead on."

The ground was a bit uneven, but negotiable. They moved forward in shuffling steps, more than once stubbing a toe on a rock placed thoughtfully in their way by some cosmic prankster. As they progressed, the air blew harder on their faces, whistling softly as the tunnel shrank in all dimensions. "It's getting narrower," he called over his shoulder. "And I'm still moving," he whispered to himself.

The tunnel t-boned into another tunnel. Jason shone the light in both directions. He stepped forward into two inches of water.

"Yikes," he said as he stepped back and ran into Ric.

"What?" Ric asked.

"Found the water," he answered, shaking his foot. "Which way?"

"Head downstream," Ric answered.

Jason bent down and put his hand in the icy water. He felt it flow in one direction. They headed to the left.

Their progress slowed as the way became so tight that they had to turn sideways to pass. Above him, Jason's hair brushed against the rock ceiling as top of the tunnel got lower as well.

"JM, can you see anything?" Ric asked.

He flipped the light around to find Ric inches from his shoulder.

"Good grief, Ric," Jason started, "do you have to stand so close? I can smell what you had for dinner three days ago."

"I doubt it," Ric snorted. "But you're certainly welcome to try."

"Give me some room, here!"

"I've been this close to you ever since…" Ric started. "Look, it's really dark. I've been hanging on to your cloak so I wouldn't get lost."

"Well, let go! God, when did the air get so close in here?"

A feeling of dread fell over him. They were surrounded by rock, tons and tons of it, above them, below them, hemming them in on either side. Sweat trickled through his hair and down his back in spite of the cold. The rock was so close to him that his breath brushed back on his cheeks in quick, hot bursts.

"JM?" Ric asked quietly.

Jason let his forehead fall against the slimy stone and gulped a breath of air. He didn't have enough wind to form words.

"Slow your breathing down, Jason," Ric told him. "We're okay. Look forward. Do you feel the air coming in from up ahead?"

Jason turned his head so that, if he could see, he would have been looking down ahead. The air was coming from in front of them, not behind them. He nodded.

"Jason?"

"Y-yes," he answered, "yes, I feel it."

"Then we'll be okay. It's a cave, Jason, not one of those tunnels," Ric said calmly. "Don't let it get to you. Listen to me. Cup your hands and put them over your mouth. Do it!"

Jason slumped, breathing faster and faster. He couldn't catch his breath, couldn't keep up. A lump was rising inside him and he knew his next breath would be his last.

"Okay, so you can't..." Ric's voice drifted in from some distant place. A hand took the flashlight away and the tunnel was illuminated once more.

Still, he couldn't breathe. He was going to die. He knew it. There wasn't enough air. The tunnel was going to come down on them. His head was spinning and he thrust a hand out against the wall to try to stop himself from falling. It was still cold and slimy and he felt a wave of nausea threaten.

"Stay with me, here..." The light went out. Jason was sinking, his body out of his control. He was being forced to walk forward a few paces, then turn away from the wall, toward the incoming breeze. Someone had him under the arms and his mouth and nose were suddenly covered. He took a breath. The air was hot. Somebody was trying to smother him. He was being suffocated. He pawed at them weakly.

"Can't breathe!" he said. Bright lights flashed in front of him in the darkness.

"Yes you can." He recognized Ric's voice and it became the only thing Jason cared about. "Breathe in and out only through your nose..."

Jason put his hand over the ones on his face.

"Just take it nice and slow..." Ric chanted, "that's right...slow breaths...focus..."

His ribs heaved with the effort it took to get enough air.

"Not so deep, JM, just take it slow... that's right, slow and easy..."

The lump in his chest began to dissipate.

"That's right, just relax and breathe...see? Nothing to it..." While Ric continued his mantra, Jason's head began to clear. He suddenly realized that he was leaning against his friend and that Ric's hands were under his arms, supporting him. The tunnel had opened up enough that he could shift and sit against one side and not be wet.

"Wha--what just happened?" he asked slowly.

"You hyperventilated," Ric answered. "You're claustrophobic and you let this place get to you."

"I am not!"

"You are to!"

"Am not!"

"Are to!"

There was a splash up ahead of them and they stopped arguing abruptly.

"What was that?" Jason asked.

"How should I know?" Ric was rustling under his cloak. "We have to go on. And you have to lead because I can't get passed you in this tunnel. Right?"

"R-right."

"And you're going to have to use that light so you can see where we're going. Right?"

"Right."

"And I'm going to hold on to your cloak so I can tell where we're going."

"Oh, all right."

"Okay, now go. Focus so you don't hyperventilate again."

"I did NOT hyperventilate!" Jason protested.

"Just go."

16 Distant Thunder

Jessie was standing in the Great Hall of Bel Haven once again. An angry Penrose stood just outside the shield she had created. The words he was mouthing would soon break through her protection and Jessie would end up with an incredible headache. Instead of letting him finish, she threw her hands up in the air and grasped the top of the dome with her fingers and dissolved the shield. Behind her, Eron fell to the floor with a thud. Quickly she turned to him, but the motion made her dizzy and quite suddenly she found herself on the floor beside him, looking up at Penrose.

"How many times must I tell you to ease off a ward like that slowly," Penrose reprimanded her softly.

"Apparently at least one more," she mumbled. "I'm okay. I think."

"Show me," he commanded.

His piercing eyes stared into hers briefly evaluating her. She felt his gentle touch on her mind, and she showed him what she had seen. He gave her a curt nod. "Sit," he said, easing her onto a nearby chair. Behind him, she heard Eron growl at Sila as she helped him to his feet. For once, she was glad the overly attentive healer was there to help him. Right now, Jessie needed a little time to gather her thoughts. Penrose registered the cuts on the back of her hands as he guided her to her seat. "Something more than a vision has happened," he whispered.

Jessie nodded. "My nephew," she whispered back. "Somehow, he released Fot."

The senior healer's eyes widened and he took in a sharp breath, but he kept his attention focused on her hands.

"I can manage, woman!" Eron snapped.

Sila was attempting to make him lie down. Jessie tried not to laugh. "You better rescue him," she told Penrose. "I'll be fine." He gave her a critical stare, then moved off to help Sila.

Jessie settled back in the hard chair. Her mind was racing through scenarios of what might have happened to bring about Fot's release. Only one person in Claxbury knew anything about the demons and she wasn't likely to tell Jason. And Jason surely would not have released Fot had he known about the danger. What mattered now was that Jason and Ric were in the portal room and that Fot would likely attack, curse or no curse. The boys knew nothing about Eormengrund. She had to get to them. She needed a plan fast and she needed help to execute it.

Eron was sitting on his bed surrounded by half a dozen healers. Blood dripped from an ugly but superficial gash across his left shoulder and his eyes were still black coals. Penrose forced his way through to his patient.

"Please, everyone, go on about your business. There is nothing more to see," he told them rather dismissively. "Sila, bring my satchel." Sila hurried off toward one of the rooms many exits as he gently probed Eron's wound. The other healers withdrew slowly, speaking to one another in hushed, frightened tones.

"I'm all right, Penrose," Eron grumbled, jerking away.

"Hold still," Penrose ordered. "I have not seen the likes of this since we left Kimala."

"We have to go after them!"

"Of course we do," he said calmly, but his eyes were smoldering. "But must you bring fear into this place? You terrify my people, Eron, in no small measure due to your insistence of remaining so visible. I have allowed this. They saw your progress. They were beginning to feel safe." He looked Eron in the eyes. "Today you have frightened them twice. I hope you have good reason."

"My vision has returned," Eron explained, "though I cannot control what I see. There are Otherworlders in the portal room. Fot has been released. Your people should be frightened. We need to move…" He swayed, placing one hand on the bed to steady himself and the other on his head. Penrose helped him sit upright again. His eyes were once again dark brown.

"Eron?" Jessie said, rising from her chair.

"Sit, Jessie. The Sword has imbibed too much tonight," Penrose stated. "I'm surprised he could see anything." Sila returned and offered him a clean cloth. "Thank you, my dear. Eron, you don't mind if I put something on it so it will heal better?" he asked.

"Do I have a choice?" Eron grumbled.

"No. Sila, palapaca, please," he directed. He took the balm from her. "Thank you. Now, fetch King Tersan," he ordered as he dabbed the goo on Eron's wound. The cloth came away black. "Poison. And it's concentrated."

A collective gasp went up from the healers gathered in the room.

"Meaning what?" Jessie said.

"Meaning an attack was made by a demon on Sword and Shield in the safety of this sanctuary where it was witnessed by many. Unfortunately, since Eron insists on staying in the Great Room, it will take no time for news of this attack to reach every person in Bel Haven."

Penrose dabbed the goo over her wounded hands. Once again, the cuts briefly turned black, then changed to a clear residue which he hastily wiped away. He cleared his throat and drew up a chair beside Eron's bed. "Jessie showed me what happened in the portal room. I know about the Otherworlders. I agree that someone must help them. Jessie is the logical choice."

Jessie nodded. "They don't understand. I have to reach them before they get killed."

"We can leave immediately," Eron added.

Penrose shook his head. "Palapaca causes sleep when combined with alcohol. You know that."

"But--"

"Even you are not a good enough horseman to make that ride in the dark while you sleep. Jessie and I will deal with the Otherworlders. I've sent for Tersan. I am releasing you into his care."

"But--"

"It's only a couple of days at most, Eron," Jessie said quietly.

"Tocar is in Il Chatel. I need to warn him." The Sword yawned mightily. "I will try to contact him through a vision but, like I said, I have no control."

"I will send a messenger tonight. Perhaps on a swift horse Tocar can be reached before the demon can fly to Il Chatel." Penrose took in a deep breath. "The time has come for the army to depart, while we hold the advantage. That means, ready or not, Eron, your time here is at an end. I must make some preparations before we depart." With that, he left the two alone. Jessie crawled into bed beside him. He took her bandaged hands in his own.

"If it is not my kinsman, it is yours." He shook his head. "Is no one safe?"

He released her and pulled her head toward his, pressing his lips against hers in a long, comforting kiss. When at last they parted, she put her head on his chest, relishing the comfort of his touch. Gently, he rubbed her back.

"It seems our time of rest has, indeed, ended," he whispered. In the next moment, he was quietly snoring.

17 Knock, Knock

It was well past dusk when Winifred pulled the van into Jessie Perrymore's drive. Up near the house, she could see the flashing red lights of the police. Her heart beat a little faster. Why had they been called to this place? They had no experience with demons, at least none that Jessie had ever mentioned. But they were on the side of good. That part, Jessie had mentioned. And they had seemed nice enough when they came to her cottage to ask about Jessie last summer.

There was a spot beside the policeman's vehicle for her to leave Caravan. She passed it by, instead circling behind Jessie's garden shed to a place that was much closer to the door. She placed her foot on the brake to command Caravan to halt. As always, it did so without protest.

"Thank you, Caravan," she said, patting the dashboard fondly. Then she picked up her cane, opened the door and disembarked.

A fine looking red-haired policeman with a flashlight in his hand made his way toward her. *Officer O'Shea*, Winifred recalled from his visit earlier in the year.

"Hello, Officer O'Shea," she said in her sweetest grandmotherly voice. "I could not help but notice your lights from my cottage. It is such a lovely evening, would you not agree?"

Officer O'Shea looked rather startled. "Ma'am?"

"Is there a problem?" Winifred asked.

"We received a 9-1-1 call from this location," he answered her. "The caller identified himself as Jason McCarthy--"

"Jason was here?" she interrupted sweetly. "He must be looking after the house in Jessie's absence. Fine young man, Jason is."

"Yes, ma'am."

"And you say he called you?" Winifred repeated.

"Yes, ma'am." O'Shea cleared his throat. "He said that he and his companion had somehow fallen under the house. Would you know anything about that, ma'am?"

"A companion? Was it Lucy? The dear girl. I imagine she misses her home."

"I wouldn't know, ma'am."

"Is Jessie back then?"

Officer O'Shea looked perplexed. "Uh, I can't say, ma'am. Mr. McCarthy did not identify the person he was with. However, he did state that perhaps Miss Perrymore had fallen beneath the building as he and his companion had. You wouldn't happen to have a key to this house, would you?"

"Why," she said, digging into her bag, "as a matter of fact, I do!" She withdrew the key and handed it to him. "May I come in with you, Officer? Jessie is a dear friend. And Jason... Such a sweet lad. Oh, but not really a lad anymore. Jason's a young man now." She winked at O'Shea. "Perhaps he was here with a young lady?"

"I wouldn't know, ma'am," he repeated, taking the key from her. "I suppose you can come in. But stay back in case there are some shenanigans going on."

Winifred did not ask what he meant by 'shenanigans' but she stood a respectful distance from the door as Officer O'Shea knocked.

"Mr. McCarthy? This is the police," he called. There was no answer. He looked at Winifred and she smiled sweetly back at him. Polly rattled in her pouch. "Mr. McCarthy," O'Shea continued, "I have a key and I'm going to open the door, okay?"

Winifred waved to him and nodded. If the demon she had seen from her living room was at large, they were in for a battle. She placed the cane squarely between her feet and prepared to throw a shield in front of him. Whether her magic would work in this world or not was a good question. Officer O'Shea turned the key and pushed the heavy wooden door open. He held his flashlight high and steady as he entered the house.

"I wonder why he does not just turn on the lights?" Winifred whispered to Polly. Polly rattled again in her pouch. "Maybe I should show him where the switch is. Oh, Officer!" she called. "Is it all right if I come in now?"

There was a terrible crash.

"Oh, hell," O'Shea said

"Officer?" Winifred called. She started toward the door, cane in hand.

Officer O'Shea's cap came flying out the door. Then came his flashlight; and his badge. They soared around the yard a few times and fell to the ground. Winifred ducked down and barreled through the door as Polly hissed a warning inside her pocket. She stopped abruptly.

Poor Officer O'Shea was sprawled out on the floor giggling helplessly as a gaggle of immature demons mercilessly tickled him.

"Open the portal," they hissed.

Bits of plastic and glass were strewn across the room. Droplets of water beaded up on the wooden floor in a haphazard pattern. Demons whizzed around in a frenzy, cackling and assaulting O'Shea. The oddly shaped shelf that once held Jessie's collection of tacky snow globes lay on its side on the floor, several dozen intact snow globes in disarray piled on the back of the shelf.

Without a word, Winifred raised her hands.

Contego ombra!

To her surprise, an umbrella of light appeared over Officer O'Shea's head. The demons crashed down on it from above him but the shield did not budge.

"It never worked that well at home," she told Polly.

Polly hissed.

"In a moment, Polly. Be patient."

Promineo!

Winifred held her hands slightly above her head, her fingers making contact with the shield. She lowered her hands and the edges of the umbrella elongated until they touched the ground, forming a protective barrier around Officer O'Shea. By this time, he had lost both of his shoes and one sock.

The demons stopped their attack to look at this unlikely heroine. A smile crossed Winifred's face as she looked them over and quite suddenly they recognized her. In an instant, they fled into the house. Winifred picked up her cane and walked over to the fallen policeman. "Are you all right, Officer?" she asked, offering a hand to him.

"Wh-what happened?" he asked.

"I believe it is obvious that you took a bit of a tumble," Winifred answered, pointing to the broken snow globes scattered across the floor. "I wonder how that shelving ended up right there in front of the door? Jessie is so proud of her collection. I would think she would be more particular. In fact, the last time I was here, that shelf was next to the fireplace...over there."

She moved to an end table, also at an odd place, and flipped on a light. The room was instantly illuminated and the damage visible.

"I love the magic of this world!" she said. She counted eleven broken snow globes. That meant eleven demons were loose. "Demons. They are a bit of a nuisance at that stage of life, but really, did you think throwing your clothing at them would help?"

"I--I--"

"Oh, it is all right, Officer," Winifred said. A siren wailed outside in the driveway. "Do not worry. Your secret is safe with me. However, you had better get dressed. I believe we have company. Here is one of your shoes…"

Officer O'Shea's face was redder than his hair. He took the shoe and began searching for his other things. Winifred removed Polly from the silk pouch. The little serpent gracefully arched her head, spreading her wings as though stretching after a satisfying sleep.

"Happy hunting," Winifred whispered.

In a flash, Polly was gone.

18 The Crystal Cave

Jason held the tiny flashlight intermittently in either hand or between his teeth, whichever way yielded the most light. They could stand normally, though the passage was only wide enough to walk single file. Behind him, Ric followed closely in nearly complete darkness, occasionally bumping him. The accidental contact was oddly reassuring.

Without warning, the wall to his right disappeared. His feet slipped and he found himself scrambling to keep his balance. Ric grabbed his cape, and yanked him back into the remaining wall.

"The wall's gone!" Jason shouted.

"I noticed!"

"It scared the hell out of me!"

"So I see!"

Jason scanned the distance in front of him with the pinpoint beam. The water ran another three or four feet that his light picked up and then disappeared. Beyond that, the light was swallowed by vast blackness. He stepped forward and the incessant wind lessened. Ric followed.

"Sounds like a waterfall ahead," he said, shining the light onto their path. "I can't tell what's beyond that."

"We're in a cavern," Ric said. "We just have to keep going until we find our way out."

"Man, I hope we don't have to go back!"

Jason's finger slipped off the light's button and they were plunged into darkness again. In the distance, there was a small amount of lighter dark. He strained to see it.

"Look!" he started. "There's our way out!"

"Where?" came Ric's answer.

"There!" He was pointing uselessly in the dark.

"I can't see it."

"There!" Jason snapped the light back on, knowing that the beam wouldn't reach the far side of the cavern but unable to resist the temptation to try. Searching for any closer sign of an exit, he started a slow, methodical scan of their surroundings.

The beam struck a stalactite. The formation was crystal-like, clear and beautiful in the middle surrounded by a crust of rock sandwiching it on the top and bottom. The beam shot inside the formation where it became trapped. Light ricocheted off the insides in a frantic unsuccessful attempt to escape. Each time the light hit the inside of the formation, it refracted and intensified producing a hypnotic display of light within its confines. The crusty layer from the top slid down until it started to push on the bottom layer. It sloughed away slowly at first, then fell away completely, leaving nothing but brilliant white light.

They stared at it, transfixed by its beauty. A slow pulse dimmed the light, then brightened it, a cycle that repeated over and over again gaining speed and brilliance until a pure white beam shot out of its center in a line so straight that it looked like a laser. It struck a second stalactite and the entire process began anew. As the second stalactite brightened, the first dimmed, the beam between them remaining a brilliant rope connecting the two formations.

As intense as the two light sources were, they were not bright enough to illuminate the huge cavern. Jason didn't care. It was such a relief to be able to see more of his surroundings than the tiny beam allowed. Every muscle in his body relaxed just a little bit.

The second crystal shot a beam to a third and then dimmed as its predecessor had. The three were in nearly a straight line.

"Wow," Jason breathed.

"I'll second that," Ric answered. "Hell of a light switch you got there."

The stream they had been walking along was now visible in the stalactites' glow. It had widened to a little over a foot as it exited the tunnel and appeared at least as deep. Barely twenty feet in front of them, the water flowed over a low spot in a rocky ledge. To the left of that, the ledge dropped level with their path.

"This way!" Jason said as he abandoned caution and strode forward.

Just as he reached the low spot, he slipped.

"Whoa!"

He waved his arms wildly trying to regain his balance. The cape wrapped his arms up and he fell four feet to another ledge, landing with one foot dangling in very cold water. He jerked his foot out and rolled to his back. Directly above him was the crystal he had ignited.

"Are you all right?" Ric asked as he stepped off the stairway Jason had missed.

"I can't believe I was so stupid." Jason did a quick damage assessment. Finding nothing but a very wet, cold foot, he stood. "I'm fine."

"Good. This is so cool."

Five crystal stalactites in an impossibly straight line were now illuminated. The last three looked dirty, like pearls unevenly formed. They had not yet shed their crusty exterior, but the beams between them were pure. The tendrils of light pulsated with a regular rhythm, flooding light toward the last one in line, arteries of some non-living entity coming to life.

"Looks like it's gonna blow!" Jason exclaimed, pointing to the last crystal.

The fifth crystal appeared to swell and shrink in rhythm with the throbbing pulse of the light feeding it. One by one, the first four dimmed into near darkness as their light drained in an orderly manner into the fifth. In a single burst, a brilliant beam shot in a straight line over the now visible lake. It struck a huge stalactite where it was absorbed. The light glowed briefly within the huge body, as the others had done, but instead of getting brighter, the giant dimmed. All six formations throbbed in sync.

"Look," Ric said. He was pointing to what was visible in the dim light. Before them a smooth surface spread further than they could see. In it, the giant stalactite was reflected. "That's some lake," he murmured. "Must have taken years to fill!"

"No kidding." Jason cocked his head to one side. "Do you hear that?"

"The only thing I hear is that waterfall."

"The wind is gone! That can't be good. Which way do we go?"

"Don't panic. I can't hear it, but I can still feel it moving. Do you see an exit?" Ric asked, turning on the narrow pathway to survey as much of the cavern as was possible.

"Only that lighter area over there." Jason pointed across the lake.

A walkway resembling a wide catwalk etched out of stone was visible for about fifty feet in front of them. It disappeared to the left, then reappeared across a short distance. Jason followed it until it met the distant shoreline. He had to imagine the connection between where the light illuminated the walkway and the lighter area in the distance that he thought was the exit.

"Do you suppose there's a place to walk all the way around?" Ric asked.

"I don't know," Jason answered. "It doesn't look like it's all that far. What I can see looks pretty level."

"We do have another option." Ric pointed in the opposite direction. "There is a path to the right of the stream as well. I saw it after you fell. That could be the way out."

"Is it like another tunnel?" Jason shivered.

"Well, it's a big black hole with rock around it. I guess it's a tunnel."

"Not to be cliché, but did you see a light?"

"No. But I didn't really look. Maybe we should."

"I don't know. That is definitely lighter over there," he said pointing.

"It looks like the ground rises that way. Logic dictates we go downhill whenever possible." Ric looked at his wrist. "Three a.m. Do you suppose the cops know where this cave is?" He poked his finger in his mouth and then held it up in the air in front of him.

"What are you doing?" Jason asked. "And I wouldn't know. The hills are riddled with caves."

"Assessing wind direction," Ric replied. "We should follow the direction the wind is coming from."

"You've watched way too many old movies."

Ric furrowed his brow and squeezed one eye shut. He stretched his arm out as far as he could and shifted his hand slightly. Jason laughed. "Okay, Master Scout, which way do we go?"

Ric shrugged. "I can't really tell. The light you're seeing over there could be moonlight. Then again, it could be some chemical reaction happening between elements."

"But to the right, we have darkness and another tunnel. That settles it." Jason pointed to the lighter area on the distant shore. "We go that-a-way."

Predictably, the path took an easy turn to the left and went slightly uphill. A mountain of a stalactite glistened in the pulsating light of the center giant. It looked as though someone had taken an enormous scoop and dipped the stone out of the lake only to deposit it on the other side of the walkway. To their right, they could see the same light reflected five feet below them in the black water of the lake. Jason kept as much distance as he could between him and the edge. His foot was still cold from his brief encounter with the water. Ric suddenly stopped and Jason halted beside him.

"Do you feel that?" he asked.

"Feel what?"

"The air…it's coming from in front of us."

"You and your air." Jason stared ahead at the light as hard as he could. "Wait--That's a good thing, right? We're going in the right direction?"

"I hope so."

Shadows subtlety shifted on the wall, pulsating more quickly now with brighter light in a throbbing, constant beat. The huge crystal had come to life, its light intensifying with each pulse.

"You don't suppose it really is going to explode?" Ric asked.

"Who knows?" Jason answered. "Who would have thought we would be attacked by a big snake with wings that smelled like flowers and garlic? Let's just get the hell out of here. We can let the cops figure it out."

"Good idea."

The mountain of stone receded and dropped away leaving them to walk over a bridge-like formation, dark water of the lake to their right and a deepening chasm on the left. A steady wind blew from the chasm's depths, the air dank, musty and chilled. Jason stopped and looked down into the darkness but he saw nothing.

"This place gives me the creeps."

There was a terrific splash in the middle of the lake. The huge crystal had shed its coating and now blazed brilliantly above them. In the next instant, light exploded from it in intense beams, shooting through the cavern to hundreds of stalactites. They shed their umbilical cords instantly, having accepted life from the giant. The cavern was bright and getting brighter.

"It looks like high noon in August!" Ric said, shielding his eyes from the light with both hands.

"Yeah," Jason agreed, "and when those little crystals get fully lit, it'll be like we're in a welding shop without eye protection! Run!"

They ran full tilt the last hundred yards to the turn in the shoreline. Silt plinked the surface of the lake like a gentle rain. It covered the walkway as well, making the ground slick under their feet. The light was getting so intense that the individual crystals were no longer visible. They made the final turn. In less than a hundred feet, they would be at the exit.

"C'mon!" Jason yelled.

Beside him, Ric slipped. He was on one knee and then sliding down the steep embankment toward the water. Jason dove after him, belly first on the rock strewn ground extending his body as far as he dared without sliding down the embankment. But he was too far away. Ric was floundering against the slick stone wall snatching at the smooth surface in an effort to regain his footing. His efforts failed and he hit the water with a mighty splash.

"Swim!" Jason shouted, panic raising the pitch of his voice half an octave. He scanned the shoreline for a place to get out. Ahead a short distance, the path dipped down to a place where the lake and the path were almost the same height. "Swim to your right!"

Ric was a poor swimmer on his best day. Jason followed him awkwardly on the shoreline, his heart pounding. At first, Ric appeared to be in control, head out of the water, progressing slowly but with certainty. But his motions became sluggish. He paused in the icy water, bobbing up and down rather than moving forward.

"Get rid of that cape!" Jason ordered. "It's pulling you down!"

Ric paused and unclasped the binding holding the garment on. The cape slid away into the depths.

"Good! Now swim!" Jason yelled.

Ric responded by starting to swim again. He was inching forward when he should be progressing by feet. Jason's heart sunk. Ric would never make it to the place where he could reach him and the shore here was still too high for Jason to reach him. Then an idea struck. "Ric, do you still have that poker?"

Ric stopped his sluggish forward movement and bobbed up and down in place. He was fiddling with something and the poker suddenly appeared.

"Hand it up here!"

Ric made some awkward motions, but held it up to Jason. Jason snatched at it, catching the thin metal utensil with his first attempt. He wrapped his fingers around it and pulled with every ounce of strength he had. Ric came up out of the water. He was just dead weight.

"You gotta help me out! Try to get your feet on the rock and walk yourself up!"

Ric shifted his weight and Jason tightened his grip. The metal slipped through his fingers, but it stopped as soon as his hands reached the tip. Certain that he had a solid hold he leaned back and braced his feet against two stalagmites that lined the pathway. Ric came halfway up the stone embankment. He slipped and his body flopped against the rock.

"It's okay!" Jason encouraged. "Get your feet under you!"

Ric heaved a sigh and turned. He was moving painfully slowly and Jason's arms were tiring. Ric shifted to get a better angle to walk up the side of the shore, taxing Jason to his maximum by pulling against him.

"That's it!" Jason called out. His muscles were on fire from the effort. "Keep walking!"

Jason put one hand over the other on the thin metal rod, trying to get closer to flesh. If he could just get hold of Ric's hand, pulling him out would be easier.

"Take my hand!" Jason shouted.

Ric took his hand off the poker and swung it toward Jason's. For one fleeting moment they touched. Contact made, connection failed. Jason watched in horror as Ric lost his grip on the poker and slammed against the stony shore again. He ended up in the lake with a splash.

"Ric!" Jason shouted.

Ric was looking up at him, defeat written across his face. Jason flipped the poker around so that the hooked end was toward his fallen comrade. "Don't you dare give up! Grab this thing!"

Ric gave a half-hearted attempt to latch onto the poker but his hand missed the metal and he floundered in the water.

"Try again!" Jason yelled, trying not to let panic set into his voice.

Ric bobbed up and down in the water. Any reserve of energy that he had was rapidly dwindling.

"Come on! One more time!" Jason yelled. "Don't you leave me here alone!"

Ric bobbed weakly.

"You can't give up! You've still got bills to pay!" he screamed.

Ric stifled a laugh. He dipped down in the water and came up with both hands in the air flailing for the poker. Jason snagged the collar of his shirt with the metal tip and pulled with every bit of energy he had. This time he put one hand over the other on the poker until he finally had Ric's hand in his own. Jason threw the poker behind him and grabbed the back of Ric's shirt. He pulled hard, then caught his belt and pulled again. One more heave and Ric's torso would be on the walkway. The lanky youth had run out of energy. Jason collected himself for one last pull.

A low pitched hum filled the cave. Pieces of silt now pelted them from above. Ric looked up at him and a glowing chunk caught him squarely on his already wounded cheek. His skin split open wide and the crystal embedded itself there. He turned to dead weight.

"Ric!" Jason shouted. He couldn't hold on any longer. Ric slid back down into the water and bobbed for a moment, then went under the surface.

"No!" Jason yelled. He shed his cape and slid down the shoreline, plunging feet first into the cold water. Ric was gone. Jason took a deep breath and dove.

The water was cloudy with silt. That, combined with the increasingly bright light above them effectively blinded Jason. He placed his hand on the lake's rocky shore to keep his bearings and kicked as hard as he could to descend. In nothing short of a miracle, he caught up with Ric's body. Taking hold under one arm, he turned and now kicked up with all his might.

Jason gasped for air when he hit the surface. Instinctively, he flipped Ric over to allow him to breathe. He didn't. Keeping them both afloat by treading water, he wrapped his lips around Ric's and breathed in once. The chest rose but Ric made no effort to continue. Jason breathed for him again and again, each time waiting for Ric to respond.

Jason temporarily gave up trying to resuscitate his friend, concentrating instead on getting them both out of the water. He put an arm across the still body and swam, one stroke, two strokes, three, until he dragged them both out of lake and onto the shore. He rolled Ric on his side, then on his back in an attempt to clear the airway. Three quick chest thrusts and Ric sputtered and coughed. Jason quickly turned him on his side. The exit was barely twenty feet away from them. They were almost home free.

"Thank you, God!" Jason said. "Say something!"

"Cold..."

"Yes!" Jason shouted. He clapped a hand on Ric's back. "Don't move." Jason staggered the short distance to his discarded cape, snatched it up.

Ric had rolled over and was on all fours.

"Man, I hope you can walk," Jason told him.

"I'll manage…"

The light from the crystals was so brilliant now that Jason could barely make out the edge of the walk. He took Ric by the arm and dragged him to his feet. Putting himself between his still coughing friend and the treacherous shore, Jason hustled them toward the exit.

Ten feet to go and the light dimmed so suddenly that Jason stumbled to a halt. He looked toward the ceiling. The crystals were pure and beautiful. A static charge prickled the hair on the back of his neck. Something big was about to happen.

"Run!" he cried.

Before he could take a step, the smaller crystals shot their light back to the huge central stalactite. It glowed brilliantly, lighting the entire cavern but not blindingly. They stopped, awestruck by its beauty. Then it came. A stream of light discharged into the depths of the lake. Hundreds of crystals lit beneath the surface transforming the black surface to a hellish fire. Back from the depths the light shot up into the central stalactite, almost instantaneously lighting every crystal in the cave.

"I can't see!" Ric said.

"Neither can I!" Jason shouted. "Keep one hand on the wall!! We're almost there!"

Sounds changed and Jason knew they had reached their destination. He let go of Ric and felt rather than saw his friend fall to the floor.

"We made it!" he laughed. "We made it!"

"I c-can't s-see anything," Ric said softly.

"Neither can I," Jason answered. "Give it a minute."

"J-JM," Ric stammered. He sucked in a breath. "I-I'm f-freezing."

Jason squinted his eyes closed and then opened them again. Their surroundings were beginning to come into focus. Light poured in from the opening that led back to the cavern.

"Here," Jason said. He took the rescued cloak and flung it around Ric.

"Th-thanks," Ric managed. "B-Better."

"You're welcome."

Light poured in from the opening that led back to the cavern and was becoming brighter every second. He didn't want to be out on the lakeshore now. The way out had to be a bit deeper in this room. "I'm going to look for the exit. I'll be right back."

The room darkened as he moved further into it. He kept his left hand on the wall as he searched for the way out. Five minutes later, he was back where he started. This exit was a room and the room was a dead end.

"And now, we're trapped like rats," Jason said aloud.

Ric didn't answer. Jason could hear him breathing evenly in the center of the room. At least it wasn't labored. All he needs is a little sleep, Jason reasoned. And maybe the light wouldn't last that long. All they had to do was wait it out.

"We'll get out of here yet, Ric," he said.

Ric snored.

A memory of garlic and lavender set off an alarm in his head. Without thinking, he dashed back out into the cavern to get the poker.

Light assaulted him, light so bright that he stumbled backward against the rocky wall. He opened his eyes to see if there was something there that he had to fight and light stabbed into his brain. He cried aloud in pain and toppled backward into the dead end room. He fell hard onto the ground.

"Ric?" Jason called weakly. "Ric, where are you?" He was blind. He could only hope the police would know to look for them here and that that thing would not. His head throbbed mercilessly and wave after wave of nausea threatened to make him vomit.

"Wonder if this is where Jessie bought it?" he mumbled before shutting his eyes to the world for perhaps the last time.

19 Polly-wanna-demon?

Winifred picked up all of the tiny plastic and glass pieces she could find and placed them on the end table. Jessie kept meticulous notes describing each captured demon and which snow globe held which demon so getting them identified should not be a monumental task. Fortunately, only eleven of the globes had broken. If they were lucky, they could resolve the problem before it became an incident. Officer O'Shea had his shoes on and was headed outside to retrieve his hat and his badge.

"It will be easier and less time consuming if I have help to re-jail them," she mumbled to herself. A whirring sound caused her to jerk back just in time to avoid being hit by one of the loose demons with Polly racing close behind it.

"I will be with you in a moment, Polly," she told her pet. She made her way into the kitchen. "Let us see, something with a lid..."

Under the sink she found a dozen canning jars with lids complete with instructions for sealing food inside them. Winifred read the directions.

"These jars keep food from spoiling," she reasoned, placing the jars on the countertop, "they should be good enough for demons. However, I do not think placing them in boiling water to establish a seal is a very nice option. A simple incantation should do. My shield seems to work, but it would be good to have assistance with incantations. Officer O'Shea seems bright. I am certain he will help if needed. Now, all we need is something to catch them in. Let's see..."

Another whirr sounded and she slammed herself up against the refrigerator as Polly now herded two demons in a mad race around the kitchen's island, under the table and through the cookware hanging from the ceiling. Pots scattered everywhere, clattering to the ground with a frightful noise, chairs overturned and even the table bucked. Polly kept the two demons ahead of her and they scooted out the door and back into the living room.

"Atta girl, Pol!" Winifred called after her. "Now, let me see…" Winifred counted her jars. "Yes, I think this will do quite nicely. We are ready for the good officer."

She headed into the living room. Headlights from the second police car glared through the front window. Beyond the glare, a car door closed and a slim woman appeared in the light. She met Officer O'Shea and they held a brief conversation.

"This just got a bit more complicated, Polly," she mused as the serpent whizzed past her again, this time herding four of the missing demons. "Ah well. No matter." She opened the front door.

"I'll check the perimeter," the woman was saying.

"Fine, Joann," Patrick answered. Joann turned to her right and proceeded to walk around the outside of the house.

"Officer O'Shea?" Winifred asked in as innocent a voice as she could muster.

O'Shea looked up at her. "Ma'am?"

"I think I found something in the kitchen. Would you come and take a look?"

"Of course." O'Shea unholstered his gun and moved cautiously toward the house.

Winifred sighed. "I don't believe you will need your weapon, Officer," she said.

"It's only a precaution," O'Shea answered. "Something attacked me in there."

Polly buzzed by, five demons now racing ahead of her. They knocked a lamp over. It crashed, sending the room into darkness. O'Shea dropped into a defensive position.

"Look out!" she cried as Polly flew by again, this time half a dozen demons in front of her. The tiny serpent was so fast she was a blur.

"What the hell was that?" Officer O'Shea shouted.

"Language, Officer. They are demons in their larval form," Winifred answered calmly. "It seems it will take a while for them to gain any size here."

"Demons?"

"Yes, dear. Come along." Without waiting for him, she waltzed into the kitchen. "You released them when you bumped into that shelving of Jessie's," she explained. "You know, I told her that something like this might happen."

"What are you talking about?"

"The demons, Officer O'Shea. You released them. I need help to put them back. Now, put your gun away. It will interfere with capturing them."

"You're kidding?" he said.

"Here." She ignored his comment and offered him a large metal tray. "Polly will herd them toward you. It should be easy. But we must hurry before they grow out of larval state."

"Huh?"

Winifred sighed. "Put away your gun. They are moving far too quickly for you to shoot one."

"Good point." Patrick put his gun back in its holster.

"There's a good lad. Now, these jars," she said, waving grandly at the array of canning jars, "seem appropriate."

O'Shea stared at the countertop. He looked confused.

"Honestly, Officer," Winifred said, her patience waning, "this is the only way to rid your world of them. If we allow them to grow—it is all too complicated to explain now and besides, it is just a theory. But right now, I need your help. You have the strength to hold the tray steady when they hit it. They'll stun themselves and we can put them into the jars. Come."

"Theory?"

Polly had seven now. She was moving so fast that Winifred could barely see her.

"Please, Patrick," Winifred said, resorting to his first name. She shoved the tray at him and one of the canning jars. "Polly will chase one so that it will run smack into the tray. Then you let it slide into the jar and I will temporarily seal it."

"Really?" he said sarcastically. But he took the tray and held it just above the jar.

Bang! Something small and snakelike appeared. It was still, but starting to move.

"Put it in the jar! Quickly!"

He poured the stunned creature into the jar and Winifred capped it. She uttered a few words and set it on the counter. "There! Now, you see, that was not so hard, was it?"

For only a moment, the demon appeared as a black snake with a bright red forked tongue and a hundred tiny hands. It folded its wings around its body and disappeared.

"What the hell was that?" Patrick asked. Polly and the herd whirled past again.

"I told you. A demon." Winifred smiled. "One down, ten to go. Now, hold that tray up," Winnie commanded.

The wind that was the herd flew by again. Polly cut one away and chased it into the tray. Thud! The winged serpent pulled up quickly, soaring above the bowl and returning to the herd that now consisted of seven demons. Patrick obediently poured the demon into the jar.

"Good show, Patrick!" Winifred exclaimed. She ducked as the herd passed again. Another thud. Another demon caught.

"You're going to have some explaining...gotcha!...to do, ma'am," Patrick said, depositing a fourth demon into its jar.

"Of course, dear," Winfred answered, capping the jar, "just as soon as we catch the rest."

For twenty more minutes, they worked until every demon in Polly's herd was captured. Polly hovered beside Winifred's head, her tiny wings moving so fast that they couldn't be seen. Two empty jars remained on the counter.

"We are not done yet, Polly," she told the serpent.

Polly was off in a shot, searching the entire house. Moments later, she returned. Alone.

"Oh my," Winifred said. "Well, where could they go?"

"Ma'am?" Patrick asked.

"It appears," she began, "that we may have a problem."

Patrick shook his head. "Ma'am, I'm not sure what just happened here, but I came out here in response to a distress call. Jason McCarthy said he had fallen under the house."

"Yes, I can see how things would appear, well, unusual," Winifred agreed with her sweetest grandma smile.

"'Unusual' is a gross understatement," Patrick said. He moved so that he blocked her path out of the house. "Is there something you would like to tell me, Miss James?"

"Young man, there are many things I could tell you and there are some things that I must tell you." She patted him lightly on the arm, then shooed him out of her way. As she headed into the living room, she turned on the overhead light.

"I'm going to have to ask you to come with me, Miss James--"

"'Miss James.' For the life of me, I cannot understand why you people need more than one name. Call me Winifred. And come along, dear, or move aside. I have things to do."

"Please, Miss James, I've helped you with, well, whatever we just did. Right now, I need for you to come down to the station and answer some questions."

"Nonsense. Time is precious, Patrick. We must recapture those demons! I can answer any questions you have right here."

"Keep your hands where I can see them, Miss James!"

Winifred turned to face him. "Why, Officer O'Shea, is there a problem?" She kept her hands where he could see them, but she started weaving a protective shield between her fingers. He stared at her hands as light danced between them.

"Stop that!" Patrick ordered.

"Stop what?" Winifred answered calmly, still weaving.

"Wh-whatever it is that you're doing with your hands!"

Winifred stopped. The shield was essentially finished. It hung suspended between them. "You said to keep my hands in sight. I have done that."

"What is it?" he asked, staring at the web.

"Just a little…" She puckered her lips and gently blew. "…magic." The shield rocketed toward Patrick knocking his cap off and sending him to the ground to join it. He looked up at her, surprise and a little fear registering on his face. "That worked well," she said with satisfaction.

"Who are you?" he breathed.

"Winifred James," she answered. "Please call me Winifred."

"O-okay." He scrambled back a bit, retrieving his cap.

She offered him a hand to assist him in standing. He took it and got to his feet. "I guess I can ask you questions here."

"That would be fine," she answered. "We have to wait for Polly to find the others."

There was a humming sound coming from near the fireplace. In the now lit room, Patrick saw something that was out of place on the floor. He strode over to the mantle and picked it up.

"What do you have there, Officer?" Winifred asked.

"A very old video recorder," he answered. "It's still recording, if memory serves." Worry furrowed his brow as he shut it off. "Winifred, do you know anyone who would want to harm Jason?"

"Jason is a lovely young man!" Winifred answered. "He should not have an enemy in the world."

Patrick shook his head and pointed to an antique wardrobe situated on the side of the room. "Is there a TV in there? Video player?"

"I believe so," Winifred answered.

Patrick opened the door, and began working with the machines inside the cabinet. "Might be evidence," he mumbled, opening the camera, "but sometimes you just have to move quickly. There..." He put the tape he had removed into the machine and touched a small black box on his shoulder. "Joann? Have you--"

Outside, a woman screamed.

Patrick drew his weapon and flew toward the front door, Winifred and Polly following in his wake. The officer stopped dead in his tracks, blocking the door with his body, preventing her from exiting.

"Stay back!" he ordered.

On the front lawn, a very tall woman stood. She was statuesque, her hair billowing around her face in the night air, a gown of soft material swirling around her perfect body. From behind Patrick, Winifred shivered. The woman had Joann firmly in her grasp. She looked straight past Patrick to Winifred.

"Wylfcynne," she hissed. She held Joann by the throat with one hand, oblivious to the strangling noises the officer was making.

"Let her go!" Patrick ordered.

"Is that all you require, little man?" the woman asked.

"Patrick, don't say anything!" Winifred pleaded.

"I said, let her go!" Patrick repeated.

The woman dropped Joann and smiled widely. She transformed in to a devilish looking creature with wings, a tail and sets of hands lining her underbelly.

"She's a demon, Patrick," Winifred started, "and legend has it that the person who releases--"

The demon shrieked. She rose into the air and swooped toward them. Polly ruffled her scales and shot out toward the demon.

"Polly! Wait!" Winifred cried.

Patrick raised his gun and aimed but before he could get a shot off, Winifred thrust his arm aside and his shot went wide. "You might harm Polly!" she shouted.

Winifred calmed herself. Her mind went into automatic setting her fingers to work. A glowing silver shield erupted from her fingertips and she threw it in front of them as the demon came in for a second run. It hit the shield so hard that Winifred found herself sitting on the ground beside a startled Patrick, but the shield held.

High above them, the demon laughed. Laughter came from two voices, not one, and faded into the night. She allowed the shield to dissipate. In the night sky, the two creatures were shadow against the moon, followed by a third, tiny spot.

20 On the Eve of War

Tersan tilted the parchment into the light and re-read the words he had just written. Letters to a six-year-old daughter were far more difficult than letters of judgement. The alliance Tersan had made with Pixil to combine their forces would not be of interest to Candra, nor would their carefully orchestrated decision to train openly at Pella Durett where their enemies could see the power of their combined forces grow. The last element of their plan, to have Sword and Shield riding at this massive army's head, was almost in place. Thus a show of power would be all that was needed to secure peace and hopefully, a bloodless victory.

In Il Chatel, Calshara's bejeweled capital, Tocar was bartering for peace. Not a single demon had been sighted since the battle on Kimala and Marand was eagerly soliciting peace. Eron was nearly ready, Jessie ever at his side. The army could move north in less than a week. If all went well, Tersan could be home with his children to celebrate Winter Solstice. He set the letter down on the desk and re-inked his quill.

Please share this with Raef. My love to you both.

He sealed Candra's letter and placed it on top of the domestic disputes he had just resolved, hoping his daughter would be satisfied with a report on the plaiting of Greystone's tail and enjoy explaining those details to her little brother. All that was left to do tonight was finish the small bottle of wine he had been nursing all evening in order to keep a clear head while doing the kingdom of Jeleste's more mundane business.

"Master Penrose," he said admiring the last dark red drop in his glass, "your cellar is exquisite." He tilted his glass to drain the last swallow. Then he rose and stretched muscles honed for battle. "Warrior by day, peacemaker by night. The price of power and privilege," he said, eyeing a second set of documents he had yet to address. "Still, better to be a king than a peasant. Rudlo!"

The door swung open and his standard bearer appeared, bowing curtly. He looked from Tersan to the documents on the table. "Majesty?"

Tersan gestured to the stack he had just completed. "See that these decisions are sent to Ellance. There is a letter for Candra as well. The rest I will tend to in Pella Durett tomorrow."

"Yes, my lord." Rudlo gathered the dispatches in one huge hand and the empty wine bottle in the other. "Another, my lord?" he offered.

Better a king... Tersan sighed. "No, not tonight."

"As you wish."

Rudlo bowed and turned to leave. He nearly ran over a hooded woman standing in the doorway. Instantly he stepped back and bowed a second time, waiting for her to speak. Moonlight shone around her slim figure obscuring her features in a soft glow. The scent of lilies filled the room. No one moved. The woman shifted slightly and candle light glinted off the Mistress Medallion clasp securing her cloak.

"Mistress Aramat?" Tersan asked.

The healer lowered her hood. White light fell on her nearly flawless porcelain skin. "Mistress Sila Atin, your Majesty," the healer answered with a dip of her head. "I have come on a mission of great urgency. Master Penrose requests your presence in the Great Hall."

"Now?" he asked through a yawn. "It is very late, madam healer."

Sila leaned close to Tersan and whispered a single word into his ear. "Demons."

Tersan grabbed his sword and hurriedly buckled it to his belt. "Where?" he demanded.

"Lord Eron has seen them, my lord," she answered reverently, "in a vision."

"A vision." Tersan rested both hands on the hilt of his sword and raised an eyebrow.

"I witnessed a wound appear across his shoulder while he stood in the Great Hall," she argued. "There was poison in it."

"Poison?" Tersan asked. He unbuckled the sword and set it on the desk.

"Only a demon can inflict this poison," she insisted, raising her voice.

"Madam!" Tersan said.

There were whispers outside the door and someone stepped away quickly.

"There is a time and a place for such news to be revealed," Tersan said sharply. "Now is not such a time!"

"I was charged to bring you to Penrose," she argued, "and you wanted to know why."

Tersan moved past her through the door in time to see a horse gallop away. A small group of people left hurriedly when they saw the king, whispering among themselves.

"I can intercept him, my lord," Rudlo offered.

"It is too late, Rudlo," Tersan said. "See to those dispatches."

"Yes, my lord."

Tersan scowled at Sila Atin and then strode quickly toward the Great Hall. Halfway across the courtyard, he heard a grunt behind him. He turned to find the healer sprawled on the ground in an undignified heap. He returned to her and helped her rise.

"Are you all right?" he asked.

"My robe was not fashioned for dashing about in the night, my lord," she answered as she smoothed the cloth across her lithe frame. He took her arm and escorted her the rest of the way to the Great Hall.

Light filled the corridor from a number of open doors. Healers spoke with hushed voices within some of the rooms, their tone fearful. Tersan ignored them, still gently guiding Sila Atin to the Great Hall. A candle flickered beside an empty bed in the center of the room. Sila sunk her fingers into Tersan's arm.

"The demon returned!" she gasped. "Lord Eron has fallen! I should not have left!"

"Calm yourself, Mistress," Tersan said. "It does not appear anything untoward has occurred. Where else would they be?"

Sila took a moment to compose herself. "This way."

They walked down an adjacent corridor, stopping in front of a door slightly ajar. Tersan knocked. It swung open to reveal Eron, alone on a narrow bed, his attention fixed on an object in his hands. Sila clutched at her chest.

"Fetch your master," Tersan commanded quietly.

"Yes, my lord," she said. She curtsied gracefully and floated down the hallway.

"How can a healer with such great talent be so naïve?" he asked, watching her with renewed appreciation.

"It's too late to chase a pretty girl tonight," Eron answered, "even for you."

"You have been away from the throne too long, my friend, if you think that all I do is bed pretty girls."

Eron snorted. "She's beautiful and brilliant, but she has no sense, though I'm not certain you need any of those qualities for a good frolic as long as the lady in question is of the same mind."

"Those days are long gone, I'm afraid." Tersan sat on the room's only chair.

"Jessie's nephew came through the portal with another young man," Eron began. "They brought Fot with them."

"I thought Fot was dead."

"Not dead, just inert. We didn't kill them because Jessie has some romantic notion that we can eventually reason with them. In addition, Wylfcynne insisted. For all I know, they're right. We've never released any of them to find out." His voice drifted and his eyes darkened. "We thought they'd be safe, imprisoned in those tiny globes and stored in Jessie's world." Eron stared at the thing in his hands.

"What are you doing?" Tersan asked.

"Rekindling my gift of vision; or trying to." Eron showed him the small stone. It was unlike anything Tersan had ever seen, as simple as a common river rock yet as intriguing as a rare gem mined from the Paranjothi mountains and cut by Ellance's finest craftsmen. "I submitted myself to Ritual in the Crystal Cave," Eron explained, "and for surviving the ordeal, the Lady gifted me with four crystals."

Light flickered on the stone's facets as Eron twisted it back and forth in his fingers. "At first, I didn't know what they were, but with Penrose's help, in time, I learned their secrets. If there is someone holding the stone whose mind I have touched or who is a blood relative, it was possible to communicate even at great distances. Penrose said there may come a time when I don't need the crystals. He was right. That day in the portal room, I lost many things." He offered it to Tersan. "Here."

For the instant that both men touched the stone, energy pulsated across its surface, leaving it unnaturally warm. As soon as Tersan alone held it, the heat faded as did its hypnotic beauty. Now, small bubbles of light churned up through the stone from its depths. Eron smiled.

"I could teach you," he said.

"Really?"

"With time, yes." He frowned. "But I have to reestablish my own skills first."

Tersan handed the gem back. "So there's a stone in the portal room?"

"No."

"Then how…?" Tersan asked.

Eron cleared his throat. "I left a part of my being there. That's the only explanation that we have for what happened."

Leather on leather rustled behind Tersan and he turned to find Jessie and Penrose, both dressed for travel.

"Tersan," Penrose started.

"Penrose, Lady Jessie," Tersan said with a nod to each of them. He handed the stone back to Eron.

"Tersan," Jessie answered. She turned to Eron. "Anything?"

"It's dark now, but Fot is gone. The way into the cave is blocked. I didn't see what happened."

"No!"

"Your shield is holding, Jess," he told her. "Jason isn't in the portal room, nor is his friend. I can only assume that they have made their way into the tunnel leading to the lake."

"That lake has a mind of its own!" she protested.

"It is not due to shed for another two weeks," Penrose assured her. "They will have a dark journey, but they will find their way."

"Jason's terrified of caves," she said.

"All paths lead to the Crystal Lake," Penrose said, "so there is little danger. From the lake, they will find their way to the mouth of the Udolphi, where we will meet them."

Eron smiled at her. "Fot managed to chase them, but you know he will not kill them," he answered, "rather let them find a way to kill themselves."

"Thank you, Eron, that's less than comforting," she said. "What about Tocar?"

Eron withdrew the stone again. Light danced across it, mesmerizing the small group. Finally, Eron spoke. "Nothing."

"Perhaps the combination of alcohol and medicine is blocking your abilities," Penrose said kindly. "I am rather surprised that you are still awake."

"He had a power nap," Jessie said, "right after you left. Then he opted to move to this room."

"It is a bit late to try to be inconspicuous," Penrose said.

"Perhaps, but I can close the door here and keep that moon-eyed healer out while Jessie is away."

"Tocar has one of your stones?" Tersan asked, pulling them back on topic.

"Yes," Jessie answered for him. She touched a finely spun chain around her neck and pulled it out of her jerkin. The stone dangling on the end of the chain appeared to have a life of its own. Gold and silver light played across its surface. "As do I."

"The fourth is in possession of Parry, the seneschal of the House of Marlandia," Penrose said, "Eron's ancestral home."

"I told Tocar that trying to reason with Marand was a fool's errand," Eron stated, "but he just had to go to Il Chatel. Now he's deep in Calshara, two days ride from the safety of the Sisters. I can't even warn him."

"A messenger has been sent," Penrose assured him, "Parry, truth be told."

"Parry's only a child!" Eron snapped. "Why did you send him?"

"The lad served in the battle for the portal. He is hardly a child, though his age would belie that. He knows more ways through the Paranjothi's than almost anyone. He was the best choice." Penrose held up a hand to silence any further protests. "And he said that if I sent another, he would go anyway."

"He is only a child," Eron repeated.

"We do what we can, Eron." Penrose spoke softly but firmly.

"The damage Fot caused has been repaired," Jessie said, taking a seat beside Eron, "I have seen it. Your visions are returning. Little time elapsed between the falling of the veil and you being able to show me your vision. The rest will return quickly as well. Believe in yourself."

"Milady, there is no more time," he told her. He turned to the others. "Is there?" he asked, though his comment was more of a statement than a question. He looked a long time at the healer, then nodded. "The Sword, albeit not the Sword who battled the king of the demons, shall ride at the head of your armies while his Shield rescues the two Otherworlders and sends them home."

69

"I will join you later," Jessie assured him. "A single horseman riding hard can catch an infantry."

"Single?" he asked.

"I am the Shield," she countered.

"And as such, you are supposed to protect," he told her, "not defend."

"You're right," she said with a sly grin. "Defending is your job."

"Milady, you take too many chances--"

"Please!"

"Tersan," Penrose said quietly as the two continued their verbal sparring, "a word."

Tersan followed the master healer out into the hallway where they could speak in private.

"I am releasing Eron into your care," he said. "He is sound of body and Jessie has shown me that his mind, indeed, is sound as well. He is whole, but he does not trust himself. As such, he can act as the figurehead we need. He will continue testing himself. That may cause you problems."

Tersan raised an eyebrow. "I can surround him with the finest warriors from Jeleste and Kimala, indeed protect him with my own life." He frowned. "However, there is the matter of verifying his visions. He can be quite unpleasant, as I have seen these past months. In this matter, I cannot help him."

Penrose nodded. "Mistress Aramat can."

"Mistress Aramat is a capable healer," Tersan agreed, "but at her age, she is fragile, perhaps too fragile to accompany the army."

Penrose smiled. "Are you asking for more help, Your Majesty?"

Tersan took in a deep breath. "I am almost certain I am not going to like your solution, Master Healer, but yes, I suppose I am."

"Good." Penrose leaned in a little closer. "My protégé, Sila Atin, will be available to assist you should Aramat be indisposed for some reason."

"Surely you have noticed the tension between Sila and Eron?" Tersan said with grim amusement. "I do not believe he is interested in her advances."

"Mooning eyes do not make one incapable." Penrose gazed back into the room at the couple still locked in a friendly battle of words. "Sila will only act if Mistress Aramat is unavailable. She has been so instructed."

"Sila does not always do what she is told," Tersan answered. "She doesn't exhibit the common sense of a girl half her age."

Penrose nodded. "I have selfishly sheltered her that is true, perhaps to her deficit. She is the most gifted healer I have ever trained. I agree, she is naive at times. But her knowledge of healing is vast. Talent such as hers can tip the scales of war in our favor. One day, I believe she will be Mistress of Bel Haven."

Tersan shook his head. "I hope that she will not have to put that considerable knowledge to use."

"As do I." He shifted his attention back to Eron. "The Sword lacks confidence. Though he will not ask for assistance, he will take it from you, his old friend. Be there for him."

Tersan nodded. "Understood."

They moved back toward the center of the room where the two were still discussing their course of action.

"Ready, Jessie?" Penrose asked.

"Take my horse," Eron offered through a yawn. "She's faster than your pony."

"I'll take them both," she answered, "in case I need them. Thanks." In one swift motion, they exchanged a kiss. Then she and Penrose melted into the darkness.

"The armies are ready, Eron," Tersan said. "Get some rest. We've got a long ride ahead of us in the morning."

"Not before we finish this." He withdrew a bottle of Penrose's wine from under the bed along with two glasses. "I was saving this to celebrate the return of my gift, and had rather hoped for other company tonight," he said, uncorking the bottle and filling the glasses. He handed one to Tersan with a laugh. "I just gave away my horse," he said, "and I believe there are only mountain ponies left in the stable."

"Now that sight will put fear into the hearts of men," Tersan laughed.

"Truly," Eron grumbled. "Manta is plains bred, a rare and fearless breed. There's not another like her from here to the Paranjothis."

"I thought Penrose had a plains-bred stallion? Surely there are others?"

"That horse is white," he informed Tersan, "Manta is black. I have to make a statement if I am to ride at the head of this army of yours and be this dark, powerful man of mystery who fearlessly combats demons and lesser mortals."

"We will find you a suitable mount," Tersan said.

Eron gazed into his wine, his eyes already glassy. "I chose to abdicate my crown," he began, "to leave the Kilmari in favor of becoming the Sword, protector of many more souls. I never knew how powerful I was until that power was ripped away from me. No one man should possess so much."

"You are the Sword, Eron." He smiled hoping his next words would be reassuring. "In order to be someone who inspires armies, *you* have been gifted with the power to back up your reputation."

Eron sighed. "I have regained enough to maintain the façade, but on the scale that is needed to battle demons…"

"You will find it again," Tersan assured him.

"You don't understand." The dark eyes met Tersan's. "Since the incident in the portal room, for the first time in my life, I am truly afraid."

Tersan leapt up, raising his glass. "To fear!" he said. "May it serve you well!"

Eron hesitated then jumped up, hoisting his glass in the air. "To fear!"

21 Tea Time

Patrick ran to Joann. The woman was sitting by the time Winifred reached them.

"I--I was just about to c-come to the d-door," she said, "when that thing grabbed me. What the hell was that, Pat?"

"Miss James?" Patrick said.

Miss James searched the sky. Polly was gone. "It appears we must take another path. Gather yourselves together and come inside," she said. "I have much to tell you."

"'You okay?" Patrick said, helping her rise. Her fingers were cold in his and she was very pale in the silvery moonlight.

"I don't know," she said. She touched her shoulder. "My com is missing."

"We'll call for backup from the car." He slipped an arm around her, his hand at her waist in case she needed help walking. They closed the short distance to the house in little time. Lights came on as they passed the front door and headed for Joann's cruiser. Miss James was bustling about, humming to herself. When she saw them open the car door and reach for the radio, she came out of the house working her fingers again.

"Please, Patrick," she said, the light between her fingers already the size of a dinner plate, "come inside and make yourselves comfortable. I am making tea for us." Her voice was stern, almost threatening.

"We can call for backup later," Patrick said. He put the mic down.

"It's protocol!" Joann protested.

"Unless you're hurt, trust me, it can wait."

They made their way back inside the house. A tea kettle was singing in the kitchen.

"Miss James--" Patrick began.

"Just Winifred."

"Do you mind if I call you Winnie?" Patrick asked. "You see, I had an aunt named Winifred who was a sour old woman. She always made me eat Brussel sprouts for Sunday dinner."

"I never recall serving you Sunday dinner," Winifred said. Her brow was furrowed. "Did I?"

"No, of course not," Patrick answered. "That was my aunt."

Winifred smiled. "I trust I do not remind you of your aunt who made you eat Brussel sprouts?"

"Hell, Winnie, I'd be hard pressed to compare you to anybody."

"Sit, sit," she repeated, waving a hand at them. She disappeared into the kitchen.

Patrick guided Joann to an overstuffed couch and steadied her as she sat. Ugly bruises were forming on her neck. She fingered them gently, wincing with even a slight touch.

"We need to get you checked out," Patrick said gently.

"I'll be fine," she answered. Her eyes flashed. "That thing caught me off guard. I want a shot at getting even."

"You're sure?"

"Oh yeah."

"Maybe we'll get a clue from this," he said as he started the VCR. "I found it running on the fireplace."

The room as it had been before Patrick's unfortunate accident was shown in tremendous detail. Two young men were engaged in sometimes intelligent, sometimes sophomoric conversation. One minute the tape showed furnishings in one position, then there was a pause and the furniture had been moved. "Looks like someone's cataloguing the contents for insurance," Joann said.

"Yeah, I think you're right." He touched the fast-forward and the tape accelerated. A young man was suddenly dancing on the now cleared floor.

"Miss James? I mean, Winnie?" he called, slowing the speed of the tape to normal. The youth was holding one of the snow globes in his hand, humming something out of a Broadway show. Winifred re-entered the room with a tray of cold French fries and some striped chocolate cookies. She stared at the screen.

"Oh dear," she said as the youth tucked the globe in his pocket.

"Is that Jason?" Patrick asked.

"Oh dear!" she repeated. She nearly dropped the tray onto the coffee table. "He has the key! Oh dear! He does not realize what he is doing!"

"That's Jason McCarthy?" Patrick asked. "What is he doing?"

Jason tucked a fireplace poker under his arm and strutted to the center of the room. He tapped it three times on the floor and started to sing. A voice behind the camera laughed and offered instructions.

"The incantation..."

Jason crooned, stepping smartly as he twirled about on the different colored patches of flooring. He wasn't half bad, though his timing needed a little bit of work.

"...the dance..."

Jason tapped on the fireplace three times. The sound of wind rushing through a small opening whistled and the camera fell, its eye now on the ceiling.

"Hang on!" the second voice yelled.

"Don't let go!"

A chill laugh emanated from the television, filling the room. There were two simultaneous screams and the wind blowing through the room appeared to reach hurricane strength. The screams diminished until the only sound was the whir of the camera itself. They kept watching the screen, waiting for something else to happen.

Something very large entered the room. Its being stole the light of day for a few moments, then the ceiling was in view again. Patrick moved to turn it off.

"Wait," Winifred said.

Less than a minute later, the darkness returned.

"Daughter," it uttered in a voice that sent chills through everyone in the room. Then it disappeared. The camera continued to film the ceiling.

"Lucy," Winifred whispered. A beeper went off in the kitchen and she quickly regained her composure. "The tea has steeped," she said. "Back in a moment."

She returned with three cups of tea on a second tray which she put down, gently this time, beside the snacks. Her hands were shaking.

"Winnie," Patrick started, "what happened? And who is Lucy?"

Winnie sat across from them on a love seat that matched the sofa they were sitting on. She took one of the cups and sipped at her tea, keeping her back straighter than anyone Patrick had ever seen even though her hands shook. When she regained her composure, she stared into her cup and spoke.

"I will answer your questions," Winnie told them, "but first, let me explain."

Patrick whipped out a pad and pen.

"What you saw out there were demons--"

"Demons?" Joann nearly yelled. She paled.

"Yes, dear, demons." She sipped her tea. "From what Jessie has told me, there are not creatures of this sort in your world--"

"'Our' world?" they repeated as one.

"Yes," Winnie said. She cleared her throat. "Patrick, when you broke those snow globes, you released them."

"They're in the snow globes." Patrick raised an eyebrow and stopped writing. "I find that rather difficult to believe."

"You just helped me recapture nine of them," she reminded him. "They are capable of changing their shape and size and all are able to fly. When they are in their larval state, they are cared for by demon chasers like Polly."

"Uh-huh." Patrick was staring and Joann elbowed him. "Hey!"

"Why aren't you writing this down?"

He shrugged. "We came here on distress call. And we haven't found McCarthy or his friend. But we have found demons. You really want me to write that down?"

"My dear, I beg to differ. We have found Jason and his friend."

Patrick walked over to the fireplace and carefully examined the stone. "Solid rock," he concluded. "The recording could be nothing more than theatrics."

73

"Patrick," Winnie started, "did you not feel something in the wind tonight? Did you look to the west of Claxbury and see anger in the sky?"

"I have to report facts, Winnie, not fantasy," he replied.

"While you were in here knocking over shelves and breaking mini jail cells," Joann said, "I was outside looking for ways to get underneath this house. I found a root cellar that led nowhere, nothing else. But that thing nearly killed me," Joann said. "I'd hardly call that fantasy."

"Yeah, and this will look great on my report." He cleared his throat. "An old video camera was found on the premises still recording. McCarthy and his companion were seen on the tape, but disappeared through a hole in the fireplace that has since been resealed. Screams were heard. On arrival, the house was in disarray, though there were no traces of blood found. Officer O'Shea was attacked by demons in their larval stage—"

"What?" Joann asked.

"—who removed his hat, his badge, his gun, his belt, both of his shoes and one sock. They tickled him mercilessly until he was rescued by an elderly neighbor whose pet demon herder chased them off."

Joann giggled. "Did that really happen?" she asked grinning widely.

"After searching the house for places where Mr. McCarthy may have fallen under the house, as he reported on his 9-1-1 call," Patrick continued with a grin, "Officer Joann Simon was attacked by a six-foot plus tall blue woman purported to be a demon from another world, who transformed into a creature with red and green eyes, wings and lots of pairs of hands and flew off into the night, joined by a second creature, also purported to be a demon. The two were followed by a demon herder a fraction of their size." He raised his eyebrows. "Oh, and did I mention the demon round-up?"

"Hmmm. I see your point," Joann mused. "The chief'll never believe this."

"Pardon me, dears, but you must convince them," Winnie insisted. She sipped the last of her tea and set her cup down. She addressed them as though they were her students. "Female demons are very powerful. They can take on nearly any form, become anything and there are only subtle ways to tell them apart from that which they imitate. So you see, they must return to their prisons." A memory played about her eyes and she blinked. The image of the teacher faded, replaced by something softer, almost romantic. "I cannot do this alone. I never could."

"Who is Lucy?" Patrick asked.

Winnie refocused on him. "She is Jessie Perrymore's daughter. It is likely they will be searching for her, though they do not know where to find her."

Patrick exchanged a look with Joann. She was rubbing her neck, a grimace on her face. "I've got a few days off coming up after this shift," she said quietly. "I will help you, Winnie." She stopped rubbing her neck and looked at Patrick. "I know you've got a long weekend planned--"

"But I let them go," Patrick interrupted. "Damn. This'll take some fast talking."

Joann cracked a smile. "You've done it before, big fella," she said with a wink. "I'm sure Samantha will understand."

"Like hell she will!"

"Language, Officer."

"Sorry. What about McCarthy and his friend?" Patrick asked.

"They are beyond our reach now," Winnie answered. "I believe they are pursued by a demon of great stature. But that demon will be unable to harm them."

"What?" both officers said in unison.

"If you release a demon, it will be sort of a slave to you and you alone until you ask it to perform one thing for you."

Patrick's mind was racing. "I asked her to let Joann go."

Winnie nodded. "But you still have control over the other one." She looked at them one at a time. "We must move with haste."

Patrick checked his watch. Their shift would end in an hour. "We need to get our paperwork done," he said, "at the station. We'll be back after that."

"Really!" Winnie huffed. "You waste precious time that we do not have time! We must find out who attacked you, Joann and who her companion is! Only then will we know what kind of danger we face."

"If we don't complete our paperwork, ma'am," Joann chimed in, "this place'll be crawling with cops in an hour. The media won't be far behind. They won't understand and that will delay us longer."

"She's right," Patrick chimed in. "We will have forty-eight hours to find McCarthy and his companion if someone files a missing person's report tonight. Time is not on our side."

Winnie's shoulders sagged and she bit her lip, her eyes darting back and forth while she stared at nothing. Finally she focused on them. "All right. Run along, you two, and do what you need to do. There is, however, one thing that you need to know. Perhaps it will hasten your return."

Patrick and Joann rose at once. Winnie gathered the tray, her normal slightly off demeanor now deadly serious.

"The demons need to feed. They will kill." She took a breath. "First for food..."

"And then?" Patrick asked.

Winnie looked him straight in the eye. "They have been known to kill for sport."

22 Whispers

"I do not know if we are in time," a voice said from some distant place.

Jason coaxed his body awake. The air around him had changed from hot and oppressive to cold and damp and rocks poked him unkindly in the back where he lay. His clothing was still damp from his impromptu swim and the blinding light from the cavern no longer lit the room where he and Ric had taken refuge. Now, he was mostly in the dark. If he squinted, he thought he could see the outline of the opening to the cavern.

"Ric?" he called softly, "is that you?"

"Jason!" a woman called out. "Thank the Lady you're alive!"

"Jessie?" Jason's heart skipped a beat. "Jessie! You're not dead!"

"Of course I'm not dead. Whatever gave you that idea?" The shadow that was Jessie bent over him. He felt a hand on his forehead and heard her relieved sigh. "He's not fevered, Penrose," she said.

"Give him a blanket anyway," an unfamiliar voice answered, "and have him drink this...half, no more."

"Thank God you've found us!" Jason exclaimed. "I thought we were lost for good! Ric!" he called. "Ric!"

"His name is Ric?" Jessie asked calmly, tucking a blanket around him.

"Yes, Ric Hawkins. You know, Ric. My roommate."

"Oh, that Ric."

"Yeah, I guess it is kind of hard to recognize him in the dark."

"Uh-huh." She held some kind of flask to his lips. "Drink."

Jason obediently drank. The liquid was thick and lukewarm. It settled in his stomach and he realized how hungry he was. Greedily, he tried to take more, but Jessie took it away.

"We have to go slowly, Jason," she said apologetically. "Penrose said only half."

"Jessie, I need your help here," Penrose called.

"I'll be right back, okay?" Jessie told him. She rubbed his back gently and left.

Jason nodded but was disappointed. He tried to focus on where Jessie had gone. Ric had to be over there with her and that Penrose person.

"Ric?" he called. He got to his feet unsteadily and took a few drunken steps forward. "Whoa, whatever that stuff is, it has quite a kick!" He sank to the ground and sat, trying to keep his eyes open. There were noises in the cave all around him. It reminded him of the inside of a conch shell, voices barely audible and likely imagined. He cocked his head and tried to concentrate to make them make sense.

"Palapaca?" Jessie's voice rose above the others, though Jason was not certain if he was hearing real words or gibberish. He was certain that he didn't much care. "That would mean--"

"Yes. Altay has more in the glade. This infection has gone far. He needs warmth," Penrose said, "and there is nothing here that is sufficient. Besides, we will lose light soon."

"Hamma can carry him back to the glade," Jessie answered. "Altay already has a fire built, I'd wager."

"Infection?" Jason asked. His tongue felt thick in his mouth and the words were beginning to sound hollow. Something was wrong. They were speaking in hushed voices. He did a quick inventory of his aches. Nothing seemed that bad. "What's palapaca?" he asked.

"You will need to ride with him, Jessie," Penrose continued without answering. "He is not alert enough to ride alone. Altay will know what to do when you reach the glade."

"Who's Hamma?" Jason repeated. He wasn't certain, but he thought he was louder this time. "And who's Altay? And whaddaya mean he's not alert enough to ride? Ride what?"

"What about Jason?" she asked hesitantly.

"Yes, what about Jason?" Jason nearly yelled. His stomach dropped like a stone. "Something bad's happened to Ric, hasn't it? Would somebody please answer me?"

"I will stay with him," Penrose said, still ignoring him. "Send Hamma back for us. We will meet you in the glade."

A shadow returned to Jason and kissed him on the forehead. "I'm sorry you and your friend got messed up in this," Jessie told him.

"I'm just glad you found us," he told her. "I called the police. They should be...coming." His head was swimming and his tongue felt very thick. He concentrated on what he was going to ask. "Jessie, what happened to Ric and who is Hamma?"

"Ric is right over there, by Penrose. Hamma is the pony who is waiting outside the entrance to this room."

"Pony?" Jason smacked his lips. The drink was making it difficult to think. "Don't they usually...bring a stretcher?"

"I'm taking Ric out to the Glade," Jessie said. "Altay is waiting for us there."

"Altay is a paramedic?" Jason asked. "Is there a helicopter to take him to the hospital?"

"Lady Jessie," Penrose said quietly, "now is not the best time."

"'Lady' Jessie?" Jason repeated.

Jessie placed a hand on his arm. "Try to relax. I'll explain everything soon. I promise. Stay here with Penrose. He is a healer, er, I mean a doctor. I gotta go."

Shadows moved around the entrance to the cave and he could hear Penrose and Jessie speaking in muffled tones to one another. Then he heard hoof beats moving away from them. He tried to see what was happening but it was too dark. He pulled the blanket tight around himself and shivered.

"Jason, is it?" Penrose asked as he came and sat beside him.

"Yes."

"My name is Penrose," he repeated. "Are you warm enough?"

"Not really," Jason answered. "That water was like ice."

Penrose wrapped a second blanket around him. He sucked in a sharp breath. "In the name of the Lady, what happened to your eyes?" he asked.

"My eyes? What's wrong with my eyes?" Jason asked, his heart beating a little faster. The pleasant buzz he had from the potion was suddenly gone.

"Nothing that cannot be fixed." Penrose began gently probing his face. "Hold still, please."

"What are you doing?" he snapped.

"Looking."

"That's kind of hard to do in the dark, isn't it?" Jason demanded. "Ow!"

"Yes, I suppose it would be hard to do in the dark."

A lump rose in Jason's throat.

"Tell me what you see," Penrose asked quietly.

"There's not much to see in this place," Jason answered, trying to keep his voice steady. "It's dark."

"Of course."

"That cave was so bright it was blinding--" he stopped speaking and started panicking. "I--I'm not blind! Oh no! Please, tell me I'm not blind! All I can see are shadows and the shadows aren't very clear! Oh, God, no!"

"Easy, Jason," Penrose said. "Sit still."

Jason looked around wildly trying to focus on anything. His eyes were as wide open as they could get and burning with the effort. He latched on to Penrose's arm and stood. He was vaguely aware that he was trembling. Penrose put one hand on top of his and held it still.

"Panic will not help you," he said softly, "but I can. I need your cooperation, Jason."

Jason swallowed hard and closed his tortured eyes. Very slowly, he sat back down on the hard floor of the cave, never releasing his grip on Penrose's arm. Tears welled up in both eyes.

"Yes, yes, I can see properly now," Penrose mused. He tried to pull his hand away from Jason without success. "I'm going to need both hands to take care of this, all right?"

Reluctantly, Jason let go. He felt himself breathing very quickly. Suddenly, he really needed to feel someone close and he grabbed at the air where Penrose had been. The healer caught his hand and held it.

"I'm blind, aren't I? I'm going to have to get a cane and a dog and learn to read Braille!"

"Hush," Penrose said.

"But you don't understand! I can't see!"

Penrose held his hand tightly. "You will be fine, Jason. You have just had an overexposure to a very bright light. I can help. Sit back for a moment. I promise this will not take long."

Jason tried to hold still on the hard rock. He was so cold now that he was shivering but his face and hands were hot and his eyes burned. He concentrated on the sounds that Penrose was making, latching on to that human contact.

"I'm going to put some drops in your eyes so I need for you to lie back. Then I'm going to put patches on them and put a bandage around your head to hold them on. It will be cool for a few moments. Ready?"

The drops cooled his burning eyes and he shut them in order to keep the medicine from running out.

"Jason, I'm going to cover your eyes now," Penrose stated. "I am not going anywhere."

The pads were also cool on his eyes, at once making them feel better and adding to the chill in his bones. Penrose seemed to sense his discomfort. Jason felt another blanket being thrown over the two already wrapping him.

"Better?" Penrose asked.

"Y-yes. Thanks."

"Good. I am going to place a bandage around your head to hold those on. Just hold still." Penrose lifted Jason's head slightly and Jason felt the bandage touch the back of his head and wrap around to the front. Penrose tied it off.

"Now I really can't see!" he cried.

"Drink this. You will feel better." Something hard again pressed against Jason's lips and Penrose held the back of his head up so he could drink. The liquid was lukewarm like the other, but this one was thicker and sweet. He drank greedily until Penrose pulled it away.

"Easy, Jason. You're going to have to sit a horse to get back to the Glade."

"A horse?"

"You are going to have to ride a horse through the cave to get out of here. Well, a pony, really. A very sure footed pony."

Jason groaned as pieces of the puzzle started falling in place. "We should have gone right when we got out of that horrible tunnel."

Penrose was quiet for a moment. "Your tunnel exited near a waterfall?" he asked.

"Yeah. A little waterfall." He heard the healer moving objects around close by.

"Yes," he answered, "I believe your assumption would be correct. The forest is not far from the waterfall. We will exit above the headwaters of the Udolphi River."

"Udolphi River?" Jason was beginning to feel a bit parrot-like.

"It is the river from which our people draw life," Penrose explained.

"I've lived in Kentucky all my life," Jason said through a yawn, "and I've never heard of the Udolphi."

"Of course," Penrose said.

Jason heard clothing rustle as the healer sat down beside him on the hard rocky floor. There was no physical contact but Jason was grateful for the company. The unmistakable scent of pipe tobacco filled the air, taking away the musty scent of the cave. It was fresh and delightful, though Jason did not long for any of it himself. His head was buzzing from whatever Penrose had given him and he was finally warm. His eyes no longer burned and he was on the verge of sleep.

"Rest now," Penrose said, sensing his feeling or knowing it. "We will be on our way soon."

Beneath the bandages, Jason closed his eyes. He was warm inside with the potion. Sleep came. He did not fight it.

How long he slept, though, he didn't know. He had an awesome dream; part nightmare, part wishful thinking, part pure amazement.

"Jason."

"Dad, just a little longer." He pulled the blankets tighter around himself.

"Jason, it is time to go. Hamma has returned."

Jason reluctantly opened his eyes to darkness. His head was buzzing contentedly and he blinked several times trying to get his eyes to focus. With a little gasp, he touched his head, confirming his reality. "It wasn't a dream, was it?"

"It is time to leave," Penrose stated. Jason felt a strong hand on his arm. "Let me help you stand."

Even with Penrose there to steady him, Jason nearly fell over. He could see nothing and sound seemed to be coming from a long way away. "I'm so tired, Penrose," he said, remembering the man's name. "Can't I sleep a little longer?"

"You will be more comfortable in the Glade," the healer answered. "We need to make haste to leave this place before the light fades. Already the way is dim."

"I'll have to take your word for it."

Penrose guided him across the rocky floor. He only stumbled twice before Penrose stopped him. Something warm and furry stood in front of him. It snorted and Jason jumped.

"Do not concern yourself," Penrose laughed, "Hamma is simply greeting you. Have you done much riding?"

Jason shook his head. "Not really. Pony rides when I was a kid."

"Ah, then this will not be that different. The hardest part is getting on. After that, all you need to do is sit."

"Right. And there's an ambulance when we get out of here?"

Penrose cleared his throat. "We are deep in the woods and will need to get out on horseback."

"They can land helicopters almost anywhere. I've seen it on cable."

"Of course." Penrose sighed but did not discuss the issue further. "Place your hand on Hamma's neck and grasp his mane firmly in your hands. That's right. Now, bend your left leg up. Good. In a moment, I'm going to put my hands under your knee and give you a boost so you can mount. I want you to swing your right leg over his back. Are you ready?"

"S-sure," Jason answered. He put his hand out and Penrose placed it on some long, stringy hair. It was just above Jason's waist in height. Penrose put his other hand beside the first. He entwined his fingers in the pony's mane.

"Now, stand with your belly to the horse and bend your left leg. On three, pull yourself up. Ready? One... two... three."

Jason swung his right leg up while he held on to the horse's mane. He nearly went over the stocky beast, but Penrose caught him before he could slide off the other side, steadying him so he could establish his balance.

"Are you all right?" Penrose asked.

"I guess." Jason wrapped his fingers tightly in the long hair. "I'm kind of dizzy."

"It is only the potion, Jason," Penrose assured him, "and the fact that you cannot see. Do not fear. I will not let you fall."

"I hope not. That water's awfully cold."

The pony moved smoothly beneath him. Penrose walked, one hand continually on the small of Jason's back to steady him. Robbed of his vision, Jason tried to put his other senses in overdrive. He smelled the cave, heard the distant sound of water trickling into the lake and felt the chill of the air. He pulled the blankets more tightly around his neck.

"We will soon be by the fire," Penrose assured him, "drinking mulled trinka."

"What is trinka?" Jason asked. "Some kind of herbal tea or something?"

"It is a treat for my people. It will warm you."

Atop his mount, Jason rocked back and forth. The horse's hooves made soft clopping noises on the stone floor. The incessant wind that had accosted them in the tunnel whispered to him, an odd counter rhythm to the hoof beats. He could hear Penrose breathing, too. The noises combined into a symphony he had never imagined before, lulling him into a trance. He shivered violently and the music ceased. Unaware, he moaned softly. Hamma stopped and he felt Penrose's hand on his forehead.

"I'd like you to drink a little more of this," the healer said. He took one of Jason's hands away from the mane and thrust a flask into it. "Take as much as you want this time," he said. "The way is not far now and you may rest when we get there."

Jason tilted the flask back and drank half of the sweet, thick liquid. Warmth rose in his face. "That's about all I can handle," he said, holding the flask out for Penrose to take, "without some food."

"More would be better, if you can," Penrose said.

"I'm afraid I might fall off," Jason answered.

Penrose laughed. "Do not concern yourself. Your balance has been excellent even though your mind is wandering."

Jason hesitantly guzzled more. A warm sensation was already building in his stomach and working its way out to the ends of his fingers and toes. His head had a nice buzz going one more time. He swayed atop his mighty steed and giggled. Penrose took the flask from him. Jason could have sworn he heard him smiling. "What was that stuff?" he asked, smacking his lips.

"A little concoction of mine," Penrose said. "Are you ready?"

"On, Scout!" he said.

The pony almost lurched forward, but Jason sat astride it without a care. The wind blew up from the bottom of the chasm that he couldn't see. He felt it on his face and arms. He waved to the little people down below. He could hear them singing to him, a chorus at once harmonic and dissonant, pure of sound and perfect of pitch. Jason sang some kind of nonsense tune with them. After what seemed an eternity, the wind slowed and stopped.

"Jason, we are nearly to the forest," Penrose was saying from some distant place. The music softened. "How are you?"

Jason felt euphoric. He would be back in civilization soon with clean sheets and pretty nurses to take care of him. "Great," he said, "never better."

"All right. We're going to be going up and down a lot of small hills inside the mountain. Lean forward when we go uphill, back when we go down and it will be easier for Hamma. All right?"

Jason nodded. "I'm ready," he told Penrose.

Jason recognized the sound of the waterfall emptying into the lake behind them. They must have passed the tunnel he and Ric had come through earlier. Jason felt a different wind on his face now. This one was fresh with the scent of fall leaves. A different music filled his mind, a lullaby preparing the masses for a long, winter's sleep.

"Ric was right," he said.

"I beg your pardon?" Penrose said.

"Ric was right," Jason repeated. "He said to follow the fresh air and that would lead us out of the cave."

They travelled in silence for quite a while, the pony easily going up and down as the path rose and fell. Sounds around him changed. They were out in the woods.

"Jason!" Jessie called.

"Jessie? Jessie! Penrose, get me off this thing!"

A hand and an arm slid around his waist and he was turned so that he could dismount. He landed on soft ground and wobbled until he regained his balance. He felt Jessie's hands on either side of his head, cradling his face. "What happened?" she asked quietly.

"He entered the cave during the cleansing," Penrose said.

"Cleansing?" Jason asked.

"I'll explain later, Jason," Jessie said. Her voice was strained.

"Where's Ric?" he asked, wiping his hands on his pant legs.

"Sleeping," Jessie answered.

"Sleeping? Well, I guess that's okay. Does he need an ambulance? Hell, I need an ambulance! I can't see!"

"Calm down, Jason," she answered evenly, though there was compassion in her voice. "Come. Altay has a fire built--"

"A fire? That's not very comforting!"

"This way," Jessie said. She led him a short distance and put his hands behind him so that he touched a flat rock. "Sit."

Jason awkwardly sat. He rearranged the blankets around his neck, pulling them tight against the cool air.

"Here," Jessie said, picking up his hand and placing a mug in it. "It has cooled enough that you can drink it without burning yourself."

"Did the other young man drink as well?" Penrose asked quietly.

"A little," Jessie answered. "Altay is with him."

Jason felt a twinge of fear. "Is there something wrong?" he asked.

There was whispering.

"Is Ric okay?" The pleasant buzz he had going from Penrose's potion was evaporating quickly. An uneasy silence fell on them and Jason imagined Jessie exchanging a look with this man. "Somebody answer me!" he demanded angrily, reaching for the bandages and trying to take them off.

"Jason, just leave the bandages for now," Penrose told him.

"We nearly got killed in there! If you've got an explanation, I want to hear it!" he said, trying to untie the knot holding the bandage on.

"You are entitled to one, son," Penrose said. He felt healer's hands over his own. "If you remove the bandages, you may do serious damage to your eyes. Would you like something to eat?"

"I'd like to go to a hospital, where I can get my eyes looked at by a doctor. A real doctor."

There was an uneasy silence. Someone poured liquid into a mug. Jason lowered his hands from the bandages and Penrose released him.

"Jessie?" he asked, a touch of panic edging into his voice.

"Jason, we're not exactly in a position where we can take you to a hospital," she said carefully.

"Why not?" he asked. The panic was growing.

"Well, because there are no hospitals here. Here's a bit of stew," she added, pushing a plate into his hands. "There's a piece of bread on the right there you can use to sop it up. Mind you, it's hot."

"I'm not hungry!" he lied, pushing the food back at her.

"All right. You don't have to eat." Jason heard her take in a big breath. He waited. "We're not in Claxbury anymore."

"Well, whatever county we're in, surely they have some facilities. Hospitals are everywhere these days," he said.

"Well, you see, we're not really in a neighboring county, Jason, at least not the way you think of it." She hesitated. "We're kind of in a different world."

"Jessie," he began, feeling rather odd to take on the role of adult with her, "don't you think you're taking this adventure thing a little too far?"

"We're in a parallel world, a different dimension."

"Right." He pulled the blankets tighter around himself with a huff. "There's no such thing."

"Yes there is. And we're in it."

"Come on, Jessie. Enough is enough. You got real quiet when I mentioned Ric. If he's injured, we need to get him to help." He swallowed. "He nearly drown in that lake and if you can't wake him up, he needs a doctor."

"Penrose is a doctor."

"Forgive me, but Penrose sounds like a quack."

"He isn't. And right now, Ric needs his care more than the finest doctor in Claxbury. We're not in our world anymore, Jason." There was a rustle of cloth and she laid her hand on top of his. "I can prove it to you."

"I'm waiting."

Jessie cleared her throat. "My house is in an air traffic pattern that's fairly active, isn't it?"

"It is."

"How far do you think you came in the cave? Half a mile? Two miles? Five miles?"

"I don't know," he said. "It's not important."

"Humor me."

He shrugged. "Not more than five."

"And that would keep us in that air traffic pattern, right?" she asked patiently.

"Probably."

"Okay, I want you to listen very carefully. Do you hear anything?"

Jason cocked his head to one side. His heart was beating so hard he couldn't hear anything else. "No," he admitted, "I don't hear anything. But that doesn't prove anything!" He was getting angrier by the minute. "For all I know, we're not even outside. I can't exactly see very well, you know."

"Okay, how about this?" She was quiet for a few minutes, then he felt the back of his neck begin to prickle. The bandages flipped off his head without anyone touching them.

"Hey!" he said.

Then they flew back on. No one touched him. Jason began to shake.

"H-how did you do that?"

"I studied and learned to manipulate things with my mind," she answered easily. "You could learn the skill, but it takes years."

Jason sat still for a minute wishing he had the plate with food on it. Instead, he drank some from the mug. It was spicy and satisfying, different from anything he had ever tasted. Stubbornly, he ignored his revelation. "What the hell was that snake thing all about?" he asked.

"I believe he's referring to Fot," Penrose offered.

Jason shivered and this time it was not from the cold. "Is that a type of animal?"

"Fot is lord of demons," she said rather more calmly than Jason thought she should. "Demons because their real name is unpronounceable. They are part substance and part energy and can easily change shape."

Jason's head was beginning to spin. "You're kidding."

"We imprisoned him and many of his fellows inside those snow globes. I thought they would be safe in my house in our world. But somehow, Fot convinced you to let him loose."

"Ric had it in his pocket when we fell through that hole. It popped out and I stepped on the damned thing!" Jason said. "I tossed it to Ric. He dropped it and it shattered. We didn't mean to break it!"

"But you did." She fell silent and Jason suddenly felt horrible. She must have sensed his discomfort. "Look, Jason, I know accidents happen. You had no way of knowing what was in that globe. It took a lot of planning and a lot of sacrifice to capture that demon and now we're faced with a big problem you unwittingly caused. We're all a little on edge because of it."

"Jessie," Penrose offered quietly, "these young men have been through a lot in the last day. Let him eat and sleep for a while. We leave for the House at first light."

"I don't want anything to eat," Jason lied. "I want to go home."

"I promise you, I will take you home at the first opportunity," Jessie said. "We are not sure where Fot is right now, but if he is guarding this portal, we aren't strong enough to make a stand against him. The other portal is two days from here."

"But the police--"

"The police aren't coming."

"But--"

"This argument has been made," Penrose interrupted. "Jason, we have come here in great haste to rescue you both on very little sleep."

"That's why we have to call EMS," Jason said stubbornly.

"I'm fine, Penrose," Jessie argued.

"The Lady forbid we need your skills, Jessie, but you had best be ready to use them. Few know the exit from the Crystal Cave, and that includes Fot. We are safe for the moment, but we all require rest, including you. Jason, I will make you this offer. If, after resting, your friend is better, we shall head for the other portal. If he is the same, we must take him to Bel Haven without delay. Agreed?"

"Do I have a choice?" Jason asked.

"Not really," Penrose said. Jason felt a hand on his shoulder. "I have done what I can here for your friend. At Bel Haven, there are many more medicines. We were not expecting what we found today."

Jessie sighed. "I could use a little sleep and..." She yawned. "...without Eron around to wake me, I might actually get some."

"Altay and I will watch over them."

Jason felt her hand on his shoulder. "Good night, Jason." And she was gone.

"Altay went to great lengths to fix this meal for you, Jason," Penrose told him. The healer took Jason's hand and put the plate into it. "Please, eat."

Jason felt around the edge of the plate until he found the bread. Hurriedly, he ate. The meal was simple, but satisfying. "Thanks," Jason managed.

"You are welcome," a woman answered. The plate disappeared from his hands.

"Come then, Jason," Penrose said. Penrose helped him rise and escorted him to a place where he recognized Ric's snoring.

"Penrose?" he said through a yawn.

"Yes?"

"What 'skills' does Jessie have that we might need?"

"She is the Shield."

"Who is Eron?"

"The Sword," he answered simply.

"Yeah. Okay. Shield. Sword." Jason lay down and closed his eyes and gave in to the warmth in his belly. The night was filled with sounds of insects and animals, a symphonic cacophony that lulled him into a sleep filled with wild disturbing dreams.

23 Of Mice and Mentors

Winifred placed the last tiny bits of plastic and glass that she had retrieved from the living room floor on the now clean stone counter in Jessie's kitchen. It was nearly three a.m. Neither Patrick nor Joann had come back and Winifred was becoming concerned.

"They said they would return," she tried to reassure herself, "and Jessie gave me the impression that police were men and women of their word. They will return." She nodded briskly and started sorting.

Jessie had painstakingly engraved the name of each demon on their tiny jails and shown Winifred each new prisoner as they arrived. Winifred was duly impressed with the collection. There were even several lesser-Fots in the group, along with minor demons who she did not know. The woman on the lawn, she feared, was a lesser-Fot, judging from the short amount of time it took for her to resume a mature status and her impressive stature. A definitive identity was possible. She got out a piece of paper, a pen and a magnifying glass from the kitchen island and began sorting through the debris.

It had been a painstaking process, but Jessie had wisely used only like colors for each prison. Winifred quickly had eleven little piles of like-colored broken pieces and, with the help of the magnifying glass and a little magic, she identified all eleven names, though she was unaware of who exactly they were. The news could have been worse. Fot himself was not among the broken vessels.

"That will do for now," she said, returning her attention to the newly re-captured demons.

She ran her finger across the bump on top of one of the lids.

"The directions say that if this bump is up, the jar is not sealed. Let us see…"

She pushed it down and it offered a satisfying click, but it immediately popped back up when she removed her finger. She got out the instructions and reread them.

"The directions say water bath the jar if it does not seal. I have already determined not to do this as it may cause irreparable damage to the creatures."

Inside their small prisons, the demons were still sleeping. She was beginning to be more than a little concerned that they would wake up.

"My shield was successful," she said thoughtfully. "Perhaps a permanent sealing spell will be as well. It would be better than attempting to cook them." Winifred took in the length of the counter with a practiced eye. "Yes, I believe I can seal all of them with just one spell. Now, where are those candles...?" She searched until she found four long and thin white tapers and holders for each. Pushing the jars carefully to the center of the island, she placed one candle at each corner and lit them all. Then she raised her hands slightly, closed her eyes and spoke in her language:

Lady of darkness, Lady of light,
Hear my prayer, this lonely night,
Demons are placed before me in jars,
Bring strength to your servant,
From heaven's purest stars.
Grant me the power to keep these souls
Out of mischief, safe from wars.

She lowered her arms. The energy within the room had shifted very subtly. Several of the lids popped, the metal bubbles now dimpled in the downward direction. A smile pulled at her lips. "Well, it may not have been my best work," she said aloud, "but I do believe I have had some success! I will have to try something different on the rest." She gathered the half pint jars that had sealed and put them in Ric's camera bag.

"Miss James?"

Patrick was staring at her.

"Patrick!" she said.

"Yes, ma'am."

Winifred looked at the clock. "It is almost dawn. Time escapes us," she said. "But Polly has not yet returned." She motioned to the demon filled jars. "They must be sealed before we continue."

"Didn't you just do that?" he asked.

"I placed a temporary seal on them when we recaptured them. Just now, I placed a more permanent seal, but it was only partially successful. Now that you are here..." she blew the candles out, then handed Patrick a book of matches. "Light the candles, say the spell and we will be ready when Polly gets back here."

"Me? If you've already done it, why do I have to?"

"Not all of them sealed, dear. This is your world, not mine. The touch of a native is needed." She stepped away from the countertop, clasped her hands and waited. Patrick just stared at her. "A basic incantation will do," she prompted.

"Well, I, um..."

"For the Lady's sake, Patrick, it's a simple incantation," she told him. "Do you not remember your training?"

Patrick shrugged. "I...I am a college graduate," he said, "I just didn't study, um, incantations?"

"Very well. You may use my spell." She took the sealed jars and placed them beside the sink. Then she rearranged the others and put the candles around them. "Light the candles; that's right. Now, you just have to repeat after me." She raised her hands in the air, palms toward the ceiling. In the ancient tongue of her race, she started:

Lady of darkness, Lady of light,
Hear my prayer, this lonely night...

Patrick cleared his throat, mirrored her stance and spoke hesitantly:

Ladybug straight, ladybug green,
Take portions magpie lengthy.

"No, no, Patrick, concentrate!"
"What the hell am I saying?"
"Mind your language, young man," Winifred scolded. Patrick looked sufficiently reprimanded and she repeated the lines once more.

Lady of darkness, Lady of light,
Hear my prayer, this lonely night...

Patrick cleared his throat and spoke.

Lady of darkness, Lady of light,
Hear my prayer, this lonely night...

"Good!" Winifred said. "Now, just a bit more. Listen carefully."

Demons are placed before me in jars,
Bring strength to your servant,
From heaven's purest stars.
Grant me the power to keep these souls
Out of mischief, safe from wars.

"That's a lot more than just a bit, Winnie," Patrick complained.
"Say it," Winifred said.
Patrick cleared his throat:

Demons are placed before me in jars,
Bring strength to your servant,

From heaven's purest stars.
Grant me the power to keep these souls
Out of mischief, safe from wars.

Popping noises emanated from the counter as the tiny dimples on each of the jars were sucked down. Patrick watched them with rapt attention.

"There," Winifred said. She beamed a smile at Patrick. "That will hold them until we can seal them in something more permanent. And the little dears are still asleep." She gathered the newly sealed jars and added them to the ones already in the bag.

"Amazing," Patrick mused.

"I have identified the demons who were in the broken globes. We have to match those we have recaptured to those who are missing. Come along."

"Yes, ma'am."

Winifred walked into the living room, the camera bag in tow. She carefully placed the remaining snow globes inside. "One, two, three..." she counted as she picked up each one and carefully placed it into the bag Patrick was holding. "With the ones we resealed, there are sixty-eight. There. All nice and secure."

Patrick cleared his throat. "Now can we go?" he asked.

"Go where, dear?"

"You said that thing would kill. I'd like to stop it before that happens."

"Of course, dear. But Polly has not returned."

"So we don't know where they went? Is that it?"

"Precisely." She motioned to the countertop where the candles were still brightly burning. "We really should let those candles burn down and go out."

"Why?"

"You really must review your incantations, young man."

He nodded but he did not look convinced. "I don't know any incantations, Winnie," he admitted. "I'll have to take your word for it."

"I need your help to find a small book."

"'Be happy to help you. What's the title?"

"It is called 'The Book of Wylfcynne'. I listed all the demons in there." Winnie started into the living room and stopped. "Oh dear."

"What?" Patrick asked.

"Lucy has the book."

"Lucy? Perrymore's daughter? Why would she have the book?"

Winnie sighed. "I had forgotten. Jessie gave it to her. It is a talisman of sorts."

"Can you remember the names?"

Something heavy knocked on the front door and Patrick walked over to open it. A whir of demon chaser nearly bowled him over as Polly flew across the room to Winnie. The little demon herder slipped into her pouch under Winnie's shirt and curled up.

"Polly?"

The serpent raised her head, shook her scales and hissed.

"Polly! Such language!"

"You're talking to a flying snake..." Patrick started. "I can't believe I'm going to ask this, but does she know where the, um..."

"Demons?" Winnie suggested.

"Yeah, that."

"Polly, you must tell us where the demons are."

Polly hissed and rattled and curled up again, though she did not put her head down.

"Polly says they are busy feeding."

"Feeding on what?" Patrick asked.

The demon herder rattled her scales and tipped her head elegantly so that her large unblinking eyes appeared almost beautiful.

"Deer." Winnie tucked the demon herder back inside her shirt. "They are in a place where there are no humans, at least not right now. And while they feed, they are extremely dangerous."

"Then we have to go now," Patrick insisted. "We can follow Polly."

"Polly has flown many miles. She must sleep."

"Can you ask her where they are?"

"Of course. Polly, where are they? Polly?"

The demon herder poked her head out of the pouch and yawned hugely. She uttered a series of humming sounds and clicks, then waited.

"They are beside a picnic table that is beside a lake," Winnie said, "and they are eating. She said they will sleep at least half a day after they are finished gorging themselves. Then they will rise and eat again before they start their search for the daughter."

"This is Kentucky," Patrick moaned. "There are thousands of lakes. Who is the daughter? Lucy Perrymore?"

"That is what I would assume, dear."

Polly made a few more noises, then sank into the pouch.

"And?" Patrick asked.

"She will take us there as soon as she has slept. She suggests that we sleep as well to prepare for the coming battle."

"I don't like the sound of that, Winnie. Do you really think we can do this without backup?"

"Would your chief take instruction from me?" she asked. When he did not answer, she continued. "If we fail to recapture them, we can make other plans. For now, though, let us keep this to ourselves."

"What about the Perrymore girl?"

"She is staying with her aunt in Claxbury." Winnie smiled. "I placed wards on that house the day Jessie left. My shielding power has worked well here. I would assume the wards would hold true as well."

"The incantations didn't," Patrick reminded her.

"We shall have to trust, Officer, that the wards will hold. Right now, those demons do not know where to find Lucy. They have no knowledge of this world."

"True."

"Now, come, let us see who we are to fight. Jessie left another list of names inside Computer, along with detailed descriptions and pictures of each demon housed here." She led the way into Jessie's study where she turned the desk chair so that Patrick could sit in it.

"Jessie showed me once how to feed Computer a piece of silver that allows it to transform images. Are you familiar with these machines, Patrick?"

"I'll do my best, ma'am," he said, slipping into the chair facing Computer. With the press of a button, the screen came into view. There was no password. "Trusting soul," he muttered.

Winifred rifled through a stack of papers piled in an orderly fashion beside Computer until she found the disc Jessie had labeled "List-O-Demons" in her scrawling handwriting. She handed Patrick "the piece of silver". He seemed to know what to do with it. Computer took the disc willingly.

"I did not recognize the demon who attacked Joann," Winnie said as lights flashed on the monitor. "A female is bad enough, but if she is a lesser-Fot, we may be in very deep trouble. Computer should tell us who they all are." She sighed. "I much prefer writing things down. It seems so much simpler."

Lights and images flashed on the screen in front of him. "What's a lesser-Fot?" he asked.

"Fot is lord of all demons," Winnie explained. "When demons start to become nearly as powerful as their leaders--"

"They call them by their leader's name. Less a little." He grinned. "That's clever."

"Clever?"

"Well, maybe practical is a better term." He looked up at her, hands empty. "Do you see the mouse?"

"No, no, no, dear," Winifred said, "Computer requires only the piece of silver."

"Yes, Winnie, I know, but I have to use the mouse to get to the disc."

Winifred shrugged. "Polly is already asleep. Demon herding can be very taxing, but I do not see that we have a choice," she said, reaching under her shirt for the tiny serpent. "Polly, we need a mouse."

Polly poked her head out of her pouch and hissed.

"Now, now, Polly--"

"Let her sleep," Patrick laughed. "It's not that kind of mouse." He opened the center drawer of the desk and withdrew an egg shaped object. "Never mind," he said.

"Oh." Winifred was frustrated. "I thought the piece of silver would be enough. It seemed to be for Jessie."

"I wonder what happened to Joann," he asked, fiddling with the keyboard.

"Why?" Winifred answered.

"She lives much closer than I do and left the station half an hour before I did."

"So you missed me?" Joann was leaning against the doorframe. She was dressed in jeans and a baggy sweatshirt. She smiled. "Sorry I'm so late. I had to call Rose and let her know what was going on. She's in St. Louis for a wedding. And then I had to make sure the cats had enough food for a few days, and a couple of clean litter boxes. They forget they're housecats if the boxes are--"

"Thanks, Joann," Patrick snipped.

She laughed. "Okay, okay. What're you doing?"

"Fetch me that bag, will you dear?" Winnie asked, pointing to the camera case containing the snow globes. Joann handed it to her. Winifred reached inside and withdrew one of the newly sealed jars. She placed it on the table beside Patrick and stared at it. Then she produced the list she had made from the snow globe debris.

"There are pictures of the little darlings on Computer. Jessie assigned them a number--"

"I got it," Patrick told her. He typed in the first name on Winnie's list and on the monitor, a greenish face came into focus and leered back at them. Beside it, the name Hree appeared.

"Hree?" Patrick asked. "Looks like a typo."

Winifred scanned the information Jessie had recorded. "He is a very minor demon," she said. "Now, let's see if he is one of our newly incarcerated prisoners."

"Hold on, Winnie. Let me pull up all their names and pictures. Make it easy on us." Patrick took all Winnie's names and matched each to a picture. "Ready," he said.

Winnie wove a tiny web over the first jar, let it descend on the top and then tapped the lid sharply. The image of a demon appeared on the side, stuck his tongue out and then disappeared.

"That was Hree," Joann said. "How did you do that?"

"Magic," Patrick answered.

One by one, they eliminated the recaptured demons from the list until only two names remained on the screen.

"Bue and Lae are the escapees, Winnie," Patrick said.

"Oh dear," Winifred repeated, "two female lesser-Fots."

"That's a bad thing, right?"

"Very bad," Winifred said. "We are in for a battle. Polly said they would sleep for a while, then eat again," she told Joann. "Best to rest while we can."

"C'mon, Patrick," Joann said, heading out the door. "Bed time."

Patrick opened his mouth to speak but thought the better of it. He followed his comrade out the door. Winifred heard them talking quietly in the hallway. Moments later, soft snoring filled the air.

24 Pella Durett

The courtyard of the House of Bel Haven was filled with its staff of healers scurrying about between the buildings and a huge cloth covered wagon. Six towering horses waited patiently in the first light of day for their instruction, oblivious to the activity around them. Boxes of supplies filled the wagon almost to its ceiling before the cloth sides were lowered to keep out the dust. Six healers took their positions on the wagon's wooden seats. The rest took positions on the massive porch. Everyone waited.

Tersan sat astride his calm grey stallion, the sun gleaming off the bright silver and gold of his armor. A mounted honor guard of twenty formed ranks behind him, ready to escort him and the Sword to Pella Durett, the southernmost fortress of Jeleste. A young page was trying to calm a great black stallion that stood riderless in the courtyard. Tersan smiled to himself. His men had found the horse that Eron wanted. He wondered if the Sword would be pleased.

As if a stage had been set, Eron swept out of the House in his trademark black leather and flowing black cape. On his brow he wore the circlet of silver that indicated his rank and around his neck, he wore the pendant of Sword and Shield that tied him to Jessie. His step was graceful and seemingly confident. Almost unnoticed beneath the cape was a long sword, sheathed in black. Tersan stifled a sigh. Never before had any Sword needed a physical weapon.

The healers parted for him to pass, bowing their heads slightly in recognition. Eron acknowledged them curtly as he made his way down the steps. The horse startled, reared up, pawed the air and then ducked his head down, nostrils flaring. Eron stopped stock still. His eyes shifted from the horse to Tersan and back to the horse. Tersan raised an eyebrow and allowed himself a tiny smile. This horse would be a challenge. Eron needed a challenge, a challenge he could win.

Heaving a huge breath, Eron strode across the courtyard and took the reins from the grateful page. Above, a bird cried and whispers raced through the ranks of the healers. Eron did not listen. His attention was fixed on his mount.

The horse cocked his head as Eron spoke and his ears pricked forward. He lifted his head and trumpeted a challenge. The man before him stood his ground, speaking words no other could hear. For a moment, the two were locked in a staring contest, each daring the other to make the next move. The reins went slack and the animal stopped his prancing. Eron stepped forward and rubbed his head, still talking to him. He blew gently into the horse's nose. Finally, the horse bent his head down so that Eron could scratch him behind the ears. He moved to the left side of the horse and smoothly mounted.

Almost immediately the horse rose halfway up to his full height and then plunged playfully downward. He sidestepped and reared, dipped his head and shook it then kicked his hind legs up. All along, Eron stayed with him. The horse arched his neck proudly and his mane and tail flashed in the bright morning sun while he pranced in place. On the porch of Bel Haven, the healers were wringing their hands in silence.

"Tersan," Eron said holding one rein in each hand and not taking his eyes off the horse, "should you not be riding this great steed?"

Tersan laughed. "My men have gone to great lengths to find you a suitable mount," he answered. "Is he not to your liking?"

"I have," Eron said, "been ill of late."

"Plains bred you wanted and plains bred you have." Tersan raised an eyebrow. "He is a fitting steed for a triumphant return to Pella Durett, would you not agree?"

"Something a little tamer would have done as well," Eron grumbled as the horse tossed his head and rose playfully in the air a second time. Effortlessly, he shifted his weight to maintain his seat.

"But another would not have been rare or fearless. I understand, though, that there are still several mountain ponies available, if you prefer a different mount."

Eron scowled at him. The horse lunged unexpectedly and the silver circlet he wore slipped to one side. He settled the horse and snatched the jewelry off his brow, tucking it under his jerkin. "I'd never hear the end of it if I lost that thing after Pixil made it for me," he said.

Tersan's eyes were twinkling. "Come along, Eron. The time has come to prepare for battle." He winked at him. "But perhaps a little fun first. Let's race."

Tersan cued Greystone with subtle pressure and they charged off across the plain at a mad gallop. Too long had his horse been kept in a paddock with the only wind in his mane not of his own making. They danced their way over mounds of grass, the horse tossing his head gaily, the man reveling in pleasure his mount took at the race. The mighty plains stallion thundered beside them, his rider looking steady though slightly uncomfortable. Quickly, they outdistanced the rest of the troop, Rudlo, the standard-bearer ten lengths behind them, the rest lagging another ten behind him. It made the small group appear disorganized and not at all impressive. Tersan did not care. For the first time in months, he was enjoying himself.

Together, the two riders passed the first of many watch towers scattered across the plain that stretched from Bel Haven to Pella Durett. A trumpet sounded clear in the morning air announcing their approach. A second trumpet sounded in the distance and a third as their approach was heralded to the fort.

Tersan pulled Greystone to a halt, ending the race. The horse rose into the air and struck at it. Tersan let the horse rear a second time, relishing the antics of his mount. Beside him, Eron worked to calm the great black stallion. The shadow that had darkened the Sword's features for so long had finally lifted.

"Having fun?" Tersan asked while they waited for the rest of the riders to catch up.

"Actually," Eron said, a smile crossing his face, "yes."

"Good."

"I am assuming the race is over?" he asked.

"It is more than half a day's ride to Pella Durett. Even a plains bred stallion could not manage to keep that pace that long."

For a long time they rode in comfortable silence. Tersan tried to put aside the exhilaration that came every time he was headed into war. He failed. He patted his horse's neck and reluctantly turned his thoughts away from the sheer joy of this morning's ride. There was something he had wanted to say for months. Now seemed an opportune time. "Eron," he began, "you delivered my people from a menace we only saw in legend, gave us time to prepare for this war against Marand at great cost. I wish to thank you for that."

"We have yet to win the war," Eron replied. "Marand is a master manipulator. He let the demons wage his war with Kimala, was carefully orchestrating it to make you keep Jeleste neutral."

"I should have seen through his falseness."

"Your mind was on other matters," Eron answered kindly. "It is not easy to lose the mother of your children."

"No, it is not." Tersan thought back to the raven-haired beauty who he had placed in the catacombs with his ancestors and to his little ones who would never know their mother. "Chantel was an extraordinary woman."

"Yes, she was." Eron now sat calmly on his horse. The great steed walked quietly beneath his rider, but his neck was still proudly arched and his clear eyes looked forward. Man and horse were as one. "Marand is now an enemy we share," he continued. "He invited Fot into his ranks and relieved me of my duties to him. I am afraid we fight two enemies, Tersan."

"Pixil has schooled my captains and myself in the ways of demons," Tersan replied. "Jelestines and Kilmari have been preparing together for war since your arrival at Bel Haven."

"My queen is a good teacher," Eron replied. As if reminded, he took the circlet from its place beneath his jerkin. "I hate this thing."

Tersan chuckled. "It is a symbol of your rank, Eron."

"I am Sword now, not king," he said, replacing the circlet, "and I do not claim to be a prince."

"As I said, Eron, my people owe you a great debt," Tersan continued. "It begins with the accolades you never received after vanquishing Fot. That single act weakened Marand's army to a point where he ceased all aggression and returned to Calshara. We have had an uneasy but pleasant peace."

"Fot is back, Tersan," Eron said sternly. "He is Marand's right hand. We ride to war, not celebration."

"An army needs heroes, Eron," Tersan argued quietly. "My people and yours have been waiting to celebrate your victory and your return for a long, long time."

"No."

Tersan shook his head. "You have defeated an enemy many thought was myth. In doing so, you have also become myth."

"Myth?" Eron snorted. "You speak like an old woman."

"A feast has been planned for our arrival and before your protest, let me tell you how important this is."

"And I may protest after that?"

"Yes." Tersan shifted in his saddle to gaze fully into Eron's face. Shadow darkened the pale features once more. "Wars are won as much by attitude as they are by weapons," Tersan continued. "Our men know Fot has returned. News such as that spreads quickly. Fewer than a hundred of my elite cavalry survived the battle for the portal unscathed. None had ever faced such enemies before. They fear them."

"With good reason."

"You defeated the commander of their forces single handedly--"

"Jessie was there!"

"Of course she was. But she is not the warrior. You are."

Eron sighed. "You give me too much credit."

"Perhaps. But the power of the enemy has grown disproportionately because demons, to us, are not a known enemy. The unknown creates doubt and doubt, in battle, can make the difference between living and dying."

"And how is celebrating my return going to change that?" Eron asked.

"As Sword, you have skills that are not possessed by ordinary people."

"Nonsense, Tersan. Everyone knows that both Sword and Shield are human. I was chosen from the ranks of anyone skilled enough to summon and wield the Sword of Light and willing to protect our people against all enemies, including demons."

Tersan looked ahead across the plain. In the distance he could see a tiny dark mound that he knew was Pella Durett. "Precisely! Very few have that gift. I certainly do not."

"All right, so I am a myth."

"We began preparing for war in spring and have been ready since mid-summer. It is common knowledge that you were gravely injured, almost killed. To see you whole again is an inspiration. We waited for this moment."

"Waited for me?"

"Penrose insisted. He wanted to give Tocar a chance to use diplomacy, too," Tersan explained. "Progress was made, but now that Fot is back, it seems that more than a show of force may be needed to maintain peace. Had we moved sooner, perhaps this show of force could have been enough to secure peace."

"The balance of power has shifted in Marand's favor," Eron answered quietly. "I am not ready to battle Fot again. I have lost all but the barest of my skills and what remains is not well controlled. I do not know if I will ever recover more."

Tersan thought back to their conversation the night before. "It does not matter. Men will succeed where Sword may not. We have great need of *you*, Eron, not your sword or your visions," he said gently. "Your presence generates fear, fear is our power, even if you could not ever produce the Sword of Light again."

Eron stared straight ahead of them and swallowed hard. The wind blew the untamed silver strands of hair out of his eyes and somewhere high above them an eagle cried. The sunlight that shone on the plain seemed to lack warmth. The time was changing and even he could feel it.

"If you were not afraid of war, my friend," Tersan added, "I would have great concern. War is the last resort of civilized men."

They rode late into the morning until the sun was high upon them and the outline of Pella Durett was clear ahead of them. In the shade of the Little Fingers, they stopped and ate a small meal, allowing the horses to rest and drink from the spring under one of the fingers. The meal was quiet but comfortable and soon they were on their way once more.

In the distance, the healers' wagon was making slower progress across the plain. They would have to take a slightly different path bypassing Pella Durett altogether and meeting them on the Durnham Plain. By late afternoon, they had reached the hill leading down and then back up to the fortress, the first of many steep hills making the fortress nearly impenetrable. Pella Durett towered above the plain. To the east, the waters of the Udolphi glistened.

"It is an impressive sight, is it not?" Tersan said.

Eron sat on his horse, his dark eyes now black and his mouth set in a straight line across his face. "Yes," he said.

"You're going to a victory celebration," Tersan told him. "At least smile."

"There is nothing to smile about, Tersan."

"Pretend."

Within the walls a trumpet sounded, pure and clear. Behind them, Rudlo answered. Men stood on the turrets, their arms raised in salutation. They raced to see their approaching leaders, most dressed in Tersan's rusty red but some in the traditional black of the Kilmari. Tersan waved to the men stationed on the turrets and a roar went up from the battlement walk. The drawbridge lowered and the army poured out of the outer walls. They formed an unruly sea of soldiers that parted to allow the approaching riders entry.

Tersan urged his horse forward. Eron did likewise and together they made their way through the throng of soldiers and well-wishers. All had come for a glimpse of their king and this man who had vanquished Fot and in whose hands their fate once again lay. Eron rode on Tersan's right. Between the horses and his cloak, the long sword he wore was nearly hidden. Still, the crowd saw it. They cheered them as they entered and spoke in whispers after they passed.

"He's not supposed to wear a sword, is he?"

"I thought his sword was magic, not metal!"

"The rumors must be true...the demon stole his power!"

If Eron heard them, he did not react. They reached a huge wooden stair where they dismounted, stretching tired muscles before passing into the keep.

Inside the impressive banquet hall of Pella Durett, more than a feast was taking place. It was a festival. Jugglers and minstrels swirled around them while busty maidens toted pitchers of ale and huge trays of food to long, wooden tables lined with soldiers. Rudlo raised a horn to his lips and blasted out six notes announcing their arrival. All noise ceased. One by one, the soldiers knelt before them as they passed to the unoccupied table at the head of the hall.

The whispers began anew as Eron swept off the cloak and unbuckled his sword. He handed both to a waiting page. The boy, not yet in is teens, practically cowered as he received them. He was careful to keep his eyes averted. Eron gave him a curt nod and took his place beside Tersan at the table.

"Soldiers of Jeleste and soldiers of Kimala," Tersan began, holding a hand up to quiet the raucous cheers as he identified both armies, "we gather here to honor our dead and welcome back the Sword of Itasha."

A single "Hail!" rang out, then all was quiet again.

"Feast now, love your women and kiss the children one last time," Tersan continued, "for tomorrow, we march to war."

A single soldier burst from the ranks. He raced toward the table where Eron stood and knelt without looking up. He held before him in both hands a battered though honed sword, as though offering it to Eron. The Sword exchanged a panicked looked with Tersan.

"Sword of Itasha," the man began, "I have sworn my allegiance to you."

"I, um, thank you," Eron said.

"My wife is heavy with child, but my oath demands that I follow you into battle and I would have it no other way." The man looked up at him. "It is said that if my Lord blesses the sword of those who serve you, they shall not perish in battle." His eyes were shining. "I--I ask that you bless my sword. I--"

"Nonsense!" Eron snapped. "You would do better to pray to the Lady. I can offer you no such assurance or blessing."

"Please, Majesty," the man pleaded. "I wish to know my unborn child."

Eron looked to Tersan as though asking for help. Then he straightened himself and spoke. "What is your name?"

"Ranit," he answered.

"Ranit, are you prepared for battle?" he asked.

"Yes, my lord."

"Do you believe the blessings of the Lady are with you and your family?"

"I do, my lord."

Eron drew in a deep breath. "I cannot grant you divine intervention to assure your safe return to your family. Ranit, I am only a man. Well-schooled, yes. Gifted, undoubtedly. But I am not omnipotent. A blessing from me comes from the heart of a man. It means well but has no power to keep you safe."

The hall was filled with whispers.

Ranit looked up at him. "Then I would have the blessing of a man."

The whispers stopped; every soul waited for his reply. Eron took the battered sword, examined it closely. He handed it back to Ranit, hilt first. "Look to your skill," he said quietly, "and trust in the Lady to bring you home safely to your child." Before anyone could speak, Eron turned and left the hall.

Letou tried to stop him, but Tersan waved him off. "Let him go, Captain," Tersan said, "let him go." He raised a mug of ale. "Music!"

25 Close Call

Something was close to Patrick's face. It wasn't anything either pleasant or unpleasant rather it was annoying. He absently batted at it with one hand and rolled over in bed. It followed him.

"Go away," he said. He pulled the covers up around his shoulders. The thing moved with him. It hissed and the hackles on the back of Patrick's neck went up. Wide awake now, he slid his hand down the side of the bed. His fingers found the cold butt of his gun and he gripped it firmly. He tested his blankets, making certain the covers wouldn't hinder his next move.

The thing pecked at him. Gripping the gun with both hands, he flew up out of bed.

"Freeze!" he ordered.

Winifred's pet floated in the air above his bed. For a second, she stared at him, then lazily floated out of the room. Patrick lowered his gun and sat down hard on the bed. He flipped the safety back on and set the weapon down.

"I see you are awake, dear."

Patrick grabbed the covers and threw them over his exposed shorts. Winnie was standing at the door, a towel in her hands and a smile on her face.

"What time is it?" he asked, fumbling for his watch. "Noon," he answered himself.

"Polly says they are stirring. It is time to go."

"How does she know?" he asked through a yawn.

"She is a demon herder."

"Oh." Patrick rubbed the back of his neck, still protecting his modesty. Winnie stood at the door, waiting. Patrick cleared his throat.

"What is it, dear?" Winnie asked.

"I, uh, I'm not accustomed to being watched while I dress."

"Oh yes. Of course." She smiled. "Matthew never minded. You remind me a bit of him, you know. Younger, of course, but, well..." She pulled the door shut.

Patrick dressed quickly. Side arm in shoulder holster, pistol in ankle holster extra clips of ammo, knife. He hoped he never had to use the knife. The weapons weren't really overkill. He'd never had to use any of them, but the mini arsenal made him feel safe. He was ready.

Joann was already in the living room when Patrick got there. A shotgun rested on her lap. He raised an eyebrow.

"I'm not taking any chances with those things," she told him.

"Understood."

Winnie breezed out of the kitchen, a picnic basket in hand. "Patrick," she started, waving to the camera bag they had left by the front door the night before, "be a dear and bring along the demons, will you? And we shall need those fireplace utensils as well."

"Fireplace utensils?" Patrick asked. "We've been trained in hand to hand combat, but not with a blunt object." He patted his gun. "We're ready."

"I'm certain you are, my dear," Winnie replied. "Those are the keys to my world that Jessie left behind. The dear girl was fascinated by magic and changed the entire set. Those who can see her work can truly appreciate their beauty. In addition, I am certain that Lae and Bue saw Jason perform the dance, use the key to open the portal--"

"So why don't we just let them go?" Patrick asked.

"We cannot let them go!" Winnie insisted.

"Why not?" Joann asked. "It sounds perfectly logical to me. Just bring them back here and send them on their way."

Winnie gave them her best mother-knows-best glare. "After what happened to you, Joann, would you really want them to be able to come and go as they please?"

Patrick looked to Joann. His fellow officer shrugged. "Joann, get the fireplace utensils, I'll get the bag."

"Good lad," Winnie said. "Patrick, remember how Polly herded the little ones through the house until we caught them?"

"That's a memory I won't soon forget," he answered.

94

"Once we find Lae and Bue, you and Joann must herd them toward me. I will capture them in a net--"

"You want us to do what?" Joann interrupted.

"If it's anything like what you used on me," Patrick said, "it may work. But two of them?"

"Really?" Joann said.

"We shall do the best we can," Winnie answered. "Now, come along. We have work to do!"

"Yes, ma'am. How far are we going?" he asked. "I'm happy to drive, but electric cars have limited range."

"We should take Caravan," Winnie told them as they started toward the front door.

"Caravan?" Joann asked.

"She named her minivan," Patrick answered.

"Ah."

"There is plenty of room," Winnie continued, "and I do not think it will mind an extra passenger or two."

"Yes, ma'am," Patrick said.

"And it will be easier to see Polly."

Without further discussion, they followed her to the garage behind the house where a cranberry colored minivan was parked. Winnie put her basket behind the driver's seat then slid in behind the wheel. The serpent hovered in front of the windshield. Patrick rode shotgun, Joann settled in behind him.

"There is food in the basket," Winnie said, "please help yourselves. Apparently Jason and his friend were planning to stay for a while. It was quite considerate of them to provide provisions for us."

They started down the long drive to the highway, Polly darting from side to side in front of them. Winnie followed her every move, jerking the wheel back and forth. The effort made Patrick wonder if he really wanted breakfast.

"Winnie, stop the car," Patrick said.

"Why?" she asked, slamming the steering wheel to the right.

"Because," Joann answered, "if you don't, every cop in the county will be looking for the drunk driver on Rte. 141."

"I am not inebriated!" Winnie protested as she ran off the driveway. She slammed on the brakes testing everyone's seat belts and threw the car into park. "I am a careful, prudent driver."

"Of course you are, Winnie," Joann said, "but you're not normally following, um..." She looked at Patrick.

"A demon herder," Patrick finished for her. He grinned. "Polly," he added.

"Yeah. You're not normally following a demon herder."

"I can do this!" Winnie took a deep breath, apparently to steady herself. She reached for the car's gearshift but before she could put it in gear, Patrick stopped her.

"Let me drive," he offered. "You tell me which way to go, all right? That way you can watch Polly and we'll get there in one piece."

"Caravan is a mighty steed," she said. "Are you certain you can handle it?"

Patrick patted the dashboard. "I'm sure we'll get along just fine, ma'am, just fine."

Winnie's eyes furrowed as if she were evaluating his abilities. He continued to smile and pat the dash. Finally, she nodded. "Be kind."

"Always," Patrick answered.

Winnie opened the door and got out, slamming it shut behind her.

"Ouch," Joann said. Patrick glanced back to find her fingering the bruises on her neck. She flashed him a grin. "Had to remind myself that all this is real."

"It is more than a little weird," he admitted. He got out, held the door open for Winnie as she got back in, then shut it and assumed his place behind the steering wheel.

"Ready?" he asked.

Winnie straightened beside him. "I am."

"Good. You watch Polly, okay? Let me know where she is?"

"Agreed."

They made their way down to the highway.

"Make a right here, dear," Winnie said.

Patrick swung right onto the highway.

"Breakfast?" Joann offered. She held a bagel for him, generously smeared with cream cheese. Patrick took it happily.

"Any chance there's coffee?"

"Hang on." He heard a thermos being opened. A disposable cup came into his peripheral vision.

"Thanks. I--"

"Turn right!" Winnie interrupted.

Patrick slowed the van and looked for the road.

"Turn right!" Winnie insisted. "Now!"

Patrick pulled over on the almost deserted highway. There was no road and little shoulder. If he left the road, there was at least a foot drop off before he'd get to uneven turf. "We can't," he said.

"But that is the way! See?" She pointed wildly. "Polly's right there! Do you not see her?"

Patrick looked to his right. Sure enough, the little serpent was hovering in the air to the right of them, waiting. "Winnie, surely Miss Perrymore told you that you have keep the van on the road," he said. "We can't go that way. This van isn't an off-road vehicle. That's a foot drop."

"But that is the way!" she protested.

"Maybe they're not that far," Joann offered. "Winnie, is there any way you can, er, ask?"

"Certainly." Winnie composed herself and motioned to her pet. Polly came down to the window and hovered outside of it. "Caravan will not tolerate this path," she said. "Are we close enough to walk?"

The serpent's neck flared, making her briefly appear twice her true size. She hissed and rattled her scales.

"Now, now, Polly. It is not kind to criticize the shortcomings of others."

Polly dipped her head and hissed.

"I see..." Winnie said.

Polly continued to hiss.

"Very well." Winnie turned to Patrick and Joann. "It is too far to walk."

"Tell her to..." Patrick hunted for words. "Can she get us closer by following a road? Something smooth like this one?"

Polly hissed again and Winnie nodded. "Go ahead then, dear," she said. "Just take a route that Caravan can follow, all right?"

Polly was off.

They traveled up into the mountains, through twists and turns, changing road after road. In the back seat, Joann logged their path so they could find their way home. She also had a road map of the state, just in case cell phone reception was unavailable. Four hours after their journey began, Polly stopped once more. She waited beside a gravel road, coming to the window to chat with Winnie.

"What now?" Patrick asked.

"A moment, dear," Winnie answered as she rolled down her window.

"Say, Joann," Patrick said as the two began to talk, "any sandwiches in that basket? And I could use something to drink, if there's any coffee left."

Joann set aside the map and began rustling in the basket.

"Polly wants to know if Caravan can traverse this road," she said.

Patrick leaned over and looked down the road. It was gravel covered with some fairly deep ruts running through the center of it. Fifty feet from the highway, the road was swallowed by a dark overgrowth of trees forming a tunnel of sorts.

"That looks like somebody's driveway," Patrick said.

"It isn't," Joann chimed in from the back seat. She held the map up so he could see it. "We're here," she said, pointing to a large green area. "On Rte. A."

"The preserve?" he said.

"Yep. Somewhere in the middle of it, if this is right."

"Great. So this leads to a ranger station or something?" he said.

"Or something." Joann folded the map and handed Patrick a sandwich. "It's not chained off so it's probably just a picnic spot."

Patrick took the food. "Looks like the road hasn't been accessed in a while. No picnickers, but hikers come from anywhere."

"Middle of the week in October," Joann said, "so my guess would be no. According to this, the road should be passable."

Polly shimmied. She zipped into the open window and curled up on Winnie's lap. In no time, she was fast asleep. Winnie clucked to her. "There's my girl," she said.

"They're this way?" Patrick asked. He threw the van into reverse and backed a short distance so that he could turn straight onto the road.

"Polly said when the road ends, turn right." She stroked the serpent. "And wake her then. There were no people," she added.

"Well, there's a bit of good news anyway."

The road turned out to be worse than Patrick first thought. Ruts crisscrossed it slowing their pace tremendously. Beside him, Winnie looked worried. Joann had taken a position between the two of them on her knees so that she could see out the front window. The ride was silent and the only one calm was Polly, who still slept on Winnie's lap. Finally, their road ended. A marker pointed to the right, indicating a campground, to the left, a lake.

"This is it," he said, turning toward the lake. "You'd better wake your partner, Winnie," Patrick said. "Joann, get ready."

"I'm way ahead of you, Pat my boy!" She was on her haunches beside the door holding the shotgun with ease. "Ready."

Polly stirred, raised her head and hissed at them, then flew out Winnie's window and headed toward the lake. Patrick turned on the headlights and slowly followed.

The almost hidden road was oppressive, dark and restrictive, the air barely moving due to the heavy undergrowth. Patrick placed his service weapon on his lap. Joann readied the shotgun. Five minutes later, the woods opened up to reveal a small nameless lake. Polly was hovering over a picnic table, waiting. They got out of the van as quietly as they could and joined her.

Ahead, in a clearing bathed by silvery light from the now risen moon, two tall, beautiful women were ripping strips of flesh from a freshly killed deer.

"This is it," he said to Joann. "You go right, I'll go left."

Joann nodded and started off to her right.

"Winnie?"

"Herd them toward me. I will be ready."

The demons stopped eating and glanced toward the van. They exchanged a knowing smile and resumed their meal. Patrick's skin prickled. He keyed the mic on his shoulder.

"Watch yourself, Joann," he said. "They're up to something."

"Roger that."

From two sides, they advanced on the demons, safety's off. Joann halted behind a picnic table, her weapon trained on the one nearest her. At that distance, Patrick thought, even an amateur could hit this large, glowing target. He stopped, one foot strategically placed in front of the other to brace himself against the kick that would come from his gun.

Back at the van, Winnie was doing something. Patrick caught her out of the corner of his eye and strained to keep both her and his quarry in sight. The demons were not the only ones glowing in the early evening darkness. Like a petal on a breeze, the older woman started forward toward them, her face set in a fierce demeanor Patrick would not have attributed to her. Around her head, the demon herder swirled, adding a brilliant amber halo to Winnie's cold silvery aura. When she got thirty feet away from them, she stopped.

"Ladies," Patrick said to the demons, "please move away from the deer. Keep your hands where we can see them." He could smell the entrails of the dead deer, could hear the smacking of their lips as they ate.

"Do you hear that?" one said to the other. "He wants us to return to those hateful little orbs."

"He is pathetic, Wylfcynne," the other said to Winnie. "Not even a Sword."

"I don't need a sword, ladies," Patrick said. He started toward them, each footfall secure on the ground before he took another step. "Now, kindly return--"

The nearest woman threw the deer's head at him, catching him squarely in the upper thigh. He slipped, fell on one knee and when he looked up again, a huge winged being was charging down on. He rolled, coming up on the other knee, his gun still in both hands but before he could fire, he found himself in the grip of something huge. His arms were pinned beside him, his mini arsenal useless in their various holders, his gun on the ground. Hot air brushed the back of his neck, then the side, then his cheek. The stench of death clung to the air along with the unlikely scent of lavender.

"I think you need to learn a little more about your enemy," the most sultry voice he had ever heard breathed into his ear. Her breath covered his face, at once intoxicating him and seducing him.

Patrick succumbed to the voice. Gunshots rang out behind him. Joann was shouting something to Winnie and Winnie was shouting back. Their voices were harsh, grating in comparison to his captor. He was all but lost in that sultry voice. His feet left the turf, his body still captive against a cold, scaly creature. Somewhere deep inside his brain an alarm was trying to sound to tell him to thrash, to try to escape, something. He was being lifted into the air. The alarm sounded louder and behind him, the creature laughed. Patrick felt his head loll to one side. His lips pulled up into a smile as he released a contented sigh.

Something whipped into his face, slapping him hard. He snapped his eyes open. One by one the many hands holding him were letting go. The laugh turned to a series of yelps and Patrick found himself falling into a silvery net. Above him, a golden streak of light attacked the blue aura of the demon, in staccato moves resembling a chicken pecking at feed.

"Polly! Get out of there!" Winnie yelled.

Patrick was lowered slowly to the ground. He landed beside his revolver. He grabbed at it and tried to concentrate on the rapidly dwindling spot that had of late released him or the twin that joined it above the lake. In an instant, they were gone.

"Damn it!" Patrick breathed. He got up, fumbled with the gun but managed to get the safety in place before attempting to reholster it. On the second try, it was put away.

"Joann!" he called, though his tongue was thick. "Joann, are you all right?"

"H-here," she said. She was stumbling toward him, her hair askew, her sweatshirt torn. There was anger in her eyes and she was trembling. Patrick took her hand. It was as cold as ice.

"That, that thing," she started, "grabbed my shotgun and threw it at me and then ripped my handgun right out of my hands! Damn it, Pat! We've got to get it back!"

"We will, dear, we will," Winnie told her. "Let me see..." A silvery orb appeared in Winnie's hand. It glowed softly as Winnie turned Joann around in a circle. "Are you injured, dear?" she asked.

"I'm still standing, aren't I?" Joann groaned.

"That's not what I asked, dear," Winnie said. "Are you injured?"

Joann's shoulders rose and fell. "Mostly my pride." She shook her head. "I'll be fine."

"Good. Come along. You can drive us back to Jessie's house while I tend to Patrick."

Patrick stumbled forward. His shirt was in tatters and his head was spinning but he was filled with a sense of euphoria that he had never had before. All he wanted to do in that moment was to be with the demon who had held him. The alarm in his head was ringing incessantly. At some deep level, he knew he was hooked on something.

"Are you injured?" Winnie asked him. She was on his left, supporting him as he walked.

"More like drunk," he answered. Every sound around him was muffled.

"Any idea where they'll go?" Joann asked as they got into the van.

"Yes, dear, I've already told you. Jessie's house." She pointed to the camera bag on the floor. "They will want to release them." She grinned. "They will be, what is the word? Pissed? Yes, pissed that their friends are not there."

Patrick sunk back in the back seat while Joann fired the van up and pulled away from the lake. Winnie was rummaging around in the picnic basket. She pulled out a jar, unscrewed the lid.

"Hold still." She dipped her finger in the jar and smeared a light oil under his nose. The scent of honeysuckle permeated the air and Patrick relaxed even further, but the sensuality of the experience was gone.

"I have been remiss in your lessons," Winnie said sadly. "But we shall fix that before your next confrontation."

"Remiss in what?" Joann said.

"They do not fear you enough to enable us to recapture them, so you will have to slay them. Do not concern yourselves overly. I can help. We simply were not well prepared this time." She smiled.

In the tiny glow shed by the van's dome light, Patrick somehow started to really trust this slightly crazy old woman.

26 Harvest

Jessie lay down on the thick bed of pine needles Altay had prepared for her. Even though the sun had just crossed the midday zenith, she needed to sleep. The full night riding to the portal was exhausting enough, but she had not dared sleep until she knew Jason was out of the Crystal Cave, safe under her watch. Or Penrose's or Altay's. She had set wards to protect them against attack, or at least warn of impending danger. Even though it was early afternoon, she fell fast asleep.

When she stirred once more, the world was dark. She looked at the stars and tried to recognize something that would tell her the time, but they were just so many twinkling lights. The ability to tell time by them was a skill she had never acquired, though she had tried. People here had no frame of reference for Gregorian calendars or Greenwich Time so she had long ago stopped wearing a watch. But she always kept track of days; Christmas and June fifth, Lucy's birthday. She hoped Lucy would forgive her for missing her birthday this year. Six months had passed since she last spoke with Lucy. Tonight, she would break the long silence. Her child was with Martha and her family. Martha...Jessie allowed herself a moment to ponder what it would be like to live her sister's life with a little more than two point five children, going to school plays and concerts, cooking for the perfect husband in suburbia.

Some things were not to be. It was just as well for her love was in Eormengrund.

The camp was quiet. Penrose stirred the fire and motioned for her to join him.

"I have sent for a wagon," he told her. "I doubt either of these young men will be able to ride to Bel Haven."

"Understood." With a laugh, she added: "Jason's got great balance, but he doesn't much care for horses. I need to check the wards." She turned and left.

There was a stillness in the air, the kind that hangs in the darkness when day has ended and night is just begun, the time of day her child came into the world. With a mother's smile, she made her way toward the mouth of the Udolphi. Washing would be a cold but welcome proposition, even if all she did was splash water on her face.

Soft mosses cushioned her every step. Too long she had been confined to Bel Haven with its rocky terrain, its schedules and rules. She had nearly forgotten what it was like to walk in the forest, free from pitying eyes or prying ones. If only she had been able to somehow get Eron through the portal, he could have recovered in her world. Then the three of them could have become a family like any normal family: Eron the doting father, Lucy the beautiful and talented daughter, she the soccer mom; make that rodeo mom or maybe dressage mom. And perhaps she would have another child, a boy this time.

"Eron, the Sword of Claxbury." Jessie smiled. "'Has a nice, homey ring to it." She shook her head. "He almost died here, where they know how to treat those wounds. Home would have been a death sentence."

A flash of light caught her eye, the kind that pricked every hair on the back of her neck. She spun around to face her would-be assailant. Two shields sprang to life from her fingertips, one to protect, the other to defend. She held them ready, searching for the source of the light.

Beyond a small grove of trees, she saw a lithe figure performing a deadly dance. Silvery light glinted off the cold metal of a long blade as it twisted at its master's command, a master dressed in black, nearly invisible behind the whirling sword. Each step taken was precisely placed as though responding to an orchestra only the swordsman could hear. The blade moved faster, its outline now blurred in the cool mountain air. Sword and master were one.

A smile crossed Jessie's lips. It was the Dance of the Sword, performed with grace on a level she had only seen Eron use. Before he was wounded, he used the dance to hone his skills with both sword and power. He had been agile and powerful, graceful and deadly, able to adapt to any circumstance. Certain Eron had found his way to her, she hurried through the grove of trees and into the meadow, allowing her shields to dissipate, a reprimand on her tongue.

"Eron, Penrose will have your head!" she scolded lightly.

The figure abruptly stopped, the sword freezing in front of its master.

"Eron?"

The figure raised the sword slowly in salutation, then stilled it and melted into shadow.

"Wait!" Jessie raced toward the place where the figure had stood but the swordsman was gone. She took three steps into the dense woods and stopped. She could easily lose her way by plummeting into the darkness with nothing for reference.

"Eron?" she repeated, this time not as loud.

Creatures of the night called to one another. No one called to her.

"Wulfhaeled?" She whispered the name of the master she never met, the man who taught Eron to fight, the Sword who died when he and Wylfcynne captured Bue. No answer.

She dared call out the name of the Kilmari legend: "Ahleri?"

She waited at the edge of the forest for him to reappear. He did not. After a long while, she made her way to the river, her mind filled with more questions than answers.

The Udolphi bent to the east and then flowed northward toward the sea. Directly ahead of her, moonlight bathed the distant plain in peace. She could make out the Giant's Fingers, the silent stones stretching upward as though some great being had fallen and turned to stone. Beyond was Bel Haven, then Pella Durett and further, the Paranjothi Mountains, Calshara and the mysterious land of the north where the demons spawned...or so legend told. Someday soon, she would bring Lucy here to share her father's land, this place of wonder. Someday when it was safe.

Jessie knelt at the river's edge. She splashed the icy water on her face, rinsing away the sweat of the previous day, trying to think. Eron was on his way to Calshara with Tersan. The swordsman in the meadow could not have been him.

"Maybe it was a ghost," she said, rising, "or just wishful thinking."

A cold wind blew down from the mountain, snatching at her cape and making her shiver. Kimala's peak shimmered in the night sky. Long ago she heard the mountain when it spoke to her. Now was no different.

The portal is vulnerable, she thought she heard it whisper, *though the battle to protect it will be waged far from here. Do not fail me, Shield.*

"I will not fail," she answered aloud. Wondering what the message meant, she made her way back to camp.

Altay was sitting between their charges, tending the fire and watching them sleep. Penrose was sleeping quietly beside them. The young healer rose and motioned for Jessie to come and take her place between them. Jessie obliged.

"How are they?"

"Ric is doing a lot better than Master Penrose expected," Altay answered. She dished something warm onto a plate and offered it and a steaming beverage mug to Jessie.

"Trinka," she said, drinking in the sweet aroma as the mug warmed her hands. "There are few things I really miss when I go back to my world." She raised the mug that had taken the chill from the darkness and sipped from it. "This is one of them."

"It is a delicacy, my lady," Altay agreed.

"That it is, Altay, that it is."

"The demon's poison had spread," Altay told her, motioning to Ric's bandaged cheek, "but the palapaca appears to have arrested it for now. We had to exhaust our entire supply--"

"All of it?" Jessie interrupted. "There was enough for twenty wounds!"

"Yes, my lady. Remember, the poison was allowed to fester for nearly a day. Palapaca has limitations. And Fot is no ordinary demon," Altay continued in an irritatingly calm voice. "Ric will need attention as soon as we reach Bel Haven, that is clear. Sending him back through the portal is not an option, at least not yet. Not until we are certain the poison has been neutralized."

"And Jason?"

"Jason may leave," she answered lightly, "as long as the healers of your world are willing to deal with whatever happened to him in the cave."

"They have no idea what they've gotten themselves in to." Jessie took up her mug once more and took a swallow of the trinka. She looked longingly toward the portal. Kimala had spoken to her but not told her what she was to do.

"There's safety in numbers," she said. "It's better not to separate."

"Agreed." Altay raised her eyebrows. "Fot has been released. Legend says the person who releases a demon has a modicum of power over it."

"They are only children!" Jessie snapped. "They don't know what they did or how to use their position to their best advantage!"

"Do you consider me a child, my lady?" Altay asked.

"Of course not!"

"Do not be angry," Altay said with a sad smile, "but by your own admission, they are older than I am."

"Our worlds are different!" Jessie protested.

"Yes, my lady, they are."

Jessie felt her face flush. "I'm sorry, Altay," she said. "It's just that, well, I chose to be here and to get involved. They didn't."

"They are involved, my lady," Altay answered gently. She had a bewitching smile. "The mountain must have had a need for them," she continued, "else they would not be here."

"The mountain...the cave..." Jessie placed her hand on Jason's chest, content to feel him breathing easily beneath her touch. Ric lay unconscious beside the fire, a pile of blankets beneath him and another over him. But he, too, seemed to be breathing easily.

"Altay," she began, "I need to return to the portal, assess any damage and repair it if it is needed. I have time to do that before we leave."

"But--"

"No buts. It's not that far. I can be there and back before morning."

"If you're going to the portal, they will want to know why you did not take them home."

Jessie frowned. "We'll cross that bridge when we come to it."

Altay stared at her for a long moment. "Be careful, my lady," she finally said.

With a nod, Jessie pulled the hood of her cloak up to hide her face. She made her way into the forest; the landmarks of this path she knew well.

It did not take long for the forest's thick canopy to steal away the moonlight. Yet even in near darkness, Jessie knew the way. She wound her way through unmarked woods, across small streams and around huge stones until she reached a small glen. The moon shone like sunlight here. Jessie's senses ignited. A ragged black hole scarred the side of the mountain. Deep within was the way home. She knew it. Fot now knew it, too. The chance they had taken seemed reasonable at the time. Now, she was not as certain.

Carefully she scanned the sky for the demon. The Kilmari would be watching. The Kilmari always watched. Surely they already knew that their greatest enemy had returned. Hugging the forest's edge, she made her way toward the hole and the stairway that lay beyond.

She estimated it took about fifteen minutes to skirt the meadow and arrive at the staircase. Once there, she used her senses to find the wards Tocar had woven over them as she cradled Eron in her arms the previous spring. The prince's spiral shield was gone, only a trace of his protective covering clinging to the yawning opening. By design, it was meant to keep demons out, not keep them from escaping. She peered into the hole and found her own shield battered but nearly in once piece. A single opening was sliced into it, a tear no wider than her thumb. She shivered, her hand throbbing as she relived Fot's tooth penetrating the barrier and her hand. A second tear, longer and wider, was in the center of the ward. That must have been the culprit for Ric's wound.

"Light!" she whispered. Fire sparked from her fingertips and she wove an intricate pattern of silver and gold, blue and green. When it filled the palm of her hand, she stopped and pursed her lips. With a puff, the shield drifted out over the hole, catching on the stone closest to her, then expanding across the rift until it caught on the other side. It continued to grow until the webbing covered the hole, visible to those with senses keen enough to see it.

"Now all I need to do is seal it," she mumbled.

"Hold fast!" a voice behind her hissed so softly Jessie barely made out the words. Cold steel pricked the back of her neck and she stiffened. Between fast moving fingers, she summoned a different kind of shield.

"State your business," the voice demanded.

Without moving her body, she raised her right hand until it hovered inches below her left shoulder. With a flip of her wrist, she tossed the defensive shield at her assailant. He grunted as it hit him. Jessie dove to her right, twisting to face him. She sent her second shield flying to encompass him. The offensive tip of his sword pricked his own chin as he now lay defenseless on the ground before her, bound by cords of energy. Jessie raised an eyebrow.

"That worked even better than in practice," she said cheerfully. She cleared her throat and rose, brushing the dirt from her hands. "Now, let's see who we've caught." She summoned a small orb of light and leaned in to her prey for a closer look.

The face that stared back was terrified. He had blue eyes and perfect teeth, chiseled features and masses of blond hair that matched his fair complexion.

"Cynthal?" The terror in his face doubled.

"Cynthal," she said, lowering her hood and summoning her power back to her. The shields vanished. "You, um, frightened me."

"L-lady Jessie?" He let his sword drop to one side and rolled up on his hands and knees gasping for breath. Jessie put a hand on his shoulder.

"Are you all right?"

"Y-yes," he said between breaths, "I-I'll--be--fine."

"I'm sorry. I've practiced that shield for a long time, but I've never had to use it."

"W-why?" he asked. He sat, one hand at his throat, the other on the ground in front of him.

"I promised Eron I could defend as well as protect," she said, letting a little pride come through in her words. "I didn't know it would work."

"N-next time I...see him," he stuttered, "I-I will let him know...it worked."

"'You sure you're all right?"

Cynthal nodded. "You stole my breath away as it tightened," he said, managing a full sentence. He took in a deep breath and looked at her. "That is all. What are you doing here, my lady?"

"Damage control," she answered. "I have to make certain this portal is sealed."

"As did I." He got to his feet, plucking up his sword in one graceful motion. "We all felt it. The power was great." He held her eyes with his own. "Has Fot returned?"

"Yes." She regarded him with her own critical eye. He appeared to be fine. "I have to go down the stairway and check on the portal, make sure there is no opening between here and my world."

"I will accompany you."

"Okay. I'll be just a minute..." She looked toward the ward she had just repaired, checking to make certain it was whole. From the edges to the center and back, she scanned it. There were no holes. "This looks good," she said. "Now..."

She made her way toward a boulder that marked the top of the hidden staircase. She touched its side in three places and a small door swung open. "Great!" she said, reaching inside the stump and withdrawing a torch. "Flame," she whispered. The torch ignited. "Ready?"

"Yes, my lady."

Together, they made their way down the stairs into the portal room, lighting torches that had hung from the stairwell unused for a long time. The way had not changed since she had been here in the spring. With each step, her pulse quickened. Debris was scattered on the steps as they came close to the bottom, making it somewhat treacherous. At last, they emerged into the portal room.

What had been a shambles was worse now. The few pieces of furniture she had left there broken were now mere splinters. The center looked as though some great hand had swept the area clean. Cynthal sucked in a huge breath behind her.

"Mother told me about Fot's capture," he said, "but I had no idea how much had been destroyed."

"This happened during his return," Jessie answered. "They are only things. They can be replaced."

She walked quickly across the room, holding the torch high and away from her body, then ran her hand across the smooth wall. Energy pricked her fingers as her hand floated over the doorway to her world.

"My lady?" Cynthal said.

"Thank goodness!" she replied. "Jason or Ric must have carried him through the portal. My world is safe."

"Jason or Ric?"

"My nephew and his friend." She sighed. "They didn't know they were bringing the lord of demons home."

"What?" Cynthal held his torch so that his face was illuminated in the light. "My Lady, how could they not know?"

"Because the demons of our world are not as obvious as Fot," she answered. "They disguise themselves as real men and women."

"I do not believe I would want to live in your world," Cynthal said.

"There is something I must do. Will you wait here?"

"As you wish, my lady."

Jessie placed the torch in a holder on the wall and touched four stones. Then she pushed. The wall gave way to a set of stairs that led to her root cellar. The air smelled different here, musty, but in a different way than the portal room. She raced up the steps and out onto the lawn, crossing quickly in the moonlight, until she came to her door. She fumbled for the hidden key, opened the door and gasped. The snow globes were gone.

"No…" she said aloud.

"Jessie? Is that you, dear?"

Jessie nearly jumped out of her skin. "Miss James?"

"How many times have I told you, you must call me Winifred?" The perky older woman appeared from the kitchen, the ever present towel in her hands. "How wonderful to see you!" she started with a smile. Her expression rapidly changed. "You are alone. What happened to Jason and his friend?"

"They released Fot--"

"Yes, dear, I know."

"Fot wounded Ric."

"Oh dear…"

"But Penrose is with them. Altay, too. He says they will be all right."

"Eron?"

"Shaky, but on his way to confront Marand with Tersan."

"Tersan! Ah, he was always a good boy."

The mantel clock chimed twice.

"Two in the morning. I've got to call Martha and let her know what's going on."

"Be brief, dear. You know how she worries."

"I hope she'll let me speak with Lucy."

"You must warn her. Other demons have been set free."

"No…" A hundred scenarios filled Jessie's mind; none of them good. "Which ones?" she asked quietly.

Winifred sucked in an uncharacteristic breath. "Bue and Lae."

Jessie's heart sank. "I'll tell her." She picked up the phone and dialed her sister's home.

"Hello?"

"Martha, it's me, Jess."

"No, honey, I'll take care of it," Martha said without bothering to cover the mouthpiece. There was a grunt of acknowledgement and the sound of a door opening and closing.

"Jessie, are you all right?" she finally asked.

"Fine."

"Where have you been? Lucy's worried sick."

"Can I talk to her?"

"She's spending the night at a friend's house. Oh, Jess, we've been so worried!"

"She's not home?"

"I, um, let her go out on an overnight. She was very excited about it. Hopefully she'll be able to take her mind off the dreams."

"Dreams?" Jessie's heart skipped a beat. "What kind of dreams?"

"Oh, you know," her sister rambled, "about damsels in distress, princes, demons, her father, that kind of thing."

Jessie groaned inwardly.

"Tell her what happened, dear" Winifred coaxed. "The short version."

Jessie nodded. Rapidly she related Eron's fall, the capture of Fot and the coming campaign to Il Chatel. "I'm sorry I missed her birthday," she finished. "Would you tell her that?"

"You're not staying?"

"No." Jessie bit her lip. "You see, Jason and his friend triggered the opening to Eormengrund and, well, it's kind of complicated, but they released Fot--"

"That really bad demon?"

"Yes, and you see, Ric was hurt badly and his only chance of survival is there."

"What? What about Jason?"

"He was hurt, but Penrose said he'll be okay. He could come home now, but it's not safe to split up."

"Oh, Jessie," Martha exclaimed with regret.

Jessie leaned her head against the kitchen wall and closed her eyes. "I made a promise."

"At what cost? First your daughter…" Martha's voice, usually so steady, cracked. "Now my son?"

An uneasy silence followed. Tears streamed down Jessie's face. She could see Martha, holding the phone away from her mouth so that the quiet sobs would remain undetected. Jessie sniffed.

"Martha," she said softly, "as soon as this campaign is over, I promise that will be all for me. I promise!"

She heard Martha swallow and in her mind, saw composure return. "I'll take care of Lucy for you," the big sister said, "just like always. And I will think of something to tell Ric's parents. Please, please, don't let anything happen to my son."

"I'll do my best. And you look out for demons."

"We love you, Jess."

"I love you, too."

Jessie hung up the phone, suddenly aware that she was crying. She plucked a tissue from the box on the countertop and blew her nose in it, snagged three more which she tucked in her bodice.

"I miss tissues," she told Winifred.

"I understand, dear," the older woman told her.

"Gotta go. Take care of yourself."

"My best to Master Penrose, and your dear Eron as well." She put her arm around Jessie's shoulders. "It will all work out, you know," she said.

"I know. It's just that I've missed so much," she said with a sniff. She honked into the tissue. "I really do have to leave now."

"I understand. We'll recapture the demons. I have help."

"Polly?"

"Polly, Patrick and Joann. They are police. Very nice, once they know what is happening."

"Police?"

"Let me worry about things here. I will make sure Lucy is safe. That's a promise. Now, run along, dear."

"Yes, Ma'am."

The way back to the root cellar and through the staircase seemed unreal. Cynthal was waiting for her. He bowed, but said nothing.

"One last thing," she said, searching the floor for the place where Eron had lain, "I have to see if there is something... There!"

Tiny flecks of gold sparkled at her from between the stones on the floor. She knelt down beside them, careful not to disturb them. She withdrew a small crystal that hung around her neck. Very cautiously, she swept the specks toward the crystal. For an instant, they lay on the clear surface, then sank inside.

"What is it, my lady?" Cynthal asked.

"Balm," Jessie answered, still working to harvest the precious light, "balm for a recovering spirit."

27 Muster

"My lord, it is dawn."

Tersan turned over in his bed and tried to ignore the headache that always accompanied too much drink and too little sleep. He took a moment to rub his temples with the heels of his hands before standing on the cold stone floor. Pella Durett was not built for comfort.

"Trinka, my lord?" the page asked.

"Water first, Garrett," Tersan croaked. The page handed him a mug filled with water. He downed it in a single draught and handed it back to the boy. Panic gripped him as he suddenly remembered his vow to Penrose. He seized the lad's hand so fiercely the boy let out a yelp. "Where's Eron?" he demanded.

"Safe on the parapet, my lord," Garrett answered quickly.

"Thank the Lady." He released the boy with a little more force than he intended. Garrett obediently stood, waiting his king's commands. Tersan looked at the mug woefully.

"Another, my lord?" Garrett guessed.

"Please."

Garrett took the mug and refilled it. "He has been there the entire night, my lord," he added rather hesitantly. "He stares to the west."

"The entire night?" Tersan asked.

"Yes, my lord." Garrett fidgeted, his eyes downcast. "I hope I did not overstep my liberties by watching him," he said.

"You have done what your king promised to do," he sighed, "but failed to do." He winked at the boy and Garrett relaxed a little. "The Sword needs a guardian. It was supposed to be me."

"I am sorry, my lord."

"It's all right. Good, in fact." Tersan walked across the room going from wobbly to steady as he moved. Garrett had set clothes out for him. He pulled on the soft jerkin and riding breeches.

"My lord?"

"What is it?"

"I thought Calshara was to the north," he said.

"It is."

"Then, begging your pardon if I am too bold, why does the Sword look to the west?"

Tersan smiled. "You will not ask that question when you are older," he answered.

"Ah, so it is a woman!" Garrett grinned.

Tersan laughed. "Apparently you are older than you look."

"I will be eleven next Solstice," he said proudly.

"Fine, fine." Tersan shrugged on the last of his garments and pulled on his boots. "Now, take me to Eron."

The walk to the parapet was longer than Tersan had remembered. Winding stairs twisted around the fortress in every conceivable direction, but Garrett seemed to know exactly where he was going. Pella Durett was alive with men and women working to feed the army. The sweet scents of bread and meat wafted up the tunnels toward them. Tersan cursed himself for drinking too much the night before. He knew his stomach would settle...eventually.

Garrett led him to a heavy wooden door but before opening it, he turned. "It is a bright day, my lord," he said.

"It seems I am again in your debt," Tersan answered. He put his hand to his forehead, ready for the onslaught of light. Garrett nodded and opened the door.

Sunlight poured over them, stabbing Tersan in the eyes in spite of the shade. He screwed his face up against it and then strode out into the daylight after the page.

Eron sat on the wall of the fortress, still looking to the west. He held a crystal in his hand but the circlet Pixil had fashioned for him was not on his brow. Garrett stopped a respectful ten feet behind him as Tersan closed the distance.

"Eron," Tersan said.

Eron kept looking across the plain. He was once again clad in his long black cape and Tersan suspected the long sword was beneath it. "They're breaking camp," he said without looking back.

Tersan joined him on the wall, careful not to get too close to the edge. "Cold night?" he asked.

"I've had colder. Your page there brought me my cloak."

"Garrett," Tersan said, "before you pack my things, go and get us something to eat. I will take that trinka now. Bring it to the war room."

"Yes, my lord." Garrett moved quickly back to the door and disappeared.

"He is a good lad," Eron said. "He stayed with me all night. Not that I needed watching."

"So he said."

In the vast courtyard below, men scurried about everywhere as tents came down and wagons were packed. Fires that had grown cold overnight were nudged into small blazes that soldiers gathered around to share a morning meal. "He wanted to know what you were looking for," Tersan said, only half interested in the answer.

"Jessie." Eron sighed. "Or Tocar, or Parry or even that blasted portal room. I gave them each one of these." He finally looked away from the horizon. "I cannot see, Tersan. I am blind."

"No. You are not blind." Tersan continued to watch the camp break. "Jessie said you weren't."

"I can't rely on random visions!"

"Then worry about it if it makes you feel better."

Eron ran a hand through his hair. "I keep telling you I am not ready to join this fight."

"Because you are nothing more than a lowly soldier?"

"That's not what I meant."

"You have always had skill with a sword, Eron, even if the sword was not part myth."

"I want it back, Tersan," he said, "I want it all back."

"Adapt," Tersan answered. "Many have had to since that day." He turned his attention away from the camp and held Eron's eyes with his own. "If Fot knew that you were so weakened, do you think he would come here to destroy you?"

"To the middle of his enemy's stronghold?" Eron asked.

Tersan laughed. "I believe you have answered my question. Save your fear, Eron, for a time when you need it to spur you onward. Do not waste it here among friends."

Eron nodded slowly. "Sage words for a young king," he said. He looked back to the west again. "About that soldier--"

"Do not concern yourself. It would not have hurt you to give your blessing, but we both know that a blessing would not keep him safe. He wanted something you could not give. You had reason not to offer it. There will always be those who look to magic to keep them safe instead of relying on their own senses. The wise who were there understood." Tersan turned his back to the camp, satisfied that the army would be ready to travel very soon. "Let's get out of this sun."

Eron smiled. "You never could resist a good pint of ale," he said, "or two."

The way to the war room rambled through the huge building. It took half an hour to reach the doors. Men dressed in the king's livery stood to one side, allowing them to enter. Another thirty or so soldiers were pouring over tables filled with maps, pointing here and there as they discussed strategy. On seeing the king and the tall, dark-haired man beside him, all talk ceased.

"Greetings, my lords!" a young man said, bowing his head slightly. His brow was filled with worry. It was unbecoming on one so young and fair. Astar's brother had become a captain in his place.

"What news, Rothen?" Tersan asked him.

"There has been no contact with Tocar, my lord," Rothen answered, "nor from Parry."

Tersan sighed. "I did not really expect to hear from either, but there is always hope Tocar would leave on his own and meet Parry along the way."

"Yes, my lord."

Eron left his side and joined the men at the table. They shifted to allow him access.

Garrett arrived with his food. "Thank you, Garrett. Are my things packed?"

"Yes, my lord," the child said.

"After you see to Lord Eron, find a place in my wagons to sleep. You have more than earned it."

"Thank you, my lord!" Garrett replied. He moved off with his bounty.

Tersan set the food aside but kept the trinka. He shook his head. "Two of Eron's kinsmen in Calshara. May the Lady protect them." Eron was out of earshot, studying the maps and asking questions. "I want one last look at where we are going before you pack away the maps. We move before mid-day."

"Yes, my lord." With catlike grace, Rothen bowed and took his leave.

Tersan joined the men surrounding the table. On it was a map detailing Calshara. Eron was pointing to Kimala and then to the Durnham Plain and Pintar Pass through the Paranjothis. Garrett handed him a mug of trinka and a plate of food. Eron thanked him. He ate and drank without looking at the offering. Gorltay and Letou explained the battle plan. The other captains backed away from the table, whispering among themselves.

"How long to move this cumbersome army?" Eron asked, not taking his eyes from the map.

"At least five days to get through the pass," Gorltay answered. "Longer if the weather turns on us. The Arandia Plain will flood if there is substantial rain, but it drains quickly."

"And it is the rainy season," Letou added.

Eron scowled. "It is too long."

"An army moves slowly, Eron," Tersan said. He nodded to his one armed captain. "Break camp, Letou."

"Yes, my lord."

"Eron, come," Tersan said. He headed out without waiting for a reply.

Tents were coming down everywhere, trees reappearing as the cloth fell. Horses were being tacked up and wagons readied. Two young pages had already brought the black and grey stallions to the main tent and they stood waiting for their riders.

Together, they walked a short distance uphill to a place where a huge dicantus tree stood. Eron leaned against a rock and surveyed the dismantling of the tent city. "Wait here for me," Tersan said.

Eron nodded. Tersan mounted his horse. Rudlo was at his side, ready to ride through the city, heralding the presence of his king. Leaving Eron, they made their way into the center of the city.

Tersan issued orders, asked questions and listened as he moved among his troops. His men were well appointed. Swords gleamed in the sunlight as they were checked and sheathed. Officers donned the red-enameled armor of Tersan's house, the golden starbursts on their shoulders matching those Tersan wore. The armor glinted in the bright sun as much as the swords had before disappearing under bright red cloaks.

The small group of Kilmari waited patiently beside their mounts, clothed plainly in black. They wore long blades or carried bows and quivers full of arrows strapped to their backs. Tersan had no doubt that there were other weapons concealed under their knee-length cloaks. Here and there he could see the shaft of a dagger that rested in its sheath above an ankle. They were a quiet company, small and deadly. Tersan was glad he would not have to battle them.

Occasionally the soldiers would point at Eron, alone in the shadow of the dicantus tree and whisper to one another. Tersan would catch a phrase here and there: "He wears a sword…" "He needs no sword!" "But look…" Tersan set his jaw as he made his way through the entire ranks of the city. In no corner were the troops not talking about Eron's sword and his refusal to give Ranit his blessing. All eyes greeted the king, but watched the solitary man on the hillside.

After making an entire round of the city, Tersan turned back toward the dicantus tree where Eron stood. As they got closer, a hush followed in their wake. When they reached the page who was holding Eron's horse, Tersan dismounted. He walked the last fifty yards up the small hill alone with a frown on his face and his brow furrowed. Eron, who had been sitting on the rock, rose to meet him.

"What?" Eron asked.

"You are wearing a blade, Eron," Tersan answered. "The Sword is not supposed to need a blade."

"I cannot reliably produce the Sword of Light, Tersan," he stated. "You know that. Would you have me walk naked into battle?"

"Don't be foolish." Tersan plucked a flower from the tree and offered it to Eron.

"What would you have me do with this?" Eron asked.

"Two days ago, in the garden at Bel Haven, you set a flower on fire."

"I was distracted by a bird, Tersan. The flower landed on the Sword and burned. That's hardly setting it on fire."

"Yes, yes I know."

"You want me to do it again?" he asked.

"I would like you to do something, well, astounding."

"Why?"

"Because every eye that has a vantage point from Pella Durett is watching you. You have to take their minds off that damned sword. They have been waiting for you to ride at the head of the army for months. We must restore their confidence."

"To see this pillar of strength that is supposed to protect them flat on his--"

"Enough, Eron!" He pointed at the flower. "You do not have to perform the Dance. Just do something, well, something they can't explain, something--"

"Something to show them that I truly am myth?"

"Yes."

"I do not think burning a flower in front of an army will give them courage."

"Then leave the blade behind."

Eron shuddered. "No."

"Then set the flower on fire."

"I have a better idea." Eron cupped the blossom in his hands. In a graceful motion, he tossed it into the air. It caught on the breeze and blew backward into the huge tree, snagging itself in between many more blossoms. A slow, even chant in a tongue Tersan had never heard before flowed from Eron's lips. He raised his arms, hands turned inward as though he was embracing the entire tree. One by one, the flowers began to twitch. A low-pitched hum resonated from the branches of the tree and birds who had made their homes there flew away in a rush.

Eron kept chanting. Activity in the camp slowed and stopped as everyone turned to watch. The Sword was swaying back and forth slowly, his hands still outstretched, his lips still moving. A light sheen of sweat formed on his forehead as he concentrated.

"Eron, don't burn the tree!" Tersan hissed.

A smile tugged at Eron's lips but he kept chanting. His feet stood solidly on the ground and his arms slowly rose until his hands were directly over his head, palms facing one another. He was chanting faster and faster, his outstretched arms moving slowly together until his palms met. He went silent, his full attention focused on the tree.

The entire camp sucked in a breath. Eron stood stock-still waiting for every eye to see him. A smile pulled at his lips and a barely noticeable tremor coursed through his body. As fast as lightning, his hands whipped down to his sides, clenched in fists so tight that veins bulged in his neck. He drew them up, keeping his elbows tight to his body until they were pointing directly at the tree. Breaths were coming fast and deep, his chest rising and falling with great effort.

"Pyradie!" he finally shouted in a whisper.

Like a snake striking, he snapped his arms out toward the tree, fingers spread wide apart. A bolt of golden light shot from his fingertips, striking the ample trunk. The leaves and flowers swayed, bending to a wind whose source was Eron. Light flew from blossom to blossom until the entire tree, leaves, trunk and flowers turned a brilliant white. It shimmered in the early morning sunlight as though attempting to rival the sun itself, glowing brilliantly with a light of its own in an eerie show of power.

Somewhere deep in the crowd someone shouted. The noise spread so quickly that soon they could hear nothing but applause and cheering. Eron dropped to his knees, his hands still extended toward the tree. He released the beam that tethered him to it and the tree returned to its normal colors, all except the flower that Tersan had plucked. That blossom floated down from its perch in the tree, drifting until it came to rest in front of Eron. He swept it off the ground. Holding it as though it were precious, he came in front of Tersan and knelt before him, offering him the blossom with his head bowed. The cheering stopped as all in the tent city waited. High above them, the cry of the eagle sounded once again. The tiny golden serpent on Tersan's armor glowed so brightly that its features melted into one another. A second time the crowd roared their approval and Tersan felt his pulse quicken as he realized he was the object of their awe.

"Good enough?" Eron whispered, looking up at Tersan.

Tersan swallowed hard. The eyes of the tiny serpents on his shoulders still glowed. Very slowly, he took the shining bloom from Eron. "By the Lady, you are myth…"

He wiped his brow with the back of his hand. "Myths don't sweat," he said. "And I'm keeping the sword."

28 Pony Rides

A fine mist descended from somewhere high up on the mountain making the air cold and damp. It hung knee-high around the camp, a shroud of water covering everything except the area around the campfire. A soft glow in the east was the only sign that the sun was rising. By mid-morning, the shapes of the trees would once again become clear. By mid-day, the mist would be gone.

Jessie held a hot mug of trinka between the palms of her hands. Steam rose lazily from the cup, bathing her face in warmth. She closed her eyes and took a moment to enjoy the heat.

"Well?" Penrose said. He was standing between the boys, his arms folded, staring at her with disapproval.

Jessie patted the prize beneath her shirt. "The crystal is half full. I hope it is enough."

"Eron has already replenished his stores, Jessie," Penrose said, "everything except his confidence. What you have retrieved," he pointed to her crystal, "may make him stronger, but it will not return him to what he once was. He must make his own journey."

"I had to reset the wards."

Penrose regarded her thoughtfully. "I had not thought of that."

"My apologies. I should have told you."

Penrose chuckled.

"Why are you laughing?"

"Because I have tasked young king Tersan with keeping Eron safe and I believe he will have his hands full."

"Tersan is no match for Fot," she argued.

"Do not underestimate him. He single handedly slayed a lesser Fot that day at the portal," Penrose said, serious once more, "never having faced its like before."

He turned away from her to look after his charges. Jessie rose and walked to the far side of the fire. Something moved in the trees. She stared into the woods to get a glimpse of whatever or whoever it was. Her heart skipped a beat. Could it be the phantom swordsman?

"Penrose," she said softly, still scanning the woods, "I saw something last night."

"Oh?"

"I thought it was Eron, practicing the Dance of the Sword," she said. "I guess I was wrong."

"Perhaps it was one of the younger Kilmari," he offered. "They often practice the Dance. There is no telling when someone else will be called on to take up the mantle of the Sword."

"True. I did meet Cynthal at the portal, but I don't think it was him. Whoever it was had precision so great that I thought it was Eron."

There was a rustling in the leaves close to the cave's entrance. A tall woman dressed in dark green emerged. She had a quiver of arrows strapped over one shoulder and carried a simple bow made of white wood. She walked purposely toward them, her identity revealed as she came closer.

"Pixil!" Jessie said, moving quickly to greet her.

"Lady Jessie," she answered with a nod, "Master Penrose. We have been trying to discover why the Cave shed early. The light will not pass through the window until the full moon and that is yet a fortnight away."

"It was probably a flashlight," Jessie said glumly.

"A what?" Penrose and Pixil asked simultaneously.

"A flashlight is a device from my world." Jessie explained. "It's just a tube with a battery in it... energy that lights up, sort of like a torch but without flame. Press a button and light comes on. They must have used one to get through the tunnel and then the cave and triggered the shedding accidently. Call it dumb luck."

"What were they doing in the cave?" the tall woman asked.

"Running from Fot." Jessie stretched, arching her back to ease the tension that had accumulated there. "They have no knowledge of this world."

Pixil picked up the mug that Penrose set aside and walked over to the fire. She helped herself to some trinka, sipping it appreciatively. Sunlight was shining through the branches of the upper trees. It caught on her coppery hair as she stared into the mug. "Then it is true," she said quietly. "It was Fot."

Jessie exchanged a look with Penrose but said nothing.

"Cynthal reported a demon exiting the cavern two nights ago. It was larger than any we have seen in a long while. We feared it might be him." She sipped the trinka again. "Marand's spies are everywhere. That news will travel faster than the demon. His minions will be bold now that Fot has returned. Travel through the plains is no longer safe."

"Surely things will not be set into motion that quickly," Jessie said. "It has only been one day."

"Sword and Shield separated in the middle of the night, Lady Jessie," Pixil answered, "after having been sequestered in Bel Haven for nearly six months. The Sword failed to protect a flower, while performing the Dance of the Sword. Tersan's army moves. I know these things. Rest assured, Marand knows as well." She set the mug down. "We are no longer safe."

"Tersan moves to the north as we speak, my lady," Penrose told her, "with the Sword."

"Eron is recovered?" she asked, wide eyed.

He smiled. "Physically, yes. His gifts have not fully returned, but his presence will put fear and doubt into the minds of our enemies."

"True." She motioned to Jason. "I understand he was exposed to the light?" she asked.

"Yes." Penrose answered. "He has some sight. The exposure was limited."

"How do you know these things?" Jessie asked.

"The mountain speaks to many," she replied with a smile. She reached into her satchel and pulled out an oddly fashioned pair of goggles. "He can use these," she said. Her eyes were twinkling. "They helped me when I was caught in the cave many years ago."

"Thank you," Jessie answered.

"You are welcome. What is this?" she said, pointing to Ric's cheek. Ugly green pus oozed through the bandage.

"By the Lady!" Penrose said, examining his patient closely. "We have exhausted our supply of palapaca. It is time to leave. Altay!"

The young healer appeared almost instantly.

"We must ride to meet the wagon. Gather the horses."

"Yes, my lord."

Pixil reached into her bag and withdrew a small jar which she handed to Penrose. "Palapaca. Every Kilmari soldier carries a small jar of it."

"Bless you, my Lady!" Penrose said, taking her offering.

A moment later, Altay returned, holding the reins of three saddled steeds, two great horses and a stout mountain pony.

"Apparently you were in scouting," Jessie mumbled. "Penrose, I think it best that we split up. We have two horses built for speed, one who is sure-footed. Altay is an accomplished horsewoman and the plains bred horses can outrun any threat. You two can transport Ric across the plains. I'll bring Jason over Orna Pass."

Pixil whistled softly. A great white horse trotted out of the forest. "You may need protection," she said. "I will accompany you. Here," she said, handing Jessie a small pouch. "If you need help, crush this. It will send a beacon and aid will come."

"Thank you, Pixil," Jessie said, tucking the pouch under her shirt. "We won't be far behind you. Now fly!"

Jessie watched them leave. When she could no longer feel the thunder of their horses' hooves on the forest floor, she leaned over and placed a hand on Jason's shoulder. Very gently, she shook him. "Jason? Jason, it's time to get up."

Jason jumped. It was very dark and someone was trying to wake him up.

"Jason?"

Something was bound around his head, keeping him from seeing. A flood of memories came back to him and he moaned.

"Tell me it was a dream," he said.

"It wasn't."

"Where's Ric?"

"Ric's going to be all right. Keep your eyes shut while I take off the bandages."

Jason's eyes no longer burned. Daylight was on the other side of his lids and he resisted the urge to look.

"I've got some rather odd goggles for you," Jessie said. "You'll be able to see through them, though it looks like they will distort your vision. Keep your eyes closed until I've got them tied on, okay?"

"Okay." He jerked a little as the first crystal was laid over his left eye. It was cool but warmed quickly. The second one wasn't as much of a shock. They completely covered his eyes. He could feel the edges making contact all around. Jessie was doing something behind his head. She was gone for a moment; he felt her hands on his shoulders.

"Okay, Jason, you can open your eyes."

Jason opened his eyes. The world had taken on a soft grey hue and everything was distorted, like a funhouse mirror, including his aunt.

"Jessie?" he asked.

"Thank goodness!" Jessie exclaimed. She leaned in and gave him a hug. "We have to go." She was holding the reins of a pony. Not really a pony, but a stout horse with short legs.

"Go where?" he asked.

"Bel Haven. Bend your knee, Jason," Jessie told him. Like Penrose had done the day before, Jessie gave him a leg-up onto the horse. Agilely, she got up behind him. The sturdy horse had no tack except the halter and a thick lead rope. "Hold on to his mane," Jessie told him. "He has a very pleasant trot, but it's hard to stay on without a saddle. I'll take the rope."

Jason wrapped his fingers in the thick mane. The horse took off at a trot.

Jessie wound her arms around his waist, using the single rope to guide the pony. Jason had a feeling the animal knew where to go for Jessie didn't force it to turn either to the right or the left. They exited the forest five minutes after they set off, now taking a windswept rock-strewn treacherous path.

Hamma chose the way for them. The little horse swayed back and forth as he trotted, a calm, gentle motion that translated to a lullaby in Jason's head. He listened for a while, appreciating a peace he had never felt before. Hamma stubbed his hoof and sharply corrected himself, jerking Jason out of his reverie. He scanned the horizon for the others.

"I don't see them up ahead."

"The horses are better suited for wider, softer trails. They have to go around while we're going in a straight line." Jessie pointed to an outcropping of stone in the distance. "We should be able to see them from there. If all goes well, we'll meet them just before we get to the plain."

They rode in silence for a while. The wind swept up from the canyon and several really large birds soared gracefully overhead searching for prey. Once in a while one would swoop down to the Udolphi and snag a fish, barely missing a beat as it soared skyward again.

"Jason," Jessie said, her voice rather urgent in his ear, "remember what I was saying last night about this being a different world?"

"Yes?"

Jessie cleared her throat. "Well, it is. Maybe you'd call it a parallel universe or another dimension."

"Really?"

"And you and Ric somehow hit on the correct sequence to open the portal in my house."

"We were just fooling around," he said absently. "Ric was cataloguing your house for insurance. I was showing him that dance sequence you taught me—"

"And you used the fireplace poker as a prop. Damn!" She sighed heavily. "You weren't supposed to be here, not now, not ever. I am so sorry."

They rode in silence until they reached the outcropping that Jessie had pointed out. The trail gave way to tundra. Green grass grew as far as Jason could see, though for him, it was more grey than green and he could see lumps of rock scattered through the plain. Behind him, Jessie shifted her position slightly and brought Hamma to a halt.

"Let's take a break," she said, sliding off. She held up her hands and helped Jason off. Hamma instantly dropped his head and began to graze. Jessie was looking directly in front of them.

"Do you see them?" Jason asked.

"Maybe. It looks like we're ahead of them. We must have made better time than I thought."

Jason took a few steps forward, glad to finally be on the ground. His legs weren't accustomed to riding and he was sore. Jessie laughed.

"What?"

"You look like a refugee from a B-western."

"Well, I haven't ridden a horse since I was six. What did you expect?"

"We can walk for a while when we get started again," she said with a smile. "It'll be good for all of us. Here." She handed him a piece of jerky. "I'm sorry there's nothing more exotic."

"That's okay." Jason bit into the salty meat. He sat on a rock and chewed.

"We'll have a proper meal when we get to the House. Here's water."

"Your house?" He took the skin she offered and poured some into his mouth. It was warm but tasted pretty much just like water.

"I'm sorry, Jason. We had to go with plan B. We're going to Bel Haven."

"Ric...?"

"Ric is very ill," she answered. "But don't worry. Penrose will have him right inside a week or two."

"Oh." Jason figured he could argue, but what would be the point?

The horses were closing in on them fast. Penrose pulled up his mount in front of them.

"How is he?" Jessie asked.

"Fading," Penrose answered. Jason's heart lurched. "Fot's poison is unlike any I have seen before. There are other antidotes at Bel Haven--"

"You can save him, can't you?" Jason asked.

"Maybe." Penrose swung down off his horse. He went over to the other white horse and waited while Pixil handed Ric down to him, then dismounted herself. Altay remained on her horse.

"There is no sign of the wagon, my lord," she told them.

"Ric?" Jason called. He made his way over to his best friend and knelt beside his limp body. Half of Ric's face was distorted into an unrecognizable mask, swelling closing one eye. Jason reached out and touched him. His skin was cold. "Ric! My god, I'm so sorry!"

Jessie, Penrose and Pixil stood a few feet away from them talking in whispers. Jason found himself crying. Ric looked so bad. They had wrapped him in a blanket. He was cold now, but his brown hair was plastered to his head and his glasses that had somehow managed to make the journey with him this far, were askew. Jason took them off and tucked them inside his own pocket.

"I'll hang onto these for you until you need them again," he said.

Ric opened his good eye. He worked his jaw but no sound came out.

"Water?" Jason asked.

He nodded. Jason retrieved a flask and squeezed some into his mouth. Ric swallowed and wiped the back of his hand across his lips.

"Remind me," he whispered, "not to come with you next time you inherit a house, okay?"

Jason nodded. He tried to swallow the huge lump in his throat but couldn't. "We're taking you to a hospital, Ric," Jason said.

"On horseback? Ha." He looked Jason in the eye. "Tell my mom I'm sorry I wasn't a better son, will you?"

"Tell her yourself."

Ric shook his head. "I don't think so…not this time…"

"Ric!"

Ric closed his eye and said no more.

Penrose was at his side in an instant. He felt Ric's face with his hand. "We must ride. Altay!"

The young healer rode the black horse to where they stood. Together, Pixil and Penrose hoisted Ric up in front of her, then remounted their own horses.

"It is not far now," he told Jason, "less than an hour's ride, if we go through the Giant's Fingers."

"The Giant's Fingers?" Jessie repeated. "Even without Fot being on the loose, that way is dangerous! Be careful."

Penrose gave her a curt nod. He put his heels to the great horse and they were off, leaving Jessie, Jason and the mountain pony behind.

"I hate you!" Jason shouted. "Ric's going to die and it's your fault!"

"I…I… Look, Jason, I can understand you being angry," Jessie started.

"Oh you can, can you?" Jason wanted to scream. "Ric's the only real friend I ever had!"

"Trust Penrose, Jason. He'll be all right."

"He looked like hell!"

"I know, but he'll be all right. Come on. I think Hamma's rested enough. Let's go."

29 The Giant's Fingers

Jason resumed his place in front of Jessie on the little horse and they followed the others at a trot. Over all, Hamma's gait was smooth, but every now and then he would swerve slightly to the left or the right to find the easiest path and throw his novice rider off balance. Jason did his best to just not fall off. The horse came to a jarring halt and Jessie was pointing.

"Look," she whispered.

Jason scanned the plain that he could see. Ahead, a streak of light surged toward the heavens.

"What is it?"

"A signal for help. Hang on!"

The little horse bolted and they were pounding across the plain.

Five minutes into their wild flight, he heard the sound of men shouting to one another. Something whirred passed his head and Jessie forced him closer to Hamma's neck.

"Keep down!" she instructed. "We're almost there!"

Seconds later, she pulled Hamma to a halt beside the great horses who were sheltered in the shadow of a huge upright stone. The rock formation continued in a rough semi-circle with many tall fingerlike stones. Jessie slid off taking Jason with her.

"Stay put!" she ordered over her shoulder.

Jason ignored her and followed.

The ground was stony, covered with a bit of sand and tough turf grass. Jessie moved swiftly between the horses, making her way over to Penrose. The healer had Pixil's bow in his hands. Her quiver lay on the ground beside him. To his right, the warrior queen was propped up against a stone with Ric's head in her lap. There was a lump as large as an egg on her head and she wasn't moving. Many things were wrong.

"Marauders," Penrose shouted angrily. He ducked as an arrow narrowly missed him. "They were on us before we knew it. I should have gone around."

"It's all right, Penrose," Jessie said, "I've got this."

Jessie spoke softly in a language Jason had never heard before. Between her fingertips, light flashed forming a round, thin dinner plate sized disc. The disc continued to grow until Jessie's form became a silhouette. With a grace Jason had never seen before in his aunt, she leapt out from behind the rock with nothing but the silvery disc between her and the marauders. She spread her arms wide. In a flash, the light shot out wherever she pointed. She turned in a circle, her shield encompassing the stones in a huge dome. Arrows bounced harmlessly to the ground.

"Theirs can't get in, ours can't get out," she mused. "Penrose, I have an idea. Can you shoot through an opening like that?"

She flicked her wrist and a window appeared in the dome of light. Penrose strung one of the arrows into the bowstring and took careful aim. He held the pose for a moment before letting the arrow fly. It soared through the opening. Jessie followed its path. "This just might work," she said.

"My Lady," Penrose started, "That was the last of our arrows."

"Then we'll have to use theirs. Jason, since you insist on being here, gather up some of those spent arrows."

"Yes, ma'am." He scurried around inside the dome gathering arrows.

Jessie stood on a rock in plain view to anyone within miles of the dome she had created. She took the pouch Pixil had given her and smashed it against one of the rock fingers. A brilliant blue light surged into the bright morning sky next to its fading twin. A ball of energy appeared between her fingers, outshining the noonday sun.

"Jason, catch." She tossed it to him. It felt as though she had tossed him air, the ball was so light. The hair on the back of his arms prickled, standing on end.

"Put it on the tip of an arrow and hand it to Penrose," she said.

Obediently, he stuck it on the end of one of the arrows and handed it over.

"I'm going to open another small hole in the dome," she told them. She was still scanning the plain. "Just shoot it through," she told Penrose.

The Healer took careful aim and let loose the arrow. It soared through the hole and a short distance from them, struck another rock where it exploded and formed a smaller dome.

"Gotcha!" Jessie cried. "Looks like one mouse is in the trap."

"Now where?" Penrose asked as Jason attached a second fireball to a second arrow.

Jessie created another hole. Another arrow flew. Another mouse was caught.

Someone shouted and a barrage of arrows hit their dome. Jessie laughed maniacally sending a chill up Jason's back. His aunt's face was no longer benevolent. With one hand, she reached down and made a motion from the ground up, lifting the edge of the dome.

"Get the arrows, Jason," she said.

Jason scurried under the dome and scooped up as many as he could find. He slipped back inside to find Penrose firing arrow after arrow at their foes. Jessie was making the fireballs like a madwoman, tossing them to Penrose and then laughing some more. Jason took a look toward their attackers. Puddles of light had formed domes in half a dozen places. Whatever was contained in the domes was invisible to Jason through his crystal glasses.

The sound of horses came from behind them and Jessie shifted her attention backward.

"The cavalry's arrived!" she shouted. She held her arm out, fingertips pointed toward the ground and raised her hand, palm upward in an arc toward the sky. The dome lifted behind them allowing a dozen people dressed like Pixil and their mounts, to enter.

"Thank the Lady," Penrose muttered. He lowered the bow. "I am not meant to be a soldier," he said. "Jason, I could use a bit of help."

Jason threaded his way across the short distance between them, glad to finally check on Ric. Above them, still on her perch, Jessie was making fireballs faster than he could see her hands move and tossing them now to the new archers.

"Get my bag," Penrose told him. Jason raced over to the horses and returned with the bag.

"Hold still," Penrose was telling Pixil. "I just want to look."

"I am fine," she said. "See to him."

Penrose reached into a small bag, extracted a few leaves and crushed them between his fingers. The fragments he sprinkled into Ric's wound.

"Palapaca is the incorrect remedy," he muttered.

"What is then?" Jason asked.

"I am not certain. Dicantus flowers are my next choice, but all I have is dried leaves. It will have to do for now."

"How--how is he?" Jason asked.

Penrose managed a small laugh. "Your friend is much stronger than I thought he would be. Demon wounds generally kill quite quickly. That he still lives is a very good sign."

Jason felt his heart sink.

"That will do for now," he told Jason.

"Where's that other healer? The cute one? Altay was her name?"

"I sent her ahead to meet the wagon. The Lady keep her safe." He retrieved Pixil's bow and rejoined the fight.

In spite of being surrounded by armed men, Jason felt quite alone. There was no one to talk to and he felt useless. The Kilmari had taken over his job of collecting arrows and there was nothing else to do for the wounded. The world was distorted through his crystal glasses. He sat beside Ric. The lanky young man was very pale, his blue lips standing out in the pale face. Jason reached out and gently placed a hand on the cold forehead. Ric shifted slightly underneath his hand and Jason let out a sigh of relief. At least he was still alive. Unwilling to break contact, he sat for a long time just maintaining contact. The sound of men grunting to one another faded. Sights were still quite real, but they were dimming.

All around him an odd rhythm began to play. He drummed on a large stone on the ground with one hand making a barely audible popping noise and he found himself humming an unfamiliar melody. The wind that blew gently through the stones harmonized with him. The tall grasses, swaying in the breeze, rubbed against one another forming a tympanic section. Without knowing he was doing it, Jason started singing.

He sang a tale of a battle long before men began recording history on paper, a tale of two warring neighbors and the star crossed lovers whose lives were bound to each other and their respective tribes in a way that forbade them to ever be happy. Or so they thought. One night they ran away on creamy white horses, to a land where no person would find them. It was a land unspoiled by the hatred their families felt for one another. And there they lived free and happy for the rest of their days.

It was a silly song, not one of great consequence, but it had a music box melody and Jason felt good singing it. The song ended and suddenly he was aware that all around him had grown silent. Penrose's great white horse nickered softly to him and Ric sighed and turned in his sleep, breathing more easily than he had been. Pixil's eyes were clear and bright, her face peaceful, the lump almost gone. Beside him, Penrose mirrored her expression. Both were staring at him.

"What?" Jason demanded.

"A siren," Penrose whispered, "you are a siren. Kimala has not had a siren for centuries."

"What's a siren?" Jason asked.

A shower of arrows answered him and the battle was on again.

For an hour more, the battle raged between the Kilmari and the marauders. For a while, Jason divided his time between the wounded and retrieving arrows. When it seemed that they would never leave this place, the rain of arrows stopped. Jason joined the archers and Jessie.

"Do you think they're gone?" Jason asked.

"I do not know," a young man about Jason's age answered. "They no longer respond."

"Jessie?" Penrose asked.

Jessie laughed. It was an almost possessed sound. "I've trapped at least twenty; marauders, Cynthal."

"Good. Then they shall be dealt with," he said with disgust.

"One way or the other," Jessie answered. "If they whine loudly enough, I might be persuaded to offer Opportunity."

"Opportunity!" the young man protested. "How could you do such a thing?"

Jessie shrugged. "The way of the Shield is mercy, Cynthal," she told him. Then she leapt off her stone perch and clapped her hands. The dome of light that had been surrounding them fell. "But, truth be told, today I have to be Shield and Sword."

"I need to get the wounded to the House," Penrose said.

"Four riders and an escort of two," Jessie said, pointing to the Kilmari. "Go."

"As you wish, my Lady."

Jason found himself being placed on Penrose's great white horse. The saddle was comfortable, the stirrups just right. Around him, the others were being helped up onto other mounts in front of the Kilmari. Cynthal stood beside Jason. "Can you ride?" he asked.

"Yes, I think so," Jason answered, grasping part of the saddle with one hand.

"Good. I will assist the Shield." He turned away and rejoined Jessie.

"What about Jessie?" Jason asked Penrose.

"She has duties," he said simply.

30 Deductive Reasoning

Patrick barely remembered the long ride back to Jessie Perrymore's place. The van pulled up to the house and the door opened letting cold, fresh air inside.

"Pat, you okay?" Joann's voice was distant, like she was talking in the next room.

"After effects of a love potion. He'll be fine after a nap, dear," Winnie replied. "Take my hand...there's a good fellow."

Patrick let her pull him out of the back seat. He was feeling no pain. Joann slung one arm around her shoulders and Winnie took the other one. Together, they crossed the short distance from the drive to the house.

The door was ajar and Patrick's instincts tried to kick in. Somewhere inside his fogged brain, an alarm was sounding.

"Take my weapon," he told Joann, his tongue thick in his mouth. "I...I shouldn't..."

She fumbled with his holster and withdrew the service revolver. "Stay here," she told them.

Patrick nodded, though he was certain she didn't see it, and slumped against the doorway.

Lights flicked on inside the house. Furniture was scattered about the room, lamps and tables lying broken on the floor, pictures ripped from the walls, their frames broken, the glass shattered.

"Oh dear," Winnie said. "They have been here." She was staring at a broken picture frame on the mantel.

"How do you know it was them?" Patrick asked. He lurched forward and sank into a loveseat that was slammed up against the front window.

"You were close to Lae, Patrick," Winnie said as she waded through the trashed pictures littering the floor. "Can you not smell it?"

Patrick sniffed the air but his mind was too fogged. "I'm afraid I'm not quite myself, Winnie," he said. "What the hell was that stuff that you gave me, anyway?"

"Mind your language, young man," Winnie said.

"Yeah, sure, whatever, sorry." Patrick's head was swimming. He blinked hard to keep his eyes open, trying to focus.

"House is clear," Joann said as she re-entered the living room. She tucked the gun in her belt and whistled. "This place is a mess," she said. She walked over to the fireplace and picked up a video camera. "Motive wasn't robbery," she said, holding the camera up to examine it. "There's two computers back there, too, and a lot of video equipment." She crinkled up her nose. "What's that smell? Kinda floral..."

"Lavender," Patrick answered. His eyelids were so heavy he couldn't keep them open any longer. It was safe here, safer than it had been in the forest. And Joann had his gun. She knew how to use it. He sat on the love seat and gave in to sleep.

"Pat? Pat, wake up! You've got to see this!"

The TV was blaring. Patrick shifted. The blanket that was covering him dropped off and he sat up quickly. His mind was clear and he wasn't hungover but he craved another whiff of the demon's breath, to feel that rush again.

"Anything that makes you feel that good can't be good for you," he said, quoting a friend who tried meth back in high school. "I won't be dipping into that well again."

Joann and Winnie were both staring at the TV housed inside an antique wardrobe on one side of the living room. He rubbed a hand over the stubble on his chin and joined them.

"Authorities tell us that the two women approached a number of children," the reporter was saying. She was dressed in a trench coat and was balancing an umbrella along with her microphone. "Apparently they were looking for someone in particular."

"Cornetta," the anchor back at the station droned, "did they harm anyone?"

"No, Mike," Cornetta answered, "but they were very suspicious. One of them reportedly had a gun and some of the children said that both women were wearing what appeared to be blood stained clothing. However, those facts have not been corroborated. Authorities are asking for the public's help in finding them."

"Thank you, Cornetta." He shifted his eyes from one screen to another one. "In other news..."

"It looks like our demons have been canvassing parks inside Claxbury," Joann said.

"I wonder what the hell for," Patrick answered.

Mike continued to talk. On the screen a picture of two slain deer appeared.

"...were not caused by accident," Mike droned. "Police are trying to..."

"It looks as though they aren't hungry anymore." Patrick stared at the screen. A toothy weatherman began gesturing to a national map behind him. Apparently, rain was in the forecast.

"Killing for sport," Joann murmured. "They could have done that in the forest."

"They must be stopped," Winnie said.

"Before they go after something other than deer," Patrick agreed. "But how?"

Winnie cleared her throat. "It will not be easy," she said. "To kill a demon, someone unskilled in the Lady's powers must attack at close range. A sword or a knife through a vulnerable spot is the only way to slay them."

"'Vulnerable spot'?" Joann repeated.

"An eye, an ear, the nose or up through the roof of their mouth," Winnie replied. "A sword is the weapon of choice."

"With a sword? That will take some doing." Patrick whistled. He pulled a long slender knife out of its sheath and turned it so it caught the light. "'Wonder if the toothpick will do?"

"It is the only way in my world," Winnie said, ignoring his last statement. "However, we do not have weapons such as yours. It appears they are capable of doing more damage than an arrow or a sword."

Patrick rolled his eyes and looked at Joann. "How's your hand-to-hand?" he asked.

"Better than my firearm rating, but neither one's stellar. You?"

"Stellar firearms, working toward it, hand to hand." He turned to Winnie. "Is there anything you can tell us about these, um, demons that'll help?"

"Bue is a lesser-Fot, in fact, she is his most powerful lieutenant," Winnie started. "Lae is her protégé. Both are extremely dangerous, but Bue has more power. We have one advantage, though--Bue has an obligation to you, Patrick. She fears the legend, as do all demons." Winnie sighed. "To Joann, though, she owes nothing."

"Great." Patrick rubbed his shoulder. "Which is which?"

The weatherman was now explaining why it was raining and how long the rain was going to last. Joann hit the remote and the screen went black.

"Your seductress was Lae," Winnie said with a wink.

Joann was grinning widely. "You talk in your sleep, big guy."

"Great. Samantha will never believe this."

"Let us get back on topic," Winnie said. "Unfortunately, you released Lae from any obligation she might have to you when you asked her to release Joann. She shall attack both of you at will."

"Okay, so we have to go after her first, right?"

"That is correct."

"Pat," Joann said, "I've taken the scanner out of my car and put it in the van. We should be able to monitor any sightings."

"What happened to Polly?" he asked.

"Polly has fed and needs to digest her dinner," Winnie told him. "We may need her services and I want her to be prepared."

"Good thinking." Patrick turned to Winnie. "I guess we start looking at the last place they were sighted, eh?"

"Yeah," Joann said. "And start sleeping in shifts until we find them."

"Jason left us food. I will be right back." Winnie left them alone in the living room.

"Joann," Patrick started, "does it seem a little odd to you that these things are hanging out around town? I mean, if it was me and I wasn't where I belonged, I'd be looking for a way to get back and to hell with killing for sport."

Joann nodded. "Good point." She screwed up her face. "How would they get back, anyway?"

"I don't know," he answered, "but I'd bet there's a rabbit hole somewhere in this house."

"They looked and couldn't find it?" she said.

"Oh, they found it, dear," Winnie said. She was again holding the picnic basket. "They saw the ritual, the dance, but they lack the portal's key."

"The fireplace utensils."

"Exactly. There is one more thing."

"Really?" Joann said almost sarcastically.

"Yes, dear. Jessie's daughter, Lucy. She knows how to open the portal and she has the Book of Wylfcynne, the original key. She is undoubtedly the daughter that Fot mentioned on that recording and she would be quite the prize to deliver to Fot."

"I'm not going to ask anything except where is she?"

"Staying with Martha and Ted McCarthy. The demons will not know her location. That is why they are looking at children, trying to find her. I have attempted to contact Martha, but she is not answering her phone."

"Keep trying."

Patrick took Winnie's basket and shepherded her out to the waiting van. "Even with their superior power right now, they really are no match for the entire Claxbury police force. Here you go." He opened the front door for Winnie, then closed it after her before climbing in the back seat himself. He put the basket on the floor. Joann slid in behind the steering wheel and fired the van up.

"Where to?" Joann asked.

"What's the last place they were spotted?"

"Effingham Place."

"And the deer?"

"Burton Street."

"Go to the park," Winnie instructed. "Demons are creatures of habit. They will return and we must protect the children. Besides, I have a feeling they might just be looking for this as well as Lucy." She patted the bag-o-demons on the floor. "We cannot let them release this army."

31 In the House

Jason wound his fingers tightly in the horse's mane to lessen his chances of falling off. The white horse named Snow ran so fast that he could barely breathe. They were in the wake of Penrose and Ric, flanked and followed by Kilmari. He caught an occasional glimpse of his friend's head as they raced across the plain but the sight was not reassuring.

The terrain shifted and they were going up a slight rise. Then the horses dove to the right, leaving Jason struggling to keep his seat. Before he could get fully upright, Snow came to a halt beside the horse he thought was carrying Ric and Penrose. Jason took a breath. Directly ahead of him, he could make out the top of something man-made against a clear blue sky. They had arrived.

A swarm of blurry people dressed in white surrounded the horses. Jason was never so glad to see someone he didn't know and wouldn't recognize tomorrow. They reached up to help him dismount. Penrose was already on the ground shouting orders and Ric was the dark blur in the middle of the white. Very quickly Jason lost sight of him.

"Swing your leg over, son," someone told him. He looked down to his left. A man was standing beside the horse, waiting to assist him. He stood up in the saddle, balanced himself and then swung his right leg over, but his left stuck in the stirrup and he lost his balance. The man caught him and helped to the ground. "Are you all right, son?" the man asked.

"Yes," Jason answered, "just a little off balance. It's distortion from the glasses. Thanks. Where'd they take Ric?" he asked.

He clapped Jason on the shoulder. "Penrose is coming, son."

Penrose hustled back through the crowd, Altay at his side. He looked intensely at Jason and Jason kept eye contact as best he could through his crystal lenses. "We need to talk."

He led Jason to a chair on the porch and motioned for him to sit before taking a seat himself. Altay stood at a respectable distance, just out of earshot. "What happened in the Cave?"

"It's a long story," Jason answered. "Can't it wait until later?"

"No, I am afraid this matter must be addressed as soon as possible, if there is indeed something to address. You mentioned getting wet?"

Jason bit his lip. "The cave was really dark when we first got there. Ric had a flashlight and I used it to look around. You know that we turned the wrong way, right?"

"Yes."

"Well, the light caught on one of the stalactites. The rock kinda sucked in the light, like it was filling a vase. It was pretty dim at first, and it had this slimy silt on it that eventually fell off. Then it was really bright and it shot a beam of light into the next stalactite."

"Go on," Penrose encouraged.

"We thought the exit was where you found us, so we headed in that direction. By the time we got to the far shore, the stalactites were all lit. They started dropping big chunks of slime into the lake. It was getting really hot so we started to run and Ric slipped and fell into the water."

"So he was totally submerged?"

"Yeah. He's not a very good swimmer, but he tried. We had that poker from Jessie's house. It was the only protection we had from that thing that tried to attack us after we got here."

"Fot. The demon." Penrose waved off a group of blurred people dressed in white.

"Well, I hooked Ric with the poker and he was almost out of the water but then the ground shook. A bunch of that silt from the crystals pelted us both. A piece of a crystal hit him in the same spot that he had that cut. It kind of glowed when it hit him and stuck to his face."

Penrose leaned forward, listening with rapt attention.

"Anyway, when he slid under the water, I dove in after him. Well, not really dove in, more like slid down the bank. He had already disappeared under the surface. I thought I would never find him, the water was so murky, but then I saw that tiny light and I swam like heck toward it. I snagged him and hightailed it to the surface."

"So the lake was entirely lit?"

"Yeah, it was, from above, anyway." Jason paused. He took a deep breath before continuing. "That water was so cold! Ric wasn't breathing when we got to the surface so I gave him mouth-to-mouth. He didn't respond so I drug him to a place where we could get out and continued the mouth to mouth. After the fifth breath or so, he sputtered and started breathing on his own." He looked intently at Penrose. "Don't you dare tell him! I know it saved his life, but he would be embarrassed if he knew another man's lips touched his."

Penrose nodded. "Your secret is safe. Then what happened?"

"We were only about twenty feet from the exit. Ric was shivering so I went back and grabbed my cape, then we made a beeline for that little room. Just before we got there, the top of the cave exploded into light and ignited the bottom of the lake. Neither one of us could see very well, so we felt our way along the wall of the cave until we got to the room."

"So the entire cave was now lit?"

"Yeah, except inside that room. I looked for an exit, but there was no way out and then I got to thinking about Fot and how he might come for us and, this is going to sound crazy, but I thought I smelled him. That poker was our only defense so I went back out and got it and hurt my eyes."

Penrose sighed. "Few have witnessed the shedding of the cave and survived to tell about it."

"Oh," was all he could think of to say.

"I had to be sure," Penrose whispered. "You have been gifted, Jason. The Lake chose you to be a Siren."

"A what?"

"A Siren," the healer repeated. "Jason, just being an Otherworlder will mark you as an enemy to some of my people. Being a Siren marks you as a significant enemy to demonkind."

"Penrose," Jason whispered back, holding the healer's gaze intently, "I don't have any idea what you're talking about."

Penrose sighed. "Just do not sing where anyone but Ric or Jessie can hear you, not until I can explain further, all right? Right now, I have things to attend to."

"Okay," Jason whispered back. "Don't sing except to Ric. Or Jessie. I got it. I don't get it, but I got it."

"Good." Penrose straightened. He straightened and motioned for the healer to join them. "Altay will take care of your needs for now. I have other things to attend to."

"Thank you."

"This way," Altay said.

Jason took a wobbly step forward and Altay slid a supporting hand under his elbow to steady him. He didn't need her support, but she was cute and paying attention to him and she smelled faintly of roses and strawberries.

"You are not accustomed to riding?" she asked.

Jason shook his head. "I've only ridden four times in my life. A pony ride when I was seven, then from the cave and off the mountain. And then that wild ride," he shook his head and looked back at his mount. "Snow's the biggest horse I've ever seen!"

"He is plains-bred, fearless and fast, not the choice of many riders. He must have liked you." She laughed. The sound was like wind chimes in a gentle breeze. "Come. I'll take you to your room."

The House was an amazing place. Inside, the cool air was permeated with a fresh sweet scent. They passed through what looked like a reception area. Jason's sneakers squeaked on the stone floor. Windows wide enough for a man to step through reached from the floor to the ceiling and massive hinged doors stood beside them ready to shutter the room against inclement weather.

Next they entered a huge area filled with neat rows of white beds; Altay called it the Great Room. The same style windows were cut into the walls and a very slight breeze swept across the room rustling the bed linens. The lack of sleep, trauma from his injuries, nearly losing his best friend and using muscles he had never known existed much less used were all beginning to take a toll on Jason. He slowed his pace, yearning to lie down on one of the beds to sleep.

"It is not far now," Altay assured him.

They passed through the room and up a narrow stairway, exiting into a long hallway. There were a number of doorways on either side. Altay led him through the first door on the left.

Jason was relieved to find Ric already in one of the three beds, lying on his side, sleeping peacefully. The same breeze he had felt in the Great Room blew through the windows here as well.

"Your friend may sleep a while longer," Altay said. "I have given him something to aid his slumber. To have suffered a wound from a demon as powerful as Fot and to have lived…"

"What?" Jason asked. He was so tired. He really didn't want any more information about demons or swords or shields. He sat in the simple wooden chair beside the bed and put his elbows on his knees and his chin on one hand. "What?" he repeated.

"Survival is rare," Altay said.

Jason reached over and touched Ric's forehead again, as much to reassure himself that he was alive as to confirm this insane reality. Ric's skin was now warm and dry. Jason breathed a sigh of relief. He felt like he could sleep for a week but what he really wanted was a shower.

"He's going to be okay, isn't he?" Jason asked.

"Yes. But there may be something different about him."

"Different?"

"He was in the water when the Crystal Lake was reborn, as you were. Persons who live through that experience are gifted, you know."

Jason groaned. "He can't carry a tune in a bucket," he whined.

"The Lake never tells what gift it gives to those who survive." Altay shrugged but there was a glimmer of mischief in her eyes. "May I offer you anything?"

"A shower would be nice."

"Shower?"

"Yeah." He sighed. Why were these people so dense? "You know, soap and water, clean clothes?"

"I will have a bath drawn for you. Is there anything else?"

"How about a pair of ruby slippers? So I can click my heels together and go home?"

Confusion crossed her creamy complexion. "I know of no such clothing," she said, "but perhaps someone else will. Are these shoes unique to your world and its magic?"

Jason laughed. "No, Altay, it was a movie… never mind."

"Is there anything else?" she asked sweetly.

He shook his head. "I'm good, thanks."

She smiled and disappeared, leaving him alone with Ric.

The chair was becoming very uncomfortable. He really wanted to stretch out on one of the beds with its crisp white linens, but he was so dirty that he really couldn't bring himself to do so. He got up, stretched, and changed to the window seat. Leaning his back against the frame, he sat inside the window itself and allowed himself to relax.

The House was located near the top of a hill with one side of the terrain leading upward and the other trailing down farther than Jason could see. His window was situated over a courtyard with a short fence made of stone. The fence wound its way around and out of sight to his right before reappearing some distance away. There, it bound a grove of blooming trees. The slight breeze bore the scent of the blossoms. He closed his eyes and inhaled. This was the source of the sweet scent in the House, he realized. Before he knew it, he was fast asleep.

"JM?"

Jason jumped.

"Whoa, there! Don't fall out the window!"

"Ric?" Jason stretched and didn't bother stifling a yawn. Ric was smiling lopsided at him. He was wearing a white robe like the healers and had a half-eaten apple in one hand. The other was lightly on Jason's arm. There was a small bandage on his face covering the cut that had been oozing pus. His skin was deep purple in color, but the swelling had gone down to the point that he was the same old Ric, just a different color.

"You were expecting someone else?" he asked, taking another bite of the apple and a step back into the room. He sat on the bed still munching. "Man, this is a great apple."

"Um, well, no, not really expecting anyone else." Jason looked critically at him. "How's the face?"

"Not bad, considering." Ric chomped the last bite of the apple. "Seems I was cut by a claw or fang or something. Penrose says I'll be fine. Marked for life," he added dramatically, "but fine. Chicks dig a guy with a scar. 'Makes me a bad boy. How are you?"

Jason got up stiffly. "Let's see…body still hurts in places I never knew I had, still wearing dopey sunglasses…" He looked at his filthy clothes. "And I need a bath and a change of clothes. I guess it wasn't a dream."

"Hardly." Ric grinned. "What's with the dopey sunglasses?"

"Remember the cave?"

"Oh yeah."

"Well, I went back into it when all the fireworks happened. 'Seems I did some damage to my eyes. These 'glasses' are supposed to let me see without causing any more damage. Speaking of which," he pulled Ric's glasses out of his pocket.

"Thanks! My insurance won't pay for another pair until February." He put them on and began to whistle.

"Why are you so happy?" Jason growled.

"I'm having a blast! You should see this place! And the women here…" He grinned and raised his eyebrows.

"For crying out loud, don't you ever think of anything else?" Jason said with a laugh.

Ric shrugged. "It never hurts to look. You are right about one thing, though."

"What?"

Ric crinkled up his nose and waved a hand in front of his face. "You really need a bath."

"Thanks."

"What are friends for? I highly recommend the blue room, sunken pool, warm water, refreshments—"

"--and it was in the blue room. Of course."

A light knock interrupted their conversation. Altay was at the door, towels in hand. "Jason, I have drawn your bath. Are you ready?"

"I suppose."

"Enjoy!" Ric called after him.

He followed her to what turned out to be a blue room with a Roman style bath. After Altay left, he shrugged off his clothes and stepped into the bath. The water was just right, hot enough to ease tense muscles, but not so hot as to be uncomfortable. He sank into the tub, ducked his head under the water a few times, rubbing his hair vigorously. Then he reclined with his head just above the water and simply did nothing.

Fifteen minutes later and feeling much better even though Altay had stolen his clothes and replaced them with a soft white robe, he returned to the room he shared with Ric. Outside, day was turning to night. Ric was standing by the window pointing excitedly.

"Your aunt is back!" he said.

Jason joined him. Jessie was dismounting below them. She had two dozen horses strung behind her, each with coats of armor slung across their backs but no riders. The young man he recognized as Cynthal slumped in the saddle on the horse beside Jessie. His aunt had her hand on his shirt, keeping him upright. There were no others. Jason's jubilation turned black. The healers surrounded Cynthal and Jessie released him. He fell off the horse into their arms. They placed him on a stretcher and carried him into the House.

"What happened?" Ric asked.

"Good question. Let's find out."

They left their room, went down the stairs and passed through the Great Room into the receiving area. A number of men and women had gathered there, their faces grim as Cynthal passed through their ranks. Most were dressed in the black leather uniform of the Kilmari. Jason caught a glimpse of him through the crowd. The youth's fair face was pale with dark blue rings under his eye and his hair was littered with debris. Penrose emerged from an antechamber door. He looked very tired. The healers stopped while he examined the young man.

"Jessie?" he said, not looking up.

"Marauders the first time." She took in a deep breath. "Marauders with a minor demon the second." She held up a small sealed vessel. Inside something glowed. "He wouldn't give me his name at first, but it's

Ket. And he won't bother us again." She examined the flask carefully, then hooked it to her belt as though it were a trophy. "We lost six Kilmari," she said.

"What of Marand's men?" Penrose said. He was probing Cynthal's wounds and frowning.

"The first group received Opportunity." She sighed. "I'm sorry, Penrose, I just can't kill unless I'm threatened. Not unless…" She closed her eyes and her body shook. "The second…the second did not receive Opportunity."

He stopped probing and looked at her. Something passed between them and he placed a hand on her arm. "We'll talk about that later," he told her quietly. Then he turned to the men carrying Cynthal. "Take him inside. I will be there shortly." He disappeared behind the wall of healers and Kilmari.

"Lady Jessie," one of the Kilmari said, "where did you leave them?"

"On the plain," she replied slowly. Her head was bowed and her eyes unfocused. She swallowed. "They are west of here but still in the shadow of the mountain. They head north to their master."

Without another word, the company exited the building.

"Jessie?" Jason said.

"Jason!" She wheeled around and embraced him so tightly he could barely breathe. Her body began to shake.

"Jessie?"

"I am so sorry!" she whispered. "It's not safe. It was never safe. What the hell was I thinking?" She pushed away from him and cradled his head in her hands, staring at him. Then she pulled Ric to her, not letting Jason go, but visibly checking him over, too. Her voice faltered and her hands were shaking as she pushed an errant strand of hair out of her face. "Tomorrow morning you head home."

"But we--"

"I just watched six friends die!" she snapped. Her voice caught. "And I killed. I'm not accustomed to killing. That's Eron's job--"

"Lady Jessie, we have prepared a meal," Altay interrupted. The young healer had joined them unnoticed until now. "Come, all of you."

After going through one small hallway, they entered a huge dining room. It was filled with long wooden tables, each with an accompanying set of benches. On the far end, one such table had been set with an abundance of food. Candles provided the only light.

"Jason," Altay said reaching for his face, "You do not need to wear the crystals in relative darkness." She lifted the smoky crystals from his eyes. "Sit. Eat."

Jason blinked a few times. The air felt good on his face after having been covered for so long and Altay smiled at him. She moved away from the table leaving the scent of strawberries in her wake. Jason stared after her.

"I see what you mean about the healers," Jason said to Ric. "She's beautiful!"

"Put your teeth back in your mouth, Jason," Jessie told him. "You can flirt later. Maybe."

They sat and ate. Though much had happened, they remained silent through the meal. Altay busied herself refilling their plates and keeping their glasses full. She split her time between them and helping others in the room. But soon they were the only diners left.

"Jason, Ric," Jessie started, when they had stopped eating and were just sipping trinka in the glow that follows a good meal, "I think I owe you both a bit more of an explanation than you've received so far."

"You have a gift for understatement," Jason replied.

Jessie cleared her throat. "When you and Ric came through the portal, you brought back a snow globe."

"Yeah?"

"Eron and I had sealed Fot in it. He is a demon of extraordinary power and our greatest enemy."

"So you said."

"Hush, Jason," Ric said. "I'd like to get up to speed on the game."

"It's no game," Jessie said. She stretched. Dark circles were forming under her red-rimmed eyes. "No, it's no game."

"So where are we?" Ric asked.

"Now? Now you are in Bel Haven. Penrose is Head of this house. We are south and east of Kimala, south of Jeleste, west of the Paranjothis and southwest of Calshara and Il Chatel, not that this information will be of benefit to you."

"Okay…" Jason said.

She smiled. "I took Fot back to our world so that he wouldn't be able to harm anyone here." She laughed. "Actually, I have no idea whether he is stronger there or here. Powers change from one reality to the next. But my powers are stronger at home, so I figured he would be safer there than here."

"Reality?" Ric asked.

"Powers?" Jason chimed in.

"Yes. Reality, parallel universe, fairy world, never-never land, and powers as in, well, whatever you want to think." She smiled. "Power comes with knowledge and study--lots of it. The doorways are open to other worlds if you know how to find them."

"More than two realities?" Jason asked.

"Yes. At least I think so. The base of our power here is in Kimala, the mountain. The Kilmari believe its heart is the Crystal Cave." She sat back on the bench and tipped her mug of trinka for a sip. "My adopted people here are involved in a power struggle and you two have unwittingly gotten caught in the middle of it."

Jason exchanged a look with Ric. "She didn't tell me this part earlier."

"Me neither," Ric answered.

Jessie laughed. "There's a lot I haven't had time to tell you and there's much more that I don't have time to tell you now. But you must know that when you freed Fot, you gained a sort of power over him."

"Power?" they said together.

"Yeah." She grinned. "He owes you. And that would give you an advantage if you were to try to put him back in his cage. He will fear you for that. And he will hunt you."

"Hunt? As in seek and destroy?"

"Yes. Well, kind of." She stared at the bottom of her empty mug as though some kind of message was written there. "He will try to force you into situations where you could harm yourselves, like he did in the Portal Room." Altay took the mug, filled it and returned it. She smiled in gratitude before the healer turned her attention to other things.

"In the spring, Eron and I and many others set a trap in the Portal Room to catch Fot. We succeeded at great cost."

"So it wasn't paprika!" Jason blurted.

"Sadly, no," Jessie answered. "Eron was lucky to have survived. His recovery is somewhat slower than I hoped. That leaves only me to put Fot back in his prison. He won't be fooled a second time. Alone, I doubt if I'm strong enough to defeat him."

"You, Jessie?" Jason asked, his eyes widening.

"I am the Shield. It is my power. Eron is the Sword. He is defender, I am protector."

"Well, that clears up nothing," Jason said.

"What happened to him?" Ric asked, ignoring his friend's comment.

Jessie touched the pendant that hung around her neck, her fingers lingering on its surface. "He rides with Tersan's army to do battle with Marand."

"Tersan?" Jason asked.

"Good guy. King of Jeleste. Marand was once an ally as well, until Fot appealed to his greed. I'm pretty sure it wasn't hard to persuade him to betray us." She set the mug down. "Marand has always lusted after pretty things and he is a pompous ass. He was involved in a property dispute with Tersan over a mine in the Paranjothi Mountains. Precious gems or something." She shook her head. "I never understood why that was so important. Anyway, Marand and Fot made a deal. Fot said he would leave Marand alone and get him the mine he was unable to acquire through normal, legal channels, and in return, Marand would help Fot get control of Kimala."

"And then he would have access to the portals?"

Jessie nodded. "We can't let that happen." She sighed. "Marand was negotiating with Tocar, Eron's brother, and we were making good progress until Fot was released, but now…" She bit her lip. "Now we have another problem that is none of your concern. You're leaving for home in the morning. Both of you."

"But Jessie, we can help!"

"Yes, I thought that at first." She shook her head. "But you could also get killed."

Jason raised his eyebrows and looked at Ric. "This Eron guy isn't strong enough to help you, is he?"

"No. He's not. At least not yet." Jessie reached over to the pitcher of steaming trinka that Altay left on the table and poured a small amount into Jason's mug before topping off her own. Steam rose from the brew and she put her head over it savoring the aroma. "I wish we had something like this at home."

Jason rolled his mug back and forth between his hands. Without looking up, he asked the question that bothered him the most. "Jessie, you've been talking about Ric and I and this Eron guy and where we are and all. There's something that's eating me."

"What?"

He cleared his throat. "Lucy. What about Lucy? She misses you terribly!"

Jessie hesitated. "I, well, I—Jason, the easiest way to tell you this is just to tell you. Eron is her father."

"Really?"

"Yes. Really." She sighed heavily. "Six months ago, I had to make a choice. I would have loved to have taken Eron home. But no medicine in our world would have saved him. Lucy knows that. So do Martha and Miss James. And bringing her here was not an option. She and I discussed that before I left."

"Mom knew and she didn't tell me? Lucy knew, too? How come I don't know?"

"It wasn't necessary for you to know," she answered bluntly. "You're my accountant and I didn't want to muddy those waters." She looked from Jason to Ric and back again. "I—I spoke with Martha last night."

"How?" they asked in unison.

"I went back through the portal and called Martha to let her know what happened to you both. She said she would contact your parents, Ric."

"Why didn't you take us back then?" Jason fumed.

"Think about it and ask me later if you haven't figured it out," she said sharply.

Jason didn't know whether to fume or be relieved. He decided to give her a bit of leeway. It had been a long few days. He nodded. "You have a point. Things are not as simple as they might be."

"You're going home in the morning."

"Are you coming with us?" Jason asked.

Jessie hesitated. She looked back and forth between them as though assessing many things. Then she rose and drained her mug. "I have things to do yet tonight. I will see you in the morning." With that, she left.

"Well, don't that just beat all?" Jason muttered.

"Don't it though?"

32 Choices

Jessie left the boys in the empty dining hall and made her way through the House trying to find Penrose. It was well after dark now and there was very little activity. When Eron was here, even when there were only the two of them, the house seemed full. Now it was horribly empty. The hallways were long and echoed hollowly with her footsteps. There was a light spilling out into her path and she hurried toward it, hoping to find Penrose there or someone who could tell her where she could find him.

"Lady Jessie? How may I help you?"

It was the Healer's Creed. She'd heard it often enough, though she wasn't expecting it right now. The voice belonged to Altay.

"Take me to Penrose," she told her.

"Of course. This way."

Altay led her to the end of the corridor and into a dimly lit room. Penrose was busily attending the room's sole occupant: Cynthal. Jessie bit her lip. He looked so very young lying motionless in that bed. His breathing was ragged. Rest was not coming to him. She took a seat beside him and took his hand in her own.

Jessie wept. She didn't know why. Perhaps it was because she had witnessed the other Kilmari dying. Perhaps it was because she had put Jason and Ric into real danger. Perhaps it was because she had not been there for Lucy the past six months. She felt like she was a player in some wicked game conceived by some thoughtless gamesman. She missed Eron so very badly; she missed Lucy even more. Today, for the first time in her life, she had been forced to kill. The fairy tale reality had changed into a very real nightmare and all she wanted to do was to somehow lasso Eron and go home to Lucy.

"He is fading," Penrose told her.

The quiet words sent her into a round of weeping. She buried her head into the healer's shoulder and sobbed until finally the tears were done. Penrose rocked her slowly back and forth and she felt secure in his arms. For a long while, they sat beside Cynthal in the light of the candle.

"I--I, hell, Penrose, I've made such a mess of things."

"Why do you say this?" he asked.

"Jason and Ric, Eron, Cynthal, Fot…" She sucked in a breath and the words came in stutters. "A-and I k-killed. Penrose, I killed!"

"Killing is part of war and we are at war."

"Yes, but I'm supposed to be the Shield. I'm supposed to prevent death." She looked directly at him. "I trapped the marauders who ambushed us, each within a shield of power. They begged for mercy. Cynthal and the other Kilmari were loath to grant it but I insisted. I gave them Opportunity."

"Mercy is the way of the Shield, whenever possible," he agreed quietly.

"As I released them, the Kilmari stripped them of their armor and boots." The events played out in her head like a horror movie. "I worked on recovering the power I had used to imprison them. It was all very routine. They were released, barefoot, onto the plain. We'd done it so many times. We were watching them, rather smugly. Penrose, I gave in to pride and that cost us dearly!" She stopped and looked up at the healer. "A second group attacked from behind us. From the west! They had a demon with them."

"You cannot save everyone," he said.

"I was arrogant! Worse than Eron ever was!"

"You captured the demon, Jessie," Penrose said. "That was your part. And you did it without Eron's aid."

She waved her hand in the air. "By the time I got done with Ket, the Kilmari were lying on the plain dead, or so I thought." She leaned on the bed and across Cynthal's unconscious form, she spoke in nearly a whisper. "I just assumed everyone was dead. The marauders scattered and I went on a hunt and destroy mission. I hunted those men down and I killed them as sure as you're standing in front of me." She gulped. "Lord help me, at the time, it felt good."

"You reacted strongly to what they had done," Penrose said. "And you could not let them escape. You did the right thing."

"I'm not looking for absolution."

"Really?"

"Well, maybe I am. I'm so mixed up." She turned away from the bed, her hand at her lips. "All I want to do is go home, crawl into my own bed and sleep for a month."

Penrose sighed. "You received the power, didn't you?"

She snapped her head around to look at him. "What power?"

"The power of the Shield; you received it and you accepted the responsibility that came along with it."

"Yes," she said. "I received it."

"By the Lady, Jessie, what are you thinking?" Penrose was staring at her with smoldering eyes. "You have vanquished a demon and have killed his allies. And you have granted mercy to some who would not have done the same for you."

"But, I never thought it would be like this!"

"Just what did you think?" He took the Cynthal's hand and pressed it between hers. "Feel this, Jessie. Blood courses through him, life courses through him. Feel the warmth. He's a real person, not some player on a board." He shook his head. "You have accused Jason and Ric of thinking our world is part of a game and you have told them that it is not. When are you going to realize that yourself?"

Jessie held on to Cynthal's hand, tightening her grip. For the third time, she wept.

33 The Siren

The day dawned sunless. The breeze that had brought with it the freshness of the dicantus flowers now carried the scent of rain. Jason lay on his back staring at the ceiling. There was nothing special about it. It was white, like the rest of the room, the curtains and the furniture. Very clean but boring. Time to get out of bed.

Jason's feet slapped the cold floor and he drew them up, now wide awake. Fumbling beneath the bed, he found the soft white boots the healers had left for him and pulled them on. He felt silly in a white robe and white boots. No one ever wore white boots. They were impractical. In the next bed, Ric was still sleeping. Jason decided to let him sleep and explore on his own.

The House was quiet, the kind of quiet that comes from familiarity. As Jason passed through the Great Room, he noticed about two dozen men and women sleeping on top of the clean white linens. They were still dressed in black leather, as though expecting to have to get up and do something again at a moment's notice. Several of the healers gathered like ghostly shadows in the corners of the room, going about their chores quietly. Jason moved on.

In the entryway, more of the black clad Kilmari stood. They gathered in groups of three or four and speaking quietly to one another. Their whispers sent a wave of energy through the air. Jason could feel it. Fear and courage permeated the air around the Kilmari. They would not willingly fail. The rhythm of their voices sounded in Jason's head. He walked in time to their musings.

The breeze blew through the huge windows, billowing long white curtains into the foyer. Like sheets snapping in a breeze, they flipped around noisily. Jason incorporated their noise into his stride. Every sound in the House belonged to him now, like a well-loved bar song. Without thinking, he began to hum.

The door to the courtyard was open and Jason walked out onto the porch, still humming. A man sat on the stair. Twinkling blue eyes peered out from under his bushy lashes. He nodded a greeting. He held an ornate pipe in one hand, filled with some kind of sweet smelling tobacco. When he sucked in on the pipe, the tobacco glowed and sent out a delightful fruity aroma, but Jason only noticed the delicate sound of leaves burning. He nodded back and stepped off into the courtyard, whistling.

Rain came. Drops splattered on the ground and he incorporated their patter into the tune he whistled. He found the tempo lively and he was dancing in time. Words transformed into song in his mind, not Singin' in the Rain, but something older and powerful, something that came from a score he had never heard in a language he did not fully understand. He jumped up on the stone wall and walked in time to the rhythm, until at last the melody made itself known to him. He stopped atop the stone wall and spread his arms in front of him. He took a very deep breath preparing to belt out a spontaneous tune that would do Rogers and Hammerstein proud.

Someone grabbed him from behind, literally knocking the wind out of him. Words, rhythm and melody deserted him. The orchestration that had been provided by all the things around him evaporated and suddenly all he heard was rain. He felt very wet. He whirled around to face the man who had been smoking on the porch.

"Why did you do that?" Jason asked angrily as he shook off the man.

"Penrose asked me to keep an eye on you, should you wander," the man replied. "My name is Caleb." One of the blue eyes winked. "Your song is not for the wind."

"Not for the wind?" The song returned, exploding in his brain. The storm roared in his head, the sounds once so gentle now crackled angrily. "My song is the wind!" he nearly yelled. His head rang with the words. Sounds were bursting in his mind in raging disorder. There was no pattern to the rhythm anymore, only a cacophony of discordant noise. He put his hands over his ears attempting to block it out; but the noise was inside his head.

"Save your song," Caleb answered. Each of his words was carefully annunciated, as though he felt the need to defend himself with them. "There are those who need it."

Something in his voice wasn't right. Jason cocked his head to one side and looked closer. Caleb was afraid; afraid of him. The storm inside his head subsided, leaving the soft patter of rain in its stead, the music disappearing to a distant place where it waited.

"What's happening to me?" Jason asked. He placed the heels of his hands on his temples and pressed hard, willing the music to stop yet at the same time he desperately wanted to release it.

"If you are willing," Caleb said kindly, "there is a need." He took Jason by the arm and led him back toward the House.

They walked past the soldiers who still gathered in the corridor. Now Jason heard the low-pitched sounds of their voices and the rustle of their clothing as they made subtle gestures toward him. The maestro inside his head was sorting the sounds into music again. Caleb picked up their pace.

When they came to the end of a long corridor, he took Jason by the shoulders and looked him in the eyes. "Please help," was all he said. He opened the door and stood aside for Jason to pass.

Silence greeted him as he entered the room and the notes in his mind softened. The young man named Cynthal was lying on the center bed of the room. Penrose was on his left, Jessie by his side and Altay stood in the corner bowing her head as though in prayer. Pixil sat on the straight-backed wooden chair beside the bed, an ugly purple bruise on her brow, her eyes rimmed with red. She looked as though she had not slept in a long time. She held Cynthal's hand in her own and her lips were moving, though she gave her words no voice. Jason noted the similarity between the two. They possessed the same aquiline nose, the same almond colored eyes, the same thin lips and strong chin, the same deep copper colored hair. Cynthal had insisted on staying to protect Jessie instead of going back to the hospital with his mother. Jason saw Jessie in a new light. Whatever her position was, it must be high indeed.

Half a dozen leather clad soldiers were standing on guard in front of the windows and at the foot of the bed. All breathed slowly, almost in unison. Jason's mind took their rhythm into the building song. Penrose exchanged a worried look with Jessie before turning to Jason.

"Jason," he began, "I…I have done what I can for Cynthal. I am afraid it is not…" He shook his head, turning his attention to the young man who was so pale he was almost lost in the white sheets. "I am afraid it is not enough."

"What can I do?" Jason asked, taking his hands away from his face. The curtains rustled. His mind shifted with the sound. "Does he need a blood transfusion or something?"

Penrose managed a short laugh. "Perhaps that would help, in your world. Here… here he is dying and there is nothing I can do to stop it." Penrose looked up at Jason, an odd hope present in his eyes. "But you might."

"Me? How?" A distant bolt of lightning struck Kimala and he waited for the accompanying thunder. It would come as a rumble, soft and comfortable, the purring of the earth.

"Jason," Jessie was saying, "you were in the cave when it shed."

"So?"

The thunder arrived, its sound reverberating in his heart. Pixil's gaze was now fixed on him, Cynthal's still hand clutched between her own. She was rubbing it slowly, skin against skin, rhythm on rhythm, chanting in his mind. They merged with sounds inside his head, building into a melody he was certain he could not much longer contain.

"You were gifted," Jessie said, "gifted with song."

Three tears ran down Pixil's cheeks and splattered on the sheet: the first was grief, the second sorrow, and the last was hope. He saw the young man's face reflect in each tear before they melted into the linens. He knew what he had to do. With great reverence, he reached out to Pixil and took the prince's limp hand from her.

Electricity surged through the prince's hand, prickling Jason's fingers and demanding he release it. He could hear the crackling power that was Cynthal. It searched for release in one form or another. Jason's heart was racing. The syncope was done, the melody complete. It was time.

A great black cloud formed over the stricken man, a roiling fast moving storm that joined with Cynthal until flesh and bone were roiling as well. The fair face darkened and lost the features that made him human. Outside, the storm battered the building, whipping the curtains into a frenzy. A peal of thunder rocked the room and the storm cloud that was Cynthal answered in kind, driving those around him to their knees. All save Jason.

At once, the music came to him, fierce and proud and unafraid. Everything around him was part of the song; the curtains, Pixil's tears now falling freely to the bed, the soldiers' breathing, the rustling of leather as they moved closer to their fallen comrade. Everything. Jason heard the song they were singing to him, soft and sweet, a lament for a fallen hero who had not yet succumbed to death, a sweet melody hoping for a miracle. In a tongue he did not know, he sang.

He found himself singing in richer tones than he had ever thought possible. He had tremendous range, singing from the depths through the heights, harmony to the sounds surrounding him, melody to the man in front of him. The hero would rise again, not yet whole, certainly changed, but not finished with life. The Lady would see to that; the Lady would gift him with many springs.

The storm that possessed Cynthal faded; color returned to his features. Jason did not stop singing. The soldier would rise and become a leader among his people, powerful and strong, a husband, a father. A second peal of thunder rumbled through his chest as the earth purred once more, taking the tempest away and leaving soft rain in its stead. The song ended.

Jason dropped the hand and staggered backward, falling into the bed beside the window. One of the Kilmari half caught him, eased him onto the bed. Cynthal opened his eyes and looked up at his mother.

"Do not weep, Mother," he whispered. He turned toward Jason. "An angel watches over me. I will be whole." With that, he closed his eyes and slept.

Jason lay back on the bed, his head sapped of everything except exquisite joy. He barely noticed Jessie pull the covers over him but he did feel the light touch of her lips on his forehead before he drifted off to sleep.

34 Coming of Age

"JM? JM? Come on. Get up. It's time to get going here."

Jason rolled over in the bed and thought seriously about going back to sleep.

"JM!"

"What?" he snapped, now fully awake. He sat up, pushed the blanket to one side and raised his eyebrows as he ran a hand over the stubble that had emerged on his chin. Ric was standing by the bed, dressed in his own clothes. He held Jason's jeans and T-shirt in one hand but as soon as Jason sat up, he threw them on the bed. "Not that I won't be happy to get rid of this goofy nightshirt, but couldn't it wait until I finish my dream?"

"Sorry." Ric grinned. "Some hot chick?"

Jason threw a pillow at him in disgust. He slid out of bed, pulled the nightshirt off and dressed. It was only as he was pulling on his socks that he noticed the bed beside him was empty. His heart lurched and he sighed heavily.

"What happened to Cynthal?" he asked.

"Cynthal?"

"Yeah." Jason pointed to the messy bed beside him. "The guy who was in that bed. What happened to him?"

"Don't know. But they're serving breakfast. Maybe he went to eat."

"Oh, I doubt it. He didn't look like he was going to get up anytime soon. I just hope he didn't, well, die."

"There's a happy thought," Ric answered. "Hurry up. I'm hungry."

"All right, all right." Jason tied his shoe and stood up. Incessant music returned in his head. He opted to ignore it. "Let's go."

They walked through the House to the dining hall, passing between many men and women who bowed their heads respectfully as they went by. From further away, they would point and then speak in hushed whispers. Even the healers avoided making eye contact.

"I don't know about you," Ric said as they took a seat in a lonely corner away from everyone, "but I will be very glad to get out of here."

"I hear ya. This is worse than being fifteen and a freshman in college."

"Surely it wasn't that bad."

"Aunt Jessie!" Jessie slid in beside Jason.

"It was every bit that bad," Ric told her. "But it has turned out okay so far."

"Glad to hear it, boy geniuses." She reached for an apple and took a big bite out of it. "I've made arrangements for Penrose and Altay to take you back to the portal today," she said around the apple.

"You're not coming home then?" Jason asked.

"As soon as this is done, I will be home for a long time, at least until Lucy is out of college." She sighed. "The army left two days ago," she explained. "I need to be with them when they reach Calshara. If we have a strong enough showing, we may have a bloodless victory."

"You're going to war?" Jason said. "Jessie, what are you thinking?"

"I'm fulfilling my obligation," she stated simply. "Don't worry. I'm well prepared."

"So was Napoleon at Waterloo," Jason told her.

Jessie rose. "I love you, Jason. I love Lucy, too. Be sure she knows that. And tell her that her father has nearly recovered entirely, will you? Please? I must go. Thank your mother for me, too."

With that, she left.

"Well, at least she isn't dead," Ric said.

"There's a comforting thought."

They ate mostly in silence. The food was filling and good, though simple. When they got down to only drinking trinka, a small group of Kilmari soldiers very slowly approached them.

"Looks like someone's not afraid to talk to us," Ric said. "Look."

Jason glanced over his shoulder, didn't immediately recognize anyone and returned to the last of his brew. He shrugged. "Do you know them?" he asked.

"No," Ric answered. "What do you suppose they want?"

"I don't know."

A young man with golden hair emerged from the group and walked slowly toward them, surrounded by what seemed to be kinsmen and Altay. He smiled widely at Jason.

"Cynthal?" Jason said.

"Jason, I believe you are called?" Cynthal answered in a voice barely above a whisper. He smiled and instantly Jason hated him. He was one of those people who was always nice, always good looking, always said and did the right thing. Jason just knew it. "Penrose tells me you brought me home from the Lady's door." He dipped his head down. "I am not yet ready to leave this world. Thank you for bringing me back."

"Well, um, yeah, sure, you're welcome," Jason mumbled. The song inside his head was starting again, joining every noise in the hall into melody. Mentally, he pushed at it until it shut up.

"You have had your say, my prince," Altay said to Cynthal. "You must return to your room now."

The golden haired man smiled another perfect smile and turned away, escorted by his honor guard. Altay stayed behind, watching his every move.

"Penrose says we will be leaving after the noon meal," she said, never taking her eyes off the perfect prince.

Jason watched Altay watch Cynthal with more than a little jealousy.

"Altay," he said, thinking this was one girl he'd never get, "what's so fascinating about him?"

"Him?" she said, her gaze still firmly attached to the prince.

"Yeah, Mr. Goodlooking there."

Altay looked away from Cynthal to Jason, her eyebrows lifted. "I beg your pardon?"

Jason pointed. "Cynthal! For crying out loud. You know, looks aren't everything."

"They are when you are assessing someone for progress," she answered smoothly.

Jason felt his face flush. He looked down at his shoes and then turned his back to her, taking his seat once more. She laughed and the song returned. This time it was not so easy to put it aside.

"I am a Healer, Jason," she said. He felt her hand light on his shoulder. "I am supposed to watch and evaluate and make certain that my charges do not push themselves further than they should."

"So Cynthal is…?"

"My charge. He no longer needs Penrose so Penrose assigned him to me. This morning, I will assign him to a lesser healer than myself." She slid into the seat beside his and grinned at him, for the first time a girl instead of a Healer. She giggled. "Cynthal is royalty, though you would never know it by his attitude. He is really very nice. However, he has many suitors and will wed royalty, not a Healer."

"There's nothing wrong with you!" Ric protested, sitting down across from them and picking up his mug of trinka.

"Of course there is nothing wrong with me!" she agreed. "But such marriages rarely happen."

"Don't sell yourself short," Ric said. Jason wanted to kick him.

Altay raised an eyebrow. "I do not wish to be the wife of a royal," she said.

It was Ric's turn to blush and Altay laughed again. The music swelled.

"Sorry. It's just that--"

"He is my charge. That is all."

"Trinka?" Jason offered her, suddenly feeling much better.

"Thank you, but I must prepare for our journey. Penrose said I could escort you to the portal."

"We're going home, then?"

Altay placed her hand on his and his heart leapt. "Yes," she said. The music took a sad turn. "I am glad you sang to him, Jason. He recovers quickly now." She squeezed his hand gently and left. Ric laughed.

"What?"

Ric rolled his eyes. "She likes you, you idiot."

Jason smiled. So many notes were vying for his attention that he couldn't think.

"What is it, JM?"

"Do you think we're doing the right thing by going home, Ric?"

"Do we have a choice?"

"We always have a choice." Crescendo, decrescendo, counterpoint; he gave up trying to silence it. "I, well, something happened to me, here."

"You mean other than finally having a girl like you?"

"Yeah," he answered without arguing. Ric raised an eyebrow.

"What happened?"

"Well, I seem to be able to do stuff. When I sing."

Ric laughed. "You learned to dance?"

"Now who's being an idiot?" he snapped.

"You're serious?" Ric raised both eyebrows, his eyes wide. "What happens when you sing?"

"I don't know how it works," he said, "but I seem to be able to influence things. Cynthal back in that room, you at the Giants Fingers."

"Me?"

"Yeah. You were in pretty bad shape. They said from a demon's wound complicated by falling into that lake."

"I feel fine now."

"I know, I know. But Cynthal? At death's door in the middle of the night and now here for breakfast only a couple hours later?"

"It's a different reality, JM. Maybe people heal faster here. Maybe it's something in the water. Who knows?"

Jason frowned. "See, I've got this music playing in my head all the time. I can't make it stop and if I went home, they'd think I was crazy."

"Have you talked to Penrose about it? Or," he winked, "Altay? Now there's a reason to stay."

"For crying out loud, Ric, would you please focus? What happens if we get home and this music won't stop and I can't get back here to figure out how to cope with it?"

"You think too much."

"They said you were changed, too, though they didn't know how."

Ric put his hand down on the table, palm up. He cupped his fingers upward as though holding a small ball. Flashes of light dashed between his fingertips, briefly connecting them with an emerald green glow. He turned his hand upside down quickly, extinguishing the light. Jason looked from Ric's hand to his face. He wasn't smiling anymore.

"I--I didn't want anyone to know," he said. "I thought it was just a little present from the lake, you know, like they said I would get. But each time I think about it, it comes and each time, it gets more intense. Look."

He raised his hand and beneath it, the cloth napkin he had been using was scorched. "That started this morning." He laughed nervously. "I thought I could use that somehow to make a little money when we got back home, you know, pay off some bills with a little magic, make a nest egg so I can go back to school for my masters."

"So we stay?" Jason said.

"I don't see that we have a choice." He bit his lip.

"What?"

"Money's tight. They've probably already fired me—"

"You work from home!"

"When I can. But I have to supplement. College wasn't cheap. The master's program won't be either. I start in January."

"Master's program? Congratulations!"

"Thanks."

"No scholarship?"

Ric blushed. "I got the paperwork in too late. There may be more money next fall."

"We'll work something out when we get back, okay? Jessie's got more money than she knows what to do with and I manage it for her. She'll pay off your college loans, get you a new car, even a house. Consider it compensation for whatever has happened to you here, okay?"

"I won't take charity."

"Compensation isn't charity."

Ric clenched his fists and lightly tapped the table. His face was red and getting redder by the second as if he was holding his breath. He kept tapping the table, each time a little harder than the last. His arms were trembling from his fists to his shoulders as he tried to stop himself. Terror filled his eyes.

"What?"

"I did it again! It's too big to hide this time! My hands are starting to burn!"

"Get rid of it!"

"I can't!"

"Why?"

"I might hurt someone!"

"Just throw it at the wall!"

Ric whirled around and opened his hands. A blast of energy flew from his fingertips and exploded against the wall cracking the plaster. Everything stopped. The occupants of the room pointed and whispered, fear on their faces. Penrose emerged from the crowd and headed quickly toward them.

"Clear your minds now, both of you," he ordered quietly. "Come with me. We need to talk."

Penrose escorted them out of the dining hall and into a long, dark tunnel. The way was cool, lit by small holes in the ceiling. Doors on either side of them were held in place by heavy metal hinges. The wood was crude, rough cut and unfinished. It smelled dank, like an old winery.

The tiny windows lighting the hallway grew further and further apart until the light all but disappeared, nearly forcing them to touch the walls to find their way. Penrose strode confidently ahead of them, never breaking stride. When they reached a fork in the tunnel, the healer halted.

"A moment," he said. He disappeared to the right, leaving them to wait in the near darkness.

"I sure hope we don't end up in another cave," Jason mumbled.

"I'm with you there, JM."

There was a flare of light. Penrose appeared with a fiery torch in his hands. "No, no, there is no cave here," Penrose told them, "only catacombs. This way." He took off down the hallway to the left.

They followed him through a series of hallways, all seemingly on the same level. The floor was even, dry and easy to negotiate. The air was sometimes dank and sometimes fresh. The scent of animals drifted their way at one turn, perfume at another and food at yet another.

After what seemed forever, Penrose halted in front of one of the old doors. He rubbed the face with his sleeve. There were runes carved in it. Penrose took his time looking at them. He made little noises and nodded his head as his fingers passed over the symbols.

"No, no, this is not it. But we're close. This way." Without looking at them, he charged off.

They followed for twenty more paces and he stopped in front of a very similar door. Once again he read over the runes; this time he was nodding. He took his torch and lit a second torch on the wall beside the door. When he turned to face them, his face was grave.

"This is the room. Wait here," he told them, "and do not attempt to enter yet. It must be prepared."

He ducked inside, pulling the heavy door almost shut behind him, blocking their view.

"How's the fiery stuff?" Jason asked.

Ric shrugged. "I'm trying not to think about it. Music?"

"Ditto."

Penrose reappeared at the door, his face somber. "Before you enter," he began, "there are a few things that you must know."

"Great," Jason said. "More secrets."

"Yes, more secrets." Penrose waved behind him. "This is a dead room. Once you walk inside, the powers that you are experiencing will cease to function."

"Yes!" Ric and Jason answered together. They almost stumbled over one another to get into the room. Penrose blocked them.

"You will temporarily lose your power."

Both of them sighed heavily. "Temporarily?" Jason repeated.

"Yes." He smiled at them. "There is another dead room on Kimala, on your way home. You will be able to retrieve your powers there, if you decide you want them back."

"I really don't want whatever this is," Ric said, "ever. I might hurt someone."

"I see." Penrose smiled annoyingly. "Jason, what about you? You've seen what good you can do. Is it something that you truly wish to lose?"

Jason shrugged. "I can't stop it in my head. It's driving me nuts!"

"I understand." He took a moment to regard them both, still preventing their entry. The song in Jason's mind was thrumming and he noted that Ric's hands were glowing green with light. "Many are gifted. Some cannot effectively use the gifts. So we bring them here and, well, shut them off I guess would be your term. Entering the dead room here gives you a chance to contemplate your power and what the possibilities are if you use it. There is one condition."

"Oh?" they responded as one.

"Until you enter the dead room on Kimala, your powers may be summoned. But if you do summon them, they will be lost to you forever."

Ric cast a sidelong glance at Jason. "I don't want the chance of it showing up when I've got a hot date or something."

"Oh, please," Jason replied, shoving his friend forward, "get in the room."

Penrose stood aside and gestured widely for them to enter. They stepped through the door and into the tiny room. Almost instantly, the music in Jason's head stopped. He breathed a sigh of relief. Ric looked at him and nodded.

"Gone?" Penrose asked.

"Gone!" they answered in unison.

"Excellent!" Penrose strode to the wall where he had left his torch. "Now, you must not attempt to summon your gifts until we reach Kimala. Understood?"

"Yes," they said.

"Good. I believe Altay has things prepared. She and I will accompany you, along with several of the Kilmari. I am afraid the way is no longer safe. Come."

They walked out into the hallway, simultaneously turned to one another, each grinning.

"Great to be normal again," Jason said.

35 The Substitute

Progress had been slow as the massive army moved across the plain and there was great unrest. The rumor that the Sword was now wearing a blade had been confirmed and, even after Eron's display of power at Pella Durett, the army whispered. He rode at the head of their forces beside the king on the great black stallion, his eyes flitting back and forth as he tried to focus on things no one else could see. The men who served him, dressed in black, were ever on the move all around Tersan's great force, like shadows in a dream. Their presence, meant to be a show of solidarity between the two peoples, only served to increase the uneasy feelings that pervaded the army.

The healers' wagon was at the edge Durnham Plain a long time before the rest of the army. When the great force arrived, the healers disembarked to tend the plethora of blisters and sunburns acquired on the first day of marching to Calshara. They worked past sunset and into the night, not pausing until each soldier who needed tending had received aid. By the time they returned to the cook tents, there was little prepared food left so they had to settle for hard bread and dried meat for their evening meal.

Sila ate quickly and returned to the scant privacy their wagon offered. She wanted to be alone for a while. This was not the life she had planned. Had it not been for the Otherworlder, it would not be the life she was living. There was always hope that things could change and Sila was going to be certain that, if the opportunity to become the Shield presented itself again, she would be there to seize it. To do so, she needed to practice, even though it was forbidden as a healer of the First Order.

She worked her fingers nimbly, forming a shield the size of her palm. Tossing it in the air, she rapidly formed a marble-sized fireball that she sent flying at it. The ball bounced harmlessly off the shield, dropping to the floor of the wagon where it exploded into fire.

"Ach!" she said, shaking her head. She kicked it and it soared out the back of the wagon and before it could hit the ground, she sent the shield out after it. The fireball was quickly consumed and the night returned to darkness.

"You should not be forming shields!" an old woman in healers' robes told her.

"Practice is allowed if a replacement is required."

"You are healer, First Order under Master Penrose, a noble and rarely achieved position." Aramat softened. "And you are no longer a child. Your time for acquiring that title has passed."

"The Otherworlder has abandoned her Sword."

"The ways of Sword and Shield are not to be judged by you, Sila Atin, you know this."

"Someone needs to be prepared to protect him, Aramat, since she is not among us."

"It is not your place to do that. You are a healer." Aramat held a hand out. "Help me up."

Reluctantly, Sila took hold of the weathered hand and pulled her colleague into the wagon.

"Honestly, you are a gifted Healer, the best of all in Bel Haven and the probable successor to Master Penrose. Why do you let this bother you so?"

"It does not bother me," Sila lied. "I just think it is good to be prepared, should the worst happen."

The older healer held her eyes for a long while as though assessing her sincerity. Finally, she shook her head and looked away. "You desire something that cannot be," the woman told her. "He has chosen another."

Sila retrieved her pallet with a huff, got out of the wagon and lay down under the stars. All around her she could hear the sounds of horses moving about in small pens and men washing dishes. In the distance, she was certain warriors were telling bawdy tales, though she could not discern their words. Resentment festered inside her. It was not dignified for a woman in her position to be with the common workers. With that last angry thought, she went to sleep.

How long she had been asleep, she did not know. Garrett, Tersan's page, was knocking furiously on the side of the wagon.

"Mistress Aramat," he called, "Mistress Aramat, you must come quickly!"

"What is it, child?" Aramat answered sleepily.

"It is the Sword, Madam," the page said. "He is in a temper such that no one has ever witnessed before."

Sila's heart leapt.

"A temper?" Aramat repeated. Her calm demeanor angered Sila. Why did she not send someone immediately?

"King Tersan has need of a Reader," the page said. "Lord Eron needs assistance."

"Lord Eron," Aramat said through a mighty yawn, "should not have come."

"Ma'am?"

"A moment, young man," she said, yawing a second time. Aramat disappeared into the wagon. Moments later, she reappeared, a satchel of medicine over her shoulder.

"I can go in your stead," Sila offered. "I am an accomplished reader."

Aramat looked at her long and hard. "It is not that I do not wish to send you so that an old woman may rest, Sila," Aramat said, "but given our conversation earlier this evening, I am not certain it is wise. I have seen things."

Sila tipped her head down slightly. "I, too, have given our conversation much thought," she lied for the second time that night. "It was not my place to say such things. I ask forgiveness." She was careful to keep her head bowed and not make eye contact with the venerable healer.

A wolf howled in the distance and was joined by his pack. Owls flew overhead, hooting and swooping down occasionally toward some poor unsuspecting mouse. The three stood in the starlight waiting for a decision to be made. Finally, Aramat removed the medication pouch.

"You have earned Penrose's trust, Sila," she said. "Tonight, because I am tired, that is good enough for me. Here." She handed the pouch to Sila.

"I will do honor to his trust," she replied.

"See that you do. Your reputation and that of Bel Haven rest always on your actions."

"This way, Madam," Garrett said.

He led her through the camp, past rows of sleeping common soldiers in lines that seemed endless. They smelled of a day's worth of walking as they snored under their roughly woven blankets. Next were the smaller tents of lesser officers. Some were still awake, talking to one another in hushed but excited tones about the prospect of war. Then were the tents of the generals, with guards standing vigilantly outside the flaps. Finally, they arrived at the largest tents in the camp, the tents of the kings.

"This way, ma'am," Garrett told her. The guards stepped aside and let them in.

The interior was richly appointed, thickly woven tapestries adorning the walls to keep out the autumn chill. Pillows were strewn on floors covered with the skins of animals. A fire burned in the center of the tent, the smoke escaping through a dedicated hole in the roof.

"Wait here, Madam Healer," Garrett said.

Sila nodded.

"About time you got here, Aramat," Tersan said as he entered the room. Sila turned to face him and the king startled. "Sila?" he asked.

"Yes, my lord," she answered, making a mental note of his mistake. "I have been sent in Aramat's stead. She is, well, not as young as she once was."

Tersan nodded. The veil covering her scar slipped and she quickly rearranged the garment to cover it. To her relief, he seemed not to notice.

"My page has informed you of Lord Eron's needs?" he asked.

"Only that a reader is needed."

"Ah." Tersan took in a huge breath and let it out, not looking at her. "He believes he has had a vision, Madam Healer. You are aware of this?"

"Yes, my lord," Sila answered.

"He was able to witness the return of Fot which was confirmed by Lady Jessie. He has not been able to summon that power of his, so he does not know if this was a dream or not. He needs clarification."

"Of course. How may I help you?"

Tersan looked closely at her face once more. "Are you a reader?"

"I am."

"You are aware of the instability of Eron's mind?"

"I am aware of the risks, my lord."

"Uh huh," he grunted. He regarded her carefully. "Very well. Eron had another vision. He says he must know if this vision was true or a dream. He will not rest until he knows the truth. That is why, Madam, I sent for you."

Sila tried not to smile. She tried not to be enthusiastic. She tried to look concerned. Tersan was going to trust her with his precious ally. The best she could do was bow her head slightly and smile. "I live to serve, my lord."

Silently, Tersan walked to the far side of the tent and pulled back a flap for Sila. With her heart racing, she passed into a small antechamber.

Eron sat beside a single candle, his face ghostly in the flickering light. He raised an earthen jug to his lips and took a long drink before placing it on the floor beside him. If he was aware of her entry, he did not say anything. Slowly she moved across the darkened room until she stood in front of him, waiting in silence. The dark eyes that had watched so many things that afternoon now stared barely blinking at the burning wick. Sila thought she saw the track of a tear on his cheek and she suppressed the urge to move closer and stroke his troubled brow as she had done so many times without his knowledge while he slept in the House. Finally he shifted his gaze toward her.

"You are gifted with the ability to Read?" he asked. The voice she remembered as rich was raspy.

"I am," she replied.

"You know what I ask of you?"

"I do."

A great cloud darkened his features. "And you are aware of the dangers you may encounter if you enter my mind?"

"I am."

He stood and took her hands in his own and her heart leapt. "I pray that what you are about to encounter was not a vision, rather a nightmare that haunts a troubled mind. I open myself to you that I may find peace in one way or another. When you enter, do not stray from the path, for I am not fully in control of a power you will never understand and I may not be able to find you to help you."

Sila's pulse quickened and she was breathing far faster than normal. She tried to form words but all she could do was nod her head.

"I am prepared," he said. "Join with me."

The dark brown eyes changed to black so quickly Sila did not have a chance to respond. Places and people flashed by her so fast she could not recognize features. She was lost in the darkness, plummeting into his mind at a speed she could not control and her physical body swooned. She was aware that her body was now being held by someone. The smell of leather from his saddle mingled with the unique aroma that was Eron himself. He had her in his arms and in his mind as well.

The images slowed and she began to recognize things. Tersan's coronation, a tall raven-haired woman with a white bow and a quiver of arrows, Lady Jessie holding a child with dark eyes and an easy smile…Sila ducked. The demon, Fot was charging at Eron, fangs bared and saliva dripping from his massive teeth. Eron stood solidly in front of him, holding in his hands the Sword of Fire. Jessie stood at his side holding a shield made of silver. Fot roared and Sila screamed as the demon lunged toward her. She shut her eyes tightly, knowing the end was coming and cowered inside of Eron's mind.

"They are only memories," Eron assured her. "Take my hand. We're almost there."

Sila opened her eyes. Eron was standing in front of her offering her his hand. She could hear the demon roaring, feel his breath on her neck and smell the horrid breath comprised of lavender and garlic. Eron's hand never wavered and she reached up to snatch it but Fot took that moment to strike at them. Terrified, she turned and ran.

The way she had come was not the way she was going. She was in a new place, filled with mystifying light and awesome noise. Rivers of molten gold surged behind a wall laden with patches of gold and silver. In the center was a tremendous silver inlay. The amount of power sacrificed to stem that tear was inspiring. On her best day, Sila could never have manufactured that amount. The Otherworlder's sacrifice was substantial, though the healer would never admit it. There were smaller silver reinforcements along the wall as well, evidence of Jessie's frantic but successful attempt to keep Eron from dying. Yet the Sword had not been idle these six months; the wall gleamed with Eron's gold. He had been busy healing himself.

However, there were still aneurysms. With a trembling hand Sila touched one of them. It was spongy, weak. Her hand came away dry. She looked closer. Droplets of gold threatened to burst through at any moment, she was certain.

"I will help," she said aloud.

In her hand, she formed a small shield. With great effort, she was able to increase the size of it such that it was just about large enough to be held by both hands. Ecstatic that she had been so successful, she slapped her patch in place and uttered an incantation. Her bandage melded with the flow of power behind the aneurysm, strengthening the weakened wall.

Intoxicated with her success, she managed a second shield, this one a bit smaller than the first. She searched the wall for another weakness. Sila found one and repeated her previous action. Soon, pale blue light joined the silver and gold emanating from the wall. Sila was very pleased. Satisfied that she had become his savior, she moved on.

She left the wall and traveled back among his memories now and suddenly she saw herself. She stopped. Her face was beautiful. Without thinking, she brushed her cheek. The scar was still there. This was a memory.

It was at the trial, the time and place when Wylfcynne passed the duties of the shield to someone younger. Eron, Penrose, Wylfcynne, and Tersan were sitting in the courtyard of Bel Haven. Eron had his back to her, his long black hair tied neatly in a single braid that reached the center of his back. He was gazing fondly at some distant place that disappeared into the darkness of Eron's memory.

"Marand sent his condolences, but will abide by our choice," Tersan said.

"There are rumors," Eron stated, "that Marand has made a deal with the demon Fot."

"Merely rumors, Eron," Tersan said.

"Then why is he not here and a part of the Choosing, as is his duty?" Eron snapped.

No one answered. "Eron is correct," Wylfcynne finally said. "Marand should be here. His lands are at much greater risk than ours from the demons."

"Let us get back to the matter at hand," Penrose stated. "As I see it, there are only two qualified candidates."

"The Otherworlder and Sila Atin?" Tersan said.

Sila was taken aback. She had actually gone this far in the selection process?

"Jessie," Eron replied from some distant place. He sighed and turned to face them. "Her name is Jessie, not 'the Otherworlder.'"

"No disrespect was intended, Eron," Tersan said. "It's just that she has an odd name."

Eron smiled. "She once said the same about you."

"Well, gentlemen, and lady," Penrose said, "it seems we have two candidates of nearly equal talent. Tersan?"

Tersan steepled his hands, his brow furrowed. "Sila Atin has great skill. She has been well schooled and is a fitting match. And she is quite a handsome woman as well," he said with a wicked smile.

Sila blushed.

"You are lucky, Eron, that the remaining candidates are women." Tersan continued. "How boring it would be to be stuck with a man."

Eron raised an eyebrow. "Tocar would have been an excellent choice," he said, "had he decided to join the competition."

"But he did not." Penrose said. "Then it is settled. Sila Atin will become shield."

"You would choose Sila Atin as well?" Eron said to Tersan.

"I agree, she would make an effective shield," Tersan said, now sitting back in his chair.

"We have come to choose my replacement," Wylfcynne said, shifting her attention between the three men. "The choice should not be so lightly made. I shudder to think that her beauty is part of your assessment."

"Sila Atin has great skill, more than Jessie," Penrose said.

Sila beamed.

"She is powerful," Eron agreed, "but over the last month, she has shown us nothing new. She simply repeats what she has learned, as if reciting from a book. Predictability will get her and anyone around her killed."

"I agree," Wylfcynne said.

"We need someone who knows how Sword and Shield intermingle and how to improvise," Eron continued.

Sila's jaw dropped.

"Jessie's powers have not yet reached their full potential," Eron continued, "and I do not think they will for quite some time."

"You would choose her over our own?" Penrose said darkly.

Eron shook his head. "I would choose the person best suited to keep our people safe. Jessie is that person. She is not the beauty Sila is, but she is a person of great sincerity and honor. Sila Atin is ignorant and arrogant. She lacks common sense. I do not wish to be coupled with an ignorant, arrogant woman who lacks common sense for the rest of my life."

The scene faded and Sila sucked in a stuttering breath.

"There you are!"

Sila jumped. Eron was standing behind her. He held his hand out and smiled grimly. "I thought I had lost you."

"Are--are you, well, real?" she nearly whispered.

"I am not memory. Take my hand." Eron's face was dark, his silver streaked hair flying about his face wildly. "Come. It is not far."

Sila took his hand, very relieved to find something substantial. She rose and followed him, gripping his hand tightly with both of her own. They stopped in short order.

The place was dark and smelled of lavender, garlic and blood. Sila cried out loud and tried to pull away, but Eron grabbed her arm and pulled her around so that she stood in front of him, holding her firmly in place.

"You are a Reader," he whispered fiercely. "Tell me what you see."

A dim light filtered in from above them. The room lightened, but the light was not enough to relieve the oppression Sila felt. The air was thick with moisture. Something was sliding, no, slithering across the floor to her right. There was a loud popping noise and a scream but Sila couldn't see what was going on.

A coppery scent replaced all others in the room and flecks of moisture dotted her face and arms. She raised her hands. They were dotted with blood. She gasped and tried to turn away, but Eron held her fast.

The thing that had occluded her view moved. Sila's stomach wrenched and she gagged. In front of her, Fot had taken partial human form, though he towered at least ten feet in the air. In his hands he held the head of a man by his long black hair. The head was dripping blood onto the floor and the neck of the body recently relieved of its master was bubbling blood. The man's face looked resigned and a tear was rolling down his cheek, last testament to a life once vital and alive.

"It was a vision. Please, my lord," she pleaded, "release me!"

Fot placed the head on a stake and laughed, the horrid breath renewing itself in the torrid air. Soft sobs from another corner of the room caught her attention and she willingly looked away from the gruesome scene only to find one nearly as bad.

A young man was tied to a chair in the corner. His face was badly bruised his left eye nearly swollen shut. Fot slithered over to him stopping inches from his face.

"I believe," he hissed, "your ambassador has failed." He laughed and the young man tried to turn away. Fot hoisted the still bleeding head over him and shook it so that the blood dripped on his shoulders. The man jerked, trying to get away but could not.

"Eron, it was not a dream! Please, let me go!" she pleaded.

"There's more," he said quietly.

A door opened and a handsome man dressed in royal robes entered the room.

"You recognize Marand?" Eron asked.

"I met him once," she answered, her voice cracking with fear.

"You did not reach an understanding?" Marand said. He made a few clucking noises with his tongue. "Pity. He worked so hard."

"We have…a messenger…from Tersan…" Fot said. The man cried out as Fot now swung the severed head and hit the boy repeatedly in the face with it. "I believe…we should…answer…"

"Yes, yes. But what to do with this mess." He pointed to the body. It had fallen on the floor. "Put it on a horse and put the head back on it. Gag the boy, bind his hands and send him back as well."

"You do not wish to kill him?" Fot asked.

"No, not yet." Marand grabbed the boy's chin and pulled it up so that he could look into his face. "Tell your masters we do not accept their proposal."

The scene faded and Sila felt herself falling into blissful darkness. The room, with all its blood and villains was gone and Sila was on the floor in the tent and someone was holding her as she wept uncontrollably. A warm cloak was thrown around her and she pulled it as tightly as she could around herself. She shook, trying to catch her breath.

"Drink," someone ordered. A warm mug was thrust in to her hands and she tried to hold it to her lips but her hands were shaking so violently that she could not drink. The same hand steadied the mug and she took a sip. Her stomach settled. She closed her eyes tightly and ran the back of her hand across her lips where the brew had slightly spilled.

"Tell me what you have seen." The voice belonged to Tersan.

Sila opened her eyes and nodded her head. It was the king who had his arms around her, the king who held the brew to her lips, the king who had given her warmth. Eron sat beside the lone candle in the room, his eyes fixed on something far in the distance.

"You do not need to go into detail," Eron told her softly. He shifted his attention to Tersan. "Suffice to say it was a vision of murder and torture."

"Who were they?" she whispered.

"The young man is Parry, my kinsman," he answered. He closed his eyes and tilted his head back, his face twisting into a tortured mask. For a moment, it looked as though he was going to weep. He leveled his gaze and raised his right arm, extending it as far as he could reach. The muscles in his fingers flexed as he focused on something unseen and closed his fingers around it. Bolts of power surged between his fingertips.

"Lord Eron," Sila asked, her voice trembling, "w-who was the other?"

"You did not recognize him?" Eron's eyes blazed and his nostrils flared. He turned his hand palm upward and the Sword of light shot up from it. He grabbed it with both hands and slammed it down and through the table, sending particles of wood and the candle flying through the air. The flaming sword disappeared and his shoulders slumped. On the floor, the candle sputtered but did not go out. Eron fell to his knees and bowed his head.

"He was Tocar, my brother."

36 The Mission

Eron took the candle in his hand and placed it on the floor beside the bed. He then started pacing. Sila watched with great concern. If the Otherworlder had worked harder to heal him, Eron may have been able to see the vision before Tocar was murdered. Tersan might have been able to send Parry more quickly and both might have escaped unscathed. Tocar would be alive now and Eron would not be suffering so. The whole situation was Jessie's fault.

"Tersan," Eron said as he made his fifth journey across the room, "I have to go. I can make it through Pintar Pass in less than a day."

"He's dead, Eron," the king replied. "You said so yourself. Going to Calshara will serve no purpose except to get you killed too."

"Tocar may be gone, but Parry is not." He stopped his pacing and looked at Tersan. "Parry is not much more than a child, Tersan. He is defenseless! There are wild things in the Paranjothis. They will smell the blood and…" He held the king's gaze evenly. "And they will attack. Parry is riding a horse that will not be able to outrun the danger, if he is able to stay on the animal."

"The Kilmari are good in such terrain," Tersan answered. "Send a unit."

"I know those mountains better than anyone! I must go."

"I cannot allow that," Tersan said. "We need you here."

"You need me. Ha." He sneered. "You need me. You know what you need, Tersan? You need to start acting like a king. Your army has been preparing for this war for months now, not days. You have been among them."

"What is your point?"

"You are depending on me to bolster their moral instead of doing that yourself, as is a king's duty. That's the only reason I'm here. For some reason, you think I will give them courage to fight."

"You do."

Eron shook his head. "Parry needs me. Kindly get out of my way."

"You will stay here, with my army," Tersan growled, "until we no longer need you."

"The Jelestines have a fool for a king," Eron replied. "You cannot keep me here."

Tersan sighed. "Very true, Eron. I cannot keep you here. All you need do is summon that damned sword and no man can stand against you. But think, man. If you leave in the middle of the night, you strike a blow to our army from which only the enemy will benefit. It will appear that you have deserted us."

Eron regarded him silently.

"There are already those who say you are weak, in need of protection yourself—"

"That is not true!"

"Agreed," Tersan continued. "But we cannot allow our enemies that image. We waited six months for you, the Sword of Itasha. If you desert us, I fear others may follow."

"I am not deserting you!"

"No. But appearances are everything."

Eron sank onto a chair, his shoulders slumped. "I hadn't thought of that," he said

"I know," Tersan offered gently. "I will send Rudlo for Parry."

"Rudlo knows the mountains," Eron agreed without looking up. "Elama knows them better."

"Then it is settled. Rudlo and Elama will go." Tersan walked over to Eron and placed a fatherly hand on his shoulder. "Do not worry. They will find him."

Eron nodded, still not looking up.

"Eron, I am sorry. I should not have let Tocar go. Marand's quarrel was with Jeleste, not Kimala."

"Tocar was a man of many talents," Eron almost whispered. He lowered his gaze again. "If there was any chance to establish a truce without bloodshed, Tocar could have done it. It is a cruel irony that he was murdered in an attempt to make a lasting peace."

Tersan turned to Sila. "I thank you for your assistance, Madame Healer. Come."

"Sila?" Eron said.

"Yes?" she answered, trying not to sound eager.

"Did you bring any of that heterra?" he asked. "I think I have need of something."

"Of course, my lord." She moved across the room to his side.

"Would you stay with me a while?" he asked her. "I may have need of your services again, should the visions return."

Tersan cleared his throat. "I will be leaving you, then. Eron, get some sleep. You will see in the morning that I was right."

"Of course," Eron replied.

There was a rustle of cloth behind them as the king exited. Sila reached into her bag and withdrew a small jar filled with blue gel. Slowly, she unwrapped the cloth that sealed it. Eron lay back on the bed, his eyes now flitting back and forth, not blinking. She dipped the cloth into the gel and reached over to work it into his brow. He snatched her hand, and pushed it away, sitting up at the side of the bed in one swift movement.

He smiled at her. "I thank you for the gift of your power, Madame Healer. I know it is a sacrifice to leave that behind, even if it is in the form of a bandage."

"It is a gift freely given," Sila said, pride swelling her head. "I do not intend to take it back."

Eron dipped his head solemnly. "Your gift will always be cherished."

Sila's heart skipped a beat. They were forever bound.

"Forgive me, I had to get rid of Tersan. He is a good king, but he tends to make spectacles of my power and we do not have time for spectacle. Will you help me?"

Sila swallowed. "I live to serve."

Eron reached for a pendant sitting on a still upright table and thrust it into her hands. "Find Elama and give her this. I have touched her mind and she has been schooled in how to use it."

"My lord?" she asked.

"Elama is going after Parry and this way I can go with her." He looked deep into her eyes, but did not intrude upon her mind. "My gift of vision is returning. I no longer need a crystal to focus, the elixir is enough. But I still require someone to be in possession of one of these crystals in order that I may communicate with them, someone whose mind I have touched."

"I will do as you ask, my lord. Now, let me give you the heterra--"

"That was a ruse, woman!" he nearly shouted. "Make haste and find Elama. Now!"

Sila recapped the heterra and tucked it back in her bag. She held the pendant in her hand and exited the room. Outside the doorway, Tersan had posted three guards. They nodded to her.

"I am to find a Kilmari woman named Elama," she said to them. "I have a message from Lord Eron."

"Elama is preparing to ride to Calshara, through the Paranjothi's," one of the guards told her. "She is in the stable area."

"Thank you." Sila said. She took two steps forward and then realized she had no idea where the horses were being kept. She turned back to the guards. "Could you show me the way?" she asked.

The three guards exchanged a look before the most senior spoke. "Madame Healer, we are assigned to watch over Lord Eron. He must not be allowed to wander the camp by himself."

Sila smiled as sweetly as she could and made her way back toward the inner chamber of the tent. "I have given him a sleeping drought," she said, raising her voice and hoping Eron would hear her. "He will go nowhere tonight."

She pushed the flap that served as a door open and beckoned them to look. Eron lay sprawled across the bed, one foot on the floor, one hand dangling off the side of the bed. As if on cue, he began to snore.

"You see," she said, "he will sleep until morning. Surely it does not require three men to watch over one who sleeps."

"No, no of course," the eldest said. "Geste, take her to the stables."

"Yes, sir."

"Many thanks," Sila said, bowing slightly.

The stables were not far. But they were far enough for Sila to make a decision. She took the pendant and hung it around her neck as she walked, her fingers never straying far from the crystal. Parry had been hurt. Parry was one of the few kinsmen Eron had left. If she tended him, she would grow in Eron's favor. She had touched Lord Eron's mind and she had been well schooled to handle any situation arising at Bel Haven. She was a healer of the First Order. Having been the last person to touch Eron's mind, she reasoned that she would be Parry's best hope of being found. She could do this.

In a makeshift courtyard, a tall woman was saddling a giant horse. She wore the black leather typical of the Kilmari. Beside her, a man was already astride a smaller horse, his face grim. Sila turned to her guide.

"Thank you, Geste," she said. "I can find my way from here."

Geste bowed to her and left. Sila approached the woman. "You are Elama?" she said.

The woman paused and stared at Sila. Apparently she did not recognize the healer. "I am," she finally answered, returning to cinch the saddle tight. "And you are?" she asked.

"Mistress Sila Atin from Bel Haven, healer, First Order under Master Penrose," Sila answered. "I have a message from Lord Eron."

"I know what I am to do, Madame Healer," Elama answered. "Tersan has told us."

"I am to come with you," Sila lied, "to tend the wounded."

"The path we take is dangerous and we must make haste," Elama said. "Are you skilled in the art of riding?"

"I will manage. Is there a suitable horse for me?"

One of the stable boys brought out a great yellow horse. He handed the lead rope to Sila with a shy smile. "He is a great horse," he told her. "He will serve you well."

The horse began to prance and snort and Sila threw the lead back to the child. "I said a suitable horse, boy!" she snapped. "Get me something I can ride!"

Elama looked around her now saddled horse, patting the animal calmly on the neck. "Hold," she told the boy. He stopped in his tracks. "Healer," she started, "we have great need of fast horses who are sure footed. The boy has brought you a suitable mount for this journey, in fact probably the best this stable has to offer. I suggest you tack him up and we will be on our way."

"'Tack him up'?" Sila replied.

"Yes. You know, saddle, bridle?"

"Let her ride mine," Rudlo said, dismounting. He walked the horse over to Sila and handed her the reins. "I will take this one."

"Rudlo, you do not understand," Elama said. "She will slow us down! We must ride swiftly if we are to save Parry."

"Lord Eron wishes her to accompany us," Rudlo said. "And she will."

"I cannot ride on that saddle," Sila said. "It is not made for a woman."

"It is simple," Elama said. "You put one leg on each side of the horse and then balance on its back."

"But I am not…" Sila searched for the correct words. "I will adapt."

Elama took one long critical look at her, then disappeared into the stable.

Rudlo motioned Sila to his own horse's side. "Here, darlin', let me help ye up." He offered her the stirrup and she stepped into it. The saddle pulled toward her and the horse skittered away. "No, do not put yer weight into the stirrup like that. Let me help ye." He offered her the stirrup again. This time she placed her foot into it and put her hands up on the saddle, pulling for all she was worth. Behind her, Rudlo placed one huge flat hand on her bottom and pushed. The action shocked her so much that she cried out in surprise, but she was on the horse. Rudlo was grinning.

"Thank you, sir," she said, glad that it was dark and he could not see the red in her cheeks.

"Lord Eron would be disappointed if he sent ye and ye were not able to come along," Rudlo told her.

"Lord Eron, Lord Eron," Elama muttered as she threw the saddle over the horse's back. "You would not be calling him 'lord' anything if you had seen him steal half a dozen pies that your mother placed on the windowsill to cool and ate them all, came in to eat lunch with blueberry stains all over his clothes and face and hands and then vomited for the next six hours." She lowered the stirrup over the cinch strap and grinned. "Ah, the wicked ways of wayward youths. There, Rudlo. You are tacked up. There is no more time for revelry. We ride."

Elama swung up onto her own horse and Rudlo gracefully mounted the still prancing yellow horse. With a shout, they were off at a gallop, Sila doing the best she could to keep up with them.

They were deep in the foothills of the Paranjothis before they stopped to give the horses a breather. All around the creatures of the night howled one last time before returning to their daytime lairs. Sila was certain that she would never walk normally again. Her legs were raw from rubbing against the soft leather saddle. When they stopped, she continued to sit on her horse.

"Get off, Healer," Elama told her. "Give the horse a break."

"I may not be able to get back on if I get off," she answered.

"Well, do it anyway," Elama said. "He needs to rest."

Sila got off the horse, instantly sorry that she had. There were blisters on her legs and they hurt so much that she could not walk straight. Elama was staring at her.

"Tell me you have some leggings on underneath that robe?" she said.

Sila shook her head. "You did not give me time to dress properly," she countered. "I am unaccustomed to riding a horse as though I was a man."

"Not done much ridin', have ye lass?" Rudlo asked. He was a gentle man even though he was unclean.

"No, not much," Sila admitted.

"Well, no matter. Have ye got any salve in that bag o yers for the blisters on yer legs?" he asked.

"Some," she answered.

"Then put it on," Elama said. "And be quick about it." She was searching through her own bags for something and pulled out a pair of silken breeches. "Put these on," she ordered, throwing them at Sila.

"Pajamas? For riding?" Sila asked.

"Silk. For keeping warm in the mountains." Elama sighed. "It will help."

"Um, thank you." Sila went behind a rock so that Rudlo could not see her and began dressing her wounds. She used almost the entire jar of hitter on her legs before she pulled the silk pants on. Elama offered her a skin of water and she drank some.

"We'll walk for a while," she said. "It will help get your circulation going again."

"I am ready to ride," Sila said.

"Perhaps, but your horse is not." Elama turned sharply and strode away.

The next hour was miserable. The path was filled with stones that the horses managed to miss, but Sila managed to trip over. Her stomach was growling now that the sun had risen and she lamented the fact that she had not eaten full rations with the rest of the healers the night before.

They reached a place where the path opened into a meadow graced by a mountain stream.

"Let the horses drink and fill your skins," Elama told her. "Then we ride."

Obediently, Sila let her horse drink. She had no skin to fill but she sated her own thirst. Elama handed her a small portion of jerky and dried fruit. She ate quickly then tried unsuccessfully to get back on her horse.

"Rudlo?" she said as sweetly as she could. He came over and once again helped her mount. The blisters were very uncomfortable, but she could tolerate it, as long as the mad gallop was over.

They rode nearly until noon, resting the horses every few hours. The way was steep and no army would be able to traverse the narrow path. Here the air was thin but the view exquisite. To the west, Kimala stood alone reaching skyward. The sun cast odd shadows across it, at this distance appearing as great black stripes across its surface. To the north, east and south, the smaller mountains in the Paranjothi range loomed at the end of a great plain.

"Calshara," Elama muttered. "I hope Parry's horse knows its way. The mountains are vast and we have only a slim chance of finding them."

"Aye, lass, but slim is better than none," Rudlo told them.

"I wonder if we should have taken the Lesser Stairs," Elama said. "The way is more difficult but it is lower."

"And there are more creatures there on the hunt. Ye cannot second guess yer choices," Rudlo answered. "We have no way of seeing which road to travel. We just have to take our best guess."

Sila fingered the pendant that she wore. She wondered if Eron had tried to reach her through it or if he could see what was happening. So far, she had heard nothing. She blushed when she thought about the salve she had put on her legs. A lady would not show such things to a gentleman. Elama noticed.

"What is it, Healer?" she asked.

"Lord Eron," she said, stumbling slightly on the words. "He said he would be able to see where we were going if we had this charm. But I have not heard from him."

Elama stared at the pendant. Her eyes narrowed. "Is it a crystal with a tiny sword embedded in its center and slightly to the right?" she asked.

"It is." Sila thought hard. She had to make this work. Reluctantly she removed the pendant and held it out to Elama. "I…I thought I would be able to see. I was in his mind tonight, helped him, and even placed some bandages in his mind to help him heal. He even said I helped him. I thought surely he would be able to communicate with me now that, that we were once one."

"What were your instructions?" Elama asked.

"To give you the crystal. But--"

"You fool!" Elama said, snatching away the pendant. "Unless you are blood kin, if he knows not who holds the crystal, he may not see! And he is not looking for you!" She pulled the pendant around her neck and instantly her eyes began to flit back and forth as Eron's had done. She sat stone still on the horse for what seemed an eternity before the spell was broken.

"Rudlo, we need to get to the Lesser Stairs as quickly as possible. You," she said to Sila, "you will answer to Lord Eron when we return. If we return. Try to keep up. We have no time to spare."

Elama gathered her reins in one hand and her horse rose on its hind legs, turning in midair. Then together they plunged down the mountain, leaving Sila to follow as best she could.

37 The Seneschal

The tired old horse tensed underneath him for what seemed the millionth time. Parry tightened his grip with his knees, wishing he were in front of Tocar instead of behind him with his hands bound around the lifeless body. He had managed to rid himself of the blindfold. Tocar was quite a bit taller and sitting up on the saddle gave his body still more height. Parry had to constantly shift just to maintain their combined balance. The scent of blood still fresh on the tunic rubbing against his face had nauseated him initially. Now, he was numb to it, though he knew that there were other creatures that were not.

The horse sidestepped to the right and Parry's body jerked. He remained mounted but something fell, hitting him in the back and landing on the horse's hindquarters and the horse jerked again. An animal roared and the horse reared and plunged, sending both riders to the rocky turf. Parry heard the distinct sound of a bone snapping and his vision turned white for a split second. His ankle was broken.

A second beast growled and he twisted his body toward the sound. The first was off to his right somewhere, chewing on something. He could not see what but he thought he knew. He had to free himself of Tocar. Working his arms, he slid down the dead man's legs, freeing himself of the body.

"I am sorry, Tocar," he said to the corpse. "You deserved better."

"Tocar is dead," someone answered in his head. *"Save yourself!"*

"Eron?"

"Yes, Parry. I am here."

"Help me! I am broken and nearly blind!"

"Understood. There is a stone behind you with a jagged edge. Reach up for it and try to sever the bond."

Parry turned around, his fingers searching the ground for the stone. He found it and began to scrape the leather thong that bound his hands against the pointed rock. After what seemed a very long time, the leather gave way and his hands were free. He fell back on the ground in short-lived relief.

There was a terrible silence as Parry waited. Beside him, Tocar's body was pulled away and the sound of growling was replaced by the sound of cloth ripping and something being chewed. Terrified, Parry pushed himself backward away from the sound, dragging his broken leg behind him.

"Eron? Eron are you there?" he whispered.

"I will not leave you. There are only two wolves," Eron replied, *"And they are...occupied. But the pack is coming."*

"Tocar!" he said, his gut twisting violently. "Eron, I--"

"Tocar is dead, Parry," Eron said firmly. *"His body serves you now. He would have it no other way."*

Parry swallowed and tried to clear his head.

"Listen carefully. There is a small outcropping of stone about twenty paces behind you. It looks like it is deep enough to hide a man inside and defensible. I can help you reach it."

Parry tried to stand. He took one step forward and his ankle refused to hold him. He collapsed onto the ground. He was not certain whether he cried on the way down but he was seeing bright light inside his head once more and he was vaguely aware that he was moaning.

"Move!" Eron commanded.

Sucking in a deep breath, Parry tried to move. He could hear the animals growling at one another, fighting over Tocar's body. Parry scrambled to his hands and knees. Keeping his injured ankle aloft, he crawled.

The way was rocky and uneven. He struggled to move forward, uncertain of where he was going, heading in a vague direction that Eron had mentioned. To his left, he thought he heard movement. A split second later, the beast was upon him.

They tumbled to the ground, the boy underneath, the beast on top growling triumphantly. Parry closed one hand on top of the other and swung at the sound with all his might, his hands meeting the beast's face. He felt a tooth dig into his arm, but his effort worked, at least for the moment. The beast was no longer on him.

"Eron!" he shouted.

"Hold still," came the answer.

The air around him came alive with energy and he stopped moving. He was relatively safe for the first time since leaving Il Chatel. He assessed his injuries; nearly blinded, broken ankle and now either bruised or broken ribs, bleeding from a gash in his arm. He was weakened from hunger and the constant drain of energy and he was cold even in the sunlight. Yet now he somehow felt a glimmer of hope. With effort, he managed to bind the wound on his arm with a combination of the leather that had once bound him and cloth ripped from an undergarment. He tied the knot with his free hand and his teeth.

"Eron?" he asked, lying back exhausted from his efforts.

"They will not bother you again. I am coming." The energy around him warmed the cold that had crept into his body. *"Sleep."*

Parry slept.

It was night when he woke. Something that had once been wet had dried on his face. When he moved, it cracked. He reached up to touch it, then remembered what it was: Tocar's blood. He tried to open his eyes, but both were swollen shut now. Beyond his lids he could see that there was a glow and he could feel the energy. Eron had said he should stay still. He shifted to his side, trying to get his injured limbs into more comfortable positions.

Voices. He heard voices. They were coming from his left, though whether it was uphill or down, north or south, he could not tell. They were angry, ready to fight. Parry squirmed. They would surely see him.

"I told ye!" a gruff male voice proclaimed. "There's a man inside that circle of fire."

"Well, I never…What's that around 'im?"

"Looks like swords, all pointy and glowing. Worth a lot of money, I'd wager."

"Wonder who left 'em here?"

"I reckon they probably belong to what's left of that fella."

Parry strained, trying to force his eyes open so he could see what he already knew they were talking about. The effort was fruitless.

"Probably put this fella inside that glowy fence there and started off for help. Old Chaptaw got 'im, I'd wager. Big mistake to leave on foot in these parts at night."

There was a moment of silence while they admired old Chaptaw's handiwork. Parry stifled a groan.

"Only pieces left of that fool."

He wanted to weep.

The voices were almost on him now. Parry curled into as tight a ball as he could and tried not to breathe. The air around him crackled.

"He don't look so tough," the first said. "He's got a set of them fancy boots, too. S'pose Marand'd give us a good price for 'im?"

"He ain't right." Footsteps shuffled closer to Parry and he cringed. "He's hurt. Too much trouble to take along."

"But he's got a nice pair o' boots!"

"And I bet there's a nice somethin' on that belt as well."

"Money?"

"Or jewels. And looky at that little bauble hangin' 'round 'is neck…"

Parry grabbed at his neck. The Seneschal crystal had become exposed. He quickly tucked it back underneath his shirt. The energy around him droned.

"Must be precious if he's goin' to that much trouble to protect it!"

Despair filled him. This was the end and he could not even stand and face death as a man. He only hoped it would come quickly. A hiss sounded over his head and he felt as though someone was above him straddling his body.

"Who're you?"

"I can be your worst nightmare," Eron answered. The whoosh of a blade sliced the air over him. It struck something solid.

"Ouch!"

"Lemme see yer hand."

Whatever the two were doing would remain a mystery to Parry. Eron laughed. His voice was muffled, as though it was very far away.

"I don't reckon I wanna die over this, Tick," the first man said.

Parry listened intently. Footsteps trod away from him and eventually died away. He let his body relax and released his knees.

"I will keep you safe," Eron told him. *"Sleep. Help is coming."*

Warmth filled his world again and he drifted to sleep.

The constant drone that had lulled him into sleeping dissipated around him, waking him instantly. He sat up, certain that this time would be the end. This time, he was ready.

"Parry?" someone called softly. He felt something cover his shoulders. "Parry, it is Elama. By the Lady, what have they done to you?"

Fingers gently probed his head, no doubt, he thought, looking for the wound that had caused so much blood. He tried to speak but the words choked in his throat. He felt the tip of a flask press gently against his battered lips. Cautiously, he drank.

"They killed Tocar," he managed, his voice trembling. "Fot tore…tore…"

"Eron told me about Tocar," Elama said, cutting him off before he had to relive the atrocity. "He sent us to find you. As luck would have it, we have a Healer with us. She will help you. This is Sila Atin."

Sila Atin touched him and he flinched. Where Elama's hands had been warm, hers were cold. She probed his face a second time, then his arm, his side and finally his ankle. Each time instinct demanded he shrink away, but he steeled himself to her touch.

"I am sorry," Sila Atin finally said, "I have used the last of the heterra on my saddle sores. It was necessary, else I could not have found you. Unfortunately, I left the encampment in rather a hurry and I therefore have nothing to offer you for comfort."

The ground beneath Parry throbbed with a single horse's hoof beats. They pounded the rocky terrain drawing closer to them. Elama was gently removing the dressing from his arm while Sila Atin wrenched his ankle. The healer let it drop on the ground, sending a bolt of pain through his head. He thought he heard men's voices quietly speaking to one another but through the fog the pain caused, the sound could just as easily have been the wind.

"You can splint his ankle, can you not?" Elama asked.

"I do not have the proper equipment. When we reach the encampment, I will be able to do that and more."

The hoof beats ceased and Parry heard boots softly touch the turf. A new person was beside him, warm and quiet. He felt the hair being brushed gently away from his brow. "I did not send her."

"Eron?" Parry said. Someone picked up his broken ankle again and pushed on it. He cried out in pain.

"Move away from my kinsman, Madam Healer," Eron growled.

"But I--" Sila Atin protested.

"I said move away!" Eron spat.

In front of him, Parry felt the air move. There was a rustling of cloth and a thud as someone landed on the ground.

"Sila Atin, you disobeyed a direct order which caused delay in the treatment of my kinsman--"

"But--"

"--and the loss of my brother's chance for burial befitting his rank."

"But I--"

"And when you are given a chance to partially redeem yourself, you offer nothing!"

"But--"

"Get out of my sight!"

Warm hands took him by the shoulder and pulled him into an embrace. He wanted to weep, but exhaustion forbade it. A gentle hand pulled his head into a warm body and held it close, not so that he would smother, but so that he would no longer fear. He realized that he was trembling. Fear, pain, anger and loss all finally caught up with him. Beneath lids that would not open, his eyes grew warm with tears. He was being rocked gently now, as a mother would hold a precious child. Tension melted away. He would live another day.

Eron entered his mind.

"I will help you sleep," he said, "and fill your mind with pleasant dreams or none at all."

"Eron..."

"When you awaken, you will be among friends."

Parry allowed himself the smallest of smiles. The ordeal was nearly at an end. He dug his fingers into Eron's cloak, making certain this man was not imagined. Too long he had been alone, fighting to stay alive.

"Sleep."

"Not yet, Eron. Please, not yet."

"Understood." Eron was gone from his mind.

A humming sound filled his head and he grew dizzy. He became vaguely aware that his arm was being re-dressed. His boot was being cut away from his foot and his ankle immobilized. The pain spiked again, but this time he knew it would be short lived. He waited for it to settle back to a dull throb.

"My Lord, let me help," Sila Atin said from some distant place. "Let him ride before me."

Parry stiffened. The thought of those cold hands on touching him caused him to shiver. He tried to fight his way up out of the fog to protest. He need not have bothered.

"Do not presume that since you helped me to distinguish vision from dream that you are anything more than what you are, madam," Eron answered.

"But my Lord--" Sila Atin protested, her voice stung by the obvious omission of her title.

"Elama," Eron said coldly, "see that she stays out of my sight."

Parry felt himself being lifted onto a horse. He was sitting in the saddle this time. Someone swung up behind him. Sleep was almost on him. He felt Eron once again in his mind.

"Sleep," Eron said.

This time, Parry slept.

38 Broken Promise

Tersan scowled at the hole burned in the back of his tent. The ruined cloth came away as ash between his fingers. Rays from the morning sun slipped in through the hole, cheering the dark space that Eron had of late occupied.

"How?" he growled.

"Sire, we had no idea," one of the sentinels said. "My men were posted on both front and back. He must have bewitched the watchmen."

"Bewitched indeed," Tersan grumbled. "It appears that the Sword is not as weak as he allowed me to believe."

"Sire?"

"He wields the Sword of Light and it appears he can still touch a mind without being noticed. Damn him." He gave the sentinel his full attention. "That healer must be complicit." Tersan strode toward the true exit. Without pausing, he barked orders. "Bring Sila Atin to me."

"She is missing, Sire."

Tersan stopped. "What?"

"She is missing, Sire," the sentinel repeated. "Madame Aramat came to us this morning. Sila Atin did not return to the healer's wagon after seeing Lord Eron the night before last." He looked straight ahead. "We have been searching for her."

"Look for her among Eron's people," Tersan growled. "He may have sent her somewhere. Or the fool may have left on her own. Either way, find her!"

The guard gave him a curt nod and left.

The cheery sunlight that had been pouring in the hole in the tent dimmed. Tersan followed the guard outside and looked skyward. Dark clouds passed over the sun and the scent of rain was in the air. Marching in it would take a toll on everything. Marching in mud would be worse.

"Break camp now!" he ordered. "And get me my horse!"

Half an hour later, with darkened skies, they were on the move again. Eron's absence did not go unnoticed, but no one dared talk to Tersan about it. The king rode alone in front of the combined armies with no one for company.

They marched into the foothills of the Paranjothis before the rain halted their progress. Setting up camp took longer than usual and Tersan yelled at anyone who came near him. When his tent was finally erected, he sequestered himself inside of it and poured over his war plans.

"Sire?" a small voice called into the tent. The voice belonged to a young boy dressed in the black leather livery of Eron's army.

"What is it, boy?" he grumbled, looking back down at his maps.

"I saw Madame Healer two nights ago. I offered her my best horse, but she would not take him. She took Master Rudlo's horse and then left with Lady Elama and Master Rudlo to find Master Parry."

Tersan looked up from his maps. He sat back, regarding the boy cautiously. "She did, did she?"

"Yes, sire. And she was not very nice."

Tersan tried unsuccessfully to keep himself from smiling. A guard burst into the tent. "Riders approaching, sire," he said, "from the north and also from the south."

"We shall have some answers soon, it appears." He rose. "Thank you, son," he said.

The boy bowed and left the tent.

"Who approaches?" he asked.

"They bear the standard of Lady Jessie from the south."

Tersan nodded. "And from the north?"

"Three riders and a horse, Sire, moving slowly; nothing more."

"Show Lady Jessie here when she arrives. Send an escort to meet the others. Perhaps it is good news."

"Yes, sire."

Tersan went back to reviewing his war plans. Nothing had changed. Satisfied that nothing would change, he had Garrett store the plans. Rain hammered the top of the tent and he wondered how his troops were bearing up under the weather. They were soldiers, though, he mused. He had been a soldier once himself. They would survive.

Jessie swept into the room, her long hair slick against her clothing. Lightning flashed outside the tent and thunder almost instantly rumbled behind her. Jessie removed her dripping cloak and handed it to Garrett.

"Thank you," she said to the page. "Where's Eron?" she asked.

"Lady Jessie," Tersan said, somewhat annoyed, "please be seated."

"Please, Tersan, let's not get lost in amenities," she answered. She was trembling and her lips were blue with cold.

"You have been riding long?" he said, waving her to take a seat.

"Since morning," she answered. "The rain is cold. Where's Eron?"

Tersan cleared his throat. "Lord Eron is no longer my charge," he answered. "Not that I did not take precaution to protect him," he added quickly. He pointed to the scorched cloth that hung to his right. "Apparently, he is making excellent progress toward becoming whole. No one saw him leave."

She wandered over to the damaged portion of the tent and took it in her hand. A smile tugged at her lips. "What happened?" Jessie asked.

"To my tent? I have no idea. No one has any idea. No one saw him leave."

Jessie turned to him; she was smiling. "I will have it mended for you," she said.

"My people have long been masters at weaving, thank you," he snapped.

"Suit yourself."

Tersan ducked his head. "Your pardon, Jessie. I meant no offense."

She was grinning now. "Eron can be a very trying man."

"He can indeed." Tersan sighed. "Jessie, he had another vision. Please, sit."

"A vision?" she repeated, the smile disappearing.

Tersan nodded. "I sent for Aramat per Eron's request. She sent Sila Atin."

"Sila is a gifted reader. But she would not have been my choice. There is too much drama in that woman."

Tersan raised an eyebrow. "Garrett, bring Lady Jessie something warm to drink and something dry to wear,'" he ordered. The page nodded and left. They were alone. "He saw Tocar murdered," Tersan said quietly. Jessie paled.

"No! Are you certain?"

"Fot killed him. Sila confirmed the vision. Eron's kinsman, Parry, witnessed the murder." Tersan stopped short of going in to gruesome details.

"Oh no." She sank into a chair.

"Marand had Parry beaten--"

"He's no older than Lucy!" She looked away from him, now staring out the hole Eron had created.

Tersan gave her time to assimilate the information. Garrett returned with a mug of something steaming. He tried to hand it to her, but she was staring straight ahead and seeing nothing. "Set it on the table, Garrett," Tersan said. The page set the mug on the table and bowed. "A blanket, please," Tersan reminded him.

Jessie's hand fell to the pendant she wore and she gripped it tightly. She closed her eyes and her brow knitted in concentration. Beneath the lids, her eyes were moving back and forth rapidly as though she was searching for something. Tersan was eerily reminded of Eron, though Eron looked with his eyes open. Finally, she shook her head and returned her attention to him. "I still can't see any of them," she said softly. "That ability was always channeled through Eron, though," she explained further. "I never could do it on my own."

"It does not matter," Tersan told her.

She nodded. "Tell me the rest," she said.

Tersan took a deep breath. "Marand put Parry and Tocar's corpse on an old horse and sent them back to us through the mountains. The way is filled with dangers enough for whole men. Eron wanted to go, but I would not let him. Like you reminded me, I did promise Penrose that I would keep him with me, under my protection. So I sent Rudlo instead."

"A good choice. He knows the mountains," Jessie agreed.

"Eron did not seem to think it was good enough. He wanted Elama to go also."

Jessie smiled. "She's a good choice, too, and for more reasons than one. She was once his seneschal. If she had his crystal, he could probably speak to her, if his power is returning. Did he send his crystal with her?"

"Well, that would clear a few things up. He was not wearing it yesterday during the march." He looked at her closely. "Does he always look at two things at one time?"

"He's seeing two different places at once?" she said, her face lighting up.

"I suppose."

She gave a short laugh. "It's rather unnerving, isn't it?"

"Yes."

The cloud darkened her face again. "Tell me more," she said, reaching for the beverage.

"Yesterday, he told me he could see Parry, but not Elama. Something was wrong but he would not tell me what it was, in fact, he was silent most of the day. He kept watching all the time watching. It was eerie. I should have known things were changing."

Jessie held the mug between her hands, warming them.

"The only thing he would tell me was that he had sent something to Elama so that he could guide her to Parry."

"Parry is now Eron's seneschal. He carries one of the crystals." She took a sip from the mug before setting it back down on the table. "If he was seeing Parry, he should have been able to see Elama as well."

"Things are becoming clearer," Tersan said. He frowned. "The stable boy said Sila Atin had gone with them to find Parry, but he did not mention the crystal." Tersan offered Jessie a smile. "Eron does not like her, you know."

"Whether he likes her or not is not an issue," she replied. "The woman has never had any common sense and now she's proven she cannot be trusted."

"That is a bold accusation, madam."

"Sila kept the crystal," Jessie replied. "If Eron could see Parry and speak to him, then he should have been able to do the same with Elama. Sila allowed them to take the wrong path, didn't she?"

Tersan shook his head. "I do not know--"

"So Eron had to leave."

The page returned with a blanket and handed it to Jessie. She pulled it tightly around herself. "Thank you," she said with a smile.

"Why can he not see you?"

"For the same reason he could not see Sila. We are not his kinsmen. However, I am certain that will change."

"There is a group of riders approaching from the north," Tersan said. "I am hopeful that it is them. They should be here shortly. Please, sit and warm yourself."

Hoof beats sounded just outside the tent's entrance. Tersan turned in time to mark Eron's entrance. The Kilmari's face was dark as he moved into the tent bearing precious cargo. He held a body close to his own, wrapped in the Sword's black cloak. Whoever it was did not struggle. Tersan held open a tent flap that separated the war room from his own bed and without a word, Eron passed into the inner chamber. Jessie followed.

"Get Aramat," Tersan called out before entering the bedchamber.

Eron pulled the cape off, letting it fall haplessly to the floor. Then, as if placing a babe on a mattress, Eron lowered his burden to Tersan's bed. Jessie gasped when she saw the beaten face.

"He will be all right, Jessie," Eron assured her, pulling a blanket over his charge. "Time will return the face we know." He pushed the hair away from the swollen brow. "But I do not know what toll this has taken on his mind." He took Parry's head between his hands and leaned over him, kissing him gently on his forehead.

"I have sent for a healer," Tersan said.

"One who knows how to treat injuries, I hope," Eron growled. He looked away from Parry, his eyes black.

"What happened?" Tersan asked.

"Sila Atin has proven her worth. It is not much."

"She is with you?" Tersan said. "Thank the Lady! She was missing."

"She is still missing," Eron growled. He raised an eyebrow. "She lost herself in the mountains."

"Why did you not send someone after her?" Tersan said.

"Because it is my belief that she did not wish to return with us," Eron said simply.

"But Eron!" Jessie exclaimed.

"We traveled quickly but not so fast that a novice like her could not keep up. As proof, I offer the old horse that carried them out of Il Chatel. That animal would not have been able to keep up had we come at a fast pace and before you ask, it brought them out of Il Chatel far enough that Parry could be saved. It was wrong to leave it to the wolves. But Sila, Sila deliberately chose a path away from ours."

"You rescued the horse from the wolves and left the healer behind?" Tersan asked.

"She chose her path," he repeated.

39 Healer's Worth

Sila let the horse wander. Every time it headed in the direction of Tersan's encampment, she steered it in another direction. She had embarrassed herself, brought shame to her profession and disgraced her family. Better to die here, in the wilderness, than to go back and face the consequences of her actions.

The mountain was unforgiving. A constant wind blew out of the north bringing with it cold rain. Sila rather welcomed it, praying it would bring her infirmities and illness. The end would come more quickly that way than if she starved to death. Eron would realize he had made a mistake, that he should not leave a woman of her worth out here in the mountains alone to die. When he came, Sila wanted to be certain that she was already dead; then he would surely grieve.

The horse nibbled at some grass here and there. It became nervous for some reason and kept trying to turn around and run back toward the camp. She pulled back on the reins of the frightened animal, trying to make it stop prancing. The action was aggravating her blisters. She had lied to Eron. There was a bit of heterra left. Why she was hording it now seemed funny and she laughed. The horse shied at her guffaw and she tried again unsuccessfully to still it.

Then Sila heard the large animals growling. They would doubtless be upon them in moments to end her miserable existence. She pulled at the horse's reins, trying to command it to stand and wait, to join her in demise. The horse ignored her. It reared and plunged, arched its back and bucked, coming down hard until it dislodged its rider. Sila landed on the wet ground with a thud and the horse thundered away.

It was just as well, she reasoned. There was no sense in sacrificing the horse for her sins. She stood, her arms out from her sides and waited for the end to come. Eron would find a piece of her, perhaps her lifeless hand and howl in despair that he had lost such a treasure. He would take her limb back to Bel Haven with reverence and speak with wisdom at her funeral. He would break down in the middle of her eulogy and need to be supported as he was led away from the podium and Penrose would fight tears and finish Eron's words for him. Then her hand would be placed in the center of an open wagon draped with flowers and escorted to Kimala, the procession extending from dawn to dusk. A funeral pyre would be built and Eron, who would have regained his composure, would light it. Holding that thought, she closed her eyes and waited for death.

And waited.

The growls became whispers somewhere far away and then simply faded into nothingness. Sila sighed and lowered her arms. If the Lady would not grant her a swift death from the beasts of the mountain, she would accept the slower death from exposure. Still, there was no point in suffering until death came. She took out the heterra and slathered the remainder over her blisters. The relief she received from the lotion was not complete but it was instant. More comfortable now, she resumed her position, closed her eyes and waited for death.

"Well, well, what 'ave we 'ere?"

A dozen armed men on horseback encircled her. She looked up at their leader, a gruff looking man with grizzled hair and an unkempt beard who was probably younger than he appeared. He smiled at her and in the last light of day Sila could see that he had no front teeth. He probably smelled bad, too.

"I am Mistress Sila Atin, from Bel Haven at Jeleste, healer, First Order under Master Penrose."

"Fancy title fer someone out 'ere in the middle of nowhere, ain't it boys?" They laughed and Sila tried very hard not to look frightened. After all, death by their hand was just as good as by anyone else's.

"She's a fine piece of woman," a huge toothless man said. "I know what to do with a woman. Give 'er to me." He started to dismount.

"I saw 'er first," a second man said. "I claim 'er."

A general argument broke out among them and Sila shivered. The riders were leering at her and she felt fear re-ignite. This was not the quiet end she had envisioned. She took a step backward, away from them and searched for an escape.

"Boys," the leader said, "we won't never get what we all deserve from this one. She may be pretty now, but she's fragile. She'll be broken by the third man."

"Then how'll we split the goods?" the huge man said.

Sila's heart pounded. These men had no respect for her or her office? All she was to them was a common stable wench to be used for their pleasure? Was that her only worth? Surely they could see that she was, indeed, a woman who should be respected.

The leader took a moment to think. "Woman with a fancy title like that might be worth some money to someone. Il Chatel'd be the place to find 'er worth."

"Il Chatel?" Sila said. She had heard of the City of Gold. Marand lived there, but surely he was with his army, lying in wait for Tersan. "I serve Penrose of Bel Haven and his allies. You will return me to him," she demanded. She could die later.

The leader brought his horse forward, slowly riding around her. She could feel his eyes evaluating every inch of her body as he completed the circle. He dismounted and came close enough to confirm her evaluation that he did, indeed, smell bad. She did not look him in the eyes, rather held her head up in the air. This man was clearly below her station. He had no right to address her in such a manner. It was time for him to follow her orders.

"You will--"

A smart slap across her face stopped her demand and she cried out in surprise and pain. Her cheek burned where his fingers landed and she rubbed the skin with one hand while staring at him.

"That's better," he said. "A woman should know when to keep 'er tongue."

"Ye could cut it out for 'er," someone in the pack said.

Sila shivered. He took hold of her chin and stared into her eyes, not allowing her to turn aside. He turned her head slightly. The scarf fell away from her face exposing her scar.

"Aw, boys, she's damaged," he said, scrutinizing the burn mark on her face. He stared at it a long time, his eyes knitting in concentration as though weighing his options. "It ain't too bad. Shouldn't cost us much."

Sila waited. In spite of the cold rain, she was sweating. She found herself thinking the scar was not really that disfiguring. It had faded quite a bit since spring. Penrose had told her as much. The man tilted her head back and forth, looking up and down her neck. When his eyes returned to hers, she did not feel more comfortable.

"Ye ain't makin' up that fancy title are ye?" he breathed into her face. "I 'ave a reputation to maintain, ye know."

"I am Mistress Sila Atin, from Bel Haven, healer, First Order under Master Penrose," she repeated, this time a bit more hesitantly. "A-and I am reader to Lord Eron, the Sword," she added.

"A reader, are ye?" The man raised an eyebrow and Sila thought she saw a glimmer of cold amusement in his eyes.

"Healers of the First Order are all readers," she explained, "but only one is reader for the Sword, Lord Eron," she lied.

The leader raised an eyebrow. "That would raise yer worth, woman, if it be true."

"It is true," she said, regaining some of her composure. He let her face go and she rubbed it where he had held her chin. "And I expect he will be here shortly to collect me."

A ripple of laughter went through the small group and Sila shifted uncomfortably.

The leader took Sila roughly with one hand and jerked her toward him. He held her head steady and forced his wet rough lips over hers while his tongue violated her mouth. He tasted of rotten meat and cheap whiskey and she tried to back away but he held her tight, forcing her to wait until he was ready to release her. When he did, she fell back, crumbling to the ground. Tears filled her eyes and she ran a hand over her now violated lips, all the while trying not to retch.

"Sweet, this one is." A chorus of cheers went up from the group. "Even if she's lying, we can sell a pretty thing like 'er, with that slight damage, at the market in Il Chatel and with the money, we can all have a good time!"

They began talking amongst themselves and the leader brought his horse straight to Sila. She shied away from him, very afraid.

"Here, Mistress Sila Atin from Bel Haven, healer of the First Order, reader to Eron," he said, throwing a skin filled with something soft but solid. "Ye walk like ye ain't never sat a horse for any distance. Got blisters?"

Sila nodded.

"That's calla butter. Use it. We got a long way to ride and I want ye in prime condition when we get there."

Sila squeezed some of the thick goo out onto her hand. She leaned over and sniffed it. The cream had no discernable aroma.

"Ye don't eat it, woman! Ye put it on the blisters." He narrowed his eyes. "Ye certain yer a healer?"

"First Order," she breathed. She looked around for a place where she could put the salve on in private. She made her way toward a bush where she would be hidden from view.

"Now see here, Healer," the leader told her, "ye can't hide from me."

"I am not attempting to hide," she said from behind the boulder, "I am merely maintaining my dignity as is fitting to a woman of my stature. Have you no chivalry?"

He laughed. "I ain't Lord Eron, woman. Suer Mantick is my name. They call me Tick."

Even though she was behind the rock, Sila turned her back to him as she raised her skirt. Very cautiously, she dabbed a bit of the salve onto one blister. It burned at first, then cooled and the pain evaporated. Steeling herself for the initial sting, she slathered it on the rest of the blisters. The ointment did its work. Amazed, she moved from behind the rock and handed Tick the unused portion.

"You must tell me what that is," she said.

"I done told ye it's calla butter," he snorted. He grinned at her and her blood ran cold. "Now, woman," he began, "you can ride with the man of your choosin'." He mounted and reached a hand down to her. "Who'll it be?"

"You," she mumbled at once. Death did not seem so fine an option now. She took his hand.

Tick hauled her up and sat her behind him on the horse. "Hold on, Mistress Sila."

Sila clung to him in spite of the smell.

Rain fell more steadily now. She did not care where they were going. She buried her head in his back and imagined he was Eron rescuing her, though she knew it was a child's dream. But Eron would come. She knew he would. He had thanked her for returning him to power. He recognized her as a healer of the First Order and a credit to her profession.

The night seemed endless. This horse was more pleasant to ride than her former mount. He was much wider, so it was easier to sit and his gait was smooth. Eron had a horse such as this. Eron would come for her. He would not let a woman of her worth be lost.

Eron needed her. Without her to confirm his vision, Parry would certainly have perished. There would have been no party sent to find him and he would have fallen prey to those creatures that supped on Tocar's corpse. Had she not also sacrificed her own power to help mend Eron's wounded mind, power that would take her years to replace? Afterward, was he not able to summon the Sword of Light?

Tersan's army still needed her. She had been among the select healers to leave Bel Haven and travel with Tersan's army. The healers were but a handful among many and they would doubtless have many charges before this war was over. They could not afford to lose even one of their number, especially one as gifted as Sila. That was why the healers rode in the center of the army, she rationalized, and why she, herself, rode in the center of the center wagon; Tersan's army protected its most prized possession.

The way to Il Chatel was long. Five hours they rode without much of a break except to rest the horses. Even men such as these knew the stupidity of not taking the time to keep their mounts fresh. Sila stayed close to Tick. She knew she would be safe there. Only money would sate this one and she intended to see that he got it. She had worth. Marand would pay for her. Marand; not some small uppity northern tribesman with too many wives and so many children that he could not name them all. The cold night was getting warmer. Sila no longer wanted to die.

Marand had stood by and watched as the demon had beheaded Tocar. He had ordered Parry to be beaten in the cruelest way, then ordered the boy to be tied behind his dead kinsman and set adrift on a very old horse. He had laughed at the thought of Eron finding them both. She shivered at the thought of it. Still, Marand was royal. He would know how to treat a woman of stature, a woman of worth. The horse stopped and she raised her head from her captor's back.

"Look, woman," Tick said.

Il Chatel, city of the golden light, shown brilliantly on the plain in front of them. Behind them, she heard the others discussing her as Eron's reader and as a healer of the First Order. They talked about their coming bounty, how much money they would enjoy when she was sold. Yes, she was a woman of great worth. Tick twisted in front of her, his burly arm around her waist and eased her to the ground. Everyone was on foot for one last stretch before entering Il Chatel. Sila took their leader to one side.

"I have more worth than you know," she told him. "Watch." With her hands out of sight of the throng of thugs, she wove a tiny shield. Tick's eyes grew large and his mouth fell open. She laughed and held the shield in her right hand, blowing gently on it so that it slammed into her left and she could recoup the power. "Marand will pay handsomely for me. See that I fall into no other's hands."

The man nodded. "Keep that to yourself, witch," he said.

Sila smiled; witch and healer. The Otherworlder could not make the same claim. Tick grabbed her by the hair this time and pulled her head back. Sila gasped but she did not have time to think much as her mouth was violated a second time. She tried to cry out, but he stifled her. He finally released her and laughed evilly.

"Too bad I can't give ye more than that, Healer," he said. "And I so want to." He leaned in toward her once more and she smelled his putrid breath but this time, he only brushed his nose against hers. He let go of her hair.

"Lord Eron will kill you if you harm me," she said risking defiance.

He laughed. "Ye have worth, Healer, aye, that's sure. But if ye were truly reader to the Sword, he would have caught us by now."

"But I am his reader!"

"Sorry, woman, but yer not." He leaned in close to her. "I don't blame ye for makin' up the story, tryin' to save yerself and all. The Sword protects his own, ye know. If what ye claim was true, me an' my band of men would be dead now."

"But--"

He put a finger on her lips. "There's a time to talk and there's a time for silence, Healer. If ye can't learn t' hold yer tongue, I'd be mor'n happy t' teach ye."

Sila slowly nodded. Her eyes were filling with tears, though she did not know why.

"There's a good girl. Now, let's get to the ride. Two hours and we'll be in the City of Gold."

He mounted his horse and held a hand down to her. Once again, she settled in behind him. This time, she did not place her head against him and pretend he was Eron. This crude man's words repeated themselves to her and slowly her mind saw the facts clearly.

Eron had dismissed her. He had summoned her to help him through a difficult time and he had not properly thanked her. She had carried the crystal into the mountains in an effort to save his kinsman. He had not used it to speak to her even though they had shared an intimate moment in his mind. He had not tried hard enough, she was certain of it. She could have shown him the way, perhaps have saved Parry from suffering further, gotten him back to camp more quickly. But no; instead he had chosen not to speak with her and the young man was subjected to more pain. This could have been avoided if Eron had only spoken to her.

And then he deserted her. He left her there in the mountains, alone and vulnerable, without food or water. True, she had not attempted to rejoin them, had allowed them to travel so far ahead of her that they were no longer in sight. Eron should have come back for her.

And now, on this, her first solo excursion away from Bel Haven, she was to be sold at market, a bauble, nothing more than a common possession. Mistress Sila Atin, from Bel Haven, healer, First Order under Master Penrose had been reduced to a possession. Where was Eron? Why had he not come?

Eron did not deserve the loyalty of a woman of her worth. Eron deserved her wrath. And she was being delivered into the hands of the man who could best help her see that Eron got what he deserved. She would become Calsharan, friend of demonkind and enemy of the Jelestines and the Kilmari. For their great army, she would set up a hospital to treat their wounds. She kept telling herself that, over and over again. Marand stood in the doorway, commanding Fot to torture… The memory haunted her and she cursed Eron for showing it to her.

Sila sat quietly behind her captor as they passed through the golden gates of Il Chatel. Eron, Tersan, even Penrose had deserted her. Now that the long ride was at an end, she prayed to the Lady for deliverance. Surely, Mistress Sila Atin from Bel Haven, healer, First Order under Master Penrose should be heard by the Goddess above all others now, in her time of most desperate need. Surely. Tick pulled his horse to a stop and pointed.

"Il Chatel Palace," he said over his shoulder.

She raised her head off of his back and looked in the direction he was pointing.

The city was built such that a single road led directly to the great palace perched on a distant hill. Even though it was near dawn, the palace was lit with thousands of lights. It glowed like a jewel against the night sky, a beacon of unfathomable wealth. Sila felt her heart leap. She did, indeed, belong in a palace as grand as that.

The band of thieves stopped in front of a shabby building and dismounted, then headed for the entry. Tick stopped too, but did not get off the horse.

"Goin' ter see the Princess, Tick?" one of the men shouted.

Tick turned the horse around and faced the man. "As a matter o' fact, I am."

"Yer wastin' yer time. Come 'ave a brew!"

"Princess'll tell us what she's worth," Tick answered. "We want a fair price, don't we?"

"Go on, then," Tick's man told him. A fat woman wearing a torn, dirty dress exploded from the building and jumped at the man and he caught her, landing a kiss on her lips. She slipped out of his arms and they walked into the dingy building together. He slapped her on the buttocks and Sila looked away disgusted.

"Be gentle with 'im, Angel!" he called after them. He turned the horse away from the road to the palace down a lonely dark street.

"Where are we going?" Sila demanded. "The palace is not this way!"

"Silence, wench," Tic told her.

"But--"

Tick turned in the saddle so quickly that Sila did not see his hand coming. He was gripping her firmly by the chin again. "I said 'silence'." He held her there, increasing the pressure until she squirmed. He let her go. "Ye'll bring more if ye ain't damaged, but don't think I won't hurt ye, wench."

Sila recoiled. Silence was in order.

Their way wandered lazily through the sleeping city. The only sounds were their horse's hooves on the spare cobblestones and an occasional squeak that Sila did not attempt to identify. The way darkened and the buildings grew closer and closer together. It seemed they were taller as well, disappearing into the darkness of the cloud covered night. Mist dampened Sila's face and she unwillingly buried her head into Tick's back to try to get some measure of warmth. Without warning, she began to cry.

The horse shied and she slipped to one side.

"Help!" she cried.

Hands pawed at her clothing, pulling her to one side and off the horse.

"Get away!" Tick said, kicking at the boys who were accosting her. He bounded off the horse and drew his sword. He slapped the broad side of it against the tallest of them and the young man winced. When the rest saw the sword, they backed off. Tick neatly grasped her arm and pulled her back toward him. "You're not hurt, are ye?" he asked.

"N-no."

"Good," he said, sheathing his sword. "Can't have my prize damaged."

"What ye got there, Tick?"

Sila snapped her head around to see who was talking. A rotund woman, her ample bosom barely contained by a low-cut dress was smiling at her. Several of her teeth were missing and she bore a smile that made the cold night seem warm in comparison.

"Nothin' fer ye, Princess," Tick answered, "least wise not 'til Marand's turned her down."

"Then why did ye make this little side journey?" Princess asked.

Tick flipped a coin to her. "Fer yer expert opinion, love." Princess caught the coin and tucked it between her breasts without taking her eyes off of him. Tick smiled. "Stand clear o' me, healer," he told Sila. "Show the princess what ye got."

Sila hesitated. "But those boys will come back!" she protested.

"Robby?" Princess said. "Naw, he's a bit o' a coward, that one. He'll not be botherin' ye again. Now stand tall, missy, so's I can have a better look at ye."

Sila stood on somewhat shaky legs in front of Princess. Princess held a torch in her hand. She moved forward slowly, holding the fire slightly ahead of her so that Sila could feel its warmth on her skin. The glow blinded her as it passed close to her face and she fought the urge to look away. Above her and behind Princess, she could hear whispers and nervous laughter.

"Hush, women," Princess said as she circled the healer "I've got work to do."

She stood in front of Sila now. She smiled a toothless grin at Tick.

"She's flawed, this one is," she said. "Got a nasty mark on her face."

"I noticed that right off," Tick said. "Tell me something I don't already know."

Princess made her way behind Sila once more. Sila kept her head high, her lips tightly shut. Without warning, she was hit on her backside. She jumped and whirled to face a grinning Princess.

"What do you think you are doing?" she demanded.

"She's angry," Princess said, still looking at Sila as though she were a side of beef instead of a woman of breeding. "'Course some men like that."

"I beg your pardon?"

"Uppity, ain't she?"

"Yep. Must be that title she's totin'," Tick said.

"Title, you say?"

"Yeah. Tell the Princess who ye are, woman."

Sila shifted her attention to Tick, her face hot with fury. "I cannot see what telling this woman my name or my title will accomplish."

Tick took a step in toward her. He gripped her upper arm in his hand, squeezing so tightly that she whimpered. He leaned in close to her ear and whispered. "Ye'll tell her because I told ye to and ye'll need no other reason. Understand?"

Sila nodded. "S-Sila Atin," she mumbled. Then she straightened, ignoring his grip on her arm. She cleared her throat. "Mistress Sila Atin from Bel Haven, healer, First Order under Master Penrose."

Princess raised an eyebrow. "A healer are ye? Impressive."

"Impressive except that she doesn't know about a simple balm like calla butter."

"Now why would ye tell me that? Yer loosin' yer touch, Tick." Princess grinned at him slyly. "I'll bet she ain't never had a man."

"Virgins bring a fair price for the first time," Tick mused.

"She's a bit on the old side to be barterin' that point, Tick."

"How dare you!" Sila said.

"Yep." Princess' eyes narrowed as she shifted her attention back to Tick. "If she's frigid, she ain't worth as much, title or no."

"Well, I never--"

"I'd need to see the rest before I can truly make you an offer."

Sila's eyes grew wide for a moment before she closed them. Her heart thumped in her chest. She had seen Penrose barter for herbs at the market in Chelsea. It always started this way.

"You ain't gonna see any more'n ye already have, love," Tick told her with a laugh. He mounted, then reached down and took Sila by the arm, swinging her up on to the horse behind him once more. "Thanks for the opinion, Princess. She's got worth. That's all I wanted to know."

He put his heels into the horse and they started forward.

"If ye change yer mind, lad..." Princess called after them.

Tick said nothing but Sila knew she would see Princess again if she would not bring a higher price elsewhere. She leaned her head into Tick's back once again, grateful that she did not have to show Princess any more than Princess had already seen.

40 At the Crossroad

A deep rumble of thunder wakened Jessie from a restless sleep. Without looking, she reached over to where Eron should have been lying, expecting to find him safe beside her. Instead, the bed was empty, the blankets still warm. The veil of sleep pulled all the way aside and she rose on an elbow, his name formed on her lips. Before she could speak it, lightning flashed and in the moment of brightness, she saw him sitting on the edge of Parry's bed, holding his kinsman's hand.

Wordlessly she pushed the covers to one side and rose from their impromptu bed on the floor. She made her way across the chill room to sit behind him. Leaning her head into his back, she put her arms loosely around him. He caught her hand and held it in his own.

"Do you ever wonder, Jessie," he said softly, "if we are doing the right thing?"

"What do you mean?" she asked without moving. He was warm and smelled of the leather he always wore even though now he was dressed only in linen.

"Tocar tried to broker a peace. What if we had done that first?"

"We can't change the past, Eron," she answered. "Don't blame yourself."

"But I do, Jessie. I do."

His body shook once and he was silent. Jessie felt a drop of water, on her hand. It was warm. She pulled him a little closer to her and nuzzled into his back. The wind tugged at the flap of the tent, flipping it lazily up against itself and letting it fall again. Cold, damp air entered their room. He placed Parry's hand back under the covers and turned to her.

"I have so few kinsmen left," he said.

"How is he?"

"Asleep. Madam Aramat saw to that."

"We should be sleeping, too."

Eron nodded. He leaned over Parry as a father would lean over a son, brushed the hair away from his forehead and kissed him. Then he led her back to the bed they shared, kissed her lightly and held her until once more, she was asleep.

Morning came. Eron was gone.

Jessie stretched and allowed herself a smile. Eron rarely stayed in bed longer than she did, at least not when he was well. While she would have preferred to awaken with him near, she was glad he had returned to his former habits. She braced herself for the cold of the room, then tossed the covers to one side and rose.

Thunder still rumbled in the distance, though there was no longer rain pounding on the tent. She glanced over to find Parry still asleep on the bed. He was breathing easily and she whispered a prayer of thanks to whichever god was listening.

Without warning, Tersan burst into the room.

"Jessie, you have to stop him!" he almost yelled.

"Stop who?"

"Eron! He's climbed halfway up the side of a mountain to a place where one old dicantus tree still blooms."

Jessie shrugged. "So?"

"Remember his failure at Bel Haven? He's preparing to do the Dance of the Sword!" he said.

"He is?" she said brightly.

"Yes!"

"Well, he does have to practice, Tersan," she reminded him as Eron had reminded her not so long ago.

"What if he fails?"

Jessie shrugged. "Then he tries again tomorrow."

"You do not understand! He is in full view of the entire army!"

Jessie let that sink in for a moment. "Let me get my cloak."

Eron reached the wide ledge that was home to a single twisted old dicantus tree. The blossoms where sparse on the weathered branches, blooming brightly in an otherwise dismal setting. With great care, he cupped one in his hand, leaning over it and breathing in its delicate aroma.

"A flower that reminds one of life," he said aloud, "at the onset of season's death. What irony."

He stepped away from the bloom and bowed to the old tree. With one hand, he unbuckled the sheathed sword that had been forged by men and withdrew the blade.

Though it had been polished and honed to a very fine edge, in the darkness of a day without sunlight, it appeared dull. Carefully, he placed it at the base of the tree, hilt against bark, tip down among the roots. Eron took a step backward and drew in a great breath. It escaped his lungs slowly and a determined smile crossed his face.

"I require a blossom, Revered One," he said to the tree apologetically.

He raised his hands up to a perfect white flower and positioned his fingers on either side of it, set to pluck it away from its sustenance. The bloom floated into his hands without resistance as though the tree was giving over its child to him for safekeeping.

He stared at the blossom, then at the tree. Wind tussled his hair, brushing it off his forehead as gently as he had brushed away Parry's scant hours earlier.

"Thank you, Revered One," he breathed. He cupped the tree's gift in both hands and whispered words in the tongue nearly all of Eormengrund had forgotten. The flower floated away from his hands into the air above his head. He watched it rise, his spirit soaring with it as they became one.

With his heart racing, he ignited the Sword of Light.

The blade felt right in his hands, an extension of who and what he was, a severed limb now restored. Intoxicated by its power, he whirled in a circle, laughing while the flower floated above him. He felt its presence rather than seeing it, heard the wind whistle through the petals, smelled the delicate perfume that defined it. He sliced at the air a hair's width beneath the bloom, buoying the blossom up on the heat rising from the blade as instinct replaced cognizance. The dance was begun.

The steps were slow at first, a thrust here, an imagined parry there, as he twirled in exact, precise grueling movements designed to test the discipline of his muscles. His body joyfully remembered each response. The fiery sword pointed systematically to his left, then right, his hands crossing and uncrossing as he fought imaginary enemies. The blossom floated on the wind he created from the motion of the sword and its heat. It danced with its own soul, flirting with Eron as though he were a suitor.

Above him a bird cried out and he laughed and lunged toward the noise, falling to the ground and rolling neatly away from the imaginary attacker, incorporating the unexpected into the dance. The flower fell with him. He turned, his body a blur of motion and passed the sword under it as it nearly touched the earth. The wind from his effort sent it aloft again and he let loose a cry of joy. In that moment, he knew he would not fail.

Jessie pulled the heavy cloak tightly around her body but the shiver that ran through her was born of excitement, not of cold. She knew the dance well, had seen it performed many times, but what Eron was doing now went beyond anything she knew, beyond anything she had ever seen him do. She found herself staring at him as open mouthed as the soldiers who formed the crowd.

"Please, Eron, do not fail," Tersan breathed beside her.

"He will not fail," she assured him quietly. "Faith has been restored."

Soldiers yelled to one another, alerting each man to the performance transpiring under the old tree. Lightning flashed and thunder crackled through the air alerting them all to the coming storm, yet no one moved. Eron's metal sword caught the lightning and sent shards of light in every direction. A chill ran up Jessie's spine. Something greater than the dance was coming.

Man and Sword of Light danced and dove on the mountain, a streak of gold with a speck of white constantly overhead. His audience watched mesmerized as he expanded the stage upon which he performed. The unstable ground yielded to him, bearing him from one side of the tree to the other, in front of it and behind it, his feet slipping on the rocky turf, yet his balance certain.

"I've never seen him move like that," Jessie whispered.

"No one moves like that!" Tersan answered. "It is amazing!"

Eron abruptly stopped. He held his fiery sword with both hands directly above his head while the blossom floated at least one man's height above him, unaffected by the brewing storm. He knelt before the old tree as the blossom drifted toward him.

"What is he up to?" Tersan asked.

"I don't know," Jessie answered.

The fiery sword disappeared and Eron lunged for the sword of metal he had been wearing. He grasped it with both hands and faced the army below him.

"He has given up!" one soldier called out.

"We are surely doomed!" another said.

"Jessie," Tersan said, "stop him!"

"No." She placed her hand on his arm. "Watch!"

Eron reared back and flung the sword into the air. It soared gracefully toward the army below. Mesmerized soldiers gaped instead of running. Eron ignited the Sword of Light and pointed it at its metal counterpart. A tendril of power flew from one weapon toward the other. At the moment they met, a bolt of lightning joined Eron's flame and the sword he had leaned upon shattered into a thousand specks of golden light.

A gasp went up from the crowd as the particles floated down to harmlessly touch them. As one, they turned once again to look at the man who stood on the mountain.

High above Eron's head, the blossom still glowed. With both hands, he raised the Sword of Light, saluting the gathering storm. The blossom that had floated above him now settled like a gemstone in a crown on top of his head. The crowd gasped as it changed from white to gold. Behind him the dicantus tree glowed bright white, then it, too, changed to gold. Eron stood motionless as the wind roared around him and the storm came upon them all.

No one moved. Then, one by one, the soldiers knelt before the man on the mountain. Eron waited until silence filled the distance between him and Tersan. He took the sword by its fiery blade, strode the short distance between them. Then he knelt and offered the hilt to Tersan.

"I am returned," he said. "I offer you my service as the true Sword of Light, the symbol, spirit and weapon of our age old alliance."

"In the name of the people of the Western Marches, I accept your support," Tersan replied in a voice that boomed over their combined armies.

Eron whipped the sword in a graceful arc until he held it once again by its hilt. The flower nestled in the crown on his head swelled to brilliant silver, then slowly it blended with the gold emanating from the sword. The two combined to create an aura that surrounded his entire body. Sword and flower vanished, but the aura around the man remained.

"He's back," Jessie breathed.

41 Stakeout

Winnie settled in on her favorite bench in Effingham Park to watch and wait. Autumn sunlight could be deceptively cold, but on this day the weather was almost hot. A slight breeze rustled the fallen leaves on the walking path in front of her. With a contented sigh, Winnie took out her needlepoint.

Joann and Patrick were positioned on the opposite side of the park so both sides of the popular walking path could be observed at once. They preferred to eat doughnuts and drink coffee in the van. Soon it would be filled with the smell of bodies and in need of airing out. Winnie wrinkled her nose at the thought.

"I do hope it doesn't cling to the upholstery," she said as she finished one thread color and reached for another. "However, I suppose, for the greater good, Caravan can handle it. Blasted beast never speaks to me."

Polly rattled in her pouch.

"No, not like you, my dear."

"Miss James!"

Winnie turned to find Anna McCarthy and her brother, Kenny, smiling at her. "Why, Anna! And Kenny! How delightful to see you!"

"You too, Miss James," Anna said.

"Come, sit." Winnie patted the bench next to her and Anna sat. Kenny's attention was drawn to a group of boys playing catch. He shrugged off his backpack and grinned.

"I'll be back," he told them before he bolted across the field to join the others.

"Men," Anna said.

Winnie laughed. "It is the same in every generation."

Anna's face became serious. "Miss James, have you seen Jason? He was supposed to come to dinner yesterday and he didn't show up. I needed to talk to him about something and it's not like him not to call or something."

"Perhaps I can help?" Winnie offered.

"I, uh, don't know. See, it's about a boy in my class."

Winnie set her stitching aside. "What about him?" she asked.

"Well, I kind of like him and I don't know how to get his attention." She blushed. "I was hoping Jason could give me some pointers. I shouldn't bother you with this."

"I was once a young woman," Winnie started, "and I once had a great love."

"You did?"

"Yes, dear," she said with a smile, "I did."

"What was his name?" Anna asked. She folded her hands and leaned her chin on them, gazing dreamily as only young girls do. Winnie smiled.

"His name was Matthew," she answered, "and he was the most handsome man that ever lived."

"How did you meet him?"

"At a competition. It was a long time ago."

"Was it love at first sight?"

A gust of wind gently disturbed Winnie's skirt. "It was for me. He had his choice of many pretty girls. I had to convince him that I was the best choice for him."

"How did you get him to pick you?" she asked.

Winnie winked at her. "I let him chase me and, when the time was right, I let him catch me."

Anna's eyes got very wide. "Do you think that would work for me?" she asked.

"I don't see why not, dear." She patted her on the knee. "Find something you both have in common and just be yourself. See if you still like him then."

"That's what Mom said, too." Anna tossed her head back. Unlike her cousin, she had long, blonde hair that shone brightly in the late afternoon sun. "I'll try it! Thanks, Miss James!"

One of the boys tossed a football to Kenny. He missed it but fell down anyway. "Mom'll kill him if he gets grass stains on his new jeans," Anna said.

"I doubt the staining of clothing is a capital offense," Winnie said. "How is Lucy getting along?" she asked.

"Okay, I guess. She keeps that Wylfcynne book with her all the time and she gets teased a lot about it. I keep telling her to leave it at home, but she insists on lugging it everywhere."

"The book is precious to her, dear."

Something moved in the trees off to Winnie's right. She rose, positioning herself between the girl and whatever it was she thought she might have seen.

"I have to go now," Anna announced. She got up and cupped her hands around her mouth. "Kenny!" she shouted. "Time to leave!"

"I will walk you home, dear," Winnie said, gathering her stitching and placing it in her bag.

"That's okay, Miss James," Anna said.

"I need to stretch my legs," she answered, "and I'd like to say hello to your parents and Lucy, as long as I am close."

Kenny ran over to them and collected his backpack. "Hey, Miss James," he said. He shrugged his pack on with a grunt. "Have you seen Jason? He went up to Jessie's house and we haven't heard from him since."

"I have not seen him, dear," Winnie replied honestly. The shadows in the trees moved again. Winnie was certain of it now. "However," she continued, shepherding the children toward the park's far exit, "there have been lights on at the Perrymore place. Perhaps the telephone is out of order."

"He has a cell," Kenny countered as they started walking. The shadows moved with them. Winnie felt the hair rise on the back of her neck.

They walked briskly out of the park, past Caravan. Patrick was sitting behind the wheel, Joann in the passenger seat watching the park intently. Winnie gave him a quick backward glance and he nodded. He placed his cup on the dashboard and got out of the car.

Winnie kept her charges close, trusting Patrick to deal with whatever was coming behind her.

42 To Kill a Demon

"What is that?"

A shadow among shadows moved with ghostly grace beyond the edge of the trees, sinking back into darkness. Patrick stiffened.

"I don't know," he answered, "but I think I'd like to find out."

"Look! It's moving again!"

The shadow appeared and split into two parts. The first flitted out of sight in the same direction Winnie had taken with the two children while the other appeared to be coming closer to them.

"Damn it, we've been made," Patrick stated.

"Shouldn't one of us go after Winnie?" Joann said.

"No. That old woman knows more about these things than we do and she can handle herself. We'll deal with this one, then help her."

"We shouldn't split up."

"It's too late now."

The shadow moved out of the trees toward the boys still playing football. It paused, waiting for them to make the first move.

"We can't confront it here," Joann stated. "There's too many people around."

"We'll have to lure it to someplace relatively safe. We can use the bag-o-demons as bait."

"That's one hell of a risk," Joann said.

"We have to take it. Be ready to drive like hell."

"Right." Joann took his place behind the wheel and started the engine. She reached under the seat for something. "Here," she said, handing him a flare and a canning jar with a lid. "You might need these."

"Here's hoping we got the easy one." He stuck the flare in a hip pocket and carried the jar. Reflexively, he checked his weapons: the blade he lovingly called an Arkansas toothpick, was ready if he got close enough to use it, both guns if not. He hustled into the darkening woods, his quarry only vaguely in sight.

On his way toward her, he made careful note of his path, where he could possibly mount an offensive without attracting attention. The way went straight through a secluded, unoccupied glen, complete with picnic table, made to order. If he could get her to follow, he had enough room to maneuver here.

The shadow was clearly visible now in the shape of a woman. She waited on the sidelines of the playing field. The boys were leaving presumably to return to their homes. They left in small groups of two or three but one boy walked alone. She moved toward him.

Patrick whistled and she swiveled around to face him. A smile crossed her face, the red and green eyes gleaming in recognition. Before she could do anything else, Patrick ran. Behind him, he could hear her coming.

When he got to the glen, he turned and waited. She was coming fast, gliding ghostlike toward him. He fingered the flare, wondering when the opportune time to try to blind her would be. The demon entered the clearing and stopped. She cast her eyes around, evaluating her surroundings before turning her attention fully to him.

She was tall, as beautiful as he remembered. Her hair flowed in the breeze, her gown clung to her body as though she had no clothing at all.

"We need not fight," she told him, her voice rich with honey. "I can make you a very wealthy man."

"No thanks." Patrick replied. He ignited the flare and dropped it, then he put the jar on the ground. "I need for you to get back into the jar, please," he said. "Consider it your obligation to me fulfilled."

"Ah, but I have already fulfilled my obligation to you," she said. She was circling him like a lioness after prey. "However, I believe we could work together," she said, moving closer. "I am an honorable partner."

"What do you have to offer?" he replied.

"As I said, I could make you a wealthy man," she repeated, her voice low and sultry. "And there are other things...things you never dreamed of..." She was moving closer, her face illuminated in the flare's garish light. He had never seen anyone so beautiful. Things were awakening inside him that were hard to control.

"What I really need is for you to get back into this jar," Patrick commanded, thinking his voice was a little shaky.

She stopped, raised an eyebrow and waited. The wind caught her hair now from behind, flipping it in delicate wisps around her face. Patrick stared into her huge, goddess-like eyes. She swayed seductively, extending her hand toward him. The scent of lavender filled his nostrils, soothing the tension in some muscles and igniting others.

"There's a good girl," he whispered as she moved toward the jar, "just a little closer…"

"I was once called Lae," she said, moving almost close enough for him to touch. "And I owe you nothing!"

In an instant, she was on him and Patrick was on the ground. He grabbed the flare and shoved it in her face scoring just enough time to escape. Scrambling to his feet, he ran for the van with all the speed he could muster.

"Things were only beginning to get interesting," she called after him. She laughed. "You cannot hide from me."

He didn't look back. Eerie laughter hastened his steps. He broke through the edge of the woods and raced into the parking lot. Daylight was gone, the sun's brightness replaced by a sliver of silver. The van's taillights glowed. Thirty feet...

"Drop!" Joann shrieked.

Patrick dropped. Something very large whooshed over him, followed by an angry cry.

"Run!" Joann yelled.

He leapt to his feet and sprinted for the van, leaping into the vehicle as Joann hit the gas. Caravan's wheels screeched and Joann laid down tracks. In an instant, they were on the road, racing westward.

Above, a tiny dot grew huge in a hurry. Lae flew directly at them but Joann didn't waver. She floored the accelerator and they raced forward.

"You wanna play chicken with me?" Joann shouted. "Then c'mon!"

Lae soared up over the top of the van, missing them by inches. They were almost to the highway.

"Perrymore's place," Patrick said. He was still catching his breath.

"Right."

Patrick flipped on the CB. They were speeding down the road under the shadow that was Lae. No one had spotted them nor seemed to care.

"Thank goodness no traffic," Joann mused.

"Yeah." Patrick checked his arsenal for the umpteenth time. He kept thinking about what Winnie had said. He would have to get past that hypnotic voice to kill her and her hypnotic breath. He thought maybe he could use her own weapon against her, make her come in close, then strike. He sighed.

"What?"

"She's got some kind of siren hold over me," Patrick explained as they raced out of town on the desolate highway. "I don't know if I can shake it."

"I'll help."

"I need it."

Lae dive bombed them, but Joann kept them on the road. Five times the demon attempted to get them to swerve off the road. Five times Joann managed to avoid her. They finally swung into Jessie's drive, flinging gravel into the air as they raced toward the house. Joann slammed on the brakes and threw the van into park.

"Ready?" she asked.

"As I'll ever be."

"On three?"

Before he could answer, something huge smashed the roof of the van. The windows in the back shattered and popped out. Lae rocked the vehicle wildly.

"Now!" he shouted.

The doors flew open and they rolled out, aiming upward toward the last place they had seen their enemy. But Lae had flown to the roof of the house. She screeched a laugh, then swooped toward Joann, knocking the policewoman to the ground on the opposite side of the van from Patrick. Joann emptied her clip as Patrick raced to join her. There was a sickening thud as flesh met flesh. Lae was leaning over Joann, her hands on either side of the woman's head.

"Stop!" Patrick yelled. He launched himself at her, knife in hand, landing squarely on her chest and knocking Joann out of her hands. With all his might, he plunged the blade into her eye.

Lae screamed. She pawed at Patrick, sending him flying against the side of the van. The demon fell backward, landing hard on her side. She tried to get up, to get airborne again.

"No you don't!" Patrick said. He raced at her again, stabbing her in the ear.

A terrible cry went up in to the night and Lae fell. This time, she did not rise.

Patrick held the knife in his hands, waiting for her to move. When she did not, he turned to Joann. His partner was sitting on the lawn, grasping her leg with one hand, her neck with the other. Tears ran down her pale face and she sucked in ragged breaths. He placed a hand on her shoulder.

"Are you all right?" he asked quietly.

"'Stupid question," she whispered, "considering something just tried to rip my head off."

"This time, you are going to the hospital," Patrick insisted.

"This time," Joann said, "I think I have to."

43 The Offering

Patrick sipped the bitter coffee in the tiny Styrofoam cup. Even four packets of real sugar and three of fake cream couldn't make the beverage any better than hot. The emergency room waiting area was small but thankfully nearly empty. Only a babe in its mother's arms wailing mournfully kept him company. A nurse dressed in bright green scrubs opened the door and walked over to the mother. They all disappeared into the treatment area, leaving Patrick and his coffee alone. A wall filled with magazines caught his eye. He picked up a copy of some financial magazine and flipped through the pages thinking he should read something, but he couldn't concentrate.

"Pat?" The nurse in green scrubs was standing at the door.

Patrick put the magazine down and rose.

"You can see your wife now," she said.

"She's not my wife," he answered as he followed her through the doors, "just a friend."

"This way," the nurse said.

Joann was lying on a gurney, an IV in her arm, bright blue ice bag on her neck. Her eyes were glazed but she waved vaguely to a plastic chair beside her. Patrick took the hint and sat.

"They won't give me coffee," she said, eyeing his cup.

"You're not missing anything," Patrick said.

"I'll be right outside," the nurse told them, "in case you need anything." She left but did not close the door. At the desk, the staff gathered. They whispered amongst themselves, pointing toward Patrick

"What's with them?" Patrick asked, shifting in the hard chair.

Joann laughed. "Have you looked in a mirror lately?"

Patrick glanced down at his clothes. He was covered in black demon's blood, his clothing torn in a number of places. He looked at his arm. Blood both dry and tacky soaked his sleeve.

"I am a bit of a mess," he admitted, setting the nasty coffee to one side. He rolled his sleeve up. There was a nasty gash there. "Great."

"They think you injured me," Joann laughed. She was giddy. The nurse took a few steps toward the room. She had a chart in her hands and paused in front of their door, apparently reading.

"And you think that's funny?" Patrick snapped.

"Hell, right now everything's kinda funny, thanks to the miracles of pharmacology." She grinned at him. "One down, one to go. Sorry I'll miss the party."

"Are you going to be all right?" he asked, rubbing his neck tiredly. The reality of what she said hit him in the gut.

"Probably," she answered. "'Glad we've got good insurance. I broke a bone in my leg. Doc says surgery to fix it, then eight weeks in a cast, a little rehab and I'll be great. I've got a story I can only tell certain people. Maybe I'll tell it anyway. Blame the fantastic on the drugs." She giggled. "Rose will believe me."

There was a knock on the door. A young woman opened it and entered, stethoscope around her neck. She wore street clothes with a lab coat over them.

"Hello, Doctor Clay," Joann said.

"They're ready for you in surgery," the petite doctor said. She looked coldly at Patrick but continued to talk to Joann. "Is there anyone you want me to call?"

"Only the cats," Joann answered. "I'll give Rose a call at a decent hour. She's in St. Louis, you know." She took hold of Clay's arm. "Did I mention I'm a police officer?" she said.

"Yes, you've told me," the doctor answered.

"Well, that's why she worries, not because of Pat." Joann looked sternly at Clay. "We had an accident," she said. "No more, no less. I am not the victim of abuse. Believe me, I know what you all are talking about out there." She nodded to the gaggle of nurses standing within earshot. "Any man who takes a hand to me wouldn't live to see the sun rise," she said loudly. "That's part of the reason I became a cop. Do you understand?"

"Um, yes."

The nurse came into the room and began unhooking various pieces of equipment from the wall and reinserting them into portable machines on the bed.

"He's got a gash on his arm, Doc," Joann continued. "Make him let you look at it." She reached over for Patrick's hand and pulled him close. "Find Winnie," she whispered. "That other thing's still out there somewhere."

"I will," he nodded. He took her hand between his own and gave her fingers a squeeze. "I'll see you soon," he said as she was wheeled out of the room, leaving Patrick and Doctor Clay standing in her wake.

"Let's have a look at that," she told him, reaching for his arm.

"I'm fine."

She had his arm, already examining the wound. "Nasty gash," she commented, still holding his arm. "Mike, get me a suture tray. And Pat, is it?"

"Yes, ma'am."

"Sit."

Patrick sat. The adrenaline that had been keeping him going was draining. He leaned his head back against the wall and let Clay work on his arm. She kept talking to him about infection and he kept nodding his head at the appropriate time. One thought filtered its way to the top of his priorities. He had to find Winnie.

"...tetanus shot?"

"I'm sorry?"

"Your last tetanus shot," Clay asked, "when was it?"

"I, uh, don't remember. We have to keep it up to date, though."

"Very good," she said.

Patrick didn't pay attention to what else she may have said. He took the prescription she offered and signed his name to the papers they held in front of him. By this time his head was pounding from lack of sleep.

"Is there anyone to drive you home?" Clay was saying from some fairly distant place.

"What?"

"Is there anyone to drive you home?" she repeated.

"No."

"Mike."

Mike appeared with a few pills encapsulated in plastic. He handed them to Patrick.

"Percocet," he said. "Take it when you get home. It'll help with the pain."

"Thanks," Patrick mumbled. "Am I done?"

"Yes."

"Thanks, Doc, Mike." He got up, stuffed the papers with instructions into his pocket and left. It was four A.M. "You have my number?"

"We do." She managed a smile. "Go home. Your partner is in good hands. Careful of that dressing when you shower."

"Yes, ma'am."

The last time he had seen Winnie she was outside the park walking with two children. They must have been rather important to her because she seemed to be guarding them and they looked vaguely familiar. He wracked his brain, trying to think where he had seen them before.

"Jessie Perrymore," he said to himself. "They were on the lawn at her sister's house. Now, where was that...?"

He recalled the neighborhood, though not the address. It wasn't far from the hospital or Effingham Park. He headed in that direction, the adrenaline returning to fuel his tired body.

Forty five minutes later, he had made three passes over the streets where he was certain the McCarthy home was. He still did not recognize the specific house, but everything was quiet. There was no sign of Winnie, not that he expected to see her at five A.M., traipsing around Martha McCarthy's neighborhood.

"Back to square one," he said to himself.

By the time he reached the Perrymore place, he had nearly run off the road twice in spite of the decent coffee he had purchased when he got gas. The gravel drive crunched under his tires as he wound through the twenty-foot thicket of trees separating the lawn from the highway.

"Aw, hell, Winnie, what're ya doing?"

Winifred James was standing beside the ruined minivan, a fiery branch in her hand. She had piled wood under the frame of the car and all around it, and was starting to light it. The fire smoldered in front of her, but only in front of her. Patrick rammed the accelerator to the floor. He got to her in seconds, threw the door open and exploded out of his car. Winnie looked up at him, tears streaking her face.

"Get in the car!" Patrick yelled.

"I see no--"

"Shut up, you fool!" He grabbed her by the waist and turned back to Joann's car, threw open the back door and stuffed her inside, slamming the door behind her. Then he slid behind the steering wheel and jammed the car into reverse. They sped away from the fire as quickly as Patrick could make the car travel, finally coming to rest a safe distance from the van. Patrick stared at the van critically.

"Looks like the fire hasn't quite caught yet," he said.

"Look here, young man, Caravan was a noble steed and deserves a decent burial!"

"Wake up and smell the coffee, Winnie," he countered. "A van is a 'thing'. It has no soul!"

"I beg to dif--"

"Does Perrymore have a fire extinguisher?" he snapped.

"What?"

"A fire extinguisher. Red, metal thing about yay long," he motioned with his hands. "Never mind. It hasn't caught yet."

He dashed out of the car toward the flames and pulled the lit tinder from beneath the van. He stomped on it until it smoldered and went out.

"That was too close," he said.

"How dare you!" Winnie said. She was manipulating her fingers again, but this time Patrick was ready. He grabbed her hands and held her still.

"You sent up a smoke signal," Patrick replied. "Let's hope no one saw it, or, if they did, that they thought it was only a leaf pile burning." Winnie looked puzzled. "I don't know where that other thing is," he said, "but this one's dead," he pointed to Lae's lifeless body. "I killed her and it would take way too long to explain what she is, that she was a threat and that there's one more out there loose, let alone make anyone believe what I'm saying."

"But we must take care of Caravan's remains!" Winnie said.

"Fine. I'll call a tow truck and they can come get it tomorrow." His head was pounding. "Winnie, if you set it on fire, it will explode. It's got gas in the tank, for crying out loud!"

Winnie looked at him, her eyes knitted.

"Do you understand?" Patrick asked. His head was pounding relentlessly now. Even rubbing his eyes with the heels of his hands didn't help.

"I should not cremate Caravan?" she said.

"Right!" Patrick laughed. "Right...thank God..." He made his way to the porch of the house and sank on swing, burying his head in his hands. The pounding was worse than ever. He looked up at Winnie.

"We've lost Joann for now," he started, "but she's going to be okay. I'm dead tired and I need a shower, but what I really need is sleep. Can I trust you and Polly to watch for Bue until I get some rest?"

Winnie held the bag-o-demons in one hand and her cane in the other. "We can do that, officer," she said quietly. "You remember where everything is?"

Patrick nodded. Half an hour later, he once again put his faith in a crazy old lady and her flying serpent and went to sleep.

Something smelled delightful. It coaxed Patrick from his sleep, setting his stomach to growling before his mind knew where he was. The bed was soft but firm, the linens fresh with a hint of the outdoors in them. He rubbed a hand across his growing beard and stretched. Stitches pulled on his left arm, yet there was no pain. His clothes were hanging from the back of the door and the mini arsenal was on the table where he had left it. He dressed quickly and made his way to the kitchen.

Winnie had fixed some sort of meal. It looked unappealing, but smelled good. He shoved a forkful of meat into his mouth. It had a spicy flavor to it unlike anything he had ever tasted. She brought him a mug of something hot. He sipped it.

"Wow. What is this?" he asked, taking another drink.

"Trinka. I'm afraid there is no more than this," she said as she joined him, "at least until I can get home again."

"Anything happen while I was sleeping?"

"It has been quiet," she answered. "I spoke with Martha. They whole family is safe in her home, including Lucy. She will call if anything happens."

Patrick nodded. "Thanks for breakfast, or whatever this meal is. Are you ready to go look for Bue?"

"Yes."

"Let's go." Patrick finished the last of his meal. Winnie snatched up her purse and the bag-o-demons and they headed to Joann's car since the Tesla's battery needed to be charged. "Where do we start to look for her?" He flipped on Joann's scanner.

"...1-7-3 Bellington Place... copy..." the radio squawked. "...Repeat...1-7-3 Bellington Place. Report of smoke by a neighbor," the radio said.

Winnie paled. "That is Martha McCarthy's home! Bue must be there!"

44 Hot Times in Claxbury

The sun had already set as they headed for the McCarthy home. Winnie clutched her cane in the front seat of Joann's vehicle. Not for the first time, was she afraid. But for the first time, she feared for Jessie's child, a child who was supposed to be safe here in a world apart from Eormengrund, safe in a house both she and Jessie had warded. She glanced nervously behind her. The camera bag containing the other demons was safe in the back seat, just as it had been one minute ago and two minutes before that.

In the distance, Claxbury's lights shone like tiny diamonds. They raced down the highways, then side streets, passed the hospital, schools and parks until they entered the subdivision where the McCarthy's lived. From the entrance, they could see the blaze. Winnie gasped.

One-seventy-three Bellington Place was on fire. A police car was parked in front of the house, its lights flashing and the neighboring homes' occupants gawked from a safe distance. Flames licked the framework around the windows of the upper floors and smoke billowed out into the night eclipsing the moon. Patrick hit the gas and they were on the lawn in seconds.

"Winnie, stay here," he told her.

Winnie waited for him to exit the car, fumbling to take the silken bag out from beneath her blouse and rouse Polly.

"Polly, if something happens to me, you must show Patrick the way," she said to the demon herder. "And tell Alvyn to let him through."

The little snake rattled and hissed. "Oh, do not worry about me," she told it. "Just try to undo what I have done, all right? Do not let Bue release the others."

The snake nodded. Winnie placed the bag so that it hung from the rear view mirror, then flung open the door. Spilling out onto the lawn, she got her feet under her and charged toward the burning structure. As she moved, she began working on a shield to keep her safe as she passed through the fire. Martha and Ted were leaning on one another, pointing hopefully at the windows. Ted's hands were bound in strips of cloth.

"Miss James!" Martha exclaimed. "Oh, Miss James, they're still in there! Anna and Kenny are still in there!"

"We tried to get them out," Ted mumbled, still staring at the windows, "but the smoke was too thick. They're stuck in their rooms, we hope. But the fire is all around them."

"Not to worry, dear," she said, patting Martha's hand. "I'll get them out."

Before they could stop her, Winnie made her way past the firefighters to the front door. She finished spinning her shield, then placed it over her head and let it cascade down her shoulders. It sealed itself under her feet. In effect, she was walking in a giant bubble. She slipped unnoticed into the burning house.

Winnie shuffled her way into the elegant living room. The costly floor to ceiling draperies had burned first, spreading the flames to the broad beams that spanned the ceiling of the two-story structure. Winnie tried to see up to the balcony and the doors beyond where the children slept, but the smoke was too thick. She knew the layout very well. Finding the stairway was an easy task. Negotiating it would be a different matter. Debris was floating to the floor all around her. One of the huge pictures in the stairwell crashed at her feet.

"Lady, protect us," she said aloud.

Though she was safe within the bubble, she could still feel the heat from the fire. Ahead of her she thought she heard someone crying. She quickened her pace.

She reached the top of the stairs and made a sharp left. Using their cries to guide her, she felt her way along the wall to Anna's door. Knowing that the smoke would probably fill the room instantly, Winnie prepared herself to open the bubble quickly to let hopefully both children in. She stopped and knocked, realizing afterward how foolish that action was.

"Mom?" Anna called. She was coughing.

"No, it's Winifred," she yelled. "Stand back!"

Slowly, she turned the knob and threw the door open.

Anna and Kenny were huddled in a corner of the room. They both had cloth over their mouths. Smoke poured in behind Winnie. She moved as quickly as she could to the two, opened the shield and snatched them into the bubble. Anna coughed and sucked in several deep breaths while Kenny stayed on all fours on the floor doing the same thing.

Anna looked up at Winnie through tear-filled eyes.

"You will be all right," Winnie cooed. She made a quick assessment of each of them. They did not appear to be hurt. Only one more to rescue. "Where's Lucy?" she asked softly.

"The police woman took her," Anna said.

"She said she'd come back for us," Kenny added, "but she didn't!"

"Police woman?" Winnie asked.

Kenny grinned widely. "She was one hell of a babe," he told her.

"Watch your language, young man," Winnie scolded.

"She *was* beautiful," Anna said with a nod. "And really tall. She talked with a funny accent, kinda like yours."

Winnie sucked in a deep breath. Bue had Lucy.

Above the crackling of the fire, she heard one of the massive beams crash to the floor outside the bedroom. The air inside the bubble was getting very warm.

"It's so hot in here!" Kenny complained.

"I know, Kenny," she said. "We shall be outside very soon. Ready?"

Kenny nodded.

"There's a good lad. Take my hands. I know you want to run, but we have to move slowly and stay together. Ready?"

They nodded. As an awkward threesome, they moved into the hallway.

Everything in the house ablaze. Fire lapped the wooden spindles of the balcony. They hugged the wall and made their way to the steps. With a crack like thunder, a second ceiling beam broke. Winnie wedged the children between herself and the wall, shielding them with her body. Half of the beam swung down into the living room, the other half banged against the balcony, striking a glancing blow against the bubble. The force of its fall took out the railing and a huge chunk of the floor they were standing on.

"Quickly!" Winnie said as she shepherded them down three steps to more solid ground.

The stairs were still pretty much whole making their escape route easier, but fire engulfed the railing. They would have to move single file.

"I will go first to make sure the stairs are still intact," she told them. "Kenny, hold on to my skirt. Anna, hold on to his shirt."

"Kind of like elephants?" Kenny said.

"Yes, dear," Winnie told them. "Do not worry. We only have to make it down a few more steps. It is not far now." She placed her hand on the wall and started down the stairs.

Though they could see to the edge of the bubble, little else was visible. She put one foot tentatively on the next step. It seemed solid enough. She tested her weight on it and it was indeed solid. She moved to the next. And the next. The stairs held. And they were on the landing.

"Thank you, Lady!" she said.

Only three more steps and they would be on the floor in the living room. Winnie relaxed a bit, preparing to bolt for the door. She stepped down without thinking and the floor gave way under her. Her foot pierced a hole in the shield and slid into the fire.

"Yeouch!" she screeched as she pulled her foot back into the bubble.

"Miss James? What's wrong?" Anna asked.

"Nothing that cannot be fixed," she said. More surprised than hurt, she repaired the hole in the shield. "We have to leave the wall now and head for the door," she said. "We are almost there!"

Winnie shuffled across the floor, striving to keep her feet on a solid surface. Her toe caught on something awkward and she tumbled forward, taking Anna and Kenny with her. They crashed in a tangled heap of arms and legs. The shield shimmered and was gone. Fire raged close around them now, the air wickedly hot.

"What the hell--?" A large man inside a different type of shield stood in front of her.

"Watch your language," Winnie gasped. The face behind the clear shield dropped its jaw. "Get the children out," she ordered.

The man scooped up Anna in one arm and Kenny in the other and disappeared into the smoke. Winnie, determined not to die, began to crawl. She made it ten feet before she started coughing uncontrollably. Something blunt ran into her leg.

"Here she is!" a muffled voice called.

Winnie felt herself being hoisted into the air. Moments later, the world was cooler. She was on the ground, the earth under her head like fresh linen. Someone slapped something entirely foreign on her face and stale air blew into her nostrils. She tried to push it away but unyielding hands held the vile smelling air firmly in place. Despite the nasty smell, she began to feel better.

"Winnie?"

Winnie opened her eyes. Patrick was standing over her, his brow deeply furrowed.

"That was a foolish thing to do! The firemen had ladders on the far side of the house. They would have gotten them out."

Winnie managed to smile. "Where are the children?"

"Anna and Kenny are with their parents."

"And Lucy?"

"They're stabilizing her."

"Stabilizing?" Winnie struggled to get up but a hand held her down.

"Take it easy, ma'am," the man holding the mask over her face drawled.

"Patrick, Bue took her."

"Took who?"

"Lucy!" Winnie snapped. She sat up despite the protests of the man holding the mask. "Oh, for the love of the Lady, get that thing off my face!"

"Please, lie down, ma'am."

"No!" Winnie summoned her power and knocked both the paramedic and Patrick back a few feet. She leapt to her feet and charged toward the ambulance, with Patrick on her heels, working up the last of her reserves into a compact circle of power that she held it in front of her as she ran.

Bue saw her coming. She smiled and reached into the ambulance, her back to Winnie as her nemesis raced forward. Winnie was almost on her when she turned around.

In one hand she had the bag of demons; in the other, Joann's gun.

"Remember me, Wylfcynne?" she breathed.

"Let the child go!" Winnie demanded.

Bue laughed. "I think not," she said. She raised the gun and fired.

There was a flash and the bullet hit the shield. It splintered the light and for the first time in her life, Winnie's shield failed.

She felt the bullet tear into her flesh and the force sent her backward into Patrick's arms. He dragged back into the yard, flipped the picnic table over and hid behind it. The man with the foul smelling air joined them.

"What the hell?" he shouted at Patrick.

"No time to explain," Patrick shouted back. "Damn it, Winnie, why are you always right?"

Winnie managed a smile. "You are going to have to follow them without me," she told him. "Take Polly and my cane. And do not mind Alvyn. He is grumpy this time of year."

"Who's Alvyn?" Patrick asked.

The man was back with his foul smelling air. He slipped an elastic band around her head so that the mask fit somewhat snugly against her face and Patrick disappeared. A second man held pressure on her shoulder. They were speaking to each other in quick, short sentences. Winnie did not understand their words, nor did she protest. She was too weak to protest.

The world was turning fuzzy. Winnie felt a prick on her arm and something cold emptied into her veins. She looked back up at Patrick. "Polly...Polly will show you," she mumbled. "She will... show..."

"All right ... Winnie?" Winnie tried to hear his response but she was losing her senses. With a fervent prayer to the Lady, she gave in to the dark.

45 One Door Closes

"Damn it!"

Bue pointed the gun at Patrick and fired. The bullet ricocheted off the swing set.

"I left an O2 tank out there," one of the paramedics said. "If--"

Before he could finish his sentence, Bue's next shot hit the oxygen tank. Instead of exploding, it became a rocket propelled by the compressed gas. The tank streaked toward Joann's tiny car. It crashed into and through the side of the vehicle before igniting the gas tank. The resulting explosion sent a huge fireball into the air.

"No!" Patrick yelled. "Damn you!"

Bue laughed.

Bullets blew chunks of wood off the table and Patrick ducked behind it, drawing his gun. He counted to three and poked his head out around the side of the table. Bue was waiting for him.

The demon held Lucy in front of her. She had the bag-o-demons in her hand.

"Let me go!" Lucy screeched. She kicked and wriggled, trying to get away.

"I do not think so," Bue answered.

Bue hit her hard across her face. The girl went limp. A hundred pairs of hands snatched Lucy up, holding her so Patrick could not get off a shot without possibly harming the girl. Bue aimed the gun at them once more. She was out of ammo. She looked at the weapon, surprise registering on her face, tried firing it one more time, then threw it away. The flames consuming Joann's car crackled.

"Name your bargain," Bue demanded. "Do you want the girl? Or maybe the old woman to be safe?"

"I want both. And that bag!" Patrick yelled. "And you back in your prison!"

Bue laughed. "You only get one, little man," she hissed. "Perhaps we shall speak again later." She retreated to the side of the ambulance, keeping Lucy in front of her. They disappeared behind the smoke billowing up from the destroyed car.

"Bue!" he yelled.

Beyond the smoking ruin of his ride, he saw a huge shadow rise and speed away.

"Damn it!" Patrick snapped. He looked at Winnie. "How bad?"

"She's stable. We'll know more when we get her in the ambulance."

"Where are you taking her?" he asked, squeezing Winnie's hand.

"Memorial."

"Tell her I'll see her soon." Patrick gave the limp hand a final squeeze then ran to one of the squad cars sitting by the curb. Before he could reach it, something whizzed by his head and dropped Winnie's cane along with a small silk pouch in front of him. Barely missing a beat, he picked up the cane, grabbed the pouch and slid behind the steering wheel. He tossed the cane and pouch on the seat beside him and fired up the engine. Then he flipped on the siren and the lights and flew back down Bellington, wondering where he would go from there. Even though the cruiser was fast, Bue had a good head start on him.

The radio crackled to life.

"O'Shea, is that you?" Chief Purdy's voice was as pudgy as he was.

"O'Shea!" he continued to drawl, "What in tarnation do you think you're doing, son?" Apparently Chief Purdy was not happy.

"Gotta love the drawl," Patrick mumbled. He picked up the handset and pressed the button. "Following a kidnap victim, Chief."

"All by your lonesome? I'll send back-up. What's your 20?"

"If that man wishes to know where we are headed," the serpent hovering over his shoulder stated, "I suggest you send him away from the Perrymore place. This is not something he would understand."

"P-P-Polly?" he said.

"No. Purdy. Chief Purdy," the radio crackled. "Son, I think you'd better just pull over and wait for assistance."

"You may not do that, Patrick," the serpent said.

"Wh-what?"

"O'Shea, pull over," Purdy insisted. Patrick imagined his jowls moving when he spoke. "That fire addled your brain, son."

Patrick slowed the cruiser and pulled to the side of the road. With one hand, he shut off the siren and the lights then put the car in park, leaving the engine running. He dragged a hand across his face, rubbing his chin tiredly.

"Let's see now," he mumbled, picking up the handset once more, "where am I?'

"You are on your way to rescue a child and possibly a world," the voice on his shoulder said.

"Not enough sleep and too much coffee," he said aloud. "I'm hearing things."

"Of course you are hearing things. I am speaking to you."

"O'Shea? What's your 20?"

Patrick held the handset in his hand. He bit his lip. The mile marker said 157. Highway AT. He hadn't made the turn off to Perrymore's house yet.

"Maybe the stress has gotten to me," he mumbled. He pressed the button and began to speak. "Chief, I'm at--"

Like a shot, Polly lunged at his hand and bit his finger. He threw the handset down and shook his hand wildly. The snake was inches from his face, black eyes glowing red. The white body twisted almost sensually in front of him and her wings were beating as fast as a hummingbird's.

"No!" she screamed, holding her position and flicking her tongue at him.

Patrick shrank back in the seat. "You're not real!" he insisted.

Almost faster than he could follow, she snapped at his head. His hat flew in to the back seat were it rested on the window ledge. Once again, she was six inches from his nose. "Was that real enough for you?" the snake hissed.

"Y-yeah."

"O'Shea!"

"Do not answer."

Patrick threw the handset on the seat beside him.

"Silence him."

"But--"

"O'Shea--" Purdy started.

"DO IT NOW!"

Patrick switched the radio off. "This is foolish," he said. "I am listening to a snake."

"I am not a snake," Polly said. She slipped under his shirt and Patrick tried to ignore the sensation as she squirmed around until her head poked out. "I am a demon herder. We are distant cousins. I suggest you ask this beast to move forward. This conversation wastes time."

Patrick laughed shortly. He threw the car into gear and pulled out onto the highway. "Talking snakes, glowing shields, demons in jars. What else could happen?"

"Bue will take the child to Jessie's house," Polly continued, ignoring his question. "Doubtless she knows the portal is there and the ritual required to open it. And Lucy has the original portal key, The Book of Wylfcynne."

Patrick sighed. "If she knew how to go home, why didn't she just leave?" he asked.

"Fot wants the child. And he wants the demons. They will remain loyal to him when he releases them and that will allow him to quickly reestablish himself. Are you that dense?"

"Apparently," he answered.

"Winifred will be all right, will she not?" Polly asked. It seemed she was genuinely concerned. "I have grown rather fond of her and good pets are difficult to find."

"The paramedic seemed to think so," Patrick answered.

Patrick stopped the car and Polly stopped speaking. They had reached Jessie's drive. He pulled his weapon out of its holster and checked the clip. It was loaded. His heart was beating faster. There would be no negotiations. He flipped off the headlights and pulled into the driveway. Patrick's pulse quickened. He parked beside Jason's VW.

"Ready?" he asked Polly.

The demon herder popped her head out of his shirt and looked at him with those beautiful eyes. "Be very careful, Patrick," she told him.

"You, too."

She rose gracefully and exited through the window. Patrick reached up, turned the dome light off and cracked the door open as quietly as he could. He dashed to the front of the old house and paused with his back against a huge tree. Peering around its trunk, he looked inside the house. A light was on. He could see shapes moving about. The front door stood wide open but there was no one guarding it. Noise was coming from inside. He cocked his head and strained to listen.

Music. A very scared girl was singing. The last strains of "Too Damned Hot" from *Kiss Me Kate* drifted out of the house. Patrick caught a glimpse of Polly on the other side of the door. He nodded to the demon herder.

"Very good, child!" Bue said. "You opened the portal on your first attempt!"

"Now!" Patrick shouted.

Together man and demon chaser burst through the door.

"Help me!" Lucy cried.

"Too late," Bue said. She snatched the girl up and threw her against the stone fireplace. Patrick shuddered, bracing himself in empathy for the girl's impact. Instead, she passed through the stone and disappeared.

Patrick lowered his gun slightly and stared.

"Help me!" Lucy called from somewhere that sounded pretty much like the place Jason McCarthy had called from in the 911 tape.

"Coming, darling," Bue said. Holding the Book of Wylfcynne in front of her, she dove through the stone fireplace, the bag-o-demons in her hand.

"What the hell--" He stood up slowly and made his way to the fireplace. Tentatively, he put his hand on the stone. It passed through and he snatched it back.

"No!" Polly said.

"If you think I was going to jump right in there without thinking first, you're out of your demon-herder mind," Patrick told her. "What the hell is that?"

"A portal to our world," Polly answered. "And you must not use this one."

"That child is down there," Patrick said. He was gathering courage to plow through it. "And I came to take her back!"

Polly rammed him with such force that his small revolver went flying to the same place his service revolver was, leaving Patrick on the floor once more.

"Hey!"

"There is a better way," Polly told him.

"But--"

"This portal is a slide," Polly continued. "Bue will be waiting for you at the other end, in our world, with her powers fully intact. It is too dangerous."

"But Lucy--!"

"Bue will not kill her because Fot wants her. He said as much when he returned to our world." Polly still hovered in front of him. "She knows the power of a mother's love and the pain she can inflict on Jessie. Jessie is a powerful leader in the war that nears. Lucy will be a tremendous weapon to use against her."

"What?"

"Come. There is another way." She zipped out the front door, leaving Patrick on the floor.

He rose slowly and retrieved his weapons before checking the fireplace once more. This time his hand met cool stone. The portal was closed.

46 Revelation

The way was not unpleasant. Jessie rode on the right hand of Tersan, Eron on the left, symbolic, steadfast, determined. They rarely spoke, looking ahead, surveilling the plains ahead of them. To the west, Kimala still rose, no longer enshrouded in clouds. The Udolphi was just out of sight, flowing north toward Jeleste. To the east, the Paranjothi range soared into the sky, Emmalie, the first of the Sister's barely visible. Beyond that, Calshara with its city of gold, Il Chatel.

Jessie sat on her mount frankly bored. She had never been much of a fan of horseback riding preferring to walk instead. This was for show. Right now, she was being a good soldier. She stifled a yawn.

On the other side of Tersan, Eron seemed content. It must be great to be able to be in two places at once, if not physically, then mentally. Kind of like playing games your phone, she reasoned. She giggled.

"Jessie?" Tersan asked.

"Nothing," she answered.

Tersan held up a hand, simultaneously stopping his mount. "We'll stop here for the night."

Jessie rolled her eyes. "Can't we go just a little further? There's still a lot of daylight."

"We have made good progress today," Tersan replied. "It takes time to move infantry, to feed them and keep them prepared for battle. That includes rest, Lady Jessie."

Eron was already off his horse. His assigned page scrambled to take the animal's reins, leaving Eron free to move about. He was in front of Jessie in an instant. Worry lined his features.

She dismounted quickly. "What is it? A vision?"

The Sword offered her a hand and quickly schooled his features. "Many visions," he told her. "Some troubling, but it is unclear."

"I can help," she assured him. Jessie looked at him long and hard. "What did you see?"

He cleared his throat. "Many visions. I told you. So many coming at once now, I have to discern which are important and which are frivolity." With that, he looked into the distance and said no more.

47 Another Door Opens

"Where?" Patrick asked as he slid behind the wheel of the cruiser.

"Winifred's cottage," Polly answered. She slipped into her pouch, curled up and went silent.

Patrick headed down the long drive and turned right. There were no lights here on the mountain and storm clouds were gathering taking away what little light that came from the sliver of the moon and the stars. Even the lines that marked the road faded and disappeared leaving only the white stripes down the middle. Lightning rippled through the sky, the mountains outlined behind the pulse of a growing storm. Rain splattered against the windshield. Patrick flipped on the wipers.

"Nothing quite like a good thunderstorm to set the stage," he said aloud. "At least we're not in Kansas."

Polly didn't answer.

Even though he had visited Winnie's home once before, the entrance to her cottage was so obscured by foliage that Patrick almost missed it. He swung into the drive and took a moment to listen to the windshield wipers, then switched on the high beams and drove the final quarter mile up to the house. Once there, he picked up Polly's pouch and Winnie's cane before bolding to relative dryness of the front porch.

The entry door was solid wood, carved into a woodland scene complete with mythical creatures. Patrick wished he had time to appreciate the intricate work. He rapped above the carving.

"Anyone home?" he asked. "Alvyn?"

Something move across the floor; it wasn't footsteps. He took a deep breath and tried the doorknob. It turned in his hand. The door swung open silently and Patrick stepped inside.

Suddenly he was struggling to breathe. He clawed at the thick, cold cord tightening around his neck. He dropped Polly's bag. Strange sucking noises were escaping his lips. The world around him dimmed. A bolt of lightning hit close to the house followed by earsplitting thunder. Patrick barely noticed.

"Alvyn," he thought he heard a woman say, "let him go. Winnie said he was okay."

Patrick dropped to his knees still clawing at the cord. Tunnel vision was all that remained of his sight.

"Alvyn!"

Pressure around his neck went slack. The cold cord landed on the floor with a thud. Patrick fell forward, barely catching himself with one hand as the other grabbed at his throat. He lapsed into a cacophony of gasps. A huge snake rose in front of him. It was strangely beautiful, pure white with dark black eyes and a brilliant flitting red tongue. It tilted its head from right to left, assessing this human's threat level. Apparently satisfied that all was well, it lowered itself to the floor and slithered to the fireplace where it crawled up onto a giant piece of driftwood where it bathed in light pouring down from at least three heat lamps. Once there, it stared at Patrick.

"Alvyn does not take kindly to strangers," Polly explained. The demon herder was gazing at the snake. "Is he not handsome?"

"Yeah, handsome," Patrick croaked.

Alvyn hissed and seemed to nod. Polly giggled like a school girl. Patrick felt like he was intruding. Polly cleared her throat and returned her attention to Patrick.

"Lady Jessie is all that stands between the demons of my world and its destruction. Eron has been sorely wounded, basically rendered ineffective, the last time we heard anything and there is no reason to think things have changed. The demons Bue took back will be after revenge. They can do grievous harm."

"I'm only interested in retrieving the girl," Patrick said.

"But if Fot releases the others, they will owe him much, even more than their allegiance. Fot will use them against us."

"It sounds like they were enemies of yours before they were sent here," Patrick countered.

"True enough." Uncharacteristically, Polly paused. Her beautiful eyes were staring at Patrick again. "I understand that your priority is to rescue Lucy. But it is my belief that the Lady has need of your help. Somehow, your assistance has been requested, else I would not have been asked to divulge the secret of entry to our world."

Patrick sighed. "I will help if I can. But the girl is my priority."

"Fair enough."

"What do I do?" he asked.

"Winifred is fond of a movie entitled: The Wizard of Oz. All you have to do is take the crystal on the mantel, hold it tightly in one hand while you lay the other on the mantel and say--"

"There's no place like home?"

"Yes, but you have to say it in our language."

"Okay."

Polly uttered five syllables in a guttural, sensual language. Patrick walked over to the mantel, grasped the crystal, tapped three times and repeated the words. The front door blew open and the wind nearly sucked him through the now transparent bricks. He tested the portal with a hand. The sensation was creepy, like fingernails on a chalkboard. Fascinated, he punched his fist in and out several times.

"I never was one for believing in fairy tales," he mused.

"The portal from Jessie's house is two days journey south and west of this one," Polly said, ignoring his comment.

"Two days! But we just left them not five miles down the road!" he protested. From the driftwood, Alvyn hissed.

"Head east and turn north when you reach the river. The Kilmari should find you."

"I hope they're the good guys," he mumbled. Like a mime, he ran his hand over the top of the opening until he finally found the margins. Somehow, the fact that the doorway was identified made him feel a bit more secure. "How will they know not to kill me?"

"Tell them who you are and that Wylfcynne sent you. They will help you."

Patrick sucked in a breath and let it out between nearly pursed lips. He stared into the opening but saw nothing but the wall. "Wylfcynne," he repeated.

"Winifred's name in our world."

"Okay, let me see if I've got it all. Head east and then north at the river, Kilmari, Wylfcynne…I need a program to keep the players straight." He looked longingly for a piece of paper to write it all down. Finding none, he shrugged. "Is there anything else?"

"No," Polly said. "I must stay here and guard the portals until Wylfcynne returns. Good luck."

Patrick nodded. "Alvyn," he said to the snake. Then he took a step forward into another world.

48 Kimala

Patrick passed through the veil of stone that was Winnie's fireplace and into a corridor of quarried stone. Huge blocks were placed precisely so that the passageway arched high above his six foot two inch frame. Though he could see no direct source of light, the way was bright and pleasant. He felt oddly at ease here, welcomed. He tucked Winnie's cane into his belt and moved forward.

The corridor wound to the right and to the left, never branching. He could smell the freshness of a forest. Behind, he could no longer see the entrance to Winnie's house. The light in front of him grew brighter with dappled pink sunlight that graced the floor and the wall to his right. A few tall trees appeared ahead of him framing a cool blue sky. He could hear a bird of prey calling, the sound echoing in what was probably a valley.

"I don't think we're in Kansas anymore," he muttered as he passed into the open air of Eormengrund.

A stone formation carved from the elements jutted out beyond his exit point, bounded by a few tall trees. He walked the short distance to a natural ledge made of stone and looked down. Beyond a descent too steep to negotiate was a lush green valley filled with towering evergreen trees and tall, golden ferns. The horizon had changed to bright pink with the rising sun. Above him, the bird called a warning again and then soared so close that he could have touched its soft white underbelly. Patrick jumped back, his heart beating a little faster.

"Definitely not Kansas."

Polly said head east, then turn north when you reach the river. He planted his hands firmly on the stone ledge and leaned out as far as he dared. Red sunlight lit a ribbon that bisected the valley below.

"Great. A river in the middle of a canyon with no discernable way to get down to it except a death slide." He straightened. "Not happening," he said simply.

To his left, the wall rose, adjoining the passage he had exited. Beyond it was a continuation of the steep decline he had just noted. Above the tunnel, the same inaccessible rock seemed to grow. The only way he could go was to the right along a fairly level path.

"That makes it easy."

Patrick turned back to look at the entry, to engrave the way back in his mind. Stone had silently filled in the opening while he wasn't looking. He raced back to the now solid wall, searching for the doorway home.

"Please," he mumbled, running his hand along the rock face, "please don't do this to me." He removed Winnie's cane from his belt and tapped three times on the wall. "There's no place like home," he chanted in as near a repeat of the language he had spoken to enter this place as he could remember.

Nothing changed.

Patrick sighed. "Okay, looks like I head toward the river. Now, let's see…put away the cane, just in case I need it for heaven knows what, check weapons…" He felt all the familiar places, then sighed. "No toothpick. Oh well. 'Guess I'm ready as I'll ever be."

The path leading away from Winnie's home curved severely to the right into unseen territory, but there was no other way to go. Wishing for hiking boots instead of sneakers, he set off.

For a while, the path was easy to negotiate. To his right was a sheer wall of rock, to his left, a steep decline. Small tufts of grass poked out here and there along the little traveled path beside rocks that made footing sometimes uneven. The way was pleasant enough; warm sunshine and a slight breeze kept him company. The path meandered about the side of the mountain, conforming to its shape. Across a chasm spanning at least a quarter of a mile, he could make out a line that marked where he would end up. Except for an occasional bird, he was alone, exposed, should anyone want to see him. That line of sight worked also in his favor.

The path made a sharp right turn and Patrick stopped dead in his tracks. Gouges in the side of the mountain indicated that this portion of the path had fallen victim to substantial rainfall. Rocks jutted out from the surface. He had no choice but to try to negotiate it.

The washout was only ten or twelve feet across. Midway, part of the path seemed intact, enough for him to stop and reestablish his bearings on a solid looking outcropping of stone. There were handholds about five feet above where the path should have been and footholds at about a foot. They jutted out far enough that an experienced rock climber would have no trouble negotiating them. But Patrick was not experienced. He had climbed two rock walls in his life, one on a cruise ship, the other in a gym.

"You didn't fall off either one," he muttered. "You can do this. Move along. You have a girl to find."

He took off his shoes and socks, tied them together and secured them through a belt loop in the center of his pants. His bare feet would feel the footholds better than his sneakers. He turned and faced the wall. With a prayer, he reached for the first holds.

Like a spider, he hugged the wall, concentrating with all his might to maintain his balance. One hand, one foot, the other hand—He paused before leaving the security of the solid path. He put weight on each of the holds making certain they would not give way under his weight. They all seemed stable. His foot left the path.

Slowly, he changed positions, reaching for the next hold and testing each one before leaving the last. He negotiated all of them until he reached the midpoint. Gratefully, he paused, turning to face the chasm.

The outcropping of stone was indeed solid and about two feet square. A strong wind would threaten the balance of a smaller person.

"I wonder how Winnie does this," he thought aloud.

He surveyed the remaining six feet. Where the path resumed, it seemed about four feet wide. Handholds and footholds on the rock face were nearly identical to what he had just negotiated. Feeling confident, but not cocky, Patrick resumed his climb.

Hand, foot, hand, test, foot... he moved slowly over the last five feet. His left foot finally touched the reestablished path and he let out a sigh of relief. He heaved himself toward the path, eager to get on with his journey.

Gravel slid under his foot. He fell forward on his shin and threw his torso onto the path, grabbing at anything that didn't move. He found a tuft of grass and held on, steadying himself, determined not to lose his balance. Somehow, Winnie's cane was in his hand and he dug it into the path with all his might. Then, he pulled.

He inched forward until he was on an elbow, then raised his knee up so that he was on steady ground. His foot slipped sending dirt and rock into the chasm, but he found purchase. With effort, he flung himself around so that his back was braced against the mountain. He watched a rivulet of gravel cascade silently downward.

After a moment or two, he caught his breath. "Winnie, you are an amazing woman," he said. He pulled his shoes and socks on, re-secured Winnie's cane and checked his weapons. Nothing was missing. He rose and resumed his journey.

The terrain had changed, though he was still painfully exposed. He was surrounded by grass above and below him yet the drop to the river not so steep on this side of the washout. He had a nagging feeling that he was being watched even though not a soul was visible. Except, of course, the birds.

"If this is supposed to be a secret path, Winnie," he said, "I'm certainly very visible."

After what seemed an eternity, he found himself looking back across the chasm at the washed out portion of the path he had successfully negotiated. There was an outline indicating where he had traveled, though had he not known where to look, it would have been very difficult to find it. He was actually looking up to it, so he was making a slow descent into the valley. Ahead, the path disappeared. Determined, he continued.

A sharp turn exposed an ancient forest. He stood in front of an archway adorned by a curtain of vines. The woods on either side of it were so thick that the only practical way to go was straight through the vines. He pulled a candy bar from his pocket and leaned against a boulder that seemed to mark the entry. He tore the wrapping open and took a bite. The chocolate was sweet, a bit melted and it reminded him how hungry he was.

"It was just after dawn when I arrived," he said, taking a second bite, "and assuming that the sun rises in the east here...To hell with the Boy Scout nonsense." He checked his watch. "It's fourteen hundred--no wonder I'm hungry!" He thought about devouring the rest of the bar but instead he carefully re-wrapped the remainder and tucked it away again. Brushing his hands against one another, he stood and gazed skyward.

"No real choice here. Have to go through the forest."

He stepped into the wood.

A tingling sensation ran throughout his body as he crossed into relative darkness. He shivered in an effort to dispel the feeling. The crystal in the top of Winnie's cane shimmered like a switch had been turned on. Blue light emanated from it, glowing rather than sending out a beam. The light was unnecessary for him to see in order to maneuver through the forest. Patrick was briefly awed, then dismissed the occurrence as normal for this place. His senses had to focus on potential real threats instead of Winnie's benign magic.

Above him, a canopy of thick greenery broke open only sporadically to let the sun in. The soles of his shoes slipped occasionally on the large flat moss covered stones, so he took care to avoid them, whenever possible choosing dirt over rock.

After a while, the trees which had been growing so thickly thinned and let in more light. Smaller versions of the giant golden ferns he had seen from Winnie's patio were scattered under the trees, adding color to the undergrowth. Woodland animals spoke to one another, announcing the presence of a stranger. Patrick tried to ignore them but their calls made him very uncomfortable. He was much more at home in the city than here.

"What have we here?" someone asked.

"Hello?" Patrick answered.

"A lost traveler," someone else answered. "And dressed in odd attire."

"Are you Kilmari?" Patrick asked.

"He knows our kind, Prytal."

"But he is not of our world," Prytal answered.

"Winnie sent me!" Patrick said. He unlatched his sidearm but left it in the holster, his hand ready to draw it at a moment's notice. "She said I was supposed to contact the Kilmari."

"Winnie?" Prytal said. "Who is Winnie?"

"Winnie. Winifred James."

Murmurs rumbled around him and he strained to see how many people were present. The only thing visible was the forest. The voices sent a chill up his spine.

"Wylfcynne!" he remembered. "Winifred is Wylfcynne."

A third voice joined the first two. "He came from Wylfcynne's portal, Prytal," a woman said quietly. "I have been watching his progress all day. He used her cane to pass through the entrance of the forest. It glowed blue."

The murmurs grew louder.

"Look, I'm not here to hurt anyone," Patrick started. "A young girl has been kidnapped and I came to find her. I just need to get to the Udolphi River and then go north to someplace called Calshara. I'd be most grateful for some assistance, if that's possible."

"What do you know of Calshara?" Prytal demanded.

Prytal was behind him now and Patrick whirled to finally put a face to the voice. His toe caught on a moss-covered stone and he found himself sprawling on the ground. His gun flew to one side and three archers appeared. Their arrows were inches from his neck. He took a deep breath and pushed them away slowly.

"A demon from your world named Bue took her," he said. "I only want to find the girl and take her home. Can you help me or not?"

The arrows were lowered and Patrick breathed an inward sigh of relief. A man stepped forward from between the archers and looked down at him. He was smaller, built like a swimmer with wide shoulders and narrow hips. The clothing he wore blended in with the trees. A triangular hat capped his blond shoulder length hair. He rather reminded Patrick of the quintessential image of Robin Hood without the tights.

"I am Prytal," he said, dipping his head slightly. "You have entered the land of the Kilmari upon the mountain of Kimala in Greater Kimala. I assume you are from the Otherworld?"

"Patrick O'Shea, or just Patrick," he answered, thrusting a hand forward. Prytal looked at it, apparently confused and Patrick pulled it back. "Winnie never told me what she called my world, but I was born there." He started looking for his gun. One of the Kilmari had picked it up and was looking down the barrel. He quickly closed his hand over the weapon and pulled it away from the young man, taking care to point it away from anything.

"Thanks," he told the man.

"Is that a weapon, Patrick?" Prytal asked.

"Yes; a very dangerous one." He flipped the safety back on and holstered it. "I came through Winifred's portal. Bue and the girl went through Jessie Perrymore's."

"Lady Jessie?" Prytal asked.

"I have no idea," Patrick answered truthfully. He was suddenly very tired. "I don't know where Bue would take the girl, but Wylfcynne seemed to think Calshara was a good starting point and that the Kilmari would help me get there. All I'm asking is for you to point me in the right direction."

Everyone but Prytal melted back into the forest. "Follow me."

Prytal led him directly downhill. The way was steep but not as steep as the descent from Winnie's patio. Patrick used the cane as a short walking stick, balancing himself in the deep forest loam. In little time, they reached a camp of sorts where several men and women were gathered around a fire chatting amicably with one another, enjoying a meal. When they saw Prytal and Patrick, they waved them to take a seat and offered them food. Patrick accepted happily and ate while Prytal explained the situation to them.

"Bue has returned," Prytal said, "and she has a girl from the Otherworld as hostage."

"Who is he?" a tall woman asked.

"He calls himself Patrick. He arrived through Wylfcynne's portal."

Patrick nodded to the woman and she smiled slightly in return.

"I've come to retrieve the girl," he told her between mouthfuls of food.

A shadow crossed the sky above them and a laugh echoed through the forest so wicked that it made Patrick's skin crawl. He stood and searched the space he could see above the trees for the source. A huge bird was flying between the sun and ground, crying out as it passed. It had a partially white underbelly graced with a very small amount of pink. The leaves at the top of the trees rustled and the thing cried out again only this time it was more of a terrified scream.

"My God, that's the girl!" Patrick yelled.

"They're headed toward the river!" The entire camp ran. Patrick ran with them.

A hundred yards from the campsite, the forest revealed a vast, slow moving river. Bue was flying over it, screeching and screaming. The girl was twisting in her grasp, her hands coming loose every so often to flail at her captor.

The demon flapped her wings a few times to gain altitude, then turned around purposely, flying so close to the water that the surface parted in her wake. She let out an ear-splitting shriek causing everyone on the ground to cover their ears and duck; everyone but Patrick. He could make out Lucy's figure, pink slippers and all. She was justifiably frightened, but she had her wits about her. A flicker of recognition registered on her face when she saw him and she started fighting with a pair of the demon's many hands. She pulled something away from Bue and threw it into the water. It looked like the bag-o-demons.

"Get that camera bag!" Patrick yelled. He raced to the river's edge ready to dive in, but the footing was too slick and he fell. One of the Kilmari had better luck. He dove in after the bag, emerging moments later with Lucy's gift. It was indeed the bag-o-demons. He handed it to Patrick.

"What is this?" Prytal asked.

"It's a long story. Where is Bue taking Lucy?" he asked, letting the name slip unintentionally.

"I do not know," Prytal answered.

Bue screamed and circled back toward them.

"Quickly, back to the forest."

Patrick scrambled to his feet and raced back into the trees. Once under the cover of the trees, they were hidden from the demon.

"What is in the bag?" Prytal asked.

"Snow globes," Patrick answered truthfully. "We can't let Bue get this bag."

"Why?"

"Because each one contains a demon like her."

Prytal's eyes widened. "Are you certain?"

Patrick nodded. He pointed to the maddened demon. "I accidently let her go, so she owes me. If she gets close enough, I'd like to ask her to release Lucy, but then she would be free to do whatever she wants to do. It's the only ace I have."

Prytal took a moment. "Understood," he finally said.

Bue was flying methodically, tacking across the river, searching for the bag Lucy had forced her to drop. Until nearly dusk, they watched, but she never got close enough for Patrick to try to get a shot off. Then the demon simply left.

"Prytal," Patrick started, "I need your help."

"There is nothing we can do now," he answered.

"Winnie said Bue would take her to Calshara, Il Chatel. How far is that?"

"Five days on the fastest of horses, longer on foot, depending on the weather." He smiled grimly. "Little can be done tonight. At first light, I will take you."

49 Northbound

Three Kilmari, clad in black leather, were waiting with Altay and Penrose in front of the stable. Each soldier was astride a tall horse. The weather had changed from stormy to a steady light, but cold rain. Altay handed each of them a cloak. Jason thought, as he pulled his around his shoulders, that he would be wet inside half an hour. He flipped the hood up over his head anyway.

"Jason, take Snow," Penrose told him, "he seems to like you. Ric, there's a quiet bay ready for you over there."

"Bay?" Ric whispered to Altay.

"The red one," she whispered back. She stopped working with her own horse. "Do you need help?" she asked.

"No," Ric answered. "I think I'm okay. Does he have a name?"

"I don't know," Altay answered.

"Then I'll call him Red."

They mounted less gracefully than the rest probably had, but were soon seated and ready to go. Penrose was animatedly talking to one of the Kilmari, waving his hands and shaking his head. The soldier finally turned away. He signaled to the others and they formed a protective circle around Rick and Jason.

"We'll ride north to the river and follow it back to the mountain," Penrose told them with a wink. "It took a little convincing, but no Giant's Fingers this time."

Jason breathed a sigh of relief. "I didn't know it, but I'm glad we're not going that way," he said with a nod to the Kilmari, "even with all the firepower."

They started back up the hill behind the House just as they had come two days prior, only this time not at breakneck speed. Once up the hill, unique and exquisite rock formations were visible. It looked as though they erupted from the earth and then were sculpted by some giant artisan. Fall blooming flowers dotted the landscape, a colorful addition to the lush grass. They passed the Giant's Fingers in the first hour, though they carefully went around the massive stones so as not to get caught up in another ambush.

By early afternoon, the rain stopped and the sky cleared to the west and south. Kimala stood alone on the plain in front of them. The center of the mountain was still engulfed in clouds, but above the fluffy collar, the highest peak soared. Trees covered the lower half, the forest extending onto the plain making it impossible to tell where the flatland truly ended and the mountain began. In the shade of a single massive tree long before they were close to the mountain, Penrose halted them.

"We will take a small meal here before continuing," he said.

Jason and Ric sat with Altay and ate. The Kilmari took turns circling the camp. They wandered ahead and came back before they ate. Even while they ate, they watched.

"They kind of give me the creeps," Jason said as two of the soldiers ate without looking at their lunch.

"They protect," Altay explained quietly. "It is their way." She was looking at them with an odd reverence.

Jason exchanged a glance with Ric who shrugged. Neither said anything more about it.

When the meal was over, they walked beside their horses for a while, more to stretch their legs than to give the animals a break. Ric took up a conversation with one of the Kilmari leaving Jason to walk beside Altay. He reached down and plucked one of the bright yellow flowers that grew along the way and handed it to her.

"Beauty for a beauty," he said lamely.

Ric groaned, but Alay blushed.

"Thank you," she said, taking the flower. She sniffed it and a bit of pollen soiled the tip of her nose.

Jason rubbed his finger across his own nose as a signal to her that something was there. She knitted her eyes. "What?"

"Here." He took a corner of his cape and gently wiped the smudge off. "Just a little pollen," he explained.

She giggled and the red deepened. "Thank you again," she repeated.

"You're welcome again."

They resumed walking, sandwiched between their guards. Ric fell back, this time to walk with Penrose.

"How did you get interested in becoming a healer?" Jason asked.

Altay shrugged. "I never thought I would be anything else. As a child, I was constantly collecting small animals who could not fend for themselves and fixing their hurts. I became accomplished at it and the Vicar of my village told Penrose about me. Penrose and I met, then spoke at length. I became apprenticed to him, as his former apprentice, Sila Atin, was accomplished enough to work without supervision." She smiled. "That was eight years ago. I hope to return to my village to serve as their healer. Penrose says I am ready."

"What do you say?" Jason asked.

Altay shrugged. "I am comfortable with the title of Healer and with the job. But with war on the horizon, the need for healers is greater here than it is at home." She twirled the flower between her fingers. "What is your calling?" she asked.

Jason looked up at the horizon. "Well, I'm a rather successful stock broker, albeit an online one." He looked at her and grinned at her confusion. "My degree is in accounting, though. I, uh, don't know your world well enough to make a comparison. Barterer maybe?"

"Oh yes, we have people who barter." She smiled at him. Jason could never remember a woman smiling at him like that before. "So you are in the business of trading?"

"Yes," he answered. "But what I really want to do is be a performer, you know a dancer or a singer. Or both. Broadway would be a great place to work. It's very exciting."

She frowned. "That is not a worthy profession," she said.

Jason laughed. "It is if you're good enough."

"Mount up, everyone," Penrose ordered.

Jason turned Snow around so that the horse was standing a bit lower than he was. He put his foot in the stirrup and stepped up. The saddle sagged toward him and he pulled himself up until he sat on the horse's back. Snow turned his head back to look at Jason, his ears laid back.

"What?" Jason asked him.

The horse shook his head.

"Hey, at least I didn't need help this time," he told him.

"Cover!" one of the Kilmari shouted.

Almost as one, eight riders went from a near standstill to a full gallop. One of the Kilmari grabbed Jason's reins and Snow kept up with the wild pace of the other horses, leaving Jason to hold on to his mane to keep his balance. The frantic ride took them swiftly over the remaining plain until they reached a half dozen boulders that marked the boundary between the trees and the grassland. The Kilmari leapt off, bows at the ready. Jason and Ric slid to the ground behind the others, craning their necks to see what was going on. It was so quiet that Jason could hear everyone breathing. Then something screamed and Jason's blood ran cold.

It was in the air, huge and black with wings that spread an unnatural distance. Beneath it was something small and white that appeared very much out of place. Jason squinted his eyes in an effort to see whatever it was better. The creature was approaching them.

"A lesser Fot," one of the Kilmari whispered. "He is bold indeed to fly so close to Kimala."

"That is not just any demon," Penrose gasped, "it is Bue!" He turned to Jason. "Did you release more than one demon?" he demanded.

"We didn't release anyone," Jason said firmly, "we broke a snow globe—"

"Only one?" Penrose snapped.

"Yes." This time it was Ric who answered. "What does it mean?"

"Bue was trapped in your world. Someone else has released her and she found her way back."

"Oh hell," they replied in unison.

Bue's massive wings flapped lazily and she gained a little altitude. The demon was carrying something in its claws. It was a small person, dressed in white with…pink slippers?

"Who…?" Ric asked.

Jason stared at the person. "Oh my God!" he whispered as his heart sank, "it's Lucy!"

The demon flew toward them, screeching as it did. It looked directly at Jason and Jason paled. Bue flew straight up and he felt her jubilation as she rose, her cry striking a nerve from his chest to his toes. She leveled off, making a lazy turn back toward Kimala. The mighty wings stroked twice more and Bue dove for them, her mouth open in an earsplitting screech that struck everyone. Jason clapped his hands over his ears trying to understand her words. He knew the intent. She was laughing at them. Lazily, she turned to the north, then sped away.

"Jason!" Penrose called.

"I'm all right," he answered, rubbing temples. "She's got Lucy!"

Penrose looked confused.

"Lucy!" Jason repeated. "My cousin! Jessie's daughter! We've got to help her!"

Penrose was taken aback, but he quickly schooled his features. "We will make camp, then decide on our course," he said.

"But-"

"She knows where we are," Penrose said, "and she will find Fot. Our plans have just become more complicated. A demon can fly much faster than the fastest horse can run," he continued when Jason started to protest. "Please, trust me."

"Ric?" he asked.

"What choice do we have?" his friend answered.

They mounted their horses and headed into the cover of the forest.

50 The Gift

Jason stretched out on the ground with his hands clasped behind his head, staring into the night. The stars were in the same patterns here, but they were more vivid, the space between them blacker than he had ever seen and that blackness was dotted by specks of light he had never seen. The Udolphi flowed a hundred yards from their camp, so wide that it made very little sound, but that sound haunted him. The horses were stirring close by and the Kilmari were speaking to one another in hushed tones that were not reassuring. Ric lay propped up on one elbow, watching them.

"JM?"

"Yeah?"

"Did you mean it about paying off my college loan?" He sounded like a kid sitting on Santa's lap at Christmas.

"Yeah. And your tuition."

"I'll pay you back."

"You already have."

Ric nodded to the Kilmari. "Don't they ever sleep?"

"I don't know. 'Sure doesn't seem like it." He pointed to two figures seemingly asleep close to them. "Penrose and Altay do, though."

"Must be nice to turn it on and turn it off again."

"We've got to convince Penrose to let us stay and hunt for Lucy."

An owl hooted somewhere deep in the woods and was answered by a wolf further away on the mountain. Ric laid back and stared into the autumn sky. "I agree. We have an obligation to your cousin."

An easy silence fell between them. Jason closed his eyes. The forest sang to him and he longed to join in the song. He resisted, instead drifting into sleep.

"Jason!"

Someone had him by the shoulder, shaking him awake. He snagged the arm at the wrist. It was Penrose. "What?" he asked sleepily.

"Get up!"

He shook off sleep. Penrose was rousing Ric. "Run for the woods!" he told them.

"Why?" both boys asked.

"Demon!"

Something very large soared over them so low that they fell to the ground, covering their heads with their hands. Behind them someone screamed. As one they turned to see it pluck Penrose off the ground. The healer squirmed in the demon's grasp, yelling obscenities as the metal of a short blade flashed in the starlight. Yet the two flew on. Mesmerized, the Otherworlders now stood where they fell, watching man and demon rise into the clear night sky. The duo circled as the alarm sounded in the camp all around them. Then the creature dove toward them, dipping so close that Jason smelled lavender and garlic.

"Fot!" Jason gasped.

Penrose squirmed wildly to get into a better position to strike. His erratic movements threw Fot off balance. The demon rose thirty, then forty feet into the air, barely clearing the tops of the trees with his unruly burden, then swooped mere inches above the ground as though he were a wave of water passing over rocks and grasses. Penrose dangled in his grasp, bouncing mercilessly off the rough terrain.

Kilmari surrounded Jason and Ric, grabbing limbs and shoving them toward the trees. They were at a dead run, leaping over downed branches and stones in a crazy zigzag pattern intended to keep them out of Fot's grasp. Jason concentrated so hard on running as fast as he could that he had no time to pay attention to where he was going. Kilmari flanked him on either side; when he stumbled, they did not let him fall. On and on into the forest they ran until Jason's lungs burned. Gasping for air, he finally had to stop and rest, leaning both hands against the trunk of a tree.

"Where is the other Otherworlder?" one of the Kilmari asked.

"Behind," his counterpart answered. "They are coming."

"How many?"

"Only two. Lesser-Fots."

"Two lesser-Fots…" He clapped Jason on the shoulder, shaking his head. "Do not concern yourself, lad," he started. "We are nearly to safety."

"P-Penrose?" he managed between gasps.

"I fear the healer is lost," the man said.

"No!"

"There is little hope, lad," he answered. "We saw him fall."

Jason managed to nod. "Ric?"

"He is coming."

"Altay?"

"The lass is already safe. She went ahead while you slept."

"Good." He pointed vaguely skyward. "One of those things up there is Fot."

The Kilmari exchanged a look but whatever they were thinking they didn't voice. Jason didn't bother to try to figure it out. He just launched into his story.

"We accidentally released him, released Fot," Jason explained, "before we knew what he was and what he would do," he added hurriedly.

They stared at him.

"He smells like garlic and lavender!" Jason insisted. "I smelled it when he tried for me and grabbed Penrose instead! It's unmistakable!"

One looked at the other and shook his head. "It does not matter whether the demon is Fot or is not," he said. "He has proven himself a deadly predator. Are you ready to move, lad?"

Jason nodded.

"Beyond that meadow is a cave that we can defend. It is too long to go around so we will have to risk running through it."

"But he'll see us!" Jason protested.

"It is a risk we must take. We will be safe on the other side. I will go first." He nodded to the Kilmari behind Jason. "Bring him when the way is clear."

The second took the first by the arm in a handshake of comradery. "Be careful."

"I do not intend to meet the Lady on this day," he said.

They were on the move again. The cave was visible barely a hundred feet from them. Jason stood at the edge of the meadow as the Kilmari began to make his way across. He sniffed the air, hoping not to smell the demon. It was fresh and clean.

"I don't think he's around," he told his guardian.

"That remains to be seen," the man responded. He held Jason back, as if the young man needed incentive not to run, but he was watching his comrade's progress. The other was nearly across the field.

A breeze swept through the glen, bringing with it the sounds of the mountain. Jason straightened as its music seeped into his mind. He clapped his hands over his ears to screen it out, to wholly ignore it. But it demanded to be heard and he found himself listening. Among the gentle tones he recognized as the forest there was a whisper of agony.

"Do you hear that?" he asked.

The Kilmari tilted his head and listened. "I hear nothing," he answered.

Jason dropped his hands to his sides and whatever it was wailed. The sound struck a nerve that ran the length of his body before he could filter it. His knees tried to buckle and it was all he could do to keep standing. The cries kept coming, staccato against the thrum of the forest.

"Lad, we must get you to safety," he said. "He is in position to defend us. Are you ready?"

The gift hit him with so many sounds that he almost sagged. He nodded because he knew if he put voice to words he needed to say, even a simple yes, his answer would be in song and somehow the Kilmari would stop him from singing. Yet he had to act. The gift demanded it.

The moaning came from a short distance to his left. The Kilmari was uphill from him, on the wrong side to stop him if he was quick enough. Adrenaline charged through his veins. The Kilmari released him.

"Stay low and run," his guardian whispered.

Jason ran.

When he was five feet away from the soldier, he let the song escape. With the first vibration, he knew it was the right thing to do. Someone was terribly broken not twenty feet from him and he knew that no matter who it was, he had to help. At once he burst into song and ran for the tortured soul.

"Jason!" the Kilmari yelled.

Jason ignored him. He was almost on the body; the moaning was so soft now that Jason knew life was ebbing away. He knelt beside the barely moving form and grasped the cold hand in his own, rubbing it gently as the words of an ancient song formed in his mind and begged to spew from his lips. The wounded head turned toward him. It was Penrose. The healer did not speak. There was life in him, life that was bound to this world by nothing greater than a thread, but life. Jason sang.

The Kilmari squatted beside Jason. He turned the stricken man's head up gently so that the pale moonlight struck the paler features of the healer. "Jason, he is all but spent," he said gently. "You must come now. It is what he would have wanted."

But the song was on Jason now and he could not stop it. Though he did not recognize the words, he knew he sang of spring and the resurgence of life. The wind that had called to him stopped now to listen, as did the creatures of the forest. They gave of themselves, channeling a piece of their being into Jason, thanking him for the song. Jason felt it rise from the earth he knelt upon, prickling through his clothing as though he had passed too close to a high voltage wire. He sent the energy through his fingertips into Penrose and the healer sucked in a huge breath.

Jason let the song swell. He still did not recognize the words but he knew what they meant. He was going to win this man's life back for him, just as surely as he had won Cynthal's and Ric's. The song all but consumed him and he had to finish it. That song commanded him now, guiding his being. The last stanza came to him and Jason did not miss a word.

For a moment, all was still. Penrose looked up at him with thanks in his eyes. The Kilmari stared serenely at them, lost in tranquility. Jason was so deeply enthralled he did not see the demon take him. Arrows whizzed by his head. He did not feel them.

"Jason!" Ric yelled.

The smell of lavender and garlic nearly smothered him. He could feel the warmth of something huge standing behind him, could hear the roar of displeasure as the last note left his lips. Penrose stirred. The spell was broken.

"Aberration!" the demon hissed.

Slowly, Jason turned to face him. The world was silent now except for the breathing of one very angry demon. Fury burned in his eyes as he bent close to Jason's face. Fot raised an arm and slammed Jason in the face. He reeled and fell to the ground.

51 Snatched

As promised, Prytal woke Patrick when the first rays of sunlight warmed Kimala's face. Food was being cooked close by, the undeniable scent of fresh cooked meat permeating the air. It was cold, but only bracingly so. Patrick stretched.

"Here," Prytal said, handing him a light cloak and a pair of boots. "I think you will find these more suitable for our journey."

"Thanks." Patrick pulled the boots on and slung the cloak over his shoulders. "Much better."

After a brief meal, they left the camp. Patrick carried the bag-o-demons by the shoulder strap. They were awkward, but not terribly heavy. He found himself in the center of six Kilmari, including Prytal. Their pace was fast and steady. He was glad to have had a night's rest before they set out.

For an entire day, they walked, rarely speaking, instead concentrating on their way. There were no sightings of Bue or Lucy, nothing to say they were following in the right direction. They stayed on the bank of the Udolphi, the path easier to negotiate there.

"When the river turns to the north," Prytal explained, "we will continue to the east." He pointed to a tiny formation in the distance. "That's where we are headed."

They kept traveling even after the sun set, no longer looking for clues, rather focused on their destination. They paused for brief meals and short rests. Each time, Patrick checked the three clips of ammo he had buckled to his belt; twelve shots in each one, seven left in the nine millimeter in his holster. Forty-three bullets. Forty-three shots in his major weapon, six in the snub nose strapped to his ankle. Forty-nine shots before he would have to resort to his fists. He could not call for back up. He was on his own. A little voice inside his head was demanding to know just what the hell he thought he was doing.

I'm saving a child, he told himself.

Day turned to night and once more they were travelling in darkness. Prytal kept them moving at least five hours after dusk. Patrick didn't mind. The less time they spent camping, the sooner he would find Lucy.

A young woman emerged from the woods. She was wearing white breeches and seemed genuinely surprised to see them. "Prytal?"

"Altay!" Prytal answered. "What brings you here?"

"We are escorting two Otherworlders to the portal," she replied. "And you?"

"We are searching for an Otherworlder as well," he answered, "with the help of another Otherworlder."

Patrick stepped forward. "Ma'am," he said with a nod. "Would one of them be named Jason McCarthy?" he asked.

"Jason, yes," Altay replied.

The peace of the night was broken by music. As one, they stopped and listened, captivated by the melody's beauty. For long moments, they stood in the moonlight listening until the song ended.

"No!" Altay whispered. She turned and ran. They followed.

Music turned to anger. Patrick could not make out the words, but the voices were strained. In the scant moonlight, he saw what he had seen in the sky above the river, only this time the demon was on the ground and a lot larger than he remembered.

"Aberration!" the demon shouted.

From ten different places in the forest, archers appeared. Patrick pointed his gun at the demon but before he could get off a shot, someone ran out from the edge of the woods and stopped directly in his line of fire.

"Fot!"

The demon turned to face the man, his red eyes glinting in the moonlight. "When I have finished with the Aberration," Fot said, "then we shall barter. Until then--"

"Now! I want to barter now!"

"Ric!" Altay shouted. "Be careful!"

Ric started to move forward toward the demon. "You said he owes me, right Altay? I released him and he owes me."

Fot laughed. "Be careful, little man," he said.

"Yes, he is in your debt," Altay replied. She was suddenly beside Patrick, a gentle hand on his arm stopping the policeman's forward motion. "But no one has ever released a demon before," she whispered to him. "Repaying the debt is only legend."

Fot laughed. "You would do well to listen to the woman-child, little man," he almost cooed as he took a step backward and to one side. There were three bodies on the ground in front of him. Two were stirring, the other was quite still. Fot spread a pair of wings so great that the sky darkened and a hundred pairs of hands appeared along his almost elegant body.

"I said I want to barter now!" Ric repeated.

Fot tilted his head to one side and flexed the wings backward, allowing the moonlight to once again shine in the meadow. He folded all his arms up so that they crossed across his belly, leaving only one pair to reach down and examine the bodies at his very human-like feet.

"Not very impressive," Fot said, picking up the still body and letting it fall like a sack of potatoes. "Not very impressive, indeed."

"You owe me, Fot," Ric said. He was slowly advancing toward the demon. As he moved, a cloud of subtle green light formed an aura around him.

Patrick squinted, still trying to get the demon in his sights but Ric kept getting in the way.

"We can make a deal, Fot." Ric stopped just out of reach of the huge creature.

"A deal?" the demon answered. His words were mesmerizing in the stillness. "What have you in mind, little man?"

"You guarantee me that you will not harm them and we'll call it even."

"No harm?" Fot laughed. "You want me not to harm them? Is that all?"

A shadow crossed the moon and Patrick looked up. Against the silvery orb a second demon was silhouetted. It was nearly as great as the one on the ground in front of them, only this one had a slender, almost sensual outline. It moved with a grace as hypnotic as Fot's voice. *Bue.*

"And you tell your followers not to hurt anybody either!" Ric added.

Fot looked up at him, eyes gleaming. "There is a limit to even my influence over others," the demon said smoothly. "I can give no guarantee that they will not harm anyone."

"Then I will not release you from your debt," Ric said.

Fot sighed. He dipped his great head to one side, the glowing red eyes looking toward the bodies on the ground and then back up at Ric once more. "My debt to you and to this, this aberration…" Fot smiled. "Perhaps I would enjoy different conditions."

"Different?" There was a note of panic in Ric's voice. Patrick shifted around so that he could get a better angle but it was dark and, though his target was very large, he didn't know where to shoot him to take best advantage of his limited ammunition.

"Yes, little man," Fot said. The demon shifted in the meadow, knowingly or not, positioning himself such that Ric was once again in the line of fire. "After all, there should be some give and take if we are to barter. Do you not agree?"

"I'm offering you a way to be paid in full! Done with us, not beholding, finished and you want to barter?"

"No little man." Fot dipped his head down and his voice softened. "I want you dead."

Fot picked up the body of the Kilmari who had tried to escort Jason across the field. He tore the dead man's arm from his body and tossed it nonchalantly to one side as though it were a petal on a flower. He then plucked the other arm off. With a sigh, he cast the body away. Ric looked like he was going to retch.

"There is little sport," Fot said, moving forward to the second body in the field, "in taking the arms from a dead man." He reached down and picked up the second body. The man moaned. "Ah, a little emotion from this one."

"Put him down!" Patrick yelled. He moved swiftly into the field. "I said, put him down."

Fot held the man in his hands and tilted his head sideways to address this newcomer. "Another Otherworlder?" Fot said casually.

"Yeah. Now put him down!"

Bue glided to the ground and landed soundlessly beside Fot. She moved with the grace of a ballerina despite her size as she made her way over to the last of the three bodies on the field.

"Bue?" Patrick said.

"Officer O'Shea, I believe?" Bue said. "And you have brought one of your weapons. How lovely!"

"Where's the girl?"

"Ankaal," she replied. She turned her attention to the body on the ground. "And this is?"

"Jason," Ric blurted.

"Another Otherworlder," she said pleasantly. "Fot, my dear, we seem to be over-run with them."

"Where's Ankaal?" Patrick demanded.

"You were in their world far longer than I," Fot said to Bue. "Are they all this impertinent?"

"Fot, you agreed to barter," Ric said. "If you don't harm them, I will release you from your obligation."

Fot lowered Penrose to the ground and let him fall. The healer managed to roll away from them but he lay still, panting. "Very well," he said. "I guarantee that I will not harm them. Do we have an accord?"

Ric moved closer to them and Penrose moaned. Jason was breathing but not conscious. "Yes, Fot, we have an accord."

Fot laughed. The sound chilled Patrick to the bone. "The young man who released me and I seem to have reached an accord, my beloved," Fot told her. "I have promised not to pull the Aberration's head from his shoulders tonight."

"So I heard, my love." She reached down and took Jason's limp body into her arms. With one hand, she petted his head as though he was a favorite cat. "Would you like for me to do it for you?" she asked.

"She can't hurt him either!" Ric yelled.

"Ah, but that was not part of our accord," Fot said. "I believe the woman child warned you not to act on impulse. You should have listened. Beloved?"

Bue sat Jason down on the ground and stood on his thighs with her hands on either side of his head.

"I believe you and I have an accord to reach as well, Bue!" Patrick yelled.

She stopped moving and turned to Fot.

"Did this Otherworlder release you, Beloved?" he asked quietly.

"Unfortunately, he did," she said.

"Pity."

"You won't harm them either, demon!" Patrick said. "Ever!"

"Oh, now there's a thinking man," Fot said. He turned to Bue. "I believe the aberration needs to be taken where he will not be harmed. Ever. Would you assist me, my love?"

Before anyone could move, Bue slid her arms under Jason's shoulders, hoisting him up so that his body rested against hers. With one massive stroke of her wings, she was aloft with Jason dangling from her belly.

"We had an accord!" Ric said.

"We still do," Fot answered. "No harm will come to him at my hands, nor will any come to that pathetic remnant of a man at your feet. We do, after all, have an accord." A smile spread across his face and the elegant head bowed. "You, on the other hand, are fair game."

"What?" Ric asked.

An instant later Fot was twenty feet in the air, roaring angrily like a bear who got too close to a bee hive. He was getting ready to swoop down on Ric. The young man dove to the ground, landing beside the healer. Penrose handed something to him that glowed blue and silver and gold. An instant later, so did Ric. Fot started his run.

"Do something!" Altay screamed.

Patrick took careful aim and fired. The gun jammed. He reached for the snub nose in the ankle holster and drew it with ease. He had just enough time to take aim.

He needn't have bothered.

Ric was beating back the monster with fireballs that he was manufacturing from thin air. Fot landed soundlessly on the ground and a great black sword appeared in his hands. He moved forward toward Ric, the sword catching the fireballs now and casting them harmlessly aside.

Fot was nearly on him.

"We had an accord!" Ric said.

"I agreed not to harm them," Fot said. "There was nothing in our agreement about you!"

Ric dropped to the ground beside Penrose and raised his hand in an arc from one side of the healer to the other. A shimmering green bubble laced with threads of blue, gold and silver appeared over them. Fot struck the bubble with his sword and the top of it sagged inches from Ric's head.

Patrick fired off all six shots, striking the demon in the chest again and again. Fot fell backward with each shot. He howled and staggered to keep his feet. He turned his attention toward Patrick and screeched so loudly that Patrick clapped his hands over his ears. Then he rose into the air and flew to the north.

Patrick raced over to the bubble. As he reached it, the glow dissipated and was gone, leaving only the healer and the lanky youth in the now still meadow. From all around in the forest, the Kilmari emerged, joining them. Ric was holding a clear crystal in his hand.

"Now will come the difficult part," Penrose croaked.

"You lied to us!" Ric shouted.

"Yes, I did. It was for your peace of mind." His eyes closed but he forced them open again. "There is no such thing as a dead room. But that trick works every time."

"What about Jason!" Ric yelled. "That demon took him!"

Penrose shook his head. "Yes, she did, but she has sworn not to harm him. And she will not. Nor will Fot. He fears the consequences of the legend too much."

"I'm going after him," Ric said.

"No."

They all looked at Penrose as though he were crazy.

"Why?" Patrick asked.

"Because, for the moment, Jason is safe. A battle line has been drawn." He closed his eyes and pain crossed his face. "Jessie and Eron need your help." He looked up at the two Otherworlders. "I do not know what you are able to do," he said, "but the Lady has summoned you. We need your help against the demons." He looked directly at Patrick. "Keep him safe," he said, nodding to Ric as he spoke. "He is part of our hope now."

"But Jason!" Ric said.

"If we win the battle, we shall have an army to search for him," Penrose said.

"But--"

"Demons can fly over vast areas of terrain," he explained softly. He placed a weak hand on Ric's arm. "The demon said the girl was on Ankaal."

"Where is that?"

"North of Il Chatel, if legend is fact," Prytal stated.

"And that's where she is taking Jason." Ric shook off Penrose's hand and stalked to the side of the meadow. He stopped beside a boulder and leaned into it, burying his head in the crook of his arm. Patrick started after him.

"Wait." Penrose motioned weakly for Patrick to join him. Reluctantly, Patrick stopped and turned his attention to Penrose. "He is barely a man," he continued, "and he now carries a heavy burden. You are an Otherworlder?"

"What was your first clue?" Patrick replied, holstering his 9mm. He was tired and hungry and he wasn't in the mood for mysteries. "Don't tell me, let me guess. The accent, right?"

Penrose stared at him for a moment in silence and Patrick got the feeling he was back in second grade with Sister Sarah reprimanding him for shooting spit wads at Ernie Phelps.

But Penrose smiled sadly instead. "I am afraid you have become involved in a war that does not concern you."

"I am a police officer. I came to rescue a little girl."

Penrose looked fully at Patrick. "Bue will retrieve Lucy and take her to Il Chatel. She is a bauble, a tool they will use against her mother."

"How far is this Il Chatel?" Patrick asked.

Penrose shook his head. "There is a war brewing between Calshara and the combined forces of Jeleste, Bel Haven and Kimala. Marand will bring the girl to the battlefield and display her as a trophy. Your best chance of retrieving her is there. He is an egotistical fop who does not think very far into his own future." He tried to smile but only one corner of his mouth rose. "For now, she is safe."

"I know the way," Prytal said.

"Good." He nodded to Altay and the girl resumed her attentions to him. "Rest now," he told Patrick. He waved a weak hand in Ric's general direction. "Make him sleep as well. In scant hours the morning will come and you will have to ride swiftly."

"What about Jason?" Patrick said.

Penrose let his head fall back against the pillow Altay had fashioned for him and closed his eyes. "Jason's fate," he whispered, "is in the hands of the Lady."

52 Cold Storage

Jason felt the wind rushing over his face. He wondered why he was holding his head out the window of Jessie's Mustang when he would surely be more comfortable behind the windshield. The road they were on was filled with twists and turns, not to mention the ups and downs that were making his stomach turn somersaults.

"Okay, Jessie," he said, trying to force his eyes open. The wind was so strong he couldn't do it. "You've convinced me. You're ready for grand prix racing." His eyelids managed to open a slit and he gasped.

Gone were the archaic dashboard with the huge numbers, the old push-button AM radio and the carnival dice hanging from the mirror. In addition, the road and even the ground were gone. All that greeted him was darkness.

Hands crossed over him, holding him snuggly to something that should have been a body, but it was cold. Scaly fingers gripped him so tightly he couldn't move. He tried to thrash. Laughter trickled down the wind to him.

"Wha--who---" He gulped. "Help!"

More fingers covered his mouth and snatched his head back until it was cradled among cold scales.

Jason heard the wings rush up and down as they rose higher. Lights winked up at him from some distant place. They were far too high for him to hear anything or make out even the shapes of buildings, let alone people, but he was fairly certain they were above a city. They plummeted toward the lights, speed increasing so fast Jason's stomach threatened to revolt. They leveled off and he could see towers and windows and people pointing toward him, but he could hear nothing. He tried to center himself, to find the music once more and let it ease his frazzled nerves.

But instead of soothing tones, all he could hear was discord and that harsh, unforgiving laughter. He struggled, trying to free his hands to cover his ears but the hands holding his own were too strong. Jason groaned. He was empty, devoid of what had recently given him life.

Penrose was right. The music had left him. His gift was forfeit.

On and on they flew into deepening darkness. Noise, not music, was caught in Jason's head and he couldn't get rid of it. It swelled until he wanted to scream. He shut his eyes tightly, trying to will it away. *It has to end soon, has to...* He drifted into sleep.

Daylight greeted him when next he was aware. Grassy plains gave way to white rock and he craned his head so that he could see the horizon. A massive stone wall was racing toward them. He tried to shout a warning, but he couldn't. The demon carrying him flew straight toward it until they were almost on it. Instead of careening to one side or the other, the demon made a gut wrenching turn skyward, holding Jason so close to the surface that his face was occasionally smacked by pine branches. The trees thinned very quickly as they rose until there was nothing but scrubby shrubs. The demon stopped their upward movement and gently landed. The hands released him and he staggered away on rubbery legs. He was cold, colder than he had been in a long, long time. Altay's cloak wasn't keeping him warm. He turned to see who or what had deposited him in this place and was met by the eyes of a demon.

"Do not sing, Aberration," the demon warned, "else I will be forced to test the legend."

"J-Jason?"

Jason whirled round. In the hazy light, a figure moved slowly toward him. He squinted, trying to make her come into focus, his eyes not quite seeing clearly after the long journey. Something about her was too familiar and the knot in his stomach tightened. Suddenly she was in his arms, weeping uncontrollably.

"Lucy?" he whispered.

"I--I was hoping it was all a b-bad dream," she whimpered.

"No such luck," he answered.

"Careful, Aberration."

Jason looked beyond his cousin. A beautiful woman stood facing him, her long hair billowing around her face in the cutting wind. She was taller than any woman he had ever seen with eyes that glowed red and green in the sparse light. As she walked toward them, her clothing clung to her body, material so sheer it had little substance. Her body was enough to make a cover model jealous. But Jason kept being drawn to her eyes, her flashing, beautiful, deadly eyes.

"Where are we?" he asked, rubbing Lucy's back gently. "And who are you? And where is the demon?"

"So many questions," she said in a sultry voice that matched her movements.

"She *is* the demon," Lucy answered. "Bue is her name." She pushed herself away from Jason slightly and brushed the tears from her eyes.

Bue stared at Jason with scrutiny, then Lucy, then Jason once more. Jason's skin crawled. He drew Lucy in to him as much for his own comfort as for hers. "Lord Fot says you all look alike," she started, "but there is a greater resemblance here. It seems we have two prizes that are dear to the Shield."

"Shield?" Lucy said.

"Jessie," Jason answered.

"Mom's here?" Lucy almost shouted. "Thank God!" She turned to look fully at Jason. "She's the Shield?" she asked.

"Yeah," Jason answered. "What do you know about it?"

Lucy nodded through her tears. "It's all in the Book of Wylfcynne here," she said. She pointed to a distant peak. "That's Kimala," she explained. He followed her finger as she pointed to a range of mountains and a huge open plain with two peaks on either side. "That's the Paranjothi range and those are the Sisters, Emmalie and Pikea. The Lady separated them because they argued too much and when they wouldn't stop, she turned them to stone." She motioned grandly with her hand to the place where they were standing. "And if I'm not mistaken, we are on top of Ankaal, guardian of the North."

"My, my, but you are well schooled for an Otherworlder," the demon said. "From here you can see many things," the demon said. She waved a hand toward the valley below them. "Oh, but wait. You humans have such limited sight." She laughed and Jason's blood ran cold. "But you will have opportunity to try while you wait here for death."

"Death?" Jason and Lucy repeated together.

"Not you, my dear," she said to Lucy. She reached out and took the girl's hand with her own that was sensually graceful. "No, not you. I have other plans for you."

Bue's hand, pristine, white and perfect changed to scaly brown fingers with red claws. Her wispy clothing melted into delicate but powerful wings and her neck elongated until she was a serpent. She never let go of Lucy and now she changed her grip, whirling the girl around so that she was slammed into the demon's torso. Fifty pairs of hands erupted from beneath the spreading wings to secure the girl to the serpent's body.

"No!" Lucy said.

"Do you not wish to see your mother?" the demon laughed. "I could grant you a peek, just before I pluck her head from her shoulders."

"Jason!"

Bue slammed Jason backward with a free hand, sending him sprawling on the gritty face of the mountain. "Do try to follow," she said with a laugh. "I promised not to harm you. Some find food here, that is, if you are truly blessed. Then you can live out your miserable life alone."

"But-"

"You are safe here, but should you try to leave this place, there are things that will kill you."

"Jason!"

Bue laughed. She took a running start at the edge of the cliff with Lucy in her grasp and leapt over it. Jason rushed over in time to see them sail away. He was cold and alone atop a mountain with an odd name in a land he did not know.

53 Preparing Marand's Prize

The city of Il Chatel was coming to life. Men trudged through the streets pulling animals laden with goods behind them, women offered food, and boys peddled firewood and girls peddled flowers. The scent of bathwater and the sweat of horses filled the air.

Sila was nearly asleep behind Tick when the thief finally stopped. The lingering reality that she was not going home to Bel Haven nor was she ever going to see Eron again loomed large. She had made mistakes that had alienated her from her people and for the first time in her life, she did not know if she would be forgiven. She would have been safe had she simply followed the others back to camp, but her romantic need to become a martyr supplanted reason. She had run away like a schoolgirl avoiding telling her parents about a bad test score. Deep in her soul, she knew she would have been forgiven. This choice was rash and irresponsible. Sadly, she realized that this bad choice was one of many bad ones she had made. There was no way to change it, not now; perhaps not ever. This was her reality and in it, she would learn to survive.

"Get off, lass," Tick said. He held his arm back so that she could use it to slide off the horse. Once on the ground, she took a moment to get her balance before Tick joined her. "Inside," he said, taking her up onto a porch in front of a sturdy but plain building.

"Where are we?" she asked.

"Not to worry." His voice was softer than it had been. "No 'arm will come to ye 'ere."

Sila limped to the door with Tick in her wake.

Inside, a woman sat behind a worn wooden counter. The floor was warped and spotted with water. He had taken her to a bath house! The sweet scent of lavender filled Sila's nostrils. Her abused body cried out for the soothing warmth of the bath.

"Two?" the woman said.

Tick shook his head. "Goods for the market," He put a few coins on the counter. "This one's special, Madame Pink. A bath, a half bed, an' somethin' nice, pretty, to wear."

Madam's eyes widened and she smiled. "Right ye are, sir! A bath fer the lady, a nap and something to show off her goods!"

"'Ave her ready by noon. I wouldn't want ter miss the auction."

"Aye, sir!"

Tick caught Sila by the arm and pulled her close to him so he could whisper to only her. "Enjoy yerself, lass, but don' even think about runnin'. I'll be outside."

"This way, miss," the woman said.

Sila followed.

The floor of the room they entered was slightly damp and a girl held linens up for Sila to inspect. Her escort scowled and snatched the towel away with one hand while she cuffed the girl with her other hand.

"'Er master paid for fresh linens, ye beggar," the woman said as she raised her hand to strike the child again.

Sila caught her arm before it could land a second blow. "The child had no way of knowing," she said, releasing the woman. When she was certain no further punishment would be administered, she nodded to the girl. "He did pay for fresh linens, child," she said with a smile. "Fetch them for me."

"Yes, mistress." The girl offered her an impromptu curtsy and scurried out of the room.

Sila looked at the water in the porcelain tub. "Is it fresh?" she asked.

"Drew it this mornin' meself," the woman replied.

"That is not what I asked and you know it."

The woman scowled. "Only been used once, miss," she said.

"My master paid for fresh water," Sila said. "I expect fresh. Please see to it that it is drawn."

The woman scowled again.

"In the meantime, I will use what is here to remove the first layer of dirt." She smiled. "We have come a long way."

Sila took her time. As promised, the attendant changed out the water and the girl brought her fresh linens. After all the time she had spent on a horse behind a very smelly thief, the scented water was particularly inviting. She disrobed and sunk into the tub.

The lotion Tick had given her had successfully healed most of her blisters. By the time she was finished bathing, the discomfort they had caused was little more than a memory. She would be whole for Marand. With a shiver she realized how well Tick knew his merchandise. With a second shiver she wondered whether she would be able to function as a slave. When the water grew cold, she reluctantly left the tub. Her clothes were gone, leaving her only a well-worn towel to swath her body.

"This way, mistress," the girl told her.

"But it is unseemly not to dress!" Sila protested.

"The bed linens are clean, unused since last washed," the girl continued. She left the room, turned to make sure Sila was following. "Please, Mistress," the girl pleaded, "else Madam will think ye displeased and punish me."

Sila opened her mouth to protest, but instead followed.

The bed was clean, comfortable and there were no bugs in it that Sila could see. She climbed under the thick pile of covers before relinquishing her towel and was soon fast asleep.

After what seemed only moments, the girl was back.

"It is time to go," she said simply.

The clothes she had worn had been taken away and replaced with a silken white gown with a pair of slippers to match.

"No undergarments?" Sila said.

"Beggin' yer pardon, mistress," the girl said with another curtsy, "but ye 'ave a beautiful body. It would be a shame not to show it to its, er, best advantage."

"How dare you!" Sila snapped. She could feel the heat rising in her face.

"I meant no disrespect, Mistress!" the girl said, cowering in front of her. "Please, try the gown on! Ye'll see!"

Sila's nostrils were flaring. "You have nothing else?"

"No, Mistress, I swear!"

"Turn around, then," Sila insisted. The girl turned.

Sila slowly picked up the gown. It had three openings and a single tie that went through the middle of it. She pulled it over her head and stuck her hands through the other holes.

The material cascaded over her, forming a second skin. The sleeves were long and hung a bit further than her wrists, an odd loop of material hanging in the hem. Where it touched her, it was luxury unknown to her, awakening a feeling deep inside that she had never known before. She tried not to smile.

"I am not certain how to tie this," she said.

"Let me 'elp," the girl said.

With her assistance, the loops in the sleeves were fashioned so that it caught between her first and second finger. The cloth swayed suggestively with her every movement. The girl stood behind her.

"Now," she said, "'old yer arms out, Mistress."

Sila held her arms out to her sides as the girl pulled the tie tight. Her breasts became round and full, accentuating every curve. Her amazement at herself must have been clear because the girl laughed.

Sila nodded. "What is your name, child?"

"Tammar."

"Tammar is a boy's name. How did you come by it?"

"My mother wanted a boy." Tammar ducked her head down. "So I was a boy until my father found out. 'E sold me to Princess." She blushed. "I--I wasn't any good as a whore. Princess sold me to Madam Pink."

"Few ladies are." Sila sat on a stool.

"I beg yer pardon, Mistress?"

"Few ladies are good solely as objects of a man's desire," Sila explained. She ran her fingers through her hair. They got caught in the tangles.

"May I 'elp with yer 'air, Mistress?" Tammar offered.

Sila hesitated. She had always hidden the scar under her hair. The girl had been right about the gown. Perhaps she would know how to fix her hair to its best advantage as well. She took in a deep breath. "Fix my hair, Tammar."

Tammar drew Sila's hair back away from her face and her scar. Sila slapped at her hand, but Tammar drew it back once again.

"It must be covered!" Sila told her, grabbing her hand.

"Ye are wrong, Mistress," Tammar said, tying the blonde trusses back. "It's just a little scar, an imperfection in an otherwise perfect face, beggin' yer pardon."

Sila let go of her hand. Perhaps she was right. Perhaps the imperfection would be enough to keep her in the palace but not solely as a plaything.

"All right, Tammar," she said.

Tammar braided the mass of golden locks into loose trusses that fell gently down her back. Sila waited in silence until the girl stopped. She turned to look at herself in the cracked mirror. For the first time since she was burned, she felt beautiful. The gown embraced her body as no other garment ever had. She felt power surge through her, power she had always known she had, power that should have made her Eron's shield. Now, she would become Marand's.

"Ye see, Mistress," Tammar said behind her, "ye are truly beautiful."

"That I am, Tammar," she said, "that I am." She dared a thought. Marand could become her tool and not the other way around: manipulate the manipulator. She could do it. She reached down and pulled on the slippers.

"Come, Tammar," she said. "It is time to leave."

Madam Pink's jaw dropped when Sila swept into the receiving room. "Tick," she said so quietly that Sila nearly missed it. She cleared her throat and called out louder this time. "Tick! Yer woman's ready."

"About time," he said as he came in from the front porch. "Uppity bi--by the Lady, what has happened here?" He stared at her from head to toe and back again, his eyes finally resting on her bosom.

"See," Tammar giggled behind her.

"Hush, Tammar," Sila snapped. She turned to Madam Pink. "I thank you for your hospitality."

"Yer welcome to use the bath anytime, Mistress," the woman replied.

"Good. Tick?"

"Ma'am?"

"Give her an extra two coins."

"Fer what?" Tick protested."

"I shall not walk into Marand's palace unattended. It would be unseemly for a woman of my stature." She turned to Tammar, touching the worn cloth of the tunic she wore. "Go and get something decent to wear. We shall wait here for you."

Tick opened his mouth but Sila shot him a look and he closed it. He dug into his bag and withdrew two coins and placed them on the counter.

"Summon a carriage," she ordered.

Tick did not move.

"Now," she said calmly. She smoothed the gown from just beneath her breasts to her hips with the palms of her hands. "You want your prize shown at its best, do you not?"

"Y-yes..."

She pulled one hand off her hip, working her fingers easily as she turned it palm upward. A tiny fireball rested in the center of her palm. "Now, I believe, would be a good time to go." She blew softly on her creation and the ball chased her captor across the room and out the door. He yelped outside and Sila smiled. She turned her attention to Madam Pink. The bath house mistress looked terrified.

"I trust you have been adequately compensated for the girl?" she asked.

"Y-yes. Please, take 'er and leave me in peace!"

Sila strode over to the counter. She put her elbows on it, leaning over far enough that she could smell Madam's fear. She summoned a second fireball. This one she tossed into the corner of the room where it hung in the air, glowing. "The next time you raise your hand to strike a child," Sila whispered, "this brothel you refer to as a bathhouse will burn to the ground."

Tammar returned to the room. She was wearing a gown similar to Sila's, though she did not yet fill it as well as her new mistress did. Tammar giggled and spun around in a circle.

"You look lovely, Tammar," she said, holding a hand out to the girl. "Come. We have a king to meet. And I have need of your strength," she added so softly that no one heard her.

54 A Face in the Crowd

Sila sat bolt upright beside Tammar. Tick had managed to find a wagon for them. It was not the grand carriage that Sila wanted, but with her newly discovered beauty, she relished the thought of being more exposed so men and women could admire her. The bravado of the morning was wearing off, replaced with fear. Memories of Bel Haven kept resurfacing. Stacking bandages in neat rows or scrubbing blood from the floor of Penrose's treatment rooms were not the most pleasant of experiences, yet there was a kind of certainty in those mundane tasks that yielded an overall feeling of security. The tips of her fingers ran over the scar on her cheek. Penrose had sat with her, easing her physical pain and mental torment while she was healing. Even in Eron's memory, her mentor had said that she, not the Otherworlder, was more qualified to become Shield. But all of that was in her past now, a past to which she was certain she could never return. The future held no such security. A tear trickled down her cheek.

"Mistress?" Tammar asked.

"It is nothing," Sila answered. She pulled her blonde coils around to conceal the scar.

"Mistress, yer hair!" Tammar protested.

Sila gently replaced the curls, allowing the scar to be in full view. "You are right, Tammar. It is a new day, a new beginning for me." She touched her new servant lightly. "But why have I brought such an innocent as you to a place as decadent as this will surely be?" she whispered.

"'Don't know what ye mean by them fancy words, my lady, but did yer ferget I was in a whorehouse?"

"I have not forgotten, child," Sila answered softly. Her mind drifted and Tocar's lifeless head appeared, blood still spurting from the torn stump that was his neck and Marand standing in the doorway smiling wickedly. "Some things I will never forget."

The palace loomed before them. Wagons lined up on the cobblestone street and Tick took his place at the end as the last wagon. Ahead of them, women disembarked and were escorted a short distance to a small raised platform. One at a time, they were made to stand, their white robes rustling slightly in the breeze while a group of three men dressed in Marand's palace livery evaluated them. After careful scrutiny, they would either present the woman's handler with a pouch presumably of coins and take them inside the palace, or send them on their way.

"We've come on a good day, woman," Tick said as they moved up in the line.

"Good for whom?" Sila dared.

Tick shifted. "Keep a civil tongue in yer head, woman," he said, "or it'll be a bad end fer all of us." He grabbed her hand and squeezed it until she wanted to cry out. "And keep that to yerself as well. Not everyone understands, hear?"

"Y-yes."

He let go of her hand and she rubbed it. Tammar gave her a quizzical look but Sila declined to answer.

"Woman and girl," a man called out. He held a hand out to Sila to help steady her as she left the wagon, then did the same for Tammar.

"Captain Kerna!" Tick said pleasantly. "I would have thought a man of your skills would be off to the war."

The captain grinned. "His majesty allowed me one more sorting before I leave. The last time I performed the sorting, seven were chosen to entertain him," he stated proudly. He looked over Sila appreciatively. "Nice," he said to Tick, "very nice."

"Best as a set, Captain," Tick told him.

Sila shot him an appreciative glance.

"A set, you say? Highly unusual."

"Worth more that way," Tick said. "The girl prepares her."

She thought she saw him wink.

"The market for women today has been very good," the captain mused. "The man himself is always looking for something, um, special. Hasn't added a face to his stable since I last did the sorting. But we don't do sets."

Sila opened her mouth to protest, but a look from Tick silenced her.

"Maybe they'll end up in the same place," Tick said. He cupped Sila's face gently in his hand. "This one is special."

"They're all special." Kerna leaned his head in close. "Marand rewards his soldiers after every battle." He chuckled. "Sometimes before. Great leader, that."

They marched to the platform and Tick helped Sila step up onto it. A rock dug into her foot and she jerked to one side, but regained her composure and took a pose she hoped looked demure. The soldiers began their evaluation.

"Nice lines," the first one said as he circled around her, looking her over much as Princess had done.

Sila blushed.

"Good bone structure, enough bosom but not too much," he added.

The red deepened.

"Speak," the second soldier ordered.

"What would you have me say, sir?" Sila asked as quietly as she was able.

"Respectful answer, intelligent, a hint of innocence, lilting tone, good pitch. Probably a good singing voice if she had a mind to."

The third approached. He placed his hands on either side of Sila's face and drew her close to him. She placed her hands lightly on his chest and waited, knowing what was coming next. When his lips touched hers, she tried not to stiffen. When his tongue entered her mouth, she allowed him entry, relaxing and mimicking his motions with her own. For a few moments, they embraced in the sunlight. His hands shifted ever so slightly on her face and she relaxed even further, expecting him to touch her elsewhere.

Abruptly, the soldier backed away from her, a smile slowly crossing his face. He lowered his arms and she let hers drift back to her sides.

"Officer material," he said. He kept staring at her and Sila held his eyes, forcing herself to smile at him. Her heart was racing, though she did not know why.

"No doubt," the first concurred, breaking the spell. "This way, miss." He held a hand out to her and Sila took it, stepping lightly off the podium. Captain Kerna handed Tick a hefty pouch. She tried to ignore it, looking to Tammar instead.

"A moment," Sila asked as quietly as she could, casting her eyes down and then back up to look at Kerna again. "Please?"

"Of course," he answered.

She nodded and walked over to Tammar. When she placed a hand on her shoulder, Sila found the girl shaking. "Listen to me," she said, turning the Tammar's face up so she could look into the terrified eyes. "Now is not the time for pride. Do as they ask. Let them touch you, if they want to. They will not harm you."

"Yer sure?"

Sila smiled. "No, but if we act alike, chances are good we will end up in the same place. Now, smile, all right?"

Tammar nodded and offered the slightest of smiles. The first soldier took her by the elbow to guide her to the platform. The three began their evaluation anew.

"Come," Captain Kerna said. He escorted her away from the sorting and into the palace. "Do not worry, Mistress," he whispered to her. "I will see to it that your servant will not be harmed."

A lump rose in Sila's throat. "Somehow, I will find a way to reward your kindness," she said.

Many women graced the grounds inside the walls. They were talking in hushed tones, excited or frightened or a combination of both. Sila and the captain moved among them, crossing a great lawn adorned with elaborately carved statues and fountains spewing tiny streams of water into elegant pools. A cool breeze tugged at her scant dress and she shivered, wishing she had a proper cloak. Kerna led her across the courtyard, winding through the carefully arranged statues until they reached an arch of stone. Beyond the arch, a group of twenty or so women stood, each dressed similarly to Sila, each beautiful.

"I must leave you now," he told her. "You have poise to match your beauty, intellect as well. Use it. I must see to your girl." He gave her hand a squeeze and left.

Sila entered the inner courtyard and prepared to wait with the others. Behind them, the door shut, closing them off from the cool autumn day. The women shuffled through a smaller arch into a chamber that

Sila had seen once before. A shiver ran through her as her eyes scanned the room for Fot. The demon was nowhere in sight. Her heart slowed down a bit.

"One moment, please," the attending soldier told them.

This time, the door behind them slammed shut. Sila sucked in a breath.

This was the room in Eron's vision. She was certain of it. Like a moth unable to avoid a flame, she sniffed the air. Blood had been split here. She gasped.

"Are you all right?" a red haired girl whispered.

Sila tried to answer, but her voice failed her. Small black dots appeared before her and her head was swimming. The girl grabbed her arm and hauled her upright. Then she slapped her.

Sila blinked at her.

"If you appear weak," the girl explained, "you will be cast out."

Sila nodded. The spots cleared. Before she could find her voice again, the doorway to the inner chamber opened and filled with a familiar figure. Sila dug her nails into the redhead's arm.

"I bid you welcome," Marand told them. He dipped his head slightly, scanning through them as he spoke. "You have been chosen from the ranks to serve my officers," he continued, walking forward into the group, "or me." He paused to touch a dark skinned beauty with admiration. "It seems the best of Il Chatel have indeed come today," he told her. "Later, my dear." He pointed to an exit on his left and an escort took the woman through that door.

"Do not fear him," Sila's new protector whispered. "He is only a man."

Another girl looked shyly away from him. Marand smiled the same smile Sila had seen in Eron's mind and she shivered. From his neck, Tocar's crystal hung. He continued to walk through the women. He pointed to one woman then another, always gesturing afterward to his guards. The chosen woman was then escorted from the room. Then he pointed to Sila's protector.

"I will not be sorted like a cow in a market place," the girl said.

Marand raised an eyebrow. He stretched his hand out to her, gently taking the luxurious braid of shining red hair between his fingers. He tilted his head to one side, his eyes fixed on her braid. The girl jerked away from him. Marand snatched the braid cruelly, jerking the girl to her knees. She shrieked, letting go of Sila to claw at Marand's hands. He had the lavish braid entwined in his fist. He smiled down at her, saying nothing.

Around the room, the women clung to one another, some looking away from the scene, others covering their faces with their hands. Sila's heart was pounding.

Marand continued to stare. He drug her face to his, stilling her head between his hands as he violated her mouth. She struggled to get away, but he held her there for what seemed an eternity. When he finally let her go, she turned her head and spat. Her lip was split from the force of his kiss, but she defiantly started at him. He jerked her forward by the glorious braid, pulled a knife from his waist and sawed it off. The girl fell back and he threw the hair at her.

"So sad," he said, clucking in disapproval. "Perhaps by the time your beauty returns you will have learned civility. Scullery for this one." He watched with mild interest as she was hauled to her feet and dragged from the room, picking his fingernails clean with the knife. He tilted his head to one side and looked at the women who were left.

"Does anyone else feel as though they are a barn yard animal?" he asked. His voice was smooth and detached. "Arrangements can be made to return you to your, shall we say, colleagues?"

No one answered.

"Fine, fine," he said. He turned and faced Sila. "And you, my dear--It cannot be!"

Sila felt her eyes widen. He reached for her carefully coiled hair, taking hold of her coiled trusses with long, fat fingers. She braced herself, shutting her eyes tightly against what she knew was the coming onslaught. Her hair was moved gently away from her neck and he held her face in his hand.

"Can it be?" he nearly whispered.

Sila dared look at him. He was staring at her. "My lord?" she said.

He took her by the chin and gently turned her face so he could look at her fully. "Long has it been since last I gazed upon you," he answered. "Your beauty has increased tenfold."

Sila felt her face warm. "M-my lord?"

"You were young when Penrose summoned me to Bel Haven," he continued, "too young, perhaps, to remember a newly crowned king in the excitement of a newly chosen sword."

"I remember you, my lord," Sila replied. "There were many at Lord Eron's testing, but you I have never forgotten."

An officer of some rank burst into the room. He bowed to Marand, speaking with eyes downcast. "My lord," the captain said, "an urgent matter has presented itself." The captain leaned close to Marand and whispered something to him. Marand nodded.

He waved to his guard and Sila obediently moved forward to follow him as others had done before her. Marand laid a hand on her arm to stop her. "No, Lady," he said with a smile. He turned to the guard. "Continue the sorting," he ordered.

He focused his attention entirely to Sila. "If you are half the healer Penrose claimed you would become, it appears I have need of your services."

"How may I serve?" Sila said without thinking.

"This way."

He walked briskly from the room. Sila followed.

55 The Healer of Il Chatel

The air was cold here. It was not the crisp bracing cold that follows the first snow of winter. It was rather the kind of cold that creates a dull, horrid ache in every joint, the kind that makes a person wonder if they will ever be warm again. Heavily filtered light seeped into the chamber from above and the smell of lavender tainted by garlic laced the air. Something lurked in the darkness, something huge and, for the moment, silent. Sila could sense its suffering. She stopped and pulled her thin garment tightly around her body trying to assuage her own fear.

"This way," Marand ordered.

"I--I cannot," she said.

He threw the torch down and grabbed her by the arms.

"You're hurting me!" she cried.

"You don't know what pain is, Healer," he hissed.

"Let go!"

"You sense him, don't you?" Marand smiled at her, but did not loosen his grip.

"Him?"

"He is injured, in need of your help."

"But--"

"Look beyond your fear! Death will be upon him if you do not act!"

"But I--"

Marand threw her away in disgust. He picked up the discarded torch while Sila rubbed her arms.

"I...I would help, if I could. But whatever is in there is not human."

"And how would you know that?" Marand asked.

"I..." Sila took a step forward, her arms forgotten. "I do not know," she answered, surprised at her own intuition.

"Of course you don't," Marand answered. "Penrose didn't tell you, did he?"

"Penrose schooled me well," she insisted.

"Penrose kept you from reaching your full potential by not telling you what he knew," Marand said. He took Sila by the arm, this time gently guiding her forward through the short hallway. When they reached the entry, Marand turned so that she could not see beyond him into the chamber. "Yes, the Master of Bel Haven knew of your gift, Sila Atin. Yet he kept that information from you."

"Penrose is a kind but stern task master who makes certain his apprentices know their subjects well before presenting them with more information that they may not understand," she spoke quickly. "Were I still among the Healers at Bel Haven, it is likely I would still be receiving this tutelage."

"There are some things he would not have you learn, even though he knows them himself." Marand touched his torch to one hidden in the darkness. It sprang to life and he placed the first beside it. Light from the flames danced across his face, illuminating his worried features. He rested his hands on Sila's shoulders.

"You *are* the woman Penrose predicted you would become," Marand told her. "You sense him and his need. You have been sent here by some divine power. Do not doubt that." He inclined his head back slightly toward the room behind him. "There lies my greatest ally," he told her, "lately escaped from a prison of unspeakable horror, an ally who has sustained a grave injury."

Sila raised up on her toes to try to see beyond Marand, but he was too tall. She rested back down on her feet again and looked into Marand's eyes. "The skills of a healer are given freely, my lord, to those in need."

"Quoted from the Healer's Creed?"

"Yes."

"And you have served lesser creatures, beasts of servitude and those meant to be slaughtered for food?"

"It is important to give comfort where it is needed," Sila said, quoting words that were not her own, "even to those creatures who are not..." She looked away from him to the floor, fear building inside her. She tried unsuccessfully to wrench away.

"Who are not human," Marand finished for her. His fingers dug into her shoulders. "Lord Fot is in great need."

"F-fot?"

"He has just returned. In the short time since his arrival, my healers have been unable to discern the cause of his wound or how to treat it, much less ease his pain. Even Bue has no answer."

"B-bue as well?"

"The Lady has delivered you to us so you may help him!"

"E-even if I knew how to treat them, I could not!"

"Stop stuttering like an ignorant child!" he hissed.

Marand released her. His jaw shook as he placed his hands, palms together, in front of him and rested his lips on the tips of his fingers. His nostrils flared with each breath and he stared into Sila's eyes, never blinking. For a long moment, he stood thus, never looking away. Air hissed out of his nose in one long breath. He lowered his hands slightly, keeping eye contact with her.

"Need I remind you of where you are?" he asked.

"The Palace of Il Chatel," she answered quickly.

"And who is master of this place?" he asked.

Sila cast her eyes to the ground, but Marand grasped her chin and made her look up at him before she could respond. "You are, my lord," she answered.

"And who is your master?" he demanded.

His voice was soft but not gentle. It was Sila's turn to take a deep breath. "Y-you are, my lord," she whispered.

"I have paid for that privilege," he said, still using that quiet, scary voice, "but I will never be your master."

"But--"

"You are your own master, Sila Atin," he told her. "You always have been."

Sila opened and closed her mouth, not able to form any words. Marand's eyes softened though she could see the worry still present behind the stare. His hands shifted from under her chin until they again rested on her shoulders.

"You are destined for greatness, my lady, grander than any healer before you."

Her mind raced back to Eron's memories and her second place finish when the Shield was chosen.

"The Otherworlder has only one skill, my lady," Marand told her, reading her thoughts. He dipped his head down, raising his eyebrows before he spoke again. "You have more than that. Many more. Remember, in addition to your skills as a shield, you also have skills as a master healer. Penrose confided in me that one day he believed you would become the Mistress of Bel Haven."

"Ha! I haven't the skill to tend the simplest of saddle sores. A common thief knew more than I."

"There are abilities you have yet to discover," he said evenly, though the muscles beside his left eye were beginning to twitch. "Think, woman. Penrose always kept you close to him. Other healers came, received instruction and returned to their homes to serve. Why would he insist that you stay with him?"

"But demons are our enemies!" she blurted out. "Fot nearly destroyed Lord Eron!"

"He wanted to control the development of your skills," Marand continued, ignoring her protest. "Why do you think he encouraged you to spend time studying to become Shield? He knew you would fail. He fears what you are destined to become, so he intentionally misdirected you."

The memory from Eron's mind shouted at her. Penrose wanted her to become Shield, not the Otherworlder. But many healers had come and gone from Bel Haven since she began her tutelage. What if that part was true? Was she in line to become Mistress of Bel Haven?

Marand jerked forward and a young girl squeezed past them in the narrow hallway. She halted just long enough for Sila to look into her terrified eyes before she bolted down the stairs.

"Come back here!" a woman behind Marand bellowed.

"Not to worry, Bue," Marand said, his attention returning to Sila. "She has nowhere to run."

"She is the Otherworlder's whelp, Marand!" Bue said. "We need her alive."

"My men are waiting at the base of the tower. As I said, she has nowhere to run."

"She must be unspoiled!"

"Unspoiled she will be." He spoke with unveiled threat. No one would dare disobey.

Marand turned away from Sila and entered the chamber. An eight foot tall woman stood in the dim light, beautiful and terrifying. "When will you learn to trust me, Bue?" He pulled Sila gently into the room. "I have brought your master aid."

Bue raised an eyebrow, then nodded. "Lord Fot's wounds are beyond my skills," she said. "Are you convinced that this woman can help?"

"If she cannot," he said, "my life is forfeit."

"So will it be." Bue answered without hesitation.

Sila gasped.

"Have faith in yourself," he whispered, "as I do."

Sila folded her arms across her chest and followed him.

Light seeped through a tiny opening high above them. It drifted across the room, widening almost to the point of disappearing as it struck the lifeless grey stones comprising the tower's wall. Tendrils of smoke drifted lazily through the light, exiting the tower in the darkness above them. Something massive lay in the center of the tower floor, silhouetted in the dim light. An appendage that looked like a wing pointed upward from a body that was easily twice Sila's height. A low moan emanated from the mass. Sila summoned all the courage she could muster and reached a trembling hand to touch Lord Fot, master of all demons. Like ice on a sensitive tooth, pain shot through her and she snatched her hand back with a gasp.

"No!" Fot thundered.

The wing slammed Sila into the shadows. She hit the wall with a thud and Marand helped her regain her footing. She stood facing the demon with Marand directly behind her. Fot writhed and the stones of the tower walls shook.

"I-I can't!" she whispered.

"Yes you can, my lady." Marand's words warmed the hair beneath her ear and sent a different kind of tingle down her spine. His hand gently massaged her neck. She leaned into his strong fingers, still terrified but quite suddenly alive. "Remember, my life?"

"O-Of course."

"I have every faith in you. Please, Lord Fot is in agony."

Sila barely lifted her head up and down. Reluctantly, she made her way to the center of the room. Each step sent a jolt through her yet her tread was light as she circled the tower until she stood in front of the demon. *Comfort where it is needed...comfort...* Sila took in a deep breath and evaluated her patient.

Fot was much larger than she had imagined. Black ichor bubbled up through his scales in three places on his chest. The blood of the demon slogged to the floor, a thick liquid reminiscent of gravy cooked too long. Within the black, speckles of brilliant red light glowed. Sila took another step forward.

"I will not harm you," she told him.

Fot threw his almost human head back and let out a pathetic roar. A wave she recognized as his pain coursed through her body. She gasped and fell back.

"Use your skills," Marand coached. "Help him."

"He is a demon!" she cried, more surprised that she had an empathic connection with him than that he was not human.

"Help him," Marand told her firmly. There was a hint of fear in his tone.

Sila bit her lip. She stepped forward, regaining the ground she had lost. Fot was staring at her now, the green and red eyes glowing dimly from beneath hooded lids. He uttered a whimper. Without thinking, Sila threw her hands up and formed a shield of bright blue light. The pain Fot emoted slid around her, dissipating into the darkness.

"You see," Marand said, "you have the skill…"

Whatever else he said was lost in tornadic wind as Fot unleashed a barrage of energy aimed at Sila. The blue shield glowed lavender as their two powers melded. She was forced backward, but this time she kept her footing and leaned into his storm. Stones cracked behind her, sending chunks of rock to the distant ground below the tower. Sunlight poured into the room, bringing with it the crisp, clean scent of autumn. Fot ceased his attack. Sila moved forward behind her shield.

Around her, the air resolved to stillness. In her periphery, she saw Bue help Marand to his feet. The Lord of Il Chatel was moving very slowly, having been caught up in Fot's pain. Whatever injuries he had sustained were not clearly visible. Sila would tend to him later.

Fot tried to throw an arm up to prevent her from touching him. It fell with a thud beside him. His eyes drifted shut.

"She has killed him!" Bue cried. "Your life is forfeit!" she snarled.

"Patience," Sila heard herself say. "He is not done yet."

With the shield around her hand, Sila reached out. The demon's temperature had drastically changed. He was hotter now than any fevered person she remembered treating. Heat rising from his body distorted the walls behind him. Energy patterns were similar in every creature she had ever treated, forming disciplined traceable patterns in a collection of auras surrounding the body. But Fot's auras were in chaotic disarray. With trembling hands, she reached out to them, untangling what she could clearly see so the auras sank back in place. She worked the bands of energy into orderly patterns running from his head to his toes making note of the places refusing to bend to her ministrations. The demon opened his eyes and looked directly into hers. In an instant, he was inside her head. She did not protest.

"I will help you," she told him.

"What do you seek in return?" he asked.

"I am a healer. I seek nothing. Let me help."

"Prepare yourself for failure, Healer," he answered, "for my energy is nearly spent and I have little control."

Sila summoned all the courage she could find. "Find control, demon, and stop wasting yourself on futile attacks," she snapped. "By the Lady, I am attempting to help you!"

Sila found herself back in the tower chamber once more, face to face with Fot. He said nothing to her. There was the slightest hint of a smile on his face. He gave her a barely discernable nod and closed his eyes. The great body went slack.

Bue gasped.

"He is asleep, Bue," Sila said. "I must complete my assessment. Please, do not interfere." She allowed her shield to dissipate and reached a hand out to actually touch the scaly body. Instinct told her what she needed to do.

Two tasks presented themselves to her. First, Fot was losing the bodily fluids the physical portion of his being needed in order to survive. She had to stem the bleeding. Second, in an attempt to heal himself, he had released his massive energy stores. Once the floodgates were opened, he was too weak to shut them. So she had to restore control to him. Without intervention, either malady would kill him. Both demanded immediate attention. Sila had to do two things at once in order to save him. She needed help.

"First things first," she mumbled. "Bue!" she ordered. "I require your assistance!"

The eight foot woman in blue was at her side in a discomforting instant.

"You must trust me," Sila said.

"I do not."

"Your master does and if you value his life, you will do exactly as I say." She stared into Bue's eyes. "If you decline, then you may not kill Marand. Fot's death will not be on his head, rather--"

"Very well," Bue said. "I will do as you say. However, I will not trust you."

"Fair enough." Sila nodded to her patient. "You must stave the energy loss."

"How?" Bue's voice was very calm.

"Enter his mind, assess the damage and the hemorrhage." She moved her fingers in a circle as she had done inside Eron's mind. A shield appeared and she plucked it from her fingers and held it in front of her. "You see? It is quite simple. Put the patch over the leak, if that is the problem. You are a healer. You can improvise if you need to."

"Communing with the Lord of Demons without his consent is forbidden," Bue answered calmly. "It bears the penalty of death."

"Not even to save his life?"

"Alas," Bue said, "no."

"Then you must attend to his blood loss while I take care of his mind."

"I have tried," she said, "but alas, to no avail."

Sila shoved her panic aside. "Then get out of my way!"

She touched Fot's forehead and tried to enter his mind. A huge wall appeared in front of her along with a giant slathering dog. The dog growled at her, baring six inch fangs. It lowered its head and came toward her. She threw her hands up just before it leapt onto her and sealed it within a bubble of power. It whimpered pathetically.

"Fot!" she shouted. "We do not have time for this! Lower your defenses! Now!"

The dog vanished, leaving the bubble empty. A hole in the wall opened and Sila stepped through it. She gasped.

A river of glowing red energy flowed before her. To her left, it curved slightly and disappeared in the distance; to her right was an awe inspiring energy fall. She raced to the base of the energy fall, thinking as she ran how she would fix it or if, indeed, it needed to be fixed. Unlike Eron's shattered mind, there was a single source releasing the energy, neat and tidy.

The wall was made of bricks and clearly scalable. The simple frock she wore tangled her foot in the first step and she fell backward with a thud. She looked around. There was no other person in sight. She slid out of the garment and, naked, started her ascent.

The stones scraped her skin unmercifully. Her fingers dug into the wall, forcing it to yield to her wishes. More than once, her foot lost its grip, throwing her face first into the stone, assaulting her skin and making her curse.

"You will not die, Demon," she told Fot. "You will not die!"

The summit was at hand, but Sila had to climb above it. A ledge presented itself beside the breach. She stood beside the flow now, her own blood dripping into the river of energy she sought to stave. Above the flow, a gate had been raised. She could see two huge chains securing it aloft. She only had to climb ten more feet to be at the very top of the wall. With an odd sense of joy, she scrambled to the top.

The chains were caught in a deep crevice. She raised her hands and formed a lever of power, lowered it until it was beneath the chain, then commanded it to be lifted. With a jerk, the gate slammed shut. Sila lost her footing on the wall and plummeted down toward the lake of energy below.

From nowhere, the dog appeared. It grabbed her by the nape of the neck and she found herself on her knees, clothed and bleeding in the tower chamber beside Fot. The demon's green and red eyes were regarding her with something akin to thanks.

"I have solved one problem, Lord Fot," she told him.

He nodded.

"Trust me again," she commanded.

The great eyes stared up at her. She placed her hand on his forehead once more. The inner turmoil was calming and she smiled.

"Sleep," she told him.

Hooded eyes closed and Fot slept.

Without fear, she probed the ichor covered scales on his chest. Black blood still oozed from his wounds, but it no longer was accompanied by specks of red power. However, this problem was not close to the surface.

"Trust your instincts," Marand encouraged. "Search your soul for what Penrose could never teach you."

Sila held her hand out over Fot, closed her eyes and searched for the cause of his wounds.

Deep in his flesh, she discovered three small twisted lumps of lead. They had torn through his muscles with such power as no weapon Sila had ever seen before. Red tendrils gripped the cylinders and then reached out into the demon's airy musculature. They gripped whatever was solid and snatched at it to try to remove the offenders. The effort caused more damage to the already damaged muscles.

"We have to get those things out of you, Fot," she said softly. "You must stop trying to heal yourself. Please."

"He sleeps," Bue told her. "He cannot hear you."

The red tendrils of power released the cylinders and Sila allowed herself a smile. "He hears me, Bue," she said. "He hears me."

She removed her hands from over the demon's body and looked directly at Bue. "I am going to remove the offending bodies," she told her. "Do not interfere."

"As you wish," Bue answered.

"I do not trust you," Sila said. "Keep your distance."

"Fair enough," Bue echoed.

Bue dipped her head down, never looking away, but she stepped away from them.

Once again, Sila placed her hands over the wounded demon, this time stopping directly over the track the first cylinder had taken into his body. With a small amount of energy, she pried open the pathway. Fot howled in pain and she slapped her hand on his forehead, sending him into a deeper sleep without his consent. He lay very still.

She sent her own energy into his body, surrounded the cylinder with it and pulled it back toward her. It fell to the floor with a clink. Fascinated, Sila picked it up and examine it in the sunlight.

"My lady," Marand said, "there is no time!"

Sila looked up at him and nodded. In moments, she extracted the other two cylinders. Fot heaved a contented sigh. His shape changed to that of a man and Sila gasped in amazement. He came aware and stared at her.

"Thank you," he said. Then he closed his eyes to sleep.

Behind her, she felt a cloak settle around her shoulders. She pulled it tight, holding it snuggly closed in front of her body. Strong hands turned her away from Fot.

"Thank you, my lady," Marand told her. "You must rest now," he added.

"I--I cannot leave my patient. Not yet."

"Bue will watch over him," he said.

"I do not trust Bue," she whispered.

"Nor do I," he whispered back. He pointed to Fot. "He has changed shapes."

"I noticed," she said.

"He is quite capable of defending himself even now." Marand pointed up to the opening that had been blown in the tower's wall. "Time has passed, my lady," he said quietly. Sila glanced upward to see the moon's bright light filter into the room. "Demons heal quickly. Please, believe me."

"It appears I have much to learn," she said.

"I will gladly teach you what I know," he said, rubbing her arms gently, "and then gift of healing that has been bestowed upon you will become clearer. But for now, you must sleep. Your chambers are prepared. Come."

Sila turned from her patient and looked to her new benefactor. There was a spark in his eyes she had never seen in any man's eyes before. She was exhausted. She allowed herself to be guided away from the tower.

56 The Gambler

Patrick watched the sun rise over the Paranjothi range. It had been three days since they left Penrose at the foot of Kimala. They traveled by horseback, something Patrick was not used to, but he was faring better than his Otherworlder counterpart. Ric rode with a pained look on his face most of the time and walked like an old man when Altay and Prytal finally let them rest. Patrick longed for a hot shower, a sharp razor, his toothbrush, a bagel with cream cheese and a hot cup of coffee. He settled for a semi-clean rag that served as a washcloth, cold water, a piece of hard bread and a cup of trinka. The trinka was not bad.

"Prytal said he'd try to find a rabbit later," Ric said as he eased himself down beside Patrick, meager breakfast in hand.

"Great."

"I've never been camping before," the lanky youth said. "Or ridden a horse. Look at me now."

"I did survival training in the army," Patrick answered. He laughed. "No horses there, though. I had a girlfriend once who liked to ride. 'Had her own horses and tried to get me interested. I couldn't see the point of getting on some creature's back just to get from here to there and back again when I had a perfectly good car that would do the same thing."

They ate in silence, enjoying the peace of the early morning. Altay and Prytal busily packed their scant equipment, all but the camera bag at Ric's feet. He reached inside of it and withdrew one of the snow globes. With a laugh, he shook the trinket, staring hard at the contents as the plastic snow slowly returned to the plastic ground.

"They hate it when you do that," he said.

"They?"

"Yeah. The demons." He pointed to the globe. "I'm pretty sure that one's cussing at me. I can't understand a word he's saying, but by the look on his face, it must be some powerful stuff."

Patrick leaned over and looked into the globe. A banner with the words "New York City" emblazoned on it was poised above the famous skyline, replicated in plastic. "I don't see anything in there except 'New York City'," he said.

"I didn't either at first. It all has to do with my gift, I suppose, or that little extra something Penrose gave me back there." He sighed. "I don't know how I'm supposed to help in this war," he said softly. "I'm not really even sure why we're getting involved except that I'm supposed to be able to help. I hope that we'll be able to find JM and Lucy."

"I came after Lucy Perrymore," Patrick answered. "As soon as I get her back, I'm headed home. The less I have to deal with these demons, the better."

Ric turned the globe back and forth, fascinated by something inside it. "Fot's not your normal demon, Patrick," he said softly.

"Define 'normal'." Patrick swallowed the last of his trinka, sad that it was gone. "In my limited experience they've either been annoying tiny flying serpents or huge bad ass bad guys." He got to his feet to return the mug to Altay but before he could move, she was holding her hand out for it. "Where are we headed again?" he asked.

Altay picked up a stick and drew a circle in the soft dirt. "That's Kimala," she said. He followed the stick as she drew a range of mountains. "That is the Paranjothi Range." She pointed with the stick to the mountains in front of them. "There."

"And we're going under it?" he said.

"Yes." She returned to her sketch and drew another circle, far to the south of the mountains, a third circle above it and a distance away from either, and a fourth circle way off to the north.

"This is Tersan's army," she explained, tapping the southernmost circle. "They will be passing through Pintar Pass, exiting by Emmalie, the eastern sister. They will camp here, on Dallow Mound before the final push against Marand and the demons." She tapped the ground again with her stick. She moved the stick directly to the north. "This is Il Chatel, Calshara's center of power."

"So that's where we're headed?" Ric asked. He was still holding the snow globe but the fascination had temporarily abated.

"Yes." She pointed to the second circle. "That is Il Chatel. Marand's city."

"And where is Lucy?" Patrick asked.

Altay shrugged. "She could be anywhere. Bue said she was at Ankaal, but Penrose seemed to think she'd be at the battlefield when the time comes to wage war."

"What's the last one?" Ric asked, pointing to the furthest circle.

"Ankaal, guardian of the North, the mountain that divides mankind from demonkind." She shook her head. "And probably where they took Jason. It is my destination."

Ric flicked his fingers and a small green fireball formed in the palm of his hand. "Take me with you," he said to her. "I owe Jason my life."

Altay shook her head. "It is too dangerous."

"You're a girl!" Ric said.

Patrick rolled his eyes.

"And your point would be what?"

"You need protection." Ric jerked a thumb toward Patrick. "He's a cop."

"'Cop'?"

"That's slang for 'policeman'," Patrick offered. She looked confused. "Back home, I enforce the law."

"A soldier?" she asked.

"Of sorts."

"So you see," Ric said, "you need us."

"I don't 'need' anyone," Altay replied. "I am the person best suited for this journey and I have to go alone because you have to meet Lord Eron and Lady Jessie as a show of force to try to stop this war before it starts." She tossed the stick to one side and went over to the horses.

"Altay!" Ric called after her.

"Let her go," Patrick said.

"But--"

"She's a woman with her marching orders," Patrick said.

"So?" Ric tucked the globe back into the bag with one hand, still cradling the ball of fire with the other.

"So you don't interfere." Patrick pointed to the fireball. "What is that?"

"Penrose said it was a shield, like the ones Jessie makes. I'm supposed to practice making them larger but he didn't give me a manual." He sighed. "How the heck am I supposed to figure out how this thing works without any kind of instruction?"

Patrick reached out to touch it. The hair on the back of his hand prickled when he got close and he snatched his hand back. Ric laughed.

"I don't think it'll hurt you," Ric said.

"Forgive me if I don't take the chance," Patrick answered.

"Are you ready?" Prytal was standing behind them, the reins of three horses in his hands.

"Can't we just walk?" Ric asked. He made a motion to toss the ball up in the air, then covered it neatly with his hand. He turned his hand palm-side up again. The ball was gone. "I'm really sore," he said softly.

"It is an easy day's ride to the entrance of the mines," Prytal answered. "After that, you may well wish you had a horse."

"An easy day," Ric muttered as he took his horse's reins from Prytal and awkwardly mounted. "He said that yesterday."

Patrick swung up onto his own horse, trying to ignore his body's complaints. Even an easy day was going to be a long day.

As promised, the way today was much easier than it had been since they left Kimala. They rode almost until dusk, making camp at the foot of the Paranjothi range. A peaceful glen emerged from the thick woods ending at a rock face with no clear way out. Patrick slid off his horse, landing on the ground gingerly. He winced sympathetically as Ric dismounted, the camera bag still slung over his shoulder. The youth walked like a refugee from a B-western.

"Hey, kid, let me take him," Patrick said, walking forward and gathering the horse from him.

"Thanks," Ric muttered.

"Ric?" Altay held a small jar in her hand.

He turned and wearily looked at her. She thrust the jar toward him and he took it from her with a sigh. Then she pointed to an opening between the old trees.

"There's a hot spring a little way back in the woods," she said softly. She motioned to Patrick. "It's large enough for a dozen men. Go and relax while there is still time. The salve is for afterward. It will ease the pain of the ride."

"Thanks," Ric mumbled.

She turned her attention to Patrick. "I am sorry we do not have a blade suitable for shaving," she apologized. She reached into her quiver and withdrew an arrow. She handed it shaft first to him. "Many of the Kilmari use the head of an arrow for that purpose."

Patrick looked at the arrow as he ran a hand over his jaw. The stubble itched unmercifully, but in a couple of days, the discomfort would be gone. "Samantha's been pestering me to grow a beard," he said, handing her back the offered pseudo-razor. "I'll live with it, thanks anyway."

He smiled at her as she took the horses' reins from him, then followed Ric into the woods.

The path led them to the base of a rocky mountain. Steam rose from the surface of a pool surrounded by huge boulders. Ric deposited the camera bag onto one of them and began to disrobe. Patrick found a flat stone beside the shore only inches high. He took his small arsenal and placed it where it was readily accessible from the water before removing his clothing just in case one of those demons showed up. With one eye on his surroundings and the other on the depth of the pool, he stepped into the water.

Warmth engulfed him, first calling attention to the blisters that had broken open and not had time to heal then easing his soreness. He allowed himself a contented sigh.

"Ow." Ric was slowly easing himself into the pool across from him.

"You okay, kid?" Patrick asked.

"I've never hurt like this before in my life!" Ric answered.

Patrick laughed. "Find a ledge and sit. Let the water do its thing."

"You sound like an ad for a hot tub."

That got a grin. "I listened to a lot of them before I bought."

Ric sat down slowly and braced his back against the side of the pool. He closed his eyes and sighed. Mist rose up around his face giving him a mystic appearance, not of peace but of power. Patrick shook the image off and relaxed.

At least half an hour later, the sun finished its decline, casting pink light on fluffy white clouds with its last breath of the day. Air filled with the chill of winter rolled gently off the mountain. Patrick splashed some water on his face, dropped beneath the surface and rubbed his hair briskly, then surfaced again. Ric hadn't moved.

"It's going to be dark soon," he said to his companion. "Altay's probably got whatever we're going to eat ready."

"I'm not hungry."

"Well I am." Patrick reluctantly left the water. He pulled on his borrowed clothes, put his weapons back in place in the two holsters and sheathed his knife. "I imagine she'd like to bathe," he said, trying a different angle.

"Fine. There's plenty of room."

"Give the woman a little privacy, will ya?"

Ric looked up at Patrick. "I'm not ready to go yet, okay?" he snapped.

"Ric--"

"This is the first time I've been comfortable in a week and I'm not about to go until I'm ready."

"I promised Penrose I'd do what I could to keep you safe," Patrick said. "Leaving you here, alone, is not my idea of keeping you safe."

Ric's hands rose out of the water. He waggled his fingers in what looked like an awkward motion. A brilliant light flashed between his hands before forming an intense ball of energy that floated in the air. He pursed his lips and blew at the ball, sending it toward Patrick. An instant later, the policeman was engulfed in the ball of light. He struggled to get free of the trap but the harder he tried, the closer the bands of energy holding him became. It was getting hard to breathe, hard to move.

"Ric!" he yelled.

The light vanished and he found himself on the ground, gasping for air. From the pool, Ric was smiling at him. "I don't think I need your protection, Pat. Go back and tell Altay that by the time she gets here, maybe I'll be finished."

"Don't get cocky," Patrick said between breaths. "You're only one man. I could have easily dropped you before that ball got here."

"Ah, but you didn't."

"What are you, twelve? I'm one of the good guys and so are you, though I'm beginning to wonder. Save your tricks for the enemy."

"What would you know about the enemy?"

"Enough to know who they are and how to kill one. You'd better figure that out, kid, if you want to keep living. And you might want to start showing a little respect to Altay. She's not a servant." He stomped back toward camp.

It was getting dark now and the creatures of the night were speaking to one another. There were fewer insects now than there had been on the plain and the wolves' howls were louder and more frequent. Patrick slowed. He estimated five minutes had passed since he left Ric and he was still simmering.

"I've met a lot of stupid kids," he muttered as he continued back toward camp. "Ric's not one of them." He stopped. "In fact, he seemed pretty bright. Damn it, Patrick! He did that on purpose and you fell for it!"

He turned on his heel and raced back to the pool.

Ric was standing by the edge, one of the snow globes poised in his hand, staring at it like it was a character out of Hamlet. Half expecting to hear the "alas, poor Yorick" soliloquy and hoping not to hear "To sleep, perchance to dream", Patrick stopped dead in his tracks.

"Don't."

"Too late," Ric said. "I have to know." He balanced the globe in one hand as though thinking about what he was going to do while the other hand toyed with his tiny shield inches from it. In one sweeping motion, he hurled the globe to the ground where it shattered against the unforgiving stone.

"Damn it!" Patrick shouted. He raced toward the youth debating in his mind which weapon to employ.

On the ground, a mist began to swirl. It was not born of the hot waters of the pool meeting the cool air of the mountain. Laughter filled the air as the mist took the shape of huge demon, wings spreading wide, head cast back on an elegant neck. Two red lights appeared in the darkness.

"Pat, get back!" Ric shouted.

"What the hell happened to the larval stage?" Patrick asked. He halted almost in reach of the towering demon. This one was much taller than the one he had killed on Jessie Perrymore's front lawn. It was quickly taking form, many arms forming along its belly along with two almost human ones long enough to reach out and pull Ric into its grasp. Patrick sucked in a deep breath and charged.

"Over here, you bag of wind!" he shouted.

"Stop!" Ric yelled.

The demon roared and reeled like a drunk trying to walk a straight line. He was huge and coming straight for Patrick. Patrick leapt up and grabbed him around his neck, trying to gain his balance so he could strike at the eyes or nose with his knife. He made an awkward stab at it before the demon grabbed him. Instinct forced him to drop the knife and fumble for his gun. Black spots encroached on the demon's face and began to supplant his vision. Patrick's feet dangled in midair while his body swayed back and forth like he was on a tire swing beside a river on a lazy summer's day.

A blaze of light swelled in his head. *Not time to walk toward the light*, he told himself. *Go away*, he told the light.

Instead of going away, the light grew in intensity. Patrick flailed at it but it was like striking a marshmallow, his fists sinking into soft pillows of squishy balls. He was falling. He tried to turn, to focus on something, anything. His body landed hard and his head fell back with a crack. Darkness filled his world.

57 Into the Darkness

The huge orange sun descended below the horizon taking with it the heat of the day. Every sound was closer and more threatening than it had been only moments before. The once cooling breeze yanked Jason's clothing sending shivers through him. A particularly hardy gust of wind billowed his shirt away from him and he snatched at the cape that had miraculously made the trip with him, closing it quickly over his chest to retain what little heat remained. He sniffed the air. There was moisture in it, he was certain. So it was that night fell on Ankaal. Jason had to find shelter.

Darker than dark, the cave's opening beckoned to him. *Not on your life*, he told it. In the moonlight, he searched for other shelter.

The meager underbrush was not enough to stop the wind. Ice crystals struck his face like so many tiny needles. He rubbed his hands up and down his arms in an attempt to get a little warmer. The motion didn't help much.

He started down the mountain, hoping to reach a tree line…or a tree. Surely if he went far enough down, there would be some kind of shelter other than that cursed cave. In short order, he was stopped by a stone ledge. It was if Ankaal had been crowned by some god and Jason was stuck behind the band. He looked over. The drop off was at least twenty feet straight down.

Moonlight bathed the vast plain below him. A ribbon of water laced dark patches together in a shimmering crazy quilt. As far as Jason could see, there was no sign of any kind of life. He was higher than any bird dared fly, above the place were wolves hunted. Even their prey had nothing to eat here. The stone was cold and hard. It stretched out in either direction as far as he could see. There were no trees, no vegetation anywhere.

Gotta find a way off this rock, he thought. He left the ledge, gathered a dozen stones into a small pile to mark his place and took off to his left.

For what seemed like hours, he walked along the unbroken crown trying to identify his path by using the moon as his reference. He had never been very good at navigating using the moon and the stars. He was tired and hungry but nothing was as uncomfortable as the cold. He was losing the feeling in his feet and had to stomp to make sure his footing was good. To his left, the wind continued to wail over the rocky ledge and to his right, nothing grew. Doggedly, he kept walking.

There's got to be a way down, he reasoned.

An hour into his walk, he stumbled over his pile of a dozen stones.

No way down…

Jason sank to his knees, shivering. He closed his eyes and ran his dry tongue over chapped lips. He looked up toward the blacker than black cave. There lay his only hope, his only chance for survival and he knew it. With a different type of determination, he started for the opening, certain now that being inside the cave was the only way to survive the night on Ankaal. Lucy had been here. She survived. If she could do it, Jason could, too. With a deep breath and not a little fear, he made his way inside.

He placed his hand on the cool, damp stone and tried to still the pounding in his chest.

You can do this, he told himself. He sidled into the darkness, leaving the wind, the lifeless plateau and the moonlight behind.

Warm air blew into his face and he relaxed a bit. *At least I won't freeze*, he told himself. The smell of sulfur tinged the warm air and he shuddered. *I wonder if this is where I descend into hell.* He laughed. *It's gonna be one heck of a descent from here.*

Water dripped somewhere close by. He shuffled his feet to move forward in the darkness and stubbed his toe.

Yeouch! he mouthed as he grabbed at the now throbbing digit. *Jason, you idiot.* He reached into his pocket and pulled out Ric's credit card flashlight. The tool clicked on; the light caught on a crystal in the cave's wall. Terrified, he snapped the light off and waited, his heart pounding. Nothing happened. He snapped the light back on and plunged into the cave.

The main tunnel quickly divided in two. The openings appeared identical in height and width, but the one on the left appeared to be the source of the warm air. Jason moved slowly into it, leaving the bone chilling cold behind him.

The floor of the tunnel descended gradually until fog blanketed the floor, concealing the surface beneath it. Jason shone the light ahead of him. Across a short distance, a fountain of fog flowed out an unseen source. He shown the light into it. The tiny beam refused to penetrate. Instead, it merely refracted the water, making the thin beam appear much thicker.

Terrific.

He resorted to small, shuffling steps so as not to reinjure his toes. This time, his path was clear.

Before long, he was standing in front of a small pool. There appeared to be no stream feeding it, nor did water bubble up from some unknown depth. It was simply there. Jason pointed the light up, almost afraid of what he would find.

There were no rock formations jutting down from the cave's roof. He flashed the light over. The pool was no more than twenty feet across, but he could not see how far it reached either right or left. Some large boulders graced the floor on an outcropping above the far wall. Further scanning revealed what looked like a fairly flattened mattress and a speck of bright pink. There was no way to get there except through the water.

"I guess I take my clothes off and wade." His face flushed and he laughed. *Like anyone's going to see you.*

He placed the flashlight between his teeth and disrobed. Folding his clothes in a tidy bundle, he tied his shoes to the top and dipped a toe into the water. He snatched back his foot, shaking it wildly. After being chilled so badly, the water seemed scalding hot. He tested it with his hand instead. It was bearable. Only twenty feet and he would be to the mattress. Twenty feet.

I can do this. I know I can.

The water was barely a foot deep and the bottom was sandy providing good footing. He held his clothes high and traversed the distance to the mattress and a blissful rest. The pink thing turned out to be a plastic barrette like the ones Lucy wore. He picked it up and placed it with his things. It was hot here, hotter than anywhere he had been in a long time. He didn't bother putting his clothes back on and then, he waited.

When nothing happened, he slipped the flashlight into his pocket and stared into the darkness. Too tired to be afraid any more, he closed his eyes. Sleep came quickly. Bue had kept her promise. For now, Jason lived.

58 A Lady's Chambers

Sila did not know how far she traveled with Marand's arm around her after they left Fot in the tower. Nor did she notice the opulence of the room to which she was escorted.

"Drink this," he told her, offering her a small challis filled with mulled wine. She willingly drank.

"This way."

Once again, she took his arm. He escorted her to a soft feather bed where he turned down the comforters for her. She vaguely remembered being helped to undress and climbing into the bed. Beyond that, time was distorted. The next thing she knew, Tammar helping her out of a warm bath and dressing her in soft clothing.

"Tammar!" she exclaimed. "How did you get here?"

"Captain Kerna brought me," she said simply. "'E's 'eading off to fight now."

"He is a soldier," Sila reminded her through a yawn.

"Yes, Mistress. Now, let me help ye back to yer room."

She allowed herself to be led once more, this time into the bedroom where warmed sheets engulfed her. For a moment, she fought sleep before giving in to its insistent call. Time passed without her.

One small corner of her mind heard the conversation between her hand maiden and her benefactor. Tammar was being very protective, insisting Marand leave at once. The insistence must have paid off. She heard the door slam and Tammar's screeching voice attempting to warble a lullaby.

"That is lovely, dear," she said tiredly when Tammar launched into the chorus for a third time. "You must teach it to me when I am more awake."

"Ye liked it?"

"Of course. Now, please, let me sleep."

Sunlight poked gently at her eyelids. Sila shifted in the bed so her head was not in the path of the beam. Five minutes later, she found herself shifting again. The third time, she gave up on sleep and sat up, blinking hard to make her surroundings come into focus. She leaned back into her bed, enjoying the sensation of finally being appreciated for her worth.

All she could really see was the inside of the curtained bed. She ran a hand over the bedclothes, reveling in the silken feel. They were far different from the coarse, starched and bleached sheets of Bel Haven. And the pillows…They were not the hard, flat pillows she was used to. Instead they were thick and covered in silk, designed to cradle her head in luxury. She yawned mightily, putting her hand over her mouth. When she touched her lips, she recoiled, startled that she felt pain.

Outside the curtains, more than one someone was moving around, trying to be quiet but failing miserably. She could see pairs of legs under the curtains. Sila giggled. Whispers and a flurry of noise answered her. The door opened and shut. Only one set of legs remained.

"Tammar?" she called. "Is that you?"

"It is, my lady."

"Help me get out of this bed, will you?" she asked, "and fetch me some heterra. I seem to have bruised my lips."

"Yes, ma'am."

Tammar pulled back the curtains and tied them to the bedpost. "Ye'll be wantin' somethin' ta eat, no doubt," she said as she moved to the foot of the bed and pulled a second curtain aside.

Sila gasped.

"What is it?" Tammar asked.

"I--I've never seen a room so beautiful!" she exclaimed.

"Aye, it is fair," Tammar answered.

"Fair?" Sila giggled again. She tossed one of the pillows at Tammar, hitting her square in the back with it. "Just fair?"

Tammar took up the pillow and held it close to her. "Beggin' yer pardon, ma'am," she started, "the room is right fair."

Sila laughed. She took another of the pillows and swung it at Tammar.

"Hey!" Tammar said.

Sila grinned and hit her again.

"Ye asked fer it," Tammar said.

The two launched into a pillow fight, giggling and dodging and striking one another with the soft feather-filled pillows until one broke. Feathers spewed out into the air and Sila kept striking until all she held was an empty sack. Tammar grinned.

"It's yer turn, my lady!" she cried.

Sila retreated but Tammar kept coming, slinging the pillow at her mistress while the two dissolved into laughter. Neither heard the light rap on the door until it became quite loud.

"Are we expecting anyone?" Sila asked. She puckered up her lips and blew at a feather that had stuck there. When it did not come off, she brushed it away, cringing slightly at the unexpected pain.

"The king's come many times," Tammar answered. "But I shooed 'im away."

"The king? Marand?" Sila lowered her head and raised her eyebrows. "And you sent him away?"

"I--I am sorry."

Sila grinned and patted the girl's cheek. "You are truly a worthy hand maiden."

"I am?" Tammar beamed.

The door burst open and Bue entered. She took in the room with one long glare, then strode through the feather strewn carpet to a claw-foot table beside the window. There, she set a crystal vase filled with purple flowers tied by a single white ribbon.

"Lord Fot sends his thanks," she said curtly. She stood in the center of the room waiting for a reply.

"It was an honor," Sila answered.

The demon remained standing.

"What is it, Bue?" Sila started, extricating herself from Tammar's terrified grip.

The demon cocked her head to one side but said nothing. "How is he?"

"Alive," she answered. Her face twisted in an ugly scowl. "He…Lord Fot…" She huffed. "Lord Fot summons--" She cleared her throat.

"Yes?" Sila said, knowing what the demon's request was but unwilling to ease her discomfort.

"Lord Fot requests your presence," she spat out. The brilliant green and red eyes fixed themselves coldly on Sila. Like a statue, she waited.

"F-Fot?" Tammar stuttered. "Is he…?"

"Lord Fot rests where your mistress left him," Bue said curtly. She continued to stare at Sila.

Sila let the demon stare until Bue finally looked away. "Convey my assurance that when I have sufficiently rested, I will come to check on my patient. If there is any change for the worse, I expect to be notified immediately. I hope that is understood?'"

Bue dipped her head once and left.

"I cured a demon," Sila said absently, "and he sent me flowers!" She leaned over the bouquet and closed her eyes, savoring the soothing scent. "Lavender! Fresh lavender! Tammar, come and smell this! Tammar?"

"D-demon?" Across the room, Tammar was sitting on the ottoman at the foot of the bed. "A d-demon?"

"Yes, Tammar, I cured a demon." She smiled as sweetly as she could. "And he wants to thank me in person."

"My lady, you canna go!"

Sila crossed the room and sat beside Tammar again. She took the girl's shaking hands in her own, her mind clicking with thoughts. "Tammar, remember what happened at the bathhouse?"

The girl was as pale as the sheets on which she sat. She turned Tammar's head so she could look into the girl's eyes.

"Madame Pink…" she started. She whimpered, but did not pull away.

"Yes, Madame Pink was your mistress," Sila urged, still holding Tammar's face. She smiled as sweetly as she could. "Go on."

"Y-ye told 'er n-not ter harm any others like me," she said.

"And you believed me when I told her not to?"

"Ye know I do. Did." She began to cry. "But 'tis a demon yer dealin' with, Lady!"

"It is indeed. You are a bright girl," she said, her eyes twinkling. "Think, Tammar."

Tammar's eyes flitted back and forth. "Oh, I don't like what yer thinking, milady!"

"And what," Sila asked pointedly, "would I be thinking?"

"That yer gonna be in league with demons!" Tammar whispered.

"Not in league, Tammar," Sila said softly as a smile crossed her face, "no, not in league at all."

Tammar whimpered but she held fast. A rap sounded on the door. The girl's eyes flitted to it and back to Sila with not a little fear in them. Sila patted her face and rose. "Answer the door, child," she said. "Nothing will harm you while you are with me." She leaned on the bedpost, her eyes unfocussed but her mind sharp. "You have bought me, but you will never be my master," she added without moving her lips.

With hesitant steps, Tammar walked to the door. Marand was standing in the entryway. He was outfitted in white, a sword's silver sheath secured at his waist. Sila quickly ducked behind a changing screen.

"Yer majesty," she heard Tammar say. She peeked around the screen to find the girl bowing before the king.

"Where is your mistress?" Marand demanded. He took three menacing steps into the room and grabbed Tammar. "I know she is no longer resting!"

"A moment, your majesty," Sila said as calmly as she could. A blue shield flared by her hand where it grew to the size of a dinner plate. She did not impede its growth.

Marand pushed Tammar aside and advanced toward the screen. Sila really wanted to throw the shield at him, encase him in a pocket of energy and hang him on the wall as a trophy. Yet there was something she wanted from him, something base and vile and insanely appealing. She calmed herself and let the shield dissipate.

"Has Lord Fot sent you?" she called, peering through the crack between the screen's partitions to check his reaction. "I am grateful for the escort. I do not know this palace."

Marand stopped abruptly. His lips curled up in a most unpleasant snarl and he placed one hand on the hilt of the sword, squeezing so hard his knuckles turned white. His jaw quivered yet his voice was quite calm.

"Fot has requested an audience with one of my slaves," he answered. As he spoke, his face returned to its proper shape. He stretched his hands in front of him and forced himself to relax. "I have come to escort you, yes."

"Ah, I see."

Behind him, Tammar held her hand over her face. Sila could not make out her expression, but she thought it was one of glee.

"Tammar, dear," she said, "come and help me."

Tammar raced across the room, offering the briefest of curtsies to Marand as she passed him. When she was behind the screen, Sila took her by the shoulders. "Matters are proceeding rapidly," she whispered. "You may be my servant, but we are no longer slaves. Trust me. I will protect you. Wait for me here."

"Yes, mistress."

"Good." She pulled the girl forward in a spontaneous moment, and planted a kiss on her forehead. Then she emerged from behind the screen without looking back. "Your Majesty," she said, sinking deeply before him. She kept her eyes lowered and waited for him to release her from her curtsey.

Marand took her hand. "Rise," he told her, helping her stand upright. There was a glimmer of satisfaction on his face. Sila took note. "This way."

59 Demon Number Sixty-eight

"Drink this."

Something hard pressed gently against Patrick's lips while a hand supported his jaw. Moisture seeped into his mouth, thick and sweet and burning. He sputtered and flailed, pushing the vessel away. Whoever was helping him lowered his hands and waited.

"You will feel better if you drink," a silken voice told him. "Here."

"Where's Ric?" Patrick demanded.

"Your traveling companion is safe," the voice told him. "Now, if you please?"

The hand and the vessel returned very gently. Patrick managed to open his eyes if only a slit. He tried to focus on his caregiver, but it was so dark he couldn't see. Instinctively, he groped for the hand holding the vessel, steadying it so that he could take a sip rather than a gulp. It burned all the way into his gut like a fine, single malt scotch and he pushed it away again.

"Slowly is fine," the silken voice continued. "There is not much. You should consume it all. Please?"

Patrick nodded. The vessel returned and he drank slowly until there was nothing left. He wiped the back of his hand across his mouth, removing the sticky remnants from his lips. A pleasant warmth was descending on him and he took a deep, appreciative breath.

"Thanks," he said thickly.

"You are welcome."

He squinted in the darkness, trying to get anything to come into focus. "Who are you?" he croaked.

"Someone who is invested in your continued survival," the voice smoothly answered. "Relax. Allow the beverage to do its work."

Patrick let his head drift backward until it met something solid. The parts of his body that were aching from his encounter with the demon were releasing their pain. In addition, he was enjoying a very pleasant buzz. He felt safe.

"You have to have a name," he said to his Good Samaritan. He was beginning to see the outline of some trees. A wolf howled in the distance. "Must be night," he added.

"It is indeed night," the silken voice replied. He was behind Patrick. "Since you feel the need for a name, you may call me Comoin."

"Comoin." Patrick grunted a bit drunkenly. "I'd rather call you Bob. D'you mind?"

"Not at all. And you are?"

"Patrick. Patrick O'Shea. Pat. Officer…" He sighed and closed his eyes. "Take your pick."

"What are you doing?"

Patrick's eyes tried to snap open. His mind registered this new voice's owner. It was Altay.

"I only seek to help," Bob told her.

"Get away from him!" she demanded.

"As you wish, Healer-Sword."

The wall Patrick was leaning against shifted and he sat down hard then failed to keep from falling backward. A small pair of hands grabbed him around the top of his arm and steadied him.

"Patrick?" Altay asked.

He squinted and she came into focus. She was holding a torch. The flickering light cast a soft glow on features that were quite pretty. She leaned over him and he patted her face clumsily. She grabbed his hand and stopped him with a huff.

"I'm okay," he said thickly. "A little drunk," he continued as she helped him to his feet. He swayed and she steadied him. "Okay, 'lot drunk. 'Bob's fault…"

"What did you give him?" Altay demanded. The torch came close to Patrick's face and he poked at it. Altay stopped him from touching the flame so he stared at it instead.

"Nectar, Lady," Bob replied. "Nothing more than nectar distilled from the orpalac flower."

"Ye-ha!"

Patrick tried to snap his head around to look for the source of the whoop. He was certain it was Ric's voice. Suddenly he remembered his close call with the demon at the pool and a lot of other unpleasant things.

225

"Ric released a demon," he said thickly. "He tricked me into leaving and when I figured it out-- I don't know what the hell he was thinking." He was having problems focusing, his pleasant buzz an annoyance now.

Altay took Patrick's head in one hand and stared into his face, evaluating his condition. After a few seconds, she seemed satisfied. She let him go and looked to Bob. A sword of light flared to life from her hand.

"I don't know what you're up to, Comoin," she said, pointing the sword menacingly at him, "but if you harm him, I will hunt you down and kill you. Understood?"

"Of course, Healer-Sword," Bob answered.

Altay waited for a moment, then handed Patrick the torch, turned on her heel and raced toward the pool. Patrick turned slowly around to thank Bob. The gratitude poised to spew from his lips died there.

An eight foot tall creature with large blinking eyes reminiscent of Lae regarded him calmly. Patrick stumbled backward, tripped over nothing and sprawled awkwardly on the ground. His torch flew in Bob's general direction. He struggled through the orpalac fog to draw some kind of weapon with which to slay the demon who was so calmly regarding him. Bob reached over him, retrieved the torch and offered the burning light to Patrick.

"You-you're one of them!" Patrick exclaimed.

"If you mean by 'one of them' a member of demonkind, then yes, verily, I am 'one of them'," Bob answered. He had an elegant head that bobbed up and down on an equally elegant neck. Though he was very tall, he was not nearly as large as the demon who had tried to kill Patrick by the pool.

"But I--you--Damn it to hell." He scrambled to his feet, his head awhirl. "You could have killed me. You didn't. Can I assume that means you won't?"

"Indeed, yes, I will not be seeking your death," Bob answered silkily. "Killing you would not be in accordance with my release agreement."

"Accordance with what?" Patrick demanded.

"With the release agreement I made with Lord Ric."

"'Lord' Ric?" Patrick's eyes narrowed. "The kid's a computer geek, not royalty."

Bob stared at him, eyes blinking unnaturally slowly. "I am afraid your words hold no meaning for me."

"Never mind." Patrick's head was starting to spin in a bad way. "Stay here."

"As you wish, Patrick."

Patrick took the torch from him and stumbled down the path toward the pool. As he moved, he felt the comfortable weight of the small gun strapped to his ankle. The sidearm was gone. It didn't really matter. He wasn't sober enough to use either. The forest ended abruptly and he found himself standing on the edge of the clearing once more with the pool in front of him.

On the boulders where he had left his clothing however long ago sat six or seven green glowing orbs. Ric perched beside them, his long legs dangling nonchalantly from his seat. He held a snow globe in his hands. The ground in front of him was littered with tiny pieces of plastic.

"I have to, Altay," he was saying. The young woman stood off to his left about twenty feet, her sword blazing brightly in her hands.

"Ric…" Patrick warned.

"Patrick!" The young man scrambled off the boulder, still holding the snow-globe. A pained look crossed Ric's face. "I swear I dropped the second globe while I was recapturing the first demon. Comoin escaped then and I had two to deal with." He was looking into the woods behind Patrick. The policeman turned to find Bob standing behind him.

"I thought I told you to wait back there," Patrick said.

"Indeed you did," the demon answered.

"He has agreed not to harm any humans," Ric explained.

"My word is my bond," Bob nodded.

Patrick warred with his brain for a moment, finally forming the question. "Why are you releasing them?"

"Yes, Ric," Altay echoed, "why *are* you releasing them?"

Ric set the final globe down carefully and turned his full attention to them. "Because their cells were dissolving," he said simply. "I could see it but no one else could. I figured if I released them, then told them not to hurt any humans, they could go home in peace and leave us alone."

Patrick nodded slowly. A hundred reasons that Ric should not have done this on his own tried to surface. Only one got through. "Hell of a gamble. You should have let us know. We could have helped, though it looks like you didn't need it."

"You would have never agreed." He picked up the last globe. It was made of glass and the water within it churned as though a storm raged inside. "There are so many wards on this one that I can barely make out the demon. I saved him for last. Demon number sixty eight." He nodded to Patrick and Altay. "I'm glad you're both here now. Ready?"

In spite of his spinning head, Patrick drew the small gun from its holster. Altay positioned herself close to the pond, her sword shining brightly. The three of them formed a triangle around the broken globes.

"Here we go…" Ric hurled the globe to the ground. It shattered into a thousand pieces. Instantly a cloud of mist sprang up from the stone. It was coppery, laced heavily with dark blue sapphire. It swirled lazily in the light of the single torch, a tiny cloud expanding rapidly with purpose.

"Sje," Bob said lightly from behind Patrick. "It is fitting that his release is last. I assume our agreement will not be intact once you are dead?" he asked.

"Your word will always be your bond," Ric answered, never taking his eyes from the mist. He waved his hands over it, his fingers moving rapidly in precise patterns. Threads of light formed a delicate web replacing the broken glass with an orb of energy. The cloud pushed gently against the webbing as though testing the strength of its new bonds.

"Who is Sje?" Patrick asked without taking his eyes off the expanding cloud.

"Before there was Fot, there was Sje," Bob answered. "He was betrayed by Fot and Bue, led into a trap set by Wulfhaeled and Wylfcynne. It seems you are familiar with the traitor Fot?"

"Yeah, I've heard of him." Patrick took a few steps closer to Ric. "Watch yourself, kid. That's got to be one really pissed off demon."

To his right, Altay moved in closer as well. She touched the top of Ric's green webbing with her sword. Rose colored coils intertwined with his green ones, doubling the threads in width. Power erupted within the netting as the demon appeared to have a moment of panic. The webbing swelled in punctuated, staccato like bursts as though someone was trying to punch their way out.

"Ric?"

"Not to worry, Pat," he answered, though sweat was beading up on his forehead.

"They all did that?" Altay asked.

"I did not," Bob answered. "I was quite cooperative."

"Actually, Altay," Ric corrected, "he's right. I'm not even sure how Comoin got out. But the rest, yeah, they all--" He jerked backward, shaking his hands wildly. "Look out!"

With a peal of thunder, the top of the webbing split open and the mist seeped through it. The head of the demon poked out, a large, humanesque head with coppery eyes shot full of blue. He levered one shoulder through the opening, then the other, then slid his entire body out of the webbing, casting it aside as though he was shedding a skin. Altay leapt between Ric and the monster while Patrick instinctively circled around so he could get a clear shot at his head even though his vision was too blurred to see clearly enough to actually shoot.

The demon stretched, clearly enjoying the sensation. Magnificent wings spread out behind him, forming a canopy over all three humans and blocking the moon's light. He held them there, flexed fully open for long moments and yawned. Then he turned away from his would be captors and headed toward the pool. He dipped a toe in the water and smiled.

"The springs of the Paranjothi still run hot," he said using the same silken tones that Fot and Bob shared. He looked back to Ric and Altay. "I do hope that whatever task you have in mind for me will wait until I have bathed? You have no idea how long I have yearned for hot water." Without waiting for their reply, he stepped into the pool.

Ric looked at Altay, then Patrick. Patrick held the gun on the demon, not letting it out of his sights.

"Comoin," the demon called calmly.

Bob cleared his throat. "Yes, my Lord Sje?"

"Have you any of that lovely orpalac nectar?" Sje dipped his wings down into the water and back out again. Droplets of water cascaded over the transparent membranes and dripped back into the pool. He let them down so that they floated on the surface of the water.

"Alas, no, my lord. I, too, was imprisoned."

Sje sat up and blinked the huge eyes at him. "I know," he said. "I also know you had a store of nectar with you when you were taken, or so you said."

Out of the corner of his eye, Patrick saw Ric and Altay exchange a shrug. The demon's eyes were in the cross-hairs of the .38, but his vision kept blurring. He doubted he would get a clean shot off.

"Orpalac helped sustain me during my captivity," Bob answered. "There was a bit left after my release, but I used it to restore the human who is now pointing at you."

Sje turned to stare at Patrick. The huge eyes did not blink, looking rather melancholy in the human-like face. "You could not spare a drop for me?" he asked.

Patrick lowered his weapon. "Had I known you wanted any, you could have had it all."

Sje sighed. "Do not take Comoin's gift so blithely, Human," he said, returning to his bath. "Orpalac is a potent restorative. I, however, prefer its recreational qualities. Even among demonkind, orpalac is rarely shared." He looked long and hard at Patrick once more. "Ahleri slept an entire day after his first tankard. I am amazed you still stand." He splashed playfully in the water. "You have no idea how totally refreshing a hot soak can be after ages in tepid water."

He continued bathing, scrubbing his scales while humming some truly dissonant tunes. The three humans and one other demon gathered at the pool's edge. Altay's sword still blazed, Ric was ready with a net of power and Patrick still held his gun in his hand, though the safety was now on. Sje stretched one more time in the water, then placed his two long arms on one of the stone's at the pool's edge and lowered his head so that it rested on top of them. He smiled at them and contentedly closed his eyes.

"You may dispense with your weapons, humans," he told them. "I am going nowhere. I have heard the bargaining power of the young shield. We shall arrange, ah, something…as soon as my soak is over."

"What?" the three said in unison.

Bob chuckled.

"I heard many things while imprisoned. The deal you struck with the young shield, Comoin," Sje said. "Caring for one human would have been enough. But you had to take them all under your care. You never have known when to stop babbling."

"I am content, my lord," Bob answered.

"That is good. Your obligation is grand."

"I hate to ask," Patrick started, "but why are you calling him 'lord'?"

"Because Sje was once lord of all demons," Bob replied.

"I thought Fot was lord of the demons?" Ric said.

"As I have explained, first there was Sje, then there was Fot." Bob shrugged. "Were you not listening, young shield?"

Sje sighed. He opened his eyes halfway and rolled them toward Ric. "Fot is despicable. He is clever but self-serving, manipulative and greedy. His list of unsavory talents is quite long. Above all else, he is a traitor."

"He is, indeed, my lord," Comoin said.

Sje leaned back in the pool. "I have no use for him."

Altay looked confused. Ric stared at the demon, his mouth open in disbelief.

"So, you'll be helping us in the war against demonkind?" Patrick asked, his mind starting to click again.

"Decidedly not," Sje said almost offhandedly. He rose and exited the pool. The water fell off his scales and wings splashing on the rocks around his feet. He looked pointedly at Ric and smiled. "What else would you have me do, young shield?"

Ric turned to Altay. "Why does he keep calling me 'Shield'?"

"Because that's what you are," Altay snapped. She let the sword evaporate.

"I thought Jessie was the Shield," Ric reasoned, "and that Eron guy was the sword."

"Eron lives?" Sje's eyes widened. He took a seat next to the recaptured demons and was examining one of the glowing pods. He stopped looking at it and looked to Ric. "Fot boasted of the Sword's demise at his hands while we were captive in the Otherworld. He spoke of him as an 'almost worthy opponent'." He sat the globe down and searched their faces. "What of Ahleri?" he said in a voice soft and caring.

The men looked at Altay and the girl bit her lip. "Ahleri must have passed long ago," she told him. "He left Il Chatel to journey northward in search of demonkind and disappeared, though some claimed to have seen him since that time. No one knows with certainty."

Sje closed his great eyes and nodded, commanding silence from them all for a long moment. Finally, he smiled. "It appears young Lord Fot is in for a few surprises."

60 Confidence

The way was almost familiar, as familiar as a dream recalled from an unknown night. Sunlight danced brilliantly in small patches on the inner walls of the long corridors, warm against Sila's skin as she passed. Her hand rested lightly on Marand's forearm, allowing him to guide her through the castle's twisting passageways. He rambled on about how lonely it was to be king and how none of the women he ever slept with was satisfying. The new horse he had acquired from somewhere was going to be the foundation for his new herd and the chef he had won in a card game was from the sea. He had the finest jewels set in precious metals and one crystal in particular that he thought would make a lovely wedding gift.

"Wedding gift?" Sila repeated.

Marand laughed. "I would shower my queen with riches," he said. Then he sighed. "Would that I could find such a woman."

"Perhaps you need to look a bit further than your bed," she replied tartly.

"I find it is a quite satisfying place to start," he answered. "More than a few have entertained me, a rare few have shown any sort of wisdom. Only one have I found worthy."

"It is not a good way to choose a queen," Sila replied.

The way took them up a flight of stairs to another corridor, this one more brightly lit than the last. Sila twirled the single stem of lavender she had removed from Fot's bouquet between her fingers, enjoying the delicate scent. Wind swept through the openings in the wall, chilling her. She stepped closer to Marand and he slid his arm around her, the cape he wore now covering them both. He was warm and smelled of perfumed water, a welcome change from Tick's sweat and, oddly, the musky scent of leather that she always associated with Eron.

"Tell me, your majesty, why you harbor a demon," she asked.

Marand hesitated. "You are a curious one, madam healer," he said. The guard leading them opened a solid wooden door at the end of the corridor and waited for them to pass before closing it behind them. They were alone in a tower. A long spiral staircase led up into darkness.

Sila stopped. "Why do you harbor a demon?" she repeated quietly.

Marand's arm slid off from around her. He gently turned her so that they were facing one another, never losing contact with her body. He smiled warmly and touched her cheek with the back of his hand. She closed her eyes, succumbing to his suggestion. He lifted her head slightly and she did not resist. The warmth of his breath touched her cheek and his lips met hers. They were soft and yielding, pressing gently on hers but not asking for anything in return. Too soon, he released her. Every nerve in her body was suddenly alive.

"If you two are quite finished," a haughty voice said from above them, "Lord Fot is ready for your audience."

Marand touched her cheek once more, not letting his eyes stray from hers. "A moment, Bue," he said, "a moment."

A door in the darkness slammed shut, presumably leaving them alone.

"You are truly the most beautiful woman I have ever met," he whispered.

Sila gulped. She gently turned her head away from him and stared at the floor she could not see, her heart racing. She bit her lip to try to focus. It seemed this man who was king wanted her as she had wanted Eron to want her. There was a demon up the stairs who needed her, an enemy of her people but not of this man. She did not care about the demon now. She did not care about Eron, either. She felt Marand's hands touching her again, the warmth of his body pressing comfortably against her own and her mind raced between the needs of her people, the needs of her patient and needs of her soul.

"I have a gift for you, if you will have it," Marand whispered. He stepped away from her so that she could see his face and bowed slightly, his hand slipping into hers. The dark blue eyes never broke contact. "But first we have an obligation to a loyal ally. Come."

This was not the tower they had visited the day before. The stairs were deceptively steep. By the time they reached the uppermost one, Sila was out of breath, but she was not certain of the cause. Marand paused in front of the door. His features blurred in the dim light but his smile shone.

"Are you ready?" he asked.

Sila nodded. He pushed the door open.

The combined scents of lavender and garlic assaulted her senses. She dropped the stem she still held and tried to make a graceful entrance. Marand chuckled softly behind her, his hands still on her waist. She felt his breath on her neck.

"His ways require a bit of acclimation," he whispered. "Well worth the effort for the support he offers us."

Sila shook off his warmth and smoothed her garment, preparing to enter the smoke filled tower. She took one deep breath and made her way in to see her patient.

Fot was reclining on a mountain of pillows, his blue scales a bit shinier today than yesterday. Before him was a massive assortment of food, bowls overflowing with fruits and vegetables, a spit of meat, several carcasses that had been reduced to skeletons and two huge platters, one filled with garlic cloves, the other with lavender. He took a sprig of lavender and chomped on it, then took up a tray of hors d'oeuvres. With a steady hand, he motioned for her to join him.

"Come, sit," he told her. When she hesitated, he added, "Please?"

Sila moved so that she was standing directly in front of him, then descended into the pit where he lay. He was decidedly more alert than he had been the previous day, the dull eyes clear now, though tired. He smiled as she took a seat on the cold hard stone in front of him.

"I would be honored if you would join me," he said. He made a motion with his right hand and Bue appeared beside him. The blue demon held a bottle in her hand and a large, intricately appointed goblet. She poured some of the contents of the bottle into the goblet and handed it to Sila. Taking the goblet required both hands.

"Thank you," Sila said.

Bue scowled and turned away.

"I offer you orpalac, the most precious of our wines," Fot explained.

Sila held the goblet up and swirled the wine around. The golden liquid formed thick legs on the glass. Without thinking, she bent her head down and closed her eyes to appreciate the bouquet. The scent was woody, not at all what she had expected.

"Sip, do not drink," Fot advised.

The goblet was cool against her lips. She took a tiny bit of the wine into her mouth, rolling it around on her tongue to appreciate the nuances. "It is good," she said. She took a sip and set the glass aside. Bue offered her a tray of morsels.

"Thank you," Sila said, taking the tray. She set it next to her on the stone and picked up a single treat. It consisted of a very delicate batter covering a slice of meat, topped by a combination of cheeses and nuts. The tidbit melted in her mouth and she gobbled down the rest to Fot's delight. Bue scowled again and disappeared back into the darkness.

"Bue is an excellent cook," he said. He held the tray of hors d'oeuvres in one hand and started to rise, his motion awkward with not a little pain.

"Don't get up," she said hastily, dropping her formality for a moment to get to the tray. She took several more of the delicacies and put them on her plate, then returned to her seat.

Marand cleared his throat and she looked up to where the king was still standing with his hands behind his back. Fot ignored him.

"Majesty?" Sila said.

"Marand was not summoned," Bue said curtly.

"Of course not, Bue," Fot replied. "However, if it is the Healer's wish, he may join us." He looked at Sila and the room fell silent.

"Um, yes, of course,…" She looked up to Marand. "Would you join us, my lord?"

Marand dipped his head and made the descent to the place where Sila now stood. For a moment, no one spoke. Finally, Marand gestured to the goblet of wine. "My thirst is great," he announced, looking at Fot.

Sila looked back and forth between the two. A silent, uncomfortable war of wills was being waged between them. Bue stood behind Fot once more, silently glowering in the dim light. She held a covered dish in her hands and waited.

"This is foolish," Sila finally said. She picked up her goblet and handed it to Marand.

"Thank you, my dear," Marand said.

"You are welcome." She turned her attention to Fot. "Your invitation was for an audience, Lord Fot," she said, "and though I truly appreciate the efforts your servant has made--" Bue made a guttural sound that sent shivers up Sila's back. She looked to the demon. "I beg your pardon, madam, but I am unsure what your relationship is with your master."

"It is of no concern, Healer," Fot replied silkily. "Please, sit."

Once again, Sila sat, this time with Marand at her side.

"I wish to thank you, on behalf of myself and demonkind," he said, his voice grave. "I owe you a great debt."

"I only did what healers do," Sila replied.

Fot shook his head. "What you did was return life to me. I sincerely doubt that any other human healer would have done the same."

"Or could have," Marand added.

Fot nodded. "Or could have," he repeated softly. He adjusted himself on the great cushions. "This is a moment that will live in the annals of human-demon history. We have found a Healer, a healer who can heal demons and not be afraid to do so." He smiled and for the first time since Sila saw him, she was not afraid. "And I hope a great ally."

Sila took the goblet and raised it in salute. Then she drained it. Almost immediately, the room around her began to spin. She staggered and Marand caught her before she fell. Fot was laughing, though there was nothing unkind in his voice.

"Not to worry," she heard Marand say. Quite suddenly she felt his face close to hers, though his words were not for her. "I shall take care of her."

"See that you do," Fot answered. There was a bit of a threat in his tone and Sila tried to focus but could not. Her head lolled against a warm shoulder as strong arms held her close. He smelled of perfumed bath water...

61 The Deal

Sje stood at the pool's edge stretching his massive wings one at a time, shaking the water off them and preening his scales like a proud peacock. He took his time while the others watched, either oblivious to their stares or enjoying them. Patrick couldn't really tell which. The dizziness he experienced from the orpalac was wearing off and being replaced by a killer hangover. All he wanted to do was find a hole somewhere and crawl into it for the next four hours. Or, better yet, a bottle of aspirin.

"Comoin," Sje said, still grooming himself.

"Yes, Lord Sje?" the blue demon answered.

"Would you be so kind as to find me a Kilmari cape? I do so hate not to blend in."

"What's he going to do with a cape?" Ric hissed.

"I don't know," Patrick answered. "He's a little too big to wear it."

"Begging your pardon, Lord, but I have sworn an oath not to harm humans."

"Or allow them to be harmed. Yes, yes, I remember your oath. Like so many of the others." He stopped. "It is not necessary that you harm a human in order to procure a piece of clothing," he said. "I merely require the clothing."

"Are you suggesting theft, my lord?"

"Theft such as this annoys but generally harms no one."

He pointed at Patrick. "Might I leave that human in your care?" he asked. "You will recall that his well-being was also a part of my oath."

"I don't need a guardian demon," Patrick told them.

Sje raised an eyebrow. With more grace than someone of his considerable size should possess, he strode forward so fast that Patrick didn't have time to draw any kind of weapon. His head was firmly in Sje's grasp and he found himself staring into copper and sapphire eyes. Sje's touch was oddly gentle.

"I will care for him in your absence," Sje answered, "though the human appears perfectly fine, considering."

"As you wish, my lord."

Bob retreated from the pool and Sje continued to stare curiously into Patrick's eyes. He thought he saw a shadow pass between them, then felt a cool breeze on his forehead. The hangover was gone. Sje released Patrick. The demon gave his wings one final smoothing and smiled.

"I, um--" Patrick started.

"I assume you are well provisioned?" Sje asked, his great eyes fixed on Altay now.

She stared at him blankly.

"Very well. I can hunt." In an instant, he spread his wings, legs flexing to spring the massive body into the air.

"No, no, wait!" Ric said. "What about the deal?"

"The 'Deal'?" Sje sighed. "Of course. The 'deal'. How foolish of me to have forgotten. I will need a moment. Perhaps two. It has been a long time."

Without waiting for reply, his huge wings folded tightly against his body and sunk into his back. The fifty pairs of hands melted into his chest and abdomen, leaving just two attached to his arms. His face was still benevolent, though there was a look of intense satisfaction playing about his lips. Patrick could have sworn he heard him giggle.

What was once a demon now stood before them as a man. In the silvery light of the moon, his blue pallor started to change, lightening until he simply appeared pale. He strode over to the pond and glanced into the calm waters, his eyes furrowed.

"Pity," he said, turning away from the water. "There was a time when I was truly good at that."

"Good at what?" Ric asked.

"Good at changing my complexion so I blend in. I have had several marriage proposals admittedly from slightly inebriated women…" He turned his head from side to side, exposing both sides of his face to them. "I am a bit pale, am I not?" he asked pointedly.

"Um, well…" Patrick started.

"Collin McGregor was paler," Ric offered.

Sje almost smiled. He turned his attention to Altay. "What say you, Healer-Sword?"

Altay cleared her throat. Her eyes were very round but she did not look away. "Were you my patient," she said slowly, "I would recommend more time in the sunlight."

Sje laughed. "Excellent! I will offer your recommendation as reason," he said, "should anyone enquire as to my pallor. Now, let us see if I can remember..." Once again, his brow furrowed. The massive body quivered and, before their eyes, the demon shrank to the size of a medium framed man. All traces of scales where gone and his bald head was now covered by an unruly shock of white hair. He stood before them, a completely nude and anatomically correct male. With a smile, he examined his hands and feet. He touched his head, smiling broadly when his fingers met his hair. "It appears I have not lost all my skills."

Altay was looking away, her face flushed in the torch light. Sje laughed at her, but he addressed his comments to Ric. "That, my dear savior, is why I need the cloak. To maintain the type of detail required to walk unnoticed among humans," he continued, holding up one hand, palm up in front of his face, examining his fingers carefully, "requires much energy."

"The others were much taller," Patrick observed.

"It is hard to get into your pubs unnoticed if you are exceptionally tall," Sje grinned. "Ahleri assured me that the extra height was threatening for some reason."

"Here." Ric tossed him the Kilmari cloak he had shed earlier when he was releasing the demons.

"Why thank you," Sje said. He threw the cloak around his shoulders and fastened it effortlessly with an intricate and beautiful knot. "Whatever will Comoin say when he returns."

"We have to discuss the matter of your favor," Ric started.

"Over food?" The coppery eyes blinked hopefully at him.

"Talk about your one-track mind," Ric muttered.

"Prytal should be back by now," Altay started. "Even if he isn't, we have some supplies--"

"Excellent!" Sje said. He started to walk in the direction of their camp, oblivious to the sharp stones he was stepping on. When he got to the edge of the clearing, he stopped.

"I fear I only know the direction of your camp," he noted. "Perhaps one of you could take the lead?"

"I, um, certainly," Altay replied. She started across the clearing, the men on her heels.

"Were the others like this?" Patrick whispered.

"He's one of a kind," Ric answered.

"I don't know whether to be thankful about that or terrified," Patrick answered.

"Me neither."

Ahead of them, Sje darted into the forest.

"Hey!" they shouted as one. They raced up to where Altay stood, staring into the darkness, her sword already glowing. Together, they plunged into the dense wood, chasing a shadow among shadows. Tree limbs smacked them across their faces, roots and slippery stones tripped them. Each time they spotted Sje, he was a little further away.

"This is foolish," Patrick said when they could no longer see the demon.

"Never trust a demon," Altay nearly whispered.

"Good lord, it's dark in here," Patrick said.

"Sje!" Ric yelled.

Nothing but the sound of insects answered him. The light from Altay's sword seemed to be absorbed by the thick undergrowth.

"It's no use," she said. "He's gone. I'm afraid if we go much further, we will be lost." She looked around. "If we're not lost already."

"Great," Ric moaned. "We'll never find him!"

"There is the matter of that favor," Patrick said. "If what Winnie said is true, he'll have to come back and settle up."

They both looked at him.

"We've got more important things to do than go chasing after this guy who may or may not be a threat, right?" he added.

The pair looked at one another and shrugged.

"Yeah, I guess you're right," Ric said grudgingly.

"I suppose we should be thankful he did not attempt to harm us," Altay added.

"Yeah, he was the biggest of all of them." Ric sighed. "I have to retrieve the demons who refused to cooperate."

"I'll come with you," Patrick told him.

"I as well."

The three picked their way through the forest, trying to retrace their steps. An hour had passed when they finally found the pool again. Ric's camera bag leaned up against one of the larger stones. The small glowing orbs that housed the demons sat like poached eggs, cracked and devoured. All were empty.

"Damn!" Ric said.

"What the hell? Where are they?" Patrick grabbed an orb and looked inside.

"It must have been Sje," Altay said. "He led us on a wild chase, then released them when we weren't looking."

Ric formed a shield, Altay produced her sword and Patrick drew his gun. Silently, they prowled the poolside looking for any sign of Sje. Patrick found his service revolver and tucked it back into his holster. That was all they found.

"Let's get back to camp," he told the others. "If we haven't been attacked by now, we probably won't be. In any event, Prytal is no match for a horde of demons."

They walked back to the campsite in silence. Laughter issued from the clearing. They stopped.

"You don't think…?" Ric started.

"Who else?" Altay answered.

"It can't be Bob," Patrick said. "I don't think Prytal would be laughing with him. C'mon."

Prytal was turning the carcass of some small animal on a spit while a pot bubbled merrily beside it. He was chatting amicably with a hooded man in a black cloak who bent over the pot, adding a pinch of something to it. With long, slow strokes, the stranger stirred the pot, reverently gazing at its contents. He dipped the large wooden spoon into the broth and held it to his lips, inhaling deeply. Then he slurped at the brew, licking his lips when he finished. He put the spoon back in the pot, withdrew something green from under his cloak and crushed the leaves into the stew.

"That will do quite nicely," he murmured. He stirred for a short time, then took another taste. He closed his eyes and shook his head slowly. Not looking at any of them, he spoke again. "It has been a long time since I have had a proper meal. Fresh vegetables and herbs are best, would you not agree?"

"I was becoming concerned about you," Prytal said to them, relief flooding his face. "Come, sit. The meal is almost ready."

Warily, they took places around the fire, eyeing the man in the cloak suspiciously. "Sage is my name," he told them with a silken voice. Patrick rolled his eyes. "Your companion has graciously invited me to share your campfire," he continued. "And, as you can see, I have not harmed him."

"'Know who your companion is, Prytal?" Patrick asked.

The Kilmari took a step back from the fire, his hand on the hilt of his sword. "I believed him to be a traveler who says he is heading to the north."

"Oh, he's going north, all right," Ric piped up.

"His name is Sje and he is a demon," Aitay told him. She cocked her head to one side. "Ric released him."

Prytal touched his sword to the cloak, pulling it back and exposing Sje's leg. The demon whirled, his hand flashing out from under the cloak, grabbing the sword as if it were nothing more than a stick of wood. He jerked it out of Prytal's hands and flung it to the ground.

"We were having such a lovely conversation," he said rather sadly. "And now you choose to point a weapon at me?" The hood fell away, revealing his handsome and somewhat less pale head. He sighed. "We were just getting to know each another, one traveler exchanging pleasantries with another. A polite and informative conversation, if I recall correctly. And now, because I am a demon you treat me thus?"

"You--you--"

He gave one huge sigh and returned to his pot. "Ahleri told me much…" he whispered. He spooned up another sample and sipped it loudly. "I believe," he said, "the stew is nearly done. What of the meat?" he asked.

Prytal was staring at him, his mouth hanging open, his eyes as wide as anyone's Patrick had ever seen. He reached down and retrieved the Kilmari's sword handing it back to him hilt first. The startled soldier shook off his surprise and took it back. For a moment, he held it in front of him, ready to fight again.

"It's okay, Prytal," Patrick said. "He may or may not be harmless, but if he wanted to hurt you, he would have done it by now."

Prytal nodded and sheathed the sword.

"It appears the meat is fully cooked," Altay said. "Help me, will you Ric?"

Together they eased the carcass off the spit and soon they were all enjoying a meal together. In the middle of it, Bob arrived. Prytal dropped his plate and drew his sword. Lumps of meat fell onto the ground and coated themselves with dirt.

"Easy," Patrick said. He gently pushed the sword aside.

"Am I to believe that no demon is a danger anymore?" Prytal asked.

"Not these two, anyway," Ric told him.

Bob held a cloak similar to Ric's in front of him, his head tilted slightly to one side. "It appears, my lord, that you have already acquired a cloak?"

"I have indeed, Comoin, courtesy of he who released me." He motioned to the newly arrived demon. "Would you sup with us?" he asked.

"I thank you, my lord, but I have already sated my hunger and my thirst."

"That is a pity." Sje smiled. "After so long a time without food, even fungus would be excellent, but we have both fresh vegetables and meat."

"I could perhaps indulge in a plate," Comoin said.

"Excellent! Here." Sje handed him a plate which he filled, then sat and ate.

"My Lord, your culinary skills have not been dulled by your interment."

"Why, thank you."

Sje sat back from the meal, apparently satisfied. The amusement that had played on his face since his release was replaced by something more serious. He cleared his throat and addressed Ric.

"The time has come for us to discuss our arrangement," he began. He looked at Altay. "I know you are traveling to the north, in search of the Aberration."

"You mean Jason, and yes," she answered, "I am."

"To the north is where my home lies. I can fly you to the place where Bue has likely taken him."

"Where is that?" Patrick asked.

"Ankaal," Sje answered almost dreamily. "It is a lone mountain, close to my home. Many say it is somewhat similar to Kimala, though few men have seen its beauty. From the summit, my people can see for many miles." He leaned forward, regarding Ric closely. "I will not agree to bring her back, nor will I agree to assist in the rescue of the aberration. If I am incorrect, I will not assist you in your search for him and I will not agree to return."

"You mean you'd just leave her there?" Ric asked. "All alone?"

"Doesn't sound like much of a deal to me," Patrick added.

"That is my offer," Sje said. "No more." He waited for a reply, the human shaped eyes still glinting copper and blue.

All three men looked at Altay. The girl glanced back and forth between them, her gaze finally settling on Sje.

"Why?" she whispered.

Sje blinked. "Why?" he repeated.

"Why would you leave me there?"

Sje raised his eyebrows. "The aberration is an aberration. You would want me to bring him back as well, would you not?" he asked with a small smile.

"Yes," she answered.

"I cannot abide him."

"Ric?" she pleaded.

"I think you should bring them both back here," he said.

"The aberration is not part of the deal." When no one said anything more, he spoke again. "I have my reasons, Healer-Sword. That is all I feel I should divulge. Do we have an accord?"

Altay regarded him with a critical eye. "Time is of great importance," she said quietly. "I do not know if Jason can survive on his own for long. He does not know the ways of the forests."

"You won't hurt her?" Ric asked.

"I will not."

"And what about the war?" Prytal asked. "Will you go and join Marand and Fot against Tersan?"

Sje raised his eyebrows. "I have listened to you speak of these men, though I do not know who they are. I have no desire to form an allegiance with any man, be he standing with Fot or against him. My only desire," he continued softly, "is to return to my home." He took in a great breath and let it out slowly. "What say you?"

Altay took in a deep breath. She looked at Ric, a frown on her face. "The climb to the summit alone would take several days," she said. "It was a fool's errand to begin with. Now, we may have a chance."

Ric glanced at Patrick. Patrick looked back to Altay. "You're sure?" he asked.

She said nothing, but nodded slowly.

"Marvelous! Then it is all settled." Sje smiled at them. "Humans can be very reasonable. I have always said so. Comoin?" he said to the other demon.

"Yes, my lord?"

"If it is not too much trouble, would you assist the humans in cleaning? I have a long way to fly in the morning--" he stretched and did not bother stifling a yawn. "--with my young passenger. She and I both need our rest."

Comoin bowed his head slightly. "As you wish, my lord."

"Wait just a minute, there, Sje," Patrick said.

Sje stopped and faced the Otherworlder. "Yes?"

"What did you do with the others?"

A wide smile crossed his face. "I released them and sent them home. They will not bother you or any other human. You have my word."

Without waiting for reply, he changed back into demon form, curled up under a huge tree and went to sleep.

62 Above and Below

The sun rose in a cold grey sky. Tiny icicles glistened on their blankets as the cold light found its way to their camp. The smell of frying meat permeated the air. Patrick wished there was coffee. He rubbed a hand across his face and braced himself for the chill that would greet him when he sat up. He dressed quickly and joined Prytal by the fire.

"The Lady has blessed us with a clear day," Prytal said as he handed Patrick a mug of trinka.

Patrick wrapped both hands around the mug savoring the heat as much as the scent. He took a sip. The trinka spread over his tongue, igniting his salivary glands. "I never thought I'd hear myself say this, but this is better than coffee."

Prytal laughed. "Lady Jessie shares your sentiments."

Just out of earshot, Altay and Ric were having an animated conversation. Bob was busying himself packing Patrick's bedding. Sje was nowhere to be seen.

"I'm not comfortable sending the girl with that demon," Patrick said as Prytal handed him a plate of food. "He's not right."

"I beg your pardon?"

"I don't trust him," he answered, biting into a crispy piece of meat. "Wow. That's really good. Isn't this the same stuff we had yesterday?"

"Yes," Prytal answered. "Sage added a few things to it."

"Speaking of the demon, where is he?"

Prytal pointed toward the hot spring. "He wanted to bathe before he left."

"You see, that's what bothers me!"

Prytal shook his head. He poured more trinka out for Ric and Altay, handing each a mug as they joined them around the fire.

"I'll be fine," Altay was saying.

"What if he leaves you in the middle of nowhere?" Ric said.

"Look, I was going to find my way there. I should think I could find my way back." She raised her eyebrows, stared at him and waited for a response.

"The camp is packed, sir," Bob said with a slight bow. "If you will not be needing me for a bit, I have some business to attend to."

"Yeah, sure, whatever," Ric told him.

"As you wish," Bob answered. He made another bow and left.

"Altay," Patrick said, "are you sure about this?"

She nodded around a mouthful of eggs. She wiped her mouth daintily on her sleeve. "I want to go," she said quietly. "And I've had every reason I shouldn't go explained to me this morning over and over again. So don't ask me not to, okay?"

"Women," Ric muttered.

Patrick snorted, but said nothing.

The meal was quickly over and Bob returned to clean and pack the cookware and utensils. He hummed happily as he worked, taking time to speak to the horses in low, even tones. They were not afraid of him.

"You know, neither one of them's right," Patrick grumbled.

"You can say that again," Ric answered.

Bob walked over to Altay and handed her a pack. "Here are two weeks' worth of supplies, Miss," he said, "and a small cook pot along with a few dishes. May they serve you well," he added with a bow.

"Thank you," Altay said.

He handed her a second, smaller pack.

"What's this?" she asked.

"Clothing," he replied. "Lord Sje requested it, I have acquired it--" He raised a hand. "No human was hurt in the acquisition."

A shadow passed above them, blocking out the sun for a moment. They looked up to find Sje soaring above the trees. Laughter trickled down to them from the treetops as the giant demon began his descent. He landed in front of them so lightly that he barely made a noise.

"Are you ready, my dear?" he asked Altay.

"I suppose as ready as I shall ever be," she said.

"Come."

Without hesitating, Altay strode over to him. She was barely a third his height but she turned her back on him to let him pick her up with his many hands. Sje cleared his throat.

"Yes, my dear, I could carry you that way," he said, reaching for her with one of his two long arms, "but it really is easier if you ride…here." Like a father hoisting his child, Sje placed Altay so that she was on his shoulders straddling his neck. She gave a little gasp of surprise, then settled in.

"Ready?"

"I--I think so."

"Splendid!"

He took two running steps, the giant wings flapped easily and they were airborne.

"You know," Ric said as the two flew straight to the north, "I think I'm jealous."

Patrick shaded his eyes with his hand. "I'm a little jealous, too."

The morning sun was brighter now and not as cold. Patrick watched until the huge body became a blip. Then he turned his attention away from the sky and nearly ran into Bob. The demon was holding all of their horses' reins in one hand, Altay's horse-turned-pack-animal's lead rope in the other.

"Good grief, Bob," Patrick said, "you could give a little warning!"

"What would you have me do, sir?" he asked.

Patrick took the reins and mounted, trying not to look too ungrateful. "Thanks," he mumbled.

"Why, you are quite welcome, sir."

Prytal swung easily into his saddle; Ric took three tries before he was finally aboard, leaning awkwardly over Red's neck before regaining his balance. He shifted his weight gingerly in the saddle.

"We are not going far, Ric," Prytal said brightly. "Once we reach the entrance to the mines, we walk."

"Right." Ric patted the bay and the huge horse turned his head so that he could be scratched behind the ears. "I get the feeling I'm going to be sorry," he said.

The journey to the cave's entrance was completed well before noon. They dismounted, handing the horses' reins back to Bob. The demon busied himself removing the riding gear and stacking it neatly beside a pile of stones. One by one, he removed their bridles and set them free. Ric took a moment to rub Red's nose one last time.

"Go on," he told the horse. "I'll see ya soon."

The horse nickered softly, then took off after the others. Bob shouldered everything the horses carried without a word. The equipment formed a mountain of supplies on his back.

"Divvy that up a little, will ya?" Patrick said.

"It is my privilege to carry them," he said, refusing to budge.

"The way is smaller than you are," Prytal explained. "You will have to meet us on the other side. You can fly, can you not?"

"Smaller?"

"Yes. I am afraid you will simply not fit," Prytal said.

"A moment." Bob lowered the huge packs of food and utensils. He furrowed his brow and started to shrink. The effort made his face very red and sweaty. He looked at his hands with surprise. "I believe I have accomplished it!" he whispered. He looked up at them, a grin almost as wide as his face flashing at them. "I did it! I really did it!"

They laughed at him and he kept smiling. Now he was a little taller than Patrick, a little shorter than Ric and a lot rounder than any of them. He leaned over to pick up the packs. When he lifted the third one, he had nowhere to put it.

"Give me that," Patrick said, taking one from his hands.

"And I'll take this one," Ric said.

Bob stood with one pack left. He raised an eyebrow and looked at Prytal.

"I think it's best you carry that one," Prytal told him, "if you're going to come with us, that is."

"As part of my contract with the young shield--"

"Stop calling me that!" Ric said.

"--I have agreed to make certain the humans come to no harm." He shouldered the pack with a grunt. "I am ready."

"Then I suppose we had best be off."

The way inside the mountain was a slit between two slivers of stone. They had to shed the packs, either dragging them behind or holding them in front of them in order to gain entry. Even in his present form, Bob had a bit of trouble squeezing through. Over one hundred feet they traveled sideways before the tunnel finally widened enough that they could walk with ease. Another hundred feet and they could walk two abreast.

"That was interesting," Patrick said.

"You say this goes all the way through to the other side?" Ric asked.

"Yes."

"And it's shorter this way?"

"To pass through should take no longer than a day."

"Good."

For the first time since arriving in Winnie's world, Patrick spent a day with no conflict. The tunnels were intricate and darker than anything he could ever imagine and it seemed like they were always going uphill, but Prytal never hesitated. He drew his sword at one point, holding it aloft in one hand while he handled a lit torch with the other. Bob seemed a little nervous, but Ric was in good spirits. The lanky youth formed a ball of energy and stuck it on the end of Prytal's sword.

"Two in one!" he proclaimed with a huge grin.

The Kilmari scowled at him. He swished the sword back and forth, but the little ball stayed firmly in place.

"Ric, would you please remove this?" he asked.

"You don't have to hold the torch that way," Ric said.

"Yes," Prytal admitted, "but the sword is heavy. Do you mind?"

Reluctantly, Ric took back the tiny ball. He rolled it between the palms of his hands until it disappeared.

They paused around what should have been noon to have a bite to eat and a little something to drink.

"How far?" Patrick asked.

"We have just passed the knees."

"Knees?" the three of them responded at once.

"Yes," Prytal answered. "We are now beneath Emmalie. We shall be camping at her base before nightfall."

The afternoon progressed as smoothly as the morning. They turned a corner and were greeted by a shaft of silvery white light. Prytal snorted.

"It appears my timing is a bit off," he said as he entered a tunnel as narrow as the western entrance had been. "Night has already fallen."

They exited the sister into a colder night than they had experienced on the Jelestine plain. A dusting of snow crunched under their boots. The underground journey had indeed been an uphill one, exiting onto the Plain of Arandia that separated the Sisters. Moonlight glistened on the snow, each tiny snowflake suckling on the light as though it were alive.

"How much further?" Patrick asked.

"We are in Calshara," Prytal answered. "Il Chatel is two days' journey to the north. From here, we must be very careful. Marand's people are everywhere."

"Any idea where they are holding Lucy Perrymore?"

"Probably the dungeons at the palace."

"May I suggest you break bread here tonight?" Bob asked. "I believe the young shield is in need of respite."

"Would you please stop calling me that?" Ric snapped.

"As you wish, my lord," Bob answered with a bow.

"For crying out loud!"

Patrick laughed. "Give it up, son," he said. "It's only a name."

"Go ahead and set up," Prytal told Bob, "but no fire."
"No fire!" Ric protested. "We'll freeze to death!"
"I will be back." The Kilmari soldier melted into the forest.
"Jason was right," Ric mumbled. "They never sleep."

63 Maggie and Amos and Altay and Sje

Jason woke with a start. A gnawing pain in his gut reminded him that his last meal was two days ago. He knew the feeling would pass. But he also knew he had to find food somewhere. Reluctantly, he rose from the now familiar bed, crossed the warm waters of the still stream and donned his clothes.

Before he reached the point where the tunnel split, he felt the cold mountain air on his face. Yesterday, he had been invigorated. Today, he was simply chilled.

For half an hour, he searched again around the cave's entry for food. The same scraggly shrubs yielded the same disappointing results. There was no food to be found. He trudged back to the cave, pulling his cloak tightly around his body.

"Bue said I would live out my life here," he said aloud more to hear the sound of his own voice than because he wondered at the length of that life. With shoulders slumped, he made his way back into the cave.

At the split, he once again felt the warmth emanating from the hot spring. He was drawn toward the meager comfort it provided. He took a step down that path but paused. Very slowly, he took Ric's flashlight out of his pocket, turned around and started down the other tunnel. The tiny beam was swallowed up by darkness only a few feet ahead of him, yet there was enough light to continue if he kept the stream of light focused on the walls.

The tunnel narrowed. All of Jason's senses went on high alert as his brain released adrenaline into his body. His heart pounded in his ears and his breaths were faster than they should be. He paused and shone the beam up. The tunnel was comfortably high and nothing looked like it was going to fall on him.

"So far, so good," he reassured himself.

In front of him, he thought he saw light. He turned off the flashlight and, sure enough, there was light ahead. He resisted the temptation to run, but he quickened his pace.

The tunnel took a hard right, more than a ninety degree turn, and emptied out into an orchard. Apples adorned the trees in various stages of ripeness. He plucked one and bit into it. Sweet juice ran down his chin and onto his neck. He didn't care. He devoured two apples before he had time to think and was reaching for a third when someone spoke to him.

"Too many apples will cause you discomfort, young man."

Jason whirled. An old man with a toothless grin was leaning on a staff watching him.

"It is not often I get visitors," he continued. "Most do not venture far from the cave. Most of the time, the only way I know I have company is by the smell."

"Smell?" Jason asked.

"Yes." The grin was plastered on his face. "Not many places to bury anyone else up here, though, not that I will be able to take care of that particular deed for much longer. I am not the man I once was."

"Smell?" Jason repeated.

The old man flashed another toothless grin. "Come if you are hungry. Here, there is abundance."

He turned away from Jason and shuffled off down a picturesque path that followed a gentle slope uphill. Jason pocketed the third apple and raced after him. When he got to the top of the rise he stopped short.

"Wow," he whispered.

Before him spread a valley. It was not strewn with trees and waterfalls and wild things, but was small and meticulously kept, much like a postcard from the Downs in England. The old man was walking easily down a wide path. An occasional note from some ditty drifted back to Jason, reminding him painfully of the loss of his gift. Then his stomach rumbled and he dismissed all other thoughts. He broke into a trot and caught up to his host. The man nodded approvingly and broke into song again. Jason felt rather like he was headed for Brigadoon.

They passed through fruit covered trees and vineyards ready for harvest before they reached a small, thatch-roofed cottage with smoke curling up out of the chimney. A round woman as old as the man exited the cottage, drying her hands on a towel. When she smiled, Jason felt like he was in his mother's kitchen. Food sprang into his mind and stayed there.

"Amos! I see we have a guest!"

"That we do, Maggie, that we do."

"He is so thin." Maggie stopped drying her hands and waved them in. "Come, young man," she said. "I've a loaf of bread in the oven that should be ready shortly. Oh, and some cheese and apples, grapes, nuts… You do like nuts, my boy?"

Jason nodded.

"Good, good! Step smartly now."

Jason stepped smartly into the cottage. It was an amazing place. No wall space was unadorned. Bunches of dried plants hung upside down in neat but disorganized rows. An overstuffed comfortable-looking couch sat in the center of the room, its front legs planted firmly on a worn but clean rag-rug. An inviting fire crackled merrily inside a plain stone hearth that jutted out into the room. To one side, he could see the bread baking in an oven, the glow of the fire casting shadows across the loaf. A kettle was nestled inside the hearth, its contents slowly bubbling. Maggie walked quickly over to it and stirred. She raised the spoon and sniffed it, then took a taste.

"Needs salt," she said.

Amos laughed. "Whatever you say, dear," he told her as she bustled around. "Young man, come. Sit."

Jason sat.

Moments later, Maggie set a plate of food in front of him. Steam rose, filling his nostrils with sumptuous scents. His hostess pulled the bread from the oven and broke it, offering half to him. He took it, juggled it between his hands until it was cool enough to handle then dipped it into his plate to sop up his stew. Nothing, not even Jessie's cooking had ever tasted so good. He ate without speaking while the old couple watched. Each time he got close to a clean plate, Maggie raced to the kitchen and filled another for him.

After what seemed an age, Jason was finally sated. He pushed himself away from the table, wiping his mouth on a cloth napkin.

"It appears the young man has had enough, Maggie," Amos said as Maggie returned with another helping of food.

"I have, Miss Maggie," Jason said. "Thank you."

"He is too thin," she replied.

"Maggie," Amos warned.

Maggie huffed. "Well, all right." She handed the plate to Amos, her attention focused on Jason. "It is time for you to return to your room," she told him. With that, she fixed a second plate for herself and sat beside Amos to eat.

"Who are you?" Jason asked.

Neither answered.

"Maggie and Amos, yeah I got that part, but who are you? Why are you here? What is this place?"

"I would love some of that cheese spread you are so fond of making," Amos said to Maggie.

"Of course, dear."

"Amos?" Jason asked.

"The apples are nearly ready for harvest," Amos said to Maggie. "Good thing. We're running low on cider."

"Crops have been bountiful this year," Maggie answered.

"I had a couple apples," Jason said. He took the one out of his pocket and offered it to Maggie.

"We shall have both white and red wine," she told Amos, ignoring Jason's offering. "Plenty of grapes. Plenty."

Amos stopped eating. His eyes widened like a child's on Christmas morning. "Ice wine?"

"The Lady willing!"

"What's ice wine?" Jason asked.

"That would be charming!" Amos answered. He dove back into his plate.

Jason stared at the couple. Neither stared back. They kept talking to one another about the harvest, the weather, their good fortune, the coming winter, their stockpile of wood, the water supply.... Anything except their visitor. Finally he reached out, picked up the apple and pocketed it.

"I, um, I'll see you in the morning, then," he said.

Maggie put a hand on Amos's, but she looked at Jason. "Very good, dear," was all she said before returning to her conversation.

Jason walked out of the cottage into the evening sun. The weather was so much more pleasant here than outside the cave on the other side of the tunnel. He wondered how a valley such as this could exist so high on a mountaintop. Reluctantly, he made his way back to the cave retracing his steps to his bed above the pool. He yawned hugely, snuggled into the mattress and fell almost instantly to sleep.

"He has to be here."

The words jarred Jason from a dreamless sleep.

"Perhaps the Aberration has met an untimely death," a silken voice answered.

"Why are you still here, Sje?" The voice belonged to a woman, a voice he knew but couldn't quite put a name to. "Your deal was to bring me here, not annoy me."

"I have fulfilled my portion of the arrangement," Sje replied. "What I do from now on is neither your concern nor your business."

"Either help or leave me alone!" the woman snapped.

"Altay?" Jason was croaking. He shook his head to try to clear it enough to focus. "Altay, is that you?"

"Did you hear that?" the woman said.

"I did, indeed. It seems demonkind's greatest enemy lives."

Jason scrambled to get up. He teetered on the edge of his bed, lost his balance and fell into the warm water of the pool. He gulped a few mouthfuls of water and came up sputtering.

"Jason!"

"Here!" Jason reached for his clothing to hastily dress. He fumbled with the neatly folded bundle and it fell with a splash into the water. The shirt spread out as it hit, his jeans sinking a bit more quickly. He snatched at both of them and hurriedly exited the pool opposite his bed. He fought with the wet jeans, dragging them up over his legs as best he could, buttoning the fly an instant before Altay's head appeared.

"Jason!" she repeated. She raced to him, a torch in one hand, the other snaking around him to pull him into a huge hug. "The Lady be praised, you are safe!"

"Good grief, Altay," he said, though he returned her hug with enthusiasm, "Bue did promise."

"Bue has a history of not keeping her promises," Sje said as he took the torch from Altay. She turned and shot him a look of mistrust. "Well, you mustn't burn the aber--young man," he finished silkily.

"Who're you?" Jason asked. Altay released him and he fought with his shirt to get it on. The warm water of the pool turned cool quickly in the open air of the cave.

"His name is Sje," Altay said.

The man inclined his head slightly. "Delighted to make your acquaintance," Sje said. There was something about his tone that did not quite ring true yet there was no threat in it.

"He brought me here."

"Wow. How'd you get up?"

Sje cleared his throat. "I believe the First Order of the day would be a meal, Jason."

Altay wheeled on him. "Your obligation has been met!" she seethed. "I would thank you to leave us alone!"

"Altay, wait," Jason said.

"Wait?" she snapped.

"I don't know how you got up here, but I've been all over this mountaintop and it looks pretty impossible to me to get down. If he can help, I suggest we let him."

Altay's eyes narrowed. "He is a demon, Jason. A really big demon."

"Oh, please, Altay, you sound like Ric." He pointed to Sje. "Where's his wings? His fangs? All those hands?"

Sje raised both eyebrows and waited for her to answer.

"Have I ever lied to you, Jason?" she demanded.

Sje shifted his attention to Jason.

"Well, not that I can recall," Jason admitted.

Sje looked back to Altay and waited.

"He's a demon!"

Sje waited for a response. The air in the cave was chilly in spite of the warm water. Jason shivered. He ran his hands up and down his arms to try to warm himself.

"Are you?" he demanded between now chattering teeth.

"Am I what?" Sje replied.

"Are you a demon?" he asked pointedly.

Sje blinked several times. Light from the torch flickered in his now coppery colored eyes shot with sapphire blue. Not the same color as Fot's, but definitely the same pattern and shape. He stumbled backward, his foot catching on a stone, sending him to the rocky floor with a clumsy thud. Sje smiled.

"I assume you have your answer?" he asked.

"Altay!"

"Oh, Jason, really," she said, placing his cloak around him. "If he wanted to hurt us, he could have done it by now. By the Lady! You're freezing!"

"Well, I should hope so! It's not exactly balmy in here, you know, and I'm kinda wet."

"What were you doing in the water?" she asked.

"Had to go through it to get to the bed," he answered, still staring at Sje.

"What bed?" Altay asked.

Jason turned. Behind him, the water stretched as far as the light reached. He slipped his hand into his pocket to retrieve the flashlight, but it was gone.

"It's just over there," he said, pointing in the direction of the ledge he had so recently vacated. "I swear it was there!"

"It's all right, Jason," Altay told him. "We all see things sometimes when we want them to be there."

"But it was there! I slept there two nights in a row!"

"It's cold in here, Jason," she continued. "Let's get out to the fire."

"There's a better place! It's a valley filled with fruit trees and well-tended vegetables and herbs! Amos and Maggie live there. I was eating apples and Amos said if I ate too many I'd get sick and then he took me to their house where Maggie fed me a really good meal with fresh bread and stew and--"

"Slow down, Jason," Altay cautioned.

"No, really! We can all go there! They're expecting me for breakfast!" He dashed down the tunnel toward the place where it split in two. No light greeted him. In fact, there was no opening. He raced to the cave's entrance, then retraced his steps searching for the tunnel. Altay followed him, torch in hand, helping him search. When they had retraced their steps back to the pool, Jason's teeth were chattering.

"It was here. I swear it was here."

Sje cleared his throat. "It appears a meal has become the second order of the day. He needs to get out of those clothes and into something dry," he said to Altay.

"I am the healer here!" she snipped back at him.

"Why, certainly you are," Sje replied.

She cleared her own throat. "Jason, you need to get out of those wet clothes and into something dry," she stated. Behind her, Sje had stripped off his cloak and was disrobing.

"What the hell is he doing?" he asked, pointing to Sje.

"I am helping to save the Aberration's life," Sje replied, "in hopes he will grant me a wish." He held the warm looking garments out for Altay to take. "And in hopes that I am not making a grievous error. I have no need of these."

He left them to stare blankly at one another.

"What was that all about?" Jason asked.

Altay was staring after him, her mouth hanging wide open. "I have no idea."

64 Reality Check

Jason reluctantly followed Altay back up the path to the summit. His legs were so heavy he wondered if Sje's clothing had weights sewn into the hems. Suddenly he did not feel at all well. First he was hot, then cold and his stomach was unsettled. All he wanted was some of his mom's good old fashioned chicken noodle soup with carrots and a lot of salt.

Frigid air whipped into the cave's opening, solidifying the fact that he really wanted to return to the warmth of his bed over the hot spring. He stopped short of the entrance to lean against the damp rock. With his back against the wall, he slid until he was sitting on the ground. Altay came back for him.

"Are you all right?" she asked. Her voice was all fuzzy, like she was speaking through a phone with a poor connection. Jason swallowed.

"Yeah. Well, no. It must have been something I ate. Amos said too many apples would make me sick."

She put her hand on his forehead, then on his cheek, worry appearing, then disappearing. "Who is Amos?"

"I assume he's Maggie's husband." He blinked slowly. "Am I gonna live?"

She rummaged around in her bag and withdrew a few dried leaves that she shoved into his hand. "Chew on these," she ordered. "You will feel better."

Jason put her offering obediently in his mouth and began to chew. They were bitter and rough against his tongue. When he tried to spit them out, she was there.

"I know they taste bad," she said soothingly. "Trust me?"

He nodded and she left him sitting there. Just beyond the cave's entrance, he could hear the two of them talking about him in little snatches of conversation.

"Hot you say?" Sje said.

"Yes. Fever. Probably from being in the cold too long. I don't know why he was in the water. There's nothing there."

"Do you have any capalla leaves?" he asked.

"Yes. He's chewing on them now."

"Good."

There was a bit of silence. "You are a healer, Altay," Sje said. "You know it is likely this is naught but a minor illness you humans get on occasion. I have seen it many times."

"Colds are rarely accompanied by hallucinations. He's seeing people."

Sje paused. "Do not make it more than it is," he said kindly. "I know of an herb that grows here on this mountain that we give the lesser demons when they are ill. Ahleri got relief from it once. The Aberration may as well."

"I wish you'd stop calling him that. His name is Jason."

"As you wish."

Jason drifted. When he woke again, the smell of soup filled his nostrils. Sje was standing over a small pot inside the cave's entry, stirring and humming. Altay was lying beside him, her head on his lap, dozing.

"Are you hungry?" Sje asked without looking up.

"Yes," Jason croaked. His voice was nearly gone.

"There is but one pot and one beverage container." He dipped some of the broth out of the pot and made his way over to where Jason sat. "Drink this slowly. It is hot."

Jason took the mug from the demon. He sniffed the contents. Finding nothing repulsive, he took a sip. The soup was hot but not hot enough to burn him. The flavor was strong, not particularly unpleasant.

"Too spicy?" Sje asked with a sigh. "My apologies. It has been a long time and Ahleri was not particular."

"It's fine," he whispered. "I just have to take it a little at a time, that's all."

Sje nodded. He stood and walked to the mouth of the cave and seemed to be looking a long way into the distance.

"What do you see?" Jason croaked.

"Men heading to war," Sje answered pleasantly. "My people are among them."

Jason shuddered. "No offense, but I have seen what you're 'people' can do to mine."

Sje sighed. "Aggression is never pleasant," he said, "for anyone." He pointed to the cup. "Drink."

Jason drank. The beverage was thick and hot and he felt much better than he had only moments before. Sje stopped looking into the distance and returned to take a seat before him. His oddly colored eyes were fixed on Jason.

"You and I can save many lives, Jason," he started, "if we work together."

"What?"

"My people will become targets within the army of Il Chatel," he replied pleasantly, "pawns used by a king who has no honor and a demon who serves only himself. You and I can stop their slaughter."

Jason laughed. "How?" he said. "We're a million miles away from anything. It would take a long time to get back there."

"I can take you," he stated.

"Okay, you can take me." He touched Altay's hair and found himself stroking her head gently. The simple motion brought him a lot of pleasure. "What about her? You can't just leave her here! Even if she finds her way to Amos and Maggie's, they're just too odd."

"Twice blessed," Sje whispered. He cleared his throat, but remained silent.

"What?" Jason asked. Altay stirred again, this time so that she was no longer using Jason as a pillow. He pulled her cloak closer around her shoulders. "Why would you help us?" he asked.

Sje sighed. "There is one among you with great powers," he said. "Or perhaps he merely possesses a great weapon. Many of my people may perish."

"Forgive me, but I think we're too late on that issue."

Sje nodded. "Tersan is a benevolent leader. So is Pixil. I would rather they be in power than Marand, who is using…It is complicated."

"Not that complicated." Jason tipped the cup up and drained the rest of the soup. "What do you propose?" he asked.

"Killing Fot," he answered evenly, "and leading my people home."

"Right." Jason looked at him. Sje was barely taller than Jason and did not seem particularly powerful. "He's a whole lot bigger than you are. How are you going to do that?"

"I will manage," he answered pleasantly. "However, I require your assistance."

"For what?"

"To convince my people that they need to go home." He was staring directly into Jason's eyes.

"How?" Jason asked.

Sje cleared his throat. "I heard you sing, albeit the sound, thankfully, was mostly absorbed by that dreadful tepid water. You are, ahem, an aberration."

"Me?"

"Sing to them. That's all you need to do. Just sing."

Jason got up and headed to the cave's entry. Beyond it he could see nothing that looked civilized. "Bue said you could see for miles," he said as Sje joined him. "I can't."

"Yet you know the war is coming."

"Yeah. Jessie and Penrose told us." He turned his attention to the demon who looked like a man. "How can one voice carry over that huge area?" he asked.

"A true aberration can, though his sacrifice will be great," Sje said. "Many lives will be saved. You have been twice blessed. Perhaps you will be saved as well."

"What do you mean?" Jason asked.

Sje took in a great breath before continuing. "Even in my time, I have never seen a true aberration. Legend has it that they can put a human army to sleep with song and drive demonkind back to their home. But the cost is great. Most do not survive. However, it appears you have been twice blessed. Your chances of surviving are greatly improved."

Jason looked to Altay, then back to Sje, shaking his head. "I don't know…"

"Marand's forces will be weakened once the demons are gone," Sje argued.

Jason cleared his throat. "There are a couple of other things you should know about, Sje," he started.

"Oh?"

"Yeah. First, I can barely talk. Surely you noticed that?"

"It will pass," the demon told him.

"I hope you're right on that count. The other thing is that I don't have any power anymore. I, um, lost it when I sang for Penrose." Jason handed him the mug. "If there's any more of that soup, I'd like seconds."

65 Strange Bedfellows

Jason sat up with a start which was a mistake since he was half naked and could see his breath. He shrugged on his shirt and pulled his cape tightly around his body. The entry to the cave was brilliant white. He shaded his eyes for what he hoped was a better look. The effort went unrewarded.

"Altay?" he called. "Sje?"

Neither answered.

He pulled on his boots and walked toward the entrance. As he got closer, the little pot came into view. A fire crackled cheerfully beneath it and its contents bubbled gently under the lid. Jason breathed a sigh of relief.

"They can't have gone far. Let's see what's cooking." Using the corner of his cape, he lifted the lid and sniffed. "Yuck," he said. "Smells worse than Ric's laundry."

A shadow crossed the mouth of the cave dimming the bright light. For a moment, it lingered there before melting into two beings.

"Jason!"

"Altay?"

"You're awake!"

Before he could respond, she had her arms wrapped around him in a huge hug. He tried to throw the cape back so he could enjoy her embrace, but by the time he did so, she had already released him and was looking back over her shoulder.

"You were right," she said cheerily. "He's awake!"

"Of course, my dear," Sje answered silkily. He walked over to the pot and crumbled a few leaves into it.

"I hope I'm not supposed to eat that," Jason said.

"No," Sje answered. He gave the contents a stir and addressed Altay with a smile. "You have done well, Healer-Sword. If we both survive the war, there are many things I would like to teach you."

"I will be honored," she answered with a bow.

"What the hell just happened?" Jason demanded.

"Trust, Jason," Altay said. She was holding his hand in her own, but smiling at Sje. "Trust."

Sje rummaged around in a meager pile of disorganized items. "Aha!" He pulled a large, flat loaf of bread from the pile along with cheese, meat and some kind of fruit. Altay busied herself with a tablecloth of sorts on which the demon placed the food.

"One last meal before we leave," Sje said. He raised their single cup in a toast. "May we all see the light of tomorrow's day!"

He took a swallow and handed the cup to Altay. "Tomorrow's day," she repeated. She took a sip and handed it to Jason.

"Tomorrow's day," he repeated, though the toast meant nothing to him. He took a sip of the beverage. It was fermented and sweet and warmed him. He handed it back to Sje. Suddenly, he was very hungry. He broke off a piece of bread, split it in two, stuffed meat on one half, then slammed the other half on top and took a bite. The meat was unknown to him, but delicious.

"Did you enjoy your sleep?" Altay asked as she finished making her own sandwich.

"Very much," Jason replied. "Where were you?"

"Hunting." She spared a smile at Sje. "It's been two days since we found you. You've barely spoken on your way out to relieve yourself or to eat."

"Two days!"

"Yes." Sje nodded toward the plain. "In that time, the armies have moved into position. It is time."

"You're leaving us here?" Jason nearly shouted.

Sje finished the last of his meal and regarded Jason with almost fear. The coppery eyes blinked slowly. His face was grave.

"You want to bargain?" Jason asked.

"It is more of a request than a bargain," Sje returned. "The Healer-Sword has told me of your gift of song. I thought I heard the discordant strains while I was still imprisoned."

"And?"

"Please, sing for me, else the explanation will merely waste time."

"What?"

"He asked you to sing, Jason," Altay repeated. "It's a simple enough request."

"Well, okay." He took in a deep breath and launched into the Birthday song. "Happy?"

Sje's face darkened. "Do not make light of this power!"

"What? You want it in the key of 'C' or something?" Jason snapped.

The copper eyes glowed. Sje leaned forward, never looking away. His nostrils flared and his normally steady hand trembled slightly as he put one fist inside the other. His knuckles were a shade lighter than his normal complexion. Jason felt his heart hammer in his chest. The demon rose and went to stand by the pot, his back to Jason.

"That wasn't very nice!" Altay scolded.

"It was stupid," Jason hissed. "Why does he want me to sing anyway?"

"He has his reasons."

"I, well, if he's asking me to sing like to cure somebody, there's nobody here to cure. Besides I just can't do that on command!"

"Why not?"

Jason put his head down close to hers. "This 'gift' that I have--it's got a mind of its own when it works and Penrose said it would never work again if I used it before I got to the Dead Room on Kimala. So I guess it's a gift I 'had'."

"The Dead Room, eh?" she said. The corners of her mouth lifted in an ever so slight smile. "What did he tell you, Jason?"

"Weren't you listening?"

"I'm still listening." She raised her eyebrows. "And I'm betting he told you what he's told a lot of gifted people whose powers grew faster than they were ready to receive them."

"What?"

She bit her lip before she spoke again. "Jason, you and Ric were gifted by the cave. We both know that."

"Hell, half of Kimala knows that!" he snorted.

"Well, if you aren't ready for it, sometimes the power gets out of control."

"Tell me about it!"

"I'm trying!"

Jason took another bite of his sandwich and washed it down with whatever was in the mug. "I'm listening."

She raised her arm in the air, her fingers gracefully extended as though she was holding something. An instant later, a fiery sword appeared. Jason gasped and she laughed.

"You see, I have been studying all my life to become Sword, should something happen to Lord Eron," she told him. She twirled in a graceful pirouette, the sword flashing as it responded to her command. She lunged at an imaginary enemy, stepped backward to avoid his blow, then in again to slice him in half. Sje applauded and she bowed to him, the sword disappearing as she rose.

"Sje taught me that last move," she explained. "Apparently, it was one of Ahleri's favorites."

"What the hell was that all about, who is Ahleri and why should I give a damn?" Jason demanded. He shook his head. "I'm sorry, Altay, that was impressive. But what does your, um, talent have to do with me?"

"You are a Siren, Jason."

"So they tell me."

"And you have not had a lot of time to acquaint yourself with your power."

"I don't have any power, remember?"

"Yes you do." She walked over to him and placed a hand on his shoulder. "Penrose told you to stop listening because you weren't ready to hear."

"He...he..."

"You needed to learn silence, just as I needed to learn to shut the sword down. It's control."

"Then…"

"You cannot return the gift," she said. "You must learn to bend it to your will when you are using it…" She smiled. "And when you are not."

"Then I can…?

"Try." She looked at him with the biggest, roundest most beautiful eyes he had ever seen. "Please?"

Jason set aside his food and closed his eyes, asking for the sounds he thought were lost forever. A thin-skinned drum thrummed in the distance. The beat was slow, methodical, somber. He felt himself swaying to the rhythm. Wind whistled viscously outside the cave bringing with it particles of moisture that slapped into the rocky face of the mountain where as they instantly froze with a miniscule crackle. Pieces of scrubby bush brushed against one another adding soft, random beats to the tympani.

Melody came behind the rhythm. He hummed the notes as words formed in his mind, words of a different race and a different time, words he could not translate, but whose meaning he understood. The notes swelled in his throat, filling his body until he felt he would burst. He placed his feet shoulder width apart but did not open the flood gate. The time was not right.

He allowed the song to trickle over the top of his dam. He spread his arms wide and let his cape billow out behind him. It snapped smartly at the back of his legs as he bobbed his head up and down to the music now accosting him from every direction.

The insistent beat pounded on the thin skinned drum in counterpoint syncopation. The pace was fast--- *one two three one two three one two one two one two three one two three one two one two…--* Notes joined in, a sultry, smoky tune that was part mystery and part darkness. The world was at odds with itself. Jason felt it now. The song was screaming, discordant and desolate. He let it loose.

There was a hand on his arm gripping him fiercely, trying to snatch his attention from the song, but the song demanded to be heard. Two hands pulled him sharply to one side and a sound he could not incorporate screeched over the song momentarily breaking his concentration.

Altay was standing in front of him, her features lost in the spell the song cast.

"Stop!" she screamed.

One two three one two three one two one two one two three…

"Jason! Enough!"

One two three one two three one two one two…

Jason concentrated. Altay's face came into focus.

"You're killing him!" she shouted.

One two three one two three one…

"Jason! Please…" she begged.

One two…

Jason shook off the rhythm, commanding it to sink back into his mind where it thrummed quietly, waiting to be released once more. This time, he confined the song to a place where he could readily retrieve it.

"I--I think I've got it under control," he told her.

She nodded and released his arm, racing toward the entrance of the cave.

One two three one two th--

"Hush," he said aloud.

The music melted away.

Feeling quite satisfied, Jason turned his attention to the mouth of the cave. Altay knelt over Sje's still form.

"What have I done?" Jason said.

He raced over to join them, unclasping his cloak as he ran. He gently raised Sje's head and lowered it on the clothing. Altay ran a hand over the pale features. The brilliant eyes were dull between the slits of skin covering them. She lifted a lid and looked beneath it.

"Help him!" Jason said.

"Help him. Right. Yes, he said this might happen." She sprinted to the fire and dragged the smelly concoction off the flames, plunking it down beside Sje. An ominous yellow smoke curled up out of the pot. It drifted toward Jason and he turned his head away nearly gagging.

"Whatever he put in that," he said through the smoke, "it smells one hundred per cent worse that it did before." He looked up at Altay. "What is it?"

She ladled a bit out on the corner of his cloak and held it under Sje's nose. "Smelling salts," she answered.

Sje coughed and pushed Altay's hands away. He sat up and shook his head, then put his hands on either side of his face. Jason looked at his cloak in disgust.

"Are you all right?" Altay asked.

"Quite," Sje answered. He turned to Jason and held the young man's gaze for a long, long time. "I am convinced that your gift is genuine, that you are a siren." Sje cocked his head to one side. "Human forces are gathering to wage war on one another. The king of Calshara has made a deal with Fot, the traitor who caused me to be imprisoned. I do not know what the agreement was but my people have become a part of this king's army. They will suffer and die for a cause that is not their own. Fot wants baubles and objects made of shiny metal. As lord of demons, my people will do his bidding."

"What does this have to do with us?" Jason asked quietly.

"In lore, a siren can chase a demon away with a song. You have proven to me that you are a siren." He cleared his throat. "I will spare you the details of my relationship with Fot and of his betrayal of me. He will be on that battlefield. I intend to challenge him to a duel. He must acquiesce. It is the way our leaders are chosen."

"You want me to sing to him so you can win?" Jason asked.

Sje laughed. The sound was pure and beautiful like wind chimes tinkling in a gentle breeze. "No," he said. "To garner the respect of my people, I must defeat him without any aid. I have no doubt that the Fot I knew is a demon I can defeat. But he is deceitful and cunning."

"So he'd cheat to win?"

"Yes." Sje took in a deep breath. "If I am defeated, I ask that you stand on the Mound of Dallow and sing over the battlefield to chase my people home, give them a chance to survive. In addition, if your song is the right one, all humans on the battlefield will cease their fighting and sleep."

"This is all in lore, right?" Jason said.

"Yes." It was Altay who answered. "You must know that there may be a cost to you."

"Please, don't tell me," Jason said. He looked at Sje. "I'll help you."

The demon nodded his thanks. "I have an obligation to an old friend to return you to your people."

"So you're not going to abandon us here on top of this forsaken mountain?" Jason asked.

"No. That was never my plan." He stood and walked to the mouth of the cave, his gait steady. Altay followed.

Jason kicked the coals of the fire around so they would burn out by themselves. Then he raced out into the winter that had claimed the top of the mountain. He shivered and drew his cloak around him again, careful not to touch the nasty smelling concoction on the corner. He could still smell it, even though the corner was at midcalf. He wiped the cloak off with a mixture of snow and gravel. On the first try, he got most of it off.

"Are you about done?" Altay asked.

"Well if you hadn't--" His mouth fell open, the comment forgotten. Altay was nestled on the shoulders of the biggest demon Jason had ever seen and the demon was reaching out to him.

"I can carry you," Sje's voice boomed from the demon's mouth, "but I would prefer that you ride instead. I will need all of my strength to fight Fot."

Jason stood anchored to the ground.

"Jason?" Sje asked.

"Come on, Jason!" Altay called. "The view is excellent!"

"Glad I'm not afraid of heights," he mumbled as he strode forward.

A moment later, he was sitting behind Altay, his hands wrapped around her waist. Sje shifted beneath them. Without warning, he raced toward the ledge. In one, two, three steps, he jumped. They fell twenty feet before the massive wings spread to catch the wind, sending them soaring away from the mountain. Jason's heart was pounding in his chest. A different song rose in him, a song of hope, of gratitude, of excitement. He stilled the sounds, storing them so he could relive them later.

66 A Change of Direction

Patrick shivered. He pulled the borrowed cloak around himself, hoping for a little more warmth and was rewarded with an extra shiver brought on by the cold cloth touching his skin. He really wanted a fire. He would have settled for a cigarette.

"Quit," he said aloud. "Don't want to go through withdrawal again."

"Quit what?" Ric asked.

"Smoking. Bad habit. I thought it used to keep me warmer. It's so damned cold here."

"Tell me about it!"

"I may be able to help, young shield."

They turned to find Bob in full demon posture, squatting above them on a huge branch like a vulture waiting for its next meal.

"I wish you wouldn't call me that!" Ric complained.

"Perhaps these would be of some use, young shield?" he said, ignoring Ric's comment. He offered them each an ordinary looking stone about the size of a melon. The stones were warm, though not hot, and round with very smooth surfaces.

"Where did you get these?" Patrick asked.

"From the hot spring on the other side of the mountain," he replied. "I do not know what length of time they will maintain their heat."

Patrick warmed his hands on the stone. "I never thought I'd feel this way about an inanimate object," he said, "but I think I'm in love."

"Go get more," Ric ordered.

"Whoa, wait here," Patrick said to Bob before turning to Ric. "Let me have a word, young shield."

"Not you, too!"

Patrick took him to one side, out of earshot of the demon. "Look, don't push him, okay?"

"He's not like us!" Ric protested.

"Well, he walked under a mountain range today, just like we did, had only a little hard bread and cheese--"

"He can hunt!"

"Yeah, but he didn't while we were under there. Did you ever think that he might be tired?"

Ric sighed. "But he offered!"

"I know he did. Let's not take advantage of him. I'd hate to piss him off."

"Okay, okay. I guess I'll just have to figure out which part of me I want to be warm and the rest can fend for themselves."

"Right."

They returned to Bob, who was now humming a discordant melody that sounded more like some poor animal caught in a trap than a lullaby.

"We, uh, think that this will be enough," Patrick told him, holding up his stone. "Right, kid?"

"Yeah. Right."

"Do demons sleep?" Patrick asked.

"We do, though I have had many years to indulge myself in that activity." He set an obviously heavy pack down on the ground in front of him. "I thought you would like more warmth," he said, opening the pack and dumping its contents on the ground before them, "so I retrieved many stones. Now, I will continue to fulfill my part of the bargain." Before either of them could speak, he spread his wings and leapt into the air.

"Don't that just beat all?" Patrick mumbled. "C'mon, kid, let's not waste old Bob's effort."

They lined a small area with the rocks, making two circles with a shared middle line and filled the empty space with long grasses that had died back for winter. Though the mattresses were not fancy, at least they were comfortable. The rest of the night was spent in companionable snoring.

"Young shield."

Patrick rolled over to find Bob, now in the form of a man, leaning over Ric trying to wake him.

"Hey, thanks for the stones," he said.

"It is my obligation to serve," Bob answered. "Young shield!" he repeated loudly.

"What? Huh?"

"I have prepared breakfast for you and your companions."

"Oh. Great. Thanks."

Bob took the lid off of a pot. A delightful aroma filled the air.

"I thought we couldn't have a fire," Ric said.

"I beg your pardon, sir?"

"Fire. You built a fire and whoever the bad guys are--"

"The Calsharans?" Bob offered.

"Yes, them. How could they miss a fire? We--"

"Hidden thus in the forest, it will be seen only by those who truly know how to look." Mischief played on his face. His smile widened as he replaced the lid on the pot. "There is no smoke for anyone to see, young shield," he said with not a little pride.

Ric squinted. He did not see it. "Sorry to have doubted you."

The food was filling though it smelled a lot better than it tasted. Bob watched them eat with interest as though evaluating their response. In the middle of the meal, Prytal showed up.

"A fire?" he said.

"Bob did it," they said in unison, pointing to the demon.

Prytal nodded. "Well done, Comoin."

The demon nodded back.

Prytal looked as though he had something to say but bit the comment back. "Is there any more?" he asked, eyeing the pot hopefully.

They spent the rest of the day hiking through the narrow pass that led to the Plain of Arandia. On occasion, Prytal would ask them to stay put while he left them to look for other things. Bob was content to stay with them, though his choice in tunes was annoying at best.

"Bob?" Ric said when the demon began a particularly discordant tune. Ric raised his eyebrows and smiled widely.

"Yes, young shield?"

"Do you think we could just enjoy a little quiet for a while?"

Bob's eyes widened. "You do not like my interpretation of--"

"Oh no, I'm sure it's fine," Patrick interrupted. "It's just that, well, we don't want to give our position away. You understand, of course."

"Of course."

Prytal suddenly appeared. "We must go!" he said in a hushed whisper. "There is no time. Hurry!"

He left their path and entered the woods that ran parallel to their course. They followed him as fast as they could run, brambles tearing first at their clothing and then at their skin as they plunged headlong downhill towards Arandia. Prytal took a slight turn and they found themselves sliding down a hillside, landing in the open on the plain. Directly ahead of them a tall stone boundary sprang up and in the distance loomed a huge rock face. What lay between the two was not visible.

"This way!" Prytal hissed.

"They'll see us," Ric said.

"They already have! Run!"

"Where's Bob?"

The demon was not behind them. In fact, he was nowhere to be seen.

"Great, just great."

"Never mind him. Run!"

Patrick and Ric shed their packs and took off running. Prytal was close behind them like a shepherd herding them. In five minutes, they reached the stone wall marking the border between the Plain of Arandia and the basin before Dallow Mound. They scrambled down the rock edge and hugged the wall, breathing hard. Below them, the terrain dropped off sharply until it finally leveled out and extended to the rock face of Dallow. There was a narrow expanse of ground adjacent to the wall that led to the stone wall as well, providing better footing and cover, but clearly it would take much longer to go around.

"A change of plans," Prytal told them. "We have to head south to the Mound of Dallow and regroup there." He pointed to the rock face. "That is the southern edge of Dallow. With any luck, Tersan's army will already be camped above."

"What about Lucy?" Patrick asked, though he knew the answer.

"We will have to find another way."

A shower of arrows interrupted him. They tucked into the rock wall, watching the arrows soar past them into the basin.

"It looks like a long way," Prytal told them, "but it is not that far. Follow the curve of the basin to the south. I shall draw their fire on the eastern side. Go!"

"Wait!" Ric shouted. "I can shield us!"

"I know you can," Prytal answered. "But we must be able to move and I do not believe you are skilled enough to maintain the shield and move at the same time."

"At least let me try!" he pleaded.

"If you fail, they will find a way to kill us inside. Go!"

Patrick grabbed Ric by the arm and shoved him forward. Prytal gathered arrows up from the ground and shot them back at their previous owners.

"Pat, help him!" Ric pleaded.

Patrick stopped. "You're right, kid. Maybe we can scare them, give us a head start."

The Calsharans were standing in the open field, no more than one hundred yards away. Patrick drew his service revolver, aimed carefully. He was relatively certain he could shoot their adversaries from here.

"What are you doing? Go!" Prytal ordered.

"I'm saving our skins," Patrick answered. "Which one do you think is the leader?"

Prytal started firing arrows again. "The third man from the right."

"Cool." Patrick's brain shifted to automatically compensate for wind and distance. "Just like fish in a barrel," he said. He squeezed the trigger. The third man from the right spun around in a circle, clutching at his shoulder. "One down…"

The Calsharans looked at their captain, not really knowing what to think about his wound. Patrick took the opportunity to take another shot. The last man on the left grabbed his knee. Prytal looked at Patrick with renewed respect.

"One more," Patrick said, "and I bet they go flying back to their side of the plain, licking their wounds." He chose a target close to the middle of the group. His shot missed its mark, ricocheting off a rock, but he had accomplished his goal. They snatched up their wounded comrades and dragged them back.

"That bought us a little time," Patrick said. "Let's not waste it."

"This way." Prytal turned straight south, abandoning the rock wall and its adjacent spit of land in favor of a more direct route. The others followed him at a trot.

There were no trees in the basin. In fact, very little grew there. In places, the ground was strewn with stones, forcing them to slow down so they could pick their way across. Other places had a sparse covering of grasses and still others, brilliantly colored wildflowers. The cold of winter had not yet touched this place. Ric was drenched in sweat, but he did not complain. After what seemed an eternity, they reached the rock wall of Dallow Mound.

"Breather," Patrick said.

Ric stopped instantly. He dropped his hands onto his knees and leaned heavily on them for a few moments, then stood up and stretched. Patrick did the same. Prytal uncorked a flask and handed it to Patrick. He was looking to the north.

"Riders."

Simultaneously Patrick and Ric turned and stared. "I don't see anything," Ric said, taking the water from Patrick and drinking.

"Neither do I," Patrick agreed.

"They are not close, but will be soon enough." He pointed to Patrick's gun. "They are after your weapon. It would be a great prize for Marand."

Patrick laughed. "It'll be a cold day in hell before they get it," he said.

Prytal looked confused.

"He means he won't give it up," Ric said.

"Very good. We will need to climb," Prytal told them. "There is no time to go around."

Ric stretched again and placed his hand on the stone wall. "I don't know how to climb," he said. "Jason kept trying to get me interested in something athletic. 'Guess I shoulda tried something."

"There is a partial stairway to the top," Prytal told them as he re-corked the flask and reattached it to his belt.

"Partial?" Ric asked.

The Kilmari nodded. "It was once carved from top to bottom, but years of rain have partially eroded it. Climbing through the ruin is not difficult, though it is time consuming."

"Better than the rock face," Patrick said.

"Yeah," Ric agreed. "Better."

67 A King's Chambers

The first thing she noticed was the soft luxury of the cloth against her skin. It moved almost as she did, comforting her in a way she had not thought possible. She stretched and turned on her side, noting the depth of the pillow beneath her head, luxury negating the anxiety she felt at not knowing exactly where she was. The pillow smelled of bath water and light perfume. Her eyes snapped open.

"Marand?"

No one answered.

A single candle flickered in a wall sconce, illuminating the room in soft, romantic light. Without knowing why, Sila rubbed a hand across her naked abdomen. She was oddly unsettled. Then again, she had never had demon's wine before. Without another thought, she reasoned the beverage was somehow responsible for her discomfort. She took time to move slowly just in case the brew had any other side effects, then clutching the coverlet to cover herself, she swung her legs out of the bed, gently brushing the silk slippers at her feet.

The king must have brought her here, sacrificing his own bed for the night so that she could rest comfortably. He probably did not want to expose her in her inebriated state to others in his court. The action was very noble of him.

A dressing gown had been neatly placed at the foot of her bed. Sila smiled. He must have summoned Tammar to help her disrobe. The girl was attentive, as always. The gown was silk, trimmed with the fine fur of some woodland creature. She quickly drew it over her head, reveling in its extravagance, then pulled on the slippers. Her gown had a cowl on it. She pulled it up so that her face was almost hidden in four or five inches of cloth and relished the heat of her own breath.

A fire crackled warmly in a huge stone hearth that comprised most of one wall. Other places in the room were cold, including where she stood. Beyond the fireplace, a window let moonlight spill into the room. She walked over to it and glanced outside.

There was a dusting of snow covering the courtyard that had only yesterday welcomed her with flowing fountains and green grasses. Now, the snow sparkled in the light of night. Nothing stirred. She placed her hand on the glass pane that held most of the cold at bay, amazed at her good fortune.

"Truly, I have been rewarded for my long suffering," she said aloud.

A light tap on the door startled her from her reverie. She cleared her throat.

"Yes?"

The door opened. Light from the hallway flooded in around a man's chiseled frame.

"Marand?" she asked.

The door closed and Calshara's king strode into the light of the candle.

"You are awake," he said. "I trust you are well rested?"

"I am."

"I have something for you, my dear." He reached behind his head and unclasped a chain. Hanging from it was a shard of crystal, uncut but exquisitely formed. It refracted the light from the candle into a hundred tiny rays as it turned slowly on its chain. "I hope it is worthy of you."

Sila stared at it for a moment, then shrunk back into her cowl to hide her features. She thought she knew where he had gotten the crystal. She knew its power if her suspicions were correct. Her mind raced.

"Majesty, listen to me closely and address me not by name," she whispered.

Marand's eyes shifted but he remained silent.

"Am I to believe you wish me to become your queen?" she asked, her mind racing.

"It is my desire," Marand answered.

She walked over to him, reached for the crystal, but did not touch it.

"Please, take this as a symbol of our betrothal."

"Where did you get this?" she asked.

"From an old and dear friend," he answered.

"Who?" she asked.

The crystal turned blood red ever so briefly, then reflected the warm yellow light once more. Sila shuddered. She shrunk back into the cowl as far as she could go letting the edges of the hood nearly obscure her vision. Then she carefully pulled her hands back into the ample sleeves and crossed her arms so that none of her flesh was showing. Marand scowled.

"No one has ever refused me!" he growled.

Sila trembled inside the robe. "I am not refusing you," she whispered, "but I must know who."

"I told you, an old friend."

Sila drew in a deep breath to steady herself. "If I am to be your queen," she dared, still whispering, "then there are things I must know. Where did you get this?"

Marand snatched the crystal back. It dangled forgotten from its chain like a cheap trinket. The veins in his neck bulged. Every muscle in his body was tensing, yet he did not move. His shoulders rose and fell as he tried to compose himself. He was not entirely successful.

"I got it from a Kilmari ambassador," he stated.

Sila gasped.

"You have an issue with that?" he demanded.

"No," Sila whispered, thinking fast. He had contained his anger so far. He wanted her to be his queen. Something inside her desperately wanted him. "Which Kilmari?" she asked.

"Why do you need to know?" he again demanded.

"Which Kilmari?"

"Fine!" He turned away from her to face the fire. She walked up behind him, careful to conceal her identity but wanting to touch him. He was seething, staring into the flames, his jaw moving. "I was too late to save him," he said without remorse.

"Save him?" Sila repeated.

"Lord Fot…"

Sila staggered. She struggled to find courage to place an understanding hand on his shoulder.

"…I was too late."

This time, the memory belonged to her. She saw the blood in the room, the head swinging by the long black hair and slamming into the youth and the door behind him opening to reveal a cool, unsurprised king.

"You did not reach an understanding?" Marand said. He made a few clucking noises with his tongue. "Pity. He worked so hard."

"Forgive me, my lord, but I must know his name," she said very softy.

"Very well." He turned to face her. "The crystal belonged to Tocar, the Kilmari ambassador. I removed it from his body after Fot killed him. The incident was, shall we say, regrettable?"

Sila put a hand over her mouth. Bile rose in her throat so much so that she wanted to find a chamber pot to relieve herself. Marand grabbed her roughly by the arm, pulling her hand away. He held up the crystal.

"If you are to become my queen," he said, "there are certain things you must accept. The execution of our enemies is one of them."

"If I am to become your queen," she whispered in return, "there are certain things you must know as well."

She waited, her heart pounding. Slowly, his grip on her arm relaxed until he finally released her. The scowl still darkened his handsome features. "What things?" he demanded.

"Patience, my lord. Where is Tammar?"

"Your servant?" he answered.

"Yes, my servant. She is the only person, besides you, who I trust."

Marand strode to the door, cracked it open and spoke to a person in the hallway. Sila returned to the window. Thoughts raced through her head. She stared at the meticulous grounds with moonlight glittering on the virgin snow. In her mind, she saw Bel Haven on a similar night, when a single horse pranced into a less grand courtyard bearing a man with a silver circlet on his brow. He removed the crown, carefully tucking it away inside his clothing, thinking no one had seen him. The horse stood alertly when he dismounted, waiting for orders and the man patted it on the neck. The door to the Great Hall opened. Light poured into the night, revealing the brother of a king.

Her heart skipped a beat.

"My lady?"

Tammar was reaching for her arm with a trembling hand. Sila turned away from the memory and smiled. "I am glad you are here. I have something you must take and keep safe for..." She met Marand's eyes, though he could not see hers. "Us."

"Of course, my lady."

"Majesty, give her the crystal," she ordered.

"She's a street urchin and probably a thief!" he snapped.

"I am to become your queen," she replied. "Trust her as I trust her."

Marand scowled. "Very well." He gave Tammar the crystal. "Your life is forfeit should this not be returned."

Tammar curtsied awkwardly.

"Keep it safe," Sila whispered, "away from me and Marand until I tell you to fetch it. Do you understand?"

"Y-yes, my lady."

"Go."

Sila tied the crystal around Tammar's neck. The girl curtsied twice and disappeared.

"Was that wise?" Marand asked.

"Yes."

"She is an urchin."

"It is only a rock for most, my lord," Sila answered as she lowered the hood. "A rock that is one of several Lord Eron can access to monitor the surroundings certain people. I am one of those people."

"Then I…"

"When in close proximity to me, he may see many things through it, as I was once his reader. His powers are returning. He is close to no longer requiring a human conduit, only the crystal."

"How did you come by this information?" he asked skeptically.

Sila took in a deep breath. "If I tell you the entire tale, will you cease questioning my loyalty to you?"

Marand appeared genuinely confused. "I would hear the tale first," he said. He placed a finger on her lips when she started to protest. "If it rings true, all things will be as you wish, my lady. I may be many things, but for my queen, I am a man of my word." He removed his finger.

"I was summoned to Lord Eron's tent six nights ago. Since his near fatal encounter with Lord Fot, he has been having terrible nightmares."

Marand chuckled.

"He bade me enter his mind to review what he feared was a vision but hoped was a nightmare."

"And you could tell the difference?"

Sila nodded. "A nightmare would not be visible to a reader. A vision can be seen." She turned away from him for a moment and bit her lip. "The damage he sustained from his battle with Fot was great. Though he had made great strides to heal himself, he was unable to find me there at first. For a time, I was alone."

"Go on."

"I wandered through his mind, seeing his memories, waiting for him to come and guide me to the place he wanted me to see. I found the source of his power, even aided in his efforts to heal himself by reinforcing aneurysms he had not fully addressed."

"Is this some fantasy?" Marand asked harshly.

"It is not," she stated. "Energy is the source of life. When I enter a mind, I am very careful not to disrupt that flow, for to do so could inflict irreparable damage on my charge."

"Go on." He sounded less than convinced.

"He finally found me and took me to his vision. I regret that it was not a nightmare, for I experienced with him his vision and it will haunt me until my death."

Marand cleared his throat. Sila ignored him and steeled herself for what came next.

"When we reached the room, Lord Fot was blocking my view. There was a horrible popping noise and Fot moved away. Blood was spewing everywhere." She stared directly into Marand's eyes. "Fot had plucked Tocar's head from his shoulders and was using it to beat poor Parry. You then entered the room."

Marand did not move.

"'You did not reach an understanding?'" she quoted. Marand fidgeted a little. "'Pity. He--'"

"Enough!" Marand snapped. "I am well aware of what I said."

"You recognize the truth?"

"Yes."

Sila cleared her throat. "The point is, Eron can see things through that crystal. Where have you been keeping it?"

Marand actually blushed. "As a trophy around my neck, though last night it was on my bed stand."

"I expect things will change now that I am your queen?"

Marand bowed slightly. "Indeed," was all he said.

"I am thinking that we may be able to use that crystal to our advantage, to feed false information to our enemies," Sila said.

"You are indeed worthy," Marand answered. He moved over to stroke her cheek lightly. She leaned into his hand, suddenly flushed. "Go to the war room and prepare the maps," she told him. "And send Tammar back to me. I will meet you there in short order."

68 Climb

By the time they reached the base of the stairs the sun was descending on the horizon. The warmth of day rapidly turned into the cold of night. Patrick wished he not shed his cloak in the mad dash across the basin. At the time, it seemed like a good idea. He looked up the stairway. Long before it ended, he lost track of the individual steps.

"Are you sure about this?" he asked Prytal.

"Tersan's army should be camped here now," the Kilmari answered. "The Mound of Dallow is the line that separates Jeleste from Calshara."

"I thought we were already in Jeleste?" Ric said.

"According to some, yes."

"So both countries claim Arandia?" Patrick offered.

"Yes, and the Sisters." He rummaged in a small pack and withdrew a loaf of hardened bread and some cheese. He broke each in thirds and handed it to them. "I regret there is not more," he said.

"Thank you," Patrick said.

The bread was dry and the cheese sharp. The meager portions left him wanting more and wondering once again where Bob was. Prytal passed the flask around. By the time each of them had taken a few swallows, it was empty. Prytal cast it aside.

"Ready?" he asked.

"Ric, you first," Patrick said.

Without comment, Ric started up the stairs.

Even though the steps were narrow and uneven, they made good progress for the first hour. They were nearly across the face of the cliff when the path turned back on itself. At the crucial place where the path turned, the stair had also melted away. Ric paused.

"I'm not sure," he said.

"Take your shoes off," Patrick told him as he tested his own Kilmari boots. He could feel the stone face with them but not quite well enough. He leaned against the rock face and took the boots off. "Those sneakers are inflexible," he said as he took the second boot off. "You'll get a better grip with your toes."

"But I--"

Arrows bounced off the wall behind them and they dropped to the relative safety of the steps. Patrick shouted as one hit him in the arm, but it, too, bounced off.

Ric laughed. "We're too high!" he said. "They can't hurt us!"

"They can if they catch us," Prytal warned. "They will make faster progress on the stairs than we did."

"Hand me your shoes," Patrick mumbled, rubbing the newly formed bruise on his arm. "Let me go first. Put your feet where I've put mine, okay?"

"I'll try. It is dark."

"We don't have a choice, son."

Patrick exchanged places with Ric.

They found themselves using hands as well as feet to negotiate their way. Patrick searched in the moonlight for shadows that indicated a hand or foot hold. This was easier than it had been on the path from Winnie's house because the stairs were still partially intact. He found one, then another and soon found himself nearly spread-eagled on the rock face. Leaning into the stone, he swung his right arm in an arc above his head, searching for something to hold on to. He found a fairly substantial outcropping about a foot above his head. His grip now secure on that piece of rock, he grappled with his left foot to find a similar spot. Without seeing where he was going, finding the place was a bit difficult, though not impossible. He pulled himself up and searched for his next hold, following the logical path that the stairs would take.

"Move to your right," Prytal instructed from at least one body length beneath him. "The stair appears to be intact there."

Patrick grunted and shifted slightly to his right. He pulled himself up twice more before his hand landed on a flat surface, then focused on the ledge. Leaning now on fully extended arms, he twisted so that he had one knee firmly on a stair. A moment later and he was steady there. He turned to look down at his companions as a volley of arrows smacked the rock beside him.

"Ric!" he yelled.

Ric was already half way through the missing stairs. The lanky young man hugged the stone when the arrows came, grunting softly as at least three found their mark, did the worst damage they could do and bounced off. He froze. Patrick could not see his face nor the lower half of his body.

"Ric!" he yelled again.

"Gimme a minute," came the muffled reply.

Seconds ticked away. Patrick looked beyond the climber to the Kilmari below. In the moonlight, Prytal shrugged.

"You must climb, lad," he called up to Ric. "The arrows will not always be so kind."

"'Weren't kind this time," Ric muttered. He swung his arm up and grabbed another handhold. Like a huge, human spider, he conquered the short distance. As soon as he could, Patrick grabbed his arm and pulled him to the stairway. Another shower of arrows sent them both slamming against the stone face.

"Yeowch!" Ric said, batting at an arrow as if it were a really big bug. "That's so annoying!" he complained.

"We have to get higher before they start doing real damage," Prytal said. He was already in front of them, snatching up fallen arrows and shooting them into the darkness below them. "Keep close to the face! Go!"

They raced to the other side of the mound as fast as Ric would allow them to go. He had to halt more and more often to catch his breath and he was starting to stumble a bit. Fortunately, there were no places on this particular leg where the stair was entirely missing. They made the switch back turn and halted.

"We are nearly to the top," Prytal said. "The end comes in the center…There!" He pointed.

Patrick could not see it. "I'll take your word for it."

A shadow crossed over the moon, stealing the silvery light. As one, they turned. A cloud, puffy and filled with layer on layer of foreboding energy threatened them. Light danced within it, skipping in chaotic patterns across its surface before diving into its depths. A rumble of thunder struck the wall, shaking the stone with its power.

"There is no time to waste!" Prytal stated. "We now race more than the Calsharans!"

Patrick summoned all the energy he had left for one final dash. Behind him, Ric was doing the same thing but the youth was faltering. He did not have the training of either of his companions and his shielding power would not help him here. Patrick grabbed his arm. "You can do this," he said.

Ric nodded, but did not look him in the eye.

The way up from here was steeper. The stairs were not broken, but whoever had crafted them had not made them even. Without the light of the moon, they found themselves using their hands as well as their feet to feel their way up. Shins scraped against rock and elbows were bruised. Still, they made progress. They made it to the center and the stair cut into the mound, more like a ladder now requiring hands and feet to climb. Patrick started up, Ric close behind.

Every ten rungs or so there was a landing that needed to be crossed before the ladder started again. Each time they reached a landing, Patrick stopped, made sure Ric and Prytal were secure before he continued.

"Looks like only three or four more sets before we get to the top," Prytal shouted to his companions. They nodded.

Lightning flashed and the accompanying thunder was so close that Ric lost his balance. His arms flailed around in a pinwheel, and he toppled backward, his arms windmilling, as he tried desperately to latch on to something. He knocked Prytal backward onto the landing but Patrick caught him by the shirt.

"Hold on!" he yelled.

"Help!" Ric screamed. Patrick held on to the shirt and pulled backward, but Ric went straight down. The policeman was suddenly on his knees, but he refused to relinquish his grip on the soft cloth of Ric's shirt. The cloth ripped. Lightning flashed again revealing the terror on Ric's face. He was torn from Patrick's grip, screaming.

"Ric!" he shouted. He slid precariously forward, but the Kilmari, now recovered, slammed him against the rock face. Somewhere below them they heard Ric scream a second time. Then, there was only the sound of the storm.

"No!" Patrick said. "Damn it!"

The two looked down. Lightning flashed, followed instantly by a tremendous clap of thunder. Stones cascaded down the hill toward them.

"We must go on!" Prytal shouted over the growing storm.

Patrick stared beneath him, hoping to see anything.

"Climb!" Prytal ordered.

Patrick sucked in a deep breath and nodded because he had to go on. He found a rung, then another and another.

The storm grew. Wind tugged at them, lightning relentlessly struck the face of the mound, sending small rivers of stone to slow their progress. The rain came first in refreshing, cold droplets, then in sheets. Patrick found his hand once again on the flat surface of a landing. He pulled himself up and sat. Without thinking twice, he reached down to help Prytal. The Kilmari took his hand and stood beside him.

"It is not far now," Prytal said, pointing up.

"I need a minute."

"It is not safe." Prytal took hold of his arm and pulled him to his feet. "The Calsharan are near. We must hurry!"

Patrick sucked in a breath and forced himself forward. Arrows whistled past his head and he instinctively dropped to the stair, hugging the face to take what little protection he could from the angle the stair offered.

"Move!" Prytal ordered. "Or they will be on us in moments!"

Using hands and feet, he scrambled, staying close to the face.

He started counting. One step, two, five, twenty…The arrows flew past him, now from both below and above. He turned to question Prytal. The Kilmari was gone.

69 Mushrooms at Two Thousand Feet

Patrick groaned. Suddenly all he wanted to do was curl up in a ball and go to sleep someplace where it was warm and the smell of Samantha's chocolate chip cookies filled the air. He let his mind wander into that scenario, shutting out the rain, the certain death of his companions and the ridiculous situation he now found himself trying to justify. It would be so much easier to simply give in to the mirage his mind offered. None of this was real, after all. None of it. If he opened his eyes, the demons, the talking snake, the glowing shields and even the girl he was after would surely all go away. Samantha would be there in that white negligee, holding a plate of cookies for him with a sweet, understanding smile across that beautiful face. He opened his eyes and realized how wrong he was.

Lucy Perrymore was his justification for being here. He was one hell of a lot of help to that girl on this chunk of rock, shivering in the rain and wishing for cookies. He looked ahead into the darkness, determined to go on.

"Damn, you, Prytal," he said softly. "I can't see what you saw."

Up. He had to climb. He started what he hoped was the last leg of this dreadful journey, cold and alone. With a moment of epiphany, he realized there were no more arrows coming at him from any direction. A good thing to be certain, yet it left him feeling oddly more alone.

Lightning still flashed, illuminating the rock face from time to time and thunder still rumbled after it struck, but the rain subsided as quickly as it had started. A cold wind blew on him now. His teeth chattered and his body shivered. He would not get frostbite from this cold. It was not as kind as that. This cold would make him suffer and claim him much later.

The tenor of the wind suddenly changed. It whistled above his head, warmer than it had been before. Patrick hugged the stone. He was nearing the top. The clouds broke and he could finally see at least some things in the moon's soft light.

The ladder opened into a huge meadow lined by trees. He scrambled up the last five rungs. He stumbled three steps and fell to his knees, his back bent, his hands resting on his thighs.

"At least the rain stopped," he said aloud as he dragged himself to his feet, "and, over there, I can get out of the wind."

He got up and started for the trees. Huge boulders lay cast about in the center of the field, just as they seemed to be everywhere he had been in this forsaken world. He negotiated his way around them toward the trees. Something blotted out the moonlight behind him. Instinct took him to the ground, drawing the gun from its holster to point at this new threat. Every muscle in his body tensed.

"Patrick?"

Patrick snorted. He lowered the gun and felt a rush as the adrenaline left his body. "Bob." He laughed, put the safety back on the gun and put it away. "Where the hell have you been?"

"I have been seeing to it that no harm came to any humans," the demon answered. "I can tell you, the task set upon me by the young shield is not an easy one. Why on this night alone, I have stopped a score of Kilmari from killing a score of Calsharans and vice versa. Not an easy task."

"You what?" Patrick said. He felt a wave of laughter coming on. The thought of a demon trying to keep two warring nations from hurting one another was too ludicrous not to be humorous.

"I have been very busy attempting to keep humans from hurting one another," Bob repeated. "And I see you are in need of food, beverage and perhaps warmth?"

"Any of the above would be fine," Patrick said. "What about Ric? And Prytal?"

"The young shield was not attempting to harm anyone when he fell," Bob replied.

"So you just let him fall?" Patrick repeated, suddenly angry.

"My agreement was not to let any harm come to any human. That includes the young shield. He waits in a safe place."

A wave of relief flooded over Patrick. "What about Prytal?"

Bob bowed his head. "His wound was too grievous to allow him to continue with you on your quest, even though he argued with me all the way to the Kilmari camp on Emmalie."

Patrick sighed. "How bad?"

"He will recover. Now, come," Bob answered. He sounded tired, but he motioned for Patrick to climb aboard his back. The memory of cookies pecked at Patrick's mind again, but he scrambled to sit astride the demon instead of giving in to the fantasy.

"Where are you taking me?" he asked wearily.

"To a place that is safe," Bob answered.

"That'll be a first," he mumbled.

In a moment, they were airborne.

Less than five minutes later, a small dot of light appeared beneath them. The forest opened to a clearing of sorts and Bob glided down to land in it. A fire burned cheerily among the boulders and a lone figure stood in front of it, warming his hands and stirring something cooking over a smokeless fire.

"I don't believe this," Patrick said. He slid off the demon's back. "Ric!" he called.

The lanky young man rushed over to greet him. Ric pulled him into a huge hug.

"Last time I saw you," he said to Ric, "you--well, it didn't look good."

"Bob caught me and brought me here," Ric explained.

"I am true to our agreement, young shield," Bob explained. "I kept you from harm."

Bob scuttled around to the other side of the fire and retrieved Patrick's cloak. With a slight nod, he handed the cloak to him. Then he took the spoon out of the pot, tasted the contents and nodded.

"My agreement with the young shield," he said, ladling stew onto plates and handing one to each of them along with a slab of something resembling bread, "was to not allow humans to be harmed. I had to wait until harm was eminent before intervening."

"You don't have to be so literal," Patrick said quietly. "Thank you for what you have done."

Patrick pulled the cloak around his shoulders, grateful for the warmth. He took the food Bob offered and sighed. "Wish I had a pint of scotch to wash this down with," he said. The stew was tasty and filling, though a bit slimy. "What is this?" he asked.

"Mushrooms," Bob announced proudly. "It is a recipe Sje is most fond of."

"It's good," Patrick answered. "Thanks."

They finished the meal in companionable silence. Bob gathered the pots and dishes and tucked them away inside a pack without cleaning them. He then doused the fire.

"Ready?" he asked.

"Ready for what?" Patrick asked, annoyed that the source of heat was gone.

"Ready to join the others," Ric said. "Bob says the army is here."

"How close?"

"An hour's journey. No more."

Patrick nodded. "I assume we can find help to go after the girl?"

"I cannot speak for this Tersan," Bob answered, "but I believe him to be a just king. Sword and Shield accompany him," he warned. "It is their child you seek."

"Understood," Patrick said. "Unfortunately, this isn't my first rodeo."

"That means he's had to deal with these situations in the past," Ric translated.

"Sword and Shield have obligations to those they serve," Bob said. "This situation will be very difficult for them."

"Understood," Patrick repeated.

70 The Making of a Warrior Queen

Sila pulled the hood of the pristine white gown up over her head so her features were again hidden deep within the folds. Tammar was waiting in her outer chambers. She opened the door and waved a hand for the girl to follow. Obediently, Tammar came, crystal in hand.

"Leave it," Sila hissed.

"But, my lady, the king said he would kill me if--"

"Leave it!" she whispered as loudly as she could. Like a wounded puppy, Tammar placed it on a table beside the door and followed her mistress into the bed chamber. Sila closed the door behind them and gestured to the tiny couch where the two sat. She took Tammar's hand in her own. "Listen carefully," she began. "We are going to war with Jeleste."

Tammar turned a bit pale.

"Lord Eron and the Otherworlder ride with King Tersan and a vast army."

"Why do we make war on them? Marand is rich!"

"Marand has his reasons," Sila said, though she was entertaining the same question. "The crystal stone in your keeping has magical properties. Through it, Lord Eron can see many things. I--We intend to show him false information."

"I see what yer thinkin'. But I'm not sure ye can do it."

"Leave those thoughts to your betters," Sila cautioned. When Tammar nodded, she continued. "There are two escorts outside this room. One will take me to Marand's war room. The other will take you to the kitchens where food is being prepared for the war council. I want you to bring a tray full of food to us."

Tammar nodded.

"Wear that stone on the outside of your clothing so that nothing is covering it. Make certain you are close enough to the maps outlining our plan of attack so that you can see them. Pause there until I dismiss you. We need to make certain Lord Eron sees the details of the map. Do you understand?"

"Yes, my lady."

Sila smiled wickedly. "Then, I want you to go into the dungeons."

"But--"

"Your escort will take you to a young woman. She is the daughter of the Otherworlder and the Sword. You will show her the crystal, make certain she touches it."

"But why?"

"I have my reasons."

"Yes, my lady."

"Now go."

Tammar curtsied and left. Sila waited for a moment, then followed, leaving her hood down so that she could see her surroundings and more importantly, so all the inhabitants of the palace could appreciate her beauty.

A short time later, she entered the bustling war room where generals poured over maps and demons watched over them. She expected all to stop and appreciate her beauty. They did not.

Lord Fot, in human form, was speaking with Marand at the front of the room. When he saw her, his eyes lit up and he bustled over to take her delicate hand into his own.

"My lady!" he exclaimed as he pressed his lips to the back of her hand. "Welcome!"

Marand worked his way around the demon and took her other hand. He bowed slightly. "My lady," he said.

"Lord Fot," she said with a nod, then turned to Marand. "Majesty."

Marand waved a hand and the room fell silent. "My captains," he said, "I have chosen my queen. Last night, in a private ceremony witnessed by the vicar of Il Chatel, we spoke our vows one to another. And then, then we spent the night consecrating our wedding vows."

Sila felt the blood rise in her face as applause and the bawdy laughter of soldiers filled the room.

"The formal ceremony joining us one to another will take place on the Mound of Dallow, after our victory there!"

A chill flew up Sila's spine. After consuming the demon's wine, Marand had not been the chivalrous gentleman of her dreams. Rather, he was just a man who had used her like every other man. Anger replaced embarrassment, the need for revenge replaced anger. Inside her mind, a door was unlocked and a new power, her new power, was revealed. He wanted her as *his* queen. Little did he know that he would soon be *her* king. She smiled sweetly at him and waited for the room to fall silent again. When she had their attention, she led him to the war map. All eyes were on her.

She released Marand's hand and slowly worked her fingers in familiar patterns until a small blue sphere of energy appeared. Her audience gasped, amazed or delighted, she could not tell which, but she did not care. With a tiny puff, she sent the sphere aloft. It floated down to the map, spellbinding captains and the king. Even the demons were smiling. It landed in the center of the map where it exploded with a tiny puff of fire. The explosion left a singe mark.

"A small demonstration of your queen's power," she began. "I will be brief. My handmaiden is in possession of a crystal that once belonged to Tocar, the Kilmari ambassador. This crystal was used by Lord Eron to communicate with his chosen people. I was once one of his chosen people. I entered his mind as his reader, sacrificed some of my power there to help him heal. I was well respected in the ranks of the Jelestine/Kilmari army until he betrayed me, left me in the wilderness to die."

Marand cleared his throat. "It is the Lady's will that you found your way to us, my dear," he said.

"Fate did, indeed, bring you to me," Fot added.

Sila smiled first at Marand, then at Fot. She paused, making certain her audience was under her spell before continuing. "My journey to Il Chatel was indeed the Lady's will." She picked up one of the pieces on the map with a slow, deliberate move. "Because I was Lord Eron's reader," she said, placing the piece distantly from where it had been, "he will be able to see everything around me when I am close to that crystal." She looked around the room noting the looks on their faces as her intentions became clear to them. "He does not know what has happened to me or that I am the catalyst of his vision here in the planning room of his enemy."

"How do you know this to be true?" one of the captains asked.

Sila quickly worked a ball of energy into her hands and threw it at him. It caught him in the chest and sent him two feet back from where he was standing. A black ring formed on his tunic.

"I beg your pardon, my queen," he said with a bow.

"You are forgiven," she said lightly. "But do not question me again else my next action will not be so kind," she lied. "Eron will see through me. But no man must utter my name while I am in close proximity to the crystal. Is that understood?"

Heads nodded and there was general agreement around the room, human and demon alike. She waved to the map. "Please, then, my captains, set the map to misdirect the Sword. My handmaiden will arrive shortly with refreshments. We must be prepared."

"My queen is clever," Marand said. He was smiling, but there was a glimmer of anger in his eyes. Sila ignored it.

Fot reached over the map and started rearranging the players. For the next fifteen minutes, Fot and Marand busied themselves rearranging everything on their war board. When Tammar arrived, Sila drew the cowl up over her head so she could not be seen.

They motioned the girl to the table, their carefully conceived deception ready for viewing. She wore the crystal around her neck as she placed a tray of delicacies on the corner of the table. Marand snatched a morsel from the tray and ate it as Fot launched into their strategy.

"The Jelestines will be expecting an ambush--" Fot barely began.

Marand gagged and spit the morsel out. He pulled a short red hair out of his mouth. "What are you trying to do, poison me?" he demanded. He swung at the tray, sending its contents flying.

Tammar shook. She lowered her eyes and curtsied. "No, majesty--of course--"

"Patience," Sila whispered. She gathered Tammar in protectively. "Do not blame the child."

"Bring me that cook!" Marand bellowed. He stared at Tammar, eyes flashing. "As a gift to my queen, I grant you your life. Now, be gone!" he ordered.

"Remember what I told you, Tammar!" Sila called after her. Tammar nodded wildly. She backed out of the room, bowing and curtsying her way to the door, bumping into a dozen captains and two or three demons as she left. They all laughed at her until finally the door slammed shut behind her.

"That was unnecessary," Sila scolded.

"Urchins need to know their place," he replied.

"She is *my* servant," she said coolly, "and you will treat her with the respect a person in her position is due." She worked a small amount of energy into a ball and cast it onto the map. It fell on the palace and burned a small hole there. "Your actions cost us our chance to mislead our enemies."

Fot laughed and Marand's face reddened. He bowed his head. "I apologize, my queen," he said.

"Good." She lowered the cowl and smiled at him. She pointed to the map once more. "Perhaps we can try again later."

"You have chosen a woman who understands war," Fot said. "How wonderfully unusual."

"It appears she understands far more than war, Fot," Marand said, regarding her with probing eyes, "far more."

71 One Man's Vision, One Little Girl's Nightmare

"No."

Jessie turned away from the spectacular view of Western Jeleste she had been enjoying from the top of the Dallow Mound. Eron stood behind her, worry creasing his aging face. His eyes flicked back and forth, seeing Jessie and what he hoped was not real. She took his hand.

"What is it?" she asked. "Another vision? Let me help."

"I will let you know if I need your help," he answered rather more sharply than he intended.

In the world of his visions, mist was churning, taking form as he watched. He silently prayed that this was a waking dream. He knew better.

"'T'was a present from my mistress, it was," a young woman was saying. She wore a bright white gown and matching slippers, though the slippers were stained with grass and dirt from the stone floor. The hem of her gown bore the same marks.

"Very pretty."

"Lucy?" he thought.

"You told me I should look at it, Tammar," Lucy said. "Give it to me." She held the crystal in front of her. It dangled from a beaded chain turning to and fro, refracting the light as it passed.

Tocar's crystal, Eron said in his mind.

"Look how it changes colors!" Lucy said. "It's clear and then--

"Ew! That looks like blood!" the other girl said.

"It can't be blood," Lucy answered, "it's only a hunk of rock. Unless it does something?"

"I don' know," Tammar answered.

"Looks like a bauble to me."

"Must be important, though." Tammar leaned close to Lucy. "I was summoned to the king's chamber for it," she reported so seriously Eron laughed.

"What do you see?" Jessie said.

"Nothing," he lied.

"King, huh?" Lucy answered. "And who would that be?"

"King Marand," the girl said with a bit of pride. "He wants to make my mistress his queen."

Lucy shifted in the darkness and Eron heard the clink of a chain. He looked down his heart sank. Lucy was chained to a huge circle of metal embedded in the floor. Eron took in a deep breath and closed his eyes, concentrating harder on his daughter than he had on anything in his life. "Lucy?" he said quietly in his mind.

"Daddy? Where are you?"

Tammar jumped back. "Who was that?" she demanded.

"It sounded like my dad," Lucy answered.

"It's bewitched! You're bewitched!" Tammar shrank away from her.

Lucy stared at the crystal, ignoring Tammar. "Daddy!" she shouted, a hint of desperation in her voice. "Help me!"

"Stay calm, Lucy. I will send help."

"A witch! You're a witch!"

"Don't be foolish. There're no such things as witches," Lucy snapped. "Well, there are, but it's just a bunch of people practicing a religion. Like Christianity or Buddhism or something."

"Princess taught me about witches," Tammar said. She was huddled against a wall, her eyes wide as a cat's in the dark. She reached a hand out to Lucy. "Gimme the crystal. I want it now!"

"What's it worth?" Lucy asked. She gripped the crystal tightly in her hand.

"I won't come and visit anymore," Tammar said.

Eron cleared his throat. In an eerie falsetto he issued a command: "Give me to her, Lucy."

"Who was that?" Tammar asked.

"Give me to her now!" he ordered. "I am bewitched and Tammar is my master!"

Eron summoned his sword. He sent a tendril of light into the crystal. The energy split into a magnificent rainbow.

"Maybe you're right," Lucy said, shrinking away from it. "Maybe it is haunted." She pointed to it. "It's all yours."

"I don't want it!"

"Well, you can't leave it here! What will your precious king say, hmmm?"

Tammar paled. She backed out of the cell, more than a little fear in her eyes. When she reached the door, she slammed it shut and her footsteps raced away.

"Daddy, help me!" Lucy cried.

"Your mother is with me," Eron said. "We will send help. Do you know where you are?"

"They must have drugged me," she said. "I don't remember."

"She's bewitched, I tell ye, bewitched!" Tammar was just outside Lucy's door again. It flew open and three burly guards burst in. Lucy tried to snatch the crystal up from the floor but Tammar was faster. The girl tucked it under her shirt and the image disappeared.

Eron shook off the vision, returning to the Mound of Dallow. Jessie was staring at him, not a little concern darkening her features.

"What?" she asked gently.

"I'm not sure," he answered. He strode into their tent and retrieved his jug.

"Eron, let me help," Jessie said. "That brew just makes you drunk. Please!"

"I have to be certain." He walked away and did not look back.

72 Little Brown Jug

Tersan reined the horse in, asking him to walk rather than run back to his tent. The sentries were in place and the perimeter, secure. The ground was slick from the torrential early evening rain. There was no point in risking damage to a good horse with a frivolous gallop in the dark even though he wanted to race as much as the horse did.

"Not now," he told himself. He clapped the Greystone's neck making wet slapping noises and turned the horse toward the center of the camp and the stable. Out of the corner of his eye, he caught a flash of light.

"What do you think, Greystone?" he asked. Tersan turned the horse in the direction of the light and tapped lightly on the animal's side, asking for a jogging trot.

The moon broke through the cloud cover making their path visible. The ground sloped upward, the grass yielding to a slightly more rocky terrain. Directly ahead of them a man stood motionless on the crest of the hill apparently staring out at whatever view was afforded there. He tipped a jug up and drank from it, then lowered the jug and dragged a hand across his face. He stumbled to a big rock and sat on it, taking another long drink. Tersan urged the horse forward, anger building.

"Soldier!" he said when he was nearly upon the man.

The man either did not hear him or did not care. Tersan dismounted.

"Soldier, stand and face your king!" he demanded.

Laughter. The man was laughing at him. Tersan strode forward.

"You are exhibiting behavior unbefitting a soldier of Jeleste or Kimala," he stated. "You will stand and face your king or you will be sent to ride with the women, your sword replaced with a paring knife, your armor with an apron."

The man took another swig. "All right," he said.

Tersan stopped dead in his tracks. "Eron?"

"I rather like peeling potatoes," Eron answered. His head was bent over the jug. This time he raised it with both hands. "No one evaluates your skill with that kind of blade." He took another swig.

"You're drunk!" Tersan said.

"Not yet, but I'm working on it." He took another slug and waved to an empty space on the rock. "I can see better when I focus less. Don't ask. Care to join me?"

Tersan looked around. Eron had chosen the spot well. No one could see them clearly here, yet strategically, it was nearly perfect. The forests that covered the northern portion of Dallow parted to reveal the Sisters and the Plain of Arandia in the distance. The encampment was totally visible behind them, yet among the standing rocks, they would not easily be seen.

Tersan took a seat next to Eron. "You've chosen your vantage point well."

"Yep." He handed Tersan the jug. "If you're gonna get drunk and you've got to maintain a facade, you gotta plan ahead."

Tersan sniffed the jug. "What is it?"

"'Little concoction of mine in a little brown jug. Makes the visions easier when I don't have to think so hard and just let it happen. Quite irresponsible according to Jessie. Happy to share, though."

Tersan tipped the jug up not knowing quite what to expect.

At first, the beverage rolled onto his tongue, a delightful mixture of flavors that made his mouth water. He swallowed. Fire burned down his throat. He sputtered and ran his tongue around his lips.

"Wow."

In the moonlight, Eron grinned. "Glad you like it. Now, give it back. I'm not yet properly inebriated."

Tersan tipped the jug up one more time before handing it back.

"I saw Lucy," Eron said, taking a giant swig. His eyes started flitting.

"Who?" Tersan asked as the jug came back to him.

"Lucy. Our daughter."

"I didn't know you had a daughter!"

"It's a secret." He kept staring at the Sisters. "Jess wanted to raise her in her world where she would be safe. I agreed after protesting. I used to see her pretty often."

"Am I to understand that the girl is no longer in the Otherworld?" Tersan asked. The concoction was already dimming his senses but he assumed that was its purpose.

"Yes. She is in Eormengrund." Eron had a head start on inebriation. "She was close to Tocar's crystal this time when I saw her. I assume she's somewhere in Calshara, probably Il Chatel." He sucked down another drink. "Saw her in a vision, talked to her. She's in a dungeon, chained to the floor. How many dungeons are there in Calshara?"

Tersan sat up a little straighter and tried to shake off the liquor. "Is that rhetorical or do you really want an answer?"

"She has to be at the palace," Eron replied.

"Why didn't you tell me?" Tersan asked.

"I just did." He stared off into the distance. "For the moment, she is safe."

"Does Jessie know?"

Eron took a large drink. "No. She knows I had this vision and a few others, but she doesn't know I've been seeing Lucy." He patted the jug. "This is the first time I've actually seen something that can give me a location. This time I saw her through Tocar's crystal. That puts her close to Marand, probably the dungeons of Il Chatel."

"I thought you weren't getting visions from that crystal?"

"Nothing important."

"Meaning?"

"Meaning most of the time I just get a quick image, nothing clear. I know that Marand has it. Last night there was a whole lot of grunting and moaning screams of, shall we say, ecstasy? It was the clearest image I had received to date. I have no desire to witness those moments so I turned my attention elsewhere."

"Identifying the person in possession of the crystal may give us an advantage. You may have a connection with one of them," Tersan said. He shuddered. "Lucy wasn't--"

"No, it was not Lucy." Eron shrugged. "It was very dark. I heard Marand speaking and the woman's voice was slurred. She was inebriated, but seemed to be enjoying herself. This morning, Marand tried to give the crystal to a woman as a wedding present. I'm fairly certain it was the same woman. It is troubling."

"He did?" Tersan snorted. "Did you recognize her?"

"I have my suspicions." He tried to hand the jug back to Tersan, but the king shook his head. "She stayed hidden, but everything about her, her voice, the way she carried herself, her height, those things all said she was Sila Atin. She served as reader to me once, as you know, so we have had a connection which would make it much easier to connect with the crystal."

"I was there. Or have you forgotten?"

"Yeah. Right. No, didn't forget." He took another swallow. "There has to be a way to get her back. But I've got to figure out exactly where she is or we have no chance."

"The palace would be a difficult place to find anything," Tersan said. "It's massive. What else did you see?"

"Just before I saw Lucy, I glimpsed Marand's war room. That woman was there, too. She is the key to those visions."

"If it is Sila Atin, she may not be acting of her own accord." Eron offered him the jug. Tersan took it. "Are you certain the visions are coming from the same stone?"

"Yes." He sighed. "My priority is to rescue my daughter, but I am not opposed to rescuing the healer as well."

"Logically," Tersan reasoned, "if the visions came from the same stone, they would have had to occur in close proximity to one another. Bedroom, war room, dungeon. This points to the palace at Il Chatel."

"True." He took a healthy swig. "This is my daughter, Tersan, and she is in great danger. I want to rescue her, but she is deep in enemy territory, unreachable without an entire army."

"The army is at your command. We will rescue your child." Tersan stared into the night sky. Far off in Ellance, his children were looking at the same stars praying to the Lady for his safe return. Their love for him was unconditional, as it always is from children so young. If it was his child chained to a dungeon floor, no power in Eormengrund would keep him from freeing them, or dying in the attempt.

A pleasant buzz descended on Tersan. It was dulling his senses. The encampment was secure for the night, the army asleep behind him. The fall rains had finally yielded to clear skies and crisp air with a gusty breeze. Moonlit shadows from tall stalks of grass undulated across the field leading to the woods, shifting like waves in an ever changing ocean. He sat and watched, mesmerized by the rhythm. Something unnatural moved.

"Did you see that?" he asked, his senses attempting to sharpen but not quite coming into focus.

"See what?" Eron asked. He set aside the jug and peered into the darkness.

"There!" Tersan pointed. He got unsteadily to his feet, still pointing. "I can't make it out."

"Probably a deer or something," Eron answered. He reached for the jug again. "'Place is rife with them."

"Can't be deer," Tersan said. "I had deer for supper. Surely they're not stupid enough to just walk into camp to be slaughtered and eaten."

"Then maybe a wolf or two?"

"Or a spy?"

"A spy wouldn't--" he belched noisily. "'Scuse me. A spy would stay to the edge of the trees. 'Tsa deer."

Tersan strained. The shadow was moving toward them. "There's something out there." He started toward his horse. Before he could mount, Eron grabbed him, and spun him around away from the horse.

"If you have to see what that is," Eron told him, "all right, I'll go with you, but on foot. You try to ride that horse in the shape I know you're in and you're gonna kill yourself."

"Fine, fine. You want east or west?"

"East. I'll try not to make too much noise but I'm not exactly sober."

Tersan nodded. He drew his sword and headed clumsily for the western edge of the forest. The shadows continued their advance, unafraid of the obvious human presence camping in the fields behind them. As the distance between them shortened, he could make out men. Two men. On the other side of the meadow, Eron's sword sprang to life.

"By the Lady, Eron, you made yourself a target," he said, breaking cover now to race for them. His gait was awkward. Combined with the rough terrain and the darkness, he had to concentrate hard on getting his feet to move forward with any sort of grace.

"Hold your position," Tersan commanded.

They stopped. Eron advanced from the east as Tersan moved in from the west.

Tersan tripped. He lost his grip on his sword. The blade shot out from his hand, falling so that the hilt snagged between two boulders, pointing straight up at his chest. In an instant, he knew he would be dead. Instead he was thrown to one side, landing hard on the rocky soil. Something pulled him to his feet. Eron came crashing toward him and shoved him aside again.

"Stop!" one of the stranger's yelled. There was a loud popping sound. Dirt puffed up from the ground by Tersan's foot. "Put your weapon down," he ordered.

"It's a demon!" Eron answered.

A second time the popping noise sounded, followed by a second puff of dirt close to Eron's feet.

"I'm wasting ammo here. Please, put the sword down."

"It's no use, Pat," the taller stranger said. "They don't understand."

"Oh. Yeah. Right."

Tersan shook his head to clear it. "There's a demon? Here?"

"Eron, right?" the taller stranger stated. "It's me! Ric! We kind of met at the Portal, remember?"

Eron shifted, still keeping his attention on the demon. "Ric returned to the Otherworld with his companion, Jason," Eron said. "They left nearly a week ago."

"Jason's up on some mountain in the north--"

"Ankaal," the demon offered silkily. "The mountain is sacred to demonkind."

"--and that demon is fulfilling his oath to me!" Ric said.

"Ankaal?" Eron repeated.

"I have sworn an oath to this young man, sir," the demon said with a bow. "Perhaps I may offer you another sign that I am not a threat?" Before their eyes, his wings disappeared along with the many hands that lined his belly. The scales melted into one another, forming a very pale colored skin that was quickly covered by clothing.

"Ew," Ric said. "That is so gross!"

The demon now appeared to be an ordinary man--a rotund ordinary man with no hair and twinkling green and red eyes. Tersan stared.

"See? If he wanted to infiltrate your army," Pat said, "he'd be able to do it without too much trouble."

Eron spoke over his shoulder, not taking his eyes off the bald man. "It's a demon, Tersan. A demon!"

"If he wanted me dead, all he had to do was let me fall."

The demon blinked his huge eyes slowly, as if he were some great benevolent being, tolerating an impertinent child.

"Hey, look," Pat started, "I'll put away my weapon. Please, leave Bob alone." He put whatever was in his hand into a pocket that seemed fashioned to hold it.

"Well, Eron? Is this person Jessie's nephew's companion?"

Eron moved closer to them.

He held the Sword of Light in front of the taller man's face. The flame went out and the sword disappeared.

"He is," he said quietly.

Tersan sheathed his sword. He looked to the man called Pat. "And you are?"

"Patrick O'Shea. I followed Lucy Perrymore to your world and I have come to take her back, but it seems we've run in to a bit of a snag." He held a hand out in the curious custom that Jessie's people gave for greeting. "Who're you," he started with a smile, "and where can I get a little of whatever it is you've been drinking?"

Tersan looked back and forth between the three men and the demon turned human, then to Eron. "It appears we have much to discuss."

73 Flashback

Jessie stopped her incessant pacing and listened intently. Gunshots; here in a world where flexing one's mind was more powerful than anything Smith, Wesson or Winchester had to offer, or so she thought. She snatched her cloak from the foot of their bed and pulled on her boots. With a cursory listen for Parry, she determined he was sleeping, wished again that he'd feel safe anywhere outside her or Eron's wingspan, and stepped out into the moonlit night.

The air was crisp, carrying with it the promise of a cold night. She ignored its greeting and searched for the person wielding the gun.

"My Lady?" her sentry said. He nervously touched the hilt of his sword. Jessie stifled the urge to ask for his assistance. Against a gun, she would have to protect him. Besides, she wasn't certain her powers were adequate to stop a bullet.

"Something I have to do by myself," she mumbled to him. By the trees, she caught a glimpse of Eron's sword. "Stay here with Parry," she instructed. "And don't let anyone follow me. Understood?"

Without waiting for his polite reply, she sprinted toward the woods.

Muzzle fire flared and she instinctively hit the ground. "Not here," she prayed, "not now!"

She threw herself behind a huge stone, one of only a few in the field. Beside her, a good sized jug sat. Something smelled oddly familiar. She picked it up, the gunfire momentarily forgotten, and sniffed.

"Eron's concoction," she said aloud. "Great."

There was silence in the meadow. She held her breath, waiting for something to happen. When she peeked around the corner, only darkness greeted her.

"Come on, Eron..." she muttered. "Fine time to go off on a drinking binge. What the...?" Tersan's mount snobbled the hair on top of her head. She rubbed the horse's nose, surprised that he was fully tacked up. High above them a greater shadow passed.

"A demon! Damn it!" She was too far away to do anything.

The demon melted into the shadows and did not appear again. Eron's sword flashed, then held still. She bit her lip, more frightened now than she had been in a long time. The horse shook its head, rattling the tack.

"Right," she said. She took a deep breath and mounted the horse.

Thinking only of Tersan and Eron, she spurred the horse into a gallop, riding low against his neck. Her fingers worked frantically, creating a shield she doubted would hold against a bullet, yet she had to try. A group of men walked out of the shadows and into the moonlight. They appeared to be no threat.

She pulled the horse up savagely, causing him to rear and snort. Then she looked to the skies for the demon. Surely he would attack her from the air. And where was this gunman? Was she dreaming?

There were five men in the group. She turned the horse toward them. Twenty seconds later, she could see their faces.

"Eron!" she shouted. She slid off the horse, holding the reins in her hand. "Are you all right?"

"Terrific," he answered. "'Been looking."

"I saw the jug." She looked to his left. "Tersan?"

"I'm fine, Jessie."

She looked to Tersan's left. The lanky young man standing there caused her eyes to open wide. "Ric?"

"I'm fine, too, um thanks, Miss Perrymore," he answered.

"What are you doing here?" she demanded.

"It's a long story," a slightly shorter man who she did not recognize said. "Jessie Perrymore, I presume?" he asked.

"Yes. And you are?"

"Patrick O'Shea, at your service," he said, extending a hand in greeting. "Officer O'Shea," he corrected himself. "Pleased to finally meet you."

"Officer?" she repeated in a whisper. She looked to his left and red and green eyes returned her gaze. Instinct took over and she loosed the shield she had prepared. It caught over the demon's head. His reaction was one not what she expected.

There was no fear.

There was no hate.

There was no defensive gesture.

He simply stopped walking and stood there looking at her with his green and red eyes and a long suffering look.

"Don't hurt him!" Ric shouted.

Jessie snapped her head around to Eron. "How much of that concoction have you had?" she snapped.

"Enough for a pleasant sensation," he answered. "Unfortunately, nothing more. Yes, I know he's a demon. Apparently there's more to this story than we are seeing."

"Miss Perrymore, please let him go!" Ric said. "He's not a threat. He's on our side. Honest!"

Tersan laid a hand on Jessie's arm. "Let him go, Jessie."

"Tersan?"

"Let him go. He kept a foolish, drunken king from running himself through with his own sword."

"He did?"

"Yes. If he had wanted to end the war before it began--"

"He could have killed you and Eron both," she finished for him. With a flick of her fingers, the net was gone. She looked at Ric. "I believe you have some explaining to do?"

"Yes, ma'am."

"Do you think we might be able to find a warmer place for such a conversation, my lady?" the demon asked. "Our way has been long and the humans, I am certain, are chilled."

"I'm sure something can be arranged," she muttered.

"My thanks, my lady," he said with a bow.

"Do you have a name, demon?" she asked.

"Certainly," he replied.

"His name is Bob," Patrick answered before Bob could speak. "The other one's too hard to pronounce."

"Bob. I can live with that."

They headed back toward camp, Jessie putting a mothering arm around Ric as they walked. "Where is Jason?" she asked.

"On a mountain named Ankaal," he answered.

"No…"

"We sent help. It's kind of complicated."

"That much I've figured out."

"Guess there's no chance of any of that shine now, is there?" Patrick whispered behind them to Tersan.

"No," the king whispered back. "But we have wine."

Half an hour later, they were settled in Tersan's tent, warming their hands by his fire. Tersan uncorked several bottles of wine and passed them around. Eron wisely chose not to take one, though both Patrick and Ric did. Jessie took the offered beverage and poured herself a glass full of it before giving the bottle to Eron.

"Go on," she said. "I have a feeling this is going to take a while."

"Keep it," he mumbled.

"So, Ric, what happened?" she asked. "How did Jason end up on Ankaal?"

Ric took a swig of the wine, made a face and swallowed. "Bue took him."

"Bue?"

"It's a long story," Patrick stated. "Maybe we can get you up to speed on what's happened in the last few days."

"He means updated," Jessie explained. "Ric, you and Jason were headed for the portal. What happened?"

"Jason McCarthy has been taken by the demon, Bue to Ankaal," Patrick started, "where she had left Lucy Perrymore--"

"Lucy was on Ankaal?" Jessie shouted. She zeroed in on Eron. "You knew, didn't you? Since when?"

Eron took a moment. "I couldn't be certain," he finally said, "but I thought I saw her enter Eormengrund at the portal. Before I could act, a lessor Fot chased her up the stairs and grabbed her. They flew off to the north."

"There's more, isn't there," Jessie stated.

"Yes. I have been able to see her journey since she arrived." He took a deep breath. "She is my daughter, too, Jessie. I have been searching for her since her arrival."

"And you didn't tell me?" Jessie fumed.

Eron shook his head slowly. "What would be the point? I could see her, but not identify where she was going. She was flown from place to place and I have no perspective from the vantage of a flying demon." He took a moment to let that sink in. "But I know where she is now."

"Where?"

"In the dungeons of Il Chatel," Eron replied. "The dungeons are connected to catacombs underneath the palace. I'm not certain you and I and a hundred Kilmari can reach her."

Jessie bit her lip.

"She is safe for now," he answered quickly. "I will find a way."

Jessie unsuccessfully held back her tears. Once she regained her composure, she returned her attention to Patrick and Ric. "What about Jason?"

"We think that when Bue retrieved Lucy from Ankaal, she left Jason there to die," Patrick said.

"Ankaal is sacred to demonkind, my lady," Bob told her. "The Guardians are said to protect the innocent. Apparently, they have done their job since your daughter has since been seen elsewhere," he added. "Do not overly concern yourself with that past."

"We sent help to JM," Ric piped up. "Altay and another demon named Sje."

For the next hour, Ric, Patrick and Bob took turns recounting their journey and the odd truce they had made with Sje and Bob. Tersan asked a few questions, Eron said nothing and Jessie tried to keep her emotions in check. When they were finally done, she drained her glass, but it was a now sober Tersan who spoke.

"There is a war council in the morning," he said. "I expect you all to be there."

"Begging your pardon, sir," Bob said, "but does that invitation include myself?"

Tersan looked to Eron, then to Jessie and then back to Bob. "I think it would be better if you did not attend, Bob," he answered. "It appears that the Otherworlders trust you. However, I have reservations."

"As you wish, my lord," Bob answered with a bow.

"Here," Eron said, handing the crystal to Tersan. "Send this to Pixil. My gift has been restored."

Tersan took the stone but regarded Eron carefully. "You're certain?"

"I am." He nodded to the stone. "If she has this, we can fight more effectively. The sooner we defeat Marand, the sooner we will be able to rescue Lucy."

"I will take it." It was Bob who spoke. "I know the way."

Tersan slowly handed him the crystal.

"My life is forfeit should I not fulfill your wishes," Bob assured him.

"Thank you," Tersan said.

With that, the demon was gone.

Reluctantly, Jessie returned to the tent she shared with Eron and Parry. She lay down on the bed, this time with him by her side and nestled her head into his chest.

"Anything?" she asked.

"She is safe," he answered, omitting the details. "She has not been harmed."

"Show me."

"I cannot. Please, trust me. She is safe."

She shed a few tears, but did not ask again.

74 A Mother's Love

It seemed the night would never end. Jessie gave up the comfort of Eron's chest. True to his word, he continued to look for their daughter, even in his sleep. Idly, she stroked his hair. Her fingers lightly touched the scar that ran the length of his skull. Eron had returned to his old ways. He no longer needed her as he had. Their child was a prisoner of their enemy in a place Eron identified. Even with his power restored, their daughter was out of reach.

She left the comfort of their bed, checking out of habit on Parry, then slipped out into the morning. A soft glow over the Pikea promised daylight soon. She nodded to the sentry as she pulled her cloak around her, careful to conceal her face. The ordinary proceedings of daily life would stop if she was recognized and right now, she wanted to be alone with her thoughts even if she had a duty to stay within the confines of the camp.

Cooks bustled about mumbling orders to the boys and girls who accompanied the army. The children scurried to and fro, bringing pots and pans and food and wood--whatever their elders required. The scent of trinka filled the air. Jessie paused beside one such campfire.

The man tending the fire was not bare headed as the rest of the cooks had been and he wore a Kilmari cloak. He was humming some horrible tune, apparently quite content that his song was discordant. Two young men attended him, one she recognized as Garrett, Tersan's page. The other, she did not know.

"Now," the man said, leaning over the various pots that sat over the fire, "add a touch of basil." He held up a few branches of the green herb. "Fresh is best," he said, plucking a few of the leaves off the stem, "however, this herb dries rather nicely and keeps well, if memory serves. Here we go." He dropped a few leaves into the pot. "Hand me that board, will you Garrett?" he said.

Both boys reached for the board the chef was pointing to. They managed to grapple over who got to hand it to him but the man simply took it and sat. He placed the remaining leaves on the board. With a long knife, he chopped them into small pieces. "Place these within the pan before you fry your meat," he said, dropping them into his skillet, "and your master will give you much praise."

"What about the trinka?" Garrett asked. "What do you do to that to make it special?"

The man laughed. "Some things are best when enjoyed simply," he answered. He took a cloth and retrieved a steaming but not boiling pot from the fire. He poured the contents into two mugs. "Go ahead," he told them, gesturing to the brew. "You have earned it."

"For us?" the boys said in unison. Their eyes were round in amazement.

"We should not," Garrett said. "Not before the lords have broken their fast."

"There is plenty," the man told them. "Trinka is best hot but not boiling. Enjoy."

Jessie stepped forward, pulling her hood back so that her face could be seen. "If you have another mug," she said, "I would like to join you."

"Of course, my lady," the man said.

"L-lady Jessie?" The boys stood and offered her their mugs.

"No, no," the man said, "there is plenty to go around. Go on, lads. Take your mugs and go gather some more wood. The fire is getting low."

The two scurried off, mugs in hand. The man poured out two more helpings of trinka.

"I dare say you have a different way of dealing with your underlings," Jessie said as she took the mug from him.

"I do indeed," he replied. He sipped at the beverage. "Yes, some things are better in their natural state. Would you not agree?"

From beneath his hood, a flash of green and red shone. Jessie nodded. "Why are you here, Bob?" she asked.

"Lord Sje has always enjoyed the company of humans," Bob answered, "even though we are at times vilified." He winked. "It's the eyes, you know."

Jessie laughed. "You're not like any other demon I've ever met," she said.

"I know." He looked after the boys who had abandoned their mugs and were now engaging in sword play with long sticks. He smiled. "Children. So innocent, so impressionable. They have so short a time to enjoy that freedom." He took a long drink. "It is in them that we must rebuild the trust…if it is ever to be rebuilt."

Jessie found herself watching him in amazement. He bustled about the campfire, stoking it himself when his helpers should have been there to do it for him. The food sizzled merrily in the frying pan and it smelled better than anything Jessie had eaten in a long time. On a flat stone a short distance from the fire, a cloth lay neatly folded in thirds. Jessie walked over to it and lifted up the top flap. There, lined up in neat rows, were a dozen stalks bearing different leaves and flowers. Some she recognized, others she did not. She picked up a flower and sniffed it. It had a delightful aroma.

"What is this?" she asked, plucking a petal from it and crushing it slightly between her fingers to further release its fragrance. She was about to put it in her mouth when Bob pulled her hand down.

"It is not for human consumption," he said. He offered her a damp cloth. "Wipe the scent from your hands, Lady Shield," he instructed.

Jessie wiped her hands and looked at him. "You really aren't like any other demon I've met," she said.

"You cannot have met many decent demons, then, Lady," he replied.

A wild thought came to Jessie. Bob handed her a plate filled with wonderful food and she set it to one side.

"I assure you, my--"

"I'll eat it in a minute," she said. "Bob, I want you to do something for me."

"If I am able," he replied. He set his pots to one side of the fire where their contents would not burn and gave her his full attention. "What is it?"

"Rescue my daughter."

"I am not certain that is possible," he answered.

"You're a demon."

"Yes?"

"You can move through places we cannot."

"True."

"Fot is gathering demons for Marand's war, isn't he?"

"I would assume."

"Then infiltrate the ranks and rescue my child! Please, help me!"

Bob held her eyes with his own now blue ones. He maintained eye contact for an uncomfortable length of time but Jessie matched him moment for moment. Finally, he turned his attention to his cooking.

"You will look after the young shield?" he asked.

"Who? Ric?"

"He is quite powerful, though he has not the knowledge to accompany the skills. He is in possession of the power you, the Sword and Wylfcynne used to trap Fot. Penrose gave it to him. But you must protect him."

"With my life," she answered truthfully.

"One more thing." He pointed to the vessel on her belt holding the demon, Ket. "I require him."

Jessie found herself without words.

"A child for a child."

"But he was responsible for the deaths of-"

"A child for a child," he repeated. "He is of no worth to you, my lady."

"If I give him to you, what will you do with him?" she asked.

"I will release him and ultimately, I shall send him home. I have no quarrel with you, nor will he. After all, he must grant me my request."

Jessie searched his face, looking into his eyes for any sign of betrayal. Slowly, she unfastened the vessel and handed it to him. "A child for a child."

Bob nodded. "See to it that my servants are fed as well," he said, waving at the two boys who had helped him. "Understand that the chance of us escaping alive is slim. However, I will do what I can."

Jessie abandoned protocol and threw her arms around him, hugging him tightly. "Thank you," she whispered. She placed a kiss on his cheek. He walked away, disappearing into the crowd of humanity of Tersan's army who he now served.

75 Mercy

"Come."

Tammar followed her mistress. They wound their way down and down into the dungeons of the palace abandoning the crisp and clear scent of early autumn snow for something far more sinister. The air did not move here, lying instead in wait to steal the essence of those who dared disturb it, pilfering each scent in order to share an exploding cornucopia of smells with every passing soul. Fine bath oils mingled with sweet perfumes and delicacies and sweat and vomit and blood. Sila steeled herself against the stench and kept moving.

The way was filled with the moans. Whether women or men, Sila could not tell yet the one thing they had in common was palpable fear that changed to hopelessness the deeper they descended. Every once in a while, she could see a wraith that was once human shifting ever so slightly within a caged room. Their impending doom imprinted the hallways more clearly than the ghosts they would surely become.

"Help me!"

Sila jumped and stopped. The Otherworlder's spawn had her hands wrapped around the bars of a small opening chiseled out of a heavy wooden door. Her face was pale and dirty, but unlike the others, there was life in her eyes, eyes strangely familiar, dark and mysterious.

"Thank you!" the spawn said when Sila stopped in front of her door. "You've got to let me out of here! Please! My father will reward you, I promise!"

"You showed her the crystal?" Sila asked.

"I did, mistress, and it spoke to 'er. At first I thought it was witchcraft, but she's only a girl!"

Sila put a hand on Tammar's shoulder. "Do not waste your time asking for mercy for this one," she whispered. "Her fate lies in Marand's hands."

"C'mon! Let me out!" the girl insisted.

A brighter, more ominous light spilled into the stone lined hallway they traversed just beyond the girl's prison. A scream filled the air, followed by soft words that Sila could not make out, but the voice she knew.

"He's nuts!" the girl cried. "And he said I'm next! You gotta help me!"

Sila strode into the room, thinking she was prepared for whatever awaited her there. She was wrong.

In the center of the room, Marand stood, a bloody sword in his hand. He was admiring the blade, running his thumb across it as though testing for sharpness. He shook his head.

"It seems I have abused the metal, Ocan. The blade has dulled," he said, thrusting it sideways at a burly man who seemed to be delighting in the events taking place before him. "Sharpen it."

"As you wish, my lord. If I may?" He handed Marand a small knife. "A gift for the artist."

"A gift you say?" Marand took the offering. The blade was barely an inch long curved like the beak of a bird of prey. It was set in plain, brown wood.

"It may not be as pretty as your swords, majesty," Ocan said, "but it is a tool worthy of a master carver."

Marand hefted it in his hand. "Good balance. I trust the metal has never tasted blood?"

"I know my master's needs," Ocan replied with a bow.

"Good." Marand waved the little knife in the air. "You know, you may be quite right." He turned to his left and for the first time, Sila saw him. She gasped.

"My dear?" Marand smiled broadly and made his way over to her. "I had no idea…"

She let him lead her over to the man who knelt on the floor in a pool of his own blood. He was barely able to hold himself upright. Tiny cuts crisscrossed his body and a dark bruise swallowed his left eye. The other still handsome eye pleaded with her for pity.

"Captain Kerna?" she asked.

"The good captain has lied to me in front of my men," Marand said casually.

"'Did not lie," the captain mumbled.

"Have you not learned?" Marand asked. He took the small knife and pressed it against the flesh on the captain's shoulder. It pressed in but did not cut.

"Wait!" Sila said.

"Wait?" Marand repeated.

"What did he say?" she asked, suddenly feeling very small.

Marand pulled the knife back. "Tell her," he said.

The captain closed his eye and licked his lips. He shifted and the chains binding him to the floor clinked. He then looked at Sila. "A demon protected them," he said.

"What?" Sila breathed.

"Followed them to the Basin after they used the weapon," he continued. "Started up the stairs. Demon--" He coughed, a harsh, dry sound.

"Give him some water," Sila said.

"That is against protocol," Ocan warned.

"Let her have what she wants," Marand answered. He stood to one side, cleaning his nails with the little knife. Sila glared at him but said nothing. Ocan dipped some water out of an old bucket and offered it to the captain. He drank.

"Thank you, my lady," he said.

"You were saying?" she asked.

"The demon prevented us from getting close enough to them to use any kind of weapon effectively," he told her.

"But he did not harm you?"

"No. That is the odd part. One of my men lost his footing on the Stair. The demon caught him and placed him on the ground inside the Basin. He should have died."

"He saved one of our soldiers?"

"Yes." His attention shifted back to Marand. "When they almost reached the top, we had been forced back to the bottom of the Stair. One of them fell. The demon plucked him out of the air and took him to the top of the mound."

"Now you see," Marand said, "no demon would do that. That is why, dear Captain, you have been brought here. You are lying."

"I speak the truth, my lord," the captain insisted.

"Lord Fot has sworn his allegiance to Calshara," Marand growled. "Perhaps you would like to tell him about this demon? He is not as patient as I."

A shadow of fear crossed the captain's face. He stared at Marand and shook his head. "The truth is as I have spoken it," he said quietly. "Even Lord Fot, in all his greatness, cannot change the truth."

"Very well, then," Marand said. "Ocan, would you be so kind as to fetch Lord Fot?"

Ocan laughed. The sound sent shivers up Sila's spine. "Wait," she said.

"My dear?"

"Is it truth you seek?" she asked pointedly.

"Of course."

"Then I have another way to retrieve it." She was looking pointedly at him and thought she saw a bit of disappointment in his eyes. "As a reader, I can enter his mind and witness his memory. It is," she said, finally realizing the power of her own ability, "it is a power granted healers of the First Order. You witnessed its use on Lord Fot."

"Really?" Marand asked with genuine interest.

"Really. With permission, the process is faster." She smiled at the captain. "Without it, there is generally damage to the patient."

"You will see that I speak the truth, my lady," he said.

"Marand?"

"Go ahead," he said, looking at her with fascination. "There's not much canvas left anyway."

She nodded and walked over to the captain. "I will not harm you," she told him. "I only seek the memory and the truth."

"I will not fight you," he told her. Awkwardly, she placed a hand on his once handsome face and plummeted into his mind. He quickly met her and led her to his memory.

A storm raged over the Mound of Dallow, lightning illuminating the sheer rock face in fractions of time. She was looking up through Kerna's eyes. Against the black clouds, a shadow revealed itself in the flashes of light. Behind her, a scream sounded and Kerna turned in time to see one of his men slip off the wall. The shadow shifted from above them to below, snatching the man from the air. In the next flash, she saw them drifting down to the basin. The one after that, the man was on the ground and the shadow gone.

Kerna looked up. He was about to shift his position on the rock face when he heard another cry. Above him, something struck the side of the mound with a thud and the shadow reappeared, this time taking on the shape of a huge winged being. It soared over the basin, visible in the sporadic light of the storm at the top of the mound. The next time lightning flashed it was gone.

"I believe you," she told him.

"There is more," he said.

She waited. The memory shifted forward in time. Kerna's men were nearly on top of the enemy, well within range for their bows.

"Fire!" the memory of Kerna commanded.

The archers let loose. One of the enemy whirled, his cry of pain muffled by a clap of thunder. Still, the man fitted an arrow to his bow. And then it happened. The shadow landed between them. It looked up.

"Climb," it said in a silky, smooth voice, reminiscent of Fot. It turned agilely on the path and faced Kerna. "I believe it would be in your best interest to return to Calshara," he told them, for the shadow was indeed a huge male demon. "I have sworn an oath to my master to protect the young shield and, alas, not to harm humans." He regarded them with two huge green and red eyes. He was a lesser Fot. Sila gasped.

"Please, cease your hostilities," he asked politely. "I grow weary of the constant rain of arrows."

Sila removed her hand from Kerna's head. She looked down at him, giving him a reassuring nod. "Release him, my husband," she said, not taking her eyes from the man. "He speaks the truth."

"But--"

"Ocan, take him to my chambers. I will care for him there until other arrangements can be made."

76 On Wing...

Lucy strained to see what was happening in the room next to hers. She knew she had no chance of seeing anything. All that was visible was the area directly in front of the tiny barred window. A figure in white glided by, followed by the girl, Tammar, who had brought her a bit of decent food and spoken kindly to her. As quickly as Tammar appeared, she was gone. Moments later, the girl was hugging the wall opposite Lucy's door, retching violently.

"Hey," Lucy asked quietly, "are you okay?"

Tammar looked up at her, pale in the scant light. She wiped her hand across her mouth and shook her head. "There're evils in this place, ye can believe that!" she whispered. "Never thought I'd say this, but I'd rather be with Princess."

"Who is that woman?" Lucy asked.

"My mistress."

"Tammar, you've got to help me get out of here!"

Tammar shook her head. "I may be the Queen's only handmaiden," she replied, "but if I did that, I don' think even she could stop 'im from bringing me down 'ere..."

Somewhere far deeper in the dungeon something moaned horribly. Tammar wrapped her arms around herself and shivered.

"You can come with me," Lucy offered. "We'll escape together!"

"Do ye promise?"

"Yes, yes, of course I promise!"

Tammar suddenly looked up the hall, her wide eyes wider still. She drew her arms around her legs and pulled them in close to her as though trying to make herself disappear. Fear turned to terror as a short, bald man appeared. He offered her a hand, which she hesitantly took.

"Your secret plot is quite safe with me, child," he told her, helping her stand.

"Ye--ye heard?

"Every word, Tammar," he answered. He rubbed her upper arms gently. "This is no place for one so innocent," he told her. "You should be in your lady's chambers, working on a tapestry, not here in this bleak and disturbing place. Go along, now."

"Go along?"

"Yes, my child, back to the palace proper. Things are about to get..." Lucy watched his shoulders rise and fall, "chaotic. Go on."

Tammar started for the room beside Lucy's, but the man turned her the other direction. "I will keep your secret," he said, "if you offer no warning."

Tammar nodded once slowly, then about twenty times in a hurry. Then she disappeared.

"Stand away from the door," the man told her calmly, "and prepare. As I have said, our departure is going to be chaotic." He took one hand and did something Lucy could not see to the lock. A tumbler clicked inside and she heard the bolt drag across the door. It opened and he slipped inside, closing it behind him.

Lucy stared at him. *On the one hand, I don't know who this man is; he could be taking me anywhere.*

The man looked out the door, checking the hallway for signs of anyone.

On the other hand, I'm in a dungeon right outside a torture chamber. How much worse can it get?

"There, all nice and quiet like nothing is happening," he told her. He pointed to the chains on her feet and shook his head. "Really. Those are so unnecessary. After all, as your friend pointed out, you are only a girl."

"Consider who put me here," she answered somewhat cockily. "He's kind of a pompous ass, isn't he?"

"Mind your language, young lady," he told her. He reached down and pulled the pin out that held the chains to the floor. One short chain hung from each band. "Marand may be pompous, but he is no fool. You would do well to respect him for what he is. Though you may feel free to loathe him, if you wish."

He touched the bands around her ankles. "Hmmm. This is somewhat of a challenge."

"They just snapped them in place," Lucy explained. "I didn't see a key or anything."

He nodded. "We may have to wait on this."

"But I can't run!"

"You will not have to."

"But how--"

"On my back," he answered. He smiled. "I am named Comoin but the Otherworlders prefer to call me Bob."

"Bob is easier to pronounce," Lucy admitted.

"So I have been told. Are you ready?"

Lucy looked around the room with the odd thought that she needed to pack. She touched her chest. The Book of Wylfcynne was still tucked under her pajamas in the waistband. She nodded. "I'm ready."

"Fine, fine." He put his hands on her shoulders. "There are a few things you must understand before we leave. First, your mother sent me."

"Mom?"

"Yes."

"I knew she would send someone!"

"Please, keep your voice down," he warned, though if he was nervous, he did not show it. "Second, I am a demon."

Lucy shrunk away from him. "I knew that, too! You've got those same eyes!"

"Very true. They do rather give me away but there is nothing that can be done about that without expending a lot of energy. You must trust me. I will not harm you."

Lucy tapped the book. "Wylfcynne seems to think otherwise," she snapped.

"Wylfcynne was wrong," he answered. "Now is not, however the time to debate this. I will tell you frankly that I can simply put you to sleep and take you from here. I would prefer, however, your assistance."

Lucy nodded. "What do I have to do?" she asked.

He turned his back to her and dropped to one knee. "Climb on my back, put your feet around my waist and your hands around my neck and hold on tightly. I have help in the depths of the dungeon, waiting for my signal. We have opened as many doors as possible."

"A diversion?" she asked.

"Yes," he said, "a diversion." He paused as she got onto his back, adjusting the chain so that the links swung freely.

Lucy tightened her hold around his neck and he swung the door open. They had to pass the room where Marand was interrogating the prisoner. Lucy stared into it and suddenly was very dizzy. The man kneeling on the floor was covered in blood, real blood and Marand was standing over him with a mad smile, holding a knife in his hand. The wraith-like woman was releasing the chains that bound the prisoner. He looked up at them, but showed only shock on his mutilated face. He looked down again.

"Can't you help him?" Lucy asked, swallowing the lump in her throat.

"The queen has intervened on his behalf," the demon assured her. "He will be safe, much safer than the others."

"He needs a doctor!"

"The queen is a healer, or so I've been told. Now hush."

They were moving very quickly through the thick air of the hallway. She tried to see everything as they passed cell after cell but Bob was moving too fast for her to take in more than a glimpse of the occupants. Light spilled into the path in front of them and she looked forward. They were about to exit the lower dungeon and enter a passage nearly twenty feet tall and fifteen feet wide. Bob paused. He raised his arms and started pounding the wall with his hands in powerful strokes. Behind them, a great noise built, as a hundred or more voices joined in joy that rapidly turned to panic.

"We are nearly free," Bob told her as he turned from the wall.

"My, my, what have we here?"

Lucy's head snapped around to see who waited in the passage in front of them.

"Fot!" she whispered. Terror filled her as Bue appeared behind him.

Bob shrugged her off his shoulders and set her to one side. Before her eyes, the demon transformed back into a demon. He said nothing to her, turning to face the pair.

"Fot!" Bob said rather congenially. "And Bue. What a pleasant surprise."

"Comoin," Fot answered. "Last time I saw you, you were entombed in a tiny bubble filled with water."

"As were you," Bob answered. He shifted protectively in front of Lucy so that she could not see the other demons.

"What are you doing here?" Fot asked.

"Stealing a child for my master," Bob answered truthfully, "and causing a little havoc as well. You will recall how I love a good party."

"Your master? Sje?"

Lucy thought she heard a touch of fear in Fot's voice.

"Sje," he replied. "Now, if you would be so kind, we have no quarrel with you."

"I cannot allow you to leave with our prize. You know that."

A sound Lucy had never heard filled the hall. It was akin to walking under a high voltage power line, only this source moved. A second, nearly identical sound came from right in front of Bob. There was a soft glow now outlining his body.

"I care little for what you will allow," Bob said. He shifted his weight back and forth, but remained stationary. Lucy hugged the wall behind him.

"And where is your master?" Fot asked.

"Quite honestly, I do not know."

There was a horrible sound of two great energies meeting. Lucy clapped her hands over her ears. She wanted to shut her eyes, too, but she had to watch. Bob ducked and twisted, managing to keep her sheltered. He let out a terrible wail and his body surged forward for an instant, then returned to his guard position. Behind her in the tunnel panic was rising. Voices were moving toward them quickly. There was more to fear behind them. Lucy placed a hand on Bob's shoulder. The great body was trembling.

"They're coming," she whispered.

He gave her the barest of nods and she climbed on his back. She could finally see the battle ground.

Fot stood before them, terrible and filled with power. He was half a foot taller than Bob. In a move so fast she barely saw it coming, he stabbed at Bob, but her champion turned the blade away, then offered a thrust of his own. He turned so that Lucy could see both demons now. Fot had shifted so that he was standing with his back to the dungeon leading to the tunnels. Bue was poised at the exit, blocking their way. Bob split his attention between the two, his head turning quickly back and forth, judging where the greatest threat would be and always turning slightly toward Fot.

A crush of humanity led by a fourth demon poured through the dungeon's opening. Even a demon of Fot's significant size could not withstand that force. He was pushed to the side, his sword poking a hole in the wall. Bue took a step toward him and was thrust into the wall as well. Ket pushed the people to one side, making a space so that Bob could bolt through the exit.

Up and up and up they raced, Ket just behind them, keeping the escaping host in check. Tammar stood against the wall in front of them too terrified to move. Bob picked her up and she screamed. They passed into Marand's throne room. A dozen people scrambled to get out of their way and he cast Tammar into that mass. Moments later, they were outside, in the courtyard.

"Hold on!" Bob warned.

In the next instant, they were off the ground. Ket appeared at their side. Lucy thought she saw him salute before he turned hard, flying in a directly opposite path away from them.

Arrows flew from a dozen directions. Lucy clung to Bob's back in terror. She wanted to bury her head in his neck, but the smooth, tightly woven scales prevented that. Suddenly Bob cried out and they veered sharply to the left. A huge arrow had pierced his left wing where it pounded against the delicate membrane that held them aloft, throwing him off-balance. The shaft was at least three inches thick with barbs attached. With each stroke of his wing, the wound grew.

Lucy flung herself sideways on his back. "Hold on to me!" she yelled. She felt a tug as he grabbed the chain attached to her ankle with one of his many hands. She inched her way out onto his wing and took hold of the arrow. The hole it made was large enough to pull the feathered portion through without causing any more damage. All she had to do was gently pull. The barbs were slippery with black ichor but she held on tight. They were losing altitude rapidly, coming close to rooftops. With all her might, she pulled and the arrow came loose in her hands. She threw it away then crawled back to her position by his head.

They soared for a while, almost clipping the roofs and an occasional tree. With a mighty effort, Bob flapped his wings and they rose high enough that all he had to do was glide, at least for a while. Moments later, they were over a mountain range. Bob flew between two peaks, and Il Chatel disappeared behind them. When the city was no longer visible, he abruptly landed.

"Bob?" Lucy asked as the demon sank into a heap under a huge pine tree.

He did not answer.

"Bob!" she demanded.

He raised his undamaged wing. "I must rest," he said to her.

"But…You're hurt!"

"I will recover. Come. You will be safe under my wing. I must rest," he repeated.

Lucy hesitated for a moment, then raced over to him. She lay down beside him suddenly very tired. The wing closed over her, enveloping her in warmth. Soon, she was asleep.

77 The Last Thread

Sila dipped the compress in cool water, wrung it out and replaced it over Tammar's forehead. In another corner of her chambers, Captain Kerna lay sleeping. She had done the best she could with the cuts Marand had made on his chest and the bruising on his face. He would heal, but his handsome body would be forever scarred.

"Tammar?" she asked gently.

The girl moaned. She raised her hand to her head. "Wh…" she started. Her head lolled back down on the pillow and she looked at Sila. "Mistress!"

"Tammar, I must be leaving you soon," Sila said. "I have brought a charge for you to care for in my absence. He knows his way around the palace and can get you safely out, should the need arise."

"Where're ye going, lady?" she asked.

"To wreak havoc upon my old masters."

"Ye will be coming back ter me, won't ye?" she asked.

"You know I will." She brushed the hair off Tammar's forehead. "Are you all right?" she asked again.

"Aye, my lady." She sat up. "Who was that girl? She said her name was Lucy, but I dunno why she was here."

"She is the Otherworlder's whelp."

"She was riding on a demon's back, lady," Tammar stated. "I thought we were allied with the demons?"

"It was a renegade," Sila replied. "Lord Fot and Bue have gone after him. He will not be a renegade for long."

"He was kind ter me," Tammar protested, "saved me from being trampled, he did!"

"He stole a prisoner from our dungeons and released countless others," Sila snapped. "Those deeds must not go unpunished."

Tammar nodded slowly. "I understand."

"We ride to war at the break of dawn," Sila said.

"War?" Tammar whispered.

"Yes. Marand has told me that Tersan wishes to be high king. He would have all of Calshara for himself. He must be stopped."

"A battlefield is no place for a lady!" Tammar protested.

"Perhaps not," Sila answered. "I am a queen. I need to show my people that I am willing to fight with them, to win their loyalty. It secures my position."

"Ye've thought 'bout it then?"

"Yes." She touched Tammar's face again. "Take care of him. He will protect you with his life."

Tammar's eyes widened. "I'm scared. Please, take me with ye!"

"You will be safer here." She gave the girl what she hoped was a reassuring smile, then rose and left the room, pulling the hood over her head to hide her face as she walked.

When she arrived at the stable, a beautiful white horse waited for her. It was appointed with a side saddle suitable for a lady of her station. Sunlight peeked over the eastern range of the Parnajothi's. The day looked to be glorious.

Marand paced the cobblestones just outside the stable. He wore a scowl on his face but offered her a cold smile.

"What news?" she whispered.

"We have lost the Otherworlder's whelp," he said. "Fot and Bue went after the renegade demon and have not returned. It took most of the night to secure the dungeon. I had to recall a legion from the ranks to recapture them and even so, some prisoners are still missing. I did not sleep well."

"There are bigger issues, husband," Sila replied. "The army is prepared?"

"Except for Fot's troops."

"They will join us after they have dealt with the traitor?" she asked.

Marand nodded slowly. "Yes, yes they will."

"Then let us proceed," she suggested. "To wait would imply weakness."

"You are wise, my queen," he told her. "Indeed, I have chosen well."

78 …and Prayer

The sounds of the forest were all around her. Wolves howled, owls hooted, the last of the crickets chirped in very slow speech to one another. A chill wind blew over the demon, tickling her nose. Lucy rubbed it and stretched.

It was odd, lying here beneath Bob's huge wing. His skin shimmered on the underside with thousands of tiny lights coursing up along the visible bony structure of the wing to the terrible hole the huge arrow had created. The light was brilliant there, layer on layer it forming new skin over the gaping wound. Lucy watched, mesmerized with the slowly shrinking hole. The tissue covering his wings was very thin and she could see right through it to the stars beyond. The moon was brilliantly white here and the stars brighter than she ever remembered seeing it, even on the mountain top where she lived near Claxbury. She sat up, squinting.

"That's the Big Dipper!" she said aloud.

Bob shifted but said nothing.

"And there's Orion! And the Seven Sisters and--"

"Hush, child," Bob whispered.

"What's wrong, Bob?" she asked.

He laughed one short wheezing guffaw. "I should think it would be obvious," he snapped.

"Well, that hole in your wing seems to be filling in nicely, if that's what you mean."

"Go to sleep!"

"I am not a child!" Lucy countered.

"Then stop acting like one." He shifted again, let out a sound between a sigh and a moan and fell silent.

"Great," Lucy said. She scrambled out from beneath the shelter of his wing, intending to argue with him but when she turned to face him, she stopped.

The brilliantly lit red and green eyes were glazed over. Even in the dark, she could tell that pain wracked his body. The wing she had been under was spread out rather awkwardly to one side and his breathing was shallow.

"I must sleep so I may heal," he said, his voice tired but this time not angry. "They will come for us, Lucy. I cannot protect you if you do not stay hidden."

"Like that glowing bandage isn't a homing beacon?"

Slowly, he retracted the wing. The glowing four inch hole disappeared beneath the folds. "It is unlikely they will find us," he said. "Ket took them on a journey far from here, toward my homeland, not away from it."

"You sleep," she told him. "I'll watch."

He laughed, this time more heartily. "All right." He laid his head down and, to Lucy's surprise, melted into the undergrowth.

"Bob!" she shouted.

The glazed eyes opened. He had not moved.

"Never mind," she said.

She began to pace, more to keep warm than anything else. What she really wanted to do was crawl back under his wing and go to sleep. Too proud to ask, she watched the moon cross the night sky. Finally, she sat, picked up a stick and dug around in the dirt, duplicating pictures she remembered from the Book of Wylfcynne with child-like precision. She rested her head on her hand, no longer able to keep her eyes fully open.

The moonlight changed to darkness and back again. She glanced up. Nothing was there so she returned to her drawing. Another shadow and this time, she thought she saw something cross the moon's face. She got up quickly and stood in the area where she thought she had last seen Bob. Panic welled up inside her. She could not see him.

"Bob?" she whispered.

Nothing.

"BOB!" she repeated as loud as she dared.

The huge boulder in front of her moved slowly and Bob's odd colored eyes appeared.

"Look!" She pointed up and he followed.

"Hurry!" he hissed, spreading his good wing, "Under here and not a sound! Our lives depend on it!"

Lucy dove under his wing and hugged his body. The images she saw through his thin skin were distorted but visible. Two demons landed gracefully in the small clearing and the smell of lavender and garlic laced the air.

"Ichor," the smooth voice that belonged to Fot declared. "He has been here."

"The whelp is still alive as well," Bue answered. She picked up the stick Lucy had been toying with. "They cannot have gone far," she said, poking at a large puddle of Bob's blood. "Marand's men found their mark," she added.

Fot looked up and nodded to the horizon. "Comoin will not be a threat to us," he said, "not until he is healed. Marand is marching to meet the enemy."

"Should I send the others back to join him?" she asked.

He looked to the ground again. "Comoin is not important. The Otherworlder's child is. She will give us a sizeable advantage as a hostage since she is offspring of both Sword and Shield. We need to find her." "

Lucy shivered.

"What about Kimala?" Bue demanded.

"We are not strong enough to take the mountain, not yet." He looked around the clearing, his eyes stopping at the place where Lucy held her breath in her hiding place. "That cursed Jelestine king joined forces with Sword and Shield..." He turned back to Bue. "The fop has trained his army well. Whoever loses the war we will then destroy and Eormengrund will be ours. We search until midday, then we rejoin Marand. "

With that, the two gracefully left the clearing.

"Did you hear that?" Lucy whispered.

"It was hard not to," Bob answered. "Fot is evil. He always has been."

"He wants to kill my parents and use me as bait!" she whimpered.

"Your parents are not easily dispatched, Lucy," he assured her. "Please, will you sleep now?"

"I'll try," Lucy whispered. Suddenly, all she wanted was to be home, safe in her bed with a rag doll to hold on to and adults talking incomprehensibly outside her door. Instead she curled up on mossy ground under a demon's wing, and fell into a restless sleep.

79 Bird's Eye View

Jason stifled a yawn. The flight had lasted far longer than he had expected it to, though in thinking back, he was not entirely surprised. To get to Ankaal initially had taken hours. The return trip should last at least as long.

Altay looked back at him. "That's Il Chatel!" she shouted excitedly, pointing to what appeared to be a city that was passing beneath them and to their left.

"Is that important?" he shouted back.

"It is the home of the enemy," she explained. "Look ahead!"

Jason looked. A mountain range rose to the far west of the city.

"The Paranjothis," she explained. "Beyond that, Jeleste."

"Great," he answered.

Sje turned suddenly and they floated to the ground, landing among the huge trees of an ancient forest. He took Jason's hand first, helping him dismount, then Altay's.

"What's wrong?" Jason asked.

"Marand's army is gone," he replied with a yawn. "I do not know what else has happened, but I would assume the battle is soon to commence."

"Then why did we stop?" Jason asked angrily.

Sje smiled. "I need to rest," he replied.

"On the eve of battle?" Jason demanded.

"Jason!" Altay said. "Use your head."

"What? Oh." He offered a sheepish smile. "Sorry."

Sje handed them the pack. "Eat. I will join you in a while." With that, he lay down, closed his eyes and slept.

Altay opened the pack and soon they were sitting against the trunk of a big tree enjoying a meal.

"Do you really think I can do it?" Jason asked. "Stop them from fighting?"

"I don't know," she answered. She leaned her head back and looked up. "I do know that when you sang to Cynthal, all of Bel Haven stopped to listen."

"Really?"

"Really." She snuggled in closer to him, her head on his shoulder. He awkwardly put his arm around her. Somehow she still smelled like strawberries and roses. He shuddered to think what he himself smelled like. Altay either did not notice or did not mind. "There was a kind of peace that fell over the whole place," she continued. "Even in the fields, they told about it."

Jason sighed. "I guess there's a chance, then," he said.

She put her hand on his other shoulder. "We all do what we can," she said, nestling against him. A stray hair tickled his nose and he sneezed. She sat up and looked at him. "Are you all right?" she asked.

"Fine," he answered, hoping she would rest her head on his shoulder again. There was something comforting about her presence, something he had never really felt before. Apparently satisfied that he was telling the truth, she resumed her position. He quickly smoothed the runaway hair down.

They sat in silence while Sje slept, dozing occasionally. The sun crossed its zenith and Jason's stomach rumbled again. He opened his mouth to apologize, but Altay was lying heavily on him, and for the first time he realized she, too, was asleep. He thought about saying something but the peace was so great, he opted for silence.

"Jason?"

Jason opened his eyes. His back was stiff from sitting for so long against the tree and his arm was totally numb.

"It's time," Altay said.

Sje stood in the center of the clearing flexing his great wings, the look on his face one of sheer delight. "Vengeance…at last." He turned to them and smiled. "I trust you rested well?" he said.

"As well as anyone can against a tree trunk," Jason said. He rubbed his arm. Pain spiked in it as the circulation returned to normal. He still felt an odd glow. Sje raised an eyebrow and smiled at him, but said nothing.

Altay was packing up the small pack, but Sje shook his head. "Only one more stop," he said to her. "We will not be needing that."

Altay nodded and put the pack down.

"It is a short flight to the Mound of Dallow, where the aberr--Jason will take his place. I have a favor to ask," he said, looking straight at Jason.

"If I can," the young man replied.

"Fine." He hesitated. "I have two reasons for joining in this fight," Sje started. "First to kill Fot, or assist in his death. I am not proud." He smiled.

"You want me to help with that?" Jason asked.

"Not really. Perhaps the young sword will assist me with that task?" he suggested, gazing now at Altay.

"If I can," she answered. "I have never fought anyone save shadows," she said.

"Your innocence will die today, then, I'm afraid," he said rather sadly. "Let us hope that will be your only loss."

Jason cleared his throat. "So whaddaya want me to do?" he asked.

"Chase the demons home." He smiled pleasantly. "On Ankaal, you proved to me that you are indeed a siren. All I want for you to do is sing."

"So you've said."

"Twice."

"Twice?"

"Well, perhaps twice." The demon took in a huge breath and let it out slowly. He shook his head. "I honestly do not know if I can defeat Fot," he said. "If I do, in full sight of my brethren, they may not, shall we say, appreciate my efforts."

Jason nodded. "So, if you win, you want me to 'encourage' them to fly back with you?"

"Yes. Something short, just to let them know what will happen. Please, do not launch into a long song until we are well away."

"Short. I can do short."

"Good." He sucked in another deep breath. "And if I fail, I want a really long, sad tune from you. Something to drive them home anyway. This is a battle we should not have joined."

Jason looked at him. "How will I know?" he asked. "I mean, whether you win or lose?"

"I will carry the young sword up into the air. You should be able to see her weapon from that distance."

"So I'll know you've won?"

"Yes."

"And if you lose?"

Sje furrowed his brow. "If the sun sets and you do not see me, you may assume I am dead."

"But what if you aren't?"

He laughed. "I shall cover my ears. Time to go."

Altay scrambled onto Sje's back, Jason right behind her. In seconds, they were off.

The air was crisp and clean and cold. Jason kept his head close to Altay's. He tried to make out the scent of flowers, but they were traveling too quickly. Still, he reveled in her warmth.

In the distance, a yawning gap appeared in the mountain range and it became two peaks instead of one. Below them, the forest was starting to give way to grassland. Ahead dark shapes started to appear on the plane. Jason leaned forward to get a better look.

Suddenly Sje turned sharply to the left. He dove down and down, back into the forest, coming abruptly to rest in a dark place. He slung the two off his back quickly and flung a wing over their heads. Above them, an ear splitting cry rang out. The scent of lavender and garlic filtered down through the trees. Jason's heart trembled.

"Do you think he saw us?" he whispered. He was shaking.

"'They', not 'he'. Bue is with him," Sje answered in a voice so quiet Jason barely heard him. "If he had seen us, he would be upon us now."

"Why not get him now?" Altay asked.

"I am no match for their combined, shall we say, talents?"

"They'll be together when we get to Dallow!" Altay protested.

"Yes, but there are two shields and will be two swords at Dallow," he said. He pulled in his wing and offered them a smile. "I shall have help." He pointed to the north. "There is something amiss not far from here," he said.

"But the battle!" Jason argued.

"Let Eron of Kimala face Lord Fot once more," Sje said. "Or the Jelestine king."

"Sure, let them fight your battles for you…" Jason said.

"Who deals the final blow does not matter." He started into the forest. "Come."

They followed.

Sje led them up a steep rise, then down again around a curving path and into a thicket of trees. A huge boulder lay to one side of the clearing. In the bright afternoon sunlight it appeared unreal.

"That moved," Altay whispered.

"How could it move?" Jason replied, though he did not doubt her. "It's gotta weigh a couple tons at least!"

"Jason?"

The boulder was calling to him.

"Jason!"

A dark haired girl emerged from under the left side of the boulder. Altay shoved Jason to one side, igniting her sword and stepping smartly in front of him. Jason rolled and was on his feet in an instant.

"Jason?"

"Lucy!" He raced toward her and drew her into a hearty embrace. "My god, I thought I'd never see you again!"

"You wouldn't believe what happened to me," she told him. She was crying. "I don't really believe it myself. This has got to be a dream and a really bad one at that."

"Comoin?" Sje spoke softly. He strode forward past the two embracing cousins until he reached the boulder. He laid a hand on it. "Comoin, it is safe. They have gone to join the battle."

The boulder melted into a demon nearly as large as Sje. He had a worn look on his face, bags under his eyes. One wing spread out at an awkward angle, a hole blown through it. Yet he smiled and tried to rise. Sje stopped him.

"Bob?" Altay said.

"Greetings, young sword," he said tiredly. He returned his attention to Sje. "I see you are well, my lord."

"And you are not." Sje started to examine the wounded wing but Comoin pushed him away.

"Do not concern yourself," he insisted. "The wound will heal."

Sje shook his head. "Not fast enough to get out of the way of Fot or Bue, should I fail. Do not resist. Please." He moved so that his body was blocking whatever it was he was doing to the injury. When he moved aside, the wing was whole. Sje smiled. "Better?" he asked.

Comoin flexed the wing. "Indeed. I am most grateful for your gift," he said.

"We fly to battle."

"He rescued me from that awful place," Lucy said. She was still clinging to Jason. Altay bowed her head and stepped to one side. The sword disappeared. "He was taking me back to my parents," Lucy continued.

"Your mother is most probably not in a safe place right now," Sje said.

"Where is she?" Lucy asked.

"Jessie'll be fine," Jason told her.

"Lady Jessie's daughter?" Altay said. She looked decidedly brighter than she had a moment before.

"She's my cousin," Jason said. He looked at Altay and she turned bright red.

Sje cleared his throat. "As amusing as this may be under other circumstances, we have little time to lose." He turned his attention to Comoin. "Jason is an--" he sighed. "A siren. I am taking him to Dallow. The young sword and I will then join the battle. At dusk, if I am not successful, he will sing."

"To chase our people home. Brilliant!" Comoin said. "I promised to take the Otherworlder back to her mother."

"Can you fly?" he asked.

"I shall manage." He sighed. "Then I must fulfill my obligation to the young shield."

Sje laughed.

"You were correct, my lord," he said, spitting his words out as though they tasted bad, "I should not have promised him to keep the humans safe. It was a monumental oath."

Sje snorted.

"I--"

"Stop!" Sje guffawed. He was laughing so hard tears welled up in his eyes.

"What, my lord?"

"That whole release thing…" he laughed, "…I.,. well it is a lie." He wiped the tears from his eyes and grinned. "You have no obligation to anyone. There is a long story associated with that but it will keep for another time."

"My lord, how could you not tell me, your most trusted servant?"

"Because I made a promise. Now, we must fly. Ready?"

Comoin held his hand out to Lucy and she reluctantly left Jason's side to scramble on board. Sje leaned down and helped Altay up, then Jason.

"You could have told me about her," she whispered to him.

"Sorry," was all he could think of to say as they rose into the sky one more time.

"Jess?"

Jessie looked up from the map she was studying in the center of Tersan's mobile war room. They had been there for hours going over and over the plan for the morning. Long before now, she had committed her part to memory, in the probability that a final attempt at negotiation would go awry.

Eron held a hand out to her. Instantly she was standing beside him in his mind, watching her daughter ride a demon through Marand's throne room followed by the demon she recognized as Ket. The two disappeared.

"Comoin rescued our daughter from Marand. We owe him much."

She was at his side in the war room once more.

"Thank the Lady," he said.

"Yes, thank her." She walked over to their bed and fell into a welcome sleep.

In the morning, soldiers and cavalry formed ranks for battle. There were no items to stow for this day would be one of war. The bulk of the support staff would remain on Dallow Mound. Jessie joined the captains as Tersan, the king, reviewed final instructions.

"Parry, you and Ric stay at the top of the Stair--"

"But I can help!" Ric protested.

Tersan held up his hand. "We have been over this," he said quietly but sternly. "You do not have the training--"

"But I have the skill!" he protested.

"Ric," Jessie said, "don't make it harder than it has to be. Lighting the signal fire is very important."

"I can help!"

"You'll be killed," Patrick said flatly. "Don't be in such a hurry to become a statistic."

Ric drew in a deep breath while Jessie held hers. Tersan could not stop him, not if he really wanted to go. Even in Claxbury, he was of age. He crossed his hands over his chest, snorted and sat back on his stool, sulking in silence.

"We will try one more time to negotiate peace without bloodshed," Tersan reminded them. "Should that fail, our goal is to trap Marand in the basin," Tersan said. "Pixil and Letou are already positioned on Emmalie and Pikea, respectively. Gorltay will take his troops to the east to join Pixil and Eron will join Letou to the east. Rothen and I will attack from the south."

"Yeah, yeah, and Pat and Jessie will find a vantage point on Emmalie and take out as many demons as possible until Pat's ammo runs out. How many times do we have to go over this?" Ric asked sullenly.

"Be quiet, Ric," Jessie warned. He huffed and went back to sulking.

"There are three remaining crystals," Eron said. "Pixil has one, Jessie has the second and you, Parry, have the third. I will join Letou on the eastern front, but will be able to coordinate everyone's movements."

"When Marand's forces pass the Sisters and exit Arandia," Tersan continued, "it is imperative that you, Ric, light the signal fire. Our entire strategy is dependent on it. Once they are through, we will close ranks behind them and put them in a defensive position. Parry will see the battle as Eron channels it to him. Am I relaying that correctly?" he asked Eron.

"Yes."

"What about Tocar's crystal?" Jessie asked.

"I have been able to see things through it as well, even though I believe it is in Marand's possession. With luck, I will be able to see what they are doing as well as our own forces."

"Patrick, if you can eliminate one or two of the demons," Tersan answered, "the seed of fear will be sewn. An unknown weapon unleashes the imagination."

"Yes, sir."

Tersan turned to Eron. "Any news from Pixil?"

Eron's eyes unfocussed and flitted back and forth for a moment. "She awaits your command," he said, returning his attention to them.

Tersan nodded. "The Lady be with us all," he said solemnly.

Flanked by Jessie and Patrick to his left, Eron on his right, Tersan led them northward. The cavalry crossed the basin in less than an hour with the infantry close on their heels. Tersan set a slow pace so that all would be rested when they reached Arandia. The gap between the Sisters was as narrow as promised. Tersan stopped.

"Only mounted soldiers from here, Rothen," he said. "We must bait the trap."

"We are prepared, my lord."

"Very good."

"Marand is cocky," Eron added. "He moves very slowly, even with demonkind as his ally. We will have ample time to get the cavalry onto Arandia."

"The woman?" Jessie asked.

"She is wearing the crown of the queen," Eron told them, "though she remains veiled."

Tersan stared straight ahead. "There is no more time for speculation. Whoever and whatever she is, we will just have to deal with her when the time comes."

"There's something a little unnerving about that," Patrick said.

Riding five abreast, they trotted into the pass. The wind blew in their faces, a biting, cold wind that was not yet winter. The horses snorted and shook their trappings, tossing their heads in the air. Jessie tightened her grip on her mare's reins. Half an hour later, they had fully descended Dallow Mound. Half an hour after that, they exited the basin at the base of the mound and entered the soft turf north of Arandia.

To the west, the sun had just reached the sheer rock wall that was Emmalie's eastern border. To the west, the marshland that spread out from Pikea's western face was exiting the shadow of its mistress. Cold air from the mountain met the warmed, moist air that rose above the marsh. An eerie fog shrouded the ground, making the terrain look ominous. The blanket wound around, oozing out onto Arandia until it met sunlight. Jessie shivered.

"Look!" Patrick pointed.

Ahead of them, reaching almost from peak to peak, Marand's army stood. Tersan held a hand up and the cavalry halted behind him. Sunlight glinted off his golden armor.

"Patrick," he ordered, "stay here with the rank. Your equestrian skills are lacking for battle."

"Yes, sir."

"Rudlo, Jessie, Eron? We go to meet an old friend."

Jessie touched her heels to the black mare. The horse sprang forward eagerly, happy to be able to race at last. The soft ground made the gallop difficult to sit as the horse worked beneath her. Tersan was right. The terrain here would tire the horses in short order, reducing their effectiveness. They would have to draw the Calsharans into the basin to use the cavalry to its greatest effect.

Behind Marand's army, a dark cloud appeared. It moved steadily to the south, as if the western wind did not exist. The leading edge reached the front of his army and dropped in front of them, forming a dark line. As one, they stopped.

"Demons," Tersan said. "We wait for Marand here."

Jessie patted her horse's neck, cooing softly. The mare tossed her head, eager to move again. "Not yet," she whispered. "Save it for the race home."

The black fringe opened and five white horses emerged. The party trotted slowly toward them, shimmering in the sunlight. They came within five feet of Tersan's party before stopping. Marand sat aboard a dull looking white steed.

"Have you come to lay claim to Calshara?" he said pleasantly.

"I do not covet your lands, Marand," Tersan answered.

"Then why are you here?" he asked in that same pleasant tone.

"To demand that you end your alliance with an ancient enemy," Tersan answered. "Renounce demonkind now and we can all go home whole."

"Oh, I think not," he replied. "However, I will give you an opportunity to surrender. You will be treated…with courtesy."

"You wish to make war on your allies," Tersan said. There was a bit of regret in his tone, like a teacher whose star pupil had decided to abandon his schooling. "Do not do this! Not only Sword and Shield stand against you and demonkind, but all of Jeleste."

"And Kimala." Marand laughed coldly. "I have sealed the witch queen's fate."

Jessie instantly clutched the crystal around her neck, searching for Eron.

He lies, Eron assured her.

"Then I have another reason to make war upon you," Tersan answered evenly, not taking his eyes off Marand, "for Pixil is a true ally and a personal friend."

"Why do you waste time with this man?" a demon beside Marand asked. "Kill them."

"Not so quickly, my friend," Marand answered. "I have long rehearsed the chivalry of war. Victory will be sweeter if opportunity is offered."

"Marand," Tersan said, "stand down and no mother shall weep tonight."

Marand laughed. He turned his mount around without saying another word and kicked the spiritless horse in the sides until it trotted back toward his lines. His demon guard and the two human captains followed in his wake.

"So it begins," Tersan said sadly.

"Jessie!"

She turned and saw it just before it struck. Her horse reared and plunged, catching her unaware. The two were parted and Jessie lay on the ground dazed. Above her, the demon roared a victory cry.

"Jessie!" someone yelled.

Shield!

Before she could act, she saw the underbelly of a grey horse soar over her. The animal rammed the demon, sending it to ground. She scrambled to get to her feet on the soggy turf. Tersan was on the demon, the grey horse standing beside him. Sunlight glinted off the small blade he had in his hand. The demon clawed at the king, too late. Tersan plunged the knife into his right eye and he screamed, then fell lifeless in front of her. Tersan leapt off the first kill of the day. He held his hand out to Jessie and pulled her to her feet. Behind them, another demon roared. Jessie whirled in time to see Eron leap off his horse, landing between them and the demon. In one motion, the demon's head lay on the ground beside his comrade.

"I'm all right," she told Tersan.

"Mount up!" Tersan ordered. "Sound retreat!"

Rudlo lifted a trumpet to his lips. Crystal clear notes filled the valley. The black fringe in front of Marand's troops floated forward as Jessie swung up onto the mare. She gave the approaching army one look over her shoulder and asked the horse to run. Four abreast, they flew back to their own ranks where they turned and waited.

81 First Blood

Sila smiled smugly. Lady Jessie, the Otherworlder who was supposed to be so powerful, had just been gracelessly unhorsed and nearly killed. The demon responsible lay bleeding on Arandia, a victim of Jeleste's king. From the line of demons in front of her, a war cry rose. It prickled the hair on the back of her neck. All around her, soldiers nervously shifted.

"They have drawn first blood! No mercy! No mercy! No mercy!" Marand chanted, pumping his fist into the air with each cry.

As one, the army joined the war cry. *No mercy! No mercy!* A thrill ran through Sila. She, too, joined in the war cry without knowing what she was doing. Never had she felt so alive.

"Form ranks!" Marand ordered over the din.

The army rearranged itself. Demons slipped back between infantry and cavalry, each one to its assigned unit. The ranks were tightly ordered, still shouting "No mercy!" as they started forward. An honor guard of sorts fell in around Marand and Sila. She threw back her hood, fully exposing herself to the brilliant sunlight. The beams caught her golden hair showering down her back and glinted off the jewels in her crown. She grasped the crystal, hoping Eron would see how powerful she had become and fear for his life.

The march was deliberate, pounding feet marching across the plain to the beat of a single huge drum. The thrill grew greater in Sila. For the first time in her life, she thought she could let go of her healer's ways and become an instrument of destruction.

Ahead, Tersan's cavalry stood. They spread out at least four deep, Tersan at the center of his line, the Otherworlder to the west, Lord Eron to the east. On Tersan's signal, they purposefully moved forward, a controlled, practiced power.

Sila pulled the rein up on her horse and leaned forward, preparing to charge, but Marand took her reins. He smiled at her. "Not yet, my queen," he said as his army shot forward all around them. "You are not trained in these ways of war." His smile broadened. "I shall remain behind to protect you."

Along with a dozen demons who will no doubt die for you, Sila thought.

"Pikemen, set!" Marand yelled.

The massive army stopped their forward motion, but continued pounding the ground with their feet. Atop her mount, Sila could feel the vibration travel through the animal and into her bones. A line of men with pointed spears formed at the front of the ranks and the huge army stopped moving, now silent, waiting. Sila looked beyond them.

A living mass of mounted horses thundered toward the waiting pikemen.

"Archers!" Marand cried. "A volley!"

More than a hundred bow strings were drawn back.

"Fire!" he ordered.

The twang of arrows leaving bows filled the still air. Some of the horses stumbled on the plain in front of them. Sila strained to see the riders. Two jet black horses and one small grey one still came.

"Another volley!" Marand ordered.

The bows were drawn. Suddenly, it was raining arrows around them. Sila quickly formed a shield, covering herself and Marand's entourage while men around them fell.

"Those cursed Kilmari!" Marand said.

The horses came within feet of the pikemen and turned.

"Fire!" Marand repeated.

The arrows again flew, hitting only a few of the retreating horses. The cavalry pulled up once more, just beyond the archers range.

"Forward!" Marand barked.

The massive army moved.

"Amaton," he called to a captain on his left, "find those archers! Show no mercy!"

"Sir," Amaton answered. He moved away, a small host of demons on his heels. They headed toward Pikea. Sila watched for a moment, holding the crystal tightly so that Eron could see the force leaving and cower in fear.

Ahead of them, Tersan was charging again.

"Pikemen set!" Marand ordered. "Archers!"

Again the army stopped, again the archers fired, again Tersan's cavalry turned and retreated. They waited now, still just out of range of the archers, but now at the pass between the Sisters. The Kilmari volley did not come. Marand laughed.

"It appears the witch queen's men are occupied," he said.

"Tersan toys with us," Sila observed.

"Yes, my dear, I believe you are correct." He smiled at her. "He knows we have the greater force. Tersan is no fool. His greatest threat is his cavalry and this ground is not good for the type of battle he wishes to fight."

"So?" she asked slowly.

"So he wishes to lure us south of the Sisters, to the basin in front of Dallow Mound, where the ground is more conducive to his style of battle." Marand sneered. "He would be a fool if he thought I did not know of his infantry waiting beyond Arandia. Tersan is no fool."

"Then we march into a trap?" Sila gasped.

"Hardly. We are superior." He laughed, then shouted, "No mercy! No mercy!"

The chant rumbled through the ranks.

"I don't believe they have many more charges in them," Tersan said, patting the stallion. Sweat covered his neck, though his flanks were still dry.

"It does not matter," Eron answered. His eyes were flitting back and forth.

"What?" Tersan asked.

"They're coming."

"What happened to Pixil?" Jessie asked.

Eron smiled grimly. "They have engaged the Calsharans from Emmalie. She is shepherding them through the pass, as planned."

"Then we have no time to lose. Rudlo? Sound retreat."

The standard bearer lifted his bugle to his lips and blew five notes. The horsemen turned and thundered back toward Dallow, glad to get to good footing once more.

Marand's army surged forward fearlessly across Arandia and through the pass between the Sword of Light glistened even in the afternoon sunlight and in the center, Tersan drew his own sword. Behind him the king's guard did the same.

Ahead of them, Marand's pikemen shouldered their weapons and marched hesitantly forward. A trumpet sounded and two groups of horsemen swept around the pikemen. They approached from both the east and the west, bearing down swiftly on the small group left to protect the retreating Jelestines.

"Easy," Tersan said to both his mount and companions. "We retreat through the pass to the other side of the Sisters in the basin, as planned. We will engage fully there."

Tersan felt the rush of war. His senses sharpened and his muscles begged to be set loose. Marand's horsemen formed a screen between them and his demon infested infantry, advancing cautiously with their small swords at the ready. Tersan schooled himself to sit still, his sword held securely in one hand, waiting.

The Calsharans stopped. These mounts not were not the same dull witted beasts Marand and his queen rode. No, these were war horses. They reared and plunged and pawed the ground, eagerly waiting for a command. Somewhere in the pack, someone shouted: "Take them!"

"Steady," Tersan commanded, "steady, let them come to us… that's right…NOW!"

As one, they turned and charged south.

82 Engaged

"Now what?"

Parry opened his eyes to find Ric staring intently at him. The Otherworlder offered no conversation. The wind here on top of Dallow whipped the Kilmari cape around him. Parry released the crystal.

"They have engaged the enemy," he said simply.

"Engaged the enemy! Well, that tells me a lot of nothing!" He turned on his heel and began to pace. From the pattern of his path, Parry assumed he had been doing quite a lot of it while Eron sent images through the crystal.

"Do you wish specific information?" he offered.

"Well, yeah!" Ric stopped.

Parry drew in a deep breath. "King Tersan has charged the enemy twice with the entire body of the cavalry. Lady Jessie was unhorsed by a demon that looks to be dead at the king's hand. Pixil was lying in wait on Emmalie but is now fully engaged with Marand. Marand has decided to advance through the pass and into the trap."

Ric shook his head. "And?" he said.

"And what?" Parry asked.

"A little more than the nutshell version would be nice."

Parry shrugged. "I do not understand," he said.

"What happened?" Ric almost demanded.

"The trap has been sprung and Marand knows it is there," Parry answered.

"What happened to Jessie? And Tersan? And where is Patrick?"

"Oh." Parry almost smiled. "Our forces sustained minimal losses, though who has fallen will not be known until the battle ends. Jessie, Patrick and Eron ride south through the pass with Tersan and his standard bearer."

"Thank you!" Ric said, though he seemed insincere.

"They are nearly through the pass," Parry continued. "Marand has placed a legion of demons at the head of his army."

"Why?"

"Because they can carve a path through our ranks and allow his soldiers through with minimal losses." He placed his hand back on the crystal.

"Patrick should be set up by now, shouldn't he?"

"They have just exited the pass and are turning to fight." He smiled. "The cavalry received a warm welcome from the waiting infantry," he said. "Patrick and Lady Jessie have broken off to the west with Rothen. Eron is on the east with Gorltay. Letou leads the western force. Tersan's cavalry is in front of Rothen's infantry. They will take the brunt of the attack in the center." He shivered.

"What?" Ric asked.

"I do not know," Parry answered truthfully. "Each time I receive an image from Calshara's new queen I feel a dreadful chill."

"That bad, eh?"

Parry nodded. "She's looking for Fot and Bue. They are not with the army."

"And that's a good thing, right?"

"I do not know."

Ric looked out over the basin to the petticoats of the Sisters. The armies were nothing more than dots from this distance, a shifting feature in a familiar landscape. To tell the armies apart was impossible. The Otherworlder stopped his pacing and leaned on one of the huge boulders overlooking the basin.

"Do all demons fly?" he asked.

"I do not know," Parry answered.

"Fot can. Bob could. Bue did." He sighed. "Sje carried Altay away like she was nothing more than a backpack."

"They are very powerful, that is true," Parry answered.

"They also have a tactical advantage. A huge one." He continued to look out over the basin. "If they can fly."

"I have been told that they are made of mostly energy and small amounts of physical material, unlike we humans, who are comprised of the opposite. They may take human form. Fighting on the ground with a set of wings on your back would be difficult."

"What else is going on?" Ric asked.

Parry held the crystal tightly. "Jessie and Patrick have abandoned their horses and have taken cover on Emmalie." He closed his eyes tightly and smiled. "The Calsharans believe they have the Kilmari on Pikea on the run. Pixil is closing ranks behind them even as she lures them forward."

"Your queen is one hell of a warrior."

"That she is." He tightened his grip on the crystal. "Eron has summoned the Sword of Light. He is hidden for now with a legion of infantry behind him on Pikea. Tersan stands in full view of the approaching army, waiting."

"Baiting them, eh?"

"Yes."

Ric nodded. "They planned this out well, didn't they?"

"Months of planning," Parry answered.

"Are any of the demons flying?" he asked.

"Not that I can see." He was touched by the queen's thoughts again and let the crystal go. "I have felt that touch before," he mused.

"What touch?"

"The queen's. I know who she is but cannot put a name to her."

"It'll come to you."

"Whether I remember or not is of little consequence right now," he admitted. "However, I would like to remember."

"Yeah, I'm sure."

Parry took hold of the crystal again. Ric looked out over the basin again.

"It will not be long now."

83 Smart Fish

Patrick was back on solid ground again, his horse unsaddled and released to its own devices, away from the battle that was about to be engaged. Half of Tersan's infantry stood to his right, ready to engage the enemy when it appeared. From his lookout, he could see Tersan's cavalry, the proud little grey stallion still dancing under his master ready to attack, and the other half of the infantry at the base of Pikea. Patrick checked his clip for what seemed the thousandth time.

"Worried, Officer?" Jessie asked him.

He looked up at her, but she was looking past him. She was rather plain, he thought, though could be quite pretty with a little make up and a different hairstyle. And she could give the gals at the precinct a run for their money in the fitness department. He looked back at the gun.

"Yes, ma'am, I am worried," he answered. "Only a fool wouldn't be."

"Glad I didn't throw in with a fool."

They were ahead of all the others, positioned on a precipice overlooking the pass at the foot of Emmalie. To their right and behind them, the sheer rock wall offered them a sort of protection, at once exposing them and any would be attackers at the same time. There was only one way up and one way down.

"I wouldn't know about that, ma'am," he told her.

"Please, call me Jessie," she asked with a smile.

Now that makes her one hell of a nice looking woman, he thought. Aloud, he said, "I will if you stop calling me 'officer' and start calling me 'Patrick'. Or 'Pat'." He smiled back at her.

She looked back to the approaching army. "Marand is sending a legion of demons through first," she said. "We'll let them get through before you open fire."

"We've got one heck of a descent back to the good guys," he said.

"Shouldn't be too much of a problem," she answered. "I know it's not particularly fair to shoot them in the back, but that is the best way to disable them so that the others can finish them off."

"All's fair," he answered, though a part of him really wanted to give some kind of warning.

She must have read his mind. "They are too dangerous, Pat. You'll see."

It was his turn to laugh. "I've never shot fish in a barrel," he told her.

"They're easier to miss than you might imagine."

Jessie pulled her crystal from beneath her jerkin and held it tightly in her hand. Her eyes shifted back and forth and her lips quivered, but she made no sound. She nodded and tucked the crystal away.

"Better than a cell phone," Patrick said with a grin.

Jessie laughed. "I don't think it'll ever catch on," she answered with a sly wink. "No camera, no text messaging, no games, no social media…Just your basic communication device."

"Some people like that," he offered.

"Not enough," she answered regretfully. She pointed down the pass again. "Looks like we're to the end of the demons. Here comes Marand's infantry." She laughed though there was little mirth in it. "The coward rides behind his army instead of before it."

Men were shouting. The battle had begun.

Patrick took careful aim and squeezed off one round. A demon shrugged his shoulders backward and fell. Without waiting to see what happened to him, Patrick chose another target. Point, aim, squeeze. A second demon fell. Then a third and a fourth and a fifth.

"I thought you said this would be hard," he told her.

"Down!" she shouted.

He reacted instantly, drawing the gun in to his chest, careful to point it away from anything important. Fire burned across his forearm and he was knocked sideways, into the stone he had been using as a bench. Instinct took over. He raised the gun and fired more than once. A yeowl answered the pops of the weapon.

"Save your ammo!" Jessie yelled. She yanked him down beside her. "Damn!" she said. "I knew that would happen!"

"Then why the hell weren't you prepared?" he asked. Blood trickled across his arm and ran down to his elbow where it dripped with a splat to the ground by his feet.

"Let me see that," she said, ignoring his question. From somewhere, she produced a strip of cloth and before he knew it, she was binding his arm. "I can't look in all directions at once," she explained. "He came straight down off the mountain. They won't try that again."

"Why not?" he asked.

"Because now we know where they are. And they're afraid of you." She gestured to the battlefield below them. "Already the demons are shifting away from us. Look."

The demon forces were shifting to the east, straight into Eron's forces. Marand's infantry, in the meantime, swung west, engaging the men protecting their escape route. Above his head, a silvery blanket had appeared. He held a hand up and touched it. It vibrated against his fingers, but did not give way.

"A shield," she explained, "so that won't happen again. Shoot while you can, Pat."

Patrick aimed seven more times. He thought he counted as many demons fall. Time was working against them. The demon forces were getting further and further away. He pulled the gun back, flipped on the safety and holstered it. "I can't be sure I'll hit them anymore," he said. "Might take our guys out with friendly fire and that's the last thing any army needs."

"Time to leave then." She grasped the crystal once more. This time the communication was very short. "Let's go."

With a wave of her hand, the shield above them evaporated. Lithely, she ran down the stone strewn path, Patrick in her wake.

A band of Kilmari soldiers fought fiercely at the foot of Emmalie, blocking the way up from the Calsharan but effectively sealing them all in place. Letou headed the infantry, his men spilling up the rocky slope, exchanging blows with the enemy. Every so often, the two at the bottom would shift, allowing fresh soldiers to join the fight. Patrick could see a hundred men lining up behind the battling swordsmen waiting to take their turn at the bottleneck that was keeping Jessie and him safe. When one of the Calsharans fell, their body was either trampled or they were thrown over the face of Emmalie to meet whatever fate chose. One man was barking orders to the rest of them. Patrick made certain he was their captain. He pushed his way through half a dozen men until he was standing beside Letou. "Captain, I have a plan," he said, amiably. "Be ready."

Letou nodded.

"Okay, you!" Patrick yelled. He drew the gun and pointed it at the Calsharan captain. "Out of our way! Please? I don't really want to hurt you."

The captain bared his teeth in a grin. He held his sword aloft and charged. Patrick squeezed off one round. The bullet found its mark in the soldier's upper chest, a wound intended to injure, not kill. Bright red blood bloomed there. His men picked him up and cast him over the cliff. Patrick swallowed hard, but the gun never wavered.

The Calsharans paused, but they did not fall back.

"C'mon, guys," Patrick told them, "I brought it for the demons, but if I have to, I'll use it on whoever gets in my way. Understand?"

A very large man shouldered his way through the others and charged. Patrick dropped him in his tracks.

"Anyone else?" he asked, hoping the answer would be no.

They fell back.

"Hurry," he mumbled to Jessie, "before they change their minds."

With Letou leading the remaining Jelestines, they raced through the opening. The soldiers formed an effective wedge that pushed to the south while Patrick covered them from behind. Men grunted and swore, wasting precious breath on unimportant words. Letou fought like the seasoned veteran he was, keeping himself at the point of his force and the men behind him in as solid a wall as he could. They drove through a thinning line of Calsharan soldiers until they reached the Jelestine line. Suddenly, Letou fell back and their forward movement halted.

"The Lady be with you," he said solemnly, then disappeared into the fray without waiting for response.

84 Shell Game

The four Jelestines who had been with them since they left Emmalie formed a tiny perimeter around them. Patrick felt at once vulnerable and useless. Unable to use the only weapon he possessed, he was forced to stand and wait.

"We need to get closer to the demons," Jessie said. She was gripping the crystal in her hand. "Tersan has his hands full in the middle of the battle. Patrick--"

"Winnie used a bubble to get your niece and nephew out of a house fire," he told her. "That might work here."

"What? When?"

"Everyone is safe," he told her. "Concentrate on today. Can you make a bubble we can travel inside?"

"Of course, but it will be more like an igloo." Her fingers worked in intricate patterns. Around the six of them, a silvery dome appeared. Sounds of battle became muffled and nearly vanished.

"Nothing like a spot light to show them where to find us," Patrick muttered. He touched the wall and pushed. It moved easily with his touch.

"It can't be helped," Jessie answered.

"I have an idea," he said. Patrick took his hand off the wall and faced her. "Can you make more than one of these?" he asked.

"I can." Jessie frowned. "Why?"

"We've got six people in here. If we go six different directions, they won't know where I am until I open fire."

A smile crossed her face slowly. "You are devious, you know."

He grinned at her. "So you can do it?"

She nodded. "Six…"

"Too many?"

"It would be…difficult. I could maintain them if I stayed still, in one place and concentrate. I've done it before."

"What about three?" he asked.

"Easier. I could move, but it would be slow."

"Slow is good," he mumbled. "Spread the fear…"

"Lady, what would you have us do?" one of the soldiers asked.

"Patrick?" she answered, turning to him.

"We need to make ourselves as big a threat as we can," he answered. "I'll stay with Jessie and we'll move through the middle. It's the shortest path and the slowest. If she can split us into three…?"

"Yes," Jessie answered slowly, "three is doable."

"Good." He nodded to soldiers. "You two go north and try to meet up with the Kilmari. And you two, south to Tersan. Jessie and I will head straight down their throats. With any luck, we'll catch Eron on the other side. Before we split, I think we need to let them know who we are."

"How?" Jessie asked.

He patted the shield. "They've already given us a wide berth," he said, pointing to the battle around them. There was a full twenty feet between the edge of the dome and the nearest enemy. A lone demon's torso was clearly visible to the west among the troops. It was headed south, toward Tersan's forces. "Let's give 'em something to think about. Lower the shield, then be ready to put it back up again in a hurry."

"How about a hole to shoot through?" she asked. "It makes us less vulnerable."

"Better yet! A tiny tank!" Patrick took the most careful aim he had ever taken in his life. He had to hit the demon and he knew it.

"Ready?" Jessie asked.

"Steady…" he answered.

"Go!" she whispered.

A hole appeared to their west. The roar of battle filled their ears and the smell of sweat and blood permeated the air. Patrick squeezed off a precious round. The demon kept moving forward unaffected. He pulled the trigger again. Nothing.

"Hurry!" Jessie shouted at him.

The army was pressing close behind them. He could feel the Jelestines shifting, watching his back. The dam was about to burst and he had the only thing that would stop it.

Abandoning his aim, he fired multiple times until over the din, the demon screeched and fell. "Now!" he shouted. The silvery shield reformed over their heads. He checked the clip. Ten left, plus one full clip.

"Damn," he muttered.

"No matter," Jessie told him. "Now we use their own fear against them."

The soldiers, who had pressed close to them in the seconds it took to shoot the demon, fell back. A maniacal grin spread over Jessie's face. The Jelestines split to their right and left and waited.

"The Lady guide you," one of them said.

Jessie nodded. In an instant, all four were gone. Jessie sagged, but recovered. Every muscle in her body was taut as she concentrated.

"I'm not so sure this was a good idea," Patrick told her. He holstered the gun and took her by the elbow. She leaned into him. "You okay?"

"Gimme a minute," she whispered. "Balance…I can do this…I've done it before…"

Patrick supported her. She bit her lip, her head bobbed up and down and her breathing calmed, though her brow remained furrowed. Gradually, she regained control.

"As long as we move slowly," she said, "I'll be okay."

"Right."

She shook her head. "The Jelestines…I've sent them to their deaths," she said.

Patrick laughed grimly. "Somebody'll write a ballad for them. Maybe us, too."

"Maybe. Let's go."

Patrick released her arm and she gave him a curt nod. "Slowly," she instructed.

They made their way into the ranks of Marand's army. The soldiers gave them a wide berth, the demons even wider. Every few minutes, they would stop, search the area for demon targets.

"Where could they have gone?" Patrick asked. "This place is big, but not that big."

Jessie shook her head. She grasped the crystal and her lips moved silently. A smile crossed her face.

"Looks like the ballad will be short," she said. "Parry said the Jelestines have joined with Pixil to the north and Tersan to the south. I've told him why and they'll stay inside the shields, drive the demons towards us. We've got them on three sides and closing in." She grinned. "We'll wait here, then spring the trap all at once."

"Lovely," he answered. "Does anyone know exactly where 'here' is?"

"We're north and west of the basin, not far from where we started."

"Wow."

"Wow?"

Patrick managed a laugh. "They moved fast!"

Demons appeared in front of them. They wielded blood encrusted human weapons, huge balls on chains and blades in excess of six feet long. The berth they gave the shield was suddenly gone and they were surrounded. Jessie took hold of the crystal again.

"Warning them?" Patrick asked.

Jessie didn't answer right away. Her eyes moved back and forth under the lids. The shield over them flared twice before settling into a slightly brighter shimmer. She turned her attention to Patrick. "Ready?"

"Steady…"

"Go!"

The hole appeared and Patrick opened fire.

Half a dozen demons were hit in the first few wild seconds. To his chagrin, a solid line reformed behind them. He fired at the line, forcing himself to aim and not waste his ammo. Behind him, Jessie held the shield like a concert shell.

"Keep firing," Jessie said. "We need to move in a circle."

Patrick moved easily with the shell as Jessie guided it slowly in a circle, firing as they turned. Demon after demon screeched loudly and fell. By the time they completed the circle, at least two dozen lay writhing on the ground. They were so close, Patrick could smell their blood.

"Round one to the humans," Patrick mumbled happily.

From behind the wounded demons, the wall reformed. Patrick checked the clip. Empty.

"Patrick…" Jessie placed a hand on his shoulder and he looked quickly behind him. Letou leapt over the body of a demon, his sword black with their blood. He killed that one and stepped onto the ground beyond it. Behind him, the Jelestines poured over the now lifeless bodies.

"All right!" Patrick cried. He ejected the spent clip and put it in his shirt pocket and reached for the last clip.

"Look out!" someone yelled.

A huge demon charged their tank. He grabbed hold of the shield's bottom edge and flipped it off of them. Patrick shoved Jessie to one side as the demon slammed into him and he fell forward on the ground, the gun skittering out of his hands. He struggled to roll onto his back but was pinned. Jessie was shouting to him. Her words were muffled by whatever was holding him to the ground. He could not breathe, could not move and now could not hear anything. Darkness would fully take him soon and he knew it.

85 Duel

Tersan slashed at the enemy soldier on the ground beside him who was attacking with a spear. The spear's shaft snapped in two and the second swipe of the king's sword cut through the leather armor into the man's chest. He gasped once. Tersan did not have time to see if he gasped again.

Two foot soldiers charged him on the left and a third was coming on the right. He loosened his grip on the horse's reins and touched his foot just behind Greystone's right front leg. The horse spun and kicked backward, catching the single threat in the throat, sending him flying. Then Greystone gathered himself and sprang forward at his master's second touch. Tersan held his sword with both hands. The blade flicked the pointed spear up and away from the charging horse, shattering its shaft and decapitating its owner. Greystone whirled, bringing the third soldier into range. The horse knocked his weapon to one side and Tersan's blade crashed down on the enemy's shoulder. There was a horrible crack and the man went down. Tersan looked up. The battlefield was getting too close for him to be effective on horseback. An opening presented itself and Greystone sprang forward into a clear field where maneuvering would be easier.

Tersan reined in the grey stallion. The horse rotated on his hind legs, snorting and tossing his head. Foam flew backward from his mouth, catching Tersan across the bridge of his nose. He scarcely noticed. Here, on a battlefield already red with blood, they were surrounded by the enemy and alone.

Greystone reared and plunged, seeking an exit in the wall that was Marand's army and Tersan worked to calm him. He patted the horse's neck and scanned the circle even as its circumference was shrinking. Half a dozen demons were among those closing in on them. Beyond the wall of soldiers, he could hear the battle raging yet here there was no battle.

"How could I have been so stupid?" he murmured.

The wall continued to close. He started the horse forward at a trot, searching for a way out. Demons moved forward with men as the noose tightened. One section had no demon in it, only men. Tersan stopped the horse. They were barely fifty feet away. He tightened his grip on the reins and beneath him, the stallion's muscles flexed.

"Now!" he shouted.

Like a cat, the horse sprang forward, galloping at break-neck speed toward the lowest section of the living wall. Marand's soldiers stood aside, apparently not willing to take on this foe. Tersan allowed himself a smile.

"Faster, Greystone!" he shouted, clinging to the horse's back with all the skill he had. In a smooth, practiced motion, they cleared the wall of soldiers.

Now he found himself in a smaller, more ominous circle. Greystone slammed to a halt in time to dodge the clutches of a demon. He turned agilely into the center of this second circle and made one lightning trip around it before stopping. Foam clung to his neck beneath the reins and he shook his head before becoming still. Tersan loosened the reins, trusting the horse's instincts. If there was an opening, Greystone would find it and Tersan would again have to use all his skills just to stay on board.

The ranks of the enemy parted. Flanked by two demons, Marand emerged. He was still mounted on the pure white horse whose mane and tail were carefully braided. The animal walked between the demons dully as though taking his master for a stroll through the park instead of being in the center of a battle. The white coat glistened pristinely in the afternoon sunlight. Greystone snorted and pawed the ground.

"Easy," Tersan whispered, patting his horse's neck gently.

"Tersan," Marand called.

"Marand," Tersan answered.

"Surrender and I may spare your life," he started.

"I think not," Tersan said.

Marand flicked a finger. An arrow screeched toward Tersan and he turned it aside easily with his sword.

"Nicely done!" Marand said, clapping his hands. "Let us try one more time. Surrender and I may spare your life."

The ongoing battle beyond the circle roared and part of the wall bulged forward then returned to its original position. Tersan shook his head. "One does not surrender to one's allies, Marand."

Marand laughed. "We no longer have an allegiance, Jelestine. Did I not make myself clear earlier?" He waved his hand in the air this time. A shower of arrows zinged in toward Tersan.

Tersan flung his shield up and caught three in it. He felt the horse shudder and when he looked down, one arrow had embedded itself in Greystone's flank. The horse whirled, throwing his rider to the ground. Tersan rolled gracefully to his feet in time to see one of Marand's men race out and try to seize the horse's reins. The horse charged him. Archers fitted arrows to their bows and took aim at the horse and Tersan whistled. The horse stopped dead and looked at his master. With a lump in his throat, Tersan whistled a second time. The horse stood quietly.

"He will not harm you," Tersan said softly.

The soldier looked at Tersan, then at Marand, then at Greystone. He approached cautiously. The horse shook his head but did not move. A trail of blood trickled from the wound. Tersan's heart raced as the soldier approached again, but the horse was well trained. He waited for the man to take hold of his reins, then followed him. The circle opened and swallowed them, leaving Tersan truly alone. Once again the sound of battle swelled beyond the circle.

"Your horse appears to be a traitor, Tersan," Marand said. "I will be happy to punish him for you. He will make an excellent meal for my officers. In fact, I will slaughter him myself."

Tersan glared at him.

"Oh, come now, Tersan, surely you would not deny your conqueror's army some spoils?" Marand laughed.

"You always were rather dull," Tersan stated. "To kill an animal such as Greystone instead of using him to improve your stock would be an error."

"Perhaps." He touched his finger to his lips and his brow furrowed. He shook his head. "But no, my officers will not be deprived of their feast." He dismounted, the saddle leaning heavily to one side as he put his weight in the stirrup. The white horse barely moved. Flanked by both soldiers and demons, he made his way across the short distance to face Tersan, concentrating on his gloves and armor as he walked. He brushed a speck of dust off of his breastplate. An arm's length from Tersan, he drew a long, perfectly forged blade from its sheath and held it up, admiring the craftsmanship. Sunlight glinted off what appeared to be virgin metal.

"You are correct in your assumption," he told Tersan, reading his thought. "I wanted the first blood drawn by this sword to be very special blood." He smiled and turned his attention from the sword to Tersan. "Your blood is very special."

Tersan shifted, holding his own blade in front of him. "Forgive me if I decline the honor."

"That is, ah, negotiable." Marand lowered his sword and moved in closer. He spoke softly so no one save Tersan could hear him. "I am prepared to offer you a way out."

"I will not negotiate with a traitor," Tersan replied.

Marand lifted an eyebrow. "You have not heard my offer, yet you decline." He removed a glove and studied his fingernails. "How uncivilized."

"I've never trusted you, Marand," Tersan returned evenly.

"Yet you wish to be High King?"

"High King?" Tersan repeated. He shook his head. "Is that what this war is all about? You think I want to be lord over you?"

"You have always coveted the mines, Tersan."

"What mines?"

"The Paranjothi Mines."

"One does not covet what one owns, Marand," he returned evenly.

"We shall see who covets what," Marand quipped.

"You fool! Fot's poisoned your mind. I have no wish to be High king. Jeleste is enough. And I can assure you that Pixil does not want more lands either. As for the mines, they were emptied of their jewels years ago."

"The Kilmari witch does not concern me," Marand said.

Tersan held his sword with both hands in front of him, never taking his eyes off Marand. "How long do you think you can trust the demons, Marand?" he asked. "A month? A year? It is they who will turn on you, not the Jelestines or the Kilmari."

"Lord Fot has pledged an oath to me," Marand said. He stared into Tersan's face waiting for a response. When he got none, he continued. "He and his mistress, Bue, should be joining us quite soon." He looked up and nodded. "Yes, quite soon."

"Marand, he will betray you! Do you not understand? Fot has no honor!"

"My dear," Marand pointed to a figure in the crowd. The woman of Eron's visions bounced up and down on her horse to get it to move forward.

"So you've decided to bring a woman into battle with you," Tersan said. "I assume you want to tell me why?"

The woman slid off the horse into the arms of a waiting soldier who helped her stand upright. She straightened her robes with both hands and then moved to within ten feet of the two kings. There, she removed the veil Eron had not been able to breach.

Marand leaned back and gestured with his left arm. "Behold, the Healer of Il Chatel!" he cried.

Sila Atin's once beautiful face now glared at him.

"Sila! We thought you were lost!" Tersan exclaimed. "We have been searching the Paranjothis for days!"

Sila tilted her head down and smiled so coldly Tersan shivered. "I have done what no other healer before me has done," she declared. She inclined her head toward him and nodded. "I have cured a demon."

"And not just any demon," Marand added. "Tell him which one, my dear."

"Lord Fot."

Beyond the ring that surrounded them, Tersan lost track of the sounds of battle.

"So you see, Tersan," Marand said, "Fot and demonkind have a new and precious ally. I will not be betrayed."

"So you have a healer for them," Tersan said. "It is she who they will protect, Marand, she who will wield power over them, not you."

"Yes, but she is my queen. Oh, the formality of a public ceremony will be observed, once this nonsense of a war is over. I have already consecrated our vows." Marand stared intently at Tersan while the Jelestine king gawked in disbelief. He touched the virgin blade to the ground, then brought it back up in salute.

"You challenge me?" Tersan asked.

"I do indeed. A duel, your army's champion, I would assume that would be you, against my army's. Ahem. That would be me."

"The battle rages all around us. Yet here, I am out-numbered," Tersan answered.

"Clearly. However, your life may be prolonged, at least for a while this way."

"And if I should win?"

Marand leaned in close to him once more. "You are the better swordsman," Marand agreed. "However, you will not win."

He nodded to Sila. The healer removed her hands from beneath her cape. She cupped them in front of her and Tersan saw a small, intensely blue sphere the size of a child's marble. She tossed it at Marand. It struck him in the chest. He spread his arms out to either side and took in a deep breath as a thin layer of blue energy covered him. He grinned at Tersan.

"And now, we fight."

Marand lunged forward, his blue-tinged sword meeting Tersan's blade with a resounding clang. Tersan met the blow with ease. The blue light started down the metal toward his hands. Sila's energy surged through him. He quickly broke contact and leapt backward. Marand laughed.

"What have you done?" Tersan demanded, shaking his stinging hands one at a time.

"You are the better swordsman," Marand replied, "so my queen has, shall we say, given me an advantage? Winning is everything."

Marand thrust at Tersan again.

Gritting his teeth against the sting, he slammed his sword against Marand's. Thrust, parry, thrust, thrust, parry. Each time the blades met, a shock shot through his body, sucking his breath from his lungs. He stumbled backward a few steps before regaining his footing. Marand charged, forcing contact and keeping it until Tersan shook violently. Every nerve in his body was alive and screaming. Sweat poured off of him, soaking the jerkin he wore beneath his armor. With all the strength he had, he threw Marand backward and away from him.

Suddenly the sword he carried was as heavy as one of his children. He saw their faces looking up at him, faces that were frozen in time a year ago. In the distance, a trumpet sounded. His army was coming for him. He got to his feet.

"You have no honor," he breathed. "And for that I will show you no mercy!"

Tersan lunged.

He thrust at Marand, using the shocks to spark him forward. Like a cat fighting an eagle, he leapt and spun, landing with the precision he had schooled into his body the many long months he had waited to go to battle. He avoided prolonged contact, preferring to strike quickly as a snake would. The swords crossed less often now and it was Marand's turn to sweat. He sliced into Marand's arm. Blood trickled down the pristine white shirt and Tersan laughed.

"A king needs a few scars," he said. "It keeps you honest."

Tersan raced backward and leapt up on a large rock. Marand followed, but the Jelestine was too fast for him. He slammed into Marand, knocking him on his backside. The virgin sword flew to one side. The point of Tersan's sword was in the center of his chest. The energy flowed up and into Tersan's body. He reveled in it as he pressed the tip into the first layer of Marand's tissue. Marand collapsed backward.

"Mercy," he begged, "have mercy!"

"Surrender." Tersan shoved the sword closer, ignoring the waves that were sapping his strength yet acting as adrenaline.

"Please!" Marand whimpered. "Allow me some dignity!" He was flat on his back now, his hands in the air above his shoulders.

Tersan lifted the sword, breaking the contact between them. He was set to deliver the final stroke when he found himself tumbling backward. He hit the boulder with his back and it knocked the wind out of him and the sword from his hand. He sucked in air and tried to keep the darkness from edging closer to him. Strong hands slid under his arms and pulled him to his feet, only to slam him to his knees again. Someone grabbed him by the hair and, when he looked up, Marand's angry eyes were staring at him.

"I have yet to christen my sword," he said, the calm in his voice at odds with the fury on his face. He took the sword and drew it across Tersan's throat, leaving a small slit in its wake. He admired his blade, now trimmed with Tersan's blood. Tersan swallowed. He looked up into the eyes of a madman.

"You will not die that easily, old friend," he said. "When this sword is covered in your blood, then your life will end. Not a moment sooner."

He smiled and Tersan shivered.

86 In the Service of the Kings

Parry shuddered.

"What?" Ric asked.

"Tersan…" he started.

"Surrounded by the bad guys and dueling with that Marand guy, right?"

"The duel is over."

Ric looked anxiously at him. "C'mon. Give."

"I beg your pardon?"

"Who won?"

Parry drew in a deep breath. "Tersan."

"All right! Score one for the good guys."

"But then she intervened."

"She?" Ric was staring into the battle as if he could see the images Eron was sending to Parry. "Jessie's there? I thought you said she was closer to Emmalie along with Pat."

"Lady Jessie and Patrick were making their way toward Lord Eron, defeating demons as they went."

"Yeah, I saw the shells from up here. Miss Perrymore and Pat are in the middle of things. I get it."

"They were traveling under a shell of energy. A demon removed the shell--"

"What? Are they okay?"

"I do not know."

Ric threw his arms up. "Well, can you find out?"

"There are many things happening at once, Ric. My view of the battle shifts and I have no control over it."

"Well then who is this woman who helped Marand? Pixil?"

"Our queen holds the northern border."

"Then who…?"

"Her name is Sila Atin," Parry answered. "We only met once, briefly." He shivered. "Her hands… her hands were as cold as a dead man's."

"You have an odd way of remembering things," Ric replied.

"It was not a pleasant experience."

"Apparently not." Ric strained to see anything.

"She is a healer of the First Order," Parry continued. "We have been searching for her for nearly a week."

"What's she doing with Marand?"

"I do not know." He sighed. "However, she intervened in the duel on Marand's behalf. Tersan was about to slay him and she threw something at Tersan."

"Threw something at him?"

"Yes, and whatever it was caught his Majesty in the chest and flung him back, away from Marand."

"That's cheating!"

Parry nodded. "Then she sent two demons to secure him while…" He stopped and swallowed hard.

"While what?" Ric demanded.

Parry bit his lip, dismissing a different image. "While Marand slit his throat."

"That bastard!" Ric cried. "Why didn't he let me go with him? I should have gone with him!"

"He is not dead," Parry said, recalling his time spent in Marand's care, "but will soon wish he was."

"That does it." Ric looked out at the field of battle. "Point me in the right direction. Two can play at this game."

"This is war, Ric. It is not a game."

"Figure of speech. That way?" he asked, pointing toward the Pikea.

"You cannot go!"

"Oh yes I can. And I will. Watch." Ric whirled his hand around his body. A shimmering light encompassed him in a dome that moved with him. "See? I'm all safe inside here. I'll be all right. Really. Point me in the right direction."

"I cannot!"

"If you don't, I'll just leave anyway." The Otherworlder stood defiantly in front of him, waiting for direction. "I can get there faster."

"How?"

"He's in the basin almost straight down from where we're standing, right?"

"He is."

"And the only thing between us and this basin is a really tall wall of rock, right?"

"Yes."

"With a staircase carved into it."

"A what?"

"A staircase. Pat and I came that way." He shrugged. "It's a broken staircase with hand holds, holes in boulders and little outcroppings of rock, like that. Pat is an accomplished climber. I followed his lead." His voice trailed off and Parry sensed not a little fear.

"Ric, it is not safe," Parry told him.

"I have to do something!"

"Killing yourself will resolve nothing."

"I have to help him. Or Pat." He sighed. "Please. I have to do something! I feel useless up here."

Parry searched his face. The Otherworlder kept eye contact, the light brown eyes not wavering. Parry nodded. He took the crystal and placed it in Ric's hand, leaving the uppermost portion of it exposed. He placed his hand tightly over Ric's.

"See what I see," he said. "Is this where you want to be?"

"W-what?" Ric whispered. "Patrick! Duck!"

The other Otherworlder ducked a passing blow from a demon. Blood dripped from a gash along his scalp and soaked through a scrap of white material binding his arm. The demon caught him with a heavy blow and he went down hard. A smile crossed the enemy's lips and he moved in for the kill. Lady Jessie threw a ball of energy at it, sending it back and Patrick came up from the ground, the gun aimed at the offender. The muzzle flashed and the image melted.

"Where did--Wait!"

Patrick's image was replaced by Tersan's. The king's armor was being ripped away. The sweat covered silken jerkin beneath it clung to his body. Two demons still restrained the king, one on each arm. A soldier pulled the cloth away from Tersan's skin and sheered it off with his sword, leaving the king naked from the waist up. Marand took his shiny sword and strode forward nonchalantly. He bent over and began to carve something into Tersan's flesh. The king's face grimaced, yet he said nothing. The scene faded.

"Wait!" Ric cried.

Eron's golden sword struck into a demon's eye. Black ichor spewed from the empty socket and the demon went slack. He was on foot, the sword flashing faster than Parry could see it move. He stopped and held very still for a moment. Then he looked directly at Parry.

"Commit the reserve. Now!"

"Yes, my lord," Parry said with a bow. The images faded and Parry started toward the signal fire. He lowered a burning torch into it and waited. From the eastern and western flanks of the mound, more fires lit. The trap was sprung. He looked off into the distance, toward the pass between the Sisters.

"What did you see?" he asked Ric, staring into the late afternoon sunlight. A flash of light and a tendril of smoke flared on each of the mountains, almost simultaneously.

"Jessie and Pat fighting off a demon, Tersan…Tersan was being carved by that bastard!"

Parry nodded.

"And then Eron ordered you to…" He looked at the fire and back at Parry. "To commit the reserve. Which you just did."

"Come." Without waiting for a reply, Parry hobbled into the grove of trees to the west of the signal fire, leaning heavily on his cane. They were almost instantly engulfed in still, silent greenery. The air was heavy with the scent of blood and smoke. There was no clearly defined path in front of him, yet Parry knew where to go. At one oddly shaped rock, he turned to his left. At a tree covered with light green moss, he turned slightly to the right. Seconds later, he stopped at an apparent dead end.

"You are certain?" he asked Ric.

"Certain that I want to help? Absolutely! I'm closer than anyone else."

Parry nodded. "This is a slide that will deliver you quickly to the base of Dallow Mound, hidden behind the stair. Do not use your skills unless you have to. Stealth is your ally if you wish to save the king." He pulled a curtain of vines to one side and a rocky outcrop appeared. He made his way through it, grateful to the wind that blew cooler air into his face. Beneath him, Tersan knelt at the mercy of Marand. Involuntarily, he gasped. The king's back was red with blood.

"Hurry!" he said.

Ric moved toward the wall. He inched over the edge and disappeared.

"The Lady keep you safe," Parry whispered. Alone and able to see the entire battlefield, he eased himself down onto a cold hard stone, suddenly not certain who would win. "The Lady keep us all safe," he prayed.

"Jessie!"

Eron's voice thundered over the battle inside Jessie's head. She ignored it and hastily prepared a blast of energy to let fly against the demon that was smothering Patrick. The blast caught the enemy neatly in his ear and he stumbled backward. The policeman lay still for a moment. Jessie threw another blast at the demon.

"Patrick!" she shouted. "Get up!"

He rolled groggily to his left and retrieved his weapon. With a not-so-steady aim, he fired twice. The demon pawed at the wound, still alive but no longer a threat. She quickly reformed the silvery shield around them both while Patrick checked his gun. His head was bleeding freely from a long cut in his scalp but he did not seem to notice.

"Patrick?" she asked.

"Damned fangs," he replied. He looked up at her. Blood dripped into his eyes. "Got any more of that cloth?" he asked.

"Jessie!" Eron demanded.

"What?" she answered aloud as she ripped a second strip of cloth from her shirt. O'Shea tried to take it from her, but she batted his hand away and examined the wound. "Head wounds bleed a lot," she said. O'Shea reached up and grabbed her hand. His eyes widened as her visions accosted him.

"Use your mind, Patrick," she told him softly. "It's like a television. You choose which vision to watch while the others play on."

"Tersan's in trouble," Eron told them. "In the basin..."

Tersan's image appeared. He was on his knees. Blood covered his heaving chest. His face was twisted in pain. The point of a sword dipped into his skin. Patrick grabbed her arm.

"My God..."

"The reserves are committed and will soon surround them," Eron said. "Tersan drew them in. We must help him."

"On our way," she answered.

"Watch your energy stores," he reminded her. "A shield is--"

"I'm watching," she snapped back.

"Good."

The image faded. "What the hell was that?"

"It's a different world, Officer." She tightened the cloth. "That will need more tending than I can give it right now."

"Yeah, I know. Some kind of poison in the fangs. Not my first rodeo."

Jessie nodded.

"It'll keep for now." He checked his gun, a look of disgust on his face. With the ease of someone accustomed to weapons, he flipped off the safety and held the gun steady. "Ready," he said, looking into the fray instead of away from it.

Jessie gave him a critical glance. He was as steady as any Kilmari she had fought with. She pointed to their collective right. "We have to move in that direction," she said over the roar of battle.

In front of them was a sea of brown fringed by green and black. Only men fought before them. She took hold of the crystal, accessing Eron's mind. The sword sliced a demon's head from its shoulders, ran two men through, then faced another demon. She switched and found Tersan again. Sucking in a deep breath, she looked at the ring surrounding the king. Demons were as thick as humans in the crowd watching the torture. Her heart skipped a beat and she changed again. To the north, Pixil was fighting the same numbers as Eron.

"They're on to you," she said to Patrick.

"On to me?" he asked, looking up at her.

"Yes. To the humans, you're a target and to the demons something to be avoided."

"Great." He looked back at her. "At least it'll be easier to get to Tersan if we don't have to fight demons. He's in pretty rough shape," he said. "There's still an army of humans and I don't have much skill with a sword. We've got to hurry!"

"I have an idea." She looped a tendril of energy into a whip and lashed out into the ranks of the enemy. They yipped when the silver whip hit them, knocking them fiercely to the ground. Jessie parted the army before them. Patrick gaped.

"Holy Moses," he breathed.

"Moses had a little help," Jessie muttered. "We'll be on our own at the end of the tunnel, but the basin is not far. Are you ready?"

Patrick holstered the gun and unsheathed his borrowed sword. Jessie cracked the whip again, the sea of men parted and they raced into the fray.

Parry purposefully abandoned his grip on the crystal and set it aside. The constant shifting between segments of battle made tracking the flow of it difficult. He hobbled to the cliff's edge where he used his own eyes to survey the valley.

A ribbon of light blazed within the western ranks of Marand's forces, extending nearly a mile until it reached the basin beyond. As he watched, the ribbon dissipated, as though something sucked it in. His eyes darted to the north. Pixil's standard was at the head of a V-shaped pathway leading toward the basin. His heart leapt as his eyes swept to the east. The division of armies was not clear. There was no flash of light, no standard bearer. The clashing armies were visible from here, but the individual players were unknown from his lofty perch.

"Do not give up, Tersan!" he said aloud. "Help is coming!"

Patrick and Jessie were on the edge of the basin. She quickly surrounded them with her shield as their presence was discovered. In the center of the basin, Tersan lifted his head and a glimmer of hope shown on his face. The demons holding the king let go of him and joined others of their kind along the perimeter of the field. They shrunk back behind their human counterparts. Marand only noticed that his gruesome play was interrupted. When he realized the two had arrived, he shoved Tersan backward. The king fell with a thud.

"My dear Jessie," Marand said, examining his sword instead of looking at her, "I see your taste in gentlemen companions has not improved." A rumble of laughter swept through the ranks that had closed behind them. "But then, what can one expect from a street urchin?" Another rumble of laughter from the ranks.

"I can pick him off from here," Patrick said, aiming the gun at Marand's head. "He's an easy target."

"One shot?" she whispered.

"If I'm lucky."

"Then wait until luck isn't a player," she answered.

"Aha." Marand finished examining the sword. "Not much room left here for more blood." He flipped the blade so he could see the other side and touched the area next to the hilt. "It appears there is only one spot left. Right next to the hilt."

"We have to get to Tersan," Jessie whispered. "I can protect him, but we have to get those soldiers away from him first."

"Dual shields?"

"Okay." She motioned and Patrick found himself alone.

"Go right. I'll draw their attention."

With small steps, they started closing the distance between them.

Marand shook his head. He looked over his shoulder at Sila. "Have you a suggestion, my dear?" he asked.

The demons who had been holding Tersan were hurriedly replaced by soldiers who dragged the king up onto his knees and securing him on either side by his arms. Tersan seemed uninterested. Sila walked forward to examine the sword. Unlike Marand, her eyes were focused on their approaching enemies. She touched the sword, looked briefly at it, then back up at Jessie and Patrick. Noise from the battle rose to their left and the ring of soldiers shifted slightly.

"There appears to be only one way to finish the christening," Sila said, staring evenly at Jessie. "Run him through."

Marand shifted his attention from the sword to Sila. "You are certain?"

"Enough of this play!" she hissed. "Do it!"

Marand smiled widely. He held the sword over his head, ready to make a downward thrust into Tersan. Patrick threw off the shield and squeezed the trigger. He heard the gun fire but found himself flying backward toward the crowd. He landed hard, the breath knocked out of him, the gun still in his hand. Sila was smiling wickedly at him.

"It is time for the healer to become a soldier," she announced. Behind her a wall of silvery light flared. Jessie had reached Tersan.

"Damn you!" Marand shouted.

"Never mind him, dear," Sila said. "We have the demons' nemesis here. See how they hide behind our brave soldiers?"

Indeed, the demons had disappeared into the ranks. Patrick had eyes only for Sila. He aimed carefully at her as she was forming a second ball of energy to throw at him. "I've never killed a person before," he told her, "let alone a woman! Please, don't make me do it!"

"Listen to how he pleads," Sila said. She held the energy ball in her hands, poised to let it fly.

"Forgive me," Patrick said. He fired.

Sila squealed. She clutched at her arm and dropped.

Without waiting, Patrick sprinted for the dome of silvery light containing Jessie and Tersan. A shower of arrows fell around him, finding their mark in his shoulder and hip. He fell and his muscles refused to allow him to rise.

"Stop!" Marand bellowed. "The queen!"

The arrows stopped.

To the north, a black standard bearing a dicantus tree adorned with brilliant white flowers waved briefly above the ranks. The line swelled and broke. A cavalry of soldiers clad in black poured into the basin, led by a woman with a flashing sword and a circlet of silver on her head. The army was distracted from Patrick. He crawled toward Jessie.

A steady hand was suddenly under his arm as he was pulled to his feet. Dragging his wounded leg, he focused on reaching the safety of the dome. Five more feet and he would be safe. Jessie waved a hand and the way opened. He collapsed next to Tersan and looked up to thank his rescuer.

"Pixil!" Jessie whispered.

"Lie still," the Kilmari queen ordered. "You have fought bravely in a cause that is not your own. Our people owe you a great debt."

"The guys at the precinct will never believe this," he mumbled. He held a hand out to her which she took. "Thanks," he told her.

"You will be safe now," she said to him with a smile he would never forget. Then she released him and turned her attention to the king. "Tersan?" she asked, placing a hand gently on his bloodied shoulder.

Tersan moaned. Pixil took her herb pouch from her shoulder and handed it to Jessie. "Use your skills," she said. "Trust that they will be enough."

"But I--"

"Only a few of us managed to break their ranks," Pixil interrupted. "Too many for you to shield. We must retreat so we may come back in greater numbers. Keep them safe."

Jessie opened her mouth to say something. Whatever her comment was, it died on her lips. "Yes, your majesty," she said.

Parry hobbled back to the boulder as fast as he could. He grabbed the crystal in time to see Lady Jessie close the bubble around herself, Patrick and Tersan. Pixil remounted her horse and whirled away from them. The Kilmari numbered less than two dozen. They formed a protective circle around the three inside the bubble. Wave after wave of soldiers attacked them. Soon, the horses were gone yet the fight continued.

Eron! Parry pleaded.

I am nearly upon them, he answered.

From the north, the Kilmari wedge had been reformed. Even from this great distance, Parry could see Marand's forces parting. Tersan's reinforcements were pounding the enemy on both the eastern and western fronts, forcing the warring parties into the basin. A cheer went up from the Kilmari guarding the bubble as relief joined them. As if someone shot them full of energy, they joined the fray, Lady Jessie's bubble now safely within friendly territory.

Marand rallied the demons. They attacked fearlessly now that Patrick was no longer a threat. The battle was at an impasse. With one exception…

Eron broke through ranks and leapt into the basin. His black leather clothing glistened with blood, his hair slicked against his forehead and there was madness on his face Parry had never witnessed before. He sliced his way through the enemy, easily finding his way into what remained of the circle. Once inside, he raced to the center and stopped.

"Marand!" he shouted over the battle. "Marand!"

Marand stopped barking orders and turned to face him, his demon guard again beside him. With his escort, he walked calmly to the center of the circle. Men on both sides stopped their fighting to watch.

"You will soon run for you precious Kimala, your tail between your legs like a beaten dog," Marand said.

"We shall see," Eron replied.

Marand snapped his fingers and held out his hand, palm up. His standard bearer placed something in his hand which he threw out into the dust. It was a bloodied circlet of silver.

"Your queen is no longer," Marand said with an evil laugh.

"Then you will see her in hell!" Eron shouted.

Faster than Parry had ever seen any man move, Eron flew at the demons. The first was missing an arm before he could draw a blade. The second was missing his head. Black ichor spewed from their bodies, showering Eron and coating Marand in black. Eron stood facing him in the circle.

"I have yet to fully christen my sword," Marand said. "Now it shall taste the blood of a Kilmari prince as well as that of a Jelestine king."

"Today you will die," Eron said, his chest heaving from the exertion he had just put forth. "As for your sword…whoever heard of feeding a piece of metal?"

He lunged.

Marand parried the stroke and returned one of his own, which Eron easily turned aside. The Kilmari prince breezed behind Marand. He turned his sword so that the flat part of it faced Marand and hit him squarely across the buttocks. The king jerked forward with a start, but recovered to face Eron once again.

Marand thrust and Eron easily parried each blow. Soldier after soldier stopped fighting to watch, all wary of those around them, but drawn to the duel between the king and Sword. In a savage move, Eron slid his blade under Marand's, grabbed the king's hand and twisted it viciously, disarming him. Eron held the tip of his sword under Marand's chin, forcing his head up. Marand's face shone eerily in the glow of the Sword of Light. Eron smiled at him. He stepped back and kicked the bloody sword toward him.

"Pick it up," Eron ordered.

Marand held his arms away from his body. "Your honor prevents you from slaying an unarmed man," he said silkily.

Eron did not answer. He took a step forward and ran him through.

Parry gasped. He let the crystal dangle from its chain and looked to the sky. Above the Sisters, two small black dots appeared. They appeared to be flying with purpose toward the basin below.

"What horrors now," he whispered as he picked up the crystal once more.

"Let me up!" Sila roared. She pushed the soldiers and demons away from her and scrambled to her feet. The Otherworlder's weapon had sliced a chunk of flesh out of her arm and it burned. She was a little dizzy, but furious. The Otherworlder would die now and at her hand. "Get out of my way!" she bellowed.

The mass of protectors parted. In front of her, Marand knelt before Eron. The Sword drew his arm back and Marand fell to the ground with a solid thud.

"No…no…please…"

The world around her went suddenly silent. Unaware, she took one step, then another, then another and another and another until she stood over him. She fell to her knees and drew him into her arms, sobbing.

"No…" she repeated over and over again. Hot tears filled her eyes and fell down her cheeks. She buried her head in his chest, searching for the smell of fresh linens and bathwater. She found it mingled with the coppery scent of his blood and the ichor of demons. Someone placed a hand on her shoulder.

"Sila?"

She gasped. Eron was offering her a hand.

"Sila, you have been through too much," he told her. "Come. Let me--"

"Murderer," she whispered. "You are a murderer!"

"He attacked us, Sila, invaded Jeleste and would have overrun Bel Haven on his way to Kimala. You know that."

"He was kind to me!" she shouted. "You were never kind!"

"Marand used people," Eron replied softly.

"Are you saying he used me?" she snapped.

"I am saying he manipulated you, yes," Eron said. "I was wrong to leave you when we recovered Parry. Now is not the time for a proper apology, though. The tide is turning. Come back with me."

Into the clearing, two huge demons flew. They landed gracefully beside the fallen king and rapidly took human form. Eron released Sila and summoned the Sword of Light once more.

"Lord Fot," he said, moving away from Sila and into the space that was rapidly clearing of all combatants, human and demon, Kilmari, Jelestine and Calsharan. Once again the collective armies held their breath. There was no sound other than a single human crying for her lost mate.

The armies fell back to the bubble where Jessie waited, oddly quiet for a battle of such scope. She had pulled the arrows from Patrick's shoulder and hip and applied palapaca to his brow. Tersan was another story. He was bleeding from dozens of cuts and, though none of them seemed deep enough to cause a big problem alone, together, they looked substantial.

"Here," Patrick said, shimmying out of his outer shirt. "Put this on him and keep him warm. He looks a mess, but he's not losing that much blood. You have to worry about shock."

Jessie cast him a sidelong look and raised both eyebrows. "Says who?"

"Says me. Look, just humor me and do it, all right? He'll keep until you can get him to a doc if you just keep him warm."

The armies parted exposing the bubble once again to the combatants. Patrick gasped.

"Bue," was all he said.

"Jessie!"

She turned around. Ric stood beside their bubble.

"Jessie, let me in!"

She waved a hand at the bubble and an opening appeared. She reached out, grabbed Ric by the arm and dragged him into the now crowded bubble.

"What the hell are you doing here?" she demanded in unison with Patrick.

Tersan managed a laugh. "He wants to help," he said very softly.

A flash of light caught all of their attentions. Fot was advancing toward Eron, his sword blazing. The Sword was being forced backward around the circle toward the waiting Bue.

"Jessie!" Ric said. "I can help him!"

She took his hand. "Can you maintain this?" she said, pointing to the bubble.

"Yes."

"Then do it."

As she stepped away from the protective bubble, her shimmering silver light was replaced by one of green with silver, gold and blue streaks. Three men watched her move into the circle to join her partner, along with every other set of eyes lining the circle.

Working quickly, she summoned a ring of power. With a skill she learned as a child, she threw the disk toward Bue, striking the blue demon in the neck. Bue howled and turned away from Eron. She prowled toward this new threat.

"Wylfcynne's heir, I presume?" Bue hissed.

"Hardly," Jessie replied, readying another lasso.

"I thought shields were limited to defense," Bue said. She leapt into the air, changing into a hideous monster instantly. Talons extended from her hands and feet, her face grew fangs that protruded from bright red lips.

Jessie only had a moment. She threw the lasso into the air but it missed completely. The blue body came crashing toward her. She dove for cover, knowing she was too late. Bue made a horrible hissing sound and veered off to Jessie's left. Seconds later, the demon was airborne again, howling.

"What--"

"Need some help?" Ric was standing outside the bubble looking quite pleased with himself.

"I--it's not--you can't--"

"It is and I can and I did and let's get on with it while we have her on the run, shall we?" he said with a maniacal smile.

"Well---okay why not?" Jessie dusted off her hands and rose. She darted across the short distance to where he stood. "But you must promise me that if we start to lose, you go back in there. Promise!"

"I promise. Happy?"

"Extremely."

In the periphery of his vision, Eron saw Jessie fall and then rise. The young Otherworlder had joined her. Together they were on the offensive. He parried the blow Fot leveled at him and turned his full attention to Fot. It was time for him, like Jessie, to go on the offensive.

Three quick slashes, three equally fast parries. He leapt forward and backward, to either side, the movements coming easily for him as he let the energy that defined him take over his body. Fot charged and he sidestepped him, making the larger combatant look clumsy in comparison. Yet Fot's movements were too fast to deal a final blow.

Fot roared in anger. He turned faster than his massive body should have allowed, using the buoyancy of his kind to fuel his movements. The Sword stood in the center of the field waiting, his weapon glowing in his hands. Though there was sweat on his brow, he was not fatigued. The world faded around them, leaving only two beings vying for supremacy. One would live to see the end of this day, the other would not. Facing one another now for the last time, they began a lethal dance.

Step right, cross over, step right, pause; cross left, step left, cross left, step left, pause. They mirrored each other's movements in perfect symmetry, each waiting for the other to glance away, to tire, to miss-step. Blades clashed, the sound thunderous throughout the basin. Eron used his smaller stature to slip beneath Fot's huge arm. He turned so quickly the demon barely had time to turn the blow aside. Fot lost then regained his footing to face Eron again.

"I am impressed, human," Fot said as they started to dance once more. "The last time I saw you, you were on your way to see your goddess."

"Perhaps the Lady will find pity for your misguided soul, Fot," Eron countered, matching him step for step. "Then again, maybe not." He turned his back on Fot and raced away from him. Fot laughed. He gave chase toward the edge of the basin. Eron was on top of the ring of stone defining its outer reaches. Too late, Fot saw the trap.

The ground sank in front of Eron. Fot was moving too fast to stop. He raced into a pit, his feet sliding out from under him as he fell. His sword clamored to the ground, hitting the stone wall with a solid clink and suddenly, Eron was on top of him, the Sword of Light at his throat.

"Say your prayers, Demon Lord," Eron said.

"Healer!" he bellowed. "Take back what is yours!"

87 End of the Line

The final descent to Dallow Mound met no resistance. A fire burned on the northern edge of the stone wall marking the boundary clearly. A young man stood beside it, leaning heavily on his cane.

Sje landed without a sound. He helped Jason and Altay dismount then turned his attention to Bob who was still circling. On Sje's signal, the second demon plummeted gracelessly toward the ground. Sje caught him, removed his precious cargo and set Lucy on the ground. He placed a hand on either of her shoulders and looked into her eyes.

"All right?" Jason heard him say quietly.

"Y-yes. That was scary."

"I know, child, I know," he said.

The youth standing by the fire limped awkwardly toward them, brandishing a dagger in one hand. He was in obvious pain, but determined. Altay stepped between him and the others.

"Parry?" she said.

The youth shifted his attention to her but continued his approach.

"Parry, stop," she said. The sword flared at her side. "Please."

Parry stopped. "I…" His hand wavered and dropped to his side. "Who are you?"

"Jason McCarthy," Jason answered, "one of the good guys." He extended a hand in greeting. Parry looked beyond him to the ladies.

"Who are you?" he repeated.

"Altay, of Bel Haven. You know me. And she is Lucy, Lady Jessie's daughter. We have come to help."

"Eron's daughter, too," Lucy piped up.

Parry clutched something in his hand. When he let it go, they saw it was a clear crystal. "I can only see through Lord Eron's eyes," he said. "I am blind. I fear he has fallen."

Sje looked up from Bob. He exchanged a silent message with Altay and she nodded. "Comoin, go home," he said to Bob. "I will meet you there."

Bob shook his head. "I must stay and protect the humans," he said.

Sje scowled. "There is no commitment, no promise! You must go home!"

Bob smiled. "I know there is no commitment, at least none that if broken binds me to hell. I have known for a long time. But I must stay until the song is begun if it is to begin. The threat approaches."

Sje drew in a great breath. "All right, then," he said. He clapped him on the shoulder then stood. "I hope to see you soon."

"Yes, my lord."

"Jason," Sje started, "I am counting on your help."

"I'm not sure I can project over that big a distance."

Sje smiled. "Your gift will allow it."

Jason stared at the copper-eyed demon. Sje looked like he had something else to say. "It's not like you not to speak freely," Jason told him. "What else is there?"

"In order to affect so many who suffer, you will become a vessel," he started, choosing his words carefully. "If the vessel ceases to be able to draw in energy to create the song, the song will take what it needs from your soul. The cost of the song may be your death."

"I really didn't want to hear that," he said.

"There may be no need for you to use your gift for demonkind," he added softly. "But for your friends…You see how the battle rages. You can save them. You have been twice blessed. That may save you." He turned to Altay. "Come. There is little time."

"Watch for my signal," Altay said to Jason. She pulled his head down and kissed him on the lips, then ran to Sje and clambered aboard. An instant later they were airborne. Two instants and they were gone.

88 Vengeance

Sila stood beside the pit, the blood of her dead king sticky on her fingers. It soaked through the white gown she wore, gluing the soft cloth to her hide. She took one look at Fot, who was about to be beheaded. She did not care about his life. She only wanted revenge.

A wicked smile crossed her lips. She raised her hands and summoned the energy she had left in Eron's mind to return to her. With a single flick of her wrist, she ripped away the gift she had given.

Eron cried out once, then dropped. His body lay crumpled on the ground, the Sword of Light gone. The tide of battle suddenly changed. Jessie ran to him but there was little she would be able to do. Sila knew this. The knowledge made her proud.

Marand's army was hers now. She had power. She was in charge. Never had she felt so alive. Bue shrieked a battle cry above her head and Fot was righting himself, retrieving his sword and rising from the pit to join her. It was time to rally her forces. But first, there was one little thing she had to do.

Very deliberately, she walked over to where Jessie now sat with Eron once again cradled in her arms, rocking him gently. No bubble of energy covered them. Jessie's eyes were as vacant as Eron's. Fot stood beside Sila, ready to finish the duel. He advanced toward them, but Sila held up a hand to stay his.

"As you wish, Healer," Fot said. "But why?"

"I have something to say, Lord Fot," she told him.

An instant later, she was once again inside Eron's head.

Jessie was working feverishly to stem the flow of energy from Eron's mind. Massive ponds of silvery light splashed on the broken walls, but gold gushed out around them. Jessie was in tears, yet she worked with such speed that even Sila was awed. When she saw Sila standing beside her, she uttered a single word.

"Why?" she whispered.

Sila laughed. "Because I can."

And then she was standing beside Fot again, looking at the two who had fallen. Fot took a step forward but paused, waiting for her command. In her mind, she saw Tocar's head briefly on a pike. The memory of that rocked her. With a wicked smile, she knew what she would do. "Take their heads. Display them so that their army can see their defeat."

"You are indeed a warrior," Fot told her. The colorless sword flared from his fingers.

"When you are done, take the Jelestine's head as well."

Fot nodded. He took a step forward and steadied himself to deliver the blow. "You were almost worthy, little man..."

Before he could act, Sila shrieked. Ric had her in a headlock, the delicate neck flexed cruelly to one side.

"Get back or I will break her neck," he shouted.

"Do it!" Sila cried.

Fot stood back, his sword still in hand. Ric forced the healer forward, half lifting her, half shoving her until she was inches from Jessie. Then he threw her into Fot while simultaneously enveloping the three into a multi-colored sphere.

"Kill them!" Sila screamed.

"Go away, bitch!" he shouted back at her.

Sila attacked the shield with her bare hands, beating on it with her fists, but the shield did not flinch. Furious, she turned to Fot as she regained her composure. "If the shield is broken, kill them."

"Jessie!" Patrick shouted from inside the bubble.

"What?" Tersan asked. He hauled himself into a sitting position, keeping his arms firmly planted across his chest and the borrowed shirt.

"Look!"

"Sila?" Tersan said.

Sila was walking toward them, determination on her face. She strode up to the bubble and placed a hand just above it. Anger twisted her face into an ugly mass and she struggled to get herself under control.

"It will not be long, Majesty, before she calls for this," she finally said, stroking the bubble as though it were made of fine silk. "And then I shall finish what my king began."

"Sila?" Tersan said. "Why?"

The protective sheen of the bubble distorted her face. She stared at him, her mouth gaping open as though she was speaking, though she did not utter a word. Then she shut it tightly, the once full lips now cruelly poised. Finally, she spoke.

"Eron lies dying. The Otherworlder will foolishly sacrifice herself for him and die in the process. I have been in his mind. I have seen it." She laughed. "When she is done, Lord Fot will take their heads and place them on pikes for all to behold. Your protection will be gone and I will have your head as well."

"I don't get a pike?" Patrick asked with not a little sarcasm. "I have a title, you know. Demon Slayer."

"It will be arranged," she replied coolly. She tilted her head and her hair cascaded around her beautiful face. Her beauty was cold. "I have you, Tersan, to thank." She curtsied, studying his reaction.

"Me?" Tersan said.

"Yes. Had you not summoned me to help him, the seed would never have been planted. Today it came to fruition."

"What did you do?" he asked.

"I, um, helped him." She smiled.

"I think she's nuts," Patrick whispered.

"You see, I gave him a present on that night, a gift from my soul, a part of me that would sustain him, make him strong, help him heal." Her smile broadened. "A gift such as that should never be given lightly for it is not meant to be retrieved. It should be revered, held sacrosanct."

"Why do the bad guys always have to gloat?" Patrick mumbled. "It's the same everywhere."

"Eron did not appreciate my gift. Still, I allowed him to keep it. He murdered my husband. I allowed him to keep it. But when he threatened my power, I decided to take back what was mine. And when I did…" She laughed. "When I did, I tore a hole in his brain. As we speak, the energy that defines him as both man and Sword is seeping from his body." She giggled.

"Sila, no!" Tersan said.

"'No' you say?" She turned cold. "He abandoned me so I was forced to become your enemy. I found other allies, then I destroyed him. Soon I will be queen over this entire land with demons at my command. And I will take Jeleste and Kimala."

"Talk about your melodrama," Patrick said.

"I shall send my forces to Ellance, capture your children and send them into slavery. Perhaps let them work in the mines or better still, introduce them to a woman I met in Il Chatel by the name of Princess." She grinned evilly. "She trades mostly girls, but I am certain there is a place in her darker corners for your son. He is still tender, is he not?"

Tersan shuddered.

Sila leaned over the bubble, now stroking it almost lovingly. "You see how the power melts away?" she said, her eyes staring dreamily at the bubble.

"You talk a good line, woman," Patrick said. "What makes you think the demons won't turn against you?"

"I healed their leader," she continued in the same far away voice.

"Yeah, well I once rescued a skunk from drowning," Patrick told her. "The ungrateful creature sprayed me when I turned him loose."

"Problems, my Queen?" Fot asked.

"Nothing that, in time, won't be solved," she answered.

A wave of nausea passed over Tersan and he sat back down in a hurry. He waved off Patrick's helping hand and waited for it to pass. High above them, a dot appeared against the grey afternoon clouds. A shimmering light accompanied the dot. Tersan blinked hard.

"The Lady help us all," he whispered.

89 Reunion

From below, they saw the great demon Sje descend into the basin. He took his time, gliding in huge, graceful circles high above them, making certain all would see him and the passenger he carried. No one save Tersan saw where he came from. All heads, though, turned to see where he would land.

A ripple of anticipation washed over the ground. Combatants stopped their fighting and pointed, regaining the nobility of fighting men by not fighting. Something important was going to happen, something important enough for them to hold their collective breath and resign themselves to the outcome. Something that offered at once hope and devastation, for Sje's purpose was unknown to them.

King Tersan, mighty leader of the combined armies of Jeleste and Kimala followed Sje's slow descent, wondering who this being was. Upon Sje's back, a person rode, though his identity was a mystery. The passenger held aloft a brilliant sword, the same sword carried always by he who was the sworn protector of the Lord of the Western Marches. He tore his eyes from the descending demon to look to the north. Huddled inside a protective bubble, he could see Sword and Shield. Lord Eron had indeed fallen. But now…now the Jelestine king dared hope one more time.

Beside the king, Officer O'Shea also watched. Though unprepared for this kind of war, he had fought well until his weapons became ineffective. Now sorely wounded, he wondered if he would live to see his lover again. He vowed to make things right, should a miracle occur, yet he did not hope. Officer O'Shea was too much of a realist to hope.

In the center of the basin, Lady Jessie and Lord Eron, who had led a great army into battle and destroyed their enemy's king, huddled in the dirt oblivious to everything around them. After defeating Marand, the heartless leader of Calshara, and nearly defeating his greatest ally, they fell into ruin at the hands of Sila Atin, now Queen Sila of Calshara. Had Ric Hawkins, the untrained shield destined to replace Lady Jessie as Shield, not formed a protective bubble around all three of them, Sword and Shield would have fallen.

The fair queen of Kimala lay upon a mound of sweet grass, her silvery crown gone along with her right eye. Healers attended her even in the midst of the battle. Soldiers formed a protective circle around her. They, too, pointed to the descending demon. Queen Pixil strained to look skyward. She prayed to the Lady for deliverance for her people. Then she closed her remaining eye.

High above them, on the Mound of Dallow, the Siren and the Seneschal peered over the edge of the cliff. Lady Jessie's daughter stood beside them. Behind them, their demon protector scanned the sky, searching for those who might harm his young charges.

Sje glided gracefully to the ground. As he landed, he swooped Altay from his back in a single, grace-filled move. An instant later, he assumed human form. Altay raced to the first bubble. She did not bother with courtesies.

"My lord," she said to the king, "we have come to assist you."

Tersan offered her a strained smile. "We welcome you. Our need is dire."

Sje ignited a magnificent glowing sword. He strolled forward and placed the brilliant sapphire tip on the bubble. Tendrils of power strengthened the webbing over the king and the officer, replacing the energy Jessie was recalling. An instant later, her silvery protection was gone. "Perhaps one day we shall exchange war stories, my friends," he told them softly. He turned away from their astonished looks to face his greatest adversary.

"Welcome back, Sje," Fot said silkily, though a crease of worry furrowed his brow. He stopped moving forward and stared at Sje. "Your servant, is dead, you know," he said casually.

"Many of my servants have died serving a false lord," Sje returned lightly. He shifted the blade such that he now held it with both hands directly in front of his body. "Only you betrayed me."

Altay placed her hand on the bubble housing Eron, Jessie and Ric. She let out a pitiful cry, then bit her lip. "Are they…are--?"

Jessie shifted and Eron let out a pained moan.

"I can't see anything wrong with him," Ric said, "apart from a couple of cuts here and there. I don't get it. 'Must have had a heart attack or something."

"I need you," Altay said to him.

"Really?"

She pointed to the circle of men and demons who stood and watched. They leaned upon their weapons, waiting for a sign. "We cannot let them interfere," she said.

"Bue's out there somewhere," Ric replied. "Tersan was right. I'm not ready for battle. If I had been, I wouldn't be holed up in here, hoping everyone will just go away and I can slink off into the dark somewhere and pretend it didn't happen."

Jessie shifted. She removed her hand from Eron's shoulder and grasped Ric's firmly in hers. "You are more than ready," she said. "Help her. Help us." She looked into his eyes, her tear streaked face set. "Believe in yourself. You are now the Shield."

Ric stared into her green eyes for a moment. "Well, if I stay in here, I'll die from hunger. Maybe you're right. Maybe it is better to go out fighting." He placed a crystal glowing with green power into her hand. "A demon named Bob taught me many things. I have no claim to this anymore," he told her. "Maybe it will help." He squeezed her hand, released it and passed out of the protection of his bubble and into battle. "Ready," he said.

On the stairs of Mount Dallow, the climbing shadow had nearly reached the summit. All eyes above it focused on the valley below, unaware of the threat approaching them. Though they could not differentiate the combatants, they would witness the duel, should they live long enough. Lucy and Parry were talking in whispers as Jason stood alone beside the still burning signal fire. Lucy left the seneschal and joined him.

"Jason?" Lucy said.

"What?"

"Even if Altay isn't able to signal," she whispered, "when one of them falls, you still have to sing."

"I don't know, Lu," he whispered back.

"She's right," Comoin said from behind them.

"What about you?" Jason snapped.

Comoin laughed. "I have heard you sing before," he said and then launched into a fair rendition of Too Damned Hot. When he finished the first two lines he made a slight bow.

"I wasn't who I am now then!" Jason protested.

"Well, that statement is about as confusing as anything I've ever heard," Lucy said.

"No matter," Comoin answered. "I will manage."

Sila Atin snarled at the demon binding the wound Patrick had inflicted on her arm. "I no longer require your aid," she told him. When he did not release her, she repelled him with a bolt of energy.

"What is happening?" she demanded.

"Lord Fot has engaged…"

"Engaged who?" she asked. "I have dispensed with that wretched sword. Who else dare challenge him? Victory is at hand!"

"A--another demon."

"Who would be so brazen? Who? Tell me now," she demanded.

The demon looked to his fellow who shrugged. "Lord Sje has returned."

"Sje?"

The demon nodded. "He was lord before Fot."

"Ah, then we need not concern ourselves," she answered. "If he was defeated once before, he shall be defeated again. Go. Help him."

"We cannot," the demon said. He smiled at her. "Our allegiance lies with the victor."

Sila scowled. "Out of my way, then. I shall deal with this myself."

"I am sorry, my lady," said the captain of Marand's guard. He tapped her expertly on the base of her skull and she fell. He caught her unconscious body before she hit the ground. "His majesty said you should be kept safe. I fear the outcome of this duel." He carried her to a waiting horse, secured her in front of him and headed north to Il Chatel.

The armies fell silent as the two great demons faced one another. Most among the humans knew Fot. Most among the demons knew Sje. Why the two were fighting was clear to all.

Step for step, the two warriors mirrored one another. Sje lunged, then parried. Fot parried then lunged. Each footstep was carefully placed. *Step right, cross-over right, step right. Step left, cross-behind, step left.*

Their eyes locked, their brains clicking to find their adversary's weakness while their bodies reacted in mindless but graceful animation.

Miss-step, lunge, parry, whirl. Their footfalls thundered on the Basin's hard ground. The grunts of effort could be heard inside the king's protective bubble. Both king and officer strained to see which demon would strike first blood, but the duo moved so quickly, neither could tell them apart.

"Get back!" Altay warned as the line of demons surged forward. She brandished her sword with authority.

"You are nothing but a child," a particularly large demon told her, "and a woman-child at that." He broke the unseen barrier and strode confidently toward her. He held a ball and chain in one hand. The lethal ball, coated with a mixture of blood, hair and cloth, swung lazily from the end of the stick.

"You have ceased fighting because Sje has returned, have you not?" Altay asked.

"The strongest of demons leads us," he told her. "Humans are of no consequence to either of them. So they shall not be to me, either."

The ball swung backward so fast it was almost a blur. Altay waited. When it was almost on her, she neatly sidestepped and sliced through the chain. The ball dropped, sinking into the soft dirt with a thunk. The demon roared and lunged at her. She held steady, her sword putting his eye out and killing him instantly.

"Anyone el--?"

The blade came so fast she did not have time to parry the blow. She was knocked backward off her feet. A shimmering curtain kept the next blow from landing on her. The second demon stepped back once, then forward, then back, then forward. Ric pelted him with balls of energy.

"A little help here?" he said without looking at her.

Altay bounced up and charged the attacking demon. He was caught off-balance in Ric's continuous barrage of hand sized energy balls. She struck once at his arm as he raised it to defend himself, severing his hand below the elbow. He yelped in pain. She hesitated.

"It's war!" Ric shouted. "No second chances!"

She wrapped both hands around the hilt of her sword.

"Forgive me," she whispered.

An instant later, the demon's head lay on the ground beside his hand.

"Anybody else?" Ric asked the quieted crowd.

There was no answer.

From the Mound of Dallow, four beings watched, still unaware of the menace from below.

"Way to go!" Jason cheered.

"You can't tell what's happening from up here!" Lucy told him.

"Maybe not with Sje and Fot," he said, pointing to a place just beyond the two whirling combatants, "but I'm pretty sure that's Altay and, if I'm not mistaken, I saw a couple of Ric's energy balls flying."

"You can't tell that from up here!" Lucy protested. "Can he, Parry?"

"I must admit, I cannot."

"I can." Comoin gazed into the distance. "He is correct, my young friends." Pain furrowed his brow. "Two of my brethren have fallen."

"I'm sorry, Bob," Jason said. "It's just that--"

"No need to apologize," Comoin said. He nodded to the field. "Soon, they will return their allegiance to my lord Sje." He sighed. "And I, too, shall be able to return home."

Sje slashed at Fot. The effort cut through his first layer of scales and a thin line of ichor beaded up around it. Fot tilted his head to one side in acknowledgment of the well placed strike.

"I see your years in confinement have done little to dull your skills, Sje," he said.

"And you have had time to hone yours," Sje answered. "But not quite enough, I fear. You always were a lazy student."

The two still circled around one another in the basin. *Thrust, parry, slash, thrust...slash, parry, thrust sidestep, touché.* Sje glanced down at his arm. "Nicely done," he said, not bothering to wipe away the black ooze. For the first time, he whirled away from Fot, moving so fast that he was behind his adversary before Fot knew what was happening.

The glowing sword was at his throat. Sje wore a pained look on his face. "Ask for forgiveness, Fot," he whispered. "I may be in the mood to grant it."

Before he could answer, a tremendous force hit them from behind, sending them sailing to the ground. Sje rolled to one side, Fot the other. Bue helped him stand.

"Your timing is impeccable, my dear," Fot said.

"Thank you," she answered.

Fear crossed Sje's face as he now faced not one but two. "There is a better way," he told them. "Work with me!"

"I have tried that before," Fot answered. "I found it...unacceptable." He turned to Bue. "Shall we?"

Inside the first bubble, Patrick rose. He helped pull Tersan to his feet. The two yelled warnings but their efforts were in vain.

"Eron!" Tersan yelled as Sje faced Bue and Fot alone, "Eron, get up! Jessie!"

Neither person inside the other bubble moved.

"JESSIE!" Patrick yelled.

Still there was no response.

"Where are the other two?" Tersan asked.

Before Patrick could shrug, Altay and Ric came running across the basin. They took up positions on either side of Sje. The huge demon smiled at them. "This is not your fight," he told them softly.

"It is now," Altay responded. Before she could say another word, the others charged.

"Now what?" Jason asked.

"It appears Bue has joined the duel," Comoin said.

"That's not fair!" Lucy protested.

"This is war, Lucy," Parry reminded her. "War is never fair."

Comoin smiled. "It appears my lord Sje has assist--"

The shadow crossed onto the summit.

"Who are you?" Jason asked.

They did not answer. Parry drew the small blade but before he could use it, Comoin flung him backward, out of harm's reach.

"Backs together!" the demon commanded.

The three huddled together beside the dying signal fire. Comoin stood between them and the men pouring over the rock wall. He produced a sword of energy and decapitated the first two over the wall. The next came with swords drawn. There was an odd sound as metal met energy but there were too many for Comoin to stop.

"If you've got any more of those daggers," Jason said to Parry over his shoulder, "I could use one!"

Lucy handed him a sturdy stick that had once been part of the fire. "Better than nothing!" she told him.

Jason jabbed at one of the attackers. The soldier easily turned the wood aside and laughed.

"I climbed all this way," he stated, looking Jason in the eye while shifting the balance of his sword between his hands, "left the glory of the fight behind and for what? Where is the honor in killing a man with a stick?"

Comoin took a step back. The man was within his reach. When the man shifted, Comoin took his head. The demon stood with his back to his charges.

Thirteen men now surrounded them.

"Not even a demon can save you now," one cackled. He raised his sword. "Charge!" he yelled.

The soldiers fell upon them in a frenzied rage. Comoin slew those who came after him but the time it took to do so was costly. Behind him, Jason swung at his attackers with the stick as Parry did on the other side with the dagger.

"Shift!" Lucy yelled. "Jason, you have to be protected! Let me!"

She shoved him in between her and Comoin. A blow struck from behind sending Parry stumbling into Jason and Jason to his knees. Lucy completed the pile, landing on top. She screamed as a sword came slashing down above her. With a solid thunk, Comoin turned it aside, but not in time to keep the blade from cutting. Lucy fell away from the pile, clutching her side. Blood oozed between her fingers and she cried out.

"You coward!" Jason raged. "She's only a girl and she didn't even have a weapon!"

Now a man possessed, he swung his club at their attackers hitting one, then two then a third before Comoin grabbed him by the collar and threw him back into safety. The demon was bleeding from a hundred places, including some well-placed slashes to his face.

"You are our hope," he said, his voice oddly weak. "Do not waste the sacrifices we have made!"

Six attackers remained. Comoin hurtled himself into two of them, effectively bowling them over. He rose, panting and another had drawn an arrow back and aimed carefully at him. Comoin blinked hard. At this range, he would be dead as soon as the arrow let loose. The archer laughed. It was the last sound he would make other than the gurgles of a dead man.

Parry hobbled over and withdrew his dagger while Comoin grabbed an attacker and threw him over the cliff.

"Help!" Jason hollered.

He was standing over Lucy holding the still burning log. Two soldiers were on either side of him, ready to attack.

Parry threw himself forward, catching the enemies' blade across his chest. He sank next to Lucy as Comoin knocked the last man twenty feet away from them. Jason stood in horrified silence. He knelt beside Lucy, placing his hand over hers. She writhed in pain and he wanted to vomit. He tore off part of his shirt and folded it hastily into a bandage which he stuffed under her hand and pressed down hard.

"Hold on," he told her through tears, "hold on…"

90 The Rightful Lord

"Look out!"

Tersan ducked as Altay slammed against the bubble. She let out a cry, but held on to her sword and rolled gamely to her feet. "Ric!" she yelled.

The king shifted his attention. Ric held a dome of energy over his head and was running toward them. Bue used both hands and slammed into his barrier. Ric staggered under the impact. He was down on one knee, but quickly regrouped and raced toward them. Sweat soaked through his shirt and he was sucking in air like a nearly drown man.

"Forget her eyes," Patrick suggested. "Go for her legs!"

"But I will be ineffective there!" she protested.

"You are the Sword!" Tersan chimed in. "You're not limited to only eyes!"

She stared in at the king, then nodded. "Ric, get me in close."

"No need to move too far," he said between breaths. Bue was on them.

Ric lifted the edge of the shield for Altay to get a poke off. Before she could move, Bue grabbed the edge of the small dome and flipped it over.

"Roll!" Tersan yelled. Ric went right, Altay left. Bue went after Altay. The girl scrambled for her sword but it evaporated when she dropped it. Bue laughed. She took Altay by the shirt and held her up off the ground. The girl's feet kicked violently but found nothing solid to vent her wrath upon. Bue laughed.

"You lose!" the demon screeched.

"Not so fast!" Ric reformed the umbrella and charged. He wedged himself under Bue's arms, forcing Altay loose. She dropped and summoned her sword.

"Move!" she yelled.

He only just got away before Bue occupied the space he had been in. The demon spread her arms wide in an effort to scoop him in to her, leaving her underbelly temporarily unprotected. In that moment, Altay's sword found its way home. It entered directly between the many sets of hands and exited Bue's back. Altay grasped the sword with both hands and ruthlessly pulled upward. An odd combination of gore and light spilled out of the demon. She looked very surprised, pawing at the wound as her life force dribbled out onto the ground. She fell with a whimper and a thud and lay motionless as the two victors stood over her now cooling corpse.

"We did it!" Ric whispered.

"I hope…we never…have to…do that again!" she said.

"Get to shelter!"

They turned to see Sje waving wildly at them.

"I will deal with this one alone."

They scrambled and ran back to the bubble containing Patrick and Tersan. Ric grabbed Altay's hand and they passed inside where they both stood bent over, catching their breath.

"I don't get it," Patrick said. "Why don't the demons attack?"

"They're waiting for their rightful leader," Tersan said. "They will follow whoever wins."

"Fickle lot…aren't they?" Ric said between gulps of air.

The duel had taken a toll on the demons. They swung the massive swords at one another with now lackluster skill, tripping over stones and their own feet while trying to kill each other. Sje wore a terrifying look on his face. Fot wore fear. Ichor flowed freely from many wounds. Sje favored his right leg, Fot his left arm. *Parry, thrust, trip, recover*…the battle had taken on a new rhythm.

Altay nodded to Ric. "I'm ready," she said. "Open this thing and let me out to help him."

Patrick placed his hand on Ric's. "No," he said. "Sje has got to do this himself, if Tersan's right about the demons. Otherwise, he will appear weak."

"But look at him!"

Sje was down. He struggled to place a hand on a boulder and pull himself up as Fot charged. The older demon bowed his head, his sword arm hanging limply at his side. He offered a weak defense, holding the sword up to ward off the death thrust that was coming. Fot swung at him, knocking the sword out of his hand.

But Sje was ready. In the time it took for Fot to knock the sword away and prepare for the killing blow, he produced a second sword and sliced his enemy in half. Ichor spewed from both halves, two fountains of black on a field of green. Sje leaned heavily on the boulder, breathing as hard as Altay and Ric.

"Now would you let me out?" Altay did not ask. She demanded. Ric dissolved a portion of the bubble and followed her out, sealing Patrick and Tersan in once more.

"Sje?" Altay cried as she ran to his side.

He waved her off, the second sword disappearing. There was more than physical pain on his face. "For a long time I have known we would meet thus," he said to her. "I did not realize so many others would be sacrificed…Are you ready?"

"Are you able to fly?" she asked.

"Well enough for this." He offered a smile. "The limp was a ruse. Come."

Altay waited while he transformed into a flying demon. She touched a long slash on his neck and he winced. "You need help," she said.

"I will heal once I am home," he replied. He held his hand out. "Let us not give them time to think."

Altay nodded. She carefully climbed aboard his shoulders one more time. His wings surged with great effort and they rose into the air.

"You are again my people!" he cried as Altay waited nervously for her cue, "The Aberration has returned! Follow me home! If we fly now, no harm will come to us!"

He flew over the entire basin, repeating his message until they were hovering in front of the Mound of Dallow. "Now!" he whispered to her.

She ignited her sword and waved it at the stone face. There was no reply.

In front of them, countless demons were taking to the sky. Some flew north, as Sje suggested. Others flew toward him, some lesser-Fots with weapons drawn.

"Do not waste your lives!" Sje pleaded with them. "Go north! We can settle all accounts there, where all will be safe!"

"Your trickery is not wasted on us," the largest of the group said. "There are riches to be had on Kimala, riches the humans keep to themselves. Fot promised them to any who followed him. What do you have to offer?"

"Life," Sje said simply. "Go north. This is ended."

The demon roared. All five raced toward them, human weapons drawn and demonic weapons powered. Sje ducked as a mace narrowly missed his skull. Altay hung on, her own sword slashing through the chain that held it to the club. The ball fell, though where it landed, neither would see.

Sje engaged in an aerial dance with the five. He dove down, skimming over the heads of the crowd below, so close that the wind from their passing ruffled the hair of the soldiers who ducked to avoid them.

"Hold on!" he yelled to Altay.

He spread his wings to halt himself in a hurry and she extended her sword. A leg of one demon was severed as he passed, a wing of another was rendered ineffective. They fell to the ground among the soldiers and Sje streaked off in the direction from which they had come. He once again reached the cliff and halted. His muscles trembled under Altay as the strain of playing the cat and mouse game continued.

"You cannot win," he told them, his voice as smooth as silk in spite of the energy he was expending to remain airborne. "Come with me to the north. In time, all will be forgiven."

"Like you forgave Fot?" the large demon said.

"Fot…Fot…" Sje's voice nearly broke. He shifted, his great wings beginning to show fatigue. "Fot had his chance a long time ago. He betrayed me to follow a path I could never condone."

"You would deny us the riches of Kimala?" he demanded.

"What use do our people have for baubles?" he asked sadly. The muscles along his back tightened. Altay patted his shoulder to let him know she was ready. "Please, follow me home."

"We won't follow you," Stayd told him. "The prize is too close at hand."

Sje hitched upward with blazing speed, then charged at Stayd. Altay's sword ripped through his underbelly. He screamed and dropped. The lord of demons turned on the other two with such speed that they could not prepare a defense. The first fell in two pieces to the ground. The second Altay stabbed through the heart, killing him instantly. The mighty wings beat thrice and they rose high above the basin. Altay reformed her sword and waved it at the cliff.

"Think they saw?" she asked.

"I do not know," Sje said. "Our time together, however, is done." He spread his wings wide and glided down to the place where Ric stood waiting for them. Altay slid off and bowed to him.

"I have been honored to know you," she told Sje.

"The honor has been mine," he returned. "Perhaps we shall meet again, young sword."

One last time, he floated into the air. He raced around the basin and headed north. One by one, demons rose from the battlefield and followed until there appeared to be a plague surging northward.

91 War Cry

Comoin gently turned Parry over. The seneschal was still breathing. The crystal had taken the impact of the blade, but he had landed head first against a huge boulder. His still blackened eye was again swollen.

Around them, their attackers moaned in agony. Comoin limped over to the first one and the man screamed as the demon picked him up. As though bearing a child, Comoin walked to the edge of the cliff.

"What are you doing?" Jason yelled.

Comoin drew the struggling soldier up over his head and heaved him back into the basin.

"Bob! Stop!"

Comoin did not stop. One by one, beginning with the soldiers who were the least wounded, he took them to the edge of the cliff and threw them over. They begged for mercy. He showed them none. Their screams echoed in Jason's head.

The last four went silently, for they were already dead. Comoin turned his attention to Jason. With purpose, the demon focused on him, limping his way across the short distance to where Jason knelt beside his quiet cousin.

"No!" Jason said, as Comoin reached out. "You can't do that! You're supposed to be one of the good guys!"

Comoin said nothing. There was pain across his battered face as he grabbed hold of Jason's arm and dragged him to the edge of the cliff.

"No! Let me go!"

Comoin held him firmly. When they reached the edge, he stopped.

"It is over," he said, releasing Jason. "Sing to save your people and send mine home."

With that, Comoin leapt from the cliff. He fell.

With a mixture of horror and relief, Jason threw himself to the ground to watch the air below. He counted to three before he saw the wings spread and Comoin take flight. He rolled onto his back and rubbed his eyes. A lump rose in his throat. He was here, on a mountain, alone, responsible for thousands of lives only wanting to save one. He got up, raced back to Lucy.

Her dark face was pale now, her open eyes vacant. The muscles holding her mouth shut relaxed and her jaw went slack.

"Don't die on me!" Jason shouted. "You can't die on me!"

Lucy did not respond. A dribble of blood trickled out of her mouth.

"No!"

"Sing, Jason," Parry said. He was oddly still.

"She's dying! Who will hold her?" He looked over to Parry. The seneschal was not moving. "You? Will you hold her while she dies so I can sing a stupid song?"

"Would that I could," Parry said. "I cannot move."

A second nerve lit up, thrilling through Jason.

"Place your cloak over her to keep her warm," Parry suggested. "But you must sing quickly or she truly will perish."

Jason stared at him. "You'd risk her life on a song?" he snarled.

"Think back to Ric and to Cynthal and to Penrose. You have the chance to save your cousin and an entire army as well. Look inside yourself. The song is there."

Jason nodded slowly. He unclasped the cloak and placed it over Lucy, patting her hand gently before rising to make the short journey to the cliff's edge alone. Far to the north of the battlefield, a small black dot struggled to join the cloud of darkness heading toward Ankaal. It was flying lower than the rest, falling a little, then recovering, then falling again. A mass of darkness engulfed it then rejoined the cloud as the throng of demons disappeared from sight.

"Godspeed," Jason said to them. The demons were safe.

Jason opened his mind and his heart. He closed his eyes, drinking in the world around him. Sounds of life came from everywhere, filling him until he thought he would burst. He spread his arms apart, his toe tapping in time to the song that was filling him. Finally a smile spread across his face and he began to sing.

Mists swirled around him, emanating from every pore in his body. They raced around Parry and Lucy, blanketing them in waves of comfort. They shifted slightly, finding a little better place to sleep, their faces radiating childlike peace. Jason felt a tear run down his face. He turned his attention to the battlefield.

The mist flowed from him now, a waterfall of peace flooding the valley below. It intermingled with the shields Jessie and Ric maintained, at once dissolving them and absorbing them, spreading their unique light through the entire battlefield. Altay's sword appeared and disappeared, her delicate rose color joining with silver gold, blue, green and a touch of Sje's sapphire. From Dallow Mound to the Plain of Arandia and halfway up Emmalie and Pikea, the mist wandered, flecks of energy from swords and shields dotting the landscape with shimmering light.

Jason's tongue was thick in his mouth. He could not stop, could not turn away from the battlefield below. His throat burned. He longed for water, yet he knew he could not stop. Above him, clouds formed and lightning rippled across the heavens. Darkness was falling in more ways than one. But the song was not ended. Long after only the truly dead were the only ones left upon the field to hear him, he continued to sing.

Behind him, Aramat stirred in the massive camp. Relief filled the old woman's soul. She pulled a blanket from the Healer's wagon and wrapped herself in it, forgetting for the moment the wounded she would shortly be tending. She put her head on her flat pillow and slept. Garrett stopped pacing in the king's tents when the mist seeped in. He curled up on a soft pile of pillows and slept. Everywhere, cooks and smithies, children servants of the army, even the horses that pulled the wagons and the wild things in the forest, all were charged with Jason's incredible peace. Sleep was universal. Sleep was healing.

Jason drew in one more breath to sing one more bittersweet note. He buckled as it resonated deep and alone in his soul, falling forward onto his hands, his head dropping down so that if he had his eyes open, he would see only his legs. Yet he held the single note. Then he collapsed onto his elbows, letting his head rest on the stone. The last note slipped into silence. The song ended. The world was quiet. He pulled himself into a ball and shut out the world around him. Now, oblivious to everything, he soundlessly wept.

He was floating on the Crystal Lake. The water lapped noiselessly against the side of his raft. An odd peace filled the unexplained void in his soul. He stretched out and closed his eyes. The hand that was on his shoulder shifted. It now encircled his chest. Warm air breathed rhythmically against his neck and the scent of roses and strawberries filled his nostrils.

"Jason?"

He opened his eyes and she shifted beneath him so he could see her face.

"Don't try to talk."

Altay's face flickered in the lightning from the storm. He smiled at her and wrapped his hand into hers. Rain splattered the ground around them. Jason turned his head to look. The fire had gone out and night had turned to day. With a start, he tried to sit up, catching himself in the cloak that someone had thrown over him. The effort made his head spin, but Altay steadied him against her chest.

"Lucy?" he croaked.

"With her parents," Altay explained. "We're a bit low on carts. They took her, then Parry and now," she said, her body shifting again, "your turn."

Jason did not protest. He remembered very little of what came next save the scent of Altay and the warmth of Tersan's tent. He nestled in her arms and slept.

92 Homeward Bound

The next several days were spent in somber reflection. The dead were gathered in the great basin at the foot of Dallow. Jelestines and Kilmaris bore each body to an individual pyre. With equal reverence, they helped the Calsharans ready their dead. Three days after the battle, the stage was set.

Each fallen soldier had one member of each army at his side. Two stood symbolically to guard him, the third, his countryman, held an unlit torch in his hand. The pyres spiraled out from the center of the basin, nearly filling it. Jason, Ric, Patrick and Altay stood guard over a shriveled mass of demons, ready to ignite the final fire for them.

Upon the spunky grey stallion, Tersan made his way to the center of the spiral, a burning torch in his hand. Beside him rode Sword and Shield. Eron's eyes no longer shifted as they once did but instead were lifeless and dull. His dark hair accentuated his pale skin but he sat his horse as a warrior would. Jessie's face, too, was drawn. Dark circles underscored her eyes. There was no sparkle left in them, yet there was no pain on her face.

They reached the center of the basin. Tersan slowly raised the burning torch. Greystone pranced in a circle, a slow, powerful salute to the dead. Tersan brought the horse to a halt and asked him to kneel. Greystone knelt, bending his exquisite head down to touch the earth. Tersan dismounted slowly, the pain of his ordeal plain on his face.

"May there never be need for another war between us," he said, holding out the torch so that Rothen, Letou and Amaton of Calshara could light their torches simultaneously from his. "May the Lady grant the dead a peaceful journey home."

Each captain turned away from the king and strode to two soldiers of other armies. Their torches were lit and they turned to the man behind them, who lit that torch.

From the top of Dallow, Parry, Lucy and Pixil watched the fire pinwheel from the center of the basin to its outermost reaches. The horses bearing Tersan, Eron and Jessie each took a separate path to the edge of the basin where they took up a sentry position. Tersan raced out to Ric, who held the torch for the demons, then returned to his place in the circle. A trumpet sounded. The innermost fire was lit. Slowly, as the soldiers left the dead to their final journey, the basin became a huge bowl filled with fire. To the east, the Calsharans assembled, to the south, the Kilmari, to the west, the Jelestines and lastly, to the north, what remained of the slain demons. Smoke rose from the pyres, individual tendrils joining together to form a single billowing cloud.

"Time to leave, dears." Aramat leaned over the three of them like the proverbial mother hen. "You need your rest." She shepherded them back to the camp as below them, the armies parted.

For two days, they traveled through Jeleste back toward Kimala. Lucy, Parry, Jason and Patrick sat in one of the healers' wagons, joined occasionally by Tersan when he became too tired to ride, talking quietly while the others rode in various combinations throughout the marching army. Each night, they camped a little further from Dallow, yet each morning the smoke from the distant pyres haunted them. It was not until Pella Durett was in sight five days later that the smoke finally vanished.

"Do you suppose it's still burning?" Ric asked Jason.

Jason shook his head. His throat still stung every time he tried to speak so he did not try very often. However, he did point to the north. "Rain," he croaked.

They reached the fortress as light mist began to dampen their clothes. By the time the horses were stalled, a light rain was falling and by the time they reached the banquet hall for a subdued victory feast, it was falling in sheets. Thunder rumbled through the stone walls of the fortress. Jason did not feel up to a party. He left Ric and headed for bed.

The scent of fresh flowers once again filled the air. Altay greeted him with a kiss. He returned the greeting awkwardly.

"Bed," he croaked.

She turned away from him, keeping his hand in hers and led him toward the curtained bed.

"Altay--"

"We are both adults," she told him, shedding her robe. "Now, hush."

Tersan stood in the empty banquet hall of Pella Durett, looking out over the plain to the east. A heavy fog covered the ground like a soft woolen blanket. He doubted very much if the air felt as comforting. He shifted slightly, repositioning his bandaged body so it would be more comfortable. He cursed Madame Aramat for not allowing him to drink last night. He thought he would have slept better for it. But now, in the first grey light of day he was glad he did not have the hangover on top of this other discomfort.

"My lord?"

The king turned away from the window. "Yes, Letou, what is it?"

Letou smiled. "Visitors."

"Father?"

Tersan's heart leapt. Candra and Raef raced across the room to meet him. He knelt to sweep them into his arms. Unbidden tears filled his eyes, tears his children would not notice. He kissed them and held them close, the pain of his ordeal supplanted. When they finally parted, his precious little girl looked at him sternly.

"Father, you have not been eating properly," she scolded.

"Oh?" he answered.

"I can tell," she told him. "A woman can always tell."

Tersan laughed. "Suppose you take me to the kitchen then," he suggested. "And then you can tell me about your trip."

They left the banquet hall, one small hand in each of his, in search of something to eat.

Jessie stood looking at the same fog covered field Tersan had just seen, except that she was looking at it around Eron. His frame nearly filled the window and he stood stock still, his right hand clenched in a knuckle-white fist held by his left. She sat on the bed clutching a pillow.

"Eron?" she said. Even his name sounded pitiful.

"I am once again a shell," he answered softly. "I have no purpose. Ergo, I have no reason to live."

"Don't be ridiculous!" she snapped. She rose, cast aside the pillow and stood behind him. She wanted so badly to comfort him, but she did not know how. The wound was too fresh and besides, there was little she had left to give save support. "We'll go back to my world," she told him. "Magic is not revered there. Your loss will be of no consequence."

"I will know, Jess."

"But it doesn't matter!" she argued. She ventured a hand on his shoulder. He did not shrug from her. Instead, he took her by the arm and pulled her in front of him, placing his arms lazily around her.

"What would I do, in your world?"

"Be my husband," she answered quickly.

He laughed. "Living requires more than that," he replied bitterly. "A man must provide for his family." He pulled her close. She could feel his breath on her ear. "I--I want a family."

Jessie turned to face him. "We have a good start."

Without looking into his eyes, she put her arms around him and held him close, holding back her tears.

"Would you kindly cut that out?"

"Cut what out?" Ric placed the ball of energy he had just formed onto a four sided pyramid he was building in the center of the floor of the room he shared with Patrick.

"It's not like you're building a house of cards, you know," Patrick told him. "Those things burn if you try to pick them up."

"Really?"

"You know, I can't wait to get back home." He ignored the growing pyramid and limped across the room to the wash stand. Scented water waited in a pitcher, along with two clean towels. He poured water into the basin, washed his face and neck and wished for a razor. "Samantha may like this," he said, rubbing his hand across the stubble that now resembled a beard. "She likes facial hair."

"And you live your life to please a woman?" Ric asked.

"The rewards," he said with a smile, "far outweigh the sacrifices."

"I wouldn't know."

"You will someday," Patrick answered, refusing to be drawn into the adolescent debate. "If you want to have a successful relationship, you have to work at pleasing all parties involved."

"This outa make me a chick magnet..." Ric added the final ball to the top of the pyramid and stood away from his creation. "After all, how many dudes can make something like that out of thin air?"

Patrick threw the towel around his shoulders, using the ends to pat his beard dry. "And what will you talk about after you're finished building your...What is that, anyway?"

Ric grinned. "It needs a catchy name."

"Right." Patrick rolled his eyes. "Why don't you just try talking to a woman? You're a bright kid."

Ric sighed. "I'm a geek, Pat, a capital-letter geek. The stuff I get excited about...well, most women don't have a use for it."

"Then find out what they do have a use for," Patrick suggested. "Find some common ground, something that interests you both." He laughed. "Or find a woman who is not 'most women'."

Ric swept his hand over the pyramid and the balls returned to the palm of his hand in rapid succession. They disappeared as soon as they hit. Ric did not flinch. He brushed his hands together and shrugged. "I'll try."

"Good luck." He looked at his watch. "Tersan's throwing a farewell breakfast," he said. "Better get a move on."

"Lucy?"

Lucy felt the hand on her back. She tried to ignore it, to return to dream-filled sleep before she lost the image of someone she had never met. The hand was gently insistent.

"Lucy, wake up. We're leaving this morning and you need to have breakfast before we go. Come on, now. I know you're awake."

Reluctantly, she responded to the voice of her mother. The man with the sandy hair and the brilliant green eyes dissipated and vanished. She rolled over. Jessie was sitting on the side of the bed dressed in leather. Behind her was the most handsome man Lucy had ever seen. A moment of déjà vu crossed her mind. She saw him in a walled garden, his head bent over a blossom. There had been pain in his face then. Things had changed little.

"Five more minutes?" she begged.

"Now," Jessie said sternly.

"All right, but I'm not getting out of this bed in front of him, even if he is my father."

That brought a smile from the man. "I'll wait outside," he said.

Lucy got the distinct impression that he did not want to leave, but it was not to see her dress. It was to stay close to them.

"My father is such a babe," she told Jessie after the door shut.

"A babe?"

"Oh, come on, Mom, don't play dumb with me." She gingerly pushed the covers to one side and rubbed her face. "Is he coming home with us this time? To stay?"

"I'm hoping to marry him."

"Whoa. That would be so cool!"

"You don't even know him!"

Lucy reached for her clothes and started dressing slowly. The wound was healing nicely. Madame Aramat said so. Still, she was sore. "All the girls will want to come to the house now," she said.

"Why?"

"To catch an eyeful of him. They'll be so jealous of me!"

"Lucy Ann Perrymore! How can you be so shallow?"

Lucy grinned. "Easy," she said. Jessie looked furious. "Mom, surely you've noticed his looks? Bad boy handsome? And that little vulnerability he showed? The loyalty to you?" She couldn't help but grin. "Nothing has changed, mind you, since the last time I saw him."

"A lot has changed," her mother told her. There was sadness in her voice. "But nothing that will prevent us from becoming a very happy normal family."

"Right." Lucy walked stiffly to the dressing table and sat down. Her hair was frightfully mussed up and she had drool crusted to her cheek. "How could you let him see me like this?" she demanded.

Jessie laughed. "He would love you if you were bald! Here. Let me help."

"I am quite capable of taking care of myself," Lucy replied, tugging her head away from her mother's touch. Jessie poured water from a pitcher on the vanity into a waiting bowl.

"Here," Jessie said, offering her a small cloth.

Five minutes later, they joined Eron in the hallway and together they made their way to the banquet hall.

Jason, Altay and Ric were already seated at the long table that ran the length of the room, engaged in animated conversation. Patrick was off in a corner, chatting with a group of Jelestine soldiers. Jessie escorted Lucy to the place where her cousin sat. When he saw them, his face flushed.

"What?" Jessie asked, worry furrowing her brow.

Altay laughed. "He's fine, my lady," she said with a wink.

"Ah," was all Jessie said to them. "Lucy, sit. Eron and I have other duties."

She left, the bad-boy hunk at her side. Lucy slid in next to Jason and Ric took his place on the other side of her.

"Nice weather we're having," he told her.

A bolt of lightning lit up the Great Hall followed by a deafening crack of thunder. Lucy clapped her hands over her ears. When no more came, she put her hands on the table and shook her head. "Nice for who?" she asked.

"'Whom'," he corrected. His face scrunched up and he huffed. "Dang!"

"What?" Jason asked.

"Never mind," Ric answered.

"Good people of Jeleste..." Tersan stood in the front of the Great hall, flanked by two children on his left and a frail looking woman with an eye patch on his right, "honored guests from Kimala..." The frail woman tipped her head in acknowledgment. "...and from the Otherworld..." Jessie stood with Eron beside the frail woman.

"Are they related?" Lucy asked Jason.

"Who?"

"That woman and my dad?"

"Pixil? I don't know. It would make sense, though. They're both Kilmari."

"...put aside the battles for a time," Tersan was saying. "It is time to rebuild. But such matters can wait at least until after breakfast." The little girl beside him tugged on his shirt. He started to bend down to hear her, then knelt instead. She held a hand up to his ear and whispered something. When she was finished, she stood back a little and waited. Tersan smiled at her. He kissed her on the forehead and stood.

"It seems my daughter has much to learn about affairs of state," he said calmly. "It seems she wants to eat." He laughed. "This may be the last time for a long time that we enjoy this fellowship. Sate your hunger, dear friends."

By noon, they were packed and ready to go. The storm abated, leaving their horses to snort cold air and return it in tiny clouds. Tersan, flanked by his ever present children on one side and healers on the other, waved from Pella Durett's steps as they climbed into various wagons for the journey to Bel Haven.

They crossed the plain slowly. Bel Haven grew from a tiny dot into the buildings that housed the healers. The journey took what was left of the day, depositing them on the steps leading to the inner sanctum shortly before sunset. The Great Hall was filled with wounded from the battle. Healers busily attended them. Penrose limped toward them, leaning heavily on a thick wooden staff.

"Welcome back," he said to them. "A meal has been prepared and your beds await. Come."

They followed him as he led them to the dining hall.

"Thank the lord," Jason whispered. "I didn't think he would make it."

Penrose turned and the procession halted. "I would not be here had it not been for you, Jason. I have not properly thanked you."

"You're alive," Jason said. Altay squeezed his hand. "That is thanks enough."

"Sirens only come to Eormengrund when there is nearly cataclysmic need," Penrose said as they seated themselves for the meal. "In legend, some have had the courage to give all of themselves in order to restore a way of life. In so doing, their physical being is sacrificed, leaving them nothing but flesh on bone. The Lady is said to take their spirit away. I am pleased that this part of the legend is inaccurate."

"On Ankaal," Altay said, "Sje said he was twice blessed. He did not explain further." She took an apple from under her shirt and set it on the table. "He wanted you to have this, Jason. I don't know why."

Jason paled but said nothing. He took the apple and tucked it away.

Penrose shook his head. "Many things are beyond my ken. I have lost a healer to unspeakable circumstances. There is apparently a lot I, too, need to learn."

The following morning, a well-appointed wagon waited outside the Great Hall. Penrose and Aramat supervised the loading of their precious human cargos for the final leg of their journey. Ric helped Lucy up, then followed her. Patrick joined them in the third seat of the wagon. Jessie and Eron sat in the second row, content to let someone else be in charge for the moment.

"Thank you, Lady Jessie," Penrose said. "There may still be hope for the return of your powers."

Jessie smiled brightly. "Eron and Lucy are all I will ever need, Penrose. Someday, you must visit my world."

"I will," he answered.

Altay pulled Jason aside. Before he could protest, she planted a kiss on his lips, a long hot kiss that left him wanting to repeat the night they spent together at Pella Durett. When they parted, he rested his forehead against hers, then brushed her cheek with the back of one hand while entwining her fingers in the other.

"Stay with me for a while," she said softly. "Penrose needs every healer he has to care for the wounded and to rehabilitate them."

"I wish I could sing for them," he said.

She laughed. "Would that you could, my love." She placed her hand on his face. "The song may return. Sje said you are twice blessed."

"I'm not sure that would work out well on Broadway. Putting your audience to sleep is not a good thing."

She bit her lip. "You're not making this easy," she said, choking back a tear. And then she was in his arms. For a while, Jason stood holding the healer. She did not weep. Rather, she held him as though he was dangling from a cliff and she was the only thing between his life and his death. The moment passed and she let him go.

"I want to stay," he told her.

"I know. Promise you will return?"

"Just try to stop me," he assured her. He kissed her again, drinking in the scent of roses and strawberries one last time.

93 The Crystal

Tammar pulled a soft blanket up over the shoulders of her mistress. Since her return to Il Chatel, Sila had said little. She was fixated on the crystal. All night she had sat holding the stone in her hand, peering into it as though there was something there to be seen. Tammar removed the bandage on her arm, cleaned the wound and replaced it with a fresh dressing. Sila did not notice.

"My lady," Tammar began. She held a tray of exotic fruit in one hand and richly spiced meats in the other, "ye must eat something."

Sila continued to stare at the stone. She gasped and smiled then stared some more. Tammar set the trays to one side.

"At least drink something," she said, pouring some wine into a vessel and offering it to her mistress.

Sila ignored her.

"Well!" Tammar set the vessel to one side and stood before Sila, her hands placed firmly on her hips. "Ye must eat! Fergive me, lady…" With the speed of a common thief, she snatched the crystal away from Sila. The queen cried out as though an appendage had been ripped away. She snatched at the crystal, her sunken eyes dully demanding its return.

"Not 'til ye've had something to eat," Tammar insisted. "Ye've got ter keep up yer strength."

"Give it to me!" Sila demanded, her voice hollow.

"No," Tammar answered. She held the crystal to one side, away from Sila. "Eat first. Drink something. I'd prefer ye got some rest."

Sila went to the trays, grabbed handfuls of fruit and crammed them into her mouth. She did the same with the meats, washing it all down by draining the vessel of wine. Food and wine were smeared across her face as she held out soiled hands to receive the crystal once more.

With a sigh, Tammar returned it to her. Her eyes widened and she laughed. The sound sent a chill down Tammar's spine.

"My lady?" she asked.

"I can see them! I know what they are doing! Best of all…" she laughed coldly again, "They do not see me!"

"My lady?"

Sila took the crystal and hung it around her neck. She looked at her hands in disgust. "Bring me water and something to wash with," she said. She looked in the mirror. "Never mind. Draw me a bath. Then summon the good captain. We have cause for celebration."

94 Last Leg

The small wagon made its way past the Giant's Fingers and back into the woods at the base of Kimala. The occupants chatted genially for most of the journey, but there were moments of comfortable silence between them as well. Jessie listened while Jason, Ric and Lucy exchanged quick-witted conversation behind her. Patrick would occasionally join in. The officer was very good with children.

Children. Jason and Ric were hardly children anymore and Lucy... Lucy was a woman in mind and body, just not in age. Where had the years gone? Stupid obligations to a fairytale land had prevented her from seeing those most precious moments.

"What is it like?"

She turned to face her lover. "What is what like?"

"The Otherworld. What's it like living there?" His voice was quiet and his eyes were scanning the hills and mountains, drinking everything in as though he would never see this his home again.

Jessie sighed. "It's very different, but very similar, too," she said. "We rely on machines to get things done, not solely our hands." She laughed. "You will be fine, my lord," she said.

"But Lucy...Do you think she will accept me as her, um, father?"

Jessie laughed again. "She said you have 'bad boy good looks' and that all her friends will be jealous."

He shifted in his seat and looked at her. "Is that good?"

"Yes."

He nodded. "I suppose if you learned the ways of my people, I can learn the ways of yours."

"We have time," she said.

They reached the entrance to the portal and disembarked. Prytal was waiting for them. He handed a small, cloth pouch to Jessie.

"Pixil sent this," he said as she took it. "Seeds for the trinka vine. They are extremely rare but the vines that grow from them never fail."

"Thank you," she said.

"Wow," Ric said. "I can see it now... trinka replaces coffee as the favored morning brew. We can set up a whole chain of trinka-houses, dollop whipped cream and cherries on top, serve it frozen on a stick--"

"They gotta grow first!" Jason interrupted.

"We have to think of a Latin name for it, don't we?" Lucy said. "My biology teacher said they use Latin because it's a dead language and nobody's going to change it."

"Wonder what 'trinka' means in Latin?" Patrick asked.

"I would think you could use anything you want when you get to that point," Lucy said. "Scientists name fungi after themselves all the time."

"Now there's a pleasant thought," Patrick grinned.

Jessie smiled. "I'm sure we can find a suitable name," she said. She tucked away the seeds, then walked up to Prytal and kissed him on the cheek. "Thank you. And thank Pixil for me, too."

"The Lady keep you all safe," he said.

"And also you," Eron returned.

Prytal bowed and disappeared back into the forest.

"This way!" Lucy announced. She fairly bounded around the boulder marking the entrance to the portal and disappeared.

"Wait for me!" Jason said. He raced behind her, Ric on his heels.

"Their recuperative powers are amazing," Patrick observed. "I guess I'll keep an eye on the young 'uns," he said with a wink. He limped around the boulder and disappeared, leaving them alone.

Eron took in a deep breath. "I suppose this is it," he said.

Jessie turned him so that she could look him straight in the eye. "Don't for a minute think that I don't want you to come with me," she said. "You are, after all, a prince. That is your birthright. A crown is a lot to give up."

"I have no desire to be a prince." He sighed. "And I can no longer be Sword."

"You are a father," she said. "All the other titles don't matter, not to your people and certainly not to Lucy or to me."

"They do to…" He smiled. "I suppose you are right. And opening the portal does not require magic per se, rather simply the casting of a spell?"

"You can always go home again. Once our children are grown, we can return."

"Children? How? When?" He took her and gave her a huge hug. "Thank you," he whispered.

She let him linger there for a moment, enjoying the smell of leather that always clung to him and thinking he was going to have to learn to bathe more frequently than once a week, else Lucy's friends would be saying something entirely different about him.

"Come on, then," she said, taking him by the hand and leading him to the stairway. "Let's go home."

95 The Sleigh Bed

Sunlight poured through the glass panes, warming the bedclothes covering his feet. Beyond the windows, unfamiliar songbirds filled the air with coy melodies promising immortality through procreation. The bed he lay in was soft but firm, luring him back into sleep. He kept his eyes closed, his body not ready yet to give over the night. With one arm, he stretched to her side of the bed, resting on her belly to feel their second child move. The unborn babe graced him with a kick before her hand met his and pressed a kiss upon it. Her breath was on his forehead and she placed a second kiss there. Then the bed shifted and he felt the soft coverlet snugged up over his shoulders.

"Go back to sleep," she whispered.

The bed shifted again. Through heavy lids, he saw her silhouette against the brightness of the new day. He pulled her pillow to him drinking in her scent. Content once again, he closed his eyes to sleep.

Sleep would not come.

Reluctantly he opened his eyes and stared down at his hands. Perhaps if he concentrated, his missing powers would somehow magically reform, leaving him whole again. He dipped his head down, the entirety of his being staring at his fingers while he searched his mind for the river that no enemy could forge, the river drained by she who was once his ally and his healer, once would-be rival of his lover, she who was now his enemy.

Nothing. There was nothing. Not even a puddle of gold was to be found. He had sworn to keep his people free and this, this was the cost. Not his people, not his love, not even his life, but his power, gone. He swallowed the lump in his throat. The Sword had died on that battlefield leaving behind simply Eron, Eron who would have to learn to live a different life now.

Give yourself time to heal, he heard Penrose say in some distant memory.

"Time to heal. What does a healer know of the ways of Swords? You cannot fathom that which I have lost."

He drew the pillow to his face. Once he had known no fear, battled an enemy of inconceivable power and won victory at a terrible price. He became aware of his own mortality. Dread then filled his mind, nearly taking him. Yet he survived. In a time dark and hopeless, he had conquered his fear and led an army into battle and on to victory only to lose who he was once more. He buried his head in the pillow and drank in one last taste of her scent. Quite suddenly he realized that she completed him. Kingdoms and champions did not matter if titles and abilities were all that remained when the wars were won. Jessie was his life now, Jessie and Lucy and their unborn child. He was born anew, not prince, not sword, but father. The thought brought a smile to his lips. It was time to abandon sleep and greet this new day.

The floor was cold against his bare feet. For a moment, he considered pulling on the slippers she had thoughtfully left by the side of the bed but decided against it. Bending over to put them on would aggravate a number of battle scarred muscles that the night's sleep had not fully rested. Besides, he had never worn slippers. There were many things here that were new to him. He rose slowly, stretching with great care until he felt fluid enough to move. He took the robe and pulled it over his abused but healing body. A songbird pecked the windowpane. He crossed the floor in an awkward gait to see what it wanted. Before he reached the window, it was gone.

The day was bright and glorious, sure to tempt children to ignore their lessons, preferring to skip instead through fields of spring flowers, the girls making necklace chains out of blossoms while dreaming of princes on white horses, the boys plucking up branches and playing at sword fighting to save the masses from evil. Life could be so simple when it was innocent.

He let his attention drift back into the room again. He had seen her manipulate this machine and the musicians inside filled the room with soft music. If he could remember the sequence of the spell, perhaps they would play for him as well.

With one hand, he caressed the box, his fingers gently probing it so as not to rudely disturb the silent players. There was a click and a light came on. Pleased with himself, he leaned on the box and closed his eyes as sultry tones filled the room. A smile touched his lips. A long time had passed since he had truly smiled. It felt good to use those muscles again.

"Eron?"

She stood in the center of the room, the warm sun bathing her in an aura he thought he would never see again. He took two short strides, willing his body to forget the trials he had seen. With gentle hands he cupped her face, tilting it upward so he could kiss her full on the lips. She leaned into the kiss, her arms resting on his shoulders, her hands entwined behind his neck. He pulled her to him, startling as his robe innocently opened and her body brushed against his. She was warm and whole and more beautiful than any woman he had ever seen. He wanted the moment to last forever. When at last he released her, she stood before him gazing into his eyes.

"Jessie," he whispered, "I love you." He placed a finger over her lips before she could speak. "I can no longer offer you what I once could," he began, lowering his finger. "I was once a king, but am no longer."

"Eron--"

"No, please, let me finish." He paused, trying to find the best words. She looked up at him, waiting for him to speak. Her actions were uncharacteristic. "I once had a crown and a sword. I had to give my crown away in order to use the sword to fight for my people."

She nodded.

"In the fight, I lost my sword."

She said nothing, but continued to gaze into his eyes. A pang of regret struck him. She would never be able to access his mind again, not to share the intimacies of his thought. An unashamed tear escaped his eye.

"You are everything to me," she told him with a smile. She rubbed the bump on her abdomen. "There is so much we have ahead of us. I look forward to the journey."

Maybe Penrose was right. Maybe in time things would return. Then again, maybe they would not. Power no longer mattered. "I have nothing to offer you." He dropped awkwardly to his knees, grasping her hand in his own. He looked into her face, hoping he would see what he needed to see.

"I--I would wed you, Lady Jessie," he said, "though I have nothing to offer."

She pulled him to his feet and slipped her hands again around his neck. Outside the windowpanes, the birds chirped merrily. The sun shone around her head forming a halo.

"Then wed me, Lord Eron," she whispered. "Wed me."

THE THANK YOU PAGE

It took a lot of years to get this story from the dream that was its beginning to the final page. Many people were very supportive in this process, but the following folks really stand out:

My family. Their undying support and patience made this possible. Barb has been wanting to read this since she first heard about it. Sue actually did read it and said it was well written, which means a whole lot because she is a woman of the world. Robyn has given silent support, most welcome because she was always there. Mom is Mom. She has always said her children could be anything they want to be. She is the quintessential wellspring of imagination. My nephews, who have waited patiently as have my brother in laws. I am truly blessed.

Help in the form of editing came from Debbie Flanagan, my sister of another mother, and Jeannine Kerr, my mentor in many worlds. They kept the grammar straight and the plot aligned. It's the details that make the difference and without these ladies, some details would surely have been missed. And without Debbie, there would be no cover art. I'll leave that to your imagination.

And then there are the two people who kept me going, one in the creative process, the other through the endless edits.

Amy Page was that constant wind that kept the edits going. It seemed an endless process to get all the pieces in place, to have the plot lines occur in the right order and not give away anything. Each time I got through an edit, I pretty much knew that I would have to go over details again and again until they were seamless. Amy was my conscience. She thought the book was my child and that I would never finish. She was wrong. I did finish. Except for putting the words on the cover. She did that for me and I thank her for it.

The last and most important influence and biggest thank you goes to Andrew Stead. Drew and I spent many nights chatting online, going over plot details and twists, speaking on occasion in person, but sending chapters back and forth. He was the first person to read this novel, my biggest supporter and will always be my cherished friend. He is a gifted writer. Someday, I'm certain he will share his works with the world. Many thanks, Drew.

Made in the USA
Lexington, KY
30 January 2018